Penguin Books
What Ho!

Pelham Grenville Wodehouse was born in 1881 in Guildford,
the son of a civil servant, and educated at Dulwich College. He
spent a brief period working for the Hong Kong and Shanghai
Bank before abandoning finance for writing, earning a living by
journalism and selling stories to magazines.

An enormously popular and prolific writer, he produced about
a hundred books. Probably best known for Jeeves, the ever-
resourceful 'gentleman's personal gentleman', and the good-
hearted young blunderer Bertie Wooster, Wodehouse created
many other comic figures, notably Lord Emsworth, the Hon.
Galahad Threepwood, Psmith and the numerous members of
the Drones Club. He was part-author and writer of fifteen straight
plays and of 250 lyrics for some thirty musical comedies. *The
Times* hailed him as a 'comic genius recognized in his lifetime
as a classic and an old master of farce'.

P. G. Wodehouse said, 'I believe there are two ways of writing
novels. One is mine, making a sort of musical comedy without
music and ignoring real life altogether; the other is going right
deep down into life and not caring a damn.'

Wodehouse married in 1914 and took American citizenship
in 1955. He was created a Knight of the British Empire in the
1975 New Year's Honours List. In a BBC interview he said that
he had no ambitions left now that he had been knighted and there
was a waxwork of him in Madame Tussaud's. He died on St
Valentine's Day, 1975, at the age of ninety-three.

P. G. Wodehouse
What Ho!

P. G. Wodehouse

What Ho!

The Best of P. G. Wodehouse

With an Introduction by
Stephen Fry

PENGUIN BOOKS

PENGUIN BOOKS

Published by the Penguin Group
Penguin Books Ltd, 80 Strand, London WC2R 0RL, England
Penguin Putnam Inc., 375 Hudson Street, New York, New York 10014, USA
Penguin Books Australia Ltd, 250 Camberwell Road, Camberwell, Victoria 3124, Australia
Penguin Books Canada Ltd, 10 Alcorn Avenue, Toronto, Ontario, Canada M4V 3B2
Penguin Books India (P) Ltd, 11 Community Centre, Panchsheel Park, New Delhi – 110 017, India
Penguin Books (NZ) Ltd, Cnr Rosedale and Airborne Roads, Albany, Auckland, New Zealand
Penguin Books (South Africa) (Pty) Ltd, 24 Sturdee Avenue, Rosebank 2196, South Africa

Penguin Books Ltd, Registered Offices: 80 Strand, London WC2R 0RL, England

www.penguin.com

9

Set in 9/11pt Monotype Trump
Phototypeset by Intype London Ltd
Printed in England by Clays Ltd, St Ives plc

Contents

Introduction

What a very, very lucky person you are. Spread out before you are the finest and funniest words from the finest and funniest writer the past century ever knew.

Doctor Sir Pelham Grenville Wodehouse (pronounced Wood-house) defies superlatives. Had his only contribution to literature been Lord Emsworth and Blandings Castle, his place in history would have been assured. Had he written of none but Mike and Psmith, he would be cherished today as the best and brightest of our comic authors. If Jeeves and Wooster had been his solitary theme, still he would be hailed as The Master. If he had given us only Ukridge, or nothing but recollections of the Mulliner family, or a pure diet of golfing stories, Wodehouse would nonetheless be considered immortal. That he gave us all those and more – so much more – is our good fortune and a testament to the most industrious, prolific and beneficent author ever to have sat down, scratched his head and banged out a sentence.

If I were to say that the defining characteristic of Wodehouse the man was his professionalism, that might make him sound rather dull. We look for eccentricity, sexual weirdness, family trauma and personal demons in our great men. Wodehouse, who knew just what was expected of authors, got used to having to apologize for a childhood that was 'as normal as rice-pudding' and a life that consisted of little more than 'sitting in front of the typewriter and cursing a bit'.

The only really controversial episode of Wodehouse's life, his broadcasts to friends from Berlin while an internee of the Germans in France and Belgium during the Second World War, is dug up from time to time by mischief makers and the ignorant. It wouldn't be worth mentioning now if it hadn't been unearthed yet again quite recently, together with wholly unjustifiable newspaper headlines in the British press linking the name Wodehouse with words like Nazi, Fascist and Traitor. Anyone who has examined the affair closely will agree with the Foreign Office official who wrote that it was unlikely

> . . . that anyone would seriously deny that 'L'Affaire Wodehouse' was very much a storm in a teacup. It is perfectly plain to any unbiased outsider that Mr Wodehouse made the celebrated broadcasts in all innocence and without any evil intent. He is reported to be of an entirely apolitical cast of mind; much of the furore of course was the result of literary jealousies.

This was written in 1947 and it expresses a view shared by Malcolm Muggeridge, who was one of the officers sent to debrief Wodehouse when Paris was liberated, and by George Orwell in his celebrated 1945 essay *In Defence of P. G. Wodehouse*: ' . . . in the case of Wodehouse, if we drive him to retire to the United States and renounce his British citizenship, we shall end by being horribly ashamed of ourselves.' The fact remains too that for decades after they were made, Wodehouse's broadcasts (which he made in order to communicate with his thousands of readers in the United States) were used by, amongst other, the CIA, as models of how to pull the wool over a captor's eyes by the use of irony. For Wodehouse's view on Fascists, one need only consult the descriptions of Sir Roderick Spode in *The Code of the Woosters* (included in this collection) to see how a political innocent may still be capable of scorching satire. Enough of all that. If the episode reveals anything it is

Wodehouse's other-worldliness – a quality that shines through in his work and a quality that in our muddied and benighted times ought in fact to be celebrated from the hilltops.

Many have sought to 'explain' Wodehouse, to psychoanalyse his world, to place his creations under the microscope of modern literary criticism. Such a project, as an article in *Punch* observed, is like 'taking a spade to a soufflé'. His world of sniffily disapproving aunts, stern and gooseberry-eyed butlers, impatient uncles, sporty young girls, natty young men who throw bread rolls in club dining rooms yet blush and stammer in the presence of the opposite sex – all these might be taken as evidence of a man stuck in a permanently pre-pubescent childhood. Beds in Wodehouse are not locations of passion and lust, they are convenient furniture to hide under when pursued. Girls are angels of perfection, or hare-brained tomboys, or stern disciplinarians who want to improve and educate, or jolly sisters who present no threat to the perfect peace offered by the state of bachelorhood. Poverty too has no place in the world of Wodehouse. A chap might be hard up, his aunt, guardian or parent might be slow in disgorging the allowance and his friends may not be susceptible to having their ears bitten for a fiver to tide a fellow over, but hardship and squalor are absent from the feast. Wodehouse wrote throughout the First World War, yet not a mention is made of it. There are no returning soldiers or references to Zeppelins or the Front. All of this would certainly seem childish, irrelevant and frivolous if it were not for the extraordinary, magical and blessed miracle of Wodehouse's prose, a prose which dispels doubt much as sunlight dispels shadows, a prose which renders any criticism, whether positive or negative, absolutely powerless and frankly silly. The prose vindicates a word often used in the discussion of Wodehouse, and that word is 'innocence'. Wodehouse himself, as mentioned earlier, was a kind of innocent, but

more importantly the fictional worlds he created were
innocent too. Evelyn Waugh compared them to Eden
before the fall, and that description – of a pre-lapsarian
idyll – recurs again and again in reviews and articles about
his work. Innocence, true *adult* innocence, is a
characteristic so rare we often call it blessed and ascribe
it only to saints. To inhabit a fictional world of true
innocence is, so far as I can tell, unique to the experience
of reading Wodehouse. It is all done with such apparent
ease, with such unforced fluency that it would be easy to
underestimate the sheer artistry and head-beatingly hard
work that went into it.

When Hugh Laurie and I had the extreme honour and
terrifying responsibility of being asked to play Bertie
Wooster and Jeeves in a series of television adaptations
we were aware of one huge problem facing us.
Wodehouse's three great achievements are Plot,
Character and Language, and the greatest of these, by
far, is Language. If we were reasonably competent then
all of us concerned in the television version could go
some way towards conveying a fair sense of the narrative
of the stories and revealing too a good deal of the
nature of their characters. The language however . . . we
could only scratch the surface of the language.
'Scratching the surface' is a phrase often used without
thought. A scratched surface, it is all too easy to forget,
is a defiled surface. Wodehouse's language lives and
breathes in its written, printed form. It oscillates
privately between the page and the reader. The moment
it is read out or interpreted it is compromised. It is, to
quote Oscar Wilde on another subject, 'like a delicate,
exotic fruit – touch it and the bloom is gone'. Scratch its
surface, in other words, and you have done it a great
disservice. Our only hope in making the television series
was that the stories and the characters might provide

enough pleasure on their own to inspire the viewer to
pick up a book and encounter The Real Thing.

Let me use an example, taken completely at random.
I flip open a book of Jeeves and Wooster short stories and
happen on Bertie and Jeeves discussing a young man
called Cyril Bassington-Bassington . . .

> 'I've never heard of him. Have *you* ever heard of him,
> Jeeves?'
> 'I am familiar with the name Bassington-
> Bassington, sir. There are three branches of the
> Bassington-Bassington family – the Shropshire
> Bassington-Bassingtons, the Hampshire Bassington-
> Bassingtons, and the Kent Bassington-Bassingtons.'
> 'England seems pretty well stocked up with
> Bassington-Bassingtons.'
> 'Tolerably so, sir.'
> 'No chance of a sudden shortage, I mean, what?'

Well, try as hard as actors might, such an exchange will
always work best on the page. It might still be amusing
when delivered as dramatic dialogue, but *no actors are
as good as the actors we each of us carry in our head*.
And that is the point really, one of the gorgeous privileges
of reading Wodehouse is that he makes us feel better
about ourselves because we derive a sense of personal
satisfaction in the laughter mutually created. The
reader, by responding in his or her own head to the rhythm
and timing on the page, has the feeling of having made
the whole thing click. Of course we yield to Wodehouse
the palm of having written it, but *our response* is what
validates the whole experience. Every comma, every 'sir'
every 'what?' is something *we* make work in the act of
reading.

'The greatest living writer of prose', 'The Master', 'the
head of my profession', 'akin to Shakespeare', 'a master of

the language' . . . if you had never read Wodehouse and
only knew about the world his books inhabit you might
be forgiven for blinking in bewilderment at the praise
that has been lavished on a 'mere' comic author by
writers like Compton Mackenzie, Evelyn Waugh, Hilaire
Belloc, Bernard Levin and Susan Hill. But once you dive
into the soufflé, once you engage with all those
miraculous verbal felicities, such adulation begins to
make sense.

Example serves better than description. Let me throw
up some more random nuggets. Particular to Wodehouse
are the transferred epithets: 'I lit a rather pleased
cigarette' or 'I pronged a moody forkful of eggs and b.'
Characteristic too are the sublimely hyperbolic similes:
'Roderick Spode. Big chap with a small moustache and
the sort of eye that can open an oyster at sixty paces' or
'The stationmaster's whiskers are of a Victorian
bushiness and give the impression of having been grown
under glass.'

Here is an example that certainly vindicates my point
about his prose working best on the page. Reading this
aloud isn't much use . . .

> 'Sir Jasper Finch-Farrowmere?' said Wilfred. 'ffinch-
> ffarrowmere,' corrected the visitor, his sensitive ear
> detecting the capitals.

Almost the very first Wodehouse story I ever read
contained this passage, which mixes typical techniques
of acutely accurate parody (romantic and detective
fiction, grand journalism, the western), comically
inappropriate simile, the extravagantly absurd and much
else besides. It was enough to get me hooked.

> 'Don't blame me, Pongo,' said Lord Ickenham, 'if Lady
> Constance takes her lorgnette to you. God bless my
> soul, though, you can't compare the lorgnettes of today

with the ones I used to know as a boy. I remember
walking one day in Grosvenor Square with my aunt
Brenda and her pug dog Jabberwocky, and a policeman
came up and said the latter ought to be wearing a
muzzle. My aunt made no verbal reply. She merely
whipped her lorgnette from its holster and looked at
the man, who gave one choking gasp and fell back
against the railings, without a mark on him but with
an awful look of horror in his staring eyes, as if he'd
seen some dreadful sight. A doctor was sent for, and
they managed to bring him around, but he was never
the same again. He had to leave the force, and
eventually drifted into the grocery business. And that
is how Sir Thomas Lipton got his start.'

I mean, what? Just occasionally Wodehouse allows
himself what could almost be termed worldly satire:

> Whatever may be said in favour of the Victorians, it is
> pretty generally admitted that few of them were to
> be trusted within reach of a trowel and a pile of bricks.

Then there is a passage like this: Lord Emsworth musing
on his feckless younger son, Freddie Threepwood.

> Unlike the male codfish, which, suddenly finding itself
> the parent of three million five hundred thousand
> little codfish, cheerfully resolves to love them all, the
> British aristocracy is apt to look with a somewhat
> jaundiced eye on its younger sons.

If you are immune to writing of this kind, then you are
fit, to use one of Wodehouse's favourite Shakespearean
quotations, only for treasons, stratagems and spoils. You
don't analyse such sunlit perfection, you just bask in its
warmth and splendour. Like Jeeves, Wodehouse stands
alone and analysis, ultimately, is useless.

*

The collection that lies before you is, like any anthology, by definition incomplete, personal and open to debate. Its source however is, I believe, unique. The selection has been made by canvassing the opinions of the membership of six different Wodehouse Societies around the world. No true Wodehousian would ever claim that his taste is better, finer and deeper than the next man's, but you can at least rest assured that these stories and excerpts have been chosen by men and women who have read, if not everything that flowed from the Master's typewriter (not everyone has access to rarer books like *The Prince and Betty*, for example, or *William Tell*) then at least close to everything. This book can be regarded as a teaser – something akin to the sampling cases that wine-merchants put together to awaken the palate. There is a representative of all the great vintages here, enough I would hope to give the first time reader a life-long love of the works and enough too to please the aficionado who wants to make a present of Wodehouse to a friend or needs one collection permanently on the bedside table. The man wrote over ninety books, after all, and if a craving comes over one during the night, it isn't always convenient to pad down to the library and pluck a specific volume from the shelf. It can be extremely useful to have a compact selection made for you. It is in this spirit that *What Ho! The Best of P. G. Wodehouse* has been put together.

Chronology with Wodehouse is not necessarily reliable or relevant, but it seems sensible to describe his creations in a more or less historical order – an order compromised by the fact that it was not uncommon for him to introduce a character in a short story and only later pick up and, as it were, run with the ball. He started writing at the end of the nineteenth century and continued until his death, manuscript on lap, on the fourteenth of February nineteen seventy-five at the age of ninety-three.

It can however be clearly stated that Wodehouse's first great creation and for some his finest, was Psmith (the 'P' is silent). Said to have been drawn from life (one Rupert D'Oyley Carte, of the Savoy Opera family) Psmith is a startling sophisticate, an expelled Old Etonian whose delicately attuned nervous system can be shocked by loud colours, celluloid cuffs and the mere mention of an inadequately pressed trouser crease. He has adopted his own brand of 'practical socialism' and retains to the end the habit of referring to everyone as 'Comrade'. Much as Jeeves was to extricate Bertie time and time again from the soup, so Psmith is the eternal saviour of stolid, dependable Mike Jackson – the Doctor Watson to Psmith's Sherlock Holmes. There is in fact a little thread of autobiography in the second Psmith novel, *Psmith in the City*. Mike, whose only real ambition is to play cricket, at which he excels to the point of genius, is denied by family ill-fortune his chance of going to Cambridge University and is forced instead to earn his crust at the 'New Asiatic Bank'. The young Wodehouse too was obliged to work for some years at the Hong Kong and Shanghai Bank in the City, until the time came when he realized that he was earning more from his writing than from his weekly stipend. Mike's salvation, however, comes not through his own achievements as a writer, but through the help of Psmith.

When Psmith and Mike meet, at Sedleigh School, we witness for the first time the authentic Wodehouse manner. The scene is a turning point in Wodehouse's writing. He develops here from a delightful and better than average writer of school stories (a huge genre in the opening years of the twentieth century) into a great comic stylist. The tones and mannerisms of Psmith might derive from character types that already existed in popular literature, but their realization and completeness is unique to Wodehouse. No one else in fiction talks like Psmith. Much of the reader's pleasure comes from delight at his sheer impertinence and an envious desire to have been able to talk like that oneself to the schoolmasters and employers who harried us in our younger days. A Wodehousian sense of the world being divided into Us (feckless youth, the hopeful and the irrepressibly optimistic) and Them (schoolmasters, bank managers, vicars, aunts and sundry other authority figures) is already established. Psmith however is distinctly pre-War (First World War, that is) and, until the later novel *Leave It To Psmith* (1925) he was unconnected to any other Wodehousian circle.

The second Wodehouse immortal to come along at this time was Stanley Featherstonehaugh Ukridge (pronounced Stanley Fanshawe Ewkridge). Ukridge keeps his pince-nez together by means of ginger-beer wire, wears pyjamas under a macintosh, calls his friends 'old horse', uses exclamations like 'Upon my Sam' and is eternally in search of funds. The master of the scam, he forever embroils his chief biographer Corky (there was one other in the novel *Love Among The Chickens*, 1906) in a series of terrible money-making schemes. Corky is himself an aspiring writer, but Wodehouse has not coloured him in as a narrator, he is not really much more than a long-suffering friend. The sums of money at stake are endearingly low and reveal both the date of the writing and the innocent existence of the heroes. It is usually half a crown that Ukridge needs and not much more. Not much more because his life has no horizons greater than the next great money-making scheme. With half a crown a man has enough to see him through. For the rest he needs no more than to borrow the top hat and morning suit 'as worn', and rely on charm. This is not yet the age of cocktails and nightclubs and sporty two-seaters. But Ukridge is for all that deeply lovable; his amorality and blithe disregard of others do not irritate. Imperishable optimism and a great spaciousness of outlook (one of Ukridge's ideals) inform the spirit

of these stories. He too is capable when occasion
demands of splendid speech:

> 'Alf Todd,' said Ukridge, soaring to an impressive burst
> of imagery, 'has about as much chance as a one-armed
> blind man in a dark room trying to shove a pound of
> melted butter into a wild cat's left ear with a red-hot
> needle.'

Wodehouse never lost his own affection for Ukridge and
continued writing about him until 1966, always setting
the stories back in a pre-Wooster epoch.

In 1915 Wodehouse published *Something Fresh*, the
first of the Blandings novels. I think he knew what he
was doing when he chose that title (*Something New* is
the American version – 'fresh' had, after all, a slightly
racy implication to the American ear . . .) for with the
creation of Blandings Castle, Wodehouse hit upon
something original, something different. He was
beginning his stride into mid-season form.

Wherever lovers of Wodehouse cluster together they
fall into debate about whether it is the Jeeves stories or
the Blandings stories that take the trophy as Wodehouse's
greatest achievements. The group will of course dispel,
muttering embarrassedly, for they know that such
questions are as pointless as wondering whether God
did a better job with the Alps or the Rockies. The question
is bound to be asked however, because each time you
read another Blandings story, the sublime nature of that
world is such as to make you gasp.

The cast of resident characters here is greater than that
of the Wooster canon. There is Lord Emsworth himself,
the amiable and dreamy peer, whose first love – pumpkins
– is soon supplanted by the truest and greatest love of
his life, The Empress of Blandings, that peerless Black
Berkshire sow, thrice winner of the silver medal for
fattest pig in Shropshire; Emsworth's sister Connie (of

whose lorgnette we heard earlier from Lord Ickenham,
another frequent guest at the Castle) who, when sorely
tried, which was often, would retire upstairs to bathe
her temples in *eau de cologne*; the Efficient Baxter,
Emsworth's secretary and a hound from hell;
Emsworth's brother Galahad the last of the Pelicans (that
breed of silk-hatted men-about-town who lived high and
were forever getting thrown out of the Criterion bar in
the eighties and nineties); the younger son Freddie, the
bane of his father's life – perhaps most especially so when
he settles down and becomes the merchant prince of
dogfood; there is Beach the butler, Sir Gregory Parsloe,
Aunts Julia and Hermione and half a dozen others, Lord
Bosham the heir, McAllister the gardener . . . the cast list
goes on and is frequently supplemented by young men
we will have met elsewhere, Ronnie Fish, Pongo
Twistleton and even Psmith himself. Blandings comes,
in the Wodehouse canon, to stand for the absolute ideal
in country houses. Its serenity and beauty are enough to
calm the most turbulent breast. It is an entire world unto
itself and, one senses, Wodehouse pours into it his
deepest feelings for England itself. Once you have drunk
from its healing spring, you will return again and again.
You must forgive my hyperbole, but Blandings is like
that, it enters a man's soul.

The young men I mention as visiting Blandings are all
members of Wodehouse's great fictional institution,
the Drones Club in Dover Street, off Piccadilly. There are
dozens of individual stories about members of the
Drones, and two principal collections, *Eggs Beans and
Crumpets* and *Young Men in Spats*. The title of the first
derives from the Drones' habit of referring to each other
as 'old egg', 'old bean', 'my dear old crumpet' and so on.
The Drones Club is a refuge for the idle young man about
town. Such beings are for the most part entirely
dependent on allowances from fat uncles. Indeed the
name Drones is a reference to the drone bee, which toils

not neither does it spin, unlike its industrious cousin, the worker. An archetypal member would be Freddie Widgeon, intensely amiable, not very bright up top and always falling in love. The only Drone who is distinctly unlikable is Oofy Prosser, the richest and meanest member. He sports pimples, Lobb shoes and the tightest wallet in London.

The second richest member of the club is, however, the most likable of all. He is Bertram Wilberforce Wooster, descendant of the Sieur de Wooster who did his bit in the crusades, and young Bertram retains the strict code of honour handed down from his ancestor, the code of the *preux chevalier*, the gentil parfit knight. Bertie Wooster is, of course, the employer of Jeeves, the supreme gentleman's personal gentleman.

Jeeves made his first appearance in 1917 in the short story 'Extricating Young Gussie' which was part of a collection called *The Man With Two Left Feet*. Wodehouse liked to mock himself for not seeing straight away that he had hit a rich seam with Jeeves, but in fact it was only two years later that he wrote four more stories. From then on he gave the world Jeeves and Wooster right up until his last complete novel, *Aunts Aren't Gentlemen* (1974).

Much has been written about Jeeves. His imperturbability, his omniscience, his unruffled insight, his orotund speech, his infallible way with a quotation . . . in short, his perfection. We all wish, sometimes, that we had such a guide, philosopher and friend. He stands alone. Others abide our question, thou art free, just about sums it up. It would be a pity, however, to overlook the character of Bertie Wooster. You will see from the mixture of complete stories and extracts offered here that Bertie is a great deal more than the silly ass or chinless wonder that people often imagine him to be. That he is loyal, kind, chivalrous, resolute and magnificently sweet-natured is apparent. But is he stupid? Jeeves is

overheard describing him once as 'mentally negligible'.
Perhaps that isn't quite fair. While not intelligent within
the meaning of the act, Bertie is desperate to learn, keen
to assimilate the wisdom of his incomparable teacher. He
does his best, he may only half know the quotations and
allusions with which he peppers his speech, but he is
biddable and anxious to improve his range of reference.
Proximity to the great brain has made him aware of the
possibilities of exerting the cerebellum. When he
struggles with a quotation or a scheme, his friends and
relations will not appreciate the great Jeevesian world
of allusion and 'the psychology of the individual' that
Bertie is trying to enter and will all too readily snap
'Talk, sense, Bertie!' – showing an impatience that we,
as readers, know to be unfair.

It is after all through Bertie's language that we
encounter Jeeves and through his eyes and ears that the
stories work. Wodehouse's genius in this canon lies in his
complete realization of Bertie as first-person narrator.
All the other stories (with the exception of Ukridge)
depend upon standard impersonal narration. The
particular joy of a Jeeves story derives from the delicious
feeling one derives from being completely in Bertie's
hands. His apparently confused way of expressing himself
both reveals character and manages, somehow, to
develop narrative with extraordinary economy and life.
Since the Jeeves stories often lead one from the other,
he will often need to repeat himself, which he manages
to do with great ingenuity. He is called upon more than
once, for example, to remind the reader about the dread
daughter of Sir Roderick Glossop. The first example
shows Bertie's way with Victorian poetry (in this case the
fragrant Felicia D. Hemans):

> I once got engaged to his daughter Honoria, a ghastly
> dynamic exhibit who read Nietzsche and had a laugh
> like waves breaking on a stern and rockbound coast.

Another description of precisely the same characteristics in Honoria gives us a very Woosteresque mixture of simile:

> Honoria . . . is one of those robust, dynamic girls with the muscles of a welter-weight and a laugh like a squadron of cavalry charging over a tin bridge.

Sometimes Bertie's speech moves towards a form of comic imagery so perfect that one could honestly call it poetic:

> As a rule, you see, I'm not lugged into Family Rows. On the occasions when Aunt is calling to Aunt like mastodons bellowing across primeval swamps . . . the clan has a tendency to ignore me.

Or . . .

> I turned to Aunt Agatha, whose demeanor was rather like that of one who, picking daisies on the railway, has just caught the Down express in the small of the back.

Included in this selection of Jeeves stories – how could it not be? – is the masterly episode where Gussie Fink-Nottle presents the prizes at Market Snodsbury grammar school. This scene is frequently included in general collections of great comic literature and has often been described as the single funniest piece of sustained writing in the language. I would urge you, however, when you have read it, to head straight for a library or bookshop and get hold of the complete novel *Right Ho, Jeeves* where you will encounter it again, fully in context, and find that it leaps even more magnificently to life.

Throughout his life, Wodehouse continued to write golfing stories. Many are collected in two books, *The Clicking of Cuthbert* and *The Heart of a Goof*. Narrated, usually to a reluctant listener, by the Oldest Member of an unnamed golf club, they stand as surely the finest collection of stories about the game ever written. Even if you are not a golfing fan and understand very little of the rules, you will find them intensely readable, with every Wodehousian quality fully realized in them. You don't, after all, get much better than this:

> The least thing upsets him on the links. He misses
> short putts because of the uproar of the butterflies in
> the adjoining meadows.

Another strand of short stories is found in the Mulliner books. Mr Mulliner is the equable, charming raconteur of The Angler's Rest, a public house situated, one imagines, on the River Thames. Mulliner appears to have an almost inexhaustible supply of young relatives (some of whom are also golfers and members of the Drones Club) whose adventures form amongst the very best examples of the art of the short story. You will see from two of the stories included here that Wodehouse, while primarily associated with England, also wrote knowledgeably about Hollywood.

I mentioned at the beginning of this introduction that the Berlin broadcasts were the only really controversial episode in Wodehouse's life. This isn't strictly true. In 1931 he caused all hell to break loose in Hollywood when he gave (again in all innocence) an interview on his life there as a writer. He had initially been invited over to the West Coast, with the offer of a princely salary, to work on screenplays. He tinkered on one script, for a film called *Rosalie*, for months and months, drawing the salary, and quietly getting on with his books and proper writing. He was foolish enough to mention this to the *Los Angeles Times* as well as disclosing the full amount he had been paid for doing virtually nothing – $104,000.

> It amazes me. They paid me $2,000 a week – and I

cannot see what they engaged me for. They were extremely nice to me, but I feel as if I have cheated them.

This endearingly frank interview was reported in the New York press. The East Coast banks that payrolled Hollywood had been itching for an excuse to control the excesses of the movie business and Wodehouse's words, it seems, became the catalyst that forced Hollywood to get out the broom and sweep itself clean. As Wodehouse's biographer, Frances Donaldson, puts it:

> . . . it has since become part of Hollywood legend, that this interview galvanized the bankers who supported the film industry into action to ensure reform – that single-handed Plum [Wodehouse's nick-name, a contraction of Pelham] rang the death-knell of all those ludicrous practices.

You would think that the satire in his short stories would have done that work on its own, but it has ever been the fate of satire that it changes nothing.

Hollywood was not the only wing of the entertainment industry that had benefited from Wodehouses's attention. To many admirers of musical comedy who have never read a novel or short story in their lives, Wodehouse has a permanent place in history as a lyricist and book writer of musicals. With his friend Guy Bolton, Wodehouse collaborated on dozens of musical comedies and straight plays. Dorothy Parker once described a Bolton-Wodehouse musical as her 'favourite indoor sport'. He wrote for some of the greatest names in Tin Pan Alley history, such as Romberg, Kern and Gershwin and liked to say that the royalties from his lyrics for 'Just My Bill' alone, a song which Jerome Kern incorporated into *Showboat*, were enough to keep him in tobacco and whisky for the rest of his life. It is fitting then that this collection should include some of his writings on the subject of theatre as well as some of the lighter verse which reveals the qualities that attracted him to the great song writers of the age.

I think I should end on a personal note. I have written it before and am not ashamed to write it again. Without Wodehouse I am not sure that I would be a tenth of what I am today – whatever that may be. In my teenage years the writings of P. G. Wodehouse awoke me to the possibilities of language. His rhythms, tropes, tricks and mannerisms are deep within me. But more than that he taught me something about good nature. It *is* enough to be benign, to be gentle, to be funny, to be kind. He mocked himself sometimes because he knew that a great proportion of his readers came from prisons and hospitals. At the risk of being sententious, isn't it true that we are all of us, for a great part of our lives, sick or imprisoned, all of us in need of this remarkable healing spirit, this balm for hurt minds?

I was fortunate enough to have received two letters and a signed photograph from the great man. I am looking at the latter now. Beneath the familiar bald head and benign grin is written in blue-black ink: 'To Stephen Fry, All the best, P. G. Wodehouse'.

Well, that is what we hope to offer you with this book: All the best.

STEPHEN FRY

Uncle Fred Flits By
(from *Young Men in Spats*)

Uncle Fred Flits By

In order that they might enjoy their afternoon luncheon coffee in peace, the Crumpet had taken the guest whom he was entertaining at the Drones Club to the smaller and less frequented of the two smoking-rooms. In the other, he explained, though the conversation always touched an exceptionally high level of brilliance, there was apt to be a good deal of sugar thrown about.

The guest said he understood.

'Young blood, eh?'

'That's right. Young blood.'

'And animal spirits.'

'And animal, as you say, spirits,' agreed the Crumpet. 'We get a fairish amount of those here.'

'The complaint, however, is not, I observe, universal.'

'Eh?'

The other drew his host's attention to the doorway, where a young man in form-fitting tweeds had just appeared. The aspect of this young man was haggard. His eyes glared wildly and he sucked at an empty cigarette-holder. If he had a mind, there was something on it. When the Crumpet called to him to come and join the party, he merely shook his head in a distraught sort of way and disappeared, looking like a character out of a Greek tragedy pursued by the Fates.

The Crumpet sighed. 'Poor old Pongo!'

'Pongo?'

'That was Pongo Twistleton. He's all broken up about his Uncle Fred.'

'Dead?'

3

'No such luck. Coming up to London again tomorrow. Pongo had a wire this morning.'

'And that upsets him?'

'Naturally. After what happened last time.'

'What was that?'

'Ah!' said the Crumpet.

'What happened last time?'

'You may well ask.'

'I do ask.'

'Ah!' said the Crumpet.

Poor old Pongo (said the Crumpet) has often discussed his Uncle Fred with me, and if there weren't tears in his eyes when he did so, I don't know a tear in the eye when I see one. In round numbers the Earl of Ickenham, of Ickenham Hall, Ickenham, Hants, lives in the country most of the year, but from time to time has a nasty way of slipping his collar and getting loose and descending upon Pongo at his flat in the Albany. And every time he does so, the unhappy young blighter is subjected to some soul-testing experience. Because the trouble with this uncle is that, though sixty if a day, he becomes on arriving in the metropolis as young as he feels – which is, apparently, a youngish twenty-two. I don't know if you happen to know what the word 'excesses' means, but those are what Pongo's Uncle Fred from the country, when in London, invariably commits.

It wouldn't so much matter, mind you, if he would confine his activities to the club premises. We're pretty broad-minded here, and if you stop short of smashing the piano, there isn't much that you can do at the Drones that will cause the raised eyebrow and the sharp intake of breath. The snag is that he will insist on lugging Pongo out in the open and there, right in the public eye, proceeding to step high, wide and plentiful.

So when, on the occasion to which I allude, he stood pink and genial on Pongo's hearth-rug, bulging with

Pongo's lunch and wreathed in the smoke of one of Pongo's cigars, and said: 'And now, my boy, for a pleasant and instructive afternoon,' you will readily understand why the unfortunate young clam gazed at him as he would have gazed at two-penn'orth of dynamite, had he discovered it lighting up in his presence.

'A what?' he said, giving at the knees and paling beneath the tan a bit.

'A pleasant and instructive afternoon,' repeated Lord Ickenham, rolling the words round his tongue. 'I propose that you place yourself in my hands and leave the programme entirely to me.'

Now, owing to Pongo's circumstances being such as to necessitate his getting into the aged relative's ribs at intervals and shaking him down for an occasional much-needed tenner or what not, he isn't in a position to use the iron hand with the old buster. But at these words he displayed a manly firmness.

'You aren't going to get me to the Dog Races again.'

'No, no.'

'You remember what happened last June.'

'Quite,' said Lord Ickenham, 'quite. Though I still think that a wiser magistrate would have been content with a mere reprimand.'

'And I won't – '

'Certainly not. Nothing of that kind at all. What I propose to do this afternoon is to take you to visit the home of your ancestors.'

Pongo did not get this.

'I thought Ickenham was the home of my ancestors.'

'It is one of the homes of your ancestors. They also resided rather nearer the heart of things, at a place called Mitching Hill.'

'Down in the suburbs, do you mean?'

'The neighbourhood is now suburban, true. It is many years since the meadows where I sported as a child were sold and cut up into building lots. But when I was a boy

5

Mitching Hill was open country. It was a vast, rolling estate belonging to your great-uncle, Marmaduke, a man with whiskers of a nature which you with your pure mind would scarcely credit, and I have long felt a sentimental urge to see what the hell the old place looks like now. Perfectly foul, I expect. Still I think we should make the pious pilgrimage.'

Pongo absolutely-ed heartily. He was all for the scheme. A great weight seemed to have rolled off his mind. The way he looked at it was that even an uncle within a short jump of the looney bin couldn't very well get into much trouble in a suburb. I mean, you know what suburbs are. They don't, as it were, offer the scope. One follows his reasoning, of course.

'Fine!' he said. 'Splendid! Topping!'

'Then put on your hat and rompers, my boy,' said Lord Ickenham, 'and let us be off. I fancy one gets there by omnibuses and things.'

Well, Pongo hadn't expected much in the way of mental uplift from the sight of Mitching Hill, and he didn't get it. Alighting from the bus, he tells me, you found yourself in the middle of rows and rows of semi-detached villas, all looking exactly alike, and you went on and you came to more semi-detached villas, and those all looked exactly alike, too. Nevertheless, he did not repine. It was one of those early spring days which suddenly change to mid-winter and he had come out without his overcoat, and it looked like rain and he hadn't an umbrella, but despite this his mood was one of sober ecstasy. The hours were passing and his uncle had not yet made a goat of himself. At the Dog Races the other had been in the hands of the constabulary in the first ten minutes.

It began to seem to Pongo that with any luck he might be able to keep the old blister pottering harmlessly about here till nightfall, when he could shoot a bit of dinner into him and put him to bed. And as Lord Ickenham had

6

specifically stated that his wife, Pongo's Aunt Jane,
had expressed her intention of scalping him with a blunt
knife if he wasn't back at the Hall by lunch time on the
morrow, it really looked as if he might get through this
visit without perpetrating a single major outrage on the
public weal. It is rather interesting to note that as he
thought this Pongo smiled, because it was the last time
he smiled that day.

All this while, I should mention, Lord Ickenham had
been stopping at intervals like a pointing dog and saying
that it must have been just about here that he plugged
the gardener in the trousers seat with his bow and arrow
and that over there he had been sick after his first cigar,
and he now paused in front of a villa which for some
unknown reason called itself The Cedars. His face was
tender and wistful.

'On this very spot, if I am not mistaken,' he said,
heaving a bit of a sigh, 'on this very spot, fifty years ago
come Lammas Eve, I . . . Oh, blast it!'

The concluding remark had been caused by the fact
that the rain, which had held off until now, suddenly
began to buzz down like a shower-bath. With no further
words, they leaped into the porch of the villa and there
took shelter, exchanging glances with a grey parrot which
hung in a cage in the window.

Not that you could really call it shelter. They were
protected from above all right, but the moisture was
now falling with a sort of swivel action, whipping in
through the sides of the porch and tickling them up
properly. And it was just after Pongo had turned up his
collar and was huddling against the door that the door
gave way. From the fact that a female of general-servant
aspect was standing there he gathered that his uncle
must have rung the bell.

This female wore a long mackintosh, and Lord
Ickenham beamed upon her with a fairish spot of suavity.

'Good afternoon,' he said.

The female said good afternoon.

'The Cedars?'

'The female said yes, it was The Cedars.

'Are the old folks at home?'

The female said there was nobody at home.

'Ah? Well, never mind. I have come,' said Lord Ickenham, edging in, 'to clip the parrot's claws. My assistant, Mr Walkinshaw, who applies the anaesthetic,' he added, indicating Pongo with a gesture.

'Are you from the bird shop?'

'A very happy guess.'

'Nobody told me you were coming.'

'They keep things from you, do they?' said Lord Ickenham, sympathetically. 'Too bad.'

Continuing to edge, he had got into the parlour by now, Pongo following in a sort of dream and the female following Pongo.

'Well, I suppose it's all right,' she said. 'I was just going out. It's my afternoon.'

'Go out,' said Lord Ickenham cordially. 'By all means go out. We will leave everything in order.'

And presently the female, though still a bit on the dubious side, pushed off, and Lord Ickenham lit the gas-fire and drew a chair up.

'So here we are my boy,' he said. 'A little tact, a little address, and here we are, snug and cosy and not catching our deaths of cold. You'll never go far wrong if you leave things to me.'

'But, dash it, we can't stop here,' said Pongo.

Lord Ickenham raised his eyebrows.

'Not stop here? Are you suggesting that we go out into that rain? My dear lad, you are not aware of the grave issues involved. This morning, as I was leaving home, I had a rather painful disagreement with your aunt. She said the weather was treacherous and wished me to take my woolly muffler. I replied that the weather was not treacherous and that I would be dashed if I took my woolly

8

muffler. Eventually, by the exercise of an iron will, I had my way, and I ask you, my dear boy, to envisage what will happen if I return with a cold in the head. I shall sink to the level of a fifth-class power. Next time I came to London, it would be with a liver pad and a respirator. No! I shall remain here, toasting my toes at this really excellent fire. I had no idea that a gas-fire radiated such warmth. I feel all in a glow.'

So did Pongo. His brow was wet with honest sweat. He is reading for the Bar, and while he would be the first to admit that he hasn't yet got a complete toe-hold on the Law of Great Britain he had a sort of notion that oiling into a perfect stranger's semi-detached villa on the pretext of pruning the parrot was a tort or misdemeanour, if not actual barratry or socage in fief or something like that. And apart from the legal aspect of the matter there was the embarrassment of the thing. Nobody is more of a whale on correctness and not doing what's not done than Pongo, and the situation in which he now found himself caused him to chew the lower lip and, as I say, perspire a goodish deal.

'But suppose the blighter who owns this ghastly house comes back?' he asked. 'Talking of envisaging things, try that one over on your pianola.'

And, sure enough, as he spoke, the front door-bell rang.

'There!' said Pongo.

'Don't say "There!" my boy,' said Lord Ickenham reprovingly. 'It's the sort of thing your aunt says. I see no reason for alarm. Obviously this is some casual caller. A ratepayer would have used his latchkey. Glance cautiously out of the window and see if you can see anybody.'

'It's a pink chap,' said Pongo, having done so.

'How pink?'

'Pretty pink.'

'Well, there you are, then. I told you so. It can't be the big chief. The sort of fellows who own houses like this are pale and sallow, owing to working in offices all day. Go and see what he wants.'

'You go and see what he wants.'

'We'll both go and see what he wants,' said Lord Ickenham.

So they went and opened the front door, and there, as Pongo had said, was a pink chap. A small young pink chap, a bit moist about the shoulder-blades.

'Pardon me,' said this pink chap, 'is Mr Roddis in?'

'No,' said Pongo.

'Yes,' said Lord Ickenham. 'Don't be silly, Douglas – of course I'm in. I am Mr Roddis,' he said to the pink chap. 'This, such as he is, is my son Douglas. And you?'

'Name of Robinson.'

'What about it?'

'My name's Robinson.'

'Oh, *your* name's Robinson? Now we've got it straight. Delighted to see you, Mr Robinson. Come right in and take your boots off.'

They all trickled back to the parlour, Lord Ickenham pointing out objects of interest by the wayside to the chap, Pongo gulping for air a bit and trying to get himself abreast of this new twist in the scenario. His heart was becoming more and more bowed down with weight of woe. He hadn't liked being Mr Walkinshaw, the anaesthetist, and he didn't like it any better being Roddis Junior. In brief, he feared the worst. It was only too plain to him by now that his uncle had got it thoroughly up his nose and had settled down to one of his big afternoons, and he was asking himself, as he had so often asked himself before, what would the harvest be?

Arrived in the parlour, the pink chap proceeded to stand on one leg and look coy.

'Is Julia here?' he asked, simpering a bit, Pongo says.

'Is she?' said Lord Ickenham to Pongo.

'No,' said Pongo.

'No,' said Lord Ickenham.

'She wired me she was coming here today.'

'Ah, then we shall have a bridge four.'

The pink chap stood on the other leg.

'I don't suppose you've ever met Julia. Bit of trouble in the family, she gave me to understand.'

'It is often the way.'

'The Julia I mean is your niece Julia Parker. Or, rather, your wife's niece Julia Parker.'

'Any niece of my wife is a niece of mine,' said Lord Ickenham heartily. 'We share and share alike.'

'Julia and I want to get married.'

'Well, go ahead.'

'But they won't let us.'

'Who won't?'

'Her mother and father. And Uncle Charlie Parker and Uncle Henry Parker and the rest of them. They don't think I'm good enough.'

'The morality of the modern young man is notoriously lax.'

'Class enough, I mean. They're a haughty lot.'

'What makes them haughty? Are they earls?'

'No, they aren't earls.'

'Then why the devil,' said Lord Ickenham warmly, 'are they haughty? Only earls have a right to be haughty. Earls are hot stuff. When you get an earl, you've got something.'

'Besides, we've had words. Me and her father. One thing led to another, and in the end I called him a perishing old – Coo!' said the pink chap, breaking off suddenly.

He had been standing by the window, and he now leaped lissomely into the middle of the room, causing Pongo, whose nervous system was by this time definitely down among the wines and spirits and who hadn't been expecting this *adagio* stuff, to bite his tongue with some severity.

11

'They're on the doorstep! Julia and her mother and father. I didn't know they were all coming.'

'You do not wish to meet them?'

'No, I don't!'

'Then duck behind the settee, Mr Robinson,' said Lord Ickenham, and the pink chap, weighing the advice and finding it good, did so. And as he disappeared the doorbell rang.

Once more, Lord Ickenham led Pongo out into the hall.

'I say!' said Pongo, and a close observer might have noted that he was quivering like an aspen.

'Say on, my dear boy.'

'I mean to say, what?'

'What?'

'You aren't going to let these bounders in, are you?'

'Certainly,' said Lord Ickenham. 'We Roddises keep open house. And as they are presumably aware that Mr Roddis has no son, I think we had better return to the old layout. You are the local vet, my boy, come to minister to my parrot. When I return, I should like to find you by the cage, staring at the bird in a scientific manner. Tap your teeth from time to time with a pencil and try to smell of iodoform. It will help to add conviction.'

So Pongo shifted back to the parrot's cage and stared so earnestly that it was only when a voice said 'Well!' that he became aware that there was anybody in the room. Turning, he perceived that Hampshire's leading curse had come back, bringing the gang.

It consisted of a stern, thin, middle-aged woman, a middle-aged man and a girl.

You can generally accept Pongo's estimate of girls, and when he says that this one was a pippin one knows that he uses the term in its most exact sense. She was about nineteen, he thinks, and she wore a black beret, a dark-green leather coat, a shortish tweed skirt, silk stockings and high-heeled shoes. Her eyes were large and

lustrous and her face like a dewy rosebud at daybreak on
a June morning. So Pongo tells me. Not that I suppose
he has ever seen a rosebud at daybreak on a June morning,
because it's generally as much as you can do to lug him
out of bed in time for nine-thirty breakfast. Still, one gets
the idea.

'Well,' said the woman, 'you don't know who I am, I'll
be bound. I'm Laura's sister Connie. This is Claude, my
husband. And this is my daughter Julia. Is Laura in?'

'I regret to say, no,' said Lord Ickenham.

The woman was looking at him as if he didn't come
up to her specifications.

'I thought you were younger,' she said.

'Younger than what?' said Lord Ickenham.

'Younger than you are.'

'You can't be younger than you are, worse luck,' said
Lord Ickenham. 'Still, one does one's best, and I am
bound to say that of recent years I have made a pretty
good go of it.'

The woman caught sight of Pongo, and he didn't seem
to please her, either.

'Who's that?'

'The local vet, clustering round my parrot.'

'I can't talk in front of him.'

'It is quite all right,' Lord Ickenham assured her. 'The
poor fellow is stone deaf.'

And with an imperious gesture at Pongo, as much as
to bid him stare less at girls and more at parrots, he got the
company seated.

'Now, then,' he said.

There was silence for a moment, then a sort of muffled
sob, which Pongo thinks proceeded from the girl. He
couldn't see, of course, because his back was turned and
he was looking at the parrot, which looked back at him
– most offensively, he says, as parrots will, using one eye
only for the purpose. It also asked him to have a nut.

The woman came into action again.

'Although,' she said, 'Laura never did me the honour to invite me to her wedding, for which reason I have not communicated with her for five years, necessity compels me to cross her threshold today. There comes a time when differences must be forgotten and relatives must stand shoulder to shoulder.'

'I see what you mean,' said Lord Ickenham. 'Like the boys of the old brigade.'

'What I say is, let bygones be bygones. I would not have intruded on you, but needs must. I disregard the past and appeal to your sense of pity.'

The thing began to look to Pongo like a touch, and he is convinced that the parrot thought so, too, for it winked and cleared its throat. But they were both wrong. The woman went on.

'I want you and Laura to take Julia into your home for a week or so, until I can make other arrangements for her. Julia is studying the piano, and she sits for the examination in two weeks' time, so until then she must remain in London. The trouble is, she has fallen in love. Or thinks she has.'

'I know I have,' said Julia.

Her voice was so attractive that Pongo was compelled to slew round and take another look at her. Her eyes, he says, were shining like twin stars and there was a sort of Soul's Awakening expression on her face, and what the dickens there was in a pink chap like the pink chap, who even as pink chaps go wasn't much of a pink chap, to make her look alike that, was frankly, Pongo says, more than he could understand. The thing baffled him. He sought in vain for a solution.

'Yesterday, Claude and I arrived in London from our Bexhill home to give Julia a pleasant surprise. We stayed, naturally, in the boarding-house where she has been living for the past six weeks. And what do you think we discovered?'

'Insects.'

'Not insects. A letter. From a young man. I found to my horror that a young man of whom I knew nothing was arranging to marry my daughter. I sent for him immediately, and found him to be quite impossible. He jellies eels!'

'Does what?'

'He is an assistant at a jellied eel shop.'

'But surely,' said Lord Ickenham, 'that speaks well for him. The capacity to jelly an eel seems to me to argue intelligence of a high order. It isn't everybody who can do it, by any means. I know if someone came to me and said 'Jelly this eel!' I should be nonplussed. And so, or I am very much mistaken, would Ramsay MacDonald and Winston Churchill.'

The woman did not seem to see eye to eye.

'Tchah!' she said. 'What do you suppose my husband's brother Charlie Parker would say if I allowed his niece to marry a man who jellies eels?'

'Ah!' said Claude, who, before we go any further, was a tall, drooping bird with a red soup-strainer moustache.

'Or my husband's brother, Henry Parker.'

'Ah!' said Claude. 'Or Cousin Alf Robbins, for that matter.'

'Exactly. Cousin Alfred would die of shame.'

The girl Julia hiccoughed passionately, so much so that Pongo says it was all he could do to stop himself nipping across and taking her hand in his and patting it.

'I've told you a hundred times, mother, that Wilberforce is only jellying eels till he finds something better.'

'What is better than an eel?' asked Lord Ickenham, who had been following this discussion with the close attention it deserved. 'For jellying purposes, I mean.'

'He is ambitious. It won't be long,' said the girl, 'before Wilberforce suddenly rises in the world.'

She never spoke a truer word. At this very moment, up he came from behind the settee like a leaping salmon.

'Julia!' he cried.

'Wilby!' yipped the girl.

And Pongo says he never saw anything more sickening
in his life than the way she flung herself into the
blighter's arms and clung there like the ivy on the old
garden wall. It wasn't that he had anything specific
against the pink chap, but this girl had made a deep
impression on him and he resented her glueing herself
to another in this manner.

Julia's mother, after just that brief moment which a
woman needs in which to recover from her natural
surprise at seeing eel-jelliers pop up from behind sofas,
got moving and plucked her away like a referee breaking
a couple of welter-weights.

'Julia Parker,' she said, 'I'm ashamed of you!'

'So am I,' said Claude.

'I blush for you.'

'Me, too,' said Claude. 'Hugging and kissing a man
who called your father a perishing old bottle-nosed
Gawd-help-us.'

'I think,' said Lord Ickenham, shoving his oar in, 'that
before proceeding any further we ought to go into
that point. If he called you a perishing old bottle-nosed
Gawd-help-us, it seems to me that the first thing to do
is to decide whether he was right, and frankly, in my
opinion.

'Wilberforce will apologize.'

'Certainly I'll apologize. It isn't fair to hold a remark
passed in the heat of the moment against a chap . . .'

'Mr Robinson,' said the woman, 'you know perfectly
well that whatever remarks you may have seen fit to
pass don't matter one way or the other. If you were
listening to what I was saying you will understand . . .'

'Oh, I know, I know. Uncle Charlie Parker and Uncle
Henry Parker and Cousin Alf Robbins and all that. Pack
of snobs!'

'What!'

'Haughty, stuck-up snobs. Them and their class distinction. Think themselves everybody just because they've got money. I'd like to know how they got it.'

'What do you mean by that?'

'Never mind what I mean.'

'If you are insinuating – '

'Well, of course, you know, Connie,' said Lord Ickenham mildly, 'he's quite right. You can't get away from that.'

I don't know if you have ever seen a bull-terrier embarking on a scrap with an Airedale and just as it was getting down nicely to its work suddenly having an unexpected Kerry Blue sneak up behind it and bite it in the rear quarters. When this happens, it lets go of the Airedale and swivels round and fixes the butting-in animal with a pretty nasty eye. It was exactly the same with the woman Connie when Lord Ickenham spoke these words.

'What!'

'I was only wondering if you had forgotten how Charlie Parker made his pile.'

'What are you talking about?'

'I know it is painful,' said Lord Ickenham, 'and one doesn't mention it as a rule, but, as we are on the subject, you must admit that lending money at two hundred and fifty per cent interest is not done in the best circles. The judge, if you remember, said so at the trial.'

'I never knew that!' cried Julia.

'Ah,' said Lord Ickenham. 'You kept it from the child? Quite right, quite right.'

'It's a lie!'

'And when Henry Parker had all that fuss with the bank it was touch and go they didn't send him to prison. Between ourselves, Connie, has a bank official, even a brother of your husband, any right to sneak fifty pounds from the till in order to put it on a hundred-to-one shot for the Grand National? Not quite playing the game, Connie. Not the straight bat. Henry, I grant you, won five thousand of the best and never looked back afterwards, but, though we applaud his judgement of form, we must surely look askance at his financial methods. As for Cousin Alf Robbins . . .'

The woman was making rummy stuttering sounds. Pongo tells me he once had a Pommery Seven which used to express itself in much the same way if you tried to get it to take a hill on high. A sort of mixture of gurgles and explosions.

'There is not a word of truth in this,' she gasped at length, having managed to get the vocal cords disentangled. 'Not a single word. I think you must have gone mad.'

Lord Ickenham shrugged his shoulders.

'Have it your own way, Connie. I was only going to say that, while the jury were probably compelled on the evidence submitted to them to give Cousin Alf Robbins the benefit of the doubt when charged with smuggling dope, everybody knew that he had been doing it for years. I am not blaming him, mind you. If a man can smuggle cocaine and get away with it, good luck to him, say I. The only point I am trying to make is that we are hardly a family that can afford to put on dog and sneer at honest suitors for our daughters' hands. Speaking for myself, I consider that we are very lucky to have the chance of marrying even into eel-jellying circles.'

'So do I,' said Julia firmly.

'You don't believe what this man is saying?'

'I believe every word.'

'So do I,' said the pink chap.

The woman snorted. She seemed over-wrought.

'Well,' she said, 'goodness knows I have never liked Laura, but I would never have wished her a husband like you!'

'Husband?' said Lord Ickenham, puzzled. 'What gives you the impression that Laura and I are married?'

There was a weighty silence, during which the parrot

threw out a general invitation to join it in a nut. Then
the girl Julia spoke.

'You'll have to let me marry Wilberforce now,' she
said. 'He knows too much about us.'

'I was rather thinking that myself,' said Lord
Ickenham. 'Seal his lips, I say.'

'You wouldn't mind marrying into a low family, would
you, darling?' asked the girl, with a touch of anxiety.

'No family could be too low for me, dearest, if it was
yours,' said the pink chap.

'After all, we needn't see them.'

'That's right.'

'It isn't one's relations that matter: it's oneselves.'

'That's right, too.'

'Wilby!'

'Julia!'

They repeated the old ivy on the garden wall act. Pongo
says he didn't like it any better than the first time, but
his distaste wasn't in it with the woman Connie's.

'And what, may I ask,' she said, 'do you propose to
marry on?'

This seemed to cast a damper. They came apart. They
looked at each other. The girl looked at the pink chap,
and the pink chap looked at the girl. You could see that a
jarring note had been struck.

'Wilberforce is going to be a very rich man some day.'

'Some day!'

'If I had a hundred pounds,' said the pink chap, 'I could
buy a half-share in one of the best milk walks in South
London tomorrow.'

'If!' said the woman.

'Ah!' said Claude.

'Where are you going to get it?'

'Ah!' said Claude.

'Where,' repeated the woman, plainly pleased with the
snappy crack and loath to let it ride without an encore,
'are you going to get it?'

'That,' said Claude, 'is the point. Where are you going to get a hundred pounds?'

'Why, bless my soul,' said Lord Ickenham jovially, 'from me, of course. Where else?'

And before Pongo's bulging eyes he fished out from the recesses of his costume a crackling bundle of notes and handed it over. And the agony of realizing that the old bounder had had all that stuff on him all this time and that he hadn't touched him for so much as a tithe of it was so keen, Pongo says, that before he knew what he was doing he had let out a sharp, whinnying cry which rang through the room like the yowl of a stepped-on puppy.

'Ah,' said Lord Ickenham. 'The vet wishes to speak to me. Yes, vet?'

This seemed to puzzle the cerise bloke a bit.

'I thought you said this chap was your son.'

'If I had a son,' said Lord Ickenham, a little hurt, 'he would be a good deal better-looking than that. No, this is the local veterinary surgeon. I may have said I *looked* on him as a son. Perhaps that was what confused you.'

He shifted across to Pongo and twiddled his hands enquiringly. Pongo gaped at him, and it was not until one of the hands caught him smartly in the lower ribs that he remembered he was deaf and started to twiddle back. Considering that he wasn't supposed to be dumb, I can't see why he should have twiddled, but no doubt there are moments when twiddling is about all a fellow feels himself equal to. For what seemed to him at least ten hours Pongo had been undergoing great mental stress, and one can't blame him for not being chatty. Anyway, be that as it may, he twiddled.

'I cannot quite understand what he says,' announced Lord Ickenham at length, 'because he sprained a finger this morning and that makes him stammer. But I gather that he wishes to have a word with me in private. Possibly my parrot has got something the matter with it which he is reluctant to mention even in sign language in front of a young unmarried girl. You know what parrots are. We will step outside.'

'*We* will step outside,' said Wilberforce.

'Yes,' said the girl Julia. 'I feel like a walk.'

'And you,' said Lord Ickenham to the woman Connie, who was looking like a female Napoleon at Moscow. 'Do you join the hikers?'

'I shall remain and make myself a cup of tea. You will not grudge us a cup of tea, I hope?'

'Far from it,' said Lord Ickenham cordially. 'This is Liberty Hall. Stick around and mop it up till your eyes bubble.'

Outside, the girl, looking more like a dewy rosebud than ever, fawned on the old buster pretty considerably.

'I don't know how to thank you!' she said. And the pink chap said he didn't, either.

'Not at all, my dear, not at all,' said Lord Ickenham.

'I think you're simply wonderful.'

'No, no.'

'You are. Perfectly marvellous.'

'Tut, tut,' said Lord Ickenham. 'Don't give the matter another thought.'

He kissed her on both cheeks, the chin, the forehead, the right eyebrow, and the tip of the nose, Pongo looking on the while in a baffled and discontented manner. Everybody seemed to be kissing this girl except him.

Eventually the degrading spectacle ceased and the girl and the pink chap shoved off, and Pongo was enabled to take up the matter of that hundred quid.

'Where,' he asked, 'did you get all that money?'

'Now, where did I?' mused Lord Ickenham. 'I know your aunt gave it to me for some purpose. But what? To pay some bill or other, I rather fancy.'

This cheered Pongo up slightly.

'She'll give you the devil when you get back,' he said, with not a little relish. 'I wouldn't be in your shoes for

something. When you tell Aunt Jane,' he said, with
confidence, for he knew his Aunt Jane's emotional
nature, 'that you slipped her entire roll to a girl, and
explain, as you will have to explain, that she was an
extraordinarily pretty girl – a girl, in fine, who looked like
something out of a beauty chorus of the better sort, I
should think she would pluck down one of the ancestral
battle-axes from the wall and jolly well strike you on
the mazzard.'

'Have no anxiety, my dear boy,' said Lord Ickenham.
'It is like your kind heart to be so concerned, but have
no anxiety. I shall tell her that I was compelled to give
the money to you to enable you to buy back some
compromising letters from a Spanish *demi-mondaine*.
She will scarcely be able to blame me for rescuing a
fondly loved nephew from the clutches of an adventuress.
It may be that she will feel a little vexed with you for a
while, and that you may have to allow a certain time to
elapse before you visit Ickenham again, but then I shan't
be wanting you at Ickenham till the ratting season starts,
so all is well.'

At this moment, there came toddling up to the gate of
The Cedars a large red-faced man. He was just going in
when Lord Ickenham hailed him.

'Mr Roddis?'

'Hey?'

'Am I addressing Mr Roddis?'

'That's me.'

'I am Mr J. G. Bulstrode from down the road,' said Lord
Ickenham. 'This is my sister's husband's brother, Percy
Frensham in the lard and imported-butter business.

The red-faced bird said he was pleased to meet them.
He asked Pongo if things were brisk in the lard and
imported-butter business, and Pongo said they were all
right, and the red-faced bird said he was glad to hear it.

'We have never met, Mr Roddis,' said Lord Ickenham,
'but I think it would be only neighbourly to inform you

that a short while ago I observed two suspicious-looking persons in your house.'

'In my house? How on earth did they get there?'

'No doubt through a window at the back. They looked to me like cat burglars. If you creep up, you may be able to see them.'

The red-faced bird crept, and came back not exactly foaming at the mouth but with the air of a man who for two pins would so foam.

'You're perfectly right. They're sitting in my parlour as cool as dammit, swigging my tea and buttered toast.'

'I thought as much.'

'And they've opened a pot of my raspberry jam.'

'Ah, then you will be able to catch them red-handed. I should fetch a policeman.'

'I will. Thank you, Mr Bulstrode.'

'Only too glad to have been able to render you this little service, Mr Roddis,' said Lord Ickenham. 'Well, I must be moving. I have an appointment. Pleasant after the rain, is it not? Come, Percy.'

He lugged Pongo off.

'So that,' he said, with satisfaction, 'is that. On these visits of mine to the metropolis, my boy, I always make it my aim, if possible, to spread sweetness and light. I look about me, even in a foul hole like Mitching Hill, and I ask myself – How can I leave this foul hole a better and happier foul hole than I found it? And if I see a chance, I grab it. Here is our omnibus. Spring aboard, my boy, and on our way home we will be sketching out rough plans for the evening. If the old Leicester Grill is still in existence, we might look in there. It must be fully thirty-five years since I was last thrown out of the Leicester Grill. I wonder who is the bouncer there now.'

Such (concluded the Crumpet) is Pongo Twistleton's Uncle Fred from the country, and you will have gathered by now a rough notion of why it is that when a telegram comes announcing his impending arrival in the great city Pongo blenches to the core and calls for a couple of quick ones.

The whole situation, Pongo says, is very complex. Looking at it from one angle, it is fine that the man lives in the country most of the year. If he didn't, he would have him in his midst all the time. On the other hand, by living in the country he generates, as it were, a store of loopiness which expends itself with frightful violence on his rare visits to the centre of things.

What it boils down to is this – Is it better to have a loopy uncle whose loopiness is perpetually on tap but spread out thin, so to speak, or one who lies low in distant Hants for three hundred and sixty days in the year and does himself proud in London for the other five? Dashed moot, of course, and Pongo has never been able to make up his mind on the point.

Naturally, the ideal thing would be if someone would chain the old hound up permanently and keep him from Jan. One to Dec. Thirty-one where he wouldn't do any harm – viz. among the spuds and tenantry. But this, Pongo admits, is a Utopian dream. Nobody could work harder to that end than his Aunt Jane, and she has never been able to manage it.

Jeeves

I — The Great Sermon Handicap

After Goodwood's over, I generally find that I get a bit restless. I'm not much of a lad for the birds and the trees and the great open spaces as a rule, but there's no doubt that London's not at its best in August, and rather tends to give me the pip and make me think of popping down into the country till things have bucked up a trifle. London, about a couple of weeks after that spectacular finish of young Bingo's which I've just been telling you about, was empty and smelled of burning asphalt. All my pals were away, most of the theatres were shut, and they were taking up Piccadilly in large spadefuls.

It was most infernally hot. As I sat in the old flat one night trying to muster up energy enough to go to bed, I felt I couldn't stand it much longer: and when Jeeves came in with the tissue-restorers on a tray I put the thing to him squarely.

'Jeeves,' I said, wiping the brow and gasping like a stranded goldfish, 'it's beastly hot.'

'The weather *is* oppressive, sir.'

'Not all the soda, Jeeves.'

'No, sir.'

'I think we've had about enough of the metrop. for the time being, and require a change. Shift-ho, I think, Jeeves, what?'

'Just as you say, sir. There is a letter on the tray, sir.'

'By Jove, Jeeves, that was practically poetry. Rhymed, did you notice?' I opened the letter. 'I say, this is rather extraordinary.'

'Sir?'

'You know Twing Hall?'

'Yes, sir.'

'Well, Mr Little is there.'

'Indeed, sir?'

'Absolutely in the flesh. He's had to take another of those tutoring jobs.'

After that fearful mix-up at Goodwood, when young Bingo Little, a broken man, had touched me for a tenner and whizzed silently off into the unknown, I had been all over the place, asking mutual friends if they had heard anything of him, but nobody had. And all the time he had been at Twing Hall. Rummy. And I'll tell you why it was rummy. Twing Hall belongs to old Lord Wickhammersley, a great pal of my guv'nor's when he was alive, and I have a standing invitation to pop down there when I like. I generally put in a week or two some time in the summer, and I was thinking of going there before I read the letter.

'And what's more, Jeeves, my cousin Claude, and my cousin Eustace – you remember them?'

'Very vividly, sir.'

'Well, they're down there, too, reading for some exam or other with the vicar. I used to read with him myself at one time. He's known far and wide as a pretty hot coach for those of fairly feeble intellect. Well, when I tell you he got *me* through Smalls, you'll gather that he's a bit of a hummer. I call this most extraordinary.'

I read the letter again. It was from Eustace. Claude and Eustace are twins, and more or less generally admitted to be the curse of the human race.

The Vicarage,
Twing, Glos.

DEAR BERTIE – Do you want to make a bit of money? I hear you had a bad Goodwood, so you probably do. Well, come down here quick and get in on the biggest sporting event of the season. I'll explain when I see you, but you can take it from me it's all right.

Claude and I are with a reading-party at old Heppenstall's. There are nine of us, not counting your pal Bingo Little, who is tutoring the kid up at the Hall.

Don't miss this golden opportunity, which may never occur again. Come and join us.

Yours,
Eustace.

I handed this to Jeeves. He studied it thoughtfully.

'What do you make of it? A rummy communication, what?'

'Very high-spirited young gentlemen, sir, Mr Claude and Mr Eustace. Up to some game, I should be disposed to imagine.'

'Yes. But what game, do you think?'

'It is impossible to say, sir. Did you observe that the letter continues over the page?'

'Eh, what?' I grabbed the thing. This was what was on the other side of the last page:

SERMON HANDICAP
RUNNERS AND BETTING
PROBABLE STARTERS

Rev. Joseph Tucker (Badgwick), scratch.
Rev. Leonard Starkie (Stapleton), scratch.
Rev. Alexander Jones (Upper Bingley),
receives three minutes.
Rev. W. Dix (Little Clickton-on-the-Wold),
receives five minutes.
Rev. Francis Heppenstall (Twing),
receives eight minutes.
Rev. Cuthbert Dibble (Boustead Parva),
receives nine minutes.
Rev. Orlo Hough (Boustead Magna),
receives nine minutes.

Rev. J. J. Roberts (Fale-by-the-Water),
receives ten minutes.
Rev. G. Hayward (Lower Bingley), receives twelve
minutes.
Rev. James Bates (Gandle-by-the-Hill), receives fifteen
minutes.

(*The above have arrived.*)

PRICES – 5–2, Tucker, Starkie; 3–1, Jones; 9–2, Dix;
6–1, Heppenstall, Dibble, Hough; 100–8 any other.

It baffled me.

'Do you understand it, Jeeves?'

'No, sir.'

'Well, I think we ought to have a look into it, anyway,
what?'

'Undoubtedly, sir.'

'Right-o, then. Pack our spare dickey and a toothbrush
in a neat brown-paper parcel, send a wire to Lord
Wickhammersley to say we're coming, and buy two
tickets on the five-ten at Paddington tomorrow.'

The five-ten was late as usual, and everybody was dressing
for dinner when I arrived at the Hall. It was only by
getting into my evening things in record time and taking
the stairs to the dining-room in a couple of bounds that
I managed to dead-heat with the soup. I slid into the
vacant chair, and found that I was sitting next to old
Wickhammersley's youngest daughter, Cynthia.

'Oh, hallo, old thing,' I said.

Great pals we've always been. In fact, there was a time
when I had an idea I was in love with Cynthia. However,
it blew over. A dashed pretty and lively and attractive
girl, mind you, but full of ideals and all that. I may be
wronging her, but I have an idea that she's the sort of girl
who would want a fellow to carve out a career and what
not. I know I've heard her speak favourably of Napoleon.

So what with one thing and another the jolly old frenzy sort of petered out, and now we're just pals. I think she's a topper, and she thinks me next door to a loony, so everything's nice and matey.

'Well, Bertie, so you've arrived?'

'Oh, yes, I've arrived. Yes, here I am. I say, I seem to have plunged into the middle of quite a young dinner-party. Who are all these coves?'

'Oh, just people from round about. You know most of them. You remember Colonel Willis, and the Spencers – '

'Of course, yes. And there's old Heppenstall. Who's the other clergyman next to Mrs Spencer?'

'Mr Hayward, from Lower Bingley.'

'What an amazing lot of clergymen there are round here. Why, there's another, next to Mrs Willis.'

'That's Mr Bates, Mr Heppenstall's nephew. He's an assistant-master at Eton. He's down here during the summer holidays, acting as locum tenens for Mr Spettigue, the rector of Gandle-by-the-Hill.'

'I thought I knew his face. He was in his fourth year at Oxford when I was a fresher. Rather a blood. Got his rowing-blue and all that.' I took another look round the table, and spotted young Bingo. 'Ah, there he is,' I said. 'There's the old egg.'

'There's who?'

'Young Bingo Little. Great pal of mine. He's tutoring your brother, you know.'

'Good gracious! Is he a friend of yours?'

'Rather! Known him all my life.'

'Then tell me, Bertie, is he at all weak in the head?'

'Weak in the head?'

'I don't mean simply because he's a friend of yours. But he's so strange in his manner.'

'How do you mean?'

'Well, he keeps looking at me so oddly.'

'Oddly? How? Give me an imitation.'

31

'I can't in front of all these people.'

'Yes, you can. I'll hold my napkin up.'

'All right, then. Quick. There!'

Considering that she had only about a second and a half to do it in, I must say it was a jolly fine exhibition. She opened her mouth and eyes pretty wide and let her jaw drop sideways, and managed to look so like a dyspeptic calf that I recognized the symptoms immediately.

'Oh, that's all right,' I said. 'No need to be alarmed. He's simply in love with you.'

'In love with me. Don't be absurd.'

'My dear old thing, you don't know young Bingo. He can fall in love with *anybody*.'

'Thank you!'

'Oh, I didn't mean it that way, you know. I don't wonder at his taking to you. Why, I was in love with you myself once.'

'Once? Ah! And all that remains now are the cold ashes? This isn't one of your tactful evenings, Bertie.'

'Well, my dear sweet thing, dash it all, considering that you gave me the bird and nearly laughed yourself into a permanent state of hiccoughs when I asked you – '

'Oh, I'm not reproaching you. No doubt there were faults on both sides. He's very good-looking, isn't he?'

'Good-looking? Bingo? Bingo good-looking? No, I say, come now, really!'

'I mean, compared with some people,' said Cynthia.

Some time after this, Lady Wickhammersley gave the signal for the females of the species to leg it, and they duly stampeded. I didn't get a chance of talking to young Bingo when they'd gone, and later, in the drawing-room, he didn't show up. I found him eventually in his room, lying on the bed with his feet on the rail, smoking a toofah. There was a notebook on the counterpane beside him.

'Hallo, old scream,' I said.

'Hallo, Bertie,' he replied, in what seemed to me rather a moody, distrait sort of manner.

'Rummy finding you down here. I take it your uncle cut off your allowance after that Goodwood binge and you had to take this tutoring job to keep the wolf from the door?'

'Correct,' said young Bingo tersely.

'Well, you might have let your pals know where you were.'

He frowned darkly.

'I didn't want them to know where I was. I wanted to creep away and hide myself. I've been through a bad time, Bertie, these last weeks. The sun ceased to shine – '

'That's curious. We've had gorgeous weather in London.'

'The birds ceased to sing – '

'What birds?'

'What the devil does it matter what birds?' said young Bingo, with some asperity. 'Any birds. The birds round about here. You don't expect me to specify them by their pet names, do you? I tell you, Bertie, it hit me hard at first, very hard.'

'What hit you?' I simply couldn't follow the blighter.

'Charlotte's calculated callousness.'

'Oh, ah!' I've seen poor old Bingo through so many unsuccessful love-affairs that I'd almost forgotten there was a girl mixed up with that Goodwood business. Of course! Charlotte Corday Rowbotham. And she had given him the raspberry, I remembered, and gone off with Comrade Butt.

'I went through torments. Recently, however, I've – er – bucked up a bit. Tell me, Bertie, what are you doing down here? I didn't know you knew these people.'

'Me? Why, I've known them since I was a kid.'

Young Bingo put his feet down with a thud.

'Do you mean to say you've known Lady Cynthia all that time?'

'Rather! She can't have been seven when I met her first.'

'Good Lord!' said young Bingo. He looked at me for the first time as though I amounted to something, and swallowed a mouthful of smoke the wrong way. 'I love that girl, Bertie,' he went on, when he'd finished coughing.

'Yes. Nice girl, of course.'

He eyed me with pretty deep loathing.

'Don't speak of her in that horrible casual way. She's an angel. An angel! Was she talking about me at all at dinner, Bertie?'

'Oh, yes.'

'What did she say?'

'I remember one thing. She said she thought you good-looking.'

Young Bingo closed his eyes in a sort of ecstasy. Then he picked up the notebook.

'Pop off now, old man, there's a good chap,' he said in a hushed, far-away voice. 'I've got a bit of writing to do.'

'Writing?'

'Poetry, if you must know. I wish the dickens,' said young Bingo, not without some bitterness, 'she had been christened something except Cynthia. There isn't a dam' word in the language it rhymes with. Ye gods, how I could have spread myself if she had only been called Jane!'

Bright and early next morning, as I lay in bed blinking at the sunlight on the dressing-table and wondering when Jeeves was going to show up with a cup of tea, a heavy weight descended on my toes, and the voice of young Bingo polluted the air. The blighter had apparently risen with the lark.

'Leave me,' I said, 'I would be alone. I can't see anybody till I've had my tea.'

'When Cynthia smiles,' said young Bingo, 'the skies are blue; the world takes on a roseate hue; birds in the

garden trill and sing, and Joy is king of everything, when
Cynthia smiles.' He coughed, changing gears. 'When
Cynthia frowns – '

'What the devil are you talking about?'

'I'm reading you my poem. The one I wrote to Cynthia
last night. I'll go on, shall I?'

'No!'

'No?'

'No. I haven't had my tea.'

At this moment Jeeves came in with the good old
beverage, and I sprang on it with a glad cry. After a couple
of sips things looked a bit brighter. Even young Bingo
didn't offend the eye to quite such an extent. By the time
I'd finished the first cup I was a new man, so much so
that I not only permitted but encouraged the poor fish
to read the rest of the bally thing, and even went so far
as to criticize the scansion of the fourth line of the fifth
verse. We were still arguing the point when the door burst
open and in blew Claude and Eustace. One of the things
which discourages me about rural life is the frightful
earliness with which events begin to break loose. I've
stayed at places in the country where they've jerked me
out of the dreamless at about six-thirty to go for a jolly
swim in the lake. At Twing, thank heaven, they know
me, and let me breakfast in bed.

The twins seemed pleased to see me.

'Good old Bertie!' said Claude.

'Stout fellow!' said Eustace. 'The Rev. told us you had
arrived. I thought that letter of mine would fetch you.'

'You can always bank on Bertie,' said Claude. 'A
sportsman to the finger-tips. Well, has Bingo told you
about it?'

'Not a word. He's been – '

'We've been talking,' said Bingo hastily, 'of other
matters.'

Claude pinched the last slice of thin bread-and-butter,
and Eustace poured himself out a cup of tea.

'It's like this, Bertie,' said Eustace, settling down cosily. 'As I told you in my letter, there are nine of us marooned in this desert spot, reading with old Heppenstall. Well, of course, nothing is jollier than sweating up the Classics when it's a hundred in the shade, but there does come a time when you begin to feel the need of a little relaxation; and, by Jove, there are absolutely no facilities for relaxation in this place whatever. And then Steggles got this idea. Steggles is one of our reading-party, and, between ourselves, rather a worm as a general thing. Still, you have to give him credit for getting this idea.'

'What idea?'

'Well, you know how many parsons there are round about here. There are about a dozen hamlets within a radius of six miles, and each hamlet has a church and each church has a parson and each parson preaches a sermon every Sunday. Tomorrow week – Sunday the twenty-third – we're running off the great Sermon Handicap. Steggles is making the book. Each parson is to be clocked by a reliable steward of the course, and the one that preaches the longest sermon wins. Did you study the race-card I sent you?'

'I couldn't understand what it was all about.'

'Why, you chump, it gives the handicaps and the current odds on each starter. I've got another one here, in case you've lost yours. Take a careful look at it. It gives you the thing in a nutshell. Jeeves, old son, do you want a sporting flutter?'

'Sir?' said Jeeves, who had just meandered in with my breakfast.

Claude explained the scheme. Amazing the way Jeeves grasped it right off. But he merely smiled in a paternal sort of way.

'Thank you, sir, I think not.'

'Well, you're with us, Bertie, aren't you?' said Claude, sneaking a roll and a slice of bacon. 'Have you studied that card? Well, tell me, does anything strike you about it?'

Of course it did. It had struck me the moment I looked at it.

'Why, it's a sitter for old Heppenstall,' I said. 'He's got the event sewed up in a parcel. There isn't a parson in the land who could give him eight minutes. Your pal Steggles must be an ass, giving him a handicap like that. Why, in the days when I was with him, old Heppenstall never used to preach under half an hour, and there was one sermon of his on Brotherly Love which lasted forty-five minutes if it lasted a second. Has he lost his vim lately, or what is it?'

'Not a bit of it,' said Eustace. 'Tell him what happened, Claude.'

'Why,' said Claude, 'the first Sunday we were here, we all went to Twing church, and old Heppenstall preached a sermon that was well under twenty minutes. This is what happened. Steggles didn't notice it, and the Rev. didn't notice it himself, but Eustace and I both spotted that he had dropped a chunk of at least half a dozen pages out of his sermon-case as he was walking up to the pulpit. He sort of flickered when he got to the gap in the manuscript, but carried on all right, and Steggles went away with the impression that twenty minutes or a bit under was his usual form. The next Sunday we heard Tucker and Starkie, and they both went well over the thirty-five minutes, so Steggles arranged the handicapping as you see on the card. You must come into this, Bertie. You see, the trouble is that I haven't a bean, and Eustace hasn't a bean, and Bingo Little hasn't a bean, so you'll have to finance the syndicate. Don't weaken! It's just putting money in all our pockets. Well, we'll have to be getting back now. Think the thing over, and phone me later in the day. And, if you let us down, Bertie, may a cousin's curse – Come on, Claude, old thing.'

The more I studied the scheme, the better it looked.

'How about it, Jeeves?' I said.

Jeeves smiled gently, and drifted out.

'Jeeves has no sporting blood,' said Bingo.

'Well, I have. I'm coming into this. Claude's quite right. It's like finding money by the wayside.'

'Good man!' said Bingo. 'Now I can see daylight. Say I have a tenner on Heppenstall, and cop; that'll give me a bit in hand to back Pink Pill with in the two o'clock at Gatwick the week after next; cop on that, put the pile on Musk-Rat for the one-thirty at Lewes, and there I am with a nice little sum to take to Alexandra Park on September the tenth, when I've got a tip straight from the stable.'

It sounded like a bit out of Smiles's *Self-Help*.

'And then,' said young Bingo, 'I'll be in a position to go to my uncle and beard him in his lair somewhat. He's quite a bit of a snob, you know, and when he hears that I'm going to marry the daughter of an earl – '

'I say, old man,' I couldn't help saying, 'aren't you looking ahead rather far?'

'Oh, that's all right. It's true nothing's actually settled yet, but she practically told me the other day she was fond of me.'

'What!'

'Well, she said that the sort of man she liked was the self-reliant, manly man with strength, good looks, character, ambition, and initiative.'

'Leave me, laddie,' I said. 'Leave me to my fried egg.'

Directly I'd got up I went to the phone, snatched Eustace away from his morning's work, and instructed him to put a tenner on the Twing flier at current odds for each of the syndicate; and after lunch Eustace rang me up to say that he had done business at a snappy seven-to-one, the odds having lengthened owing to a rumour in knowledgeable circles that the Rev. was subject to hay-fever, and was taking big chances strolling in the

paddock behind the Vicarage in the early mornings. And
it was dashed lucky, I thought next day, that we had
managed to get the money on in time, for on the Sunday
morning old Heppenstall fairly took the bit between his
teeth, and gave us thirty-six solid minutes on Certain
Popular Superstitions. I was sitting next to Steggles in
the pew, and I saw him blench visibly. He was a little rat-
faced fellow, with shifty eyes and a suspicious nature.
The first thing he did when he emerged into the open air
was to announce, formally, that anyone who fancied the
Rev. could now be accommodated at fifteen-to-eight on,
and he added, in a rather nasty manner, that if he had
his way, this sort of in-and-out running would be brought
to the attention of the Jockey Club, but that he supposed
that there was nothing to be done about it. This ruinous
price checked the punters at once, and there was little
money in sight. And so matters stood till just after lunch
on Tuesday afternoon, when, as I was strolling up and
down in front of the house with a cigarette, Claude
and Eustace came bursting up the drive on bicycles,
dripping with momentous news.

'Bertie,' said Claude, deeply agitated, 'unless we take
immediate action and do a bit of quick thinking, we're
in the cart.'

'What's the matter?'

'G. Hayward's the matter,' said Eustace morosely. 'The
Lower Bingley starter.'

'We never even considered him,' said Claude.
'Somehow or other, he got overlooked. It's always the
way. Steggles overlooked him. We all overlooked him.
But Eustace and I happened by the merest fluke to be
riding through Lower Bingley this morning, and there
was a wedding on at the church, and it suddenly struck
us that it wouldn't be a bad move to get a line on G.
Hayward's form, in case he might be a dark horse.'

'And it was jolly lucky we did,' said Eustace. 'He
delivered an address of twenty-six minutes by Claude's

39

stop-watch. At a village wedding, mark you! What'll we do when he really extends himself!'

'There's only one thing to be done, Bertie,' said Claude. 'You must spring some more funds, so that we can hedge on Hayward and save ourselves.'

'But – '

'Well, it's the only way out.'

'But I say, you know, I hate the idea of all that money we put on Heppenstall being chucked away.'

'What else can you suggest? You don't suppose the Rev. can give this absolute marvel a handicap and win, do you?'

'I've got it!' I said.

'What?'

'I see a way by which we can make it safe for our nominee. I'll pop over this afternoon, and ask him as a personal favour to preach that sermon of his on Brotherly Love on Sunday.'

Claude and Eustace looked at each other, like those chappies in the poem, with a wild surmise.

'It's a scheme,' said Claude.

'A jolly brainy scheme,' said Eustace. 'I didn't think you had it in you, Bertie.'

'But even so,' said Claude, 'fizzer as that sermon no doubt is, will it be good enough in the face of a four-minute handicap?'

'Rather!' I said. 'When I told you it lasted forty-five minutes, I was probably understating it. I should call it – from my recollection of the thing – nearer fifty.'

'Then carry on,' said Claude.

I toddled over in the evening and fixed the thing up. Old Heppenstall was most decent about the whole affair. He seemed pleased and touched that I should have remembered the sermon all these years, and said he had once or twice had an idea of preaching it again, only it had seemed to him, on reflection, that it was perhaps a trifle long for a rustic congregation.

'And in these restless times, my dear Wooster,' he said, 'I fear that brevity in the pulpit is becoming more and more desiderated by even the bucolic churchgoer, who one might have supposed would be less afflicted with the spirit of hurry and impatience than his metropolitan brother. I have had many arguments on the subject with my nephew, young Bates, who is taking my old friend Spettigue's cure over at Gandle-by-the-Hill. His view is that a sermon nowadays should be a bright, brisk, straight-from-the shoulder address, never lasting more than ten or twelve minutes.'

'Long?' I said. 'Why, my goodness! You don't call that Brotherly Love sermon of yours *long*, do you?'

'It takes fully fifty minutes to deliver.'

'Surely not?'

'Your incredulity, my dear Wooster, is extremely flattering – far more flattering, of course, than I deserve. Nevertheless, the facts are as I have stated. You are sure that I would not be well advised to make certain excisions and eliminations? You do not think it would be a good thing to cut, to prune? I might, for example, delete the rather exhaustive excursus into the family life of the early Assyrians?'

'Don't touch a word of it, or you'll spoil the whole thing,' I said earnestly.

'I am delighted to hear you say so, and I shall preach the sermon without fail next Sunday morning.'

What I have always said, and what I always shall say, is, that this ante-post betting is a mistake, an error, and a mug's game. You can never tell what's going to happen. If fellows would only stick to the good old SP there would be fewer young men go wrong. I'd hardly finished my breakfast on the Saturday morning, when Jeeves came to my bedside to say that Eustace wanted me on the telephone.

'Good Lord, Jeeves, what's the matter, do you think?'

I'm bound to say I was beginning to get a bit jumpy by this time.

'Mr Eustace did not confide in me, sir.'

'Has he got the wind up?'

'Somewhat vertically, sir, to judge by his voice.'

'Do you know what I think, Jeeves? Something's gone wrong with the favourite.'

'Which is the favourite, sir?'

'Mr Heppenstall. He's gone to odds on. He was intending to preach a sermon on Brotherly Love which would have brought him home by lengths. I wonder if anything's happened to him.'

'You could ascertain, sir, by speaking to Mr Eustace on the telephone. He is holding the wire.'

'By Jove, yes!'

I shoved on a dressing gown, and flew downstairs like a mighty, rushing wind. The moment I heard Eustace's voice I knew we were for it. It had a croak of agony in it.

'Bertie?'

'Here I am.'

'Deuce of a time you've been. Bertie, we're sunk. The favourite's blown up.'

'No!'

'Yes. Coughing in his stable all last night.'

'What!'

'Absolutely! Hay-fever.'

'Oh, my sainted aunt!'

'The doctor is with him now, and it's only a question of minutes before he's officially scratched. That means the curate will show up at the post instead, and he's no good at all. He is being offered at a hundred-to-six, but no takers. What shall we do?'

I had to grapple with the thing for a moment in silence.

'Eustace.'

'Hallo?'

'What can you get on G. Hayward?'

'Only four to one now. I think there's been a leak, and

Steggles has heard something. The odds shortened late last night in a significant manner.'

'Well, four to one will clear us. Put another fiver all round on G. Hayward for the syndicate. That'll bring us out on the right side of the ledger.'

'If he wins.'

'What do you mean? I thought you considered him a cert, bar Heppenstall.'

'I'm beginning to wonder,' said Eustace gloomily, 'if there's such a thing as a cert, in this world. I'm told the Rev. Joseph Tucker did an extraordinarily fine trial gallop at a mothers' meeting over at Badgwick yesterday. However, it seems our only chance. So-long.'

Not being one of the official stewards, I had my choice of churches next morning, and naturally I didn't hesitate. The only drawback to going to Lower Bingley was that it was ten miles away, which meant an early start, but I borrowed a bicycle from one of the grooms and tooled off. I had only Eustace's word for it that G. Hayward was such a stayer, and it might have been that he had showed too flattering form at that wedding where the twins had heard him preach; but any misgivings I may have had disappeared the moment he got into the pulpit. Eustace had been right. The man was a trier. He was a tall, rangy-looking greybeard, and he went off from the start with a nice, easy action, pausing and clearing his throat at the end of each sentence, and it wasn't five minutes before I realized that here was the winner. His habit of stopping dead and looking round the church at intervals was worth minutes to us, and in the home stretch we gained no little advantage owing to his dropping his pince-nez and having to grope for them. At the twenty-minute mark he had merely settled down. Twenty-five minutes saw him going strong. And when he finally finished with a good burst, the clock showed thirty-five minutes fourteen seconds. With the handicap which he had been given, this seemed to me to make the event easy for him, and it was with much *bonhomie* and goodwill to all men that I hopped on to the old bike and started back to the Hall for lunch.

Bingo was talking on the phone when I arrived.

'Fine! Splendid! Topping!' he was saying. 'Eh? Oh, we needn't worry about him. Right-o, I'll tell Bertie.' He hung up the receiver and caught sight of me. 'Oh, hallo, Bertie; I was just talking to Eustace. It's all right, old man. The report from Lower Bingley has just got in. G. Hayward romps home.'

'I knew he would. I've just come from there.'

'Oh, were you there? I went to Badgwick. Tucker ran a splendid race, but the handicap was too much for him. Starkie had a sore throat and was nowhere. Roberts, of Fale-by-the-Water, ran third. Good old G. Hayward!' said Bingo affectionately, and we strolled out on to the terrace.

'Are all the returns in, then?' I asked.

'All except Gandle-by-the-Hill. But we needn't worry about Bates. He never had a chance. By the way, poor old Jeeves loses his tenner. Silly ass!'

'Jeeves? How do you mean?'

'He came to me this morning, just after you had left, and asked me to put a tenner on Bates for him. I told him he was a chump, and begged him not to throw his money away, but he would do it.'

'I beg your pardon, sir. This note arrived for you just after you had left the house this morning.'

Jeeves had materialized from nowhere, and was standing at my elbow.

'Eh? What? Note?'

'The Reverend Mr Heppenstall's butler brought it over from the Vicarage, sir. It came too late to be delivered to you at the moment.'

Young Bingo was talking to Jeeves like a father on the subject of betting against the form-book. The yell I gave made him bite his tongue in the middle of a sentence.

'What the dickens is the matter?' he asked, not a little peeved.

'We're dished! Listen to this!'

I read him the note:

> The Vicarage,
> Twing, Glos.
>
> MY DEAR WOOSTER – As you may have heard, circumstances over which I have no control will prevent my preaching the sermon on Brotherly Love for which you made such a flattering request. I am unwilling, however, that you shall be disappointed, so, if you will attend divine service at Gandle-by-the-Hill this morning, you will hear my sermon preached by young Bates, my nephew. I have lent him the manuscript at his urgent desire, for, between ourselves, there are wheels within wheels. My nephew is one of the candidates for the headmastership of a well-known public school, and the choice has narrowed down between him and one rival.
>
> Late yesterday evening James received private information that the head of the Board of Governors of the school proposed to sit under him this Sunday in order to judge of the merits of his preaching, a most important item in swaying the Board's choice. I acceded to his plea that I lend him my sermon on Brotherly Love, of which, like you, he apparently retains a vivid recollection. It would have been too late for him to compose a sermon of suitable length in place of this brief address which – mistakenly, in my opinion – he had designed to deliver to his rustic flock, and I wished to help the boy.
>
> Trusting that his preaching of the sermon will supply you with as pleasant memories as you say you have of mine, I remain,
>
> Cordially yours,
> F. Heppenstall.

PS – The hay-fever has rendered my eyes unpleasantly weak for the time being, so I am dictating this letter to my butler, Brookfield, who will convey it to you.

I don't know when I've experienced a more massive silence than the one that followed my reading of this cheery epistle. Young Bingo gulped once or twice, and practically every known emotion came and went on his face. Jeeves coughed one soft, low, gentle cough like a sheep with a blade of grass stuck in its throat, and then stood gazing serenely at the landscape. Finally young Bingo spoke.

'Great Scott!' he whispered hoarsely. 'An SP job!'

'I believe that is the technical term, sir,' said Jeeves.

'So you had inside information, dash it!' said young Bingo.

'Why, yes, sir,' said Jeeves. 'Brookfield happened to mention the contents of the note to me when he brought it. We are old friends.'

Bingo registered grief, anguish, rage, despair and resentment.

'Well, all I can say,' he cried, 'is that it's a bit thick! Preaching another man's sermon! Do you call that honest? Do you call that playing the game?'

'Well, my dear old thing,' I said, 'be fair. It's quite within the rules. Clergymen do it all the time. They aren't expected always to make up the sermons they preach.'

Jeeves coughed again, and fixed me with an expressionless eye.

'And in the present case, sir, if I may be permitted to take the liberty of making the observation, I think we should make allowances. We should remember that the securing of this headmastership meant everything to the young couple.'

'Young couple? What young couple?'

'The Reverend James Bates, sir, and Lady Cynthia. I am informed by her ladyship's maid that they have been engaged to be married for some weeks – provisionally, so to speak; and his lordship made his consent conditional on Mr Bates securing a really important and remunerative position.'

Young Bingo turned a light green.

'Engaged to be married!'

'Yes, sir.'

There was a silence.

'I think I'll go for a walk,' said Bingo.

'But, my dear old thing,' I said, 'it's just lunch-time. The gong will be going any minute now.'

'I don't want any lunch!' said Bingo.

2 — Jeeves and the Impending Doom

It was the morning of the day on which I was slated to pop down to my Aunt Agatha's place at Woollam Chersey in the county of Herts for a visit of three solid weeks; and, as I seated myself at the breakfast table, I don't mind confessing that the heart was singularly heavy. We Woosters are men of iron, but beneath my intrepid exterior at that moment there lurked a nameless dread.

'Jeeves,' I said, 'I am not the old merry self this morning.'

'Indeed, sir?'

'No, Jeeves. Far from the old merry self.'

'I am sorry to hear that, sir.'

He uncovered the fragrant eggs and b., and I pronged a moody forkful.

'Why – this is what I keep asking myself, Jeeves – why has my Aunt Agatha invited me to her country seat?'

'I could not say, sir.'

'Not because she is fond of me.'

'No, sir.'

'It is a well-established fact that I give her a pain in the neck. How it happens I cannot say, but every time our paths cross, so to speak, it seems to be a mere matter of time before I perpetrate some ghastly floater and have her hopping after me with her hatchet. The result being that she regards me as a worm and an outcast. Am I right or wrong, Jeeves?'

'Perfectly correct, sir.'

'And yet now she has absolutely insisted on my scratching all previous engagements and buzzing down to Woollam Chersey. She must have some sinister reason

of which we know nothing. Can you blame me, Jeeves,
if the heart is heavy?'

'No, sir. Excuse me, sir, I fancy I heard the front-door
bell.'

He shimmered out, and I took another listless stab at
the e. and bacon.

'A telegram, sir,' said Jeeves, re-entering the presence.

'Open it, Jeeves, and read contents. Who is it from?'

'It is unsigned, sir.'

'You mean there's no name at the end of it?'

'That is precisely what I was endeavouring to convey,
sir.'

'Let's have a look.'

I scanned the thing. It was a rummy communication.
Rummy. No other word.

As follows:

> Remember when you come here absolutely vital meet
> perfect strangers.

We Woosters are not very strong in the head, particularly
at breakfast-time; and I was conscious of a dull ache
between the eyebrows.

'What does it mean, Jeeves?'

'I could not say, sir.'

'It says "come here". Where's here?'

'You will notice the message was handed in at
Woollam Chersey, sir.'

'You're absolutely right. At Woollam, as you very
cleverly spotted, Chersey. This tells us something,
Jeeves.'

'What, sir?'

'I don't know. It couldn't be from my Aunt Agatha, do
you think?'

'Hardly, sir.'

'No; you're right again. Then all we can say is that
some person unknown, resident at Woollam Chersey,

considers it absolutely vital for me to meet perfect strangers. But why should I meet perfect strangers, Jeeves?'

'I could not say, sir.'

'And yet, looking at it from another angle, why shouldn't I?'

'Precisely, sir.'

'Then what it comes to is that the thing is a mystery which time alone can solve. We must wait and see, Jeeves.'

'The very expression I was about to employ, sir.'

I hit Woollam Chersey at about four o'clock, and found Aunt Agatha in her lair, writing letters. And, from what I know of her, probably offensive letters, with nasty postscripts. She regarded me with not a fearful lot of joy.

'Oh, there you are, Bertie.'

'Yes, here I am.'

'There's a smut on your nose.'

I plied the handkerchief.

'I am glad you have arrived so early. I want to have a word with you before you meet Mr Filmer.'

'Who?'

'Mr Filmer, the Cabinet Minister. He is staying in the house. Surely even you must have heard of Mr Filmer?'

'Oh, rather,' I said, though as a matter of fact the bird was completely unknown to me. What with one thing and another, I'm not frightfully up in the personnel of the political world.

'I particularly wish you to make a good impression on Mr Filmer.'

'Right-ho.'

'Don't speak in that casual way, as if you supposed that it was perfectly natural that you would make a good impression upon him. Mr Filmer is a serious-minded man of high character and purpose, and you are just the type

of vapid and frivolous wastrel against which he is most
likely to be prejudiced.'

Hard words, of course, from one's own flesh and blood,
but well in keeping with past form.

'You will endeavour, therefore, while you are here not
to display yourself in the *role* of a vapid and frivolous
wastrel. In the first place, you will give up smoking during
your visit.'

'Oh, I say!'

'Mr Filmer is president of the Anti-Tobacco League.
Nor will you drink alcoholic stimulants.'

'Oh, dash it!'

'And you will kindly exclude from your conversation
all that is suggestive of the bar, the billiard room, and
the stage door. Mr Filmer will judge you largely by your
conversation.'

I rose to a point of order.

'Yes, but why have I got to make an impression on this
– on Mr Filmer?'

'Because,' said the old relative, giving me the eye, 'I
particularly wish it.'

Not, perhaps, a notably snappy come-back as come-
backs go; but it was enough to show me that that was more
or less that; and I beetled out with an aching heart.

I headed for the garden, and I'm dashed if the first
person I saw wasn't young Bingo Little.

Bingo Little and I have been pals practically from birth.
Born in the same village within a couple of days of one
another, we went through kindergarten, Eton, and Oxford
together; and, grown to riper years we have enjoyed in
the old metrop. full many a first-class binge in each other's
society. If there was one fellow in the world, I felt, who
could alleviate the horrors of this blighted visit of mine,
that bloke was young Bingo Little.

But how he came to be there was more than I could
understand. Some time before, you see, he had married
the celebrated authoress, Rosie M. Banks; and the last I

had seen of him he had been on the point of
accompanying her to America on a lecture tour. I
distinctly remembered him cursing rather freely because
the trip would mean his missing Ascot.

Still, rummy as it might seem, here he was. And aching
for the sight of a friendly face, I gave tongue like a
bloodhound.

'Bingo!'

He spun round; and, by Jove, his face wasn't friendly
after all. It was what they call contorted. He waved his
arms at me like a semaphore.

'Sh!' he hissed. 'Would you ruin me?'

'Eh?'

'Didn't you get my telegram?'

'Was that *your* telegram?'

'Of course it was my telegram.'

'Then why didn't you sign it?'

'I did sign it.'

'No, you didn't. I couldn't make out what it was all
about.'

'Well, you got my letter.'

'What letter?'

'My letter.'

'I didn't get any letter.'

'Then I must have forgotten to post it. It was to tell
you that I was down here tutoring your Cousin Thomas,
and that it was essential that, when we met, you should
treat me as a perfect stranger.'

'But why?'

'Because, if your aunt supposed that I was a pal of
yours, she would naturally sack me on the spot.'

'Why?'

Bingo raised his eyebrows.

'Why? Be reasonable, Bertie. If you were your aunt,
and you knew the sort of chap you were, would you let a
fellow you knew to be your best pal tutor your son?'

This made the old head swim a bit, but I got his

meaning after a while, and I had to admit that there was
much rugged good sense in what he said. Still, he hadn't
explained what you might call the nub or gist of the
mystery.

'I thought you were in America,' I said.

'Well, I'm not.

'Why not?'

'Never mind why not. I'm not.'

'But why have you taken a tutoring job?'

'Never mind why, I have my reasons. And I want you
to get it into your head, Bertie – to get it right through
the concrete – that you and I must not be seen hobnobbing.
Your foul cousin was caught smoking in the shrubbery
the day before yesterday, and that has made my position
pretty tottery, because your aunt said that, if I had
exercised an adequate surveillance over him, it couldn't
have happened. If, after that, she finds out I'm a friend
of yours, nothing can save me from being shot out. And
it is vital that I am not shot out.'

'Why?'

'Never mind why.'

At this point he seemed to think he heard somebody
coming, for he suddenly leaped with incredible agility into
a laurel bush. And I toddled along to consult Jeeves about
these rummy happenings.

'Jeeves,' I said, repairing to the bedroom, where he was
unpacking my things, 'you remember that telegram?'

'Yes, sir.'

'It was from Mr Little. He's here, tutoring my young
Cousin Thomas.'

'Indeed, sir?'

'I can't understand it. He appears to be a free agent, if
you know what I mean; and yet would any man who
was a free agent wantonly come to a house which
contained my Aunt Agatha?'

'It seems peculiar, sir.'

'Moreover, would anybody of his own free will and as

53

a mere pleasure-seeker tutor my Cousin Thomas, who is notoriously a tough egg and a fiend in human shape?'

'Most improbable, sir.'

'These are deep waters, Jeeves.'

'Precisely, sir.'

'And the ghastly part of it all is that he seems to consider it necessary, in order to keep his job, to treat me like a long-lost leper. Thus killing my only chance of having anything approaching a decent time in this abode of desolation. For do you realize, Jeeves, that my aunt says I mustn't smoke while I'm here?'

'Indeed, sir?'

'Nor drink.'

'Why is this, sir?'

'Because she wants me – for some dark and furtive reason which she will not explain – to impress a fellow named Filmer.'

'Too bad, sir. However, many doctors, I understand, advocate such abstinence as the secret of health. They say it promotes a freer circulation of the blood and insures the arteries against premature hardening.'

'Oh, do they? Well, you can tell them next time you see them that they are silly asses.'

'Very good, sir.'

And so began what, looking back along a fairly eventful career, I think I can confidently say was the scaliest visit I have ever experienced in the course of my life. What with the agony of missing the lifegiving cocktail before dinner; the painful necessity of being obliged, every time I wanted a quiet cigarette, to lie on the floor in my bedroom and puff the smoke up the chimney; the constant discomfort of meeting Aunt Agatha round unexpected corners; and the fearful strain on the morale of having to chum with the Right Hon. A. B. Filmer, it was not long before Bertram was up against it to an extent hitherto undreamed of.

I played golf with the Right Hon. every day, and it was
only by biting the Wooster lip and clenching the fists
till the knuckles stood out white under the strain that I
managed to pull through. The Right Hon. punctuated
some of the ghastliest golf I have ever seen with a flow of
conversation which, as far as I was concerned, went
completely over the top; and, all in all, I was beginning
to feel pretty sorry for myself when, one night as I was
in my room listlessly donning the soup-and-fish in
preparation for the evening meal, in trickled young Bingo
and took my mind off my own troubles.

For when it is a question of a pal being in the soup, we
Woosters no longer think of self; and that poor old Bingo
was knee-deep in the bisque was made plain by his mere
appearance – which was that of a cat which has just been
struck by a half-brick and is expecting another shortly.

'Bertie,' said Bingo, having sat down on the bed and
diffused silent gloom for a moment, 'how is Jeeves's
brain these days?'

'Fairly strong on the wing, I fancy. How is the grey
matter, Jeeves? Surging about pretty freely?'

'Yes, sir.'

'Thank Heaven for that,' said young Bingo, 'for I
require your soundest counsel. Unless right-thinking
people take strong steps through the proper channels, my
name will be mud.'

'What's wrong, old thing?' I asked, sympathetically.

Bingo plucked at the coverlet.

'I will tell you,' he said. 'I will also now reveal why I
am staying in this pest-house, tutoring a kid who
requires not education in the Greek and Latin languages
but a swift slosh on the base of the skull with a black-
jack. I came here, Bertie, because it was the only thing I
could do. At the last moment before she sailed to
America, Rosie decided that I had better stay behind and
look after the Peke. She left me a couple of hundred quid
to see me through till her return. This sum, judiciously

expended over the period of her absence, would have been enough to keep Peke and self in moderate affluence. But you know how it is.'

'How what is?'

'When someone comes slinking up to you in the club and tells you that some cripple of a horse can't help winning even if it develops lumbago and the botts ten yards from the starting-post. I tell you, I regarded the thing as a cautious and conservative investment.'

'You mean you planked the entire capital on a horse?'

Bingo laughed bitterly.

'If you could call the thing a horse. If it hadn't shown a flash of speed in the straight, it would have got mixed up with the next race. It came in last, putting me in a dashed delicate position. Somehow or other I had to find the funds to keep me going, so that I could win through till Rosie's return without her knowing what had occurred. Rosie is the dearest girl in the world; but if you were a married man, Bertie, you would be aware that the best of wives is apt to cut up rough if she finds that her husband has dropped six weeks' housekeeping money on a single race. Isn't that so, Jeeves?'

'Yes, sir. Women are odd in that respect.'

'It was a moment for swift thinking. There was enough left from the wreck to board the Peke out at a comfortable home. I signed him up for six weeks at the Kosy Komfort Kennels at Kingsbridge, Kent, and tottered out, a broken man, to get a tutoring job. I landed the kid Thomas. And here I am.'

It was a sad story, of course, but it seemed to me that, awful as it might be to be in constant association with my Aunt Agatha and young Thos, he had got rather well out of a tight place.

'All you have to do,' I said, 'is to carry on here for a few weeks more, and everything will be oojah-cum-spiff.'

Bingo barked bleakly.

'A few weeks more! I shall be lucky if I stay two days. You remember I told you that your aunt's faith in me as a guardian of her blighted son was shaken a few days ago by the fact that he was caught smoking. I now find that the person who caught him smoking was the man Filmer. And ten minutes ago young Thomas told me that he was proposing to inflict some hideous revenge on Filmer for having reported him to your aunt. I don't know what he is going to do, but if he does it, out I inevitably go on my left ear. Your aunt thinks the world of Filmer, and would sack me on the spot. And three weeks before Rosie gets back!'

I saw all.

'Jeeves,' I said.

'Sir?'

'I see all. Do you see all?'

'Yes, sir.

'Then flock round.'

'I fear, sir – '

Bingo gave a low moan.

'Don't tell me, Jeeves,' he said, brokenly, 'that nothing suggests itself.'

'Nothing at the moment, I regret to say sir.'

Bingo uttered a stricken woofle like a bull-dog that has been refused cake.

'Well, then, the only thing I can do, I suppose,' he said sombrely, 'is not to let the pie-faced little thing out of my sight for a second.'

'Absolutely,' I said. 'Ceaseless vigilance, eh, Jeeves?'

'Precisely, sir.'

'But meanwhile, Jeeves,' said Bingo in a low, earnest voice, 'you will be devoting your best thought to the matter, won't you?'

'Most certainly, sir.'

'Thank you, Jeeves.'

'Not at all, sir.'

*

I will say for young Bingo that, once the need for action arrived, he behaved with an energy and determination which compelled respect. I suppose there was not a minute during the next two days when the kid Thos was able to say to himself, 'Alone at last!' But on the evening of the second day Aunt Agatha announced that some people were coming over on the morrow for a spot of tennis, and I feared that the worst must now befall.

Young Bingo, you see, is one of those fellows who, once their fingers close over the handle of a tennis racket, fall into a sort of trance in which nothing outside the radius of the lawn exists for them. If you came up to Bingo in the middle of a set and told him that panthers were devouring his best friend in the kitchen garden, he would look at you and say, 'Oh, ah?' or words to that effect. I knew that he would not give a thought to young Thomas and the Right Hon. till the last ball had bounced, and, as I dressed for dinner that night, I was conscious of an impending doom.

'Jeeves,' I said, 'have you ever pondered on Life?'

'From time to time, sir, in my leisure moments.'

'Grim, isn't it, what?'

'Grim, sir?'

'I mean to say, the difference between things as they look and things as they are.'

'The trousers perhaps a half-inch higher, sir. A very slight adjustment of the braces will effect the necessary alteration. You were saying, sir?'

'I mean, here at Woollam Chersey we have apparently a happy, care-free country-house party. But beneath the glittering surface, Jeeves, dark currents are running. One gazes at the Right Hon. wrapping himself round the salmon mayonnaise at lunch, and he seems a man without a care in the world. Yet all the while a dreadful fate is hanging over him, creeping nearer and nearer. What exact steps do you think the kid Thomas intends to take?'

'In the course of an informal conversation which I had with the young gentleman this afternoon, sir, he informed me that he had been reading a romance entitled *Treasure Island*, and had been much struck by the character and actions of a certain Captain Flint. I gathered that he was weighing the advisability of modelling his own conduct on that of the Captain.'

'But, good heavens, Jeeves! If I remember *Treasure Island*, Flint was the bird who went about hitting people with a cutlass. You don't think young Thomas would bean Mr Filmer with a cutlass?'

'Possibly he does not possess a cutlass, sir.'

'Well, with anything.'

'We can but wait and see, sir. The tie, if I might suggest it, sir, a shade more tightly knotted. One aims at the perfect butterfly effect. If you will permit me – '

'What do ties matter, Jeeves, at a time like this? Do you realize that Mr Little's domestic happiness is hanging in the scale?'

'There is no time, sir, at which ties do not matter.'

I could see the man was pained, but I did not try to heal the wound. What's the word I want? Preoccupied. I was too preoccupied, don't you know. And *distrait*. Not to say care worn. I was still care worn when, next day at half-past two, the revels commenced on the tennis lawn. It was one of those close, baking days, with thunder rumbling just round the corner; and it seemed to me that there was a brooding menace in the air.

'Bingo,' I said, as we pushed forth to do our bit in the first doubles, 'I wonder what young Thos will be up to this afternoon, with the eye of authority no longer on him?'

'Eh?' said Bingo, absently. Already the tennis look had come into his face, and his eye was glazed. He swung his racket and snorted a little.

'I don't see him anywhere,' I said.

'You don't what?'

'See him.'

'Who?'

'Young Thos.'

'What about him?'

I let it go.

The only consolation I had in the black period of the opening of the tourney was the fact that the Right Hon. had taken a seat among the spectators and was wedged in between a couple of females with parasols. Reason told me that even a kid so steeped in sin as young Thomas would hardly perpetrate any outrage on a man in such a strong strategic position. Considerably relieved, I gave myself up to the game; and was in the act of putting it across the local curate with a good deal of vim when there was a roll of thunder and the rain started to come down in buckets.

We all stampeded for the house, and had gathered in the drawing room for tea, when suddenly Aunt Agatha, looking up from a cucumber sandwich, said:

'Has anybody seen Mr Filmer?'

It was one of the nastiest jars I have ever experienced. What with my fast serve zipping sweetly over the net and the man of God utterly unable to cope with my slow bending return down the centre-line, I had for some little time been living, as it were, in another world. I now came down to earth with a bang: and my slice of cake, slipping from my nerveless fingers, fell to the ground and was wolfed by Aunt Agatha's spaniel, Robert. Once more I seemed to become conscious of an impending doom.

For this man Filmer, you must understand, was not one of those men who are lightly kept from the tea table. A hearty trencherman, and particularly fond of his five o'clock couple of cups and bite of muffin, he had until this afternoon always been well up among the leaders in the race for the food-trough. If one thing was certain, it was that only the machinations of some enemy could be

keeping him from being in the drawing room now,
complete with nose-bag.

'He must have got caught in the rain and be sheltering
somewhere in the grounds,' said Aunt Agatha. 'Bertie,
go out and find him. Take a raincoat to him.'

'Right-ho!' I said. My only desire in life now was to
find the Right Hon. And I hoped it wouldn't be merely
his body.

I put on a raincoat and tucked another under my arm,
and was sallying forth, when in the hall I ran into Jeeves.

'Jeeves,' I said, 'I fear the worst. Mr Filmer is missing.'

'Yes, sir.'

'I am about to scour the grounds in search of him.'

'I can save you the trouble, sir. Mr Filmer is on the
island in the middle of the lake.'

'In this rain? Why doesn't the chump row back?'

'He has no boat, sir.'

'Then how can he be on the island?'

'He rowed there, sir. But Master Thomas rowed after
him and set his boat adrift. He was informing me of the
circumstances a moment ago, sir. It appears that Captain
Flint was in the habit of marooning people on islands,
and Master Thomas felt that he could pursue no more
judicious course than to follow his example.'

'But, good Lord, Jeeves! The man must be getting
soaked.'

'Yes, sir. Master Thomas commented upon that aspect
of the matter.'

It was a time for action.

'Come with me, Jeeves!'

'Very good, sir.'

I buzzed for the boathouse.

My Aunt Agatha's husband, Spenser Gregson, who is
on the Stock Exchange, had recently cleaned up to an
amazing extent in Sumatra Rubber; and Aunt Agatha, in
selecting a country estate, had lashed out on an
impressive scale. There were miles of what they call

rolling parkland, trees in considerable profusion well
provided with doves and what not cooing in no uncertain
voice, gardens full of roses, and also stables, out-houses,
and messuages, the whole forming a rather fruity *tout
ensemble*. But the feature of the place was the lake.

It stood to the east of the house, beyond the rose garden,
and covered several acres. In the middle of it was an
island. In the middle of the island was a building known
as the Octagon. And in the middle of the Octagon, seated
on the roof and spouting water like a public fountain, was
the Right Hon. A. B. Filmer. As we drew nearer, striking
a fast clip with self at oars and Jeeves handling the tiller-
ropes, we heard cries of gradually increasing volume, if
that's the expression I want; and presently, up aloft,
looking from a distance as if he were perched on top of
the bushes, I located the Right Hon. It seemed to me that
even a Cabinet Minister ought to have had more sense
than to stay right out in the open like that when there
were trees to shelter under.

'A little more to the right, Jeeves.'

'Very good, sir.'

I made a neat landing.

'Wait here, Jeeves.'

'Very good, sir. The head gardener was informing me
this morning, sir, that one of the swans had recently
nested on this island.'

'This is no time for natural history gossip, Jeeves,' I
said, a little severely, for the rain was coming down
harder than ever and the Wooster trouser-legs were
already considerably moistened.

'Very good, sir.'

I pushed my way through the bushes. The going was
sticky and took about eight and eleven pence off the
value of my Sure-Grip tennis shoes in the first two yards:
but I persevered, and presently came out in the open and
found myself in a sort of clearing facing the Octagon.

This building was run up somewhere in the last

century, I have been told, to enable the grandfather of the late owner to have some quiet place out of earshot of the house where he could practise the fiddle. From what I know of fiddlers, I should imagine that he had produced some fairly frightful sounds there in his time, but they can have been nothing to the ones that were coming from the roof of the place now. The Right Hon., not having spotted the arrival of the rescue-party, was apparently trying to make his voice carry across the waste of waters to the house; and I'm not saying it was not a good sporting effort. He had one of those highish tenors, and his yowls seemed to screech over my head like shells.

I thought it about time to slip him the glad news that assistance had arrived, before he strained a vocal cord.

'Hi!' I shouted, waiting for a lull.

He poked his head over the edge.

'Hi,' he bellowed, looking in every direction but the right one, of course.

'Hi!'

'Hi!'

'Hi!'

'Hi!'

'Oh!' he said, spotting me at last.

'What-ho!' I replied, sort of clinching the thing.

I suppose the conversation can't be said to have touched a frightfully high level up to this moment; but probably we should have got a good deal brainier very shortly – only just then, at the very instant when I was getting ready to say something good, there was a hissing noise like a tyre bursting in a nest of cobras, and out of the bushes to my left there popped something so large and white and active that, thinking quicker than I have ever done in my puff, I rose like a rocketing pheasant, and, before I knew what I was doing, had begun to climb for life. Something slapped against the wall about an inch below my right ankle, and any doubts I may have had about remaining below vanished. The lad who bore 'mid

snow and ice the banner with the strange device
'Excelsior!' was the model for Bertram.

'Be careful!' yipped the Right Hon.

I was.

Whoever built the Octagon might have constructed it
especially for this sort of crisis. Its walls had grooves at
regular intervals which were just right for the hands and
feet, and it wasn't very long before I was parked up on
the roof beside the Right Hon., gazing down at one of the
largest and shortest-tempered swans I had ever seen. It
was standing below, stretching up a neck like a hosepipe,
just where a bit of brick, judiciously bunged, would catch
it amidships.

I bunged the brick and scored a bull's-eye.

The Right Hon. didn't seem any too well pleased.

'Don't tease it!' he said.

'It teased me,' I said.

The swan extended another eight feet of neck and gave
an imitation of steam escaping from a leaky pipe. The
rain continued to lash down with what you might call
indescribable fury, and I was sorry that in the agitation
inseparable from shinning up a stone wall at practically
a second's notice I had dropped the raincoat which I had
been bringing with me for my fellow-rooster. For a
moment I thought of offering him mine, but wiser
counsels prevailed.

'How near did it come to getting you?' I asked.

'Within an ace,' replied my companion, gazing down
with a look of marked dislike. 'I had to make a very
rapid spring.'

The Right Hon. was a tubby little chap who looked as
if he had been poured into his clothes and had forgotten
to say 'When!' and the picture he conjured up, if you
know what I mean, was rather pleasing.

'It is no laughing matter,' he said, shifting the look of
dislike to me.

'Sorry.'

'I might have been seriously injured.'

'Would you consider bunging another brick at the bird?'

'Do nothing of the sort. It will only annoy him.'

'Well, why not annoy him? He hasn't shown such a dashed lot of consideration for our feelings.'

The Right Hon. now turned to another aspect of the matter.

'I cannot understand how my boat, which I fastened securely to the stump of a willow-tree, can have drifted away.'

'Dashed mysterious.'

'I begin to suspect that it was deliberately set loose by some mischievous person.'

'Oh, I say, no, hardly likely, that. You'd have seen them doing it.'

'No, Mr Wooster. For the bushes form an effective screen. Moreover, rendered drowsy by the unusual warmth of the afternoon, I dozed off for some little time almost immediately I reached the island.'

This wasn't the sort of thing I wanted his mind dwelling on, so I changed the subject.

'Wet, isn't it, what?' I said.

'I had already observed it,' said the Right Hon. in one of those nasty, bitter voices. 'I thank you, however, for drawing the matter to my attention.'

Chit-chat about the weather hadn't gone with much of a bang, I perceived. I had a shot at Bird Life in the Home Counties.

'Have you ever noticed,' I said, 'how a swan's eyebrows sort of meet in the middle?'

'I have had every opportunity of observing all that there is to observe about swans.'

'Gives them a sort of peevish look, what?'

'The look to which you allude has not escaped me.'

'Rummy,' I said, rather warming to my subject, 'how bad an effect family life has on a swan's disposition.'

'I wish you would select some other topic of conversation than swans.'

'No, but, really, it's rather interesting. I mean to say, our old pal down there is probably a perfect ray of sunshine in normal circumstances. Quite the domestic pet, don't you know. But purely and simply because the little woman happens to be nesting – '

I paused. You will scarcely believe me, but until this moment, what with all the recent bustle and activity, I had clean forgotten that, while we were treed up on the roof like this, there lurked all the time in the background one whose giant brain, if notified of the emergency and requested to flock round, would probably be able to think up half-a-dozen schemes for solving our little difficulties in a couple of minutes.

'Jeeves!' I shouted.

'Sir?' came a faint respectful voice from the great open spaces.

'My man,' I explained to the Right Hon. 'A fellow of infinite resource and sagacity. He'll have us out of this in a minute. Jeeves!'

'Sir?'

'I'm sitting on the roof.'

'Very good, sir.'

'Don't say "Very good". Come and help us. Mr Filmer and I are treed, Jeeves.'

'Very good, sir.'

'Don't keep saying "Very good". It's nothing of the kind. The place is alive with swans.'

'I will attend to the matter immediately, sir.'

I turned to the Right Hon. I even went so far as to pat him on the back. It was like slapping a wet sponge.

'All is well,' I said. 'Jeeves is coming.'

'What can he do?'

I frowned a trifle. The man's tone had been peevish, and I didn't like it.

'That,' I replied with a touch of stiffness, 'we cannot

say until we see him in action. He may pursue one course, or he may pursue another. But on one thing you can rely with the utmost confidence – Jeeves will find a way. See, here he comes stealing through the undergrowth, his face shining with the light of pure intelligence. There are no limits to Jeeves's brain-power. He virtually lives on fish.'

I bent over the edge and peered into the abyss.

'Look out for the swan, Jeeves.'

'I have the bird under close observation, sir.'

The swan had been uncoiling a further supply of neck in our direction; but now he whipped round. The sound of a voice speaking in his rear seemed to affect him powerfully. He subjected Jeeves to a short, keen scrutiny; and then, taking in some breath for hissing purposes, gave a sort of jump and charged ahead.

'Look out, Jeeves!'

'Very good, sir.'

Well, I could have told that swan it was no use. As swans go, he may have been well up in the ranks of the intelligentsia; but, when it came to pitting his brains against Jeeves, he was simply wasting his time. He might just as well have gone home at once.

Every young man starting life ought to know how to cope with an angry swan, so I will briefly relate the proper procedure. You begin by picking up the raincoat which somebody has dropped; and then, judging the distance to a nicety, you simply shove the raincoat over the bird's head; and, taking the boat-hook which you have prudently brought with you, you insert it underneath the swan and heave. The swan goes into a bush and starts trying to unscramble itself; and you saunter back to your boat, taking with you any friends who may happen at the moment to be sitting on roofs in the vicinity. That was Jeeves's method, and I cannot see how it could have been improved upon.

The Right Hon. showing a turn of speed of which I

would not have believed him capable, we were in the boat in considerably under two ticks.

'You behaved very intelligently, my man,' said the Right Hon. as we pushed away from the shore.

'I endeavour to give satisfaction, sir.'

The Right Hon. appeared to have said his say for the time being. From that moment he seemed to sort of huddle up and meditate. Dashed absorbed he was. Even when I caught a crab and shot about a pint of water down his neck he didn't seem to notice it.

It was only when we were landing that he came to life again.

'Mr Wooster.'

'Oh, ah?'

'I have been thinking of that matter of which I spoke to you some time back – the problem of how my boat can have got adrift.'

I didn't like this.

'The dickens of a problem,' I said. 'Better not bother about it any more. You'll never solve it.'

'On the contrary, I have arrived at a solution, and one which I think is the only feasible solution. I am convinced that my boat was set adrift by the boy Thomas, my hostess's son.'

'Oh, I say, no! Why?'

'He had a grudge against me. And it is the sort of thing only a boy, or one who is practically an imbecile, would have thought of doing.'

He legged it for the house; and I turned to Jeeves, aghast. Yes, you might say aghast.

'You heard, Jeeves?'

'Yes, sir.'

'What's to be done?'

'Perhaps Mr Filmer, on thinking the matter over, will decide that his suspicions are unjust.'

'But they aren't unjust.'

'No, sir.'

'Then what's to be done?'

'I could not say, sir.'

I pushed off rather smartly to the house and reported to Aunt Agatha that the Right Hon. had been salved; and then I toddled upstairs to have a hot bath, being considerably soaked from stem to stern as the result of my rambles. While I was enjoying the grateful warmth, a knock came at the door.

It was Purvis, Aunt Agatha's butler.

'Mrs Gregson desires me to say, sir, that she would be glad to see you as soon as you are ready.'

'But she has seen me.'

'I gather that she wishes to see you again, sir.'

'Oh, right-ho.'

I lay beneath the surface for another few minutes; then, having dried the frame, went along the corridor to my room. Jeeves was there, fiddling about with underclothing.

'Oh, Jeeves,' I said, 'I've just been thinking. Oughtn't somebody to go and give Mr Filmer a spot of quinine or something? Errand of mercy, what?'

'I have already done so, sir.'

'Good. I wouldn't say I like the man frightfully, but I don't want him to get a cold in the head.' I shoved on a sock. 'Jeeves,' I said, 'I suppose you know that we've got to think of something pretty quick? I mean to say, you realize the position? Mr Filmer suspects young Thomas of doing exactly what he did do, and if he brings home the charge Aunt Agatha will undoubtedly fire Mr Little, and then Mrs Little will find out what Mr Little has been up to, and what will be the upshot and outcome, Jeeves? I will tell you. It will mean that Mrs Little will get the goods on Mr Little to an extent to which, though only a bachelor myself, I should say that no wife ought to get the goods on her husband if the proper give and take of married life – what you might call the essential balance, as it were – is to be preserved. Women bring these things up, Jeeves. They do not forget and forgive.'

'Very true, sir.'

'Then how about it?'

'I have already attended to the matter, sir.'

'You have?'

'Yes, sir. I had scarcely left you when the solution of the affair presented itself to me. It was a remark of Mr Filmer's that gave me the idea.'

'Jeeves, you're a marvel!'

'Thank you very much, sir.'

'What was the solution?'

'I conceived the notion of going to Mr Filmer and saying that it was you who had stolen his boat, sir.'

The man flickered before me. I clutched a sock in a feverish grip.

'Saying – what?'

'At first Mr Filmer was reluctant to credit my statement. But I pointed out to him that you had certainly known that he was on the island – a fact which he agreed was highly significant. I pointed out, furthermore, that you were a light-hearted young gentleman, sir, who might well do such a thing as a practical joke. I left him quite convinced, and there is now no danger of his attributing the action to Master Thomas.'

I gazed at the blighter spellbound.

'And that's what you consider a neat solution?' I said.

'Yes, sir. Mr Little will now retain his position as desired.'

'And what about me?'

'You are also benefited, sir.'

'Oh, I am, am I?'

'Yes, sir. I have ascertained that Mrs Gregson's motive in inviting you to this house was that she might present you to Mr Filmer with a view to your becoming his private secretary.'

'What!'

'Yes, sir. Purvis, the butler, chanced to overhear Mrs Gregson in conversation with Mr Filmer on the matter.'

'Secretary to that super fatted bore! Jeeves, I could never have survived it.'

'No, sir. I fancy you would not have found it agreeable. Mr Filmer is scarcely a congenial companion for you. Yet, had Mrs Gregson secured the position for you, you might have found it embarrassing to decline to accept it.'

'Embarrassing is right!'

'Yes, sir.'

'But I say, Jeeves, there's just one point which you seem to have overlooked. Where exactly do I get off?'

'Sir?'

'I mean to say, Aunt Agatha sent word by Purvis just now that she wanted to see me. Probably she's polishing up her hatchet at this very moment.'

'It might be the most judicious plan not to meet her, sir.'

'But how can I help it?'

'There is a good, stout waterpipe running down the wall immediately outside this window, sir. And I could have the two-seater waiting outside the park gates in twenty minutes.'

I eyed him with reverence.

'Jeeves,' I said, 'you are always right. You couldn't make it five, could you?'

'Let us say ten, sir.'

'Ten it is. Lay out some raiment suitable for travel, and leave the rest to me. Where is this waterpipe of which you speak so highly?'

3 — Jeeves and the Song of Songs

Another day had dawned all hot and fresh and, in
pursuance of my unswerving policy at that time, I was
singing 'Sonny Boy' in my bath, when there was a soft
step without and Jeeves's voice came filtering through
the woodwork.

'I beg your pardon, sir.'

I had just got to that bit about the Angels being lonely,
where you need every ounce of concentration in order to
make the spectacular finish, but I signed off courteously.

'Yes, Jeeves? Say on.'

'Mr Glossop, sir.'

'What about him?'

'He is in the sitting room, sir.'

'Young Tuppy Glossop?'

'Yes, sir.'

'In the sitting room?'

'Yes, sir.'

'Desiring speech with me?'

'Yes, sir.'

'H'm!'

'Sir?'

'I only said H'm.'

And I'll tell you why I said H'm. It was because the
man's story had interested me strangely. The news that
Tuppy was visiting me at my flat, at an hour when he
must have known that I would be in my bath and
consequently in a strong strategic position to heave a wet
sponge at him, surprised me considerably.

I hopped out with some briskness and, slipping a
couple of towels about the limbs and torso, made for the

sitting room. I found young Tuppy at the piano, playing 'Sonny Boy' with one finger.

'What ho!' I said, not without a certain hauteur.

'Oh, hullo, Bertie,' said young Tuppy. 'I say, Bertie, I want to see you about something important.'

It seemed to me that the bloke was embarrassed. He had moved to the mantelpiece, and now he broke a vase in rather a constrained way.

'The fact is, Bertie, I'm engaged.'

'Engaged?'

'Engaged,' said young Tuppy, coyly dropping a photograph frame into the fender. 'Practically, that is.'

'Practically?'

'Yes. You'll like her, Bertie. Her name is Cora Bellinger. She's studying for Opera. Wonderful voice she has. Also dark, flashing eyes and a great soul.'

'How do you mean, practically?'

'Well, it's this way. Before ordering the trousseau, there is one little point she wants cleared up. You see, what with her great soul and all that, she has a rather serious outlook on life: and the one thing she absolutely bars is anything in the shape of hearty humour. You know, practical joking and so forth. She said if she thought I was a practical joker she would never speak to me again. And unfortunately she appears to have heard about that little affair at the Drones – I expect you have forgotten all about that, Bertie?'

'I have not!'

'No, no, not forgotten exactly. What I mean is, nobody laughs more heartily at the recollection than you. And what I want you to do, old man, is to seize an early opportunity of taking Cora aside and categorically denying that there is any truth in the story. My happiness, Bertie, is in your hands, if you know what I mean.'

Well, of course, if he put it like that, what could I do? We Woosters have our code.

'Oh, all right,' I said, but far from brightly.

'Splendid fellow!'

'When do I meet this blighted female?'

'Don't call her "this blighted female", Bertie, old man.
I have planned all that out. I will bring her round here
today for a spot of lunch.'

'What!'

'At one-thirty. Right. Good. Fine. Thanks. I knew I
could rely on you.'

He pushed off, and I turned to Jeeves, who had
shimmered in with the morning meal.

'Lunch for three today, Jeeves,' I said.

'Very good, sir.'

'You know, Jeeves, it's a bit thick. You remember my
telling you about what Mr Glossop did to me that night at
the Drones?'

'Yes, sir.'

'For months I have been cherishing dreams of getting
a bit of my own back. And now, so far from crushing
him into the dust, I've got to fill him and fiancée with
rich food and generally rally round and be the good angel.'

'Life is like that, sir.'

'True, Jeeves. What have we here?' I asked, inspecting
the tray.

'Kippered herrings, sir.'

'And I shouldn't wonder,' I said, for I was in thoughtful
mood, 'if even herrings haven't troubles of their own.'

'Quite possibly, sir.'

'I mean, apart from getting kippered.'

'Yes, sir.'

'And so it goes on, Jeeves, so it goes on.'

I can't say I exactly saw eye to eye with young Tuppy in
his admiration for the Bellinger female. Delivered on
the mat at one-twenty-five, she proved to be an
upstanding light-heavyweight of some thirty summers,
with a commanding eye and a square chin which I,
personally, would have steered clear of. She seemed to

me a good deal like what Cleopatra would have been after
going in too freely for the starches and cereals. I don't
know why it is, but women who have anything to do with
Opera, even if they're only studying for it, always appear
to run to surplus poundage.

Tuppy, however, was obviously all for her. His whole
demeanour, both before and during lunch, was that of
one striving to be worthy of a noble soul. When Jeeves
offered him a cocktail, he practically recoiled as from a
serpent. It was terrible to see the change which love had
effected in the man. The spectacle put me off my food.

At half-past two, the Bellinger left to go to a singing
lesson. Tuppy trotted after her to the door, bleating and
frisking a goodish bit, and then came back and looked at
me in a goofy sort of way.

'Well, Bertie?'

'Well, what?'

'I mean, isn't she?'

'Oh, rather,' I said, humouring the poor fish.

'Wonderful eyes?'

'Oh, rather.'

'Wonderful figure?'

'Oh, quite.'

'Wonderful voice?'

Here I was able to intone the response with a little
more heartiness. The Bellinger, at Tuppy's request, had
sung us a few songs before digging in at the trough, and
nobody could have denied that her pipes were in great
shape. Plaster was still falling from the ceiling.

'Terrific,' I said.

Tuppy sighed, and, having helped himself to about four
inches of whisky and one of soda, took a deep, refreshing
draught.

'Ah!' he said. 'I needed that.'

'Why didn't you have it at lunch?'

'Well, it's this way,' said Tuppy. 'I have not actually
ascertained what Cora's opinions are on the subject of

taking of slight snorts from time to time, but I thought it more prudent to lay off. The view I took was that laying off would seem to indicate the serious mind. It is touch-and-go, as you might say, at the moment, and the smallest thing may turn the scale.'

'What beats me is how on earth you expect to make her think you've got a mind at all – let alone a serious one.'

'I have my methods.'

'I bet they're rotten.'

'You do, do you?' said Tuppy warmly. 'Well, let me tell you, my lad, that that's exactly what they're anything but. I am handling this affair with consummate generalship. Do you remember Beefy Bingham who was at Oxford with us?'

'I ran into him only the other day. He's a parson now.'

'Yes. Down in the East End. Well, he runs a Lads' Club for the local toughs – you know the sort of thing – cocoa and backgammon in the reading room and occasional clean, bright entertainments in the Oddfellows' Hall: and I've been helping him. I don't suppose I've passed an evening away from the backgammon board for weeks. Cora is extremely pleased. I've got her to promise to sing on Tuesday at Beefy's next clean, bright entertainment.'

'You have?'

'I absolutely have. And now mark my devilish ingenuity, Bertie. I'm going to sing, too.'

'Why do you suppose that's going to get you anywhere?'

'Because the way I intend to sing the song I intend to sing will prove to her that there are great deeps in my nature, whose existence she has not suspected. She will see that rough, unlettered audience wiping the tears out of its bally eyes and she will say to herself "What ho! The old egg really has a soul!" For it is not one of your mouldy comic songs, Bertie. No low buffoonery of that sort for me. It is all about Angela being lonely and what not – '

I uttered a sharp cry.

'You don't mean you're going to sing "Sonny Boy"?'

'I jolly well do.'

I was shocked. Yes, dash it, I was shocked. You see, I held strong views on 'Sonny Boy'. I considered it a song only to be attempted by a few of the elect in the privacy of the bathroom. And the thought of it being murdered in open Oddfellows' Hall by a man who could treat a pal as young Tuppy had treated me that night at the Drones sickened me. Yes, sickened me.

I hadn't time, however, to express my horror and disgust, for at this juncture Jeeves came in.

'Mrs Travers has just rung up on the telephone, sir. She desired me to say that she will be calling to see you in a few minutes.'

'Contents noted, Jeeves,' I said. 'Now listen, Tuppy – '

I stopped. The fellow wasn't there.

'What have you done with him, Jeeves?' I asked.

'Mr Glossop has left, sir.'

'Left? How can he have left? He was sitting there – '

'That is the front door closing now, sir.'

'But what made him shoot off like that?'

'Possibly Mr Glossop did not wish to meet Mrs Travers, sir.'

'Why not?'

'I could not say, sir. But undoubtedly at the mention of Mrs Travers' name he rose very swiftly.'

'Strange, Jeeves.'

'Yes, sir.'

I turned to a subject of more moment.

'Jeeves,' I said. 'Mr Glossop proposes to sing "Sonny Boy" at an entertainment down in the East End next Tuesday.'

'Indeed, sir?'

'Before an audience consisting mainly of costermongers, with a sprinkling of whelk-stall owners, purveyors of blood-oranges, and minor pugilists.'

'Indeed, sir?'

'Make a note to remind me to be there. He will infallibly get the bird, and I want to witness his downfall.'

'Very good, sir.'

'And when Mrs Travers arrives, I shall be in the sitting room.'

Those who know Bertram Wooster best are aware that in his journey through life he is impeded and generally snootered by about as scaly a platoon of aunts as was ever assembled. But there is one exception to the general ghastliness – viz., my Aunt Dahlia. She married old Tom Travers the year Blue-bottle won the Cambridgeshire, and is one of the best. It is always a pleasure to me to chat with her, and it was with a courtly geniality that I rose to receive her as she sailed over the threshold at about two fifty-five.

She seemed somewhat perturbed, and snapped into the agenda without delay. Aunt Dahlia is one of those big, hearty women. She used to go in a lot for hunting, and she generally speaks as if she had just sighted a fox on a hillside half a mile away.

'Bertie,' she cried, in a manner of one encouraging a bevy of hounds to renewed efforts. 'I want your help.'

'And you shall have it, Aunt Dahlia,' I replied suavely. 'I can honestly say that there is no one to whom I would more readily do a good turn than yourself; no one to whom I am more delighted to be – '

'Less of it,' she begged, 'less of it. You know that friend of yours, young Glossop?'

'He's just been lunching here.'

'He has, has he? Well, I wish you'd poisoned his soup.'

'We didn't have soup. And, when you describe him as a friend of mine, I wouldn't quite say the term absolutely squared with the facts. Some time ago, one night when we had been dining together at the Drones – '

At this point Aunt Dahlia – a little brusquely, it seemed to me – said that she would rather wait for the story of my life till she could get it in book-form. I could see now that she was definitely not her usual sunny self, so I shelved my personal grievances and asked what was biting her.

'It's that young hound Glossop,' she said.

'What's he been doing?'

'Breaking Angela's heart.' (Angela. Daughter of above. My cousin. Quite a good egg.)

'Breaking Angela's heart?'

'Yes . . . Breaking . . . Angela's HEART!'

'You say he's breaking Angela's heart?'

She begged me in rather a feverish way to suspend the vaudeville cross-talk stuff.

'How's he doing that?' I asked.

'With his neglect. With his low, callous, double-crossing duplicity.'

'Duplicity is the word, Aunt Dahlia,' I said. 'In treating of young Tuppy Glossop, it springs naturally to the lips. Let me just tell you what he did to me one night at the Drones. We had finished dinner – '

'Ever since the beginning of the season, up till about three weeks ago, he was all over Angela. The sort of thing which, when I was a girl, we should have described as courting – '

'Or wooing?'

'Wooing or courting, whichever you like.'

'Whichever *you* like, Aunt Dahlia,' I said courteously.

'Well, anyway, he haunted the house, lapped up daily lunches, danced with her half the night, and so on, till naturally the poor kid, who's quite off her oats about him, took it for granted that it was only a question of time before he suggested that they should feed for life out of the same crib. And now he's gone and dropped her like a hot brick, and I hear he's infatuated with some girl he met at a Chelsea tea-party – a girl named – now, what was it?'

'Cora Bellinger.'

'How do you know?'

'She was lunching here today.'

'He brought her?'

'Yes.'

'What's she like?'

'Pretty massive. In shape, a bit on the lines of the Albert Hall.'

'Did he seem very fond of her?'

'Couldn't take his eyes off the chassis.'

'The modern young man,' said Aunt Dahlia, 'is a congenital idiot and wants a nurse to lead him by the hand and some strong attendant to kick him regularly at intervals of a quarter of an hour.'

I tried to point out the silver lining.

'If you ask me. Aunt Dahlia,' I said, 'I think Angela is well out of it. This Glossop is a tough baby. One of London's toughest. I was trying to tell you just now what he did to me one night at the Drones. First having got me in a sporting mood with a bottle of the ripest, he betted I wouldn't swing myself across the swimming-bath by the ropes and rings. I knew I could do it on my head, so I took him on, exulting in the fun, so to speak. And when I'd done half the trip and was going as strong as dammit, I found he had looped the last rope back against the rail, leaving me no alternative but to drop into the depths and swim ashore in correct evening costume.'

'He did?'

'He certainly did. It was months ago, and I haven't got really dry yet. You wouldn't want your daughter to marry a man capable of a thing like that?'

'On the contrary, you restore my faith in the young hound. I see that there must be lots of good in him, after all. And I want this Bellinger business broken up, Bertie.'

'How?'

'I don't care how. Any way you please.'

'But what can I do?'

'Do? Why, put the whole thing before your man Jeeves.

Jeeves will find a way. One of the most capable fellers I ever met. Put the thing squarely up to Jeeves and tell him to let his mind play round the topic.'

'There may be something in what you say, Aunt Dahlia,' I said thoughtfully.

'Of course there is,' said Aunt Dahlia. 'A little thing like this will be child's play to Jeeves. Get him working on it, and I'll look in tomorrow to hear the result.'

With which, she biffed off, and I summoned Jeeves to the presence.

'Jeeves,' I said, 'you have heard all?'

'Yes, sir.'

'I thought you would. My Aunt Dahlia has what you might call a carrying voice. Has it ever occurred to you that, if all other sources of income failed, she could make a good living calling the cattle home across the Sands of Dee?'

'I had not considered the point, sir, but no doubt you are right.'

'Well, how do we go? What is your reaction? I think we should do our best to help and assist.'

'Yes, sir.'

'I am fond of my Aunt Dahlia and I am fond of my cousin Angela. Fond of them both, if you get my drift. What the misguided girl finds to attract her in young Tuppy, I cannot say, Jeeves, and you cannot say. But apparently she loves the man – which shows it can be done, a thing I wouldn't have believed myself – and is pining away like – '

'Patience on a monument, sir.'

'Like Patience, as you very shrewdly remark, on a monument. So we must cluster round. Bend your brain to the problem, Jeeves. It is one that will tax you to the uttermost.'

Aunt Dahlia blew in on the morrow, and I rang the bell for Jeeves. He appeared looking brainier than one could have believed possible – sheer intellect shining from every feature – and I could see at once that the engine had been turning over.

'Speak, Jeeves,' I said.

'Very good, sir.'

'You have brooded?'

'Yes, sir.'

'With what success?'

'I have a plan, sir, which I fancy may produce satisfactory results.'

'Let's have it,' said Aunt Dahlia.

'In affairs of this description, madam, the first essential is to study the psychology of the individual.'

'The what of the individual?'

'The psychology, madam.'

'He means the psychology,' I said. 'And by psychology, Jeeves, you imply – ?'

'The natures and dispositions of the principals in the matter, sir.'

'You mean, what they're like?'

'Precisely, sir.'

'Does he talk like this to you when you're alone, Bertie?' asked Aunt Dahlia.

'Sometimes. Occasionally. And, on the other hand, sometimes not. Proceed, Jeeves.'

'Well, sir, if I may say so, the thing that struck me most forcibly about Miss Bellinger when she was under my observation was that hers was a somewhat hard and intolerant nature. I could envisage Miss Bellinger applauding success. I could not so easily see her pitying and sympathizing with failure. Possibly you will recall, sir, her attitude when Mr Glossop endeavoured to light her cigarette with his automatic lighter? I thought I detected a certain impatience at his inability to produce the necessary flame.'

'True, Jeeves. She ticked him off.'

'Precisely, sir.'

'Let me get this straight,' said Aunt Dahlia, looking a bit fogged. 'You think that, if he goes on trying to light her cigarettes with his automatic lighter long enough, she will eventually get fed up and hand him the mitten? Is that the idea?'

'I merely mentioned the episode, madam, as an indication of Miss Bellinger's somewhat ruthless nature.'

'Ruthless,' I said, 'is right. The Bellinger is hard-boiled. Those eyes. That chin. I could read them. A woman of blood and iron, if ever there was one.'

'Precisely, sir. I think, therefore, that, should Miss Bellinger be a witness of Mr Glossop appearing to disadvantage in public, she would cease to entertain affection for him. In the event, for instance, of his failing to please the audience on Tuesday with his singing – '

I saw daylight.

'By Jove, Jeeves! You mean if he gets the bird, all will be off?'

'I shall be greatly surprised if such is not the case, sir.'

I shook my head.

'We cannot leave this thing to chance, Jeeves. Young Tuppy, singing "Sonny Boy", is the likeliest prospect for the bird that I can think of – but, no – you must see for yourself that we can't simply trust to luck.'

'We need not trust to luck, sir. I would suggest that you approach your friend, Mr Bingham, and volunteer your services as a performer at his forthcoming entertainment. It could readily be arranged that you sang immediately before Mr Glossop. I fancy, sir, that, if Mr Glossop were to sing "Sonny Boy" directly after you, too, had sung "Sonny Boy", the audience would respond satisfactorily. By the time Mr Glossop began to sing, they would have lost their taste for that particular song and would express their feelings warmly.'

'Jeeves,' said Aunt Dahlia, 'you're a marvel!'

'Thank you, madam.'

83

'Jeeves,' I said, 'you're an ass!'

'What do you mean, he's an ass?' said Aunt Dahlia hotly. 'I think it's the greatest scheme I ever heard.'

'Me sing "Sonny Boy" at Beefy Bingham's clean, bright entertainment? I can see myself!'

'You sing it daily in your bath, sir. Mr Wooster,' said Jeeves, turning to Aunt Dahlia, 'has a pleasant, light baritone – '

'I bet he has,' said Aunt Dahlia.

I froze the man with a look.

'Between singing "Sonny Boy" in one's bath, Jeeves, and singing it before a hall full of assorted blood-orange merchants and their young, there is a substantial difference.'

'Bertie,' said Aunt Dahlia, 'you'll sing, and like it!'

'I will not.'

'Bertie!'

'Nothing will induce – '

'Bertie,' said Aunt Dahlia firmly, 'you will sing "Sonny Boy" on Tuesday, the third *prox,* and sing it like a lark at sunrise, or may an aunt's curse – '

'I won't.'

'Think of Angela!'

'Dash Angela!'

'Bertie!'

'No, I mean, hang it all!'

'You won't?'

'No, I won't.'

'That is your last word, is it?'

'It is. Once and for all, Aunt Dahlia, nothing will induce me to let out so much as a single note.'

And so that afternoon I sent a pre-paid wire to Beefy Bingham, offering my services in the cause, and by nightfall the thing was fixed up. I was billed to perform next but one after the intermission. Following me, came Tuppy. And, immediately after him, Miss Cora Bellinger, the well-known operatic soprano.

'Jeeves,' I said that evening – and I said it coldly – 'I shall be obliged if you will pop round to the nearest music-shop and procure me a copy of "Sonny Boy". It will now be necessary for me to learn both verse and refrain. Of the trouble and nervous strain which this will involve, I say nothing.'

'Very good, sir.'

'But this I do say – '

'I had better be starting immediately, sir, or the shop will be closed.'

'Ha!' I said.

And I meant it to sting.

Although I had steeled myself to the ordeal before me and had set out full of the calm, quiet courage which makes men do desperate deeds with careless smiles, I must admit that there was a moment, just after I had entered the Oddfellows' Hall at Bermondsey East and run an eye over the assembled pleasure-seekers, when it needed all the bulldog pluck of the Woosters to keep me from calling it a day and taking a cab back to civilization. The clean, bright entertainment was in full swing when I arrived, and somebody who looked as if he might be the local undertaker was reciting 'Gunga Din'. And the audience, though not actually chi-yiking in the full technical sense of the term, had a grim look which I didn't like at all. The mere sight of them gave me the sort of feeling Shadrach, Meshach and Abednego must have had when preparing to enter the burning, fiery furnace.

Scanning the multitude, it seemed to me that they were for the nonce suspending judgement. Did you ever tap on the door of one of those New York speakeasy places and see the grille snap back and a Face appear? There is one long, silent moment when its eyes are fixed on yours and all your past life seems to rise up before you. Then you say that you are a friend of Mr Zinzinheimer and he told you they would treat you right if you mentioned

his name, and the strain relaxes. Well, these
costermongers and whelkstallers appeared to me to be
looking just like that Face. Start something, they seemed
to say, and they would know what to do about it. And I
couldn't help feeling that my singing 'Sonny Boy' would
come, in their opinion, under the head of starting
something.

'A nice, full house, sir,' said a voice at my elbow. It
was Jeeves, watching the proceedings with an indulgent
eye.

'You here, Jeeves?' I said, coldly.

'Yes, sir. I have been present since the
commencement.'

'Oh?' I said. 'Any casualties yet?'

'Sir?'

'You know what I mean, Jeeves,' I said sternly, 'and
don't pretend you don't. Anybody got the bird yet?'

'Oh, no, sir.'

'I shall be the first, you think?'

'No, sir. I see no reason to expect such a misfortune. I
anticipate that you will be well received.'

A sudden thought struck me.

'And you think everything will go according to
plan?'

'Yes, sir.'

'Well, I don't,' I said. 'And I'll tell you why I don't. I've
spotted a flaw in your beastly scheme.'

'A flaw, sir?'

'Yes. Do you suppose for a moment that, if when Mr
Glossop hears me singing that dashed song, he'll come
calmly on a minute after me and sing it too? Use your
intelligence, Jeeves. He will perceive the chasm in his
path and pause in time. He will back out and refuse to go
on at all.'

'Mr Glossop will not hear you sing, sir. At my advice,
he has stepped across the road to the Jug and Bottle, an
establishment immediately opposite the hall, and he

intends to remain there until it is time for him to appear on the platform.'

'Oh?' I said.

'If I might suggest it, sir, there is another house named the Goat and Grapes only a short distance down the street. I think it might be a judicious move – '

'If I were to put a bit of custom in their way?'

'It would ease the nervous strain of waiting, sir.'

I had not been feeling any too pleased with the man for having let me in for this ghastly binge, but at these words, I'm bound to say, my austerity softened a trifle. He was undoubtedly right. He had studied the psychology of the individual, and it had not led him astray. A quiet ten minutes at the Goat and Grapes was exactly what my system required. To buzz off there and inhale a couple of swift whisky-and-sodas was with Bertram Wooster the work of a moment.

The treatment worked like magic. What they had put into the stuff, besides vitriol, I could not have said; but it completely altered my outlook on life. That curious, gulpy feeling passed. I was no longer conscious of the sagging sensation at the knees. The limbs ceased to quiver gently, the tongue became loosened in its socket, and the backbone stiffened. Pausing merely to order and swallow another of the same, I bade the barmaid a cheery good night, nodded affably to one or two fellows in the bar whose faces I liked, and came prancing back to the hall, ready for anything.

And shortly afterwards I was on the platform with about a million bulging eyes goggling up at me. There was a rummy sort of buzzing in my ears, and then through the buzzing I heard the sound of a piano starting to tinkle: and, commending my soul to God, I took a good, long breath and charged in.

Well, it was a close thing. The whole incident is a bit blurred, but I seem to recollect a kind of murmur as I hit the refrain. I thought at the time it was an attempt on the part of the many-headed to join in the chorus, and at the moment it rather encouraged me. I passed the thing over the larynx with all the vim at my disposal, hit the high note, and off gracefully into the wings. I didn't come on again to take a bow. I just receded and oiled round to where Jeeves awaited me among the standees at the back.

'Well, Jeeves,' I said, anchoring myself at his side and brushing the honest sweat from the brow, 'they didn't rush the platform.'

'No, sir.'

'But you can spread it about that that's the last time I perform outside my bath. My swan-song, Jeeves. Anybody who wants to hear me in future must present himself at the bathroom door and shove his ear against the keyhole. I may be wrong, but it seemed to me that towards the end they were hotting up a trifle. The bird was hovering in the air. I could hear the beating of its wings.'

'I did detect a certain restlessness, sir, in the audience. I fancy they have lost their taste for that particular melody.'

'Eh?'

'I should have informed you earlier, sir, that the song had already been sung twice before you arrived.'

'What!'

'Yes, sir. Once by a lady and once by a gentleman. It is a very popular song, sir.'

I gaped at the man. That, with this knowledge, he could calmly have allowed the young master to step straight into the jaws of death, so to speak, paralysed me. It seemed to show that the old feudal spirit had passed away altogether. I was about to give him my views on the matter in no uncertain fashion, when I was stopped by the spectacle of young Tuppy lurching on to the platform.

Young Tuppy had the unmistakable air of a man who has recently been round to the Jug and Bottle. A few cheery cries of welcome, presumably from some of his

backgammon-playing pals who felt that blood was
thicker than water, had the effect of causing the genial
smile on his face to widen till it nearly met at the back.
He was plainly feeling about as good as a man can feel
and still remain on his feet. He waved a kindly hand to
his supporters, and bowed in a regal sort of manner, rather
like an Eastern monarch acknowledging the plaudits of
the mob.

Then the female at the piano struck up the opening
bars of 'Sonny Boy', and Tuppy swelled like a balloon,
clasped his hands together, rolled his eyes up at the ceiling
in a manner denoting Soul, and began. I think the populace
was too stunned for the moment to take immediate steps.
It may seem incredible, but I give you my word that
young Tuppy got right through the verse without so much
as a murmur. Then they all seemed to pull themselves
together.

A costermonger, roused, is a terrible thing. I had never
seen the proletariat really stirred before, and I'm bound
to say it rather awed me. I mean, it gave you some idea of
what it must have been like during the French
Revolution. From every corner of the hall there proceeded
simultaneously the sort of noise which you hear, they
tell me, at one of those East End boxing places when the
referee disqualifies the popular favourite and makes
the quick dash for life. And then they passed beyond mere
words and began to introduce the vegetable motive.

I don't know why, but somehow I had got it into my
head that the first thing thrown at Tuppy would be a
potato. One gets these fancies. It was, however, as a matter
of fact, a banana, and I saw in an instant that the choice
had been made by wiser heads than mine. These blokes
who have grown up from childhood in the knowledge of
how to treat a dramatic entertainment that doesn't please
them are aware by a sort of instinct just what to do for
the best, and the moment I saw the banana splash on
Tuppy's shirt-front I realized how infinitely more

effective and artistic it was than any potato could have been.

Not that the potato school of thought had not also its supporters. As the proceedings warmed up, I noticed several intelligent-looking fellows who threw nothing else.

The effect on young Tuppy was rather remarkable. His eyes bulged and his hair seemed to stand up, and yet his mouth went on opening and shutting, and you could see that in a dazed, automatic way he was still singing 'Sonny Boy'. Then, coming out of his trance, he began to pull for the shore with some rapidity. The last seen of him, he was beating a tomato to the exit by a short head.

Presently the tumult and the shouting died. I turned to Jeeves.

'Painful, Jeeves,' I said. 'But what would you?'

'Yes, sir.'

'The surgeon's knife, what?'

'Precisely, sir.'

'Well, with this happening beneath her eyes, I think we may definitely consider the Glossop-Bellinger romance off.'

'Yes, sir.'

At this point old Beefy Bingham came out on to the platform.

'Ladies and gentlemen,' said old Beefy.

I supposed that he was about to rebuke his flock for the recent expression of feeling. But such was not the case. No doubt he was accustomed by now to the wholesome give-and-take of these clean, bright entertainments and had ceased to think it worth while to make any comment when there was a certain liveliness.

'Ladies and gentlemen,' said old Beefy, 'the next item on the programme was to have been Songs by Miss Cora Bellinger, the well-known operatic soprano. I have just received a telephone-message from Miss Bellinger, saying that her car has broken down. She is, however, on her way here in a cab and will arrive shortly. Meanwhile, our friend Mr Enoch Simpson will recite "Dangerous Dan McGrew".'

I clutched at Jeeves.

'Jeeves! You heard?'

'Yes, sir.'

'She wasn't there!'

'No, sir.'

'She saw nothing of Tuppy's Waterloo.'

'No, sir.'

'The whole bally scheme has blown a fuse.'

'Yes, sir.'

'Come, Jeeves,' I said, and those standing by wondered, no doubt, what had caused that clean-cut face to grow so pale and set. 'I have been subjected to a nervous strain unparalleled since the days of the early Martyrs. I have lost pounds in weight and permanently injured my entire system. I have gone through an ordeal, the recollection of which will make me wake up screaming in the night for months to come. And all for nothing. Let us go.'

'If you have no objection, sir, I would like to witness the remainder of the entertainment.'

'Suit yourself, Jeeves,' I said moodily. 'Personally, my heart is dead and I am going to look in at the Goat and Grapes for another of their cyanide specials and then home.'

It must have been about half-past ten, and I was in the old sitting room sombrely sucking down a more or less final restorative, when the front-door bell rang, and there on the mat was young Tuppy. He looked like a man who has passed through some great experience and stood face to face with his soul. He had the beginnings of a black eye.

'Oh, hullo, Bertie,' said young Tuppy.

He came in and hovered about the mantelpiece as if he were looking for things to fiddle with and break.

'I've just been singing at Beefy Bingham's entertainment,' he said after a pause.

'Oh?' I said. 'How did you go?'

'Like a breeze,' said young Tuppy. 'Held them spellbound.'

'Knocked 'em, eh?'

'Cold,' said young Tuppy. 'Not a dry eye.'

And this, mark you, a man who had had a good upbringing and had, no doubt, spent years at his mother's knee being taught to tell the truth.

'I suppose Miss Bellinger is pleased?'

'Oh, yes. Delighted.'

'So now everything's all right?'

'Oh, quite.'

Tuppy paused.

'On the other hand, Bertie – '

'Yes?'

'Well, I've been thinking things over. Somehow I don't believe Miss Bellinger is the mate for me after all.'

'You don't?'

'No, I don't.'

'Why don't you?'

'Oh, I don't know. These things sort of flash on you. I respect Miss Bellinger, Bertie. I admire her. But – er – well, I can't help feeling now that a sweet, gentle girl – er – like your cousin Angela, for instance, Bertie, – would – er – in fact – well, what I came round for was to ask if you would 'phone Angela and find out how she reacts to the idea of coming out with me tonight to the Berkeley for a segment of supper and a spot of dancing.'

'Go ahead. There's the 'phone.'

'No, I'd rather you asked her, Bertie. What with one thing and another, if you paved the way – You see, there's just a chance that she may be – I mean, you know how misunderstandings occur – and – well, what I'm driving at, Bertie, old man, is that I'd rather you surged round and did a bit of paving, if you don't mind.'

I went to the 'phone and called up Aunt Dahlia's.

'She says come right along,' I said.

'Tell her,' said Tuppy in a devout sort of voice, 'that I will be with her in something under a couple of ticks.'

He had barely biffed, when I heard a click in the keyhole and a soft padding in the passage without.

'Jeeves,' I called.

'Sir?' said Jeeves, manifesting himself.

'Jeeves, a remarkably rummy thing has happened. Mr Glossop has just been here. He tells me that it is all off between him and Miss Bellinger.'

'Yes, sir.'

'You don't seem surprised.'

'No, sir. I confess I had anticipated some such eventuality.'

'Eh? What gave you that idea?'

'It came to me, sir, when I observed Miss Bellinger strike Mr Glossop in the eye.'

'Strike him!'

'Yes, sir.'

'In the eye?'

'The right eye, sir.'

I clutched the brow.

'What on earth made her do that?'

'I fancy she was a little upset, sir, at the reception accorded to her singing.'

'Great Scott! Don't tell me she got the bird, too?'

'Yes, sir.'

'But why? She's got a red-hot voice.'

'Yes, sir. But I think the audience resented her choice of a song.'

'Jeeves!' Reason was beginning to do a bit of tottering on its throne. 'You aren't going to stand there and tell me that Miss Bellinger sang "Sonny Boy" too!'

'Yes, sir. And rashly, in my opinion – brought a large doll on to the platform to sing it to. The audience affected

93

to mistake it for a ventriloquist's dummy, and there was some little disturbance.'

'But, Jeeves, what a coincidence!'

'Not altogether, sir. I ventured to take the liberty of accosting Miss Bellinger on her arrival at the hall and recalling myself to her recollection. I then said that Mr Glossop had asked me to request her that as a particular favour to him – the song being a favourite of his – she would sing "Sonny Boy". And when she found that you and Mr Glossop had also sung the song immediately before her, I rather fancy that she supposed that she had been made the victim of a practical pleasantry by Mr Glossop. Will there be anything further, sir?'

'No, thanks.'

'Good night, sir.'

'Good night, Jeeves,' I said reverently.

4 — Gussie Presents the Prizes

Everything was in train. Jeeves's morbid scruples about lacing the chap's orange juice had put me to a good deal of trouble, but I had surmounted every obstacle in the old Wooster way. I had secured an abundance of the necessary spirit, and it was now lying in its flask in the drawer of the dressing-table. I had also ascertained that the jug, duly filled, would be standing on a shelf in the butler's pantry round about the hour of one. To remove it from that shelf, sneak it up to my room, and return it, laced, in good time for the midday meal would be a task calling, no doubt, for address, but in no sense an exacting one.

It was with something of the emotions of one preparing for a treat for a deserving child that I finished my tea and rolled over for that extra spot of sleep which just makes all the difference when there is man's work to be done and the brain must be kept clear for it.

And when I came downstairs an hour or so later, I knew how right I had been to formulate this scheme for Gussie's bucking up. I ran into him on the lawn, and I could see at a glance that if ever there was a man who needed a snappy stimulant, it was he. All nature, as I have indicated, was smiling, but not Augustus Fink-Nottle. He was walking round in circles, muttering something about not proposing to detain us long, but on this auspicious occasion feeling compelled to say a few words.

'Ah, Gussie,' I said, arresting him as he was about to start another lap. 'A lovely morning, is it not?'

Even if I had not been aware of it already, I could have divined from the abruptness with which he damned the lovely morning that he was not in merry mood. I addressed myself to the task of bringing the roses back into his cheeks.

'I've got good news for you, Gussie.'

He looked at me with a sudden sharp interest.

'Has Market Snodsbury Grammar School burned down?'

'Not that I know of.'

'Have mumps broken out? Is the place closed on account of measles?'

'No, no.'

'Then what do you mean you've got good news?'

I endeavoured to soothe.

'You mustn't take it so hard, Gussie. Why worry about a laughably simple job like distributing prizes at a school?'

'Laughably simple, eh? Do you realize I've been sweating for days and haven't been able to think of something to say yet, except that I won't detain them long. You bet I won't detain them long. I've been timing my speech, and it lasts five seconds. What the devil am I to say, Bertie? What do you say when you're distributing prizes?'

I considered. Once, at my private school, I had won a prize for Scripture knowledge, so I suppose I ought to have been full of inside stuff. But memory eluded me.

Then something emerged from the mists.

'You say the race is not always to the swift.'

'Why?'

'Well, it's a good gag. It generally gets a hand.'

'I mean, why isn't it? Why isn't the race to the swift?'

'Ah, there you have me. But the nibs say it isn't.'

'But what does it mean?'

'I take it it's supposed to console the chaps who haven't won prizes.'

'What's the good of that to me? I'm not worrying about them. It's the ones that have won prizes that I'm

worrying about, the little blighters who will come up on
the platform. Suppose they make faces at me.'

'They won't.'

'How do you know they won't? It's probably the first
thing they'll think of. And even if they don't – Bertie,
shall I tell you something?'

'What?'

'I've a good mind to take that tip of yours and have a
drink.'

I smiled. He little knew, about summed up what I was
thinking.

'Oh, you'll be all right,' I said.

He became fevered again.

'How do you know I'll be all right? I'm sure to blow
up in my lines.'

'Tush!'

'Or drop a prize.'

'Tut!'

'Or something. I can feel it in my bones. As sure as
I'm standing here, something is going to happen this
afternoon which will make everybody laugh themselves
sick at me. I can hear them now. Like hyenas . . . Bertie!'

'Hullo?'

'Do you remember that kids' school we went to before
Eton?'

'Quite. It was there I won my Scripture prize.'

'Never mind about your Scripture prize. I'm not
talking about your Scripture prize. Do you recollect the
Bosher incident?'

I did, indeed. It was one of the high spots of my youth.

'Major-General Sir Wilfred Bosher came to distribute
the prizes at that school,' proceeded Gussie in a dull,
toneless voice. 'He dropped a book. He stooped to pick it
up. And, as he stooped, his trousers split up the back.'

'How we roared!'

Gussie's face twisted.

'We did, little swine that we were. Instead of remaining

97

silent and exhibiting a decent sympathy for a gallant officer at a peculiarly embarrassing moment, we howled and yelled with mirth. I loudest of any. That is what will happen to me this afternoon, Bertie. It will be a judgement on me for laughing like that at Major-General Sir Wilfred Bosher.'

'No, no, Gussie, old man. Your trousers won't split.'

'How do you know they won't? Better men than I have split their trousers. General Bosher was a D. S. O., with a fine record of service on the north-western frontier of India, and his trousers split. I shall be a mockery and a scorn. I know it. And you, fully cognizant of what I am in for, babbling about good news. What news could possibly be good to me at this moment except the information that bubonic plague had broken out among the scholars of Market Snodsbury Grammar School, and that they were all confined to their beds with spots?'

The moment had come for me to speak. I laid a hand gently on his shoulder. He brushed it off. I laid it on again. He brushed it off once more. I was endeavouring to lay it on for the third time, when he moved aside and desired, with a certain petulance, to be informed if I thought I was a ruddy osteopath.

I found his manner trying, but one has to make allowances. I was telling myself that I should be seeing a very different Gussie after lunch.

'When I said I had good news, old man, I meant about Madeline Bassett.'

The febrile gleam died out of his eyes, to be replaced by a look of infinite sadness.

'You can't have good news about her. I've dished myself there completely.'

'Not at all. I am convinced that if you take another whack at her, all will be well.'

And, keeping it snappy, I related what had passed between the Bassett and myself on the previous night.

'So all you have to do is play a return date, and you

cannot fail to swing the voting. You are her dream man.'

He shook his head.

'No.'

'What?'

'No use.'

'What do you mean?'

'Not a bit of good trying.'

'But I tell you she said so in so many words – '

'It doesn't make any difference. She may have loved me once. Last night will have killed all that.'

'Of course it won't.'

'It will. She despises me now.'

'Not a bit of it. She knows you simply got cold feet.'

'And I should get cold feet if I tried again. It's no good, Bertie. I'm hopeless, and there's an end of it. Fate made me the sort of chap who can't say "bo" to a goose.'

'It isn't a question of saying "bo" to a goose. The point doesn't arise at all. It is simply a matter of – '

'I know, I know. But it's no good. I can't do it. The whole thing is off. I am not going to risk a repetition of last night's fiasco. You talk in a light way of taking another whack at her, but you don't know what it means. You have not been through the experience of starting to ask the girl you love to marry you and then suddenly finding yourself talking about the plumlike external gills of the newly-born newt. It's not a thing you can do twice. No, I accept my destiny. It's all over. And now, Bertie, like a good chap, shove off. I want to compose my speech. I can't compose my speech with you mucking around. If you are going to continue to muck around, at least give me a couple of stories. The little hell hounds are sure to expect a story or two.'

'Do you know the one about – '

'No good. I don't want any of your off-colour stuff from the Drones' smoking-room. I need something clean. Something that will be a help to them in their after lives.

Not that I care a damn about their after lives, except that I hope they'll all choke.'

'I heard a story the other day. I can't quite remember it, but it was about a chap who snored and disturbed the neighbours, and it ended, "It was his adenoids that adenoid them."''

He made a weary gesture.

'You expect me to work that in, do you, into a speech to be delivered to an audience of boys, every one of whom is probably riddled with adenoids? Damn it, they'd rush the platform. Leave me, Bertie. Push off. That's all I ask you to do. Push off . . . Ladies and gentlemen,' said Gussie, in a low, soliloquizing sort of way, 'I do not propose to detain this auspicious occasion long – '

It was a thoughtful Wooster who walked away and left him at it. More than ever I was congratulating myself on having had the sterling good sense to make all my arrangements so that I could press a button and set the things moving at an instant's notice.

Until now, you see, I had rather entertained a sort of hope that when I had revealed to him the Bassett's mental attitude, Nature would have done the rest, bracing him up to such an extent that artificial stimulants would not be required. Because, naturally, a chap doesn't want to have to sprint about country houses lugging jugs of orange juice, unless it is absolutely essential.

But now I saw that I must carry on as planned. The total absence of pep, ginger, and the right spirit which the man had displayed during these conversational exchanges convinced me that the strongest measure would be necessary. Immediately upon leaving him, therefore, I proceeded to the pantry, waited till the butler had removed himself elsewhere, and nipped in and secured the vital jug. A few moments later, after a wary passage of the stairs, I was in my room. And the first thing I saw there was Jeeves, fooling about with trousers.

He gave the jug a look which – wrongly, as it was to

turn out – I diagnosed as censorious. I drew myself up a bit. I intended to have no rot from the fellow.

'Yes, Jeeves?'

'Sir?'

'You have the air of one about to make a remark, Jeeves.'

'Oh, no, sir. I note that you are in possession of Mr Fink-Nottle's orange juice. I was merely about to observe that in my opinion it would be injudicious to add spirit to it.'

'That is a remark, Jeeves, and it is precisely – '

'Because I have already attended to the matter, sir.'

'What?'

'Yes, sir. I decided, after all, to acquiesce in your wishes.'

I stared at the man, astounded. I was deeply moved. Well, I mean, wouldn't any chap who had been going about thinking that the old feudal spirit was dead and then suddenly found it wasn't, have been deeply moved?

'Jeeves,' I said, 'I am touched.'

'Thank you, sir.'

'Touched and gratified.'

'Thank you very much, sir.'

'But what caused this change of heart?'

'I chanced to encounter Mr Fink-Nottle in the garden, sir, while you were still in bed, and we had a brief conversation.'

'And you came away feeling that he needed a bracer?'

'Very much so, sir. His attitude struck me as defeatist.'

I nodded.

'I felt the same. "Defeatist" sums it up to a nicety. Did you tell him his attitude struck you as defeatist?'

'Yes, sir.'

'But it didn't do any good?'

'No, sir.'

'Very well, then, Jeeves. We must act. How much gin did you put in the jug?'

'A liberal tumblerful, sir.'

'Would that be a normal dose for an adult defeatist, do you think?'

'I fancy it should prove adequate, sir.'

'I wonder. We must not spoil the ship for a ha'porth of tar. I think I'll add just another fluid ounce or so.'

'I would not advocate it, sir. In the case of Lord Brancaster's parrot – '

'You are falling into your old error, Jeeves, of thinking that Gussie is a parrot. Fight against this. I shall add the oz.'

'Very good, sir.'

'And, by the way, Jeeves, Mr Fink-Nottle is in the market for bright, clean stories to use in his speech. Do you know any?'

'I know a story about two Irishmen, sir.'

'Pat and Mike?'

'Yes, sir.'

'Who were walking along Broadway?'

'Yes, sir.'

'Just what he wants. Any more?'

'No, sir.'

'Well, every little helps. You had better go and tell it to him.'

'Very good, sir.'

He passed from the room, and I unscrewed the flask and tilted into the jug a generous modicum of its contents. And scarcely had I done so, when there came to my ears the sound of footsteps without. I had only just time to shove the jug behind the photograph of Uncle Tom on the mantelpiece before the door opened and in came Gussie, curveting like a circus horse.

'What-ho, Bertie,' he said. 'What-ho, what-ho, what-ho, and again what-ho. What a beautiful world this is, Bertie. One of the nicest I ever met.'

I stared at him speechless. We Woosters are as quick

as lightning, and I saw at once that something had happened.

I mean to say, I told you about him walking round in circles. I recorded what passed between us on the lawn. And if I portrayed the scene with anything like adequate skill, the picture you will have retained of this Fink-Nottle will have been that of a nervous wreck, sagging at the knees, green about the gills, and picking feverishly at the lapels of his coat in an ecstasy of craven fear. In a word, defeatist. Gussie, during that interview, had, in fine, exhibited all the earmarks of one licked to a custard.

Vastly different was the Gussie who stood before me now. Self-confidence seemed to ooze from the fellow's every pore. His face was flushed, there was a jovial light in his eyes, the lips were parted in a swashbuckling smile. And when with a genial hand he sloshed me on the back before I could sidestep, it was as if I had been kicked by a mule.

'Well, Bertie,' he proceeded, as blithely as a linnet without a thing on his mind, 'you will be glad to hear that you were right. Your theory has been tested and proved correct. I feel like a fighting cock.'

My brain ceased to reel. I saw all.

'Have you been having a drink?'

'I have. As you advised. Unpleasant stuff. Like medicine. Burns your throat, too, and makes one as thirsty as the dickens. How anyone can mop it up, as you do, for pleasure, beats me. Still, I would be the last to deny that it tunes up the system. I could bite a tiger.'

'What did you have?'

'Whisky. At least, that was the label on the decanter, and I have no reason to suppose that a woman like your aunt – staunch, true-blue, British – would deliberately deceive the public. If she labels her decanters Whisky, then I consider that we know where we are.'

'A whisky and soda, eh? You couldn't have done better.'

'Soda?' said Gussie thoughtfully. 'I knew there was something I had forgotten.'

'Didn't you put any soda in it?'

'It never occurred to me. I just nipped into the dining-room and drank out of the decanter.'

'How much?'

'Oh, about ten swallows. Twelve, maybe. Or fourteen. Say sixteen medium-sized gulps. Gosh, I'm thirsty.'

He moved over to the wash-stand and drank deeply out of the water bottle. I cast a covert glance at Uncle Tom's photograph behind his back. For the first time since it had come into my life, I was glad that it was so large. It hid its secret well. If Gussie had caught sight of that jug of orange juice, he would unquestionably have been on to it like a knife.

'Well, I'm glad you're feeling braced,' I said.

He moved buoyantly from the wash-stand, and endeavoured to slosh me on the back again. Foiled by my nimble footwork, he staggered to the bed and sat down upon it.

'Braced? Did I say I could bite a tiger?'

'You did.'

'Make it two tigers. I could chew holes in a steel door. What an ass you must have thought me out there in the garden. I see now you were laughing in your sleeve.'

'No, no.'

'Yes,' insisted Gussie. 'That very sleeve,' he said, pointing. 'And I don't blame you. I can't imagine why I made all that fuss about a potty job like distributing prizes at a rotten little country grammar school. Can you imagine, Bertie?'

'No.'

'Exactly. Nor can I imagine. There's simply nothing to it. I just shin up on the platform, drop a few gracious words, hand the little blighters their prizes, and hop down again, admired by all. Not a suggestion of split trousers from start to finish. I mean, why should anybody split his trousers? I can't imagine. Can you imagine?'

'No.'

'Nor can I imagine. I shall be a riot. I know just the sort of stuff that's needed – simple, manly, optimistic stuff straight from the shoulder. This shoulder,' said Gussie, tapping. 'Why I was so nervous this morning I can't imagine. For anything simpler than distributing a few footling books to a bunch of grimy-faced kids I can't imagine. Still, for some reason I can't imagine, I was feeling a little nervous, but now I feel fine, Bertie – fine, fine, fine – and I say this to you as an old friend. Because that's what you are, old man, when all the smoke has cleared away – an old friend. I don't think I've ever met an older friend. How long have you been an old friend of mine, Bertie?'

'Oh, years and years.'

'Imagine! Though, of course, there must have been a time when you were a new friend . . . Hullo, the luncheon gong. Come on, old friend.'

And, rising from the bed like a performing flea, he made for the door.

I followed rather pensively. What had occurred was, of course, so much velvet, as you might say. I mean, I had wanted a braced Fink-Nottle – indeed, all my plans had had a braced Fink-Nottle as their end and aim – but I found myself wondering a little whether the Fink-Nottle now sliding down the banister wasn't, perhaps, a shade too braced. His demeanour seemed to me that of a man who might quite easily throw bread about at lunch.

Fortunately, however, the settled gloom of those around him exercised a restraining effect upon him at the table. It would have needed a far more plastered man to have been rollicking at such a gathering. I had told the Bassett that there were aching hearts in Brinkley Court, and it now looked probable that there would shortly be aching tummies. Anatole, I learned, had retired to his bed with a fit of the vapours, and the meal now before us had been cooked by the kitchen maid – as C3 a performer as ever wielded a skillet.

This, coming on top of their other troubles, induced in the company a pretty unanimous silence – a solemn silence, as you might say – which even Gussie did not seem prepared to break. Except, therefore, for one short snatch of song on his part, nothing untoward marked the occasion, and presently we rose, with instructions from Aunt Dahlia to put on festal raiment and be at Market Snodsbury not later than 3.30. This leaving me ample time to smoke a gasper or two in a shady bower beside the lake, I did so, repairing to my room round about the hour of three.

Jeeves was on the job, adding the final polish to the old topper, and I was about to appraise him of the latest developments in the matter of Gussie, when he forestalled me by observing that the latter had only just concluded an agreeable visit to the Wooster bedchamber.

'I found Mr Fink-Nottle seated here when I arrived to lay out your clothes, sir.'

'Indeed, Jeeves? Gussie was in here, was he?'

'Yes, sir. He left only a few moments ago. He's driving to the school with Mr and Mrs Travers in the large car.'

'Did you give him your story of the two Irishmen?'

'Yes, sir. He laughed heartily.'

'Good. Had you any other contributions for him?'

'I ventured to suggest that he might mention to the young gentlemen that education is a drawing out, not a putting in. The late Lord Brancaster was much addicted to presenting prizes at schools, and he invariably employed this dictum.'

'And how did he react to that?'

'He laughed heartily, sir.'

'This surprised you, no doubt? This practically incessant merriment, I mean.'

'Yes, sir.'

'You thought it odd in one who, when you last saw him, was well up in Group A of the defeatists.'

'Yes, sir.'

'There is a ready explanation, Jeeves. Since you last saw him, Gussie has been on a bender. He's as tight as an owl.'

'Indeed, sir?'

'Absolutely. His nerve cracked under the strain, and he sneaked into the dining-room and started mopping the stuff up like a vacuum cleaner. Whisky would seem to be what he filled the radiator with. I gather that he used up most of the decanter. Golly, Jeeves, it's lucky he didn't get at that laced orange juice on top of that, what?'

'Extremely, sir.'

I eyed the jug. Uncle Tom's photograph had fallen into the fender, and it was standing there right out in the open, where Gussie couldn't have helped seeing it. Mercifully, it was empty now.

'It was a most prudent act on your part, if I may say so, sir, to dispose of the orange juice.'

I stared at the man.

'What? Didn't you?'

'No, sir.'

'Jeeves, let us get this clear. Was it not you who threw away that o.j.?'

'No, sir. I assumed, when I entered the room and found the pitcher empty, that you had done so.'

We looked at each other, awed. Two minds with but a single thought.

'I very much fear, sir – '

'So do I, Jeeves.'

'It would seem almost certain – '

'Quite certain. Weigh the facts. Sift the evidence. The jug was standing on the mantelpiece, for all eyes to behold. Gussie had been complaining of thirst. You found him in here, laughing heartily. I think that there can be little doubt, Jeeves, that the entire contents of that jug are at this moment reposing on top of the existing cargo in that already brilliantly lit man's interior. Disturbing, Jeeves.'

'Most disturbing, sir.'

'Let us face the position, forcing ourselves to be calm. You inserted in that jug – shall we say a tumblerful of the right stuff?'

'Fully a tumblerful, sir.'

'And I added of my plenty about the same amount.'

'Yes, sir.'

'And in two shakes of a duck's tail Gussie, with all that lapping about inside him, will be distributing the prizes at Market Snodsbury Grammar School before an audience of all that is fairest and most refined in the country.'

'Yes, sir.'

'It seems to me, Jeeves, that the ceremony may be one fraught with considerable interest.'

'Yes, sir.'

'What, in your opinion, will the harvest be?'

'One finds it difficult to hazard a conjecture, sir.'

'You mean imagination boggles?'

'Yes, sir.'

I inspected my imagination. He was right. It boggled.

'And yet, Jeeves,' I said, twiddling a thoughtful steering wheel, 'there is always the bright side.'

Some twenty minutes had elapsed, and having picked the honest fellow up outside the front door, I was driving in the two-seater to the picturesque town of Market Snodsbury. Since we had parted – he to go to his lair and fetch his hat, I to remain in my room and complete the formal costume – I had been doing some close thinking.

The results of this I now proceeded to hand on to him.

'However dark the prospect may be, Jeeves, however murkily the storm clouds may seem to gather, a keen eye can usually discern the blue bird. It is bad, no doubt, that Gussie should be going, some ten minutes from now, to distribute prizes in a state of advanced intoxication, but we must never forget that these things cut both ways.'

'You imply, sir – '

'Precisely. I am thinking of him in his capacity of wooer. All this ought to have put him in rare shape for offering his hand in marriage. I shall be vastly surprised if it won't turn him into a sort of caveman. Have you ever seen James Cagney in the movies?'

'Yes, sir.'

'Something on those lines.'

I heard him cough, and sniped him with a sideways glance. He was wearing that informative look of his.

'Then you have not heard, sir?'

'Eh?'

'You are not aware that a marriage has been arranged and will shortly take place between Mr Fink-Nottle and Miss Bassett?'

'What?'

'Yes, sir.'

'When did this happen?'

'Shortly after Mr Fink-Nottle had left your room, sir.'

'Ah! In the post-orange juice era?'

'Yes, sir.'

'But are you sure of your facts? How do you know?'

'My informant was Mr Fink-Nottle himself, sir. He appeared anxious to confide in me. His story was somewhat incoherent, but I had no difficulty in apprehending its substance. Prefacing his remarks with the statement that this was a beautiful world, he laughed heartily and said that he became formally engaged.'

'No details?'

'No, sir.'

'But one can picture the scene.'

'Yes, sir.'

'I mean, imagination doesn't boggle.'

'No, sir.'

And it didn't. I could see exactly what must have happened. Insert a liberal dose of mixed spirits in a normally abstemious man, and he becomes a force. He does not stand around, twiddling his fingers and stammering. He acts. I had no doubt that Gussie must have reached for the Bassett and clasped her to him like a stevedore handling a sack of coals. And one could readily envisage the effect of that sort of thing on a girl of romantic mind.

'Well, well, well, Jeeves.'

'Yes, sir.'

'This is splendid news.'

'Yes, sir.'

'You see now how right I was.'

'Yes, sir.'

'It must have been rather an eye-opener for you, watching me handle this case.'

'Yes, sir.'

'The simple, direct method never fails.'

'No, sir.'

'Whereas the elaborate does.'

'Yes, sir.'

'Right-ho, Jeeves.'

We had arrived at Market Snodsbury Grammar School. It had, I understood, been built somewhere in the year 1416, and as with so many of these ancient foundations, there still seemed to brood over its Great Hall, where the afternoon's festivities were to take place, not a little of the fug of the centuries. It was the hottest day of the summer, and though somebody had opened a tentative window or two, the atmosphere remained distinctive and individual.

In this hall the youth of Market Snodsbury had been eating its daily lunch for a matter of five hundred years, and the flavour lingered. The air was sort of heavy and languorous, if you know what I mean, with the scent of Young England and boiled beef and carrots.

Aunt Dahlia, who was sitting with a bevy of the local nibs in the second row, sighted me as I entered and waved to me to join her, but I was too smart for that. I wedged myself in among the standees at the back, leaning up against a chap who, from the aroma, might have been a corn chandler or something of that order. The essence of strategy on these occasions is to be as near the door as possible.

The hall was gaily decorated with flags and coloured paper, and the eye was further refreshed by the spectacle of a mixed drove of boys, parents, and what not, the former running a good deal to shiny faces and Eton collars, the latter stressing the black-satin note rather when female, and looking as if their coats were too tight, if male. And presently there was some applause – sporadic, Jeeves has since told me it was – and I saw Gussie being steered by a bearded bloke in a gown to a seat in the middle of the platform.

And I confess that as I beheld him and felt that there but for the grace of God went Bertram Wooster, a shudder ran through the frame. It all reminded me so vividly of the time I had addressed that girls' school.

Of course, looking at it dispassionately, you may say that for horror and peril there is no comparison between an almost human audience like the one before me and a mob of small girls with pigtails down their backs, and this, I concede, is true. Nevertheless, the spectacle was enough to make me feel like a fellow watching a pal going over Niagara Falls in a barrel, and the thought of what I had escaped caused everything for a moment to go black and swim before my eyes.

When I was able to see clearly once more, I perceived that Gussie was now seated. He had his hands on his knees, with his elbows out at right angles, like a nigger minstrel of the old school about to ask Mr Bones why a

chicken crosses the road, and he was staring before him
with a smile so fixed and pebble-beached that I should
have thought that anybody could have guessed that there
sat one in whom the old familiar juice was plashing up
against the back of the front teeth.

In fact, I saw Aunt Dahlia, who, having assisted at so
many hunting dinners in her time, is second to none as a
judge of the symptoms, give a start and gaze long and
earnestly. And she was just saying something to Uncle
Tom on her left when the bearded bloke stepped to the
footlights and started making a speech. From the fact that
he spoke as if he had a hot potato in his mouth without
getting the raspberry from the lads in the ringside seats,
I deduced that he must be the head master.

With his arrival in the spotlight, a sort of perspiring
resignation seemed to settle on the audience. Personally,
I snuggled up against the chandler and let my attention
wander. The speech was on the subject of the doings of
the school during the past term, and this part of a prize-
giving is always apt to fail to grip the visiting stranger. I
mean, you know how it is. You're told that J. B. Brewster
has won an Exhibition for Classics at Cat's, Cambridge,
and you feel that it's one of those stories where you can't
see how funny it is unless you really know the fellow.
And the same applies to G. Bullett being awarded the
Lady Jane Wix Scholarship at the Birmingham College
of Veterinary Science.

In fact, I and the corn chandler, who was looking a bit
fagged I thought, as if he had had a hard morning
chandling the corn, were beginning to doze lightly when
things suddenly brisked up, bringing Gussie into the
picture for the first time.

'Today,' said the bearded bloke, 'we are happy to
welcome as the guest of the afternoon Mr Fitz-Wattle – '

At the beginning of the address, Gussie had subsided
into a sort of daydream, with his mouth hanging open.
About half-way through, faint signs of life had begun to

show. And for the last few minutes he had been trying
to cross one leg over the other and failing and having
another shot and failing again. But only now did he
exhibit any real animation. He sat up with a jerk.

'Fink-Nottle,' he said, opening his eyes.

'Fitz-Nottle.'

'Fink-Nottle.'

'I should say Fink-Nottle.'

'Of course you should, you silly ass,' said Gussie
genially. 'All right, get on with it.'

And closing his eyes, he began trying to cross his legs
again.

I could see that this little spot of friction had rattled
the bearded bloke a bit. He stood for a moment of
fumbling at the fungus with a hesitating hand. But they
make these headmasters of tough stuff. The weakness
passed. He came back nicely and carried on.

'We are all happy, I say, to welcome as the guest of the
afternoon Mr Fink-Nottle, who has kindly consented to
award the prizes. This task, as you know, is one that
should have devolved upon that well-beloved and vigorous
member of our board of governors, the Rev. William
Plomer, and we are all, I am sure, very sorry that illness
at the last moment should have prevented him from being
here today. But, if I may borrow a familiar metaphor from
the – if I may employ a homely metaphor familiar to you
all – what we lose on the swings we gain on the
roundabouts.'

He paused, and beamed rather freely, to show that this
was comedy. I could have told the man it was no use.
Not a ripple. The corn chandler leaned against me and
muttered 'Whoddidesay?' but that was all.

It's always a nasty jar to wait for the laugh and find
that the gag hasn't got across. The bearded bloke was
visibly discomposed. At that, however, I think he would
have got by, had he not, at this juncture, unfortunately
stirred Gussie up again.

'In other words, though deprived of Mr Plomer, we have with us this afternoon Mr Fink-Nottle. I am sure Mr Fink-Nottle's name is one that needs no introduction to you. It is, I venture to assert, a name that is familiar to us all.'

'Not to you,' said Gussie.

And the next moment I saw what Jeeves had meant when he had described him as laughing heartily. 'Heartily' was absolutely the *mot juste*. It sounded like a gas explosion.

'You didn't seem to know it so dashed well, what, what?' said Gussie. And, reminded apparently by the word 'what' of the word 'Wattle,' he repeated the latter some sixteen times with a rising inflection.

'Wattle, Wattle, Wattle,' he concluded. 'Right-ho. Push on.'

But the bearded bloke had shot his bolt. He stood there, licked at last; and, watching him closely, I could see that he was now at the crossroads. I could spot what he was thinking as clearly as if he had confided it to my personal ear. He wanted to sit down and call it a day, I mean, but the thought that gave him pause was that, if he did, he must then either uncork Gussie or take the Fink-Nottle speech as read and get straight on to the actual prize-giving.

It was a dashed tricky thing, of course, to have to decide on the spur of the moment. I was reading in the paper the other day about those birds who are trying to split the atom, the nub being that they haven't the foggiest as to what will happen if they do. It may be all right. On the other hand, it may not be all right. And pretty silly a chap would feel, no doubt, if, having split the atom, he suddenly found the house going up in smoke and himself torn limb from limb.

So with the bearded bloke. Whether he was abreast of the inside facts in Gussie's case, I don't know, but it was obvious to him by this time that he had run into something pretty hot. Trial gallops had shown that Gussie had his own way of doing things. Those interruptions had been enough to prove to the perspicacious that here, seated on the platform at the big binge of the season, was one who, if pushed forward to make a speech, might let himself go in a rather epoch-making manner.

On the other hand, chain him up and put a green-baize cloth over him, and where were you? The proceeding would be over about half an hour too soon.

It was, as I say, a difficult problem to have to solve, and, left to himself, I don't know what conclusion he would have come to. Personally, I think he would have played it safe. As it happened, however, the thing was taken out of his hands, for at this moment, Gussie, having stretched out his arms and yawned a bit, switched on that pebble-beached smile again and tacked down to the edge of the platform.

'Speech,' he said affably.

He then stood with his thumbs in the armholes of his waistcoat, waiting for the applause to die down.

It was some time before this happened, for he had got a very fine hand indeed. I suppose it wasn't often that the boys of Market Snodsbury Grammar School came across a man public-spirited enough to call their head master a silly ass, and they showed their appreciation in no uncertain manner. Gussie may have been one over the eight, but as far as the majority of those present were concerned he was sitting on top of the world.

'Boys,' said Gussie, 'I mean ladies and gentlemen and boys, I do not detain you long, but I suppose on this occasion to feel compelled to say a few auspicious words. Ladies – and boys and gentlemen – we have all listened with interest to the remarks of our friend here who forgot to shave this morning – I don't know his name, but then he didn't know mine – Fitz-Wattle, I mean, absolutely absurd – which squares things up a bit – and we are all sorry that the Reverend What-ever-he-was-called should be dying of adenoids, but after all, here today, gone tomorrow, and all flesh is as grass, and what not, but that wasn't what I wanted to say. What I wanted to say was this – and I say it confidently – without fear of contradiction – I say, in short, I am happy to be here on this auspicious occasion and I take much pleasure in kindly awarding the prizes, consisting of the handsome books you see laid out on that table. As Shakespeare says, there are sermons in books, stones in the running brooks, or, rather, the other way about, and there you have it in a nutshell.'

It went well, and I wasn't surprised. I couldn't quite follow some of it, but anybody could see that it was real ripe stuff, and I was amazed that even the course of treatment he had been taking could have rendered so normally tongue-tied a dumb brick as Gussie capable of it.

It just shows, what any member of Parliament will tell you, that if you want real oratory, the preliminary noggin is essential. Unless pie-eyed, you cannot hope to grip.

'Gentlemen,' said Gussie, 'I mean ladies and gentlemen and, of course, boys, what a beautiful world this is. A beautiful world, full of happiness on every side. Let me tell you a little story. Two Irishmen, Pat and Mike, were walking along Broadway, and one said to the other, "Begorrah, the race is not always to the swift," and the other replied, "Faith and begob, education is a drawing out, not a putting in."'

I must say it seemed to me the rottenest story I had ever heard, and I was surprised that Jeeves should have considered it worth while shoving into a speech. However, when I taxed him with this later, he said that Gussie had altered the plot a good deal, and I dare say that accounts for it.

At any rate, that was the *conte* as Gussie told it, and when I say that it got a very fair laugh, you will understand what a popular figure he had become with the multitude. There might be a bearded bloke or so on the platform and a small section in the second row who were wishing the speaker would conclude his remarks and resume his seat, but the audience as a whole was for him solidly.

There was applause, and a voice cried: 'Hear, hear!'

'Yes,' said Gussie, 'it is a beautiful world. The sky is blue, the birds are singing, there is optimism everywhere. And why not, boys and ladies and gentlemen? I'm happy, you're happy, we're all happy, even the meanest Irishman that walks along Broadway. Though, as I say, there were two of them – Pat and Mike, one drawing out, the other putting in. I should like you boys, taking the time from me, to give three cheers for this beautiful world. All together, now.'

Presently the dust settled down and the plaster stopped falling from the ceiling, and he went on.

'People who say it isn't a beautiful world don't know what they are talking about. Driving here in the car today to award the kind prizes, I was reluctantly compelled to tick off my host on this very point. Old Tom Travers. You will see him sitting there in the second row next to the large lady in beige.'

He pointed helpfully, and the hundred or so Market Snodsburyians who craned their necks in the direction indicated were able to observe Uncle Tom blushing prettily.

'I ticked him off properly, the poor fish. He expressed the opinion that the world was in a deplorable state. I said, "Don't talk rot, old Tom Travers." "I am not accustomed to talk rot," he said. "Then, for a beginner," I said, "you do it dashed well." And I think you will admit, boys and ladies and gentlemen, that was telling him.'

The audience seemed to agree with him. The point went big. The voice that had said, 'Hear, hear,' said 'Hear,

hear' again, and my corn chandler hammered the floor vigorously with a large-size walking stick.

'Well, boys,' resumed Gussie, having shot his cuffs and smirked horribly, 'this is the end of the summer term, and many of you, no doubt, are leaving the school. And I don't blame you, because there's a froust in here you could cut with a knife. You are going out into the great world. Soon many of you will be walking along Broadway. And what I want to impress upon you is that, however much you may suffer from adenoids, you must all use every effort to prevent yourselves becoming pessimists and talking rot like old Tom Travers. There in the second row. The fellow with a face rather like a walnut.'

He paused to allow those wishing to do so to refresh themselves with another look at Uncle Tom, and I found myself musing in some little perplexity. Long association with the members of the Drones has put me pretty well in touch with the various ways in which an overdose of the blushful Hippocrene can take the individual, but I had never seen anyone react quite as Gussie was doing.

There was a snap about his work which I had never witnessed before, even in Barmy Fotheringay-Phipps on New Year's Eve.

Jeeves, when I discussed the matter with him later, said it was something to do with inhibitions, if I caught the word correctly, and the suppression of, I think he said, the ego. What he meant, I gathered, was that, owing to the fact that Gussie had just completed a five years' stretch of blameless seclusion among the newts, all the goofiness which ought to have been spread out thin over those five years and had been bottled up during that period came to the surface on this occasion in a lump – or, if you prefer to put it that way, like a tidal wave.

There may be something in this. Jeeves generally knows.

Anyway, be that as it may, I was dashed glad I had had

the shrewdness to keep out of that second row. It might be unworthy of the prestige of a Wooster to squash in among the proletariat in the standing-room-only section, but at least, I felt, I was out of the danger zone. So thoroughly had Gussie got it up his nose by now that it seemed to me that had he sighted me he might have become personal about even an old school friend.

'If there's one thing in the world I can't stand,' proceeded Gussie, 'it's a pessimist. Be optimists, boys. You all know the difference between an optimist and a pessimist. An optimist is a man who – well, take the case of two Irishmen, walking along Broadway. One is an optimist and one is a pessimist, just as one's name is Pat and the other Mike . . . Why, hullo, Bertie; I didn't know you were here.'

Too late, I endeavoured to go to earth behind the chandler, only to discover that there was no chandler there. Some appointment, suddenly remembered – possibly a promise to his wife that he would be home to tea – had caused him to ooze away while my attention was elsewhere, leaving me right out in the open.

Between me and Gussie, who was now pointing in an offensive manner, there was nothing but a sea of interested faces looking up at me.

'Now, there,' boomed Gussie, continuing to point, 'is an instance of what I mean. Boys and ladies and gentlemen, take a good look at that object standing up there at the back – morning coat, trousers as worn, quiet grey tie, and carnation in buttonhole – you can't miss him. Bertie Wooster, that is, and as foul a pessimist as ever bit a tiger. I tell you I despise that man. And why do I despise him? Because, boys and ladies and gentlemen, he is a pessimist. His attitude is defeatist. When I told him I was going to address you this afternoon, he tried to dissuade me. And do you know why he tried to dissuade me? Because he said my trousers would split up the back.'

The cheers that greeted this were the loudest yet. Anything about splitting trousers went straight to the simple hearts of the young scholars of Market Snodsbury Grammar School. Two in the row in front of me turned purple, and a small lad with freckles seated beside them asked me for my autograph.

'Let me tell you a story about Bertie Wooster.'

A Wooster can stand a good deal, but he cannot stand having his name bandied in a public place. Picking my feet up softly, I was in the very process of executing a quiet sneak for the door, when I perceived that the bearded bloke had at last decided to apply the closure.

Why he hadn't done so before is beyond me. Spell-bound, I take it. And, of course, when a chap is going like a breeze with the public, as Gussie had been, it's not so dashed easy to chip in. However, the prospect of hearing another of Gussie's anecdotes seemed to have done the trick. Rising rather as I had risen from my bench at the beginning of that painful scene with Tuppy in the twilight, he made a leap for the table, snatched up a book and came bearing down on the speaker.

He touched Gussie on the arm, and Gussie, turning sharply and seeing a large bloke with a beard apparently about to bean him with a book, sprang back in an attitude of self-defence.

'Perhaps, as time is getting on, Mr Fink-Nottle, we had better – '

'Oh, ah,' said Gussie, getting the trend. He relaxed. 'The prizes, eh? Of course, yes. Right-ho. Yes, might as well be shoving along with it. What's this one?'

'Spelling and dictation – P. K. Purvis,' announced the bearded bloke.

'Spelling and dictation – P. K. Purvis,' echoed Gussie, as if he were calling coals. 'Forward, P. K. Purvis.'

Now that the whistle had been blown on his speech, it seemed to me that there was no longer any need for the strategic retreat which I had been planning. I had no

wish to tear myself away unless I had to. I mean, I had told
Jeeves that this binge would be fraught with interest, and
it was fraught with interest. There was a fascination
about Gussie's methods which gripped and made one
reluctant to pass the thing up provided personal
innuendoes were steered clear of. I decided, accordingly,
to remain, and presently there was musical squeaking
and P. K. Purvis climbed the platform.

The spelling-and-dictation champ was about three foot
six in his squeaking shoes, with a pink face and sandy
hair. Gussie patted his hair. He seemed to have taken an
immediate fancy to the lad.

'You P. K. Purvis?'

'Sir, yes, sir.'

'It's a beautiful world, P. K. Purvis.'

'Sir, yes, sir.'

'Ah, you've noticed it, have you? Good. You married,
by any chance?'

'Sir, no, sir.'

'Get married, P. K. Purvis,' said Gussie earnestly. 'It's
the only life . . . Well, here's your book. Looks rather
bilge to me from a glance at the title page, but, such as it
is, here you are.'

P. K. Purvis squeaked off amidst sporadic applause, but
one could not fail to note that the sporadic was followed
by a rather strained silence. It was evident that Gussie
was striking something of a new note in Market
Snodsbury scholastic circles. Looks were exchanged
between parent and parent. The bearded bloke had the
air of one who has drained the bitter cup. As for Aunt
Dahlia, her demeanour now told only too clearly that
her last doubts had been resolved and her verdict was in.
I saw her whisper to the Bassett, who sat on her right, and
the Bassett nodded sadly and looked like a fairy about to
shed a tear and add another star to the Milky Way.

Gussie, after the departure of P. K. Purvis, had fallen
into a sort of daydream and was standing with his mouth

open and his hands in his pockets. Becoming abruptly aware that a fat kid in knickerbockers was at his elbow, he started violently.

'Hullo!' he said, visibly shaken. 'Who are you?'

'This,' said the bearded bloke, 'is R. V. Smethurst.'

'What's he doing here?' asked Gussie suspiciously.

'You are presenting him with the drawing prize, Mr Fink-Nottle.'

This apparently struck Gussie as a reasonable explanation. His face cleared.

'That's right, too,' he said . . . 'Well, here it is, cocky. You off?' he said, as the kid prepared to withdraw.

'Sir, yes, sir.'

'Wait, R. V. Smethurst. Not so fast. Before you go, there is a question I wish to ask you.'

But the bearded bloke's aim now seemed to be to rush the ceremonies a bit. He hustled R. V. Smethurst off stage rather like a chucker-out in a pub regretfully ejecting an old and respected customer, and started paging G. G. Simmons. A moment later the latter was up and coming, and conceive my emotion when it was announced that the subject on which he had clicked was Scripture knowledge. One of us, I mean to say.

G. G. Simmons was an unpleasant, perky-looking stripling, mostly front teeth and spectacles, but I gave him a big hand. We Scripture-knowledge sharks stick together.

Gussie, I was sorry to see, didn't like him. There was in his manner, as he regarded G. G. Simmons, none of the chumminess which had marked it during his interview with P. K. Purvis or, in a somewhat lesser degree, with R. V. Smethurst. He was cold and distant.

'Well, G. G. Simmons.'

'Sir, yes, sir.'

'What do you mean – sir, yes, sir? Dashed silly thing to say. So you've won the Scripture-knowledge prize, have you?'

'Sir, yes, sir.'

'Yes,' said Gussie, 'you look just the sort of little tick who would. And yet,' he said, pausing and eyeing the child keenly, 'how are we to know that this has all been open and above board? Let me test you, G. G. Simmons. What was What's-His-Name – the chap who begat Thingummy? Can you answer me that, Simmons?'

'Sir, no, sir.'

Gussie turned to the bearded bloke.

'Fishy,' he said. 'Very fishy. This boy appears to be totally lacking in Scripture knowledge.'

The bearded bloke passed a hand across his forehead.

'I can assure you, Mr Fink-Nottle, that every care was taken to ensure a correct marking and that Simmons outdistanced his competitors by a wide margin.'

'Well, if you say so,' said Gussie doubtfully. 'All right, G. G. Simmons, take your prize.'

'Sir, thank you, sir.'

'But let me tell you that there's nothing to stick on side about in winning a prize for Scripture knowledge. Bertie Wooster – '

I don't know when I've had a nastier shock. I had been going on the assumption that, now that they had stopped him making his speech, Gussie's fangs had been drawn, as you might say. To duck my head down and resume my edging toward the door was with me the work of a moment.

'Bertie Wooster won the Scripture-knowledge prize at a kids' school we were at together, and you know what he's like. But, of course, Bertie frankly cheated. He succeeded in scrounging that Scripture-knowledge trophy over the heads of better men by means of some of the rawest and most brazen swindling methods ever witnessed even at a school where such things were common. If that man's pockets, as he entered the examination-room, were not stuffed to bursting-point with lists of the kings of Judah – '

I heard no more. A moment later I was out in God's air, fumbling with a fevered foot at the self-starter of the old car.

The engine raced. The clutch slid into position. I tooted and drove off.

My ganglions were still vibrating as I ran the car into the stables of Brinkley Court, and it was a much shaken Bertram who tottered up to his room to change into something loose. Having donned flannels, I lay down on the bed for a bit, and I suppose I must have dozed off, for the next thing I remember is finding Jeeves at my side.

I sat up. 'My tea, Jeeves?'

'No, sir. It is nearly dinner-time.'

The mists cleared away.

'I must have been asleep.'

'Yes, sir.'

'Nature taking its toll of the exhausted frame.'

'Yes, sir.'

'And enough to make it.'

'Yes, sir.'

'And now it's nearly dinner-time, you say? All right. I am in no mood for dinner, but I suppose you had better lay out the clothes.'

'It will not be necessary, sir. The company will not be dressing tonight. A cold collation has been set out in the dining-room.'

There was a pause.

'Well, Jeeves,' I said, 'it was certainly one of those afternoons, what?'

'Yes, sir.'

'I cannot recall one more packed with incident. And I left before the finish.'

'Yes, sir. I observed your departure.'

'You couldn't blame me for withdrawing.'

'No, sir. Mr Fink-Nottle had undoubtedly become embarrassingly personal.'

'Was there much more of it after I went?'

'No, sir. The proceedings terminated very shortly. Mr Fink-Nottle's remarks with reference to Master G. G. Simmons brought about an early closure.'

'But he had finished his remarks about G. G. Simmons.'

'Only temporarily, sir. He resumed them immediately after your departure. If you recollect, sir, he had already proclaimed himself suspicious of Master Simmons's bona fides, and he now proceeded to deliver a violent verbal attack upon the young gentleman, asserting that it was impossible for him to have won the Scripture-knowledge prize without systematic cheating on an impressive scale. He went so far as to suggest that Master Simmons was well known to the police.'

'Golly, Jeeves!'

'Yes, sir. The words did create a considerable sensation. The reaction of those present to this accusation I should describe as mixed. The young students appeared pleased and applauded vigorously, but Master Simmons's mother rose from her seat and addressed Mr Fink-Nottle in terms of strong protest.

'Did Gussie seem taken aback? Did he recede from his position?'

'No, sir. He said that he could see it all now; and hinted at a guilty liaison between Master Simmons's mother and the head master, accusing the latter of having cooked the marks, as his expression was, in order to gain favour with the former.'

'You don't mean that?'

'Yes, sir.'

'Egad, Jeeves! And then – '

'They sang the national anthem, sir.'

'Surely not?'

'Yes, sir.'

'At a moment like that?'

'Yes, sir.'

'Well, you were there and you know, of course, but I should have thought the last thing Gussie and this woman would have done in the circs. would have been to start singing duets.'

'You misunderstand me, sir. It was the entire company who sang. The head master turned to the organist and said something to him in a low tone. Upon which the latter began to play the national anthem, and the proceedings terminated.'

'I see. About time, too.'

'Yes, sir. Mrs Simmons's attitude had become unquestionably menacing.'

I pondered. What I had heard was, of course, of a nature to excite pity and terror, not to mention alarm and despondency, and it would be paltering with the truth to say that I was pleased about it. On the other hand, it was all over now, and it seemed to me that the thing to do was not to mourn over the past but to fix the mind on the bright future. I mean to say, Gussie might have lowered the existing Worcestershire record for goofiness and definitely forfeited all chance of becoming Market Snodsbury's favourite son, but you can't get away from the fact that he had proposed to Madeline Bassett, and you had to admit that she had accepted him.

I put this to Jeeves.

'A frightful exhibition,' I said, 'and one which will very possibly ring down history's pages. But we must not forget, Jeeves, that Gussie, though now doubtless looked upon in the neighbourhood as the world's worst freak, is all right otherwise.'

'No, sir.'

I did not quite get this.

'When you say "No, sir," do you mean "Yes, sir"?'

'No, sir. I mean "No, sir."'

'He is not all right otherwise?'

'No, sir.'

'But he's betrothed.'

'No longer, sir. Miss Bassett has severed the engagement.'

5 — Roderick Spode Gets His Comeuppance

I wouldn't say that Jeeves was actually smirking, but there was a definite look of quiet satisfaction on his face, and I suddenly remembered what this sickening scene with Gussie had caused me to forget – viz. that the last time I had seen him he had been on his way to the telephone to ring up the Secretary of the Junior Ganymede Club. I sprang to my feet eagerly. Unless I had misread that look, he had something to report.

'Did you connect with the Sec., Jeeves?'

'Yes, sir. I have just finished speaking to him.'

'And did he dish the dirt?'

'He was most informative, sir.'

'Has Spode a secret?'

'Yes, sir.'

I smote the trouser leg emotionally.

'I should have known better than to doubt Aunt Dahlia. Aunts always know. It's a sort of intuition. Tell me all.'

'I fear I cannot do that, sir. The rules of the club regarding the dissemination of material recorded in the book are very rigid.'

'You mean your lips are sealed?'

'Yes, sir.'

'Then what was the use of telephoning?'

'It is only the details of the matter which I am precluded from mentioning, sir. I am at perfect liberty to tell you that it would greatly lessen Mr Spode's potentiality for evil, if you were to inform him that you know all about Eulalie, sir.'

'Eulalie?'

'Eulalie, sir.'

'That would really put the stopper on him?'

'Yes, sir.'

I pondered. It didn't sound much to go on.

'You're sure you can't go a bit deeper into the subject?'

'Quite sure, sir. Were I to do so, it is probable that my resignation would be called for.'

'Well, I wouldn't want that to happen, of course.' I hated to think of a squad of butlers forming a hollow square while the Committee snipped his buttons off. 'Still, you really are sure that if I look Spode in the eye and spring this gag, he will be baffled? Let's get this quite clear. Suppose you're Spode, and I walk up to you and say "Spode, I know all about Eulalie," that would make you wilt?'

'Yes, sir. The subject of Eulalie, sir, is one which the gentleman, occupying the position he does in the public eye, would, I am convinced, be most reluctant to have ventilated.'

I practised it for a bit. I walked up to the chest of drawers with my hands in my pockets, and said, 'Spode, I know all about Eulalie.' I tried again, waggling my finger this time. I then had a go with folded arms, and I must say it still didn't sound too convincing.

However, I told myself that Jeeves always knew.

'Well, if you say so, Jeeves. Then the first thing I had better do is find Gussie and give him this life-saving information.'

'Sir?'

'Oh, of course, you don't know anything about that, do you? I must tell you, Jeeves, that, since we last met, the plot has thickened again. Were you aware that Spode has long loved Miss Bassett?'

'No, sir.'

'Well, such is the case. The happiness of Miss Bassett is very dear to Spode, and now that her engagement has gone phut for reasons highly discreditable to the male contracting party, he wants to break Gussie's neck.'

'Indeed, sir?'

'I assure you. He was in here just now, speaking of it, and Gussie, who happened to be under the bed at the time, heard him. With the result that he now talks of getting out of the window and going to California. Which, of course, would be fatal. It is imperative that he stays on and tries to effect a reconciliation.'

'Yes, sir.'

'He can't effect a reconciliation, if he is in California.'

'No, sir.'

'So I must go and try to find him. Though, mark you, I doubt if he will be easily found at this point in his career. He is probably on the roof, wondering how he can pull it up after him.'

My misgivings were proved abundantly justified. I searched the house assiduously, but there were no signs of him. Somewhere, no doubt, Totleigh Towers hid Augustus Fink-Nottle, but it kept its secret well. Eventually, I gave it up, and returned to my room, and stap my vitals if the first thing I beheld on entering wasn't the man in person. He was standing by the bed, knotting sheets.

The fact that he had his back to the door and that the carpet was soft kept him from being aware of my entry till I spoke. My 'Hey!' – a pretty sharp one, for I was aghast at seeing my bed thus messed about – brought him spinning round, ashen to the lips.

'Woof!' he exclaimed. 'I thought you were Spode!'

Indignation succeeded panic. He gave me a hard stare. The eyes behind the spectacles were cold. He looked like an annoyed turbot.

'What do you mean, you blasted Wooster,' he demanded, 'by sneaking up on a fellow and saying "Hey!" like that? You might have given me heart failure.'

'And what do you mean, you blighted Fink-Nottle,' I

demanded in my turn, 'by mucking up my bed linen after I specifically forbade it? You have sheets of your own. Go and knot those.'

'How can I? Spode is sitting on my bed.'

'He is?'

'Certainly he is. Waiting for me. I went there after I left you, and there he was. If he hadn't happened to clear his throat, I'd have walked right in.'

I saw that it was high time to set this disturbed spirit at rest.

'You needn't be afraid of Spode, Gussie.'

'What do you mean, I needn't be afraid of Spode? Talk sense.'

'I mean just that. Spode, *qua* menace, if *qua* is the word I want, is a thing of the past. Owing to the extraordinary perfection of Jeeves's secret system, I have learned something about him which he wouldn't care to have generally known.'

'What?'

'Ah, there you have me. When I said I had learned it, I should have said that Jeeves had learned it, and unfortunately Jeeves's lips are sealed. However, I am in a position to slip it across the man in no uncertain fashion. If he attempts any rough stuff, I will give him the works.'

I broke off, listening. Footsteps were coming along the passage. 'Ah!' I said. 'Someone approaches. This may quite possibly be the blighter himself.'

An animal cry escaped Gussie.

'Lock that door!'

I waved a fairly airy hand.

'It will not be necessary,' I said. 'Let him come. I positively welcome this visit. Watch me deal with him, Gussie. It will amuse you.'

I had guessed correctly. It was Spode, all right. No doubt he had grown weary of sitting on Gussie's bed, and had felt that another chat with Bertram might serve to vary the monotony. He came in, as before, without knocking, and as he perceived Gussie, uttered a wordless exclamation of triumph and satisfaction. He then stood for a moment, breathing heavily through the nostrils.

He seemed to have grown a bit since our last meeting, being now about eight foot six, and had my advices *in re* getting the bulge on him proceeded from a less authoritative source, his aspect might have intimidated me quite a good deal. But so sedulously had I been trained through the years to rely on Jeeves's lightest word that I regarded him without a tremor.

Gussie, I was sorry to observe, did not share my sunny confidence. Possibly I had not given him a full enough explanation of the facts in the case, or it may have been that, confronted with Spode in the flesh, his nerve had failed him. At any rate, he now retreated to the wall and seemed, as far as I could gather, to be trying to get through it. Foiled in this endeavour, he stood looking as if he had been stuffed by some good taxidermist, while I turned to the intruder and gave him a long, level stare, in which surprise and hauteur were nicely blended.

'Well, Spode,' I said, 'what is it now?'

I had put a considerable amount of top spin on the final word, to indicate displeasure, but it was wasted on the man. Giving the question a miss like the deaf adder of Scripture, he began to advance slowly, his gaze concentrated on Gussie. The jaw muscles, I noted, were working as they had done on the occasion when he had come upon me toying with Sir Watkyn Bassett's collection of old silver: and something in his manner suggested that he might at any moment start beating his chest with a hollow drumming sound, as gorillas do in moments of emotion.

'Ha!' he said.

Well, of course, I was not going to stand any rot like that. This habit of his of going about the place saying 'Ha!' was one that had got to be checked, and checked promptly.

'Spode!' I said sharply, and I have an idea that I rapped the table.

He seemed for the first time to become aware of my presence. He paused for an instant, and gave me an unpleasant look.

'Well, what do *you* want?'

I raised an eyebrow or two.

'What do I want? I like that. That's good. Since you ask, Spode, I want to know what the devil you mean by keeping coming into my private apartment, taking up space which I require for other purposes and interrupting me when I am chatting with my personal friends. Really, one gets about as much privacy in this house as a strip-tease dancer. I assume that you have a room of your own. Get back to it, you fat slob, and stay there.'

I could not resist shooting a swift glance at Gussie, to see how he was taking all this, and was pleased to note on his face the burgeoning of a look of worshipping admiration, such as a distressed damsel of the Middle Ages might have directed at a knight on observing him getting down to brass tacks with the dragon. I could see that I had once more become to him the old Daredevil Wooster of our boyhood days, and I had no doubt that he was burning with shame and remorse as he recalled those sneers and jeers of his.

Spode, also, seemed a good deal impressed, though not so favourably. He was staring incredulously, like one bitten by a rabbit. He seemed to be asking himself if this could really be the shrinking violet with whom he had conferred on the terrace.

He asked me if I had called him a slob, and I said I had.

'A fat slob?'

'A fat slob. It is about time,' I proceeded, 'that some public-spirited person came along and told you where you got off. The trouble with you, Spode, is that just because you have succeeded in inducing a handful of half-wits to disfigure the London scene by going about in black shorts, you think you're someone. You hear them shouting, "Heil, Spode!" and you imagine it is the Voice of the People. That is where you make your bloomer. What the Voice of the People is saying is: "Look at that frightful ass Spode swanking about in footer bags! Did you ever in your puff see such a perfect perisher?"'

He did what is known as struggling for utterance.

'Oh?' he said. 'Ha! Well, I will attend to you later.'

'And I,' I retorted, quick as a flash, 'will attend to you now.' I lit a cigarette. 'Spode,' I said, unmasking my batteries, 'I know your secret!'

'Eh?'

'I know all about – '

'All about what?'

It was to ask myself precisely that question that I had paused. For, believe me or believe me not, in this tense moment, when I so sorely needed it, the name which Jeeves had mentioned to me as the magic formula for coping with this blister had completely passed from my mind. I couldn't even remember what letter it began with.

It's an extraordinary thing about names. You've probably noticed it yourself. You think you've got them, I mean to say, and they simply slither away. I've often wished I had a quid for every time some bird with a perfectly familiar map has come up to me and Hallo-Woostered, and had me gasping for air because I couldn't put a label to him. This always makes one feel at a loss, but on no previous occasion had I felt so much at a loss as I did now.

'All about what?' said Spode.

'Well, as a matter of fact,' I had to confess, 'I've forgotten.'

A sort of gasping gulp from up-stage directed my attention to Gussie again, and I could see that the significance of my words had not been lost on him. Once more he tried to back: and as he realized that he had already gone as far as he could go, a glare of despair came into his eyes. And then, abruptly, as Spode began to advance upon him, it changed to one of determination and stern resolve.

I like to think of Augustus Fink-Nottle at the moment. He showed up well. Hitherto, I am bound to say, I had never regarded him highly as a man of action. Essentially the dreamer type, I should have said. But now he couldn't have smacked into it with a prompter gusto if he had been a rough-and-tumble fighter on the San Francisco waterfront from early childhood.

Above him, as he stood glued to the wall, there hung a fairish-sized oil-painting of a chap in knee-breeches and a three-cornered hat gazing at a female who appeared to be chirruping to a bird of sorts – a dove, unless I am mistaken, or a pigeon. I had noticed it once or twice since I had been in the room, and had, indeed, thought of giving it to Aunt Dahlia to break instead of the Infant Samuel at Prayer. Fortunately, I had not done so, or Gussie would not now have been in a position to tear it from its moorings and bring it down with a nice wristy action on Spode's head.

I say 'fortunately', because if ever there was a fellow who needed hitting with oil paintings, that fellow was Roderick Spode. From the moment of our first meeting, his every word and action had proved abundantly that this was the stuff to give him. But there is always a catch in these good things, and it took me only an instant to see that this effort of Gussie's, though well meant, had achieved little of constructive importance. What he should have done, of course, was to hold the picture sideways, so as to get the best out of the stout frame. Instead of which, he had used the flat of the weapon, and Spode came through the canvas like a circus rider going through a paper hoop. In other words, what had promised to be a decisive blow had turned out to be merely what Jeeves would call a gesture.

It did, however, divert Spode from his purpose for a few seconds. He stood there blinking, with the thing round his neck like a ruff, and the pause was sufficient to enable me to get into action.

Give us a lead, make it quite clear to us that the party has warmed up and that from now on anything goes, and we Woosters do not hang back. There was a sheet lying on the bed where Gussie had dropped it when disturbed at his knotting, and to snatch this up and envelop Spode in it was with me the work of a moment. It is a long time since I studied the subject, and before committing myself definitely I should have to consult Jeeves, but I have an idea that ancient Roman gladiators used to do much the same sort of thing in the arena, and were rather well thought of in consequence.

I suppose a man who has been hit over the head with a picture of a girl chirruping to a pigeon and almost immediately afterwards emmeshed in a sheet can never really retain the cool, intelligent outlook. Any friend of Spode's, with his interests at heart, would have advised him at this juncture to keep quite still and not stir till he had come out of the cocoon. Only thus, in a terrain so liberally studded with chairs and things, could a purler have been avoided.

He did not do this. Hearing the rushing sound caused by Gussie exiting, he made a leap in its general direction and took the inevitable toss. At the moment when Gussie, moving well, passed through the door, he was on the ground, more inextricably entangled than ever.

My own friends, advising me, would undoubtedly have recommended an immediate departure at this point, and looking back, I can see that where I went wrong was in pausing to hit the bulge which, from the remarks that were coming through at that spot, I took to be Spode's head, with a china vase that stood on the mantelpiece not far from where the Infant Samuel had been. It was a strategical error. I got home all right and the vase broke into a dozen pieces, which was all to the good – for the more of the property of a man like Sir Watkyn Bassett that was destroyed, the better – but the action of dealing this buffet caused me to overbalance. The next moment, a hand coming out from under the sheet had grabbed my coat.

It was a serious disaster, of course, and one which might well have caused a lesser man to feel that it was no use going on struggling. But the whole point about the Woosters, as I have had occasion to remark before, is that they are not lesser men. They keep their heads. They think quickly, and they act quickly. Napoleon was the same. I have mentioned that at the moment when I was preparing to inform Spode that I knew his secret, I had lighted a cigarette. This cigarette, in its holder, was still between my lips. Hastily removing it, I pressed the glowing end on the ham-like hand which was impeding my getaway.

The results were thoroughly gratifying. You would have thought that the trend of recent events would have put Roderick Spode in a frame of mind to expect anything and be ready for it, but this simple manoeuvre found him unprepared. With a sharp cry of anguish, he released the coat, and I delayed no longer. Bertram Wooster is a man who knows when and when not to be among those present. When Bertram Wooster sees a lion in his path, he ducks down a side street. I was off at an impressive speed, and would no doubt have crossed the threshold with a burst which would have clipped a second or two off Gussie's time, had I not experienced a head-on collision with a solid body which happened to be entering at the moment. I remember thinking, as we twined our arms about each other, that at Totleigh Towers, if it wasn't one thing, it was bound to be something else.

I fancy that it was the scent of *eau-de-Cologne* that still clung to her temples that enabled me to identify this solid body as that of Aunt Dahlia, though even without it the rich, hunting-field expletive which burst from her lips would have put me on the right track. We came down in a tangled heap, and must have rolled inwards to some extent, for the next thing I knew, we were colliding with the sheeted figure of Roderick Spode, who when last seen had been at the other end of the room. No doubt the explanation is that we had rolled nor'-nor'-east and he had been rolling sou'-sou'-west, with the result that we had come together somewhere in the middle.

Spode, I noticed, as Reason began to return to her throne, was holding Aunt Dahlia by the left leg, and she didn't seem to be liking it much. A good deal of breath had been knocked out of her by the impact of a nephew on her midriff, but enough remained to enable her to expostulate, and this she was doing with all the old fire.

'What is this joint?' she was demanding heatedly. 'A loony bin? Has everybody gone crazy? First I meet Spink-Bottle racing along the corridor like a mustang. Then you try to walk through me as if I were thistledown. And now the gentleman in the burnous has started tickling my ankle – a thing that hasn't happened to me since the York and Ainsty Hunt Ball of the year nineteen-twenty-one.'

These protests must have filtered through to Spode, and presumably stirred his better nature, for he let go, and she got up, dusting her dress.

'Now, then,' she said, somewhat calmer. 'An explanation, if you please, and a categorical one. What's the idea? What's it all about? Who the devil's that inside the winding-sheet?'

I made the introductions.

'You've met Spode, haven't you? Mr Roderick Spode, Mrs Travers.'

Spode had now removed the sheet, but the picture was still in position, and Aunt Dahlia eyed it wonderingly.

'What on earth have you got that thing round your

neck for?' she asked. Then, in more tolerant vein: 'Wear it if you like, of course, but it doesn't suit you.'

Spode did not reply. He was breathing heavily. I didn't blame him, mind you – in his place, I'd have done the same – but the sound was not agreeable, and I wished he wouldn't. He was also gazing at me intently, and I wished he wouldn't do that, either. His face was flushed, his eyes were bulging, and one had the odd illusion that his hair was standing on end – like quills upon the fretful porpentine, as Jeeves once put it when describing to me the reactions of Barmy Fotheringay-Phipps on seeing a dead snip, on which he had invested largely, come in sixth in the procession at the Newmarket Spring Meeting.

I remember once, during a temporary rift with Jeeves, engaging a man from the registry office to serve me in his stead, and he hadn't been with me a week when he got blotto one night and set fire to the house and tried to slice me up with a carving knife. Said he wanted to see the colour of my insides, of all bizarre ideas. And until this moment I had always looked on that episode as the most trying in my experience. I now saw that it must be ranked second.

This bird of whom I speak was a simple, untutored soul and Spode a man of good education and upbringing, but it was plain that there was one point at which their souls touched. I don't suppose they would have seen eye to eye on any other subject you could have brought up, but in the matter of wanting to see the colour of my insides their minds ran on parallel lines. The only difference seemed to be that whereas my employee had planned to use a carving knife for his excavations, Spode appeared to be satisfied that the job could be done all right with the bare hands.

'I must ask you to leave us, madam,' he said.

'But I've only just come,' said Aunt Dahlia.

'I am going to thrash this man within an inch of his life.'

It was quite the wrong tone to take with the aged relative. She has a very clannish spirit and, as I have said, is fond of Bertram. Her brow darkened.

'You don't touch a nephew of mine.'

'I am going to break every bone in his body.'

'You aren't going to do anything of the sort. The idea! ... Here you!'

She raised her voice sharply as she spoke the concluding words, and what had caused her to do so was the fact that Spode at this moment made a sudden move in my direction.

Considering the manner in which his eyes were gleaming and his moustache bristling, not to mention the gritting teeth and the sinister twiddling of the fingers, it was a move which might have been expected to send me flitting away like an adagio dancer. And had it occurred somewhat earlier, it would undoubtedly have done so. But I did not flit. I stood where I was, calm and collected. Whether I folded my arms or not, I cannot recall, but I remember that there was a faint, amused smile upon my lips.

For that brief monosyllable 'you' had accomplished what a quarter of an hour's research had been unable to do – viz. the unsealing of the fount of memory. Jeeves's words came back to me with a rush. One moment, the mind a blank: the next, the fount of memory spouting like nobody's business. It often happens this way.

'One minute, Spode,' I said quietly. 'Just one minute. Before you start getting above yourself, it may interest you to learn that I know all about Eulalie.'

It was stupendous. I felt like one of those chaps who press buttons and explode mines. If it hadn't been that my implicit faith in Jeeves had led me to expect solid results, I should have been astounded at the effect of this pronouncement on the man. You could see that it had got right in amongst him and churned him up like an egg whisk. He recoiled as if he had run into something hot, and a look of horror and alarm spread slowly over his face.

The whole situation recalled irresistibly to my mind something that had happened to me once up at Oxford, when the heart was young. It was during Eights Week, and I was sauntering on the riverbank with a girl named something that has slipped my mind, when there was a sound of barking and a large, hefty dog came galloping up, full of beans and buck and obviously intent on mayhem. And I was just commending my soul to God, and feeling that this was where the old flannel trousers got about thirty bob's worth of value bitten out of them, when the girl, waiting till she saw the whites of its eyes, with extraordinary presence of mind suddenly opened a coloured Japanese umbrella in the animal's face. Upon which, it did three back somersaults and retired into private life.

Except that he didn't do any back somersaults, Roderick Spode's reactions were almost identical with those of this nonplussed hound. For a moment, he just stood gaping. Then he said 'Oh?' Then his lips twisted into what I took to be his idea of a conciliatory smile. After that, he swallowed six – or it may have been seven – times, as if he had taken aboard a fish bone. Finally, he spoke. And when he did so, it was the nearest thing to a cooing dove that I have ever heard – and an exceptionally mild-mannered dove, at that.

'Oh, do you?' he said.

'I do,' I replied.

If he had asked me what I knew about her, he would have had me stymied, but he didn't.

'Er – how did you find out?'

'I have my methods.'

'Oh?' he said.

'Ah,' I replied, and there was silence again for a moment.

I wouldn't have believed it possible for so tough an egg

to sidle obsequiously, but that was how he now sidled up to me. There was a pleading look in his eyes.

'I hope you will keep this to yourself, Wooster? You will keep it to yourself, won't you, Wooster?'

'I will – '

'Thank you, Wooster.'

' – provided,' I continued, 'that we have no more of these extraordinary exhibitions on your part of – what's the word?'

He sidled a bit closer.

'Of course, of course. I'm afraid I have been acting rather hastily.' He reached out a hand and smoothed my sleeve. 'Did I rumple your coat, Wooster? I'm sorry. I forgot myself. It shall not happen again.'

'It had better not. Good Lord! Grabbing fellows' coats and saying you're going to break chaps' bones. I never heard of such a thing.'

'I know, I know. I was wrong.'

'You bet you were wrong. I shall be very sharp on that sort of thing in the future, Spode.'

'Yes, yes, I understand.'

'I have not been at all satisfied with your behaviour since I came to this house. The way you were looking at me at dinner. You may think people don't notice these things, but they do.'

'Of course, of course.'

'And calling me a miserable worm.'

'I'm sorry I called you a miserable worm, Wooster. I spoke without thinking.'

'Always think, Spode. Well, that is all. You may withdraw.'

'Good night, Wooster.'

'Good night, Spode.'

He hurried out with bowed head, and I turned to Aunt Dahlia, who was making noises like a motor-bicycle in the background.

Blandings

1 — Lord Emsworth and the Girl Friend

The day was so warm, so fair, so magically a thing of sunshine and blue skies and bird-song that anyone acquainted with Clarence, ninth Earl of Emsworth, and aware of his liking for fine weather, would have pictured him going about the place on this summer morning with a beaming smile and an uplifted heart. Instead of which, humped over the breakfast table, he was directing at a blameless kippered herring a look of such intense bitterness that the fish seemed to sizzle beneath it. For it was August Bank Holiday, and Blandings Castle on August Bank Holiday became, in his lordship's opinion, a miniature Inferno.

This was the day when his park and grounds broke out into a noisome rash of swings, roundabouts, marquees, toy balloons and paper bags; when a tidal wave of the peasantry and its squealing young engulfed those haunts of immemorial peace. On August Bank Holiday he was not allowed to potter pleasantly about his gardens in an old coat: forces beyond his control shoved him into a stiff collar and a top hat and told him to go out and be genial. And in the cool of the quiet evenfall they put him on a platform and made him make a speech. To a man with a day like that in front of him fine weather was a mockery.

His sister, Lady Constance Keeble, looked brightly at him over the coffee-pot.

'What a lovely morning!' she said.

Lord Emsworth's gloom deepened. He chafed at being called upon – by this woman of all others – to behave as if everything was for the jolliest in the jolliest of all possible worlds. But for his sister Constance and her hawk-like vigilance, he might, he thought, have been able at least to dodge the top hat.

'Have you got your speech ready?'

'Yes.'

'Well, mind you learn it by heart this time and don't stammer and dodder as you did last year.'

Lord Emsworth pushed plate and kipper away. He had lost his desire for food.

'And don't forget you have to go to the village this morning to judge the cottage gardens.'

'All right, all right, all right,' said his lordship testily. 'I've not forgotten.'

'I think I will come to the village with you. There are a number of those Fresh Air London children staying there now, and I must warn them to behave properly when they come to the Fête this afternoon. You know what London children are. McAllister says he found one of them in the gardens the other day, picking his flowers.'

At any other time the news of this outrage would, no doubt, have affected Lord Emsworth profoundly. But now, so intense was his self-pity, he did not even shudder. He drank coffee with the air of a man who regretted that it was not hemlock.

'By the way, McAllister was speaking to me again last night about that gravel path through the yew alley. He seems very keen on it.'

'Glug!' said Lord Emsworth – which, as any philologist will tell you, is the sound which peers of the realm make when stricken to the soul while drinking coffee.

Concerning Glasgow, that great commercial and manufacturing city in the county of Lanarkshire in Scotland, much has been written. So lyrically does the *Encyclopaedia Britannica* deal with the place that it covers twenty-seven pages before it can tear itself away and go on to Glass, Glastonbury, Glatz, and Glauber. The only aspect of it, however, which immediately concerns the present historian is the fact that the citizens it breeds are apt to be grim, dour, persevering, tenacious men; men with red whiskers who know what they want and mean to get it. Such a one was Angus McAllister, head-gardener at Blandings Castle.

For years Angus McAllister had set before himself as his earthly goal the construction of a gravel path through the Castle's famous yew alley. For years he had been bringing the project to the notice of his employer, though in anyone less whiskered the latter's unconcealed loathing would have caused embarrassment. And now, it seemed, he was at it again.

'Gravel path!' Lord Emsworth stiffened through the whole length of his stringy body. Nature, he had always maintained, intended a yew alley to be carpeted with a mossy growth. And, whatever Nature felt about it, he personally was dashed if he was going to have men with Clydeside accents and faces like dissipated potatoes coming along and mutilating that lovely expanse of green velvet. 'Gravel path, indeed! Why not asphalt? Why not a few hoardings with advertisements of liver pills and a filling-station? That's what the man would really like.'

Lord Emsworth felt bitter, and when he felt bitter he could be terribly sarcastic.

'Well, I think it is a very good idea,' said his sister. 'One could walk there in wet weather then. Damp moss is ruinous to shoes.'

Lord Emsworth rose. He could bear no more of this. He left the table, the room and the house and, reaching the yew alley some minutes later, was revolted to find it infested by Angus McAllister in person. The head-gardener was standing gazing at the moss like a high priest of some ancient religion about to stick the gaff into the human sacrifice.

'Morning, McAllister,' said Lord Emsworth coldly.

'Good morrrrning, your lorrudsheep.'

There was a pause. Angus McAllister, extending a foot that looked like a violin-case, pressed it on the moss.

The meaning of the gesture was plain. It expressed contempt, dislike, a generally anti-moss spirit: and Lord Emsworth, wincing, surveyed the man unpleasantly through his pince-nez. Though not often given to theological speculation, he was wondering why Providence, if obliged to make head-gardeners, had found it necessary to make them so Scotch. In the case of Angus McAllister, why, going a step farther, have made him a human being at all? All the ingredients of a first-class mule simply thrown away. He felt that he might have liked Angus McAllister if he had been a mule.

'I was speaking to her leddyship yesterday.'

'Oh?'

'About the gravel path I was speaking to her leddyship.'

'Oh?'

'Her leddyship likes the notion fine.'

'Indeed! Well . . .'

Lord Emsworth's face had turned a lively pink, and he was about to release the blistering words which were forming themselves in his mind when suddenly he caught the head-gardener's eye and paused. Angus McAllister was looking at him in a peculiar manner, and he knew what that look meant. Just one crack, his eye was saying – in Scotch, of course – just one crack out of you and I tender my resignation. And with a sickening shock it came home to Lord Emsworth how completely he was in this man's clutches.

He shuffled miserably. Yes, he was helpless. Except for that kink about gravel paths, Angus McAllister was a head-gardener in a thousand, and he needed him. He could not do without him. That, unfortunately, had been proved by experiment. Once before, at the time when they were grooming for the Agricultural Show that pumpkin which had subsequently romped home so gallant a winner, he had dared to flout Angus McAllister. And Angus had resigned, and he had been forced to plead – yes, plead – with him to come back. An employer cannot hope to do this sort of thing and still rule with an iron hand. Filled with the coward rage that dares to burn but does not dare to blaze, Lord Emsworth coughed a cough that was undisguisedly a bronchial white flag.

'I'll – er – I'll think it over, McAllister.'

'Mphm.'

'I have to go to the village now. I will see you later.'

'Mphm.'

'Meanwhile, I will – er – think it over.'

'Mphm.'

The task of judging the floral displays in the cottage gardens of the little village of Blandings Parva was one to which Lord Emsworth had looked forward with pleasurable anticipation. It was the sort of job he liked. But now, even though he had managed to give his sister Constance the slip and was free from her threatened society, he approached the task with a downcast spirit. It is always unpleasant for a proud man to realize that he is no longer captain of his soul; that he is to all intents and purposes ground beneath the number twelve heel of a Glaswegian head-gardener; and, brooding on this, he judged the cottage gardens with a distrait eye. It was only when he came to the last on his list that anything like animation crept into his demeanour.

This, he perceived, peering over its rickety fence, was not at all a bad little garden. It demanded closer inspection. He unlatched the gate and pottered in. And a dog, dozing behind a water-butt, opened one eye and looked at him. It was one of those hairy, nondescript dogs, and its gaze was cold, wary and suspicious, like that of a stockbroker who thinks someone is going to play the confidence trick on him.

Lord Emsworth did not observe the animal. He had pottered to a bed of wallflowers and now, stooping, he took a sniff at them.

As sniffs go, it was an innocent sniff, but the dog for

some reason appeared to read into it criminality of a high order. All the indignant householder in him woke in a flash. The next moment the world had become full of hideous noises, and Lord Emsworth's preoccupation was swept away in a passionate desire to save his ankles from harm.

As these chronicles of Blandings Castle have already shown, he was not at his best with strange dogs. Beyond saying 'Go away, sir!' and leaping to and fro with an agility surprising in one of his years, he had accomplished little in the direction of a reasoned plan of defence when the cottage door opened and a girl came out.

'Hoy!' cried the girl.

And on the instant, at the mere sound of her voice, the mongrel, suspending hostilities, bounded at the new-comer and writhed on his back at her feet with all four legs in the air. The spectacle reminded Lord Emsworth irresistibly of his own behaviour when in the presence of Angus McAllister.

He blinked at his preserver. She was a small girl, of uncertain age – possibly twelve or thirteen, though a combination of London fogs and early cares had given her face a sort of wizened motherliness which in some odd way caused his lordship from the first to look on her as belonging to his own generation. She was the type of girl you see in back streets carrying a baby nearly as large as herself and still retaining sufficient energy to lead one little brother by the hand and shout recrimination at another in the distance. Her cheeks shone from recent soaping, and she was dressed in a velveteen frock which was obviously the pick of her wardrobe. Her hair, in defiance of the prevailing mode, she wore drawn tightly back into a short pigtail.

'Er – thank you,' said Lord Emsworth.

'Thank you, sir,' said the girl.

For what she was thanking him, his lordship was not able to gather. Later, as their acquaintance ripened, he was to discover that this strange gratitude was a habit with his new friend. She thanked everybody for everything. At the moment, the mannerism surprised him. He continued to blink at her through his pince-nez.

Lack of practice had rendered Lord Emsworth a little rusty in the art of making conversation to members of the other sex. He sought in his mind for topics.

'Fine day.'

'Yes, sir. Thank you, sir.'

'Are you' – Lord Emsworth furtively consulted his list – 'are you the daughter of – ah – Ebenezer Sprockett?' he asked, thinking, as he had often thought before, what ghastly names some of his tenantry possessed.

'No, sir. I'm from London, sir.'

'Ah? London, eh? Pretty warm it must be there.' He paused. Then, remembering a formula of his youth: 'Er – been out much this Season?'

'No, sir.'

'Everybody out of town now, I suppose? What part of London?'

'Drury Line, sir.'

'What's your name? Eh, what?'

'Gladys, sir. Thank you, sir. This is Ern.'

A small boy had wandered out of the cottage, a rather hard-boiled specimen with freckles, bearing surprisingly in his hand a large and beautiful bunch of flowers. Lord Emsworth bowed courteously and with the addition of this third party to the *tête-à-tête*, felt more at his ease.

'How do you do?' he said. 'What pretty flowers.'

With her brother's advent Gladys, also, had lost diffidence and gained conversational aplomb.

'A treat, ain't they?' she agreed eagerly. 'I got 'em for 'im up at the big 'ahse. Coo! The old josser the plice belongs to didn't arf chase me. 'E found me picking 'em and 'e sharted somefin at me and come runnin' after me,

but I copped 'im on the shin wiv a stone and 'e stopped
to rub it and I come away.'

Lord Emsworth might have corrected her impression
that Blandings Castle and its gardens belonged to Angus
McAllister, but his mind was so filled with admiration
and gratitude that he refrained from doing so. He looked
at the girl almost reverently. Not content with controlling
savage dogs with a mere word, this super-woman
actually threw stones at Angus McAllister – a thing which
he had never been able to nerve himself to do in an
association which had lasted nine years – and, what was
more, copped him on the shin with them. What
nonsense, Lord Emsworth felt, the papers talked about
the Modern Girl. If this was a specimen, the Modern Girl
was the highest point the sex had yet reached.

'Ern,' said Gladys, changing the subject, 'is wearin'
'air-oil todiy.'

Lord Emsworth had already observed this and had,
indeed, been moving to windward as she spoke.

'For the Feet,' explained Gladys.

'For the feet?' It seemed unusual.

'For the Feet in the pork this afternoon.'

'Oh, you are going to the Fête?'

'Yes, sir, thank you, sir.'

For the first time, Lord Emsworth found himself
regarding that grisly social event with something
approaching favour.

'We must look out for one another there,' he said
cordially. 'You will remember me again? I shall be
wearing' – he gulped – 'a top hat.'

'Ern's going to wear a stror penamaw that's been give
'im.'

Lord Emsworth regarded the lucky young devil with
frank envy. He rather fancied he knew that panama. It
had been his constant companion for some six years and
then had been torn from him by his sister Constance
and handed over to the vicar's wife for her rummage sale.

He sighed.

'Well, good-bye.'

'Good-bye, sir. Thank you, sir.'

Lord Emsworth walked pensively out of the garden and, turning into the little street, encountered Lady Constance.

'Oh, there you are, Clarence.'

'Yes,' said Lord Emsworth, for such was the case.

'Have you finished judging the gardens?'

'Yes.'

'I am just going into this end cottage here. The vicar tells me there is a little girl from London staying there. I want to warn her to behave this afternoon. I have spoken to the others.'

Lord Emsworth drew himself up. His pince-nez were slightly askew, but despite this his gaze was commanding and impressive.

'Well, mind what you say,' he said authoritatively. 'None of your district-visiting stuff, Constance.'

'What do you mean?'

'You know what I mean. I have the greatest respect for the young lady to whom you refer. She behaved on a certain recent occasion – on two recent occasions – with notable gallantry and resource, and I won't have her bally-ragged. Understand that!'

The technical title of the orgy which broke out annually on the first Monday in August in the park of Blandings Castle was the Blandings Parva School Treat, and it seemed to Lord Emsworth, wanly watching the proceedings from under the shadow of his top hat, that if this was the sort of thing schools looked on as pleasure he and they were mentally poles apart. A function like the Blandings Parva School Treat blurred his conception of Man as Nature's Final Word.

The decent sheep and cattle to whom this park normally belonged had been hustled away into regions unknown, leaving the smooth expanse of turf to children whose vivacity scared Lord Emsworth and adults who appeared to him to have cast aside all dignity and every other noble quality which goes to make a one hundred per cent British citizen. Look at Mrs Rossiter over there, for instance, the wife of Jno. Rossiter, Provisions, Groceries and Homemade Jams. On any other day of the year, when you met her, Mrs Rossiter was a nice, quiet, docile woman who gave at the knees respectfully as you passed. Today, flushed in the face and with her bonnet on one side, she seemed to have gone completely native. She was wandering to and fro drinking lemonade out of a bottle and employing her mouth, when not so occupied, to make a devastating noise with what he believed was termed a squeaker.

The injustice of the thing stung Lord Emsworth. This park was his own private park. What right had people to come and blow squeakers in it? How would Mrs Rossiter like it if one afternoon he suddenly invaded her neat little garden in the High Street and rushed about over her lawn, blowing a squeaker?

And it was always on these occasions so infernally hot. July might have ended in a flurry of snow, but directly the first Monday in August arrived and he had to put on a stiff collar, out came the sun, blazing with tropic fury.

Of course, admitted Lord Emsworth, for he was a fair-minded man, this cut both ways. The hotter the day, the more quickly his collar lost its starch and ceased to spike him like a javelin. This afternoon, for instance, it had resolved itself almost immediately into something which felt like a wet compress. Severe as were his sufferings, he was compelled to recognize that he was that much ahead of the game.

A masterful figure loomed at his side.

'Clarence!'

Lord Emsworth's mental and spiritual state was now

such that not even the advent of his sister Constance could add noticeably to his discomfort.

'Clarence, you look a perfect sight.'

'I know I do. Who wouldn't in a rig-out like this? Why in the name of goodness you always insist . . .'

'Please don't be childish, Clarence. I cannot understand the fuss you make about dressing for once in your life like a reasonable English gentleman and not like a tramp.'

'It's this top hat. It's exciting the children.'

'What on earth do you mean, exciting the children?'

'Well, all I can tell you is that just now, as I was passing the place where they're playing football – Football! In weather like this! – a small boy called out something derogatory and threw a portion of a coconut at it.'

'If you will identify the child,' said Lady Constance warmly, 'I will have him severely punished.'

'How the dickens,' replied his lordship with equal warmth, 'can I identify the child? They all look alike to me. And if I did identify him, I would shake him by the hand. A boy who throws coconuts at top hats is fundamentally sound in his views. And stiff collars . . .'

'Stiff! That's what I came to speak to you about. Are you aware that your collar looks like a rag? Go in and change it at once.'

'But, my dear Constance . . .'

'At once, Clarence. I simply cannot understand a man having so little pride in his appearance. But all your life you have been like that. I remember when we were children . . .'

Lord Emsworth's past was not of such a purity that he was prepared to stand and listen to it being lectured on by a sister with a good memory.

'Oh, all right, all right, all right,' he said. 'I'll change it, I'll change it.'

'Well, hurry. They are just starting tea.'

Lord Emsworth quivered.

'Have I got to go into that tea-tent?'

'Of course you have. Don't be so ridiculous. I do wish you would realize your position. As master of Blandings Castle . . .'

A bitter, mirthless laugh from the poor peon thus ludicrously described drowned the rest of the sentence.

It always seemed to Lord Emsworth, in analysing these entertainments, that the August Bank Holiday Saturnalia at Blandings Castle reached a peak of repulsiveness when tea was served in the big marquee. Tea over, the agony abated, to become acute once more at the moment when he stepped to the edge of the platform and cleared his throat and tried to recollect what the deuce he had planned to say to the goggling audience beneath him. After that, it subsided again and passed until the following August.

Conditions during the tea hour, the marquee having stood all day under a blazing sun, were generally such that Shadrach, Meshach and Abednego, had they been there, could have learned something new about burning fiery furnaces. Lord Emsworth, delayed by the revision of his toilet, made his entry when the meal was half over and was pleased to find that his second collar almost instantaneously began to relax its iron grip. That, however, was the only gleam of happiness which was to be vouchsafed him. Once in the tent, it took his experienced eye but a moment to discern that the present feast was eclipsing in frightfulness all its predecessors.

Young Blandings Parva, in its normal form, tended rather to the stolidly bovine than the riotous. In all villages, of course, there must of necessity be an occasional tough egg – in the case of Blandings Parva the names of Willie Drake and Thomas (Rat-Face) Blenkiron spring to the mind – but it was seldom that the local infants offered anything beyond the power of a curate to control. What was giving the present gathering its striking

resemblance to a reunion of *sansculottes* at the height of
the French Revolution was the admixture of the Fresh
Air London visitors.

About the London child, reared among the tin cans
and cabbage stalks of Drury Lane and Clare Market,
there is a breezy insouciance which his country cousin
lacks. Years of back-chat with annoyed parents and
relatives have cured him of any tendency he may have
had towards shyness, with the result that when he
requires anything he grabs for it, and when he is amused
by any slight peculiarity in the personal appearance of
members of the governing classes he finds no difficulty
in translating his thoughts into speech. Already, up and
down the long tables, the curate's unfortunate squint was
coming in for hearty comment, and the front teeth of one
of the school-teachers ran it a close second for popularity.
Lord Emsworth was not, as a rule, a man of swift
inspirations, but it occurred to him at this juncture that
it would be a prudent move to take off his top hat before
his little guests observed it and appreciated its humorous
possibilities.

The action was not, however, necessary. Even as he
raised his hand a rock cake, singing through the air like
a shell, took it off for him.

Lord Emsworth had had sufficient. Even Constance,
unreasonable woman though she was, could hardly
expect him to stay and beam genially under conditions
like this. All civilized laws had obviously gone by the
board and Anarchy reigned in the marquee. The curate
was doing his best to form a provisional government
consisting of himself and the two school-teachers, but
there was only one man who could have coped
adequately with the situation and that was King Herod,
who – regrettably – was not among those present. Feeling
like some aristocrat of the old *regime* sneaking away from
the tumbril, Lord Emsworth edged to the exit and
withdrew.

Outside the marquee the world was quieter, but only comparatively so. What Lord Emsworth craved was solitude, and in all the broad park there seemed to be but one spot where it was to be had. This was a red-tiled shed, standing beside a small pond, used at happier times as a lounge or retiring-room for cattle. Hurrying thither, his lordship had begun to revel in the cool, cow-scented dimness of its interior when from one of the dark corners, causing him to start and bite his tongue, there came the sound of a subdued sniff.

He turned. This was persecution. With the whole park to mess about in, why should an infernal child invade this one sanctuary of his? He spoke with angry sharpness. He came of a line of warrior ancestors and his fighting blood was up.

'Who's that?'

'Me, sir. Thank you, sir.'

Only one person of Lord Emsworth's acquaintance was capable of expressing gratitude for having been barked at in such a tone. His wrath died away and remorse took its place. He felt like a man who in error has kicked a favourite dog.

'God bless my soul!' he exclaimed. 'What in the world are you doing in a cow-shed?'

'Please, sir, I was put.'

'Put? How do you mean, put? Why?'

'For pinching things, sir.'

'Eh? What? Pinching things? Most extraordinary. What did you – er – pinch?'

'Two buns, two jem-sengwiches, two apples and a slicer cake.'

The girl had come out of her corner and was standing correctly at attention. Force of habit had caused her to intone the list of the purloined articles in the sing-song voice in which she was wont to recite the multiplication-table at school, but Lord Emsworth could see that she was deeply moved. Tear-stains glistened on her face, and no Emsworth had ever been able to watch unstirred a woman's tears. The ninth Earl was visibly affected.

'Blow your nose,' he said, hospitably extending his handkerchief.

'Yes, sir. Thank you, sir.'

'What did you say you had pinched? Two buns . . .'

' . . . Two jem-sengwiches, two apples and a slicer cake.'

'Did you eat them?'

'No, sir. They wasn't for me. They was for Ern.'

'Ern? Oh, ah, yes. Yes, to be sure. For Ern, eh?'

'Yes, sir.'

'But why the dooce couldn't Ern have – er – pinched them for himself? Strong, able-bodied young feller, I mean.'

Lord Emsworth, a member of the old school, did not like this disposition on the part of the modern young man to shirk the dirty work and let the woman pay.

'Ern wasn't allowed to come to the treat, sir.'

'What! Not allowed? Who said he mustn't?'

'The lidy, sir.'

'What lidy?'

'The one that come in just after you'd gorn this morning.'

A fierce snort escaped Lord Emsworth. Constance! What the devil did Constance mean by taking it upon herself to revise his list of guests without so much as a . . . Constance, eh? He snorted again. One of these days Constance would go too far.

'Monstrous!' he cried.

'Yes, sir.'

'High-handed tyranny, by Gad. Did she give any reason?'

'The lidy didn't like Ern biting 'er in the leg, sir.'

'Ern bit her in the leg?'

'Yes, sir. Pliying 'e was a dorg. And the lidy was cross

159

and Ern wasn't allowed to come to the treat, and I told 'im I'd bring 'im back somefing nice.'

Lord Emsworth breathed heavily. He had not supposed that in these degenerate days a family like this existed. The sister copped Angus McAllister on the shin with stones, the brother bit Constance in the leg . . . It was like listening to some grand old saga of the exploits of heroes and demigods.

'I thought if I didn't 'ave nothing myself it would make it all right.'

'Nothing?' Lord Emsworth started. 'Do you mean to tell me you have not had tea?'

'No, sir. Thank you, sir. I thought if I didn't 'ave none, then it would be all right Ern 'aving what I would 'ave 'ad if I 'ad 'ave 'ad.'

His lordship's head, never strong, swam a little. Then it resumed its equilibrium. He caught her drift.

'God bless my soul!' said Lord Emsworth. 'I never heard anything so monstrous and appalling in my life. Come with me immediately.'

'The lidy said I was to stop 'ere, sir.'

Lord Emsworth gave vent to his loudest snort of the afternoon.

'Confound the lidy!'

'Yes, sir. Thank you, sir.'

Five minutes later Beach, the butler, enjoying a siesta in the housekeeper's room, was roused from his slumbers by the unexpected ringing of a bell. Answering its summons, he found his employer in the library, and with him a surprising young person in a velveteen frock, at the sight of whom his eyebrows quivered and, but for his iron self-restraint, would have risen.

'Beach!'

'Your lordship?'

'This young lady would like some tea.'

'Very good, your lordship.'

'Buns, you know. And apples, and jem – I mean jam-sandwiches, and cake, and that sort of thing.'

'Very good, your lordship.'

'And she has a brother, Beach.'

'Indeed, your lordship?'

'She will want to take some stuff away for him.' Lord Emsworth turned to his guest. 'Ernest would like a little chicken, perhaps?'

'Coo!'

'I beg your pardon?'

'Yes, sir. Thank you, sir.'

'And a slice or two of ham?'

'Yes, sir. Thank you, sir.'

'And – he has no gouty tendency?'

'No, sir. Thank you, sir.'

'Capital! Then a bottle of that new lot of port, Beach. It's some stuff they've sent me down to try,' explained his lordship. 'Nothing special, you understand,' he added apologetically, 'but quite drinkable. I should like your brother's opinion of it. See that all that is put together in a parcel, Beach, and leave it on the table in the hall. We will pick it up as we go out.'

A welcome coolness had crept into the evening air by the time Lord Emsworth and his guest came out of the great door of the castle. Gladys, holding her host's hand and clutching the parcel, sighed contentedly. She had done herself well at the tea-table. Life seemed to have nothing more to offer.

Lord Emsworth did not share this view. His spacious mood had not yet exhausted itself.

'Now, is there anything else you can think of that Ernest would like?' he asked. 'If so, do not hesitate to mention it. Beach, can you think of anything?'

The butler, hovering respectfully, was unable to do so.

'No, your lordship. I ventured to add – on my own

responsibility, your lordship – some hard-boiled eggs and
a pot of jam to the parcel.'

'Excellent! You are sure there is nothing else?'

A wistful look came into Gladys's eyes.

'Could he 'ave some flarze?'

'Certainly,' said Lord Emsworth. 'Certainly, certainly,
certainly. By all means. Just what I was about to suggest
my – er – what *is* flarze?'

Beach, the linguist, interpreted.

'I think the young lady means flowers, your lordship.'

'Yes, sir. Thank you, sir. Flarze.'

'Oh?' said Lord Emsworth. 'Oh? Flarze?' he said
slowly. 'Oh, ah, yes. Yes. I see. H'm!'

He removed his pince-nez, wiped them thoughtfully,
replaced them, and gazed with wrinkling forehead at the
gardens that stretched gaily out before him. Flarze! It
would be idle to deny that those gardens contained flarze
in full measure. They were bright with Achillea, Bignonia
Radicans, Campanula, Digitalis, Euphorbia, Funkia,
Gypsophila, Helianthus, Iris, Liatris, Monarda, Phlox
Drummondi, Salvia, Thalictrum, Vinca and Yucca. But
the devil of it was that Angus McAllister would have a
fit if they were picked. Across the threshold of this Eden
the ginger whiskers of Angus McAllister lay like a flaming
sword.

As a general rule, the procedure for getting flowers out
of Angus McAllister was as follows. You waited till he
was in one of his rare moods of complaisance, then you
led the conversation gently round to the subject of
interior decoration, and then, choosing your moment,
you asked if he could possibly spare a few to be put in
vases. The last thing you thought of doing was to charge
in and start helping yourself.

'I – er . . .' said Lord Emsworth.

He stopped. In a sudden blinding flash of clear vision
he had seen himself for what he was – the spineless,
unspeakably unworthy descendant of ancestors who,

though they may have had their faults, had certainly
known how to handle employees. It was 'How now,
varlet!' and 'Marry come up, thou malapert knave!' in
the days of previous Earls of Emsworth. Of course, they
had possessed certain advantages which he lacked. It
undoubtedly helped a man in his dealings with the
domestic staff to have, as they had had, the rights of
the high, the middle and the low justice – which meant,
broadly, that if you got annoyed with your head-gardener
you could immediately divide him into four head-
gardeners with a battle-axe and no questions asked – but
even so, he realized that they were better men than he
was and that, if he allowed craven fear of Angus
McAllister to stand in the way of this delightful girl and
her charming brother getting all the flowers they
required, he was not worthy to be the last of their line.

Lord Emsworth wrestled with his tremors.

'Certainly, certainly, certainly,' he said, though not
without qualm. 'Take as many as you want.'

And so it came about that Angus McAllister, crouched
in his potting-shed like some dangerous beast in its den,
beheld a sight which first froze his blood and then sent it
boiling through his veins. Flitting to and fro through his
sacred gardens, picking his sacred flowers, was a small
girl in a velveteen frock. And – which brought apoplexy
a step closer – it was the same small girl who two days
before had copped him on the shin with a stone. The
stillness of the summer evening was shattered by a roar
that sounded like boilers exploding, and Angus McAllister
came out of the potting-shed at forty-five miles per hour.

Gladys did not linger. She was a London child, trained
from infancy to bear herself gallantly in the presence of
alarms and excursions, but this excursion had been so
sudden that it momentarily broke her nerve. With a
horrified yelp she scuttled to where Lord Emsworth stood
and, hiding behind him, clutched the tails of his
morning-coat.

'Oo-er!' said Gladys.

Lord Emsworth was not feeling so frightfully good himself. We have pictured him a few moments back drawing inspiration from the nobility of his ancestors and saying, in effect, 'That for McAllister!', but truth now compels us to admit that this hardy attitude was largely due to the fact that he believed the head-gardener to be a safe quarter of a mile away among the swings and roundabouts of the Fête. The spectacle of the man charging vengefully down on him with gleaming eyes and bristling whiskers made him feel like a nervous English infantryman at the Battle of Bannockburn. His knees shook and the soul within him quivered.

And then something happened, and the whole aspect of the situation changed.

It was, in itself, quite a trivial thing, but it had an astoundingly stimulating effect on Lord Emsworth's morale. What happened was that Gladys, seeking further protection, slipped at this moment a small, hot hand into his.

It was a mute vote of confidence, and Lord Emsworth intended to be worthy of it.

'He's coming,' whispered his lordship's Inferiority Complex agitatedly.

'What of it?' replied Lord Emsworth stoutly.

'Tick him off,' breathed his lordship's ancestors in his other ear.

'Leave it to me,' replied Lord Emsworth.

He drew himself up and adjusted his pince-nez. He felt filled with a cool masterfulness. If the man tendered his resignation, let him tender his damned resignation.

'Well, McAllister?' said Lord Emsworth coldly.

He removed his top hat and brushed it against his sleeve.

'What is the matter, McAllister?'

He replaced his top hat.

'You appear agitated, McAllister.'

He jerked his head militantly. The hat fell off. He let it lie. Freed from its loathsome weight he felt more masterful than ever. It had just needed that to bring him to the top of his form.

'This young lady,' said Lord Emsworth, 'has my full permission to pick all the flowers she wants, McAllister. If you do not see eye to eye with me in this matter, McAllister, say so and we will discuss what you are going to do about it, McAllister. These gardens, McAllister, belong to me, and if you do not – er – appreciate that fact you will, no doubt, be able to find another employer – ah – more in tune with your views. I value your services highly, McAllister, but I will not be dictated to in my own garden, McAllister. Er – dash it,' added his lordship, spoiling the whole effect.

A long moment followed in which Nature stood still, breathless. The Achillea stood still. So did the Bignonia Radicans. So did the Campanula, the Digitalis, the Euphorbia, the Funkia, the Gypsophila, the Helianthus, the Iris, the Liatris, the Monarda, the Phlox Drummondi, the Salvia, the Thalictrum, the Vinca and the Yucca. From far off in the direction of the park there sounded the happy howls of children who were probably breaking things, but even these seemed hushed. The evening breeze had died away.

Angus McAllister stood glowering. His attitude was that of one sorely perplexed. So might the early bird have looked if the worm ear-marked for its breakfast had suddenly turned and snapped at it. It had never occurred to him that his employer would voluntarily suggest that he sought another position, and now that he had suggested it, Angus McAllister disliked the idea very much. Blandings Castle was in his bones. Elsewhere, he would feel an exile. He fingered his whiskers, but they gave him no comfort.

He made his decision. Better to cease to be a Napoleon than be a Napoleon in exile.

'Mphm,' said Angus McAllister.

'Oh, and by the way, McAllister,' said Lord Emsworth,
'that matter of the gravel path through the yew alley.
I've been thinking it over, and I won't have it. Not on any
account. Mutilate my beautiful moss with a beastly gravel
path? Make an eyesore of the loveliest spot in one of the
finest and oldest gardens in the United Kingdom?
Certainly not. Most decidedly not. Try to remember,
McAllister, as you work in the gardens of Blandings
Castle, that you are not back in Glasgow, laying out
recreation grounds. That is all, McAllister. Er – dash it
– that is all.'

'Mphm,' said Angus McAllister.

He turned. He walked away. The potting-shed
swallowed him up. Nature resumed its breathing. The
breeze began to blow again. And all over the gardens birds
who had stopped on their high note carried on according
to plan.

Lord Emsworth took out his handkerchief and dabbed
with it at his forehead. He was shaken, but a novel sense
of being a man among men thrilled him. It might seem
bravado, but he almost wished – yes, dash it, he almost
wished – that his sister Constance would come along and
start something while he felt like this.

He had his wish.

'Clarence!'

Yes, there she was, hurrying towards him up the garden
path. She, like McAllister, seemed agitated. Something
was on her mind.

'Clarence!'

'Don't keep saying "Clarence!" as if you were a dashed
parrot,' said Lord Emsworth haughtily. 'What the dickens
is the matter, Constance?'

'Matter? Do you know what the time is? Do you know
that everybody is waiting down there for you to make
your speech?'

Lord Emsworth met her eye sternly.

'I do not,' he said. 'And I don't care. I'm not going to make any dashed speech. If you want a speech, let the vicar make it. Or make it yourself. Speech! I never heard such dashed nonsense in my life.' He turned to Gladys. 'Now, my dear,' he said, 'if you will just give me time to get out of these infernal clothes and this ghastly collar and put on something human, we'll go down to the village and have a chat with Ern.'

2 — *PGW's Notes for a Sequel to* Lord Emsworth and the Girl Friend

Central Idea

Lord Emsworth and the Girl Friend meet again. She is now a tweeny at Blandings and they have an affecting reunion. I see her as coming into library with wood and Lord Emsworth springing up and saying 'Allow me' and then the recognition.

This recognition should come at a moment when Lord E is in some sort of trouble, and he confides in her and they work together through the story.

I seem to see her engaged to jealous valet, or something, and the course of the story places her in a position where he is angry with her, thinking she has been carrying on with someone else, and she cannot square herself except by giving Lord E away. This she nobly refuses to do. Then the story ought to build up to Lord E finding out about her self-sacrifice and confessing to his crime, whatever it is, and dominating situation.

The crime would presumably be helping young lover of whom Lady Constance disapproves. It is young lover who makes valet jealous. I see story leading up to girl friend telling lover of something she has done to help him and he kisses her gratefully, which valet sees.

Notes

Just groping. How wd it be if lover was the local vet, who has saved life of Empress, which of course makes Lord E his firm friend. He has also saved life of heroine's dog. Heroine should be one of Lord E's numerous nieces. Then you would get a nice love story, with strong

snobbish motive. In end, vet might turn out to be very
rich, or something that would conciliate heroine's
mother.

Lord E could get hero into house as his secretary.
Though wait, if he is vet, he is presumably well known
to all. Might be better not to make him a professional vet.

3 — The Crime Wave at Blandings

The day on which Lawlessness reared its ugly head at
Blandings Castle was one of singular beauty. The sun
shone down from a sky of cornflower blue, and what one
would really like would be to describe in leisurely detail
the ancient battlements, the smooth green lawns, the
rolling parkland, the majestic trees, the well-bred bees
and the gentlemanly birds on which it shone.

But those who read thrillers are an impatient race.
They chafe at scenic rhapsodies and want to get on to
the rough stuff. When, they ask, did the dirty work start?
Who were mixed up in it? Was there blood, and, if so,
how much? And – most particularly – where was
everybody and what was everybody doing at whatever
time it was? The chronicler who wishes to grip must
supply this information at the earliest possible moment.

The wave of crime, then, which was to rock one of
Shropshire's stateliest homes to its foundations broke
out towards the middle of a fine summer afternoon, and
the persons involved in it were disposed as follows:

Clarence, ninth Earl of Emsworth, the castle's owner
and overlord, was down in the potting-shed, in
conference with Angus McAllister, his head-gardener, on
the subject of sweet peas.

His sister, Lady Constance, was strolling on the terrace
with a swarthy young man in spectacles, whose name
was Rupert Baxter and who had at one time been Lord
Emsworth's private secretary.

Beach, the butler, was in a deck-chair outside the back
premises of the house, smoking a cigar and reading
Chapter Sixteen of *The Man With The Missing Toe*.

George, Lord Emsworth's grandson, was prowling through the shrubbery with the airgun which was his constant companion.

Jane, his lordship's niece, was in the summer-house by the lake.

And the sun shone serenely down – on, as we say, the lawns, the battlements, the trees, the bees, the best type of bird and the rolling parkland.

Presently Lord Emsworth left the potting-shed and started to wander towards the house. He had never felt happier. All day his mood had been one of perfect contentment and tranquillity, and for once in a way Angus McAllister had done nothing to disturb it. Too often, when you tried to reason with that human mule, he had a way of saying 'Mphm' and looking Scotch and then saying 'Grmph' and looking Scotch again, and after that just fingering his beard and looking Scotch without speaking, which was intensely irritating to a sensitive employer. But this afternoon Hollywood yes-men could have taken his correspondence course, and Lord Emsworth had none of that uneasy feeling, which usually came to him on these occasions, that the moment his back was turned his own sound, statesmanlike policies would be shelved and some sort of sweet pea New Deal put into practice as if he had never spoken a word.

He was humming as he approached the terrace. He had his programme all mapped out. For perhaps an hour, till the day had cooled off a little, he would read a Pig book in the library. After that he would go and take a sniff at a rose or two and possibly do a bit of snailing. These mild pleasures were all his simple soul demanded. He wanted nothing more. Just the quiet life, with nobody to fuss him.

And now that Baxter had left, he reflected buoyantly, nobody did fuss him. There had, he dimly recalled, been some sort of trouble a week or so back – something about some man his niece Jane wanted to marry and his sister Constance didn't want her to marry – but that had apparently all blown over. And even when the thing had been at its height, even when the air had been shrill with women's voices and Connie had kept popping out at him and saying 'Do *listen*, Clarence!' he had always been able to reflect that, though all this was pretty unpleasant, there was nevertheless a bright side. He had ceased to be the employer of Rupert Baxter.

There is a breed of granite-faced, strong-jawed business man to whom Lord Emsworth's attitude towards Rupert Baxter would have seemed frankly inexplicable. To these Titans a private secretary is simply a Hey-you, a Hi-there, a mere puppet to be ordered hither and thither at will. The trouble with Lord Emsworth was that it was he and not his secretary who had been the puppet. Their respective relations had always been those of a mild reigning monarch and the pushing young devil who has taken on the dictatorship. For years, until he had mercifully tendered his resignation to join an American named Jevons, Baxter had worried Lord Emsworth, bossed him, bustled him, had always been after him to do things and remember things and sign things. Never a moment's peace. Yes, it was certainly delightful to think that Baxter had departed for ever. His going had relieved this Garden of Eden of its one resident snake.

Still humming, Lord Emsworth reached the terrace. A moment later, the melody had died on his lips and he was rocking back on his heels as if he had received a solid punch on the nose.

'God bless my soul!' he ejaculated, shaken to the core.

His pince-nez, as always happened when he was emotionally stirred, had leaped from their moorings. He recovered them and put them on again, hoping feebly that the ghastly sight he had seen would prove to have been an optical illusion. But no. However much he blinked, he could not blink away the fact that the man over there talking to his sister Constance was Rupert Baxter in person. He stood gaping at him with a horror which would have been almost excessive if the other had returned from the tomb.

Lady Constance was smiling brightly, as women so often do when they are in the process of slipping something raw over on their nearest and dearest.

'Here is Mr Baxter, Clarence.'

'Ah,' said Lord Emsworth.

'He is touring England on his motor-bicycle, and finding himself in these parts, of course, he looked us up.'

'Ah,' said Lord Emsworth.

He spoke dully, for his soul was heavy with foreboding. It was all very well for Connie to say that Baxter was touring England, thus giving the idea that in about five minutes the man would leap on his motor-bicycle and dash off to some spot a hundred miles away. He knew his sister. She was plotting. Always ardently pro-Baxter, she was going to try to get Blandings Castle's leading incubus back into office again. Lord Emsworth would have been prepared to lay the odds on this in the most liberal spirit. So he said 'Ah.'

The monosyllable, taken in conjunction with the sagging of her brother's jaw and the glare of agony behind his pince-nez, caused Lady Constance's lips to tighten. A disciplinary light came into her fine eyes. She looked like a female lion-tamer about to assert her personality with one of the troupe.

'Clarence!' she said sharply. She turned to her companion. 'Would you excuse me for a moment, Mr Baxter. There is something I want to talk to Lord Emsworth about.'

She drew the pallid peer aside, and spoke with sharp rebuke.

'Just like a stuck pig!'

'Eh?' said Lord Emsworth. His mind had been

wandering, as it so often did. The magic word brought it back. 'Pigs? What about pigs?'

'I was saying that you were looking like a stuck pig. You might at least have asked Mr Baxter how he was.'

'I could see how he was. What's he doing here?'

'I told you what he was doing here.'

'But how does he come to be touring England on motor-bicycles? I thought he was working for an American fellow named something or other.'

'He has left Mr Jevons.'

'What!'

'Yes. Mr Jevons had to return to America, and Mr Baxter did not want to leave England.'

Lord Emsworth reeled. Jevons had been his sheet-anchor. He had never met that genial Chicagoan, but he had always thought kindly and gratefully of him, as one does of some great doctor who has succeeded in isolating and confining a disease germ.

'You mean the chap's out of a job?' he cried aghast.

'Yes. And it could not have happened at a more fortunate time, because something has got to be done about George.'

'Who's George?'

'You have a grandson of that name,' explained Lady Constance with the sweet, frozen patience which she so often used when conversing with her brother. 'Your heir, Bosham, if you recollect, has two sons, James and George. George, the younger, is spending his summer holidays here. You may have noticed him about. A boy of twelve with auburn hair and freckles.'

'Oh, George? You mean George? Yes, I know George. He's my grandson. What about him?'

'He is completely out of hand. Only yesterday he broke another window with that airgun of his.'

'He needs a mother's care?' Lord Emsworth was vague, but he had an idea that that was the right thing to say.

'He needs a tutor's care, and I am glad to say that Mr

Baxter has very kindly consented to accept the position.'

'What!'

'Yes. It is all settled. His things are at the Emsworth Arms, and I am sending down for them.'

Lord Emsworth sought feverishly for arguments which would quash this frightful scheme.

'But he can't be a tutor if he's galumphing all over England on a motor-bicycle.'

'I had not overlooked that point. He will stop galumphing over England on a motor-bicycle.'

'But – '

'It will be a wonderful solution of a problem which was becoming more difficult every day. Mr Baxter will keep George in order. He is so firm.'

She turned away, and Lord Emsworth resumed his progress towards the library.

It was a black moment for the ninth Earl. His worst fears had been realized. He knew just what all this meant. On one of his rare visits to London he had once heard an extraordinarily vivid phrase which had made a deep impression upon him. He had been taking his after-luncheon coffee at the Senior Conservative Club and some fellows in an adjoining nest of armchairs had started a political discussion, and one of them had said about something or other that, mark his words, it was the 'thin end of the wedge'. He recognized what was happening now as the thin end of the wedge. From Baxter as a temporary tutor to Baxter as a permanent secretary would, he felt, be so short a step that the contemplation of it chilled him to the bone.

A short-sighted man whose pince-nez have gone astray at the very moment when vultures are gnawing at his bosom seldom guides his steps carefully. Anyone watching Lord Emsworth totter blindly across the terrace would have foreseen that he would shortly collide with something, the only point open to speculation being with what he would collide. This proved to be a

small boy with ginger hair and freckles who emerged
abruptly from the shrubbery carrying an airgun.

'Coo!' said the small boy. 'Sorry, Grandpapa.'

Lord Emsworth recovered his pince-nez and, having
adjusted them on the old spot, glared balefully.

'George! Why the dooce don't you look where you're
going?'

'Sorry, Grandpapa.'

'You might have injured me severely.'

'Sorry, Grandpapa.'

'Be more careful another time.'

'OK, big boy.'

'And don't call me "big boy".'

'Right ho, Grandpapa. I say,' said George, shelving the
topic, 'who's the bird talking to Aunt Connie?'

He pointed – a vulgarism which a good tutor would
have corrected – and Lord Emsworth, following the
finger, winced as his eye rested once more upon Rupert
Baxter. The secretary – already Lord Emsworth had
mentally abandoned the qualifying 'ex' – was gazing out
over the rolling parkland, and it seemed to his lordship
that his gaze was proprietorial. Rupert Baxter, flashing
his spectacles over the grounds of Blandings Castle, wore
– or so it appeared to Lord Emsworth – the smug air of
some ruthless monarch of old surveying conquered
territory.

'That is Mr Baxter,' he replied.

'Looks a bit of a blister,' said George critically.

The expression was new to Lord Emsworth, but he
recognized it at once as the ideal description of Rupert
Baxter. His heart warmed to the little fellow, and he might
quite easily at this moment have given him sixpence.

'Do you think so?' he said lovingly.

'What's he doing here?'

Lord Emsworth felt a pang. It seemed brutal to dash
the sunshine from the life of this admirable boy. Yet
somebody had got to tell him.

'He is going to be your tutor.'

'Tutor?'

The word was a cry of agony forced from the depths of the boy's soul. A stunned sense that all the fundamental decencies of life were being outraged had swept over George. His voice was thick with emotion.

'Tutor?' he cried. '*Tew*-tor? Ter-YEW-tor? In the middle of the summer holidays? What have I got to have a tutor for in the middle of the summer holidays? I do call this a bit off. I mean, in the middle of the summer holidays. Why do I want a tutor? I mean to say, in the middle of – '

He would have spoken at greater length, for he had much to say on the subject, but at this point Lady Constance's voice, musical but imperious, interrupted his flow of speech.

'Gee-orge.'

'Coo! Right in the middle – '

'Come here, George. I want you to meet Mr Baxter.'

'Coo!' muttered the stricken child again and, frowning darkly, slouched across the terrace. Lord Emsworth proceeded to the library, a tender pity in his heart for this boy who by his crisp summing-up of Rupert Baxter had revealed himself so kindred a spirit. He knew just how George felt. It was not always easy to get anything into Lord Emsworth's head, but he had grasped the substance of his grandson's complaint unerringly. George, about to have a tutor in the middle of the summer holidays, did not want one.

Sighing a little, Lord Emsworth reached the library and found his book.

There were not many books which at a time like this could have diverted Lord Emsworth's mind from what weighed upon it, but this one did. It was Whiffle on *The Care Of The Pig* and, buried in its pages, he forgot everything. The chapter he was reading was that noble one about swill and bran-mash, and it took him completely out of the world, so much so that when some twenty minutes later the door suddenly burst open it was as if a bomb had been exploded under his nose. He dropped Whiffle and sat panting. Then, although his pince-nez had followed routine by flying off, he was able by some subtle instinct to sense that the intruder was his sister Constance, and an observation beginning with the words 'Good God, Connie!' had begun to leave his lips, when she cut him short.

'Clarence,' she said, and it was plain that her nervous system, like his, was much shaken, 'the most dreadful thing has happened!'

'Eh?'

'That man is here.'

'What man?'

'That man of Jane's. The man I told you about.'

'What man did you tell me about?'

Lady Constance seated herself. She would have preferred to have been able to do without tedious explanations, but long association with her brother had taught her that his was a memory that had to be refreshed. She embarked, accordingly, on these explanations, speaking wearily, like a schoolmistress to one of the duller members of her class.

'The man I told you about – certainly not less than a hundred times – was a man Jane met in the spring, when she went to stay with her friends the Leighs in Devonshire. She had a silly flirtation with him, which, of course, she insisted in magnifying into a great romance. She kept saying they were engaged. And he hasn't a penny. Nor prospects. Nor, so I gathered from Jane, a position.'

Lord Emsworth interrupted at this point to put a question.

'Who,' he asked courteously, 'is Jane?'

Lady Constance quivered a little.

'Oh, Clarence! Your niece Jane.'

'Oh, my *niece* Jane? Ah! Yes. Yes, of course. My niece Jane. Yes, of course, to be sure. My – '

'Clarence, please! For pity's sake! Do stop doddering and listen to me. For once in your life I want you to be firm.'

'Be what?'

'Firm. Put your foot down.'

'How do you mean?'

'About Jane. I had been hoping that she had got over this ridiculous infatuation – she has seemed perfectly happy and contented all this time – but no. Apparently they have been corresponding regularly, and now the man is here.'

'Here?'

'Yes.'

'Where?' asked Lord Emsworth, gazing in an interested manner about the room.

'He arrived last night and is staying in the village. I found out by the merest accident. I happened to ask George if he had seen Jane, because I wanted Mr Baxter to meet her, and he said he had met her going towards the lake. So I went down to the lake, and there I discovered her with a young man in a tweed coat and flannel knickerbockers. They were kissing one another in the summer-house.'

Lord Emsworth clicked his tongue.

'Ought to have been out in the sunshine,' he said, disapprovingly.

Lady Constance raised her foot quickly, but instead of kicking her brother on the shin merely tapped the carpet with it. Blood will tell.

'Jane was defiant. I think she must be off her head. She insisted that she was going to marry this man. And, as I say, not only has he not a penny, but he is apparently out of work.'

'What sort of work does he do?'

'I gather that he has been a land-agent on an estate in Devonshire.'

'It all comes back to me,' said Lord Emsworth. 'I remember now. This must be the man Jane was speaking to me about yesterday. Of course, yes. She asked me to give him Simmons's job. Simmons is retiring next month. Good fellow,' said Lord Emsworth sentimentally. 'Been here for years and years. I shall be sorry to lose him. Bless my soul, it won't seem like the same place without old Simmons. Still,' he said, brightening, for he was a man who could make the best of things, 'no doubt this new chap will turn out all right. Jane seems to think highly of him.'

Lady Constance had risen slowly from her chair. There was incredulous horror on her face.

'Clarence! You are not telling me that you have promised this man Simmons's place?'

'Eh? Yes, I have. Why not?'

'Why not! Do you realize that directly he gets it he will marry Jane?'

'Well, why shouldn't he? Very nice girl. Probably make him a good wife.'

Lady Constance struggled with her feelings for a space.

'Clarence,' she said, 'I am going out now to find Jane. I shall tell her that you have thought it over and changed your mind.'

'What about?'

'Giving this man Simmons's place.'

'But I haven't.'

'Yes, you have.'

And so, Lord Emsworth discovered as he met her eye, he had. It often happened that way after he and Connie had talked a thing over. But he was not pleased about it.

'But, Connie, dash it all – '

'We will not discuss it any more, Clarence.'

Her eye played upon him. Then she moved to the door and was gone.

Alone at last, Lord Emsworth took up his Whiffle on *The Care Of The Pig* in the hope that it might, as had happened before, bring calm to the troubled spirit. It did, and he was absorbed in it when the door opened once more.

His niece Jane stood on the threshold.

Lord Emsworth's niece was the third prettiest girl in Shropshire. In her general appearance she resembled a dewy rose, and it might have been thought that Lord Emsworth, who yielded to none in his appreciation of roses, would have felt his heart leap up at the sight of her.

This was not the case. His heart did leap, but not up. He was a man with certain definite views about roses. He preferred them without quite such tight lips and determined chins. And he did not like them to look at him as if he were something slimy and horrible which they had found under a flat stone.

The wretched man was now fully conscious of his position. Under the magic spell of Whiffle he had been able to thrust from his mind for a while the thought of what Jane was going to say when she heard the bad news; but now, as she started to advance slowly into the room in that sinister, purposeful way characteristic of so many of his female relations, he realized what he was in for, and his soul shrank into itself like a salted snail.

Jane, he could not but remember, was the daughter of his sister Charlotte, and many good judges considered Lady Charlotte a tougher egg even than Lady Constance, or her younger sister, Lady Julia. He still quivered at some of the things Charlotte had said to him in her time; and, eyeing Jane apprehensively, he saw no reason for supposing that she had not inherited quite a good deal of the maternal fire.

The girl came straight to the point. Her mother, Lord Emsworth recalled, had always done the same.

'I should like an explanation, Uncle Clarence.'

Lord Emsworth cleared his throat unhappily.

'Explanation, my dear?'

'Explanation was what I said.'

'Oh, explanation? Ah, yes. Er – what about?'

'You know jolly well what about. That agent job. Aunt Constance says you've changed your mind. Have you?'

'Er . . . Ah . . . Well . . .'

'Have you?'

'Ah . . . Well . . . Er . . .'

'HAVE you?'

'Well . . . Er . . . Ah . . . Yes.'

'Worm!' said Jane. 'Miserable, crawling, cringing, gelatine-backboned worm!'

Lord Emsworth, though he had been expecting something along these lines, quivered as if he had been harpooned.

'That', he said, attempting a dignity which he was far from feeling, 'is not a very nice thing to say . . .'

'If you only knew the things I would like to say! I'm holding myself in. So you've changed your mind, have you? Ha! Does a sacred promise mean nothing to you, Uncle Clarence? Does a girl's whole life's happiness mean nothing to you? I never would have believed that you could have been such a blighter.'

'I am not a blighter.'

'Yes, you are. You're a life-blighter. You're trying to blight my life. Well, you aren't going to do it. Whatever happens, I mean to marry George.'

Lord Emsworth was genuinely surprised.

'Marry George? But Connie told me you were in love with this fellow you met in Devonshire.'

'His name is George Abercrombie.'

'Oh, ah?' said Lord Emsworth, enlightened. 'Bless my soul, I thought you meant my grandson, George, and it puzzled me. Because you couldn't marry him, of course. He's your brother or cousin or something. Besides, he's too young for you. What would George be? Ten? Eleven?'

He broke off. A reproachful look had hit him like a
shell.

'Uncle Clarence!'

'My dear?'

'Is this a time for drivelling?'

'My dear!'

'Well, is it? Look in your heart and ask yourself. Here
I am, with everybody spitting on their hands and dashing
about trying to ruin my life's whole happiness, and instead
of being kind and understanding and sympathetic you
start talking rot about young George.'

'I was only saying – '

'I heard what you were saying, and it made me sick.
You really must be the most callous man that ever
lived. I can't understand you of all people behaving like
this, Uncle Clarence. I always thought you were fond
of me.'

'I am fond of you.'

'It doesn't look like it. Flinging yourself into this foul
conspiracy to wreck my life.'

Lord Emsworth remembered a good one.

'I have your best interests at heart, my dear.'

It did not go very well. A distinct sheet of flame shot
from the girl's eyes.

'What do you mean, my best interests? The way Aunt
Constance talks, and the way you are backing her up,
anyone would think that George was someone in a straw
hat and a scarlet cummerbund that I'd picked up on the
pier at Blackpool. The Abercrombies are one of the oldest
families in Devonshire. They date back to the Conquest,
and they practically ran the Crusades. When your
ancestors were staying at home on the plea of war work
of national importance and wangling jobs at the base, the
Abercrombies were out fighting the Paynim.'

'I was at school with a boy named Abercrombie,' said
Lord Emsworth musingly.

'I hope he kicked you. No, no, I don't mean that. I'm

sorry. The one thing I'm trying to do is to keep this little talk free of – what's the word?'

Lord Emsworth said he did not know.

'Acrimony. I want to be calm and cool and sensible. Honestly, Uncle Clarence, you would love George. You'll be a sap if you give him the bird without seeing him. He's the most wonderful man on earth. He got into the last eight at Wimbledon this year.'

'Did he, indeed? Last eight what?'

'And there isn't anything he doesn't know about running an estate. The very first thing he said when he came into the park was that a lot of the timber wanted seeing to badly.'

'Blast his impertinence,' said Lord Emsworth warmly. 'My timber is in excellent condition.'

'Not if George says it isn't. George knows timber.'

'So do I know timber.'

'Not so well as George does. But never mind about that. Let's get back to this loathsome plot to ruin my life's whole happiness. Why can't you be a sport, Uncle Clarence, and stand up for me? Can't you understand what this means to me? Weren't you ever in love?'

'Certainly I was in love. Dozens of times. I'll tell you a very funny story – '

'I don't want to hear funny stories.'

'No, no. Quite. Exactly.'

'All I want is to hear you saying that you will give George Mr Simmons's job, so that we can get married.'

'But your aunt seems to feel so strongly – '

'I know what she feels strongly. She wants me to marry that ass Roegate.'

'Does she?'

'Yes, and I'm not going to. You can tell her from me that I wouldn't marry Bertie Roegate if he were the only man in the world – '

'There's a song of that name,' said Lord Emsworth, interested. 'They sang it during the War. No, it wasn't

"man". It was "girl". "If you were the only . . ." How did
it go? Ah, yes. "If you were the only girl in the world and
I was the only boy . . .'"

'Uncle Clarence!'

'My dear?'

'Please don't sing. You're not in the taproom of the
Emsworth Arms now.'

'I have never been in the taproom of the Emsworth
Arms.'

'Or at a smoking-concert. Really, you seem to have
the most extraordinary idea of the sort of attitude that's
fitting when you're talking to a girl whose life's happiness
everybody is sprinting about trying to ruin. First you
talk about young George, then you start trying to tell
funny stories, and now you sing comic songs.'

'It wasn't a comic song.'

'It was, the way you sang it. Well?'

'Eh?'

'Have you decided what you are going to do about
this?'

'About what?'

The girl was silent for a moment, during which
moment she looked so like her mother that Lord
Emsworth shuddered.

'Uncle Clarence,' she said in a low, trembling voice,
'you are not going to pretend that you don't know what
we've been talking about all this time? Are you or are
you not going to give George that job?'

'Well – '

'Well?'

'Well – '

'We can't stay here for ever, saying "Well" at one
another. Are you or are you not?'

'My dear, I don't see how I can. Your aunt seems to
feel so very strongly . . .'

He spoke mumblingly, avoiding his companion's eye,
and he had paused, searching for words, when from the

drive outside there arose a sudden babble of noise. Raised
voices were proceeding from the great open spaces. He
recognized his sister Constance's penetrating soprano,
and mingling with it his grandson George's treble 'Coo'.
Competing with both, there came the throaty baritone of
Rupert Baxter. Delighted with the opportunity of changing
the subject, he hurried to the window.

'Bless my soul! What's all that?'

The battle, whatever it may have been about, had
apparently rolled away in some unknown direction, for
he could see nothing from the window but Rupert Baxter,
who was smoking a cigarette in what seemed a rather
overwrought manner. He turned back, and with infinite
relief discovered that he was alone. His niece had
disappeared. He took up Whiffle on *The Care Of The Pig*
and had just started to savour once more the perfect
prose of that chapter about swill and bran-mash, when
the door opened. Jane was back. She stood on the
threshold, eyeing her uncle coldly.

'Reading, Uncle Clarence?'

'Eh? Oh, ah, yes. I was just glancing at Whiffle on *The
Care Of The Pig*!'

'So you actually have the heart to read at a time like
this? Well, well! Do you ever read Western novels, Uncle
Clarence?'

'Eh? Western novels? No. No, never.'

'I'm sorry. I was reading one the other day, and I hoped
that you might be able to explain something that puzzled
me. What one cowboy said to another cowboy.'

'Oh, yes?'

'This cowboy – the first cowboy – said to the other
cowboy – the second cowboy – "Gol dern ye. Hank
Spivis, for a sneaking, ornery, low-down, double-crossing,
hornswoggling skunk." Can you tell me what a
sneaking, ornery, low-down, double-crossing,
hornswoggling skunk is, Uncle Clarence?'

'I'm afraid I can't, my dear.'

'I thought you might know.'

'No.'

'Oh.'

She passed from the room, and Lord Emsworth resumed his Whiffle.

But it was not long before the volume was resting on his knee while he stared before him with a sombre gaze. He was reviewing the recent scene and wishing that he had come better out of it. He was a vague man, but not so vague as to be unaware that he might have shown up in a more heroic light.

How long he sat brooding, he could not have said. Some little time, undoubtedly, for the shadows on the terrace had, he observed as he glanced out of the window, lengthened quite a good deal since he had seen them last. He was about to rise and seek consolation from a ramble among the flowers in the garden below, when the door opened – it seemed to Lord Emsworth, who was now feeling a little morbid, that that blasted door had never stopped opening since he had come to the library to be alone – and Beach, the butler, entered.

He was carrying an airgun in one hand and in the other a silver salver with a box of ammunition on it.

Beach was a man who invested all his actions with something of the impressiveness of a high priest conducting an intricate service at some romantic altar. It is not easy to be impressive when you are carrying an airgun in one hand and a silver salver with a box of ammunition on it in the other, but Beach managed it. Many butlers in such a position would have looked like sportsmen setting out for a day with the birds, but Beach still looked like a high priest. He advanced to the table at Lord Emsworth's side and laid his cargo upon it as if the gun and the box of ammunition had been a smoked offering and his lordship a tribal god.

Lord Emsworth eyed his faithful servitor sourly. His

manner was that of a tribal god who considers the smoked offering not up to sample.

'What the devil's all this?'

'It is an airgun, m'lord.'

'I can see that, dash it. What are you bringing it here for?'

'Her ladyship instructed me to convey it to your lordship – I gathered for safe keeping, m'lord. The weapon was until recently the property of Master George.'

'Why the dooce are they taking his airgun away from the poor boy?' demanded Lord Emsworth hotly. Ever since the lad had called Rupert Baxter a blister he had been feeling a strong affection for his grandson.

'Her ladyship did not confide in me on that point, m'lord. I was merely instructed to convey the weapon to your lordship.'

At this moment, Lady Constance came sailing in to throw light on the mystery.

'Ah, I see Beach has brought it to you. I want you to lock that gun up somewhere, Clarence. George is not to be allowed to have it any more.'

'Why not?'

'Because he is not to be trusted with it. Do you know what happened? He shot Mr Baxter!'

'What!'

'Yes. Out on the drive just now. I noticed that the boy's manner was sullen when I introduced him to Mr Baxter, and said that he was going to be his tutor. He disappeared into the shrubbery, and just now, as Mr Baxter was standing on the drive, George shot him from behind a bush.'

'Good!' cried Lord Emsworth, then prudently added the word 'gracious'.

There was a pause. Lord Emsworth took up the gun and handled it curiously.

'Bang!' he said, pointing it at a bust of Aristotle which stood on a bracket by the bookshelves.

'Please don't wave the thing about like that, Clarence. It may be loaded.'

'Not if George has just shot Baxter with it. No,' said Lord Emsworth, pulling the trigger, 'it's not loaded.' He mused a while. An odd, nostalgic feeling was creeping over him. Far-off memories of his boyhood had begun to stir within him. 'Bless my soul,' he said. 'I haven't had one of these things in my hand since I was a child. Did you ever have one of these things, Beach?'

'Yes, m'lord, when a small lad.'

'Bless my soul, I remember my sister Julia borrowing mine to shoot her governess. You remember Julia shooting the governess, Connie?'

'Don't be absurd, Clarence.'

'It's not absurd. She did shoot her. Fortunately women wore bustles in those days. Beach, don't you remember my sister Julia shooting the governess?'

'The incident would, no doubt, have occurred before my arrival at the castle, m'lord.'

'That will do, Beach,' said Lady Constance. 'I do wish, Clarence,' she continued as the door closed, 'that you would not say that sort of thing in front of Beach.'

'Julia did shoot the governess.'

'If she did, there is no need to make your butler a confidant.'

'Now, what was that governess's name? I have an idea it began with – '

'Never mind what her name was or what it began with. Tell me about Jane. I saw her coming out of the library. Had you been speaking to her?'

'Yes. Oh, yes. I spoke to her.'

'I hope you were firm.'

'Oh, very firm. I said "Jane . . ." But listen, Connie, damn it, aren't we being a little hard on the girl? One doesn't want to ruin her whole life's happiness, dash it.'

'I knew she would get round you. But you are not to give way an inch.'

'But this fellow seems to be a most suitable fellow. One of the Abercrombies and all that. Did well in the Crusades.'

'I am not going to have my niece throwing herself away on a man without a penny.'

'She isn't going to marry Roegate, you know. Nothing will induce her. She said she wouldn't marry Roegate if she were the only girl in the world and he was the only boy.'

'I don't care what she said. And I don't want to discuss the matter any longer. I am now going to send George in, for you to give him a good talking-to.'

'I haven't time.'

'You have time.'

'I haven't. I'm going to look at my flowers.'

'You are not. You are going to talk to George. I want you to make him see quite clearly what a wicked thing he has done. Mr Baxter was furious.'

'It all comes back to me,' cried Lord Emsworth, 'Mapleton!'

'What *are* you talking about?'

'Her name was Mapleton. Julia's governess.'

'Do stop about Julia's governess. Will you talk to George?'

'Oh, all right, all right.'

'Good. I'll go and send him to you.'

And presently George entered. For a boy who had just stained the escutcheon of a proud family by shooting tutors with airguns, he seemed remarkably cheerful. His manner was that of one getting together with an old crony for a cosy chat.

'Hallo, Grandpapa,' he said breezily.

'Hallo, my boy,' replied Lord Emsworth, with equal affability.

'Aunt Connie said you wanted to see me.'

'Eh? Ah! Oh! Yes.' Lord Emsworth pulled himself together. 'Yes, that's right. Yes, to be sure. Certainly I want to see you. What's all this, my boy, eh? Eh, what? What's all this?'

'What's all what, Grandpapa?'

'Shooting people and all that sort of thing. Shooting Baxter and all that sort of thing. Mustn't do that, you know. Can't have that. It's very wrong and – er – very dangerous to shoot at people with a dashed great gun. Don't you know that, hey? Might put their eye out, dash it.'

'Oh, I couldn't have hit him in the eye, Grandpapa. His back was turned and he was bending over, tying his shoelace.'

Lord Emsworth started.

'What! Did you get Baxter in the seat of the trousers?'

'Yes, Grandpapa.'

'Ha, ha . . . I mean, disgraceful . . . I – er – I expect he jumped?'

'Oh, yes, Grandpapa. He jumped like billy-o.'

'Did he, indeed? How this reminds me of Julia's governess. Your Aunt Julia once shot her governess under precisely similar conditions. She was tying her shoelace.'

'Coo! Did *she* jump?'

'She certainly did, my boy.'

'Ha, ha!'

'Ha, ha!'

'Ha, ha!'

'Ha, h-Ah . . . Er – well, just so,' said Lord Emsworth, a belated doubt assailing him as to whether this was quite the tone. 'Well, George, I shall of course impound this – er – instrument.'

'Right ho, Grandpapa,' said George, with the easy amiability of a boy conscious of having two catapults in his drawer upstairs.

'Can't have you going about the place shooting people.'

'OK, Chief.'

Lord Emsworth fondled the gun. That nostalgic feeling was growing.

'Do you know, young man, I used to have one of these things when I was a boy.'

'Coo! Were guns invented then?'

'Yes, I had one when I was your age.'

'Ever hit anything, Grandpapa?'

Lord Emsworth drew himself up a little haughtily.

'Certainly I did. I hit all sorts of things. Rats and things. I had a very accurate aim. But now I wouldn't even know how to load the dashed affair.'

'This is how you load it, Grandpapa. You open it like this and shove the slug in here and snap it together again like that and there you are.'

'Indeed? Really? I see. Yes. Yes, of course, I remember now.'

'You can't kill anything much with it,' said George, with a wistfulness which betrayed an aspiration to higher things. 'Still, it's awfully useful for tickling up cows.'

'And Baxter.'

'Yes.'

'Ha, ha!'

'Ha, ha!'

Once more, Lord Emsworth forced himself to concentrate on the right tone.

'We mustn't laugh about it, my boy. It's no joking matter. It's very wrong to shoot Mr Baxter.'

'But he's a blister.'

'He is a blister,' agreed Lord Emsworth, always fair-minded. 'Nevertheless . . . Remember, he is your tutor.'

'Well, I don't see why I've got to have a tutor right in the middle of the summer holidays. I sweat like the dickens all through the term at school,' said George, his voice vibrant with self-pity, 'and then plumb spank in the middle of the holidays they slosh a tutor on me. I call it a bit thick.'

Lord Emsworth might have told the little fellow that thicker things than that were going on in Blandings Castle, but he refrained. He dismissed him with a kindly, sympathetic smile and resumed his fondling of the airgun.

Like so many men advancing into the sere and yellow of life, Lord Emsworth had an eccentric memory. It was not to be trusted an inch as far as the events of yesterday or the day before were concerned. Even in the small matter of assisting him to find a hat which he had laid down somewhere five minutess ago it was nearly always useless. But by way of compensation for this it was a perfect encyclopaedia on the remote past. It rendered his boyhood an open book to him.

Lord Emsworth mused on his boyhood. Happy days, happy days. He could recall the exact uncle who had given him the weapon, so similar to this one, with which Julia had shot her governess. He could recall brave, windswept mornings when he had gone prowling through the stable yard in the hope of getting a rat – and many a fine head had he secured. Odd that the passage of time should remove the desire to go and pop at things with an airgun . . .

Or did it?

With a curious thrill that set his pince-nez rocking gently on his nose, Lord Emsworth suddenly became aware that it did not. All that the passage of time did was to remove the desire to pop temporarily – say for forty years or so. Dormant for a short while – we'll call it fifty years – that desire, he perceived, still lurked unquenched. Little by little it began to stir within him now. Slowly but surely, as he sat there fondling the gun, he was once more becoming a potential popper.

At this point, the gun suddenly went off and broke the bust of Aristotle.

It was enough. The old killer instinct had awakened. Reloading with the swift efficiency of some hunter of the woods, Lord Emsworth went to the window. He was a little uncertain as to what he intended to do when he got there, except that he had a clear determination to loose off at something. There flitted into his mind what his grandson George had said about tickling up cows, and this served to some extent to crystallize his aims. True, cows were not plentiful on the terrace of Blandings Castle. Still, one might have wandered there. You never knew with cows.

There were no cows. Only Rupert Baxter. The ex-secretary was in the act of throwing away a cigarette.

Most men are careless in the matter of throwing away cigarettes. The world is their ashtray. But Rupert Baxter had a tidy soul. He allowed the thing to fall to the ground like any ordinary young man, it is true, but immediately he had done so his better self awakened. He stooped to pick up the object that disfigured the smooth flagged stones, and the invitation of that beckoning trousers' seat would have been too powerful for a stronger man than Lord Emsworth to resist.

He pulled the trigger, and Rupert Baxter sprang into the air with a sharp cry. Lord Emsworth reseated himself and took up Whiffle on *The Care Of The Pig*.

Everyone is interested nowadays in the psychology of the criminal. The chronicler, therefore, feels that he runs no risk of losing his grip on the reader if he pauses at this point to examine and analyse the workings of Lord Emsworth's mind after the perpetration of the black act which has just been recorded.

At first, then, all that he felt as he sat turning the pages of his Whiffle was a sort of soft warm glow, a kind of tremulous joy such as he might have experienced if he had just been receiving the thanks of the nation for some great public service.

It was not merely the fact that he had caused his late employee to skip like the high hills that induced this glow. What pleased him so particularly was that it had been such a magnificent shot. He was a sensitive man, and though in his conversation with his grandson George he had tried to wear the mask, he had not been able completely to hide his annoyance at the boy's careless assumption that in his airgun days he had been an indifferent marksman.

'Did you ever hit anything, Grandpapa?' Boys say these things with no wish to wound, but nevertheless they pierce the armour. 'Did you ever hit anything, Grandpapa?' forsooth! He would have liked to see George stop putting finger to trigger for forty-seven years and then, first crack out of the box, pick off a medium-sized secretary at a distance like that! In rather a bad light, too.

But after he had sat for a while, silently glowing, his mood underwent a change. A gunman's complacency after getting his man can never remain for long an unmixed complacency. Sooner or later there creeps in the thought of Retribution. It did with Lord Emsworth. Quite suddenly, whispering in his ear, he heard the voice of Conscience say:

'What if your sister Constance learns of this?'

A moment before this voice spoke, Lord Emsworth had been smirking. He now congealed, and the smile passed from his lips like breath off a razor blade, to be succeeded by a tense look of anxiety and alarm.

Nor was this alarm unjustified. When he reflected how scathing and terrible his sister Constance could be when he committed even so venial a misdemeanour as coming down to dinner with a brass paper-fastener in his shirt front instead of the more conventional stud, his imagination boggled at the thought of what she would do in a case like this. He was appalled. Whiffle on *The Care Of The Pig* fell from his nerveless hand, and he sat looking like a dying duck. And Lady Constance, who now entered, noted the expression and was curious as to its cause.

'What is the matter, Clarence?'

'Matter?'

'Why are you looking like a dying duck?'

'I am not looking like a dying duck,' retorted Lord Emsworth with what spirit he could muster.

'Well,' said Lady Constance, waiving the point, 'have you spoken to George?'

'Certainly. Yes, of course I've spoken to George. He was in here just now and I – er – spoke to him.'

'What did you say?'

'I said' – Lord Emsworth wanted to make this very clear – 'I said that I wouldn't even know how to load one of those things.'

'Didn't you give him a good talking-to?'

'Of course I did. A very good talking-to. I said "Er – George, you know how to load those things and I don't, but that's no reason why you should go about shooting Baxter."'

'Was that all you said?'

'No. That was just how I began. I – '

Lord Emsworth paused. He could not have finished the sentence if large rewards had been offered to him to do so. For, as he spoke, Rupert Baxter appeared in the doorway, and he shrank back in his chair like some Big Shot cornered by G-men.

The secretary came forward limping slightly. His eyes behind their spectacles were wild and his manner emotional. Lady Constance gazed at him wonderingly.

'Is something the matter, Mr Baxter?'

'Matter?' Rupert Baxter's voice was taut and he quivered in every limb. He had lost his customary suavity and was plainly in no frame of mind to mince his words. 'Matter? Do you know what has happened? That infernal boy has shot me *again*!'

'What!'

'Only a few minutes ago. Out on the terrace.'

Lord Emsworth shook off his palsy.

'I expect you imagined it,' he said.

'Imagined it!' Rupert Baxter shook from spectacles to shoes. 'I tell you I was on the terrace, stooping to pick up my cigarette, when something hit me on the . . . something hit me.'

'Probably a wasp,' said Lord Emsworth. 'They are very plentiful this year. I wonder,' he said chattily, 'if either of you are aware that wasps serve a very useful purpose. They keep down the leather-jackets, which, as you know, inflict serious injury upon – '

Lady Constance's concern became mixed with perplexity.

'But it could not have been George, Mr Baxter. The moment you told me of what he had done, I confiscated his airgun. Look, there it is on the table now.'

'Right there on the table,' said Lord Emsworth, pointing helpfully. 'If you come over here, you can see it clearly. Must have been a wasp.'

'You have not left the room, Clarence?'

'No. Been here all the time.'

'Then it would have been impossible for George to have shot you, Mr Baxter.'

'Quite,' said Lord Emsworth. 'A wasp, undoubtedly. Unless, as I say, you imagined the whole thing.'

The secretary stiffened.

'I am not subject to hallucinations, Lord Emsworth.'

'But you are, my dear fellow. I expect it comes from exerting your brain too much. You're always getting them.'

'Clarence!'

'Well, he is. You know that as well as I do. Look at that time he went grubbing about in a lot of flower-pots because he thought you had put your necklace there.'

'I did not – '

'You did, my dear fellow. I dare say you've forgotten it, but you did. And then, for some reason best known to yourself, you threw the flower-pots at me through my bedroom window.'

Baxter turned to Lady Constance, flushing darkly. The episode to which his former employer had alluded was one of which he never cared to be reminded.

'Lord Emsworth is referring to the occasion when your diamond necklace was stolen, Lady Constance. I was led to believe that the thief had hidden it in a flowerpot.'

'Of course, Mr Baxter.'

'Well, have it your own way,' said Lord Emsworth agreeably. 'But bless my soul, I shall never forget waking up and finding all those flower-pots pouring in through the window and then looking out and seeing Baxter on the lawn in lemon-coloured pyjamas with a wild glare in his – '

'Clarence!'

'Oh, all right. I merely mentioned it. Hallucinations – he gets them all the time,' he said stoutly, though in an undertone.

Lady Constance was cooing to the secretary like a mother to her child.

'It really is impossible that George should have done this, Mr Baxter. The gun has never left this – '

She broke off. Her handsome face seemed to turn suddenly to stone. When she spoke again the coo had gone out of her voice and it had become metallic.

'Clarence!'

'My dear?'

Lady Constance drew in her breath sharply.

'Mr Baxter, I wonder if you would mind leaving us for a moment. I wish to speak to Lord Emsworth.'

The closing of the door was followed by a silence, followed in its turn by an odd, whining noise like gas escaping from a pipe. It was Lord Emsworth trying to hum carelessly.

'Clarence!'

'Yes? Yes, my dear?'

The stoniness of Lady Constance's expression had become more marked with each succeeding moment. What had caused it in the first place was the recollection, coming to her like a flash, that when she had entered this room she had found her brother looking like a dying duck. Honest men, she felt, do not look like dying ducks. The only man whom an impartial observer could possibly mistake for one of these birds *in extremis* is the man with crime upon his soul.

'Clarence, was it you who shot Mr Baxter?'

Fortunately there had been that in her manner which led Lord Emsworth to expect the question. He was ready for it.

'Me? Who, me? Shoot Baxter? What the dooce would I want to shoot Baxter for?'

'We can go into your motives later. What I am asking you now is – Did you?'

'Of course I didn't.'

'The gun has not left the room.'

'Shoot Baxter, indeed! Never heard anything so dashed absurd in my life.'

'And you have been here all the time.'

'Well, what of it? Suppose I have? Suppose I had wanted to shoot Baxter? Suppose every fibre in my being had egged me on, dash it, to shoot the feller? How could I have done it, not even knowing how to load the contrivance?'

'You used to know how to load an airgun.'

'I used to know a lot of things.'

'It's quite easy to load an airgun. I could do it myself.'

'Well, I didn't.'

'Then how do you account for the fact that Mr Baxter was shot by an airgun which had never left the room you were in?'

Lord Emsworth raised pleading hands to heaven.

'How do you know he was shot with this airgun? God bless my soul, the way women jump to conclusions is

199

enough to . . . How do you know there wasn't another
airgun? How do you know the place isn't bristling with
airguns? How do you know Beach hasn't an airgun? Or
anybody?'

'I scarcely imagine that Beach would shoot Mr Baxter.'

'How do you know he wouldn't? He used to have an
airgun when he was a small lad. He said so. I'd watch
the man closely.'

'Please don't be ridiculous, Clarence.'

'I'm not being half as ridiculous as you are. Saying I
shoot people with airguns. Why should I shoot people
with airguns? And how do you suppose I could have
potted Baxter at that distance?'

'What distance?'

'He was standing on the terrace, wasn't he? He
specifically stated that he was standing on the terrace.
And I was up here. It would take a most expert marksman
to pot the fellow at a distance like that. Who do you think
I am? One of those chaps who shoot apples off their son's
heads?'

The reasoning was undeniably specious. It shook Lady
Constance. She frowned undecidedly.

'Well, it's very strange that Mr Baxter should be so
convinced that he was shot.'

'Nothing strange about it at all. There wouldn't be
anything strange if Baxter was convinced that he was a
turnip and had been bitten by a white rabbit with pink
eyes. You know perfectly well, though you won't admit
it, that the fellow's a raving lunatic.'

'Clarence!'

'It's no good saying "Clarence". The fellow's potty to
the core, and always has been. Haven't I seen him on the
lawn at five o'clock in the morning in lemon-coloured
pyjamas, throwing flower-pots in at my window? Pooh!
Obviously, the whole thing is the outcome of the man's
diseased imagination. Shot, indeed! Never heard such
nonsense. And now', said Lord Emsworth, rising firmly,

'I'm going out to have a look at my roses. I came to this room to enjoy a little quiet reading and meditation, and ever since I got here there's been a constant stream of people in and out, telling me they're going to marry men named Abercrombie and saying they've been shot and saying I shot them and so on and so forth . . . Bless my soul, one might as well try to read and meditate in the middle of Piccadilly Circus. Tchah!' said Lord Emsworth, who had now got near enough to the door to feel safe in uttering this unpleasant exclamation. 'Tchah!' he said, and adding 'Pah!' for good measure made a quick exit.

But even now his troubled spirit was not to know peace. To reach the great outdoors at Blandings Castle, if you start from the library and come down the main staircase, you have to pass through the hall. To the left of this hall there is a small writing-room. And outside this writing-room Lord Emsworth's niece Jane was standing.

'Yoo-hoo,' she cried. 'Uncle Clarence.'

Lord Emsworth was in no mood for yoo-hooing nieces. George Abercrombie might enjoy chatting with this girl. So might Herbert, Lord Roegate. But he wanted solitude. In the course of the afternoon he had had so much female society thrust upon him that if Helen of Troy had appeared in the doorway of the writing-room and yoo-hooed at him, he would merely have accelerated his pace.

He accelerated it now.

'Can't stop, my dear, can't stop.'

'Oh, yes you can, old Sure-shot,' said Jane, and Lord Emsworth found that he could. He stopped so abruptly that he nearly dislocated his spine. His jaw had fallen and his pince-nez were dancing on their string like leaves in the wind.

'Two-Gun Thomas, the Marksman of the Prairie – He never misses. Kindly step this way, Uncle Clarence,' said Jane, 'I would like a word with you.'

*

Lord Emsworth stepped that way. He followed the girl into the writing-room and closed the door carefully behind him.

'You – you didn't see me?' he quavered.

'I certainly did see you,' said Jane. 'I was an interested eye-witness of the whole thing from start to finish.'

Lord Emsworth tottered to a chair and sank into it, staring glassily at his niece. Any Chicago business man of the modern school would have understood what he was feeling and would have sympathized with him.

The thing that poisons life for gunmen and sometimes makes them wonder moodily if it is worth while going on is this tendency of the outside public to butt in at inconvenient moments. Whenever you settle some business dispute with a commercial competitor by means of your sub-machine-gun, it always turns out that there was some officious witness passing at the time, and there you are, with a new problem confronting you.

And Lord Emsworth was in worse case than his spiritual brother of Chicago would have been, for the latter could always have solved his perplexities by rubbing out the witness. To him this melancholy pleasure was denied. A prominent Shropshire landowner, with a position to keep up in the county, cannot rub out his nieces. All he can do, when they reveal that they have seen him wallowing in crime, is to stare glassily at them.

'I had a front seat for the entire performance,' proceeded Jane. 'When I left you, I went into the shrubbery to cry my eyes out because of your frightful cruelty and inhumanity. And while I was crying my eyes out, I suddenly saw you creep to the window of the library with a hideous look of low cunning on your face and young George's airgun in your hand. And I was just wondering if I couldn't find a stone and bung it at you, because it seemed to me that something along those lines was what you had been asking for from the start, when you raised the gun and I saw that you were taking aim.

The next moment there was a shot, a cry, and Baxter
weltering in his blood on the terrace. And as I stood there,
a thought floated into my mind. It was – What will Aunt
Constance have to say about this when I tell her?'

Lord Emsworth emitted a low, gargling sound, like the
death rattle of that dying duck to which his sister had
compared him.

'You – you aren't going to tell her?'

'Why not?'

An ague-like convulsion shook Lord Emsworth.

'I implore you not to tell her, my dear. You know what
she's like. I should never hear the end of it.'

'She would give you the devil, you think?'

'I do.'

'So do I. And you thoroughly deserve it.'

'My dear!'

'Well, don't you? Look at the way you've been
behaving. Working like a beaver to ruin my life's
happiness.'

'I don't want to ruin your life's happiness.'

'You don't? Then sit down at this desk and dash off a
short letter to George, giving him that job.'

'But – '

'What did you say?'

'I only said, "But – "'

'Don't say it again. What I want from you, Uncle
Clarence, is prompt and cheerful service. Are you ready?
"Dear Mr Abercrombie . . ."'

'I don't know how to spell it,' said Lord Emsworth,
with the air of a man who has found a way out
satisfactory to all parties.

'I'll attend to the spelling. A-b, ab, e-r, er; c-r-o-m,
crom; b-i-e, bie. The whole constituting the word
"Abercrombie", which is the name of the man I love. Got
it?'

'Yes,' said Lord Emsworth sepulchrally. 'I've got it.'

'Then carry on. "Dear Mr Abercrombie. Pursuant" –

one p, two u's – spread 'em about a bit, an r, an s, and an ant – "Pursuant on our recent conversation – "'

'But I've never spoken to the man in my life.'

'It doesn't matter. It's just a form. "Pursuant on our recent conversation, I have much pleasure in offering you the post of land-agent at Blandings Castle, and shall be glad if you will take up your duties immediately. Yours faithfully, Emsworth." E-m-s-w-o-r-t-h.'

Jane took the letter, pressed it lovingly on the blotting-pad and placed it in the recesses of her costume. 'Fine,' she said. 'That's that. Thanks awfully, Uncle Clarence. This has squared you nicely for your recent foul behaviour in trying to ruin my life's happiness. You made a rocky start, but you've come through magnificently at the finish.'

Kissing him affectionately, she passed from the room, and Lord Emsworth, slumped in his chair, tried not to look at the vision of his sister Constance which was rising before his eyes. What Connie was going to say when she learned that in defiance of her direct commands he had given this young man . . .

He mused on Lady Constance, and wondered if there were any other men in the world so sister pecked as he. It was weak of him, he knew, to curl up into an apologetic ball when assailed by a mere sister. Most men reserved such craven conduct for their wives. But it had always been so, right back to those boyhood days which he remembered so well. And too late to alter it now, he supposed.

The only consolation he was able to enjoy in this dark hour was the reflection that, though things were bad, they were unquestionably less bad than they might have been. At the least, his fearful secret was safe. That rash moment of recovered boyhood would never now be brought up against him. Connie would never know whose hand it was that had pulled the fatal trigger. She might suspect, but she could never know. Nor could

Baxter ever know. Baxter would grow into an old, white-haired, spectacled pantaloon, and always this thing would remain an insoluble mystery to him.

Dashed lucky, felt Lord Emsworth, that the fellow had not been listening at the door during the recent conversation . . .

It was at this moment that a sound behind him caused him to turn and, having turned, to spring from his chair with a convulsive leap that nearly injured him internally. Over the sill of the open window, like those of a corpse emerging from the tomb to confront its murderer, the head and shoulders of Rupert Baxter were slowly rising. The evening sun fell upon his spectacles, and they seemed to Lord Emsworth to gleam like the eyes of a dragon.

Rupert Baxter had not been listening at the door. There had been no necessity for him to do so. Immediately outside the writing-room window at Blandings Castle there stands a rustic garden seat, and on this he had been sitting from beginning to end of the interview which has just been recorded. If he had been actually in the room, he might have heard a little better, but not much.

When two men stand face to face, one of whom has recently shot the other with an airgun and the second of whom has just discovered who it was that did it, it is rarely that conversation flows briskly from the start. One senses a certain awkwardness – what the French call *gêne*. In the first half-minute of this encounter the only thing that happened in a vocal way was that Lord Emsworth cleared his throat, immediately afterwards becoming silent again. And it is possible that his silence might have prolonged itself for some considerable time, had not Baxter made a movement as if about to withdraw. All this while he had been staring at his former employer, his face an open book in which it was easy for the least discerning eye to read a number of disconcerting emotions. He now took a step backwards, and Lord Emsworth's aphasia left him.

'Baxter!'

There was urgent appeal in the ninth Earl's voice. It was not often that he wanted Rupert Baxter to stop and talk to him, but he was most earnestly desirous of detaining him now. He wished to soothe, to apologize, to explain. He was even prepared, should it be necessary, to offer the man his old post of private secretary as the price of his silence.

'Baxter! My dear fellow!'

A high tenor voice, raised almost to A in Alt by agony of soul, has a compelling quality which it is difficult even for a man in Rupert Baxter's mental condition to resist. Rupert Baxter had not intended to halt his backward movement, but he did so, and Lord Emsworth, reaching the window and thrusting his head out, was relieved to see that he was still within range of the honeyed word.

'Er – Baxter,' he said, 'could you spare me a moment?'

The secretary's spectacles flashed coldly.

'You wish to speak to me, Lord Emsworth?'

'That's exactly it,' assented his lordship, as if he thought it a very happy way of putting the thing. 'Yes, I wish to speak to you.' He paused, and cleared his throat again. 'Tell me, Baxter- – tell me, my dear fellow – were you – er – were you sitting on that seat just now?'

'I was.'

'Did you, by any chance, overhear my niece and myself talking?'

'I did.'

'Then I expect – I fancy – perhaps – possibly – no doubt you were surprised at what you heard?'

'I was astounded,' said Rupert Baxter, who was not going to be fobbed off with any weak verbs at a moment like this.

Lord Emsworth cleared his throat for the third time.

'I want to tell you all about that,' he said.

'Oh?' said Rupert Baxter.

'Yes. I – ah – welcome this opportunity of telling you all about it,' said Lord Emsworth, though with less pleasure in his voice than might have been expected from a man welcoming an opportunity of telling somebody all about something. 'I fancy that my niece's remarks may – er – possibly have misled you.'

'Not at all.'

'They may have put you on the wrong track.'

'On the contrary.'

'But, if I remember correctly, she gave the impression – by what she said – my niece gave the impression by what she said – anybody overhearing what my niece said would have received the impression that I took deliberate aim at you with the gun.'

'Precisely.'

'She was quite mistaken,' said Lord Emsworth warmly. 'She has got hold of the wrong end of the stick completely. Girls say such dashed silly things . . . cause a lot of trouble . . . upset people. They ought to be more careful. What actually happened, my dear fellow, was that I was glancing out of the library window . . . with the gun in my hand . . . and without knowing it I must have placed my finger on the trigger . . . for suddenly . . . without the slightest warning . . . you could have knocked me down with a feather . . . the dashed thing went off. By accident.'

'Indeed?'

'Purely by accident. I should not like you to think that I was aiming at you.'

'Indeed?'

'And I should not like you to tell – er – anybody about the unfortunate occurrence in a way that would give her . . . I mean them . . . the impression that I aimed at you.'

'Indeed?'

Lord Emsworth could not persuade himself that his companion's manner was encouraging. He had a feeling that he was not making headway.

'That's how it was,' he said, after a pause.

'I see.'

'Pure accident. Nobody more surprised than myself.'

'I see.'

So did Lord Emsworth. He saw that the time had come to play his last card. It was no moment for shrinking back and counting the cost. He must proceed to that last fearful extremity which he had contemplated.

'Tell me, Baxter,' he said, 'are you doing anything just now, Baxter?'

'Yes,' replied the other, with no trace of hesitation. 'I am going to look for Lady Constance.'

A convulsive gulp prevented Lord Emsworth from speaking for an instant.

'I mean,' he quavered, when the spasm had spent itself, 'I gathered from my sister that you were at liberty at the moment – that you had left that fellow what's-his-name – the American fellow – and I was hoping, my dear Baxter,' said Lord Emsworth, speaking thickly, as if the words choked him, 'that I might be able to persuade you to take up – to resume – in fact, I was going to ask you if you would care to become my secretary again.'

He paused and, reaching for his handkerchief, feebly mopped his brow. The dreadful speech was out, and its emergence had left him feeling spent and weak.

'You were?' cried Rupert Baxter.

'I was,' said Lord Emsworth hollowly.

A great change for the better had come over Rupert Baxter. It was as if those words had been a magic formula, filling with sweetness and light one who until that moment had been more like a spectacled thunder-cloud than anything human. He ceased to lower darkly. His air of being on the point of shooting out forked lightning left him. He even went so far as to smile. And if the smile was a smile that made Lord Emsworth feel as if his vital organs were being churned up with an egg-whisk, that was not his fault. He was trying to smile sunnily.

'Thank you,' he said. 'I shall be delighted.'

Lord Emsworth did not speak.

'I was always happy at the Castle.'

Lord Emsworth did not speak.

'Thank you very much,' said Rupert Baxter. 'What a beautiful evening.'

He passed from view, and Lord Emsworth examined the evening. As Baxter had said, it was beautiful, but it did not bring the balm which beautiful evenings usually brought to him. A blight seemed to hang over it. The setting sun shone bravely on the formal garden over which he looked, but it was the lengthening shadows rather than the sunshine that impressed themselves upon Lord Emsworth.

His heart was bowed down with weight of woe. Oh, says the poet, what a tangled web we weave when first we practise to deceive, and it was precisely the same, Lord Emsworth realized, when first we practise to shoot airguns. Just one careless, offhand pop at a bending Baxter, and what a harvest, what a retribution! As a result of that single idle shot he had been compelled to augment his personal staff with a land-agent, which would infuriate his sister Constance, and a private secretary, which would make his life once again the inferno it had been in the old, bad Baxter days. He could scarcely have got himself into more trouble if he had gone blazing away with a machine-gun.

It was with a slow and *distrait* shuffle that he eventually took himself from the writing-room and proceeded with his interrupted plan of going and sniffing at his roses. And so preoccupied was his mood that Beach, his faithful butler, who came to him after he had been smiling at them for perhaps half an hour, was obliged to speak twice before he could induce him to remove his nose from a Gloire de Dijon.

'Eh?'

'A note for you, m'lord.'

'A note? Who from?'

'Mr Baxter, m'lord.'

If Lord Emsworth had been less care worn, he might have noticed that the butler's voice had not its customary fruity ring. It had a dullness, a lack of tone. It was the voice of a butler who has lost the bluebird. But, being in the depths and so in no frame of mind to analyse the voice-production of butlers, he merely took the envelope from its salver and opened it listlessly, wondering what Baxter was sending him notes about.

The communication was so brief that he was enabled to discover this at a glance.

LORD EMSWORTH – After what has occurred, I must reconsider my decision to accept the post of secretary which you offered me.

I am leaving the Castle immediately.

R. Baxter

Simply that, and nothing more.

Lord Emsworth stared at the thing. It is not enough to say that he was bewildered. He was nonplussed. If the Gloire de Dijon at which he had recently been sniffing had snapped at his nose and bitten the tip off, he could scarcely have been more taken aback. He could make nothing of this.

As in a dream, he became aware that Beach was speaking.

'Eh?'

'My month's notice, m'lord.'

'Your what?'

'My month's notice, m'lord.'

'What about it?'

'I was saying that I wish to give my month's notice, m'lord.'

A weak irritation at all this chattering came upon Lord Emsworth. Here he was, trying to grapple with this

frightful thing which had come upon him, and Beach
would insist on weakening his concentration by
babbling.

'Yes, yes, yes,' he said. 'I see. All right. Yes, yes.'

'Very good, m'lord.'

Left alone, Lord Emsworth faced the facts. He
understood now what had happened. The note was no
longer mystic. What it meant was that for some reason
that trump card of his had proved useless. He had
thought to stop Baxter's mouth with bribes, and he
had failed. The man had seemed to accept the olive
branch, but later there must have come some sharp
revulsion of feeling, causing him to change his mind.
No doubt a sudden twinge of pain in the wounded area
had brought the memory of his wrongs flooding back
upon him, so that he found himself preferring vengeance
to material prosperity. And how he was going to blow the
gaff. Even now the whole facts in the case might have
been placed before Lady Constance. And even now, Lord
Emsworth felt with a shiver, Connie might be looking
for him.

The sight of a female form coming through the rose
bushes brought him the sharpest shudder of the day, and
for an instant he stood panting like a dog. But it was not
his sister Constance. It was his niece Jane.

Jane was in excellent spirits.

'Hullo, Uncle Clarence,' she said. 'Having a look at
the roses? I've sent that letter off to George, Uncle
Clarence. I got the boy who cleans the knives and boots
to take it. Nice chap. His name is Cyril.'

'Jane,' said Lord Emsworth, 'a terrible, a ghastly thing
has happened. Baxter was outside the window of the
writing-room when we were talking, and he heard
everything.'

'Golly! He didn't?'

'He did. Every word. And he means to tell your
aunt.'

'How do you know?'

'Read this.'

Jane took the note.

'H'm,' she said, having scanned it. 'Well, it looks to me, Uncle Clarence, as if there is only one thing for you to do. You must assert yourself.'

'Assert myself?'

'You know what I mean. Get tough. When Aunt Constance comes trying to bully you, stick your elbows out and put your head on one side and talk back at her out of the corner of your mouth.'

'But what shall I say?'

'Good heavens, there are a hundred things you can say. "Oh, yeah?" "Is zat so?" "Hey, just a minute," "Listen, baby," "Scram" . . .'

'Scram?'

'It means "Get the hell outa here".'

'But I can't tell Connie to get the hell outa here.'

'Why not? Aren't you master in your own house?'

'No,' said Lord Emsworth.

Jane reflected.

'Then I'll tell you what to do. Deny the whole thing.'

'Could I, do you think?'

'Of course you could. And then Aunt Constance will ask me, and I'll deny the whole thing. Categorically. We'll both deny it categorically. She'll have to believe us. We'll be two to one. Don't you worry, Uncle Clarence. Everything'll be all right.'

She spoke with the easy optimism of Youth, and when she passed on a few moments later seemed to be feeling that she was leaving an uncle with his mind at rest. Lord Emsworth could hear her singing a gay song.

He felt no disposition to join in the chorus. He could not bring himself to share her sunny outlook. He looked into the future and still found it dark.

There was only one way of taking his mind off this dark future, only one means of achieving a momentary forgetfulness of what lay in store. Five minutes later, Lord Emsworth was in the library, reading Whiffle on *The Care Of The Pig*.

But there is a point beyond which the magic of the noblest writer ceases to function. Whiffle was good – no question about that – but he was not good enough to purge from the mind such a load of care as was weighing upon Lord Emsworth's. To expect him to do so was trying him too high. It was like asking Whiffle to divert and entertain a man stretched upon the rack.

Lord Emsworth was already beginning to find a difficulty in concentrating on that perfect prose, when any chance he might have had of doing so was removed. Lady Constance appeared in the doorway.

'Oh, here you are, Clarence,' said Lady Constance.

'Yes,' said Lord Emsworth in a low, strained voice.

A close observer would have noted about Lady Constance's manner, as she came into the room, something a little nervous and apprehensive, something almost diffident, but to Lord Emsworth, who was not a close observer, she seemed pretty much as usual, and he remained gazing at her like a man confronted with a ticking bomb. A dazed sensation had come upon him. It was in an almost detached way that he found himself speculating as to which of his crimes was about to be brought up for discussion. Had she met Jane and learned of the fatal letter? Or had she come straight from an interview with Rupert Baxter in which that injured man had told all?

He was so certain that it must be one of these two topics that she had come to broach that her manner as she opened the conversation filled him with amazement. Not only did it lack ferocity, it was absolutely chummy. It was as if a lion had come into the library and started bleating like a lamb.

'All alone, Clarence?'

Lord Emsworth hitched up his lower jaw, and said Yes, he was all alone.

'What are you doing? Reading?'

Lord Emsworth said Yes, he was reading.

'I'm not disturbing you, am I?'

Lord Emsworth, though astonishment nearly robbed him of speech, contrived to say that she was not disturbing him. Lady Constance walked to the window and looked out.

'What a lovely evening.'

'Yes.'

'I wonder you aren't out of doors.'

'I was out of doors. I came in.'

'Yes. I saw you in the rose garden.' Lady Constance traced a pattern on the window-sill with her finger. 'You were speaking to Beach.'

'Yes.'

'Yes, I saw Beach come up and speak to you.'

There was a pause. Lord Emsworth was about to break in by asking his visitor if she felt quite well, when Lady Constance spoke again. That apprehension in her manner, that nervousness, was now well marked. She traced another pattern on the window-sill.

'Was it important?'

'Was what important?'

'I mean, did he want anything?'

'Who?'

'Beach.'

'Beach?'

'Yes. I was wondering what he wanted to see you about.'

Quite suddenly there flashed upon Lord Emsworth the recollection that Beach had done more than merely hand him Baxter's note. With it – dash it, yes, it all came back to him – with it he had given his month's notice. And it just showed, Lord Emsworth felt, what a morass of trouble he was engulfed in that the fact of this superb butler

handing in his resignation had made almost no
impression on him. If such a thing had happened only
as recently as yesterday, it would have constituted a major
crisis. He would have felt that the foundations of his
world were rocking. And he had scarcely listened. 'Yes,
yes,' he had said, if he remembered correctly. 'Yes, yes,
yes. All right.' Or words to that effect.

Bending his mind now on the disaster, Lord Emsworth
sat stunned. He was appalled. Almost since the
beginning of time, this super-butler had been at the
Castle, and now he was about to melt away like snow
in the sunshine – or as much like snow in the sunshine
as was within the scope of a man who weighed sixteen
stone in the buff. It was frightful. The thing was a
nightmare. He couldn't get on without Beach. Life
without Beach would be insupportable.

He gave tongue, his voice sharp and anguished.

'Connie! Do you know what's happened? Beach has
given notice!'

'What!'

'Yes! His month's notice. He's given it. Beach has. And
not a word of explanation. No reason. No – '

Lord Emsworth broke off. His face suddenly hardened.
What seemed the only possible solution of the mystery
had struck him. Connie was at the bottom of this. Connie
must have been coming the *grande dame* on the butler,
wounding his sensibilities.

Yes, that must be it. It was just the sort of thing she
would do. If he had caught her being the Old English
Aristocrat once, he had caught her a hundred times. That
way of hers of pursing the lips and raising the eyebrows
and generally doing the daughter-of-a-hundred-earls stuff.
Naturally no butler would stand it.

'Connie,' he cried, adjusting his pince-nez and staring
keenly and accusingly, 'what have you been doing to
Beach?'

Something that was almost a sob burst from Lady

Constance's lips. Her lovely complexion had paled, and in some odd way she seemed to have shrunk.

'I shot him,' she whispered.

Lord Emsworth was a little hard of hearing.

'You did what?'

'I shot him.'

'Shot him?'

'Yes.'

'You mean, *shot* him?'

'Yes, yes, yes! I shot him with George's airgun.'

A whistling sigh escaped Lord Emsworth. He leaned back in his chair, and the library seemed to be dancing old country dances before his eyes. To say that he felt weak with relief would be to understate the effect of this extraordinary communication. His relief was so intense that he felt absolutely boneless. Not once but many times during the past quarter of an hour he had said to himself that only a miracle could save him from the consequences of his sins, and now the miracle had happened. No one was more alive than he to the fact that women are abundantly possessed of crust, but after this surely even Connie could not have the crust to reproach him for what he had done.

'Shot him?' he said, recovering speech.

A fleeting touch of the old imperiousness returned to Lady Constance.

'Do stop saying "Shot him?" Clarence! Isn't it bad enough to have done a perfectly mad thing, without having to listen to you talking like a parrot? Oh, dear! Oh, dear!'

'But what did you do it for?'

'I don't know. I tell you I don't know. Something seemed suddenly to come over me. It was as if I had been bewitched. After you went out, I thought I would take the gun to Beach – '

'Why?'

'I ... I ... Well, I thought it would be safer with him

than lying about in the library. So I took it down to his pantry. And all the way there I kept remembering what a wonderful shot I had been as a child – '

'What?' Lord Emsworth could not let this pass. 'What do you mean, you were a wonderful shot as a child? You've never shot in your life.'

'I have. Clarence, you were talking about Julia shooting Miss Mapleton. It wasn't Julia – it was I. She had made me stay in and do my rivers of Europe over again, so I shot her. I was a splendid shot in those days.'

'I bet you weren't as good as me,' said Lord Emsworth, piqued. 'I used to shoot rats.'

'So used I to shoot rats.'

'How many rats did you ever shoot?'

'Oh, Clarence, Clarence! Never mind about the rats.'

'No,' said Lord Emsworth, called to order. 'No, dash it. Never mind the rats. Tell me about this Beach business.'

'Well, when I got to the pantry, it was empty, and I saw Beach outside by the laurel bush, reading in a deck-chair – '

'How far away?'

'I don't know. What does it matter? About six feet, I suppose.'

'Six feet? Ha!'

'And I shot him. I couldn't resist it. It was like some horrible obsession. There was a sort of hideous picture in my mind of how he would jump. So I shot him.'

'How do you know you did? I expect you missed him.'

'No. Because he sprang up. And then he saw me at the window and came in, and I said, "Oh, Beach, I want you to take this airgun and keep it," and he said, "Very good, m'lady."'

'He didn't say anything about you shooting him?'

'No. And I have been hoping and hoping that he had not realized what had happened. I have been in an agony of suspense. But now you tell me that he has given his notice, so he must have done. Clarence,' cried Lady Constance, clasping her hands like a persecuted heroine, 'you see the awful position, don't you? If he leaves us he will spread the story all over the county and people will think I'm mad. I shall never be able to live it down. You must persuade him to withdraw his notice. Offer him double wages. Offer him anything. He must not be allowed to leave. If he does, I shall never . . . Sh!'

'What do you mean, Sh . . . Oh, ah,' said Lord Emsworth, at last observing that the door was opening.

It was his niece Jane who entered.

'Oh, hallo, Aunt Constance,' she said. 'I was wondering if you were in here. Mr Baxter's looking for you.'

Lady Constance was *distraite*.

'Mr Baxter?'

'Yes. I heard him asking Beach where you were. I think he wants to see you about something,' said Jane.

She directed at Lord Emsworth a swift glance, accompanied by a fleeting wink. 'Remember!' said the glance. 'Categorically!' said the wink.

Footsteps sounded outside. Rupert Baxter strode into the room.

At an earlier point in this chronicle, we have compared the aspect of Rupert Baxter, when burning with resentment, to a thunder-cloud, and it is possible that the reader may have formed a mental picture of just an ordinary thunder-cloud, the kind that rumbles a bit but does not really amount to anything very much. It was not this kind of cloud that the secretary resembled now, but one of those which burst over cities in the tropics, inundating countrysides while thousands flee. He moved darkly towards Lady Constance, his hands outstretched. Lord Emsworth he ignored.

'I have come to say goodbye, Lady Constance,' he said.

There were not many statements that could have

roused Lady Constance from her preoccupation, but this one did. She ceased to be the sportswoman brooding on memories of shikari, and stared aghast.

'Goodbye?'

'Goodbye.'

'But, Mr Baxter, you are not leaving us?'

'Precisely.'

For the first time, Rupert Baxter deigned to recognize that the ninth Earl was present.

'I am not prepared', he said bitterly, 'to remain in a house where my chief duty appears to be to act as a target for Lord Emsworth and his airgun.'

'What!'

'Exactly.'

In the silence which followed these words, Jane once more gave her uncle that glance of encouragement and stimulation – that glance which said 'Be firm!' To her astonishment, she perceived that it was not needed. Lord Emsworth was firm already. His face was calm, his eye steady, and his pince-nez were not even quivering.

'The fellow's potty,' said Lord Emsworth in a clear resonant voice. 'Absolutely potty. Always told you he was. Target for my airgun? Pooh! Pah! What's he talking about?'

Rupert Baxter quivered. His spectacles flashed fire.

'Do you deny that you shot me, Lord Emsworth?'

'Certainly I do.'

'Perhaps you will deny admitting to this lady here in the writing-room that you shot me?'

'Certainly I do.'

'Did you tell me that you had shot Mr Baxter, Uncle Clarence?' said Jane. 'I didn't hear you.'

'Of course I didn't.'

'I thought you hadn't. I should have remembered it.'

Rupert Baxter's hands shot ceilingwards, as if he were calling upon heaven to see justice done.

'You admitted it to me personally. You begged me not

to tell anyone. You tried to put matters right by engaging me as your secretary, and I accepted the position. At this time I was perfectly willing to forget the entire affair. But when, not half an hour later . . .'

Lord Emsworth raised his eyebrows. Jane raised hers.

'How very extraordinary,' said Jane.

'Most,' said Lord Emsworth.

He removed his pince-nez and began to polish them, speaking soothingly the while. But his manner, though soothing, was very resolute.

'Baxter, my dear fellow,' he said, 'there's only one explanation of all this. It's just what I was telling you. You've been having these hallucinations of yours again. I never said a word to you about shooting you. I never said a word to my niece about shooting you. Why should I, when I hadn't? And as for what you say about engaging you as my secretary, the absurdity of the thing is manifest on the very face of it. There is nothing on earth that would induce me to have you as my secretary. I don't want to hurt your feelings, but I'd rather be dead in a ditch. Now, listen, my dear Baxter, I'll tell you what to do. You just jump on that motor-bicycle of yours and go on touring England where you left off. And soon you will find that the fresh air will do wonders for that pottiness of yours. In a day or two you won't know . . .'

Rupert Baxter turned and stalked from the room.

'Mr Baxter!' cried Lady Constance.

Her intention of going after the fellow and pleading with him to continue inflicting his beastly presence on the quiet home life of Blandings Castle was so plain that Lord Emsworth did not hesitate.

'Connie!'

'But, Clarence!'

'Constance, you will remain where you are. You will not stir a step.'

'But, Clarence!'

'Not a dashed step. You hear me? Let him scram!'

Lady Constance halted, irresolute. Then suddenly she met the full force of the pince-nez and it was as if she – like Rupert Baxter – had been struck by a bullet. She collapsed into a chair and sat there twisting her rings forlornly.

'Oh, and, by the way, Connie,' said Lord Emsworth, 'I've been meaning to tell you. I've given that fellow Abercrombie that job he was asking for. I thought it all over carefully, and decided to drop him a line saying that pursuant on our recent conversation I was offering him Simmons's place. I've been making enquiries, and I find he's a capital fellow.'

'He's a baa-lamb,' said Jane.

'You hear? Jane says he's a baa-lamb. Just the sort of chap we want about the place.'

'So now we're going to get married.'

'So now they're going to get married. An excellent match, don't you think, Connie?'

Lady Constance did not speak. Lord Emsworth raised his voice a little.

'DON'T YOU, CONNIE?'

Lady Constance leaped in her seat as if she had heard the Last Trump.

'Very,' she said. 'Oh, very.'

'Right,' said Lord Emsworth. 'And now I'll go and talk to Beach.'

In the pantry, gazing sadly out on the stable yard, Beach the butler sat sipping a glass of port. In moments of mental stress, port was to Beach what Whiffle was to his employer, or, as we must now ruefully put it, his late employer. He flew to it when Life had got him down, and never before had Life got him down as it had now.

Sitting there in his pantry, that pantry which so soon would know him no more, Beach was in the depths. He mourned like some fallen monarch about to say goodbye to all his greatness and pass into exile. The die was cast.

The end had come. Eighteen years, eighteen happy years, he had been in service at Blandings Castle, and now he must go forth, never to return. Little wonder that he sipped port. A weaker man would have swigged brandy.

Something tempestuous burst open the door, and he perceived that his privacy had been invaded by Lord Emsworth. He rose, and stood staring. In all the eighteen years during which he had held office, his employer had never before paid a visit to the pantry.

But it was not simply the other's presence that caused his gooseberry eyes to dilate to their full width, remarkable though that was. The mystery went deeper than that. For this was a strange, unfamiliar Lord Emsworth, a Lord Emsworth who glared where once he had blinked, who spurned the floor like a mettlesome charger, who banged tables and spilled port.

'Beach,' thundered this changeling, 'what the dooce is all this dashed nonsense?'

'M'lord?'

'You know what I mean. About leaving me. Have you gone off your head?'

A sigh shook the butler's massive frame.

'I fear that in the circumstances it is inevitable, m'lord.'

'Why? What are you talking about? Don't be an ass, Beach. Inevitable, indeed! Never heard such nonsense in my life. Why is it inevitable? Look me in the face and answer me that.'

'I feel it is better to tender my resignation than to be dismissed, m'lord.'

It was Lord Emsworth's turn to stare.

'Dismissed?'

'Yes, m'lord.'

'Beach, you're tight.'

'No, m'lord. Has not Mr Baxter spoken to you, m'lord?'

'Of course he's spoken to me. He's been gassing away half the afternoon. What's that got to do with it?'

Another sigh, seeming to start at the soles of his flat feet, set the butler's waistcoat rippling like corn in the wind.

'I see that Mr Baxter has not yet informed you, m'lord. I assumed that he would have done so before this. But it is a mere matter of time, I fear, before he makes his report.'

'Informed me of what?'

'I regret to say, m'lord, that in a moment of uncontrollable impulse I shot Mr Baxter.'

Lord Emsworth's pince-nez flew from his nose. Without them he could see only indistinctly, but he continued to stare at the butler, and in his eyes there appeared an expression which was a blend of several emotions. Amazement would have been chief of these, had it not been exceeded by affection. He did not speak, but his eyes said 'My brother!'

'With Master George's airgun, m'lord, which her ladyship left in my custody. I regret to say, m'lord, that upon receipt of the weapon I went out into the grounds and came upon Mr Baxter walking near the shrubbery. I tried to resist the temptation m'lord, but it was too keen. I was seized with an urge which I have not experienced since I was a small lad, and, in short, I – '

'Plugged him?'

'Yes, m'lord.'

Lord Emsworth could put two and two together.

'So that's what he was talking about in the library. That's what made him change his mind and send me that note . . . How far was he away when you shot him?'

'A matter of a few feet, m'lord. I endeavoured to conceal myself behind a tree, but he turned very sharply, and I was so convinced that he had detected me that I felt I had no alternative but to resign my situation before he could make his report to you, m'lord.'

'And I thought you were leaving because my sister Connie shot you!'

'Her ladyship did not shoot me, m'lord. It is true that the weapon exploded accidentally in her ladyship's hand, but the bullet passed me harmlessly.'

Lord Emsworth snorted.

'And she said she was a good shot! Can't even hit a sitting butler at six feet. Listen to me, Beach. I want no more of this nonsense of you resigning. Bless my soul, how do you suppose I could get on without you? How long have you been here?'

'Eighteen years, m'lord.'

'Eighteen years! And you talk of resigning! Of all the dashed absurd ideas!'

'But I fear, m'lord, when her ladyship learns – '

'Her ladyship won't learn. Baxter won't tell her. Baxter's gone.'

'Gone, m'lord?'

'Gone, for ever.'

'But I understood, m'lord – '

'Never mind what you understood. He's gone. A few feet away, did you say?'

'M'lord?'

'Did you say Baxter was only a few feet away when you got him?'

'Yes, m'lord.'

'Ah!' said Lord Emsworth.

He took the gun absently from the table and absently slipped a slug into the breech. He was feeling pleased and proud, as champions do whose pre-eminence is undisputed. Connie had missed a mark like Beach – practically a haystack – at six feet. Beach had plugged Baxter – true – and so had young George – but only with the muzzle of the gun almost touching the fellow. It had been left for him, Clarence, ninth Earl of Emsworth, to do the real shooting . . .

A damping thought came to diminish his complacency. It was as if a voice had whispered in his ear the word 'Fluke!' His jaw dropped a little, and he stood for a while, brooding. He felt flattened and discouraged.

Had it been merely a fluke, that superb shot from the library window? Had he been mistaken in supposing that the ancient skill still lingered? Would he – which was what the voice was hinting – under similar conditions miss nine times out of ten?

A stuttering, sputtering noise broke in upon his reverie. He raised his eyes to the window. Out in the stable yard, Rupert Baxter was starting up his motor-bicycle.

'Mr Baxter, m'lord.'

'I see him.'

An overwhelming desire came upon Lord Emsworth to put this thing to the test, to silence for ever that taunting voice.

'How far away would you say he was, Beach?'

'Fully twenty yards, m'lord.'

'Watch!' said Lord Emsworth.

Into the sputtering of the bicycle there cut a soft pop. It was followed by a sharp howl. Rupert Baxter, who had been leaning on the handle-bars, rose six inches with his hand to his thigh.

'There!' said Lord Emsworth.

Baxter had ceased to rub his thigh. He was a man of intelligence, and he realized that anyone on the premises of Blandings Castle who wasted time hanging about and rubbing thighs was simply asking for it. To one trapped in this inferno of Blandings Castle instant flight was the only way of winning to safety. The sputtering rose to a crescendo, diminished, died away altogether. Rupert Baxter had gone on, touring England.

Lord Emsworth was still gazing out of the window raptly, as if looking at the X which marked the spot. For a long moment Beach stood staring reverently at his turned back. Then, as if performing some symbolic rite in keeping with the dignity of the scene, he reached for his glass of port and raised it in a silent toast.

Peace reigned in the butler's pantry. The sweet air of the summer evening poured in through the open window. It was as if Nature had blown the All Clear.

Blandings Castle was itself again.

4 — Pig-hoo-o-o-o-ey!

Thanks to the publicity given to the matter by *The Bridgnorth, Shifnal, and Albrighton Argus* (with which is incorporated *The Wheat-Growers' Intelligencer and Stock Breeders' Gazetteer*), the whole world today knows that the silver medal in the Fat Pigs class at the eighty-seventh annual Shropshire Agricultural Show was won by the Earl of Emsworth's black Berkshire sow, Empress of Blandings.

Very few people, however, are aware how near that splendid animal came to missing the coveted honour.

Now it can be told.

This brief chapter of Secret History may be said to have begun on the night of the eighteenth of July, when George Cyril Wellbeloved (twenty-nine), pig-man in the employ of Lord Emsworth, was arrested by Police-Constable Evans of Market Blandings for being drunk and disorderly in the tap-room of the Goat and Feathers. On July the nineteenth, after first offering to apologize, then explaining that it had been his birthday, and finally attempting to prove an alibi, George Cyril was very properly jugged for fourteen days without the option of a fine.

On July the twentieth, Empress of Blandings, always hitherto a hearty and even a boisterous feeder, for the first time on record declined all nourishment. And on the morning of July the twenty-first, the veterinary surgeon called in to diagnose and deal with this strange asceticism, was compelled to confess to Lord Emsworth that the thing was beyond his professional skill.

Let us just see, before proceeding, that we have got these dates correct:

July 18. – Birthday Orgy of Cyril Wellbeloved.
July 19. – Incarceration of Ditto.
July 20. – Pig Lays off the Vitamins.
July 21. – Veterinary Surgeon Baffled.
Right.

The effect of the veterinary surgeon's announcement on Lord Emsworth was overwhelming. As a rule, the wear and tear of our complex modern life left this vague and amiable peer unscathed. So long as he had sunshine, regular meals, and complete freedom from the society of his younger son Frederick, he was placidly happy. But there were chinks in his armour, and one of these had been pierced this morning. Dazed by the news he had received, he stood at the window of the great library of Blandings Castle, looking out with unseeing eyes.

As he stood there, the door opened. Lord Emsworth turned; and having blinked once or twice, as was his habit when confronted suddenly with anything, recognized in the handsome and imperious-looking woman who had entered, his sister, Lady Constance Keeble. Her demeanour, like his own, betrayed the deepest agitation.

'Clarence,' she cried, 'an awful thing has happened!'
Lord Emsworth nodded dully.
'I know. He's just told me.'
'What! Has he been here?'
'Only this moment left.'
'Why did you let him go? You must have known I would want to see him.'
'What good would that have done?'
'I could at least have assured him of my sympathy,' said Lady Constance stiffly.
'Yes, I suppose you could,' said Lord Emsworth, having

considered the point. 'Not that he deserves any
sympathy. The man's an ass.'

'Nothing of the kind. A most intelligent young man,
as young men go.'

'Young? Would you call him young? Fifty, I should
have said, if a day.'

'Are you out of your senses? Heacham fifty?'

'Not Heacham. Smithers.'

As frequently happened to her when in conversation
with her brother, Lady Constance experienced a swimming
sensation in the head.

'Will you kindly tell me, Clarence, in a few simple
words, what you imagine we are talking about?'

'I'm talking about Smithers. Empress of Blandings is
refusing her food, and Smithers says he can't do anything
about it. And he calls himself a vet!'

'Then you haven't heard? Clarence, a dreadful thing
has happened. Angela has broken off her engagement to
Heacham.'

'And the Agricultural Show on Wednesday week!'

'What on earth has that got to do with it?' demanded
Lady Constance, feeling a recurrence of the swimming
sensation.

'What has it got to do with it?' said Lord Emsworth
warmly. 'My champion sow, with less than ten days to
prepare herself for a most searching examination in
competition with all the finest pigs in the county, starts
refusing her food – '

'Will you stop maundering on about your insufferable
pig and give your attention to something that really
matters? I tell you that Angela – your niece Angela – has
broken off her engagement to Lord Heacham and
expresses her intention of marrying that hopeless ne'er-
do-well, James Belford.'

'The son of old Belford, the parson?'

'Yes.'

'She can't. He's in America.'

'He is not in America. He is in London.'

'No,' said Lord Emsworth, shaking his head sagely. 'You're wrong. I remember meeting his father two years ago out on the road by Meeker's twenty-acre field, and he distinctly told me the boy was sailing for America next day. He must be there by this time.'

'Can't you understand? He's come back.'

'Oh? Come back? I see. Come *back*?'

'You know there was once a silly sentimental sort of affair between him and Angela; but a year after he left she became engaged to Heacham and I thought the whole thing was over and done with. And now it seems that she met this young man Belford when she was in London last week, and it has started all over again. She tells me she has written to Heacham and broken the engagement.'

There was a silence. Brother and sister remained for a space plunged in thought. Lord Emsworth was the first to speak.

'We've tried acorns,' he said. 'We've tried skim milk. And we've tried potato-peel. But, no, she won't touch them.'

Conscious of two eyes raising blisters on his sensitive skin, he came to himself with a start.

'Absurd! Ridiculous! Preposterous!' he said, hurriedly. 'Breaking the engagement? Pooh! Tush! What nonsense! I'll have a word with that young man. If he thinks he can go about the place playing fast and loose with my niece and jilting her without so much as a – '

'Clarence!'

Lord Emsworth blinked. Something appeared to be wrong, but he could not imagine what. It seemed to him that in his last speech he had struck just the right note – strong, forceful, dignified.

'Eh?'

'It is Angela who has broken the engagement.'

'Oh, Angela?'

'She is infatuated with this man Belford. And the point is, what are we to do about it?'

Lord Emsworth reflected.

'Take a strong line,' he said firmly. 'Stand no nonsense. Don't send 'em a wedding-present.'

There is no doubt that, given time, Lady Constance would have found and uttered some adequately corrosive comment on this imbecile suggestion; but even as she was swelling preparatory to giving tongue, the door opened and a girl came in.

She was a pretty girl, with fair hair and blue eyes which in their softer moments probably reminded all sorts of people of twin lagoons slumbering beneath a southern sky. This, however, was not one of those moments. To Lord Emsworth, as they met his, they looked like something out of an oxy-acetylene blow-pipe; and, as far as he was capable of being disturbed by anything that was not his younger son Frederick, he was disturbed. Angela, it seemed to him, was upset about something; and he was sorry. He liked Angela.

To ease a tense situation, he said:

'Angela, my dear, do you know anything about pigs?'

The girl laughed. One of those sharp, bitter laughs which are so unpleasant just after breakfast.

'Yes, I do. You're one.'

'Me?'

'Yes, you. Aunt Constance says that, if I marry Jimmy, you won't let me have my money.'

'Money? Money?' Lord Emsworth was mildly puzzled. 'What money? You never lent me any money.'

Lady Constance's feelings found vent in a sound like an overheated radiator.

'I believe this absent-mindedness of yours is nothing but a ridiculous pose, Clarence. You know perfectly well that when poor Jane died she left you Angela's trustee.'

'And I can't touch my money without your consent till I'm twenty-five.'

'Well, how old are you?'

'Twenty-one.'

'Then what are you worrying about?' asked Lord Emsworth, surprised. 'No need to worry about it for another four years. God bless my soul, the money is quite safe. It is in excellent securities.'

Angela stamped her foot. An unladylike action, no doubt, but how much better than kicking an uncle with it, as her lower nature prompted.

'I have told Angela,' explained Lady Constance, 'that, while we naturally cannot force her to marry Lord Heacham, we can at least keep her money from being squandred by this wastrel on whom she proposes to throw herself away.'

'He isn't a wastrel. He's got quite enough money to marry me on, but he wants some capital to buy a partnership in a – '

'He is a wastrel. Wasn't he sent abroad because – '

'That was two years ago. And since then – '

'My dear Angela, you may argue until – '

'I'm not arguing. I'm simply saying that I'm going to marry Jimmy, if we both have to starve in the gutter.'

'What gutter?' asked his lordship, wrenching his errant mind away from thoughts of acorns.

'Any gutter.'

'Now, please listen to me, Angela.'

It seemed to Lord Emsworth that there was a frightful amount of conversation going on. He had the sensation of having become a mere bit of flotsam upon a tossing sea of female voices. Both his sister and his niece appeared to have much to say, and they were saying it simultaneously and fortissimo. He looked wistfully at the door.

It was smoothly done. A twist of the handle, and he was where beyond those voices there was peace. Galloping gaily down the stairs, he charged out into the sunshine.

His gaiety was not long-lived. Free at last to concentrate itself on the really serious issues of life, his mind grew sombre and grim. Once more there descended upon him the cloud which had been oppressing his soul before all this Heacham-Angela-Belford business began. Each step that took him nearer to the sty where the ailing Empress resided seemed a heavier step than the last. He reached the sty; and, draping himself over the rails, peered moodily at the vast expanse of pig within.

For, even though she had been doing a bit of dieting of late, Empress of Blandings was far from being an ill-nourished animal. She resembled a captive balloon with ears and a tail, and was as nearly circular as a pig can be without bursting. Nevertheless, Lord Emsworth, as he regarded her, mourned and would not be comforted. A few more square meals under her belt, and no pig in all Shropshire could have held its head up in the Empress's presence. And now, just for lack of those few meals, the supreme animal would probably be relegated to the mean obscurity of an 'Honourably Mentioned'. It was bitter, bitter.

He became aware that somebody was speaking to him; and, turning, perceived a solemn young man in riding breeches.

'I say,' said the young man.

Lord Emsworth, though he would have preferred solitude, was relieved to find that the intruder was at least one of his own sex. Women are apt to stray off into side-issues, but men are practical and can be relied on to stick to the fundamentals. Besides, young Heacham probably kept pigs himself and might have a useful hint or two up his sleeve.

'I say, I've just ridden over to see if there was anything I could do about this fearful business.'

'Uncommonly kind and thoughtful of you, my dear fellow,' said Lord Emsworth, touched. 'I fear things look very black.'

'It's an absolute mystery to me.'

'To me, too.'

'I mean to say, she was all right last week.'

'She was all right as late as the day before yesterday.'

'Seemed quite cheery and chirpy and all that.'

'Entirely so.'

'And then this happens – out of a blue sky, as you might say.'

'Exactly. It is insoluble. We have done everything possible to tempt her appetite.'

'Her appetite? Is Angela ill?'

'Angela? No, I fancy not. She seemed perfectly well a few minutes ago.'

'You've seen her this morning, then? Did she say anything about this fearful business?'

'No. She was speaking about some money.'

'It's all so dashed unexpected.'

'Like a bolt from the blue,' agreed Lord Emsworth. 'Such a thing has never happened before. I fear the worst. According to the Wolff-Lehmann feeding standards, a pig, if in health, should consume daily nourishment amounting to fifty-seven thousand eight hundred calories, these to consist of proteins four pounds five ounces, carbohydrates twenty-five pounds – '

'What has that got to do with Angela?'

'Angela?'

'I came to find out why Angela has broken off our engagement.'

Lord Emsworth marshalled his thoughts. He had a misty idea that he had heard something mentioned about that. It came back to him.

'Ah, yes, of course. She has broken off the engagement, hasn't she? I believe it is because she is in love with someone else. Yes, now that I recollect, that was distinctly stated. The whole thing comes back to me quite clearly. Angela has decided to marry someone else. I knew there

was some satisfactory explanation. Tell me, my dear
fellow, what are your views on linseed meal?'

'What do you mean, linseed meal?'

'Why, linseed meal,' said Lord Emsworth, not being
able to find a better definition. 'As a food for pigs.'

'Oh, curse all pigs!'

'What!' There was a sort of astounded horror in Lord
Emsworth's voice. He had never been particularly fond
of young Heacham, for he was not a man who took much
to his juniors, but he had not supposed him capable of
anarchistic sentiments like this. 'What did you say?'

'I said, "Curse all pigs!" You keep talking about pigs.
I'm not interested in pigs. I don't want to discuss
pigs. Blast and damn every pig in existence!'

Lord Emsworth watched him, as he strode away, with
an emotion that was partly indignation and partly relief
– indignation that a landowner and a fellow son of
Shropshire could have brought himself to utter such
words, and relief that one capable of such utterance was
not going to marry into his family. He had always in his
woollen-headed way been very fond of his niece Angela,
and it was nice to think that the child had such solid
good sense and so much cool discernment. Many girls of
her age would have been carried away by the glamour
of young Heacham's position and wealth; but she,
divining with an intuition beyond her years that he was
unsound on the subject of pigs, had drawn back while
there was still time and refused to marry him.

A pleasant glow suffused Lord Emsworth's bosom, to
be frozen out a few moments later as he perceived his
sister Constance bearing down upon him. Lady
Constance was a beautiful woman, but there were times
when the charm of her face was marred by a rather curious
expression; and from nursery days onward his lordship
had learned that this expression meant trouble. She was
wearing it now.

'Clarence,' she said, 'I have had enough of this
nonsense of Angela and young Belford. The thing cannot
be allowed to go drifting on. You must catch the two
o'clock train to London.'

'What! Why?'

'You must see this man Belford and tell him that, if
Angela insists on marrying him, she will not have a
penny for four years. I shall be greatly surprised if that
piece of information does not put an end to the whole
business.'

Lord Emsworth scratched meditatively at the
Empress's tank-like back. A mutinous expression was
on his mild face.

'Don't see why she shouldn't marry the fellow,' he
mumbled.

'Marry James Belford?'

'I don't see why not. Seems fond of him and all that.'

'You never have had a grain of sense in your head,
Clarence. Angela is going to marry Heacham.'

'Can't stand that man. All wrong about pigs.'

'Clarence, I don't wish to have any more discussion
and argument. You will go to London on the two o'clock
train. You will see Mr Belford. And you will tell him
about Angela's money. Is that quite clear?'

'Oh, all right,' said his lordship moodily. 'All right, all
right, all right.'

The emotions of the Earl of Emsworth, as he sat next day
facing his luncheon-guest, James Bartholomew Belford,
across a table in the main dining-room of the Senior
Conservative Club, were not of the liveliest and most
agreeable. It was bad enough to be in London at all on
such a day of golden sunshine. To be charged, while
there, with the task of blighting the romance of two young
people for whom he entertained a warm regard was
unpleasant to a degree.

For, now that he had given the matter thought, Lord

Emsworth recalled that he had always liked this boy
Belford. A pleasant lad, with, he remembered now, a
healthy fondness for that rural existence which so
appealed to himself. By no means the sort of fellow who,
in the very presence and hearing of Empress of Blandings,
would have spoken disparagingly and with oaths of pigs
as a class. It occurred to Lord Emsworth, as it has
occurred to so many people, that the distribution of
money in this world is all wrong. Why should a man
like pig-despising Heacham have a rent roll that ran into
the tens of thousands, while this very deserving youngster
had nothing?

These thoughts not only saddened Lord Emsworth –
they embarrassed him. He hated unpleasantness, and it
was suddenly borne in upon him that, after he had broken
the news that Angela's bit of capital was locked up and
not likely to get loose, conversation with his young friend
during the remainder of lunch would tend to be
somewhat difficult.

He made up his mind to postpone the revelation.
During the meal, he decided, he would chat pleasantly
of this and that; and then, later, while bidding his guest
good-bye, he would spring the thing on him suddenly
and dive back into the recesses of the club.

Considerably cheered at having solved a delicate
problem with such adroitness, he started to prattle.

'The gardens at Blandings,' he said, 'are looking
particularly attractive this summer. My head-gardener,
Angus McAllister, is a man with whom I do not always
find myself seeing eye to eye, notably in the matter of
hollyhocks, on which I consider his views subversive to
a degree; but there is no denying that he understands
roses. The rose garden – '

'How well I remember that rose garden,' said James
Belford, sighing slightly and helping himself to Brussels
sprouts. 'It was there that Angela and I used to meet on
summer evenings.'

Lord Emsworth blinked. This was not an encouraging start, but the Emsworths were a fighting clan. He had another try.

'I have seldom seen such a blaze of colour as was to be witnessed there during the month of June. Both McAllister and I adopted a very strong policy with the slugs and plant lice, with the result that the place was a mass of flourishing Damasks and Ayrshires and – '

'Properly to appreciate roses,' said James Belford, 'you want to see them as a setting for a girl like Angela. With her fair hair gleaming against the green leaves she makes a rose garden seem a veritable Paradise.'

'No doubt,' said Lord Emsworth. 'No doubt. I am glad you liked my rose garden. At Blandings, of course, we have the natural advantage of loamy soil, rich in plant food and humus; but, as I often say to McAllister, and on this point we have never had the slightest disagreement, loamy soil by itself is not enough. You must have manure. If every autumn a liberal mulch of stable manure is spread upon the beds and the coarser parts removed in the spring before the annual forking – '

'Angela tells me,' said James Belford, 'that you have forbidden our marriage.'

Lord Emsworth choked dismally over his chicken. Directness of this kind, he told himself with a pang of self-pity, was the sort of thing young Englishmen picked up in America. Diplomatic circumlocution flourished only in a more leisurely civilization, and in those energetic and forceful surroundings you learned to Talk Quick and Do It Now, and all sorts of uncomfortable things.

'Er – well, yes, now you mention it, I believe some informal decision of that nature was arrived at. You see, my dear fellow, my sister Constance feels rather strongly – '

'I understand. I suppose she thinks I'm a sort of prodigal.'

'No, no, my dear fellow. She never said that. Wastrel was the term she employed.'

'Well, perhaps I did start out in business on those lines. But you can take it from me that when you find yourself employed on a farm in Nebraska belonging to an apple-jack-nourished patriarch with strong views on work and a good vocabulary, you soon develop a certain liveliness.'

'Are you employed on a farm?'

'I was employed on a farm.'

'Pigs?' said Lord Emsworth in a low, eager voice.

'Among other things.'

Lord Emsworth gulped. His fingers clutched at the table-cloth.

'Then perhaps, my dear fellow, you can give me some advice. For the last two days my prize sow, Empress of Blandings, has declined all nourishment. And the Agricultural Show is on Wednesday week. I am distracted with anxiety.'

James Belford frowned thoughtfully.

'What does your pig-man say about it?'

'My pig-man was sent to prison two days ago. Two days!' For the first time the significance of the coincidence struck him. 'You don't think that can have anything to do with the animal's loss of appetite?'

'Certainly. I imagine she is missing him and pining away because he isn't there.'

Lord Emsworth was surprised. He had only a distant acquaintance with George Cyril Wellbeloved, but from what he had seen of him he had not credited him with this fatal allure.

'She probably misses his afternoon call.'

Again his lordship found himself perplexed. He had had no notion that pigs were such sticklers for the formalities of social life.

'His call?'

'He must have had some special call that he used when he wanted her to come to dinner. One of the first things you learn on a farm is hog-calling. Pigs are temperamental. Omit to call them, and they'll starve rather than put on the nose-bag. Call them right, and they will follow you to the ends of the earth with their mouths watering.'

'God bless my soul! Fancy that.'

'A fact, I assure you. These calls vary in different parts of America. In Wisconsin, for example, the words "Poig, Poig, Poig" bring home – in both the literal and the figurative sense – the bacon. In Illinois, I believe they call "Burp, Burp, Burp", while in Iowa the phrase "Kus, Kus, Kus" is preferred. Proceeding to Minnesota, we find "Peega, Peega, Peega" or, alternatively, "Oink, Oink, Oink", whereas in Milwaukee, so largely inhabited by those of German descent, you will hear the good old Teuton "Komm Schweine, Komm Schweine". Oh, yes, there are all sorts of pig-calls, from the Massachusetts "Phew, Phew, Phew" to the "Loo-ey, Loo-ey, Looey" of Ohio, not counting various local devices such as beating on tin cans with axes or rattling pebbles in a suit-case. I knew a man out in Nebraska who used to call his pigs by tapping on the edge of the trough with his wooden leg.'

'Did he, indeed?'

'But a most unfortunate thing happened. One evening, hearing a woodpecker at the top of a tree, they started shinning up it; and when the man came out he found them all lying there in a circle with their necks broken.'

'This is no time for joking,' said Lord Emsworth, pained.

'I'm not joking. Solid fact. Ask anybody out there.'

Lord Emsworth placed a hand to his throbbing forehead.

'But if there is this wide variety, we have no means of knowing which call Wellbeloved . . .'

'Ah,' said James Belford, 'but wait. I haven't told you all. There is a master-word.'

'A what?'

240

'Most people don't know it, but I had it straight from
the lips of Fred Patzel, the hog-calling champion of the
Western States. What a man! I've known him to bring
pork chops leaping from their plates. He informed me
that, no matter whether an animal has been trained to
answer to the Illinois "Burp" or the Minnesota "Oink",
it will always give immediate service in response to this
magic combination of syllables. It is to the pig world what
the Masonic grip is to the human. "Oink" in Illinois or
"Burp" in Minnesota, and the animal merely raises its
eyebrows and stares coldly. But go to either state and call
"Pig-hoo-oo-ey!" . . .'

The expression on Lord Emsworth's face was that of a
drowning man who sees a lifeline.

'It that the master-word of which you spoke?'

'That's it.'

'Pig – !'

' – hoo-oo-ey.'

'Pig-hoo-o-ey!'

'You haven't got it quite right. The first syllable should
be short and staccato, the second long and rising into a
falsetto, high but true.'

'Pig-hoo-o-o-ey.'

'Pig-hoo-o-o-ey.'

'Pig-hoo-o-o-ey!' yodelled Lord Emsworth, flinging his
head back and giving tongue in a high, penetrating tenor
which caused ninety-three Senior Conservatives,
lunching in the vicinity, to congeal into living statues
of alarm and disapproval.

'More body to the "hoo",' advised James Belford.

'Pig-hoo-o-o-ey!'

The Senior Conservative Club is one of the few places
in London where lunchers are not accustomed to getting
music with their meals. White-whiskered financiers
gazed bleakly at bald-headed politicians, as if asking
silently what was to be done about this. Bald-headed
politicians stared back at white-whiskered financiers,

replying in the language of the eye that they did not know. The general sentiment prevailing was a vague determination to write to the Committee about it.

'Pig-hoo-o-o-oey!' carolled Lord Emsworth. And, as he did so, his eye fell on the clock over the mantelpiece. Its hands pointed to twenty minutes to two.

He started convulsively. The best train in the day for Market Blandings was the one which left Paddington station at two sharp. After that there was nothing till the five-five.

He was not a man who often thought; but, when he did, to think was with him to act. A moment later he was scudding over the carpet, making for the door that led to the broad staircase.

Throughout the room which he had left, the decision to write in strong terms to the Committee was now universal; but from the mind, such as it was, of Lord Emsworth the past, with the single exception of the word 'Pig-hoo-o-o-oey!', had been completely blotted.

Whispering the magic syllables, he sped to the cloakroom and retrieved his hat. Murmuring them over and over again, he sprang into a cab. He was still repeating them as the train moved out of the station; and he would doubtless have gone on repeating them all the way to Market Blandings had he not, as was his invariable practice when travelling by rail, fallen asleep after the first ten minutes of the journey.

The stopping of the train at Swindon Junction woke him with a start. He sat up, wondering, after his usual fashion on these occasions, who and where he was. Memory returned to him, but a memory that was, alas, incomplete. He remembered his name. He remembered that he was on his way home from a visit to London. But what it was that you said to a pig when inviting it to drop in for a bite of dinner he had completely forgotten.

*

It was the opinion of Lady Constance Keeble, expressed verbally during dinner in the brief intervals when they were alone, and by means of silent telepathy when Beach, the butler, was adding his dignified presence to the proceedings, that her brother Clarence, in his expedition to London to put matters plainly to James Belford, had made an outstanding idiot of himself.

There had been no need whatever to invite the man Belford to lunch; but, having invited him to lunch, to leave him sitting, without having clearly stated that Angela would have no money for four years, was the act of a congenital imbecile. Lady Constance had been aware ever since their childhood days that her brother had about as much sense as a –

Here Beach entered, superintending the bringing-in of the savoury, and she had been obliged to suspend her remarks.

This sort of conversation is never agreeable to a sensitive man, and his lordship had removed himself from the danger zone as soon as he could manage it. He was now seated in the library, sipping port and straining a brain which Nature had never intended for hard exercise in an effort to bring back that word of magic of which his unfortunate habit of sleeping in trains had robbed him.

'Pig – '

He could remember as far as that; but of what avail was a single syllable? Besides, weak as his memory was, he could recall that the whole gist or nub of the thing lay in the syllable that followed. The 'pig' was a mere preliminary.

Lord Emsworth finished his port and got up. He felt restless, stifled. The summer night seemed to call to him like some silver-voiced swineherd calling to his pig. Possibly, he thought, a breath of fresh air might stimulate his brain-cells. He wandered downstairs; and, having dug a shocking old slouch hat out of the cupboard where he hid it to keep his sister Constance from impounding and burning it, he strode heavily out into the garden.

He was pottering aimlessly to and fro in the parts adjacent to the rear of the castle when there appeared in his path a slender female form. He recognized it without pleasure. Any unbiased judge would have said that his niece Angela, standing there in the soft, pale light, looked like some dainty spirit of the Moon. Lord Emsworth was not an unbiased judge. To him Angela merely looked like Trouble. The march of civilization has given the modern girl a vocabulary and an ability to use it which her grandmother never had. Lord Emsworth would not have minded meeting Angela's grandmother a bit.

'Is that you, my dear?' he said nervously.

'Yes.'

'I didn't see you at dinner.'

'I didn't want any dinner. The food would have choked me. I can't eat.'

'It's precisely the same with my pig,' said his lordship. 'Young Belford tells me – '

Into Angela's queenly disdain there flashed a sudden animation.

'Have you seen Jimmy? What did he say?'

'That's just what I can't remember. It began with the word "Pig" – '

'But after he had finished talking about you, I mean. Didn't he say anything about coming down here?'

'Not that I remember.'

'I expect you weren't listening. You've got a very annoying habit, Uncle Clarence,' said Angela maternally, 'of switching your mind off and just going blah when people are talking to you. It gets you very much disliked on all sides. Didn't Jimmy say anything about me?'

'I fancy so. Yes, I am nearly sure he did.'

'Well, what?'

'I cannot remember.'

There was a sharp clicking noise in the darkness. It was caused by Angela's upper front teeth meeting her lower front teeth; and was followed by a sort of wordless exclamation. It seemed only too plain that the love and respect which a niece should have for an uncle were in the present instance at a very low ebb.

'I wish you wouldn't do that,' said Lord Emsworth plaintively.

'Do what?'

'Make clicking noises at me.'

'I will make clicking noises at you. You know perfectly well, Uncle Clarence, that you are behaving like a bohunkus.'

'A what?'

'A bohunkus,' explained his niece coldly, 'is a very inferior sort of worm. Not the kind of worm that you see on lawns, which you can respect, but a really degraded species.'

'I wish you would go in, my dear,' said Lord Emsworth. 'The night air may give you a chill.'

'I won't go in. I came out here to look at the moon and think of Jimmy. What are you doing out here, if it comes to that?'

'I came here to think. I am greatly exercised about my pig, Empress of Blandings. For two days she has refused her food, and young Belford says she will not eat until she hears the proper call or cry. He very kindly taught it to me, but unfortunately I have forgotten it.'

'I wonder you had the nerve to ask Jimmy to teach you pig-calls, considering the way you're treating him.'

'But – '

'Like a leper, or something. And all I can say is that, if you remember this call of his, and it makes the Empress eat, you ought to be ashamed of yourself if you still refuse to let me marry him.'

'My dear,' said Lord Emsworth earnestly, 'if through young Belford's instrumentality Empress of Blandings

is induced to take nourishment once more there is
nothing I will refuse him – nothing.'

'Honour bright?'

'I give you my solemn word.'

'You won't let Aunt Constance bully you out of it?'

Lord Emsworth drew himself up.

'Certainly not,' he said proudly. 'I am always ready to
listen to your Aunt Constance's views, but there are
certain matters where I claim the right to act according
to my own judgement.' He paused and stood musing. 'It
began with the word "Pig – "'

From somewhere near at hand music made itself heard.
The servants' hall, its day's labours ended, was
refreshing itself with the housekeeper's gramophone. To
Lord Emsworth the strains were merely an additional
annoyance. He was not fond of music. It reminded him
of his younger son Frederick, a flat but persevering
songster both in and out of the bath.

'Yes, I can distinctly recall as much as that. Pig –
Pig – '

'WHO – '

Lord Emsworth leaped in the air. It was as if an electric
shock had been applied to his person.

'WHO stole my heart away?' howled the
gramophone. 'WHO – ?

The peace of the summer night was shattered by a
triumphant shout.

'Pig-HOO-o-o-o-ey!'

A window opened. A large, bald head appeared. A
dignified voice spoke.

'Who is there? Who is making that noise?'

'Beach!' cried Lord Emsworth. 'Come out here at
once.'

'Very good, your lordship.'

And presently the beautiful night was made still more
lovely by the added attraction of the butler's presence.

'Beach, listen to this.'

'Very good, your lordship.'

'Pig-hoo-o-o-o-ey!'

'Very good, your lordship.'

'Now you do it.'

'I, your lordship?'

'Yes. It's a way you call pigs.'

'I do not call pigs, your lordship,' said the butler coldly.

'What do you want Beach to do it for?' asked Angela.

'Two heads are better than one. If we both learn it, it will not matter should I forget it again.'

'By Jove, yes! Come on, Beach. Push it over the thorax,' urged the girl eagerly. 'You don't know it, but this is a matter of life and death. At-a-boy, Beach! Inflate the lungs and go to it.'

It had been the butler's intention, prefacing his remarks with the statement that he had been in service at the castle for eighteen years, to explain frigidly to Lord Emsworth that it was not his place to stand in the moonlight practising pig-calls. If, he would have gone on to add, his lordship saw the matter from a different angle, then it was his, Beach's, painful duty to tender his resignation, to become effective one month from that day.

But the intervention of Angela made this impossible to a man of chivalry and heart. A paternal fondness for the girl, dating from the days when he had stooped to enacting – and very convincingly, too, for his was a figure that lent itself to the impersonation – the role of a hippopotamus for her childish amusement, checked the words he would have uttered. She was looking at him with bright eyes, and even the rendering of pig-noises seemed a small sacrifice to make for her sake.

'Very good, your lordship,' he said in a low voice, his face pale and set in the moonlight. 'I shall endeavour to give satisfaction. I would merely advance the suggestion, your lordship, that we move a few steps farther away from the vicinity of the servants' hall. If I were to be

247

overheard by any of the lower domestics, it would
weaken my position as a disciplinary force.'

'What chumps we are!' cried Angela, inspired. 'The
place to do it is outside the Empress's sty. Then, if it
works, we'll see it working.'

Lord Emsworth found this a little abstruse, but after a
moment he got it.

'Angela,' he said, 'you are a very intelligent girl. Where
you get your brains from, I don't know. Not from my
side of the family.'

The bijou residence of the Empress of Blandings looked
very snug and attractive in the moonlight. But beneath
even the beautiful things of life there is always an
underlying sadness. This was supplied in the present
instance by a long, low trough, only too plainly full to the
brim of succulent mash and acorns. The fast, obviously,
was still in progress.

The sty stood some considerable distance from the
castle walls, so that there had been ample opportunity
for Lord Emsworth to rehearse his little company during
the journey. By the time they had ranged themselves
against the rails, his two assistants were letter-perfect.

'Now,' said his lordship.

There floated out upon the summer night a strange
composite sound that sent the birds roosting in the trees
above shooting off their perches like rockets. Angela's
clear soprano rang out like the voice of the village
blacksmith's daughter. Lord Emsworth contributed a
reedy tenor. And the bass notes of Beach probably did
more to startle the birds than any other one item in the
programme.

They paused and listened. Inside the Empress's boudoir
there sounded the movement of a heavy body. There
was an inquiring grunt. The next moment the sacking
that covered the doorway was pushed aside, and the
noble animal emerged.

'Now!' said Lord Emsworth again.

Once more that musical cry shattered the silence of the night. But it brought no responsive movement from Empress of Blandings. She stood there motionless, her nose elevated, her ears hanging down, her eyes everywhere but on the trough where, by rights, she should now have been digging in and getting hers. A chill disappointment crept over Lord Emsworth, to be succeeded by a gust of petulant anger.

'I might have known it,' he said bitterly. 'That young scoundrel was deceiving me. He was playing a joke on me.'

'He wasn't,' cried Angela indignantly. 'Was he, Beach?'

'Not knowing the circumstances, miss, I cannot venture an opinion.'

'Well, why has it no effect, then?' demanded Lord Emsworth.

'You can't expect it to work right away. We've got her stirred up, haven't we? She's thinking it over, isn't she? Once more will do the trick. Ready, Beach?'

'Quite ready, miss.'

'Then when I say three. And this time, Uncle Clarence, do please for goodness' sake not yowl like you did before. It was enough to put any pig off. Let it come out quite easily and gracefully. Now, then. One, two – three!'

The echoes died away. And as they did so a voice spoke.

'Community singing?'

'Jimmy!' cried Angela, whisking round.

'Hullo, Angela. Hullo, Lord Emsworth. Hullo, Beach.'

'Good evening, sir. Happy to see you once more.'

'Thanks. I'm spending a few days at the Vicarage with my father. I got down here by the five-five.'

Lord Emsworth cut peevishly in upon these civilities.

'Young man,' he said, 'what do you mean by telling me that my pig would respond to that cry? It does nothing of the kind.'

'You can't have done it right.'

'I did it precisely as you instructed me. I have had,

moreover, the assistance of Beach here and my niece
Angela – '

'Let's hear a sample.'

Lord Emsworth cleared his throat.

'Pig-hoo-o-o-o-ey!'

James Belford shook his head.

'Nothing like it,' he said. 'You want to begin the "Hoo"
in a low minor of two quarter notes in four-four time.
From this build gradually to a higher note, until at last
the voice is soaring in full crescendo, reaching F sharp
on the natural scale and dwelling for two retarded half-
notes, then breaking into a shower of accidental grace-
notes.'

'God bless my soul!' said Lord Emsworth, appalled. 'I
shall never be able to do it.'

'Jimmy will do it for you,' said Angela. 'Now that he's
engaged to me, he'll be one of the family and always
popping about here. He can do it every day till the show
is over.'

James Belford nodded.

'I think that would be the wisest plan. It is doubtful if
an amateur could ever produce real results. You need a
voice that has been trained on the open prairie and that
has gathered richness and strength from competing with
tornadoes. You need a manly, sunburned, wind-scorched
voice with a suggestion in it of the crackling of corn
husks and the whisper of evening breezes in the fodder.
Like this!'

Resting his hands on the rail before him, James Belford
swelled before their eyes like a young balloon. The
muscles on his cheekbones stood out, his forehead
became corrugated, his ears seemed to shimmer. Then,
at the very height of the tension, he let it go like, as the
poet beautifully puts it, the sound of a great Amen.

'Pig-HOOOOO-OOO-OOO-O-O-ey!'

They looked at him, awed. Slowly, fading off across
hill and dale, the vast bellow died away. And suddenly,

as it died, another, softer sound succeeded it. A sort of gulpy, gurgly, plobby, squishy, wofflesome sound, like a thousand eager men drinking soup in a foreign restaurant. And, as he heard it, Lord Emsworth uttered a cry of rapture.

The Empress was feeding.

5 — *Extract from* Something New

(This extract from the American edition was omitted from the English edition, *Something Fresh*)

Breakfast at Blandings Castle was an informal meal. There was food and drink in the long dining-hall for such as were energetic enough to come down and get it; but the majority of the house party breakfasted in their rooms, Lord Emsworth, whom nothing in the world would have induced to begin the day in the company of a crowd of his relations, most of whom he disliked, setting them the example.

When, therefore, Baxter, yielding to Nature after having remained awake until the early morning, fell asleep at nine o'clock, nobody came to rouse him. He did not ring his bell, so he was not disturbed; and he slept on until half past eleven, by which time, it being Sunday morning and the house party including one bishop and several of the minor clergy, most of the occupants of the place had gone off to church.

Baxter shaved and dressed hastily, for he was in a state of nervous apprehension. He blamed himself for having lain in bed so long. When every minute he was away might mean the loss of the scarab, he had passed several hours in dreamy sloth. He had wakened with a presentiment. Something told him the scarab had been stolen in the night, and he wished now that he had risked all and kept guard.

The house was very quiet as he made his way rapidly to the hall. As he passed a window he perceived Lord Emsworth, in an un-Sabbatarian suit of tweeds and

bearing a garden fork – which must have pained the
hishop – bending earnestly over a flower bed; but he was
the only occupant of the grounds, and indoors there
was a feeling of emptiness. The hall had that Sunday-
morning air of wanting to be left to itself, and
disapproving of the entry of anything human until lunch
time, which can be felt only by a guest in a large house
who remains at home when his fellows have gone to
church.

The portraits on the walls, especially the one of the
late Countess of Emsworth in the character of Venus
rising from the sea, stared at Baxter as he entered, with
cold reproof. The very chairs seemed distant and
unfriendly; but Baxter was in no mood to appreciate their
attitude. His conscience slept. His mind was occupied,
to the exclusion of all other things, by the scarab and its
probable fate. How disastrously remiss it had been of
him not to keep guard last night! Long before he opened
the museum door he was feeling the absolute certainty
that the worst had happened.

It had. The card which announced that here was an
Egyptian scarab of the reign of Cheops of the Fourth
Dynasty, presented by J. Preston Peters, Esquire, still lay
on the cabinet in its wonted place; but now its neat
lettering was false and misleading. The scarab was gone.

For all that he had expected this, for all his premonition
of disaster, it was an appreciable time before the Efficient
Baxter rallied from the blow. He stood transfixed, goggling
at the empty place.

Then his mind resumed its functions. All, he
perceived, was not yet lost. Baxter the watchdog must
retire, to be succeeded by Baxter the sleuthhound. He had
been unable to prevent the theft of the scarab, but he might
still detect the thief.

For the Doctor Watsons of this world, as opposed to
the Sherlock Holmeses, success in the province of

detective work must always be, to a very large extent, the result of luck. Sherlock Holmes can extract a clew from a wisp of straw or a flake of cigar ash; but Doctor Watson has to have it taken out for him and dusted, and exhibited clearly, with a label attached.

The average man is a Doctor Watson. We are wont to scoff in a patronizing manner at that humble follower of the great investigator; but as a matter of fact we should have been just as dull ourselves. We should not even have risen to the modest height of a Scotland Yard bungler.

Baxter was a Doctor Watson. What he wanted was a clew; but it is so hard for the novice to tell what is a clew and what is not. And then he happened to look down – and there on the floor was a clew that nobody could have overlooked.

Baxter saw it, but did not immediately recognize it for what it was. What he saw, at first, was not a clew, but just a mess. He had a tidy soul and abhorred messes, and this was a particularly messy mess. A considerable portion of the floor was a sea of red paint. The can from which it had flowed was lying on its side near the wall. He had noticed that the smell of paint had seemed particularly pungent, but had attributed this to a new freshet of energy on the part of Lord Emsworth. He had not perceived that paint had been spilled.

'Pah!' said Baxter.

Then suddenly, beneath the disguise of the mess, he saw the clew. A footmark! No less. A crimson footmark on the polished wood! It was as clear and distinct as though it had been left there for the purpose of assisting him. It was a feminine footmark, the print of a slim and pointed shoe.

This perplexed Baxter. He had looked on the siege of the scarab as an exclusively male affair. But he was not perplexed long. What could be simpler than that Mr Peters should have enlisted female aid? The female of the species is more deadly than the male. Probably she makes a better purloiner of scarabs. At any rate, there the footprint was, unmistakably feminine.

Inspiration came to him. Aline Peters had a maid! What more likely than that secretly she should be a hireling of Mr Peters, on whom he had now come to look as a man of the blackest and most sinister character? Mr Peters was a collector; and when a collector makes up his mind to secure a treasure, he employs, Baxter knew, every possible means to that end.

Baxter was now in a state of great excitement. He was hot on the scent and his brain was working like a buzz saw in an ice box. According to his reasoning, if Aline Peters' maid had done this thing there should be red paint in the hall marking her retreat, and possibly a faint stain on the stairs leading to the servants' bedrooms.

He hastened from the museum and subjected the hall to a keen scrutiny. Yes; there was red paint on the carpet. He passed through the green-baize door and examined the stairs. On the bottom step there was a faint but conclusive stain of crimson!

He was wondering how best to follow up this clew when he perceived Ashe coming down the stairs. Ashe, like Baxter, and as the result of a night disturbed by anxious thoughts, had also overslept himself.

There are moments when the giddy excitement of being right on the trail causes the amateur – or Watsonian – detective to be incautious. If Baxter had been wise he would have achieved his object – the getting a glimpse of Joan's shoes – by a devious and snaky route. As it was, zeal getting the better of prudence, he rushed straight on. His early suspicion of Ashe had been temporarily obscured. Whatever Ashe's claims to be a suspect, it had not been his footprint Baxter had seen in the museum.

'Here, you!' said the Efficient Baxter excitedly.

'Sir?'

'The shoes!'

'I beg your pardon?'

'I wish to see the servants' shoes. Where are they?'

'I expect they have them on, sir.'

'Yesterday's shoes, man – yesterday's shoes. Where are they?'

'Where are the shoes of yesteryear?' murmured Ashe. 'I should say at a venture, sir, that they would be in a large basket somewhere near the kitchen. Our genial knife-and-shoe boy collects them, I believe, at early dawn.'

'Would they have been cleaned yet?'

'If I know the lad, sir – no.'

'Go and bring that basket to me. Bring it to me in this room.'

The room to which he referred was none other than the private sanctum of Mr Beach, the butler, the door of which, standing open, showed it to be empty. It was not Baxter's plan, excited as he was, to risk being discovered sifting shoes in the middle of a passage in the servants' quarters.

Ashe's brain was working rapidly as he made for the shoe cupboard, that little den of darkness and smells, where Billy, the knife-and-shoe boy, better known in the circle in which he moved as Young Bonehead, pursued his menial tasks. What exactly was at the back of the Efficient Baxter's mind prompting these maneuvers he did not know; but that there was something he was certain.

He had not yet seen Joan this morning, and he did not know whether or not she had carried out her resolve of attempting to steal the scarab on the previous night; but this activity and mystery on the part of their enemy must have some sinister significance. He gathered up the shoe basket thoughtfully.

He staggered back with it and dumped it down on the floor of Mr Beach's room. The Efficient Baxter stooped eagerly over it. Ashe, leaning against the wall, straightened the creases in his clothes and sticked disgustedly at an inky spot which the journey had transferred from the basket to his coat.

'We have here, sir,' he said, 'a fair selection of our various foot coverings.'

'You did not drop any on your way?'

'Not one, sir.'

The Efficient Baxter uttered a grunt of satisfaction and bent once more to his task. Shoes flew about the room. Baxter knelt on the floor beside the basket and dug like a terrier at a rat hole. At last he made a dive and with an exclamation of triumph rose to his feet. In his hand he held a shoe.

'Put those back,' he said.

Ashe began to pick up the scattered footgear.

'That's the lot, sir,' he said, rising.

'Now come with me. Leave the basket there. You can carry it back when you return.'

'Shall I put back that shoe, sir?'

'Certainly not. I shall take this one with me.'

'Shall I carry it for you, sir?'

Baxter reflected.

'Yes. I think that would be best.'

Trouble had shaken his nerve. He was not certain that there might not be others besides Lord Emsworth in the garden; and it occurred to him that, especially after his reputation for eccentric conduct had been so firmly established by his misfortunes that night in the hall, it might cause comment should he appear before them carrying a shoe.

Ashe took the shoe and, doing so, understood what before had puzzled him. Across the toe was a broad splash of red paint. Though he had nothing else to go on, he saw all. The shoe he held was a female shoe. His own researches in the museum had made him aware of the presence there of red paint. It was not difficult to build up on these data a pretty accurate estimate of the position of affairs.

'Come with me,' said Baxter.

He left the room. Ashe followed him.

In the garden Lord Emsworth, garden fork in hand, was dealing summarily with a green young weed that had incautiously shown its head in the middle of a flower bed. He listened to Baxter's statement with more interest than he usually showed in anybody's statements. He resented the loss of the scarab, not so much on account of its intrinsic worth as because it had been the gift of his friend Mr Peters.

'Indeed!' he said, when Baxter had finished. 'Really? Dear me! It certainly seems – It is extremely suggestive. You are certain there was red paint on this shoe?'

'I have it with me. I brought it on purpose to show you.' He looked at Ashe, who stood in close attendance. 'The shoe!'

Lord Emsworth polished his glasses and bent over the exhibit.

'Ah!' he said. 'Now let me look at – This, you say, is the – Just so; just so! Just – My dear Baxter, it may be that I have not examined this shoe with sufficient care, but – Can you point out to me exactly where this paint is that you speak of?'

The Efficient Baxter stood staring at the shoe with a wild, fixed stare. Of any suspicion of paint, red or otherwise, it was absolutely and entirely innocent!

The shoe became the center of attraction, the cynosure of all eyes. The Efficient Baxter fixed it with the piercing glare of one who feels that his brain is tottering. Lord Emsworth looked at it with a mildly puzzled expression. Ashe Marson examined it with a sort of affectionate interest, as though he were waiting for it to do a trick of some kind. Baxter was the first to break the silence.

'There was paint on this shoe,' he said vehemently. 'I tell you there was a splash of red paint across the toe. This man here will bear me out in this. You saw paint on this shoe?'

'Paint, sir?'

'What! Do you mean to tell me you did not see it?'

'No, sir; there was no paint on this shoe.'

'This is ridiculous. I saw it with my own eyes. It was a broad splash right across the toe.'

Lord Emsworth interposed.

'You must have made a mistake, my dear Baxter. There is certainly no trace of paint on this shoe. These momentary optical delusions are, I fancy, not uncommon. Any doctor will tell you – '

'I had an aunt, your lordship,' said Ashe chattily, 'who was remarkably subject – '

'It is absurd! I cannot have been mistaken,' said Baxter. 'I am positively certain the toe of this shoe was red when I found it.'

'It is quite black now, my dear Baxter.'

'A sort of chameleon shoe,' murmured Ashe.

The goaded secretary turned on him.

'What did you say?'

'Nothing, sir.'

Baxter's old suspicion of this smooth young man came surging back to him.

'I strongly suspect you of having had something to do with this.'

'Really, Baxter,' said the earl, 'that is surely the least probable of solutions. This young man could hardly have cleaned the shoe on his way from the house. A few days ago, when painting in the museum, I inadvertently splashed some paint on my own shoe. I can assure you it does not brush off. It needs a very systematic cleaning before all traces are removed.'

'Exactly, your lordship,' said Ashe. 'My theory, if I may – '

'Yes?'

'My theory, your lordship, is that Mr Baxter was deceived by the light-and-shade effects on the toe of the shoe. The morning sun, streaming in through the

window, must have shone on the shoe in such a manner
as to give it a momentary and fictitious aspect of redness.
If Mr Baxter recollects, he did not look long at the shoe.
The picture on the retina of the eye consequently had not
time to fade. I myself remember thinking at the moment
that the shoe appeared to have a certain reddish tint. The
mistake – '

'Bah!' said Baxter shortly.

Lord Emsworth, now thoroughly bored with the whole
affair and desiring nothing more than to be left alone
with his weeds and his garden fork, put in his word.
Baxter, he felt, was curiously irritating these days. He
always seemed to be bobbing up. The Earl of Emsworth
was conscious of a strong desire to be free from his
secretary's company. He was efficient, yes – invaluable
indeed – he did not know what he should do without
Baxter; but there was no denying that his company tended
after a while to become a trifle tedious. He took a fresh
grip on his garden fork and shifted it about in the air as a
hint that the interview had lasted long enough.

'It seems to me, my dear fellow,' he said, 'the only
explanation that will square with the facts. A shoe that
is really smeared with red paint does not become black
of itself in the course of a few minutes.'

'You are very right, your lordship,' said Ashe
approvingly. 'May I go now, your lordship?'

'Certainly – certainly; by all means.'

'Shall I take the shoe with me, your lordship?'

'If you do not want it, Baxter.'

The secretary passed the fraudulent piece of evidence
to Ashe without a word; and the latter, having included
both gentlemen in a kindly smile, left the garden.

On returning to the butler's room, Ashe's first act was
to remove a shoe from the top of the pile in the basket.
He was about to leave the room with it, when the sound
of footsteps in the passage outside halted him.

'I do not in the least understand why you wish me to

come here, my dear Baxter,' said a voice, 'and you are completely spoiling my morning, but – '

For a moment Ashe was at a loss. It was a crisis that called for swift action, and it was a little hard to know exactly what to do. It had been his intention to carry the paint-splashed shoe back to his own room, there to clean it at his leisure; but it appeared that his strategic line of retreat was blocked. Plainly, the possibility – nay, the certainty – that Ashe had substituted another shoe for the one with the incriminating splash of paint on it had occurred to the Efficient Baxter almost directly the former had left the garden.

The window was open. Ashe looked out. There were bushes below. It was a makeshift policy, and one which did not commend itself to him as the ideal method, but it seemed the only thing to be done, for already the footsteps had reached the door. He threw the shoe out of the window, and it sank beneath the friendly surface of the long grass round a wistaria bush.

Ashe turned, relieved, and the next moment the door opened and Baxter walked in, accompanied – with obvious reluctance – by his bored employer.

Baxter was brisk and peremptory.

'I wish to look at those shoes again,' he said coldly.

'Certainly, sir,' said Ashe.

'I can manage without your assistance,' said Baxter.

'Very good, sir.'

Leaning against the wall, Ashe watched him with silent interest, as he burrowed among the contents of the basket, like a terrier digging for rats. The Earl of Emsworth took no notice of the proceedings. He yawned plaintively, and pottered about the room. He was one of Nature's potterers.

The scrutiny of the man whom he had now placed definitely as a malefactor irritated Baxter. Ashe was looking at him in an insufferably tolerant manner, as if he were an indulgent father brooding over his infant son while engaged in some childish frolic. He lodged a protest.

'Don't stand there staring at me!'

'I was interested in what you were doing, sir.'

'Never mind! Don't stare at me in that idiotic way.'

'May I read a book, sir?'

'Yes, read if you like.'

'Thank you, sir.'

Ashe took a volume from the butler's slenderly stocked shelf. The shoe-expert resumed his investigations in the basket. He went through it twice, but each time without success. After the second search he stood up and looked wildly about the room. He was as certain as he could be of anything that the missing piece of evidence was somewhere within those four walls. There was very little cover in the room, even for so small a fugitive as a shoe. He raised the tablecloth and peered beneath the table.

'Are you looking for Mr Beach, sir?' said Ashe. 'I think he has gone to church.'

Baxter, pink with his exertions, fastened a baleful glance upon him.

'You had better be careful,' he said.

At this point the Earl of Emsworth, having done all the pottering possible in the restricted area, yawned like an alligator.

'Now, my dear Baxter – ' he began querulously.

Baxter was not listening. He was on the trail. He had caught sight of a small closet in the wall, next to the mantelpiece, and it had stimulated him.

'What is in this closet?'

'That closet, sir?'

'Yes, this closet.' He rapped the door irritably.

'I could not say, sir. Mr Beach, to whom the closet belongs, possibly keeps a few odd trifles there. A ball of string, perhaps. Maybe an old pipe or something of that kind. Probably nothing of value or interest.'

'Open it.'

'It appears to be locked, sir.'

'Unlock it.'

'But where is the key?'

Baxter thought for a moment.

'Lord Emsworth,' he said, 'I have my reasons for thinking that this man is deliberately keeping the contents of this closet from me. I am convinced that the shoe is in there. Have I your leave to break open the door?'

The earl looked a little dazed, as if he were unequal to the intellectual pressure of the conversation.

'Now, my dear Baxter,' said the earl impatiently, 'please tell me once again why you have brought me in here. I cannot make head or tail of what you have been saying. Apparently you accuse this young man of keeping his shoes in a closet. Why should you suspect him of keeping his shoes in a closet? And if he wishes to do so, why on earth should not he keep his shoes in a closet? This is a free country.'

'Exactly, your lordship,' said Ashe approvingly. 'You have touched the spot.'

'It all has to do with the theft of your scarab, Lord Emsworth. Somebody got into the museum and stole the scarab.'

'Ah, yes; ah, yes – so they did. I remember now. You told me. Bad business that, my dear Baxter. Mr Peters gave me that scarab. He will be most deucedly annoyed if it's lost. Yes, indeed.'

'Whoever stole it upset the can of red paint and stepped in it.'

'Devilish careless of them. It must have made the dickens of a mess. Why don't people look where they are walking?'

'I suspect this man of shielding the criminal by hiding her shoe in this closet.'

'Oh, it's not his own shoes that this young man keeps in closets?'

'It is a woman's shoe, Lord Emsworth.'

'The deuce it is! Then it was a woman who stole the

scarab? Is that the way you figure it out? Bless my soul,
Baxter, one wonders what women are coming to
nowadays. It's all this movement, I suppose. The Vote,
and all that – eh? I recollect having a chat with the
Marquis of Petersfield some time ago. He is in the
Cabinet, and tells me it is perfectly infernal the way these
women carry on. He said sometimes it got to such a
pitch, with them waving banners and presenting
petitions, and throwing flour and things at a fellow, that
if he saw his own mother coming toward him, with a
hand behind her back, he would run like a rabbit. Told
me so himself.'

'So,' said the Efficient Baxter, cutting in on the flow of
speech, that I wish to do is to break open this closet.'

'Eh? Why?'

'To get the shoe.'

'The shoe? . . . Ah, yes, I recollect now. You were
telling me.'

'If your lordship has no objection.'

'Objection, my dear fellow? None in the world. Why
should I have any objection? Let me see! What is it you
wish to do?'

'This,' said Baxter shortly.

He seized the poker from the fireplace and delivered
two rapid blows on the closet door. The wood was
splintered. A third blow smashed the flimsy lock. The
closet, with any skeletons it might contain, was open for
all to view.

It contained a corkscrew, a box of matches, a paper-
covered copy of a book entitled 'Mary, the Beautiful
Mill-Hand,' a bottle of embrocation, a spool of cotton,
two pencil-stubs, and other useful and entertaining
objects. It contained, in fact, almost everything except a
paint-splashed shoe, and Baxter gazed at the collection
in dumb disappointment.

'Are you satisfied now, my dear Baxter,' said the earl,
'or is there any more furniture that you would like to

break? You know, this furniture breaking is becoming a positive craze with you, my dear fellow. You ought to fight against it. The night before last, I don't know how many tables broken in the hall; and now this closet. You will ruin me. No purse can stand the constant drain.'

Baxter did not reply. He was still trying to rally from the blow. A chance remark of Lord Emsworth's set him off on the trail once more. Lord Emsworth, having said his say, had dismissed the affair from his mind and begun to potter again. The course of his pottering had brought him to the fireplace, where a little pile of soot on the fender caught his eye. He bent down to inspect it.

'Dear me!' he said. 'I must remember to tell Beach to have his chimney swept. It seems to need it badly.'

No trumpet-call ever acted more instantaneously on old war-horse than this simple remark on the Efficient Baxter. He was still convinced that Ashe had hidden the shoe somewhere in the room, and, now that the closet had proved an alibi, the chimney was the only spot that remained unsearched. He dived forward with a rush, nearly knocking Lord Emsworth off his feet, and thrust an arm up into the unknown. The startled peer, having recovered his balance, met Ashe's respectfully pitying gaze.

'We must humor him,' said the gaze, more plainly than speech.

Baxter continued to grope. The chimney was a roomy chimney, and needed careful examination. He wriggled his hand about clutchingly. From time to time soot fell in gentle showers.

'My dear Baxter!'

Baxter was baffled. He withdrew his hand from the chimney, and straightened himself. He brushed a bead of perspiration from his face with the back of his hand. Unfortunately, he used the sooty hand, and the result was too much for Lord Emsworth's politeness. He burst into a series of pleased chuckles.

'Your face, my dear Baxter! Your face! It is positively covered with soot – positively! You must go and wash it. You are quite black. Really, my dear fellow, you present rather an extraordinary appearance. Run off to your room.'

Against this crowning blow the Efficient Baxter could not stand up. It was the end.

'Soot!' he murmured weakly. 'Soot!'

'Your face is covered, my dear fellow – quite covered.'

'It certainly has a faintly sooty aspect, sir,' said Ashe.

His voice roused the sufferer to one last flicker of spirit.

'You will hear more of this,' he said. 'You will – '

At this moment, slightly muffled by the intervening door and passageway, there came from the direction of the hall a sound like the delivery of a ton of coal. A heavy body bumped down the stairs, and a voice which all three recognized as that of the Honorable Freddie uttered an oath that lost itself in a final crash and a musical splintering sound, which Baxter for one had no difficulty in recognizing as the dissolution of occasional china.

Even if they had not so able a detective as Baxter with them, Lord Emsworth and Ashe would have been at no loss to guess what had happened. Doctor Watson himself could have deduced it from the evidence. The Honorable Freddie had fallen downstairs.

6 — Almost Entirely About Flower-pots

I

The Efficient Baxter prowled feverishly up and down the yielding carpet of the big drawing-room. His eyes gleamed behind their spectacles, his dome-like brow was corrugated. Except for himself, the room was empty. As far as the scene of the disaster was concerned, the tumult and the shouting had died. It was going on vigorously in practically every other part of the house, but in the drawing-room there was stillness, if not peace.

Baxter paused, came to a decision, went to the wall and pressed the bell.

'Thomas,' he said when that footman presented himself a few moments later.

'Sir?'

'Send Susan to me.'

'Susan, sir?'

'Yes, Susan,' snapped the Efficient One, who had always a short way with the domestic staff. 'Susan, Susan, Susan . . . The new parlourmaid.'

'Oh, yes, sir. Very good, sir.'

Thomas withdrew, outwardly, all grave respectfulness, inwardly piqued, as was his wont, at the airy manner in which the secretary flung his orders about at the castle. The domestic staff at Blandings lived in a perpetual state of smouldering discontent under Baxter's rule.

'Susan,' said Thomas when he arrived in the lower regions, 'you're to go up to the drawing-room. Nosey Parker wants you.'

The pleasant-faced young woman whom he addressed laid down her knitting.

'Who?' she asked.

'Mister Blooming Baxter. When you've been here a little longer you'll know that he's the feller that owns the place. How he got it I don't know. Found it,' said Thomas satirically, 'in his Christmas stocking, I expect. Anyhow, you're to go up.'

Thomas's fellow-footman, Stokes, a serious-looking man with a bald forehead, shook that forehead solemnly.

'Something's the matter,' he asserted. 'You can't tell me that wasn't a scream we heard when them lights was out. Or,' he added weightily, for he was a man who looked at every side of a question, 'a shriek. It was a shriek or scream. I said so at the time. "There," I said, "listen!" I said. "That's somebody screaming," I said. "Or shrieking." Something's up.'

'Well, Baxter hasn't been murdered, worse luck,' said Thomas. 'He's up there screaming or shrieking for Susan. "Send Susan to me!"' proceeded Thomas, giving an always popular imitation. '"Susan, Susan, Susan." So you'd best go, my girl, and see what he wants.'

'Very well.'

'And, Susan,' said Thomas, a tender note creeping into his voice, for already, brief as had been her sojourn at Blandings, he had found the new parlourmaid making a deep impression on him, 'if it's a row of any kind . . .'

'Or description,' interjected Stokes.

'Or description,' continued Thomas, accepting the word, 'if 'e's 'arsh with you for some reason or other, you come right back to me and sob out your troubles on my chest, see? Lay your little 'ead on my shoulder and tell me all about it.'

The new parlourmaid, primly declining to reply to this alluring invitation, started on her journey upstairs; and Thomas, with a not unmanly sigh, resumed his interrupted game of halfpenny nap with colleague Stokes.

*

The Efficient Baxter had gone to the open window and was gazing out into the night when Susan entered the drawing-room.

'You wished to see me, Mr Baxter?'

The secretary spun round. So softly had she opened the door, and so noiselessly had she moved when inside the room, that it was not until she spoke that he had become aware of her arrival. It was a characteristic of this girl Susan that she was always apt to be among those present some time before the latter became cognizant of the fact.

'Oh, good evening, Miss Simmons. You came in very quietly.'

'Habit,' said the parlourmaid.

'You gave me quite a start.'

'I'm sorry. What was it,' she asked, dismissing in a positively unfeeling manner the subject of her companion's jarred nerves, 'that you wished to see me about?'

'Shut that door.'

'I have. I always shut doors.'

'Please sit down.'

'No, thank you, Mr Baxter. It might look odd if anyone should come in.'

'Of course. You think of everything.'

'I always do.'

Baxter stood for a moment, frowning.

'Miss Simmons,' he said, 'when I thought it expedient to instal a private detective in this house, I insisted on Wragge's sending you. We had worked together before . . .'

'Sixteenth of December, 1918, to January twelve, 1919, when you were secretary to Mr Horace Jevons, the American millionaire,' said Miss Simmons as promptly as if he had touched a spring. It was her hobby to remember dates with precision.

'Exactly. I insisted upon your being sent because I knew from experience that you were reliable. At that time I looked on your presence here merely as a precautionary measure. Now, I am sorry to say . . .'

'Did someone steal Lady Constance's necklace tonight?'

'Yes!'

'When the lights went out just now?'

'Exactly.'

'Well, why couldn't you say so at once? Good gracious, man, you don't have to break the thing gently to me.'

The Efficient Baxter, though he strongly objected to being addressed as 'man', decided to overlook the solecism.

'The lights suddenly went out,' he said. 'There was a certain amount of laughter and confusion. Then a piercing shriek . . .'

'I heard it.'

'And immediately after Lady Constance's voice crying that her jewels had been snatched from her neck.'

'Then what happened?'

'Still greater confusion, which lasted until one of the maids arrived with a candle. Eventually the lights went on again, but of the necklace there was no sign whatever.'

'Well? Were you expecting the thief to wear it as a watch-chain or hang it from his teeth?'

Baxter was finding his companion's manner more trying every minute, but he preserved his calm.

'Naturally the doors were barred and a complete search instituted. And extremely embarrassing it was. With the single exception of the scoundrel who has been palming himself off as McTodd, all those present were well-known members of Society.'

'Well-known members of Society might not object to getting hold of a twenty-thousand-pound necklace. But still with the McTodd fellow there, you oughtn't to have had far to look. What had he to say about it?'

'He was among the first to empty his pockets.'

'Well, then, he must have hidden the thing somewhere.'

'Not in this room. I have searched assiduously.'

'H'm.'

There was a silence.

'It is baffling,' said Baxter, 'baffling.'

'It is nothing of the kind,' replied Miss Simmons tartly. 'This wasn't a one-man job. How could it have been? I should be inclined to call it a three-man job. One to switch off the lights, one to snatch the necklace, and one to – was that window open all the time? I thought so – and one to pick up the necklace when the second fellow threw it out on to the terrace.'

'Terrace!'

The word shot from Baxter's lips with explosive force. Miss Simmons looked at him curiously.

'Thought of something?'

'Miss Simmons,' said the Efficient One impressively, 'everybody was assembled in here waiting for the reading to begin, but the pseudo-McTodd was nowhere to be found. I discovered him eventually on the terrace in close talk with the Halliday girl.'

'His partner,' said Miss Simmons, nodding. 'We thought so all along. And let me add my little bit. There's a fellow down in the servants' hall that calls himself a valet, and I'll bet he didn't know what a valet was till he came here. I thought he was a crook the moment I set eyes on him. I can tell 'em in the dark. Now, do you know whose valet he is? This McTodd fellow's!'

Baxter bounded to and fro like a caged tiger.

'And with my own ears,' he cried excitedly, 'I heard the Halliday girl refuse to come to the drawing-room to listen to the reading. She was out on the terrace throughout the whole affair. Miss Simmons, we must act! We must act!'

'Yes, but not like idiots,' replied the detective frostily.

'What do you mean?'

'Well, you can't charge out, as you looked as if you
wanted to just then, and denounce these crooks where
they sit. We've got to go carefully.'

'But meanwhile they will smuggle the necklace away!'

'They won't smuggle any necklace away, not while
I'm around. Suspicion's no good. We've made out a nice
little case against the three of them, but it's no use unless
we catch them with the goods. The first thing we have to
do is to find out where they've hidden the stuff. And
that'll take patience. I'll start by searching that girl's room.
Then I'll search the valet fellow's room. And if the stuff
isn't there it'll mean they've hidden it out in the open
somewhere.'

'But this McTodd fellow. This fellow who poses as
McTodd. He may have it all the while.'

'No. I'll search his room, too, but the stuff won't be
there. He's the fellow who's going to get it in the end,
because he's got that place out in the woods to hide it in.
But they wouldn't have had time to slip it to him yet. That
necklace is somewhere right here. And if,' said Miss
Simmons with grim facetiousness, 'they can hide it from
me, they may keep it as a birthday present.'

2

How wonderful, if we pause to examine it, is Nature's
inexorable law of compensation. Instead of wasting time
in envy of our mental superiors, we would do well to
reflect that these gifts of theirs which excite our wistful
jealousy are ever attended by corresponding penalties. To
take an example that lies to hand, it was the very fact
that he possessed a brain like a buzz-saw that rendered
the Efficient Baxter a bad sleeper. Just as he would be
dropping off, bing! would go that brain of his, melting the
mists of sleep like snow in a furnace.

This was so even when life was running calmly for
him and without excitement. Tonight, his mind, bearing

the load it did, firmly declined even to consider the
question of slumber. The hour of two, chiming from
the clock over the stables, found him as wide awake as
ever he was at high noon.

Lying in bed in the darkness, he reviewed the situation
as far as he had the data. Shortly before he retired, Miss
Simmons had made her report about the bedrooms.
Though subjected to the severest scrutiny, neither
Psmith's boudoir nor Cootes's attic nor Eve's little nook
on the third floor had yielded up treasure of any
description. And this, Miss Simmons held, confirmed her
original view that the necklace must be lying concealed in
what might almost be called a public spot – on some
window-ledge, maybe, or somewhere in the hall . . .

Baxter lay considering this theory. It did appear to be
the only tenable one; but it offended him by giving the
search a frivolous suggestion of being some sort of round
game like Hunt the Slipper or Find the Thimble. As a
child he had held austerely aloof from these silly
pastimes, and he resented being compelled to play them
now. Still . . .

He sat up thinking. He had heard a noise.

The attitude of the majority of people towards noises in
the night is one of cautious non-interference. But Rupert
Baxter was made of sterner stuff. The sound had seemed
to come from downstairs somewhere – perhaps from
that very hall where, according to Miss Simmons, the
stolen necklace might even now be lying hid. Whatever
it was, it must certainly not be ignored. He reached for
the spectacles which lay ever ready to his hand on the
table beside him: then climbed out of bed, and, having
put on a pair of slippers and opened the door, crept forth
into the darkness. As far as he could ascertain by holding
his breath and straining his ears, all was still from cellar
to roof; but nevertheless he was not satisfied. He
continued to listen. His room was on the second floor,

one of a series that ran along a balcony overlooking the hall; and he stood, leaning over the balcony rail, a silent statue of Vigilance.

The noise which had acted so electrically upon the Efficient Baxter had been a particularly noisy noise; and only the intervening distance and the fact that his door was closed had prevented it sounding to him like an explosion. It had been caused by the crashing downfall of a small table containing a vase, a jar of potpourri, an Indian sandalwood box of curious workmanship, and a cabinet-size photograph of the Earl of Emsworth's eldest son, Lord Bosham; and the table had fallen because Eve, *en route* across the hall in quest of her precious flower-pot, had collided with it while making for the front door. Of all indoor sports – and Eve, as she stood pallidly among the ruins, would have been the first to endorse this dictum – the one which offers the minimum of pleasure to the participant is that of roaming in pitch darkness through the hall of a country-house. Easily navigable in the daytime, these places become at night mere traps for the unwary.

Eve paused breathlessly. So terrific had the noise sounded to her guilty ears that every moment she was expecting doors to open all over the castle, belching forth shouting men with pistols. But as nothing happened, courage returned to her, and she resumed her journey. She found the great door, ran her fingers along its surface, and drew the chain. The shooting back of the bolts occupied but another instant, and then she was out on the terrace running her hardest towards the row of flower-pots.

Up on his balcony, meanwhile, the Efficient Baxter was stopping, looking, and listening. The looking brought no results, for all below was black as pitch; but the listening proved more fruitful. Faintly from down in the well of the hall there floated up to him a peculiar sound like something rustling in the darkness. Had he reached the balcony a moment earlier, he would have heard the rattle of the chain and the click of the bolts; but these noises had occurred just before he came out of his room. Now all that was audible was this rustling.

He could not analyse the sound, but the fact that there was any sound at all in such a place at such an hour increased his suspicions that dark doings were towards which would pay for investigation. With stealthy steps he crept to the head of the stairs and descended.

One uses the verb 'descend' advisedly, for what is required is some word suggesting instantaneous activity. About Baxter's progress from the second floor to the first there was nothing halting or hesitating. He, so to speak, did it now. Planting his foot firmly on a golf-ball which the Hon. Freddie Threepwood, who had been practising putting in the corridor before retiring to bed, had left in his casual fashion just where the steps began, he took the entire staircase in one majestic, vol-planing sweep. There were eleven stairs in all separating his landing from the landing below, and the only ones he hit were the third and tenth. He came to rest with a squattering thud on the lower landing, and for a moment or two the fever of the chase left him.

The fact that many writers in their time have commented at some length on the mysterious manner in which Fate is apt to perform its work must not deter us now from a brief survey of this latest manifestation of its ingenious methods. Had not his interview with Eve that afternoon so stimulated the Hon. Freddie as to revive in him a faint yet definite desire to putt, there would have been no golf-ball waiting for Baxter on the stairs. And had he been permitted to negotiate the stairs in a less impetuous manner, Baxter would not at this juncture have switched on the light.

It had not been his original intention to illuminate the theatre of action, but after that Lucifer-like descent from

the second floor to the first he was taking no more
chances. 'Safety First' was Baxter's slogan. As soon,
therefore, as he had shaken off a dazed sensation of mental
and moral collapse, akin to that which comes to the man
who steps on the teeth of a rake and is smitten on the
forehead by the handle, he rose with infinite caution to
his feet and, feeling his way down by the banisters, groped
for the switch and pressed it. And so it came about that
Eve, heading for home with her precious flower-pot in
her arms, was stopped when at the very door by a sudden
warning flood of light. Another instant, and she would
have been across the threshold of disaster.

For a moment paralysis gripped her. The light had
affected her like someone shouting loudly and
unexpectedly in her ear. Her heart gave one convulsive
bound, and she stood frozen. Then, filled with a blind
desire for flight, she dashed like a hunted rabbit into the
friendly shelter of a clump of bushes.

Baxter stood blinking. Gradually his eyes adjusted
themselves to the light, and immediately they had done
so he was seized by a fresh frenzy of zeal. Now that all
things were made visible to him he could see that that
faint rustling sound had been caused by a curtain
flapping in the breeze, and that the breeze which made
the curtain flap was coming in through the open front
window.

Baxter wasted no time in abstract thought. He acted
swiftly and with decision. Straightening his spectacles
on his nose, he girded up his pyjamas and galloped out
into the night.

The smooth terrace slept under the stars. To a more poetic
man than Baxter it would have seemed to wear that
faintly reproachful air which a garden always assumes
when invaded at unseemly hours by people who ought
to be in bed. Baxter, never fanciful, was blind to this. He

was thinking, thinking. That shaking-up on the stairs had
churned into activity the very depths of his brain and he
was at the fever-point of his reasoning powers. A thought
had come like a full-blown rose, flushing his brow. Miss
Simmons, arguing plausibly, had suggested that the
stolen necklace might be concealed in the hall. Baxter,
inspired, fancied not. Whoever it was that had been at
work in the hall just now had been making for the garden.
It was not the desire to escape which had led him – or
her – to open the front door, for the opening had been
done before he, Baxter, had come out on to the balcony
– otherwise he must have heard the shooting of the bolts.
No. The enemy's objective had been the garden. In other
words, the terrace. And why? Because somewhere on the
terrace was the stolen necklace.

Standing there in the starlight, the Efficient Baxter
endeavoured to reconstruct the scene, and did so with
remarkable accuracy. He saw the jewels flashing down.
He saw them picked up. But there he stopped. Try as he
might, he could not see them hidden. And yet that they
had been hidden – and that within a few feet of where
he was now standing – he felt convinced.

He moved from his position near the door and began
to roam restlessly. His slippered feet padded over the soft
turf.

Eve peered out from her clump of bushes. It was not easy
to see any great distance, but Fate, her friend, was still
with her. There had been a moment that night when
Baxter, disrobing for bed, had wavered absently between
his brown and his lemon-coloured pyjamas, little recking
of what hung upon the choice. Fate had directed his hand
to the lemon-coloured, and he had put them on; with the
result that he shone now in the dim light like the white
plume of Navarre. Eve could follow his movements
perfectly, and, when he was far enough away from his
base to make the enterprise prudent, she slipped out and

raced for home and safety. Baxter at the moment was leaning on the terrace wall, thinking, thinking, thinking.

It was possibly the cool air, playing about his bare ankles, that at last chilled the secretary's dashing mood and brought the disquieting thought that he was doing something distinctly dangerous in remaining out here in the open like this. A gang of thieves are ugly customers, likely to stick at little when a valuable necklace is at stake, and it came to the Efficient Baxter that in his light pyjamas he must be offering a tempting mark for any marauder lurking – say in those bushes. And at the thought, the summer night, though pleasantly mild, grew suddenly chilly. With an almost convulsive rapidity he turned to re-enter the house. Zeal was well enough, but it was silly to be rash. He covered the last few yards of his journey at a rare burst of speed.

It was at this point that he discovered that the lights in the hall had been switched off and that the front door was closed and bolted.

3

It is the opinion of most thoughtful students of life that happiness in this world depends chiefly on the ability to take things as they come. An instance of one who may be said to have perfected this attitude is to be found in the writings of a certain eminent Arabian author who tells of a traveller who, sinking to sleep one afternoon upon a patch of turf containing an acorn, discovered when he woke that the warmth of his body had caused the acorn to germinate and that he was now some sixty feet above the ground in the upper branches of a massive oak. Unable to descend, he faced the situation equably. 'I cannot,' he observed, 'adapt circumstances to my will: therefore I shall adapt my will to circumstances. I decide to remain here.' Which he did.

Rupert Baxter, as he stood before the barred door of Blandings Castle, was very far from imitating this admirable philosopher. To find oneself locked out of a country-house at half-past two in the morning in lemon-coloured pyjamas can never be an unmixedly agreeable experience, and Baxter was a man less fitted by nature to endure it with equanimity than most men. His was a fiery and an arrogant soul, and he seethed in furious rebellion against the intolerable position into which Fate had manoeuvred him. He even went so far as to give the front door a petulant kick. Finding, however, that this hurt his toes and accomplished no useful end, he addressed himself to the task of ascertaining whether there was any way of getting in – short of banging the knocker and rousing the house, a line of action which did not commend itself to him. He made a practice of avoiding as far as possible the ribald type of young man of which the castle was now full, and he had no desire to meet them at this hour in his present costume. He left the front door and proceeded to make a circuit of the castle walls; and his spirits sank even lower. In the Middle Ages, during that stormy period of England's history when walls were built six feet thick and a window was not so much a window as a handy place for pouring molten lead on the heads of visitors, Blandings had been an impregnable fortress. But in all its career it can seldom have looked more of a fortress to anyone than it did now to the Efficient Baxter.

One of the disadvantages of being a man of action, impervious to the softer emotions, is that in moments of trial the beauties of Nature are powerless to soothe the anguished heart. Had Baxter been of a dreamy and poetic temperament he might now have been drawing all sorts of balm from the loveliness of his surroundings. The air was full of the scent of growing things; strange, shy creatures came and went about him as he walked; down in the woods a nightingale had begun to sing; and there was something grandly majestic in the huge bulk of the

castle as it towered against the sky. But Baxter had
temporarily lost his sense of smell; he feared and disliked
the strange, shy creatures; the nightingale left him cold;
and the only thought the towering castle inspired in him
was that it looked as if a fellow would need half a ton of
dynamite to get into it.

Baxter paused. He was back now near the spot from
which he had started, having completed two laps
without finding any solution of his difficulties. The idea
in his mind had been to stand under somebody's window
and attract the sleeper's attention with soft, significant
whistles. But the first whistle he emitted had sounded
to him in the stillness of early morn so like a steam siren
that thereafter he had merely uttered timid, mouse-like
sounds which the breezes had carried away the moment
they crept out. He proposed now to halt for a while and
rest his lips before making another attempt. He proceeded
to the terrace wall and sat down. The clock over the
stables struck three.

To the restless type of thinker like Rupert Baxter, the
act of sitting down is nearly always the signal for
the brain to begin working with even more than its
customary energy. The relaxed body seems to invite
thought. And Baxter, having suspended for the moment
his physical activities – and glad to do so, for his slippers
hurt him – gave himself up to tense speculation as to the
hiding-place of Lady Constance Keeble's necklace. From
the spot where he now sat he was probably, he reflected,
actually in a position to see that hiding-place – if only,
when he saw it, he were able to recognize it for what it
was. Somewhere out here – in yonder bushes or in some
unsuspected hole in yonder tree – the jewels must have
been placed. Or . . .

Something seemed to go off inside Baxter like a
touched spring. One moment, he was sitting limply,
keenly conscious of a blister on the sole of his left foot;
the next, regardless of the blister, he was off the wall

and racing madly along the terrace in a flurry of flying slippers. Inspiration had come to him.

Day dawns early in the summer months, and already a sort of unhealthy pallor had begun to manifest itself in the sky. It was still far from light, but objects hitherto hidden in the gloom had begun to take on uncertain shape. And among these there had come into the line of Baxter's vision a row of fifteen flower-pots.

There they stood, side by side, round and inviting, each with a geranium in its bed of mould. Fifteen flower-pots. There had originally been sixteen, but Baxter knew nothing of that. All he knew was that he was on the trail.

The quest for buried treasure is one which right through the ages has exercised an irresistible spell over humanity. Confronted with a spot where buried treasure may lurk, men do not stand upon the order of their digging; they go at it with both hands. No solicitude for his employer's geraniums came to hamper Rupert Baxter's researches. To grasp the first flower-pot and tilt out its contents was with him the work of a moment. He scrabbled his fingers through the little pile of mould . . .

Nothing.

A second geranium lay broken on the ground . . .

Nothing.

A third . . .

The Efficient Baxter straightened himself painfully. He was unused to stooping, and his back ached. But physical discomfort was forgotten in the agony of hope frustrated. As he stood there, wiping his forehead with an earth-stained hand, fifteen geranium corpses gazed up at him in the growing light, it seemed with reproach. But Baxter felt no remorse. He included all geraniums, all thieves, and most of the human race in one comprehensive black hatred.

All that Rupert Baxter wanted in this world now was bed. The clock over the stables had just struck four, and he was aware of an overpowering fatigue. Somehow or other, if he had to dig through the walls with his bare hands, he must get into the house. He dragged himself painfully from the scene of carnage and blinked up at the row of silent windows above him. He was past whistling now. He stooped for a pebble, and tossed it up at the nearest window.

Nothing happened. Whoever was sleeping up there continued to sleep. The sky had turned pink, birds were twittering in the ivy, other birds had begun to sing in the bushes. All Nature, in short, was waking – except the unseen sluggard up in that room.

He threw another pebble . . .

It seemed to Rupert Baxter that he had been standing there throwing pebbles through a nightmare eternity. The whole universe had now become concentrated in his efforts to rouse that log-like sleeper; and for a brief instant fatigue left him, driven away by a sort of Berserk fury. And there floated into his mind, as if from some previous existence, a memory of somebody once standing near where he was standing now and throwing a flower-pot in at a window at someone. Who it was that had thrown the thing at whom, he could not at the moment recall; but the outstanding point on which his mind focused itself was the fact that the man had had the right idea. This was no time for pebbles. Pebbles were feeble and inadequate. With one voice the birds, the breezes, the grasshoppers, the whole chorus of Nature waking to another day seemed to shout to him, 'Say it with flower-pots!'

4

The ability to sleep soundly and deeply is the prerogative, as has been pointed out earlier in this straightforward narrative of the simple home-life of the English upper classes, of those who do not think quickly. The Earl of Emsworth, who had not thought quickly since the occasion in the summer of 1874 when he had heard his father's footsteps approaching the stable-loft in which he, a lad of fifteen, sat smoking his first cigar, was an excellent sleeper. He started early and finished late. It was his gentle boast for more than twenty years he had never missed his full eight hours. Generally he managed to get something nearer ten.

But then, as a rule, people did not fling flower-pots through his window at four in the morning.

Even under this unusual handicap, however, he struggled bravely to preserve his record. The first of Baxter's missiles, falling on a settee, produced no change in his regular breathing. The second, which struck the carpet, caused him to stir. It was the third, colliding sharply with his humped back, that definitely woke him. He sat up in bed and stared at the thing.

In the first moment of his waking, relief was, oddly enough, his chief emotion. The blow had roused him from a disquieting dream in which he had been arguing with Angus McAllister about early spring bulbs, and McAllister, worsted verbally, had hit him in the ribs with a spud. Even in his dream Lord Emsworth had been perplexed as to what his next move ought to be; and when he found himself awake and in his bedroom he was at first merely thankful that the necessity for making a decision had at any rate been postponed. Angus McAllister might on some future occasion smite him with a spud, but he had not done it yet.

There followed a period of vague bewilderment. He looked at the flower-pot. It had no message for him.

He had not put it there. He never took flower-pots to bed. Once, as a child, he had taken a dead pet rabbit, but never a flower-pot. The whole affair was completely inscrutable; and his lordship, unable to solve the mystery, was on the point of taking the statesmanlike course of going to sleep again, when something large and solid whizzed through the open window and crashed against the wall, where it broke, but not into such small fragments that he could not perceive that in its prime it, too, had been a flower-pot. And at this moment his eyes fell on the carpet and then on the settee; and the affair passed still farther into the realm of the inexplicable. The Hon. Freddie Threepwood, who had a poor singing-voice but was a game trier, had been annoying his father of late by crooning a ballad ending in the words:

> It is not raining at all:
> It's raining vi-o-lets.

It seemed to Lord Emsworth now that matters had gone a step farther. It was raining flower-pots.

The customary attitude of the Earl of Emsworth towards all mundane affairs was one of vague detachment; but this phenomenon was so remarkable that he found himself stirred to quite a little flutter of excitement and interest. His brain still refused to cope with the problem of why anybody should be throwing flower-pots into his room at this hour – or, indeed, at any hour; but it seemed a good idea to go and ascertain who this peculiar person was.

He put on his glasses and hopped out of bed and trotted to the window. And it was while he was on his way there that memory stirred in him, as some minutes ago it had stirred in the Efficient Baxter. He recalled that odd episode of a few days back, when that delightful girl, Miss What's-her-name, had informed him that his secretary had been throwing flower-pots at that poet fellow,

McTodd. He had been annoyed, he remembered, that
Baxter should so far have forgotten himself. Now, he
found himself more frightened than annoyed. Just as
every dog is permitted one bite without having its sanity
questioned, so, if you consider it in a broad-minded way,
may every man be allowed to throw one flower-pot. But
let the thing become a habit, and we look askance. This
strange hobby of his appeared to be growing on Baxter
like a drug, Lord Emsworth did not like it at all. He had
never before suspected his secretary of an unbalanced
mind, but now he mused, as he tiptoed cautiously to the
window, that the Baxter sort of man, energetic, restless
type, was just the kind that does go off his head. Just
some such calamity as this, his lordship felt, he might
have foreseen. Day in, day out, Rupert Baxter had been
exercising his brain ever since he had come to the castle
– and now he had gone and sprained it. Lord Emsworth
peeped timidly out from behind the curtain.

His worst fears were realized. It was Baxter sure
enough; and a tousled, wild-eyed Baxter incredibly clad
in lemon-coloured pyjamas.

Lord Emsworth stepped back from the window. He had
seen sufficient. The pyjamas had in some curious way
set the coping-stone on his dismay, and he was now in a
condition approximating to panic. That Baxter should
be so irresistibly impelled by his strange mania as actually
to omit to attire himself decently before going out on
one of these flower-pot-hurling expeditions of his seemed
to make it all so sad and hopeless. The dreamy peer was
no poltroon, but he was past his first youth, and it came
to him very forcibly that the interviewing and pacifying of
secretaries who ran amok was young man's work. He
stole across the room and opened the door. It was his
purpose to put this matter into the hands of an agent.
And so it came about that Psmith was aroused some few
minutes later from slumber by a touch on the arm and

sat up to find his host's pale face peering at him in the weird light of early morning.

'My dear fellow,' quavered Lord Emsworth.

Psmith, like Baxter was a light sleeper; and it was only a moment before he was wide awake and exerting himself to do the courtesies.

'Good morning,' he said pleasantly. 'Will you take a seat?'

'I am extremely sorry to be obliged to wake you, my dear fellow,' said his lordship, 'but the fact of the matter is, my secretary, Baxter, has gone off his head.'

'Much?' inquired Psmith, interested.

'He is out in the garden in his pyjamas, throwing flower-pots through my window.'

'Flower-pots?'

'Flower-pots!'

'Oh, flower-pots!' said Psmith, frowning thoughtfully, as if he had expected it would be something else. 'And what steps are you proposing to take? That is to say,' he went on, 'unless you wish him to continue throwing flower-pots.'

'My dear fellow . . .!'

'Some people like it,' explained Psmith. 'But you do not? Quite so, quite so. I understand perfectly. We all have our likes and dislikes. Well, what would you suggest?'

'I was hoping that you might consent to go down – er – having possibly armed yourself with a good stout stick – and induce him to desist and return to bed.'

'A sound suggestion in which I can see no flaw,' said Psmith approvingly. 'If you will make yourself at home in here – pardon me for issuing invitations to you in your own house – I will see what can be done. I have always found Comrade Baxter a reasonable man, ready to welcome suggestions from outside sources, and I have no doubt that we shall easily be able to reach some arrangement.'

He got out of bed, and, having put on his slippers, and his monocle, paused before the mirror to brush his hair.

'For,' he explained, 'one must be natty when entering the presence of a Baxter.'

He went to the closet and took from among a number of hats a neat Homburg. Then, having selected from a bowl of flowers on the mantelpiece a simple white rose, he pinned it in the coat of his pyjama suit and announced himself ready.

5

The sudden freshet of vicious energy which had spurred the Efficient Baxter on to his recent exhibition of marksmanship had not lasted. Lethargy was creeping back on him even as he stooped to pick up the flower-pot which had found its billet on Lord Emsworth's spine. And, as he stood there after hurling that final missile, he had realized that that was his last shot. If that produced no results, he was finished.

And, as far as he could gather, it had produced no results whatever. No head had popped inquiringly out of the window. No sounds of anybody stirring had reached his ears. The place was as still as if he had been throwing marsh-mallows. A weary sigh escaped from Baxter's lips. And a moment later he was reclining on the ground with his head propped against the terrace, a beaten man.

His eyes closed. Sleep, which he had been denying to himself for so long, would be denied no more. When Psmith arrived, daintily swinging the Hon. Freddie Threepwood's niblick like a clouded cane, he had just begun to snore.

Psmith was a kindly soul. He did not like Rupert Baxter, but that was no reason why he should allow him to continue lying on turf wet with the morning dew, thus courting lumbago and sciatica. He prodded Baxter in the stomach with the niblick, and the secretary sat up, blinking. And with returning consciousness came a burning sense of grievance.

'Well, you've been long enough,' he growled. Then, as he rubbed his red-rimmed eyes and was able to see more clearly, he perceived who it was that had come to his rescue. The spectacle of Psmith of all people beaming benignly down at him was an added offence. 'Oh, it's you?' he said morosely.

'I in person,' said Psmith genially. 'Awake, beloved! Awake, for morning in the bowl of night has flung the stone that puts the stars to flight; and lo! the hunter of the East has caught the Sultan's turret in a noose of light. The Sultan himself,' he added, 'you will find behind yonder window, speculating idly on your motives for bunging flower-pots at him. Why, if I may venture the question, *did* you?'

Baxter was in no confiding mood. Without replying, he rose to his feet and started to trudge wearily along the terrace to the front door. Psmith fell into step beside him.

'If I were you,' said Psmith, 'and I offer the suggestion in the most cordial spirit of goodwill, I would use every effort to prevent this passion for flinging flower-pots from growing upon me. I know you will say that you can take it or leave it alone; that just one more pot won't hurt you; but can you stop at one? Isn't it just that first insidious flower-pot that does all the mischief? Be a man, Comrade Baxter!' He laid his hand appealingly on the secretary's shoulder. 'The next time the craving comes on you, fight it. Fight it! Are you, the heir of the ages, going to become a slave to a habit? Tush! You know and I know that there is better stuff in you than that. Use your will-power, man, use your will-power.'

Whatever reply Baxter might have intended to make to this powerful harangue – and his attitude as he turned

on his companion suggested that he had much to say –
was checked by a voice from above.

'Baxter! My dear fellow!'

The Earl of Emsworth, having observed the secretary's
awakening from the safe observation-post of Psmith's
bedroom, and having noted that he seemed to be
exhibiting no signs of violence, had decided to make his
presence known. His panic had passed, and he wanted to
go into first causes.

Baxter gazed wanly up at the window.

'I can explain everything, Lord Emsworth.'

'What?' said his lordship, leaning farther out.

'I can explain everything,' bellowed Baxter.

'It turns out after all,' said Psmith pleasantly, 'to be
very simple. He was practising for the Jerking The
Geranium event at the next Olympic Games.'

Lord Emsworth adjusted his glasses.

'Your face is dirty,' he said, peering down at his
dishevelled secretary. 'Baxter, my dear fellow, your face
is dirty.'

'I was digging,' replied Baxter sullenly.

'What?'

'Digging!'

'The terrier complex,' explained Psmith. 'What,' he
asked kindly, turning to his companion, 'were you
digging for? Forgive me if the question seems an
impertinent one, but we are naturally curious.'

Baxter hesitated.

'What were you digging for?' asked Lord Emsworth.

'You see,' said Psmith. '*He* wants to know.'

Not for the first time since they had become
associated, a mad feeling of irritation at his employer's
woolly persistence flared up in Rupert Baxter's bosom.
The old ass was always pottering about asking questions.
Fury and want of sleep combined to dull the secretary's
normal prudence. Dimly he realized that he was

imparting Psmith, the scoundrel who he was convinced was the ringleader of last night's outrage, valuable information; but anything was better than to have to stand here shouting up at Lord Emsworth. He wanted to get it over and go to bed.

'I thought Lady Constance's necklace was in one of the flower-pots,' he shrilled.

'What?'

The secretary's powers of endurance gave out. This maddening inquisition, coming on top of the restless night he had had, was too much for him. With a low moan he made one agonized leap for the front door and passed through it to where beyond these voices there was peace.

Psmith, deprived thus abruptly of his stimulating society, remained for some moments standing near the front door, drinking in with grave approval the fresh scents of the summer morning. It was many years since he had been up and about as early as this, and he had forgotten how delightful the first beginnings of a July day can be. Unlike Baxter, on whose self-centred soul these things had been lost, he revelled in the soft breezes, the singing birds, the growing pinkness of the eastern sky. He awoke at length from his reverie to find that Lord Emsworth had toddled down and was tapping him on the arm.

'*What* did he say?' inquired his lordship. He was feeling like a man who has been cut off in the midst of an absorbing telephone conversation.

'Say?' said Psmith. 'Oh, Comrade Baxter? Now, let me think. What *did* he say?'

'Something about something being in a flower-pot,' prompted his lordship.

'Ah, yes. He said he thought that Lady Constance's necklace was in one of the flower-pots.'

'What!'

Lord Emsworth, it should be mentioned, was not completely in touch with recent happenings in his home.

His habit of going early to bed had caused him to miss the sensational events in the drawing-room: and, as he was a sound sleeper, the subsequent screams – or, as Stokes the footman would have said, shrieks – had not disturbed him. He stared at Psmith, aghast. For a while the apparent placidity of Baxter had lulled his first suspicions, but now they returned with renewed force.

'Baxter thought my sister's necklace was in a flower-pot?' he gasped.

'So I understood him to say.'

'But why should my sister keep her necklace in a flower-pot?'

'Ah, there you take me into deep waters.'

'The man's mad,' cried Lord Emsworth, his last doubts removed. 'Stark, staring mad! I thought so before, and now I'm convinced of it.'

His lordship was no novice in the symptoms of insanity. Several of his best friends were residing in those palatial establishments set in pleasant parks and surrounded by high walls with broken bottles on them, to which the wealthy and aristocratic are wont to retire when the strain of modern life becomes too great. And one of his uncles by marriage, who believed that he was a loaf of bread, had made his first public statement on the matter in the smoking-room of this very castle. What Lord Emsworth did not know about lunatics was not worth knowing.

'I must get rid of him,' he said. And at the thought the fair morning seemed to Lord Emsworth to take on a sudden new beauty. Many a time had he toyed wistfully with the idea of dismissing his efficient but tyrannical secretary, but never before had that sickeningly competent young man given him any reasonable cause to act. Hitherto, moreover, he had feared his sister's wrath should he take the plunge. But now . . . Surely even Connie, pig-headed as she was, could not blame him for dispensing with the services of a secretary who thought she kept her necklaces in flower-pots, and went out into the garden in the early dawn to hurl them at his bedroom window.

His demeanour took on a sudden buoyancy. He hummed a gay air.

'Get rid of him,' he murmured, rolling the blessed words round his tongue. He patted Psmith genially on the shoulder. 'Well, my dear fellow,' he said, 'I suppose we had better be getting back to bed and seeing if we can't get a little sleep.'

Psmith gave a little start. He had been somewhat deeply immersed in thought.

'Do not,' he said courteously, 'let me keep you from the hay if you wish to retire. To me – you know what we poets are – this lovely morning has brought inspiration. I think I will push off to my little nook in the woods, and write a poem about something.'

He accompanied his host up the silent stairs, and they parted with mutual good will at their respective doors. Psmith, having cleared his brain with a hurried cold bath, began to dress.

As a rule, the donning of his clothes was a solemn ceremony over which he dwelt lovingly; but this morning he abandoned his customary leisurely habit. He climbed into his trousers with animation, and lingered but a moment over the tying of his tie. He was convinced that there was that before him which would pay for haste.

Nothing in this world is sadder than the frequency with which we suspect our fellows without just cause. In the happenings of the night before, Psmith had seen the hand of Edward Cootes. Edward Cootes, he considered, had been indulging in what – in another – he would certainly have described as funny business. Like Miss Simmons, Psmith had quickly arrived at the conclusion that the necklace had been thrown out of the drawing-room window by one of those who made up the audience at his reading: and it was his firm belief that it had been picked up and hidden by Mr Cootes. He had been trying to think ever since where that persevering man could have concealed it, and Baxter had provided the clue. But Psmith saw clearer than Baxter. The secretary, having disembowelled fifteen flower-pots and found nothing, had abandoned his theory. Psmith went further, and suspected the existence of a sixteenth. And he proposed as soon as he was dressed to sally downstairs in search of it.

He put on his shoes, and left the room, buttoning his waistcoat as he went.

6

The hands of the clock over the stables were pointing to half-past five when Eve Halliday, tiptoeing furtively, made another descent of the stairs. Her feelings as she went were very different from those which had caused her to jump at every sound when she had started on this same journey three hours earlier. Then, she had been a prowler in the darkness and, as such, a fitting object of suspicion: now, if she happened to run into anybody, she was merely a girl who, unable to sleep, had risen early to take a stroll in the garden. It was a distinction that made all the difference.

Moreover, it covered the facts. She had not been able to sleep – except for an hour when she had dozed off in a chair by her window; and she certainly proposed to take a stroll in the garden. It was her intention to recover the necklace from the place where she had deposited it, and bury it somewhere where no one could possibly find it. There it could lie until she had a chance of meeting and talking to Mr Keeble, and ascertaining what was the next step he wished taken.

Two reasons had led Eve, after making her panic dash back into the house after lurking in the bushes while Baxter patrolled the terrace, to leave her precious flower-pot on the sill of the window beside the front door. She had read in stories of sensation that for purposes of concealment the most open place is the best place: and, secondly, the nearer the front door she put the flower-pot, the less distance would she have to carry it when the time came for its removal. In the present excited conditions of the household, with every guest an amateur detective, the spectacle of a girl tripping downstairs with a flower-pot in her arms would excite remark.

Eve felt exhilarated. She was not used to getting only one hour's sleep in the course of a night, but excitement and the reflection that she had played a difficult game and won it against odds bore her up so strongly that she was not conscious of fatigue: and so uplifted did she feel that as she reached the landing above the hall she abandoned her cautious mode of progress and ran down the remaining stairs. She had the sensation of being in the last few yards of a winning race.

The hall was quite light now. Every object in it was plainly visible. There was the huge dinner-gong: there was the long leather settee: there was the table which she had upset in the darkness. And there was the sill of the window by the front door. But the flower-pot which had been on it was gone.

The Drones

1 — Bingo and the Peke Crisis

A Bean was showing his sore legs to some Eggs and Piefaces in the smoking-room of the Drones Club, when a Crumpet came in. Having paused at the bar to order an Annie's Night Out, he made his way to the group.

'What,' he asked, 'is the trouble?'

It was a twice – or even more than that – told tale, but the Bean embarked upon it without hesitation.

'That ass Bingo Little. Called upon me at my residence the day before yesterday with a ravening Pekinese, and tried to land me with it.'

'Said he had brought it as a birthday present,' added one of the Eggs.

'That was his story,' assented the Bean. 'It doesn't hold water for an instant. It was not my birthday. And if it had been, he should have been well enough acquainted with my psychology to know that I wouldn't want a blasted, man-eating Peke with teeth like needles and a disposition that led it to take offence at the merest trifle. Scarcely had I started to deflect the animal to the door, when it turned like a flash and nipped me in the calf. And if I hadn't had the presence of mind to leap on to a table, the outcome might have been even more serious. Look!' said the Bean. 'A nasty flesh wound.'

The Crumpet patted his shoulder and, giving as his reason the fact that he was shortly about to lunch, asked the other to redrape the limb.

'I don't wonder that the episode has left you in something of a twitter,' he said. 'But I am in a position to give you a full explanation. I saw Bingo last night, and he told me all. And when you have heard the story, you will, I feel sure, agree with me that he is more to be pitied than censured. *Tout comprendre,'* said the Crumpet, who had taken French at school, *'c'est tout pardonner.'*

You are all, he proceeded, more or less familiar with Bingo's circumstances, and I imagine that you regard him as one of those rare birds who are absolutely on velvet. He eats well, sleeps well and is happily married to a charming girl well provided with the stuff – Rosie M. Banks, the popular female novelist, to wit – and life for him, you feel, must be one grand, sweet song.

But it seems to be the rule in this world that though you may have goose, it is never pure goose. In the most apparently Grade A ointment there is always a fly. In Bingo's case it is the fact that he seldom, if ever, has in his possession more than the merest cigarette money. Mrs Bingo seems to feel that it is best that this should be so. She is aware of his fondness for backing horses which, if they finish at all, come in modestly at the tail of the procession, and she deprecates it. A delightful girl – one of the best, and the tree, as you might say, on which the fruit of Bingo's life hangs – she is deficient in sporting blood.

So on the morning on which this story begins it was in rather sombre mood that he seated himself at the breakfast-table and speared a couple of eggs and a rasher of ham. Mrs Bingo's six Pekes frolicked about his chair, but he ignored their civilities. He was thinking how bitter it was that he should have an absolute snip for the two o'clock at Hurst Park that afternoon and no means of cashing in on it. For his bookie, a man who seemed never to have heard of the words 'Service and Co-operation', had informed him some time back that he was no longer prepared to accept mere charm of manner as a substitute for money down in advance.

He had a shot, of course, at bracing the little woman

for a trifle, but without any real hope of accomplishing anything constructive. He is a chap who knows when he is chasing rainbows.

'I suppose, my dear old in-sickness-and-in-health-er,' he began diffidently, 'you wouldn't care for me to make a little cash for jam today?'

'How do you mean?' said Mrs Bingo who was opening letters behind the coffee apparatus.

'Well, it's like this. There's a horse – '

'No, precious, you know I don't like you to bet.'

'I would hardly call this betting. Just reaching out and gathering in the stuff is more the way I would describe it. This horse, you see, is called Pimpled Charlie – '

'What an odd name.'

'Most peculiar. And when I tell you that last night I dreamed that I was rowing in a boat on the fountain in Trafalgar Square with Oofy Prosser, you will see its extraordinary significance.'

'Why?'

'Oofy's name,' said Bingo in a low, grave voice, 'is Alexander Charles, and what we were talking about in the boat was whether he ought not to present his collection of pimples to the nation.'

Mrs Bingo laughed a silvery laugh.

'You *are* silly!' she said indulgently, and Bingo knew that hope, never robust, must now be considered dead. If this was the attitude she proposed to take towards what practically amounted to a divine revelation, there was little to be gained by pursuing the subject. He cheesed it, accordingly, and the conversation turned to the prospects of Mrs Bingo having a fine day for her journey. For this morning she was beetling off to Bognor Regis to spend a couple of weeks with her mother.

And he had just returned to his meditations after dealing with this topic, when he was jerked out of them by a squeal of ecstasy from behind the coffee-pot, so piercing in its timbre that it dislodged half an egg from

his fork. He looked up and saw that Mrs Bingo was
brandishing a letter, beaming the while like billy-o.

'Oh, sweetie-pie,' she cried, for it is in this fashion that
she often addresses him, 'I've heard from Mr Purkiss!'

'This Purkiss being who?'

'You've never met him. He's an old friend of mine. He
lives quite near here. He owns a children's magazine
called *Wee Tots*.'

'So what?' said Bingo, still about six parasangs from
getting the gist.

'I didn't like to tell you before, darling, for fear it might
not come to anything, but some time ago he happened
to mention to me that he was looking out for a new editor
for *Wee Tots*, and I asked him to try you. I told him you
had had no experience, of course, but I said you were
awfully clever, and he would be there to guide you, and
so on. Well, he said he would think it over, but that his
present idea was to make a nephew of his the editor. But
now I've had this letter from him, saying that the nephew
has been county-courted by his tailor, and this has made
Mr Purkiss think his nature is too frivolous, and he wants
to see you and have a talk. Oh, Bingo, I'm sure he
means to give you the job.'

Bingo had to sit for a moment to let this sink in. Then
he rose and kissed Mrs Bingo tenderly.

'My little helpmeet!' he said.

He was extraordinarily bucked. The appointment, he
presumed, carried with it something in the nature of a
regular salary, and a regular salary was what he had been
wanting for years. Judiciously laid out on those tips from
above which he so frequently got in the night watches,
he felt, such a stipend could speedily be built up into a
vast fortune. And, even apart from the sordid angle, the
idea of being an editor, with all an editor's unexampled
opportunities for putting on dog and throwing his weight
about, enchanted him. He looked forward with a bright
enthusiasm to getting fellow-members of the Drones to

send in contributions to the Kiddies' Korner, and then bunging them back as not quite up to his standard.

'He has been staying with his wife with an aunt at Tunbridge Wells, and he is coming back this morning, and he wants you to meet him under the clock at Charing Cross at twelve. Can you be there?'

'I can,' said Bingo. 'And not only there, but there with my hair in a braid.'

'You will be able to recognize him, he says, because he will be wearing a grey tweed suit and a Homburg hat.'

'I,' said Bingo, with a touch of superiority, 'shall be in a morning coat and the old topper.'

Once again he kissed Mrs Bingo, even more tenderly than before. And pretty soon after that it was time for her to climb aboard the car which was to take her to Bognor Regis. He saw her off at the front door, and there were unshed tears in her eyes as she made her farewells. For the poignancy of departure was intensified by the fact that, her mother's house being liberally staffed with cats, she was leaving the six Pekes behind her.

'Take care of them while I'm away,' she murmured brokenly, as the animals barged into the car and got shot out again by Bagshaw, the butler. 'You will look after them, won't you, darling?'

'Like a father,' said Bingo. 'Their welfare shall be my constant concern.'

And he spoke sincerely. He liked those Pekes. His relations with them had always been based on a mutual affection and esteem. They licked his face, he scratched their stomachs. Pleasant give and take, each working for each.

'Don't forget to give them their coffee-sugar every night.'

'Trust me,' said Bingo, 'to the death.'

'And call in at Boddington and Biggs's for Ping-Poo's harness. They are mending it. Oh, and by the way,' said Mrs Bingo, opening her bag and producing currency, 'when you go to Boddington and Biggs, will you pay their bill. It will save me writing out a cheque.'

She slipped him a couple of fivers, embraced him fondly and drove off, leaving him waving on the front steps.

I mention this fact of his waving particularly, because it has so important a bearing on what followed. You cannot wave a hand with a couple of fivers in it without them crackling. And a couple of fivers cannot crackle in the hand of a man who has received direct information from an authoritative source that a seven-to-one shot is going to win the two o'clock race at Hurst Park without starting in his mind a certain train of thought. The car was scarcely out of sight before the Serpent had raised its head in this Garden of Eden – the Little home was one of those houses that stand in spacious grounds along the edge of Wimbledon Common – and was whispering in Bingo's ear: 'How about it, old top?'

Now at ordinary times and in normal circumstances, Bingo is, of course, the soul of honesty and would never dream of diverting a Bond Street firm's legitimate earnings into more private and personal channels. But here, the Serpent pointed out, and Bingo agreed with him, was plainly a special case.

There could be no question, argued the Serpent, of doing down Boddington and Biggs. That could be dismissed right away. All it meant, if Bingo deposited these fivers with his bookie, to go on Pimpled Charlie's nose for the two o'clock, was that Boddington and his boy-friend would collect tomorrow instead of today. For if by some inconceivable chance Pimpled Charlie failed to click, all he, Bingo, had to do was to ask for a small advance on his salary from Mr Purkiss, who by that time would have become his employer. Probably, said the Serpent, Purkiss would himself suggest some such arrangement. He pointed out to Bingo that it was not likely that he would have much difficulty in fascinating the man. Quite apart from the morning coat and the

sponge-bag trousers, that topper of his was bound to
exercise a spell. Once let Purkiss get a glimpse of it, and
there would be very little sales-resistance from him. The
thing, in short, was as good as in the bag.

It was with the lightest of hearts, accordingly, that Bingo
proceeded to London an hour later, lodged the necessary
with his bookie, whose office was in Oxford Street, and
sauntered along to Charing Cross Station, arriving under
the clock as its hands pointed to five minutes to twelve.
And promptly at the hour a stout elderly man in a grey
tweed suit and a Homburg hat rolled up.

The following conversation then took place.

'Mr Little?'

'How do you do?'

'How do you do? Lovely day.'

'Beautiful.'

'You are punctual, Mr Little.'

'I always am.'

'A very admirable trait.'

'What ho!'

And it was at this moment, just as everything was
going as smooth as syrup and Bingo could see the awe
and admiration burgeoning in his companion's eyes as
they glued themselves on the topper, that out of the
refreshment-room, wiping froth from his lips, came
B. B. Tucker, Gents' Hosier and Bespoke Shirt Maker, of
Bedford Street, Strand, to whom for perhaps a year and a
quarter Bingo had owed three pounds, eleven and
fourpence for goods supplied.

It just shows you how mental exhilaration can destroy
a man's clear, cool judgement. When this idea of meeting
under the clock at Charing Cross had been mooted, Bingo,
all above himself at the idea of becoming editor of a
powerful organ for the chicks, had forgotten prudence
and right-hoed without a second thought. It was only
now that he realized what madness it had been to allow

himself to be lured within a mile of Charing Cross. The
locality was literally stiff with shops where in his
bachelor days he had run up little accounts, and you
never knew when the proprietors of these shops were not
going to take it into their heads, as B. B. Tucker had plainly
done, to step round to the station refreshment-room for
a quick one.

He was appalled. He knew how lacking in tact and
savoir-faire men like B. B. Tucker are. When they see an
old patron chatting with a friend, they do not just nod
and smile and pass by. They come right up and start
talking about how a settlement would oblige, and all that
sort of rot. And if Purkiss was the sort of person who
shrank in horror from nephews who got county-courted
by their tailors, two minutes of B. B. Tucker, Bingo felt,
would undo the whole effect of the topper.

And the next moment, just as Bingo had anticipated,
up he came.

'Oh, Mr Little,' he began.

It was a moment for the swiftest action. There was a
porter's truck behind Bingo, and most people would have
resigned themselves to the fact that retreat was cut off.
But Bingo was made of sterner stuff.

'Well, good-bye, Purkiss,' he said, and, springing
lightly over the truck, was gone with the wind. Setting
a course for the main entrance, he passed out of the station
at a good rate of speed and was presently in the
Embankment gardens. There he remained until he
considered that B. B. Tucker had had time to blow over,
after which he returned to the old spot under the clock,
in order to resume his conference with Purkiss at the
point where it had been broken off.

Well, in one respect, everything was fine because
B. B. Tucker had disappeared. But in another respect the
posish was not so good. Purkiss also had legged it. He had
vanished like snow off a mountain-top, and after pacing
up and down for half an hour Bingo was forced to the

conclusion that he wasn't coming back. Purkiss had called it a day? Now that he had leisure to think, he remembered that as he had hurdled the truck he had seen the man shoot an odd glance at him, and it occurred to him that Purkiss might have gone off thinking him a bit eccentric. He feared the worst. An aspirant to an editorial chair, he knew, does not win to success by jumping over trucks in the presence of his prospective proprietor.

Moodily, he went off and had a spot of lunch, and he was just getting outside his coffee when the result of the two o'clock came through on the tape. Pimpled Charlie had failed to finish in the first three. Providence, in other words, when urging him to put his chemise on the animal, had been pulling his leg. It was not the first time that this had happened.

And by the afternoon post next day there arrived a letter from Purkiss which proved that his intuition had not deceived him. He read it, and tore it into a hundred pieces. Or so he says. Eight, more likely. For it was the raspberry. Purkiss, wrote Purkiss, had given the matter his consideration and had decided to make other arrangements with regard to the editorship of *Wee Tots*.

To say that Bingo was distrait as he dined that night would not be to overstate the facts. There was, he could see, a lot which he was going to find it difficult to explain to Mrs Bingo on her return, and it was not, moreover, going to be any too dashed good when he had explained it. She would not be pleased about the ten quid. That alone would cast a cloud upon the home. Add the revelation that he had mucked up his chance of becoming Ye Ed., and you might say that the home would be more or less in the melting-pot.

And so, as I say, he was distrait. The six Pekes accompanied him into the library and sat waiting for their coffee-sugar, but he was too preoccupied to do the square thing by the dumb chums. His whole intellect was riveted on the problem of how to act for the best.

And then – gradually – he didn't know what first put the idea into his head – it began to steal over Bingo that there was something peculiar about these six Pekes.

It was not in their appearance or behaviour. They looked the same as usual, and they behaved the same as usual. It was something subtler than that. And then, suddenly, like a wallop on the base of the skull, it came to him.

There were only five of them.

Now, to the lay mind, the fact that in a house containing six Pekes only five had rolled up at coffee-sugar-time would not have seemed so frightfully sinister. The other one is off somewhere about its domestic duties, the lay mind would have said – burying a bone, taking a refreshing nap, or something of the sort. But Bingo knew Pekes. Their psychology was an open book to him. And he was aware that if only five of them had clustered round when there was coffee-sugar going, there could be only five on the strength. The sixth must be A.W.O.L.

He had been stirring his coffee when he made the discovery, and the spoon fell from his nerveless fingers. He gazed at the Shape Of Things To Come, all of a doodah.

This was the top. He could see that. Everything else was by comparison trifling, even the trousering of Boddington and Biggs's ten quid. Mrs Bingo loved these Pekes. She had left them with him as a sacred charge. And at the thought of what would ensue when the time came for him to give an account of his stewardship and he had to confess that he was in the red, imagination boggled. There would be tears . . . reproaches . . . oh-how-could-you's . . . Why, dash it, felt Bingo, with a sudden start that nearly jerked his eyeballs out of their sockets, it was quite possible that, taking a line through that unfortunate ten quid business, she might even go

so far as to suppose that he had snitched the missing
animal and sold it for gold.

Shuddering strongly, he leaped from his chair and rang
the bell. He wished to confer with Bagshaw and learn if
by any chance the absentee was down in the kitchen. But
Bagshaw was out for the evening. A parlour maid
answered the bell, and when she had informed him that
the downstairs premises were entirely free from Pekes,
Bingo uttered a hollow groan, grabbed his hat and started
out for a walk on Wimbledon Common. There was just
a faint chance – call it a hundred to eight – that the little
blighter might have heard the call of the wild and was
fooling about somewhere out in the great open spaces.

How long he wandered, peering about him and uttering
chirruping noises, he could not have said, but it was a
goodish time, and his rambles took him far afield. He had
halted for a moment in quite unfamiliar territory to light
a cigarette, and was about to give up the search, and totter
home, when suddenly he stiffened in every limb and
stood goggling, the cigarette frozen on his lips.

For there, just ahead of him in the gathering dusk, he
had perceived a bloke of butlerine aspect. And this butler,
if butler he was, was leading on a leash a Peke so identical
with Mrs Bingo's gang that it could have been signed
up with the troupe without exciting any suspicions
whatever. Pekes, as you are probably aware, are either
beige and hairy or chestnut and hairy. Mrs Bingo's were
chestnut and hairy.

The sight brought new life to Bingo. His razor-like
intelligence had been telling him for some time that the
only possible solution of the impasse was to acquire
another Peke and add it to the strength, and the snag
about that was, of course, that Pekes cost money – and of
money at the moment he possessed but six shillings and
a little bronze.

His first impulse was to leap upon this butler and
choke the animal out of him with his bare hands. Wiser

counsels, however, prevailed, and he contented himself with trailing the man like one of those fellows you read about who do not let a single twig snap beneath their feet. And presently the chap left the Common and turned into a quiet sort of road and finished up by going through a gate into the garden of a sizeable house. And Bingo, humming nonchalantly, walked on past till he came to some shops. He was looking for a grocer's and eventually he found one and, going in, invested a portion of his little capital in a piece of cheese, instructing the man behind the counter to give him the ripest and breeziest he had in stock.

For Bingo, as I said before, knew Pekes, and he was aware that, while they like chicken, are fond of suet pudding and seldom pass up a piece of milk chocolate if it comes their way, what they will follow to the ends of the earth and sell their souls for is cheese. And it was his intention to conceal himself in the garden till the moment of the animal's nightly airing, and then come out and make a dicker with it by means of the slab which he had just purchased.

Ten minutes later, accordingly, he was squatting in a bush, waiting for zero hour.

It is not a vigil to which he cares to look back. The experience of sitting in a bush in a strange garden, unable to smoke and with no company but your thoughts and a niffy piece of cheese, is a testing one. Ants crawled up his legs, beetles tried to muscle in between his collar and his neck, and others of God's creatures, taking advantage of the fact that he had lost his hat, got in his hair. But eventually his resolution was rewarded. A french window was thrown open, and the Peke came trotting out into the pool of light from the lamps within, followed by a stout, elderly man. And conceive Bingo's emotion when he recognized in this stout, elderly exhibit none other than old Pop Purkiss.

The sight of him was like a tonic. Until this moment

Bingo had not been altogether free from those things of Conscience . . . not psalms . . . yes, qualms. He had had qualms about the lay-out. From time to time there crept over him a certain commiseration for the bloke whose household pet he was about to swipe. A bit tough on the poor bounder, he had felt. These qualms now vanished. After the way he had let him down, Purkiss had forfeited all claim to pity. He was a man who deserved to be stripped of every Peke in his possession.

The question, however, that exercised Bingo a bit at this juncture was how was this stripping to be done. If it was the man's intention to follow hard on the animal's heels till closing time, it was difficult to see how he was to be de-Peked without detection.

But his luck was in. Purkiss had apparently been entertaining himself with a spot of music on the radio, for when he emerged it was playing a gay rumba. And now, as radios do, it suddenly broke off in the middle, gave a sort of squawk and began to talk German. And Purkiss turned back to fiddle with it.

It gave Bingo just the time he needed. He was out of the bush in a jiffy, like a leopard bounding from its lair. There was one anxious moment when the Peke drew back with raised eyebrows and a good deal of that To-what-am-I-indebted-for-this-visit stuff, but fortunately the scent of the cheese floated to its nostrils before it could utter more than a *sotto voce* whoofle, and from then on everything went with a swing. Half a minute later, Bingo was tooling along the road with the Peke in his arms. And eventually he reached the Common, struck a spot which he recognized and pushed home.

Mrs Bingo's Pekes were all in bed when he got there, and when he went and sprang the little stranger on them he was delighted with the ready affability with which they made him one of themselves. Too often, when you introduce a ringer into a gaggle of Pekes, there ensues a scrap like New Year's Eve in Madrid; but tonight, after a certain amount of tentative sniffing, the home team issued their O.K., and he left them all curled up in their baskets like so many members of the Athenaeum. He then went off to the library, and rang the bell. He wished, if Bagshaw had returned, to take up with him the matter of a stiff whisky and soda.

Bagshaw had returned, all right. He appeared, looking much refreshed from his evening out, and biffed off and fetched the fixings. And it was as he was preparing to depart that he said:

'Oh, about the little dog, sir.'

Bingo gave a jump that nearly upset his snifter.

'Dog?' he said, in his emotion putting in about five d's at the beginning of the word. 'What dog?' he said, inserting about seven w's in the 'what'.

'Little Wing-Fu, sir. I was unable to inform you earlier, as you were not in the house when Mrs Little's message arrived. Mrs Little telephoned shortly after luncheon, instructing me to send Wing-Fu by rail to Bognor Regis Station. It appears that there is an artist gentleman residing in the vicinity who paints animals' portraits, and Mrs Little wished to have Wing-Fu's likeness done. I dispatched the little fellow in a hamper, and on my return to the house found a telegram announcing his safe arrival. It occurred to me that I had better mention the matter to you, as it might have caused you some anxiety, had you chanced to notice that one of the dogs was missing. Good night, sir,' said Bagshaw, and popped off.

He left Bingo, as you may well suppose, chafing quite a goodish deal. Thanks to Mrs Bingo's lack of a sense of what was fitting having led her to conduct these operations through an underling instead of approaching him, Bingo, in her absence the head of the house, he had imperilled his social standing by becoming a dogstealer. And all for nothing.

Remembering the agonies he had gone through in that bush – not only spiritual because of the qualms of

310

conscience, but physical because of the ants, the beetles
and the unidentified fauna which had got in his hair,
you can't blame him for being pretty sick about the whole
thing. He had a sense of grievance. Why, he asked, had he
not been informed of what was going on? Was he a cipher?
And, anyway, where was the sense of pandering to Wing-
Fu's vanity by having his portrait painted? He was quite
sidey enough already.

And the worst of it was that though he could see that
everything now pointed to some swift, statesmanlike
move on his part, he was dashed if he could think of one.
It was in a pretty dark mood that he swallowed a second
snort and trudged up to bed.

But there's nothing like sleeping on a thing. He got the
solution in his bath next morning. He saw that it was
all really quite simple. All he had to do was to take
Purkiss's Peke back to the Purkiss shack, slip it in
through the garden gate, and there he would be, quit of
the whole unpleasant affair.

And it was only when towelling himself after the tub
that he suddenly realized that he didn't know the name
of Purkiss's house – not even the name of the road it was
in – and that he had tacked to and fro so assiduously on
his return journey that he couldn't possibly find his way
back to it.

And, what was worse, for it dished the idea of looking
him up in the telephone book, he couldn't remember
Purkiss's name.

Oh, yes, he knows it now, all right. It is graven on his
heart. If you stopped him on the street today and said, 'Oh,
by the way, Bingo, what is the name of the old blister who
owns *Wee Tots*?' he would reply like a flash: 'Henry
Cuthbert Purkiss.' But at that moment it had clean gone.
You know how it is with names. Well, when I tell you
that during breakfast he was convinced that it was
Winterbottom and that by lunch-time he had switched
to Benjafield, you will see how far the evil had spread.

And, as you will recall, his only documentary evidence no longer existed. With a peevishness which he now regretted, he had torn the fellow's letter into a hundred pieces. Or at least eight.

At this juncture, Bingo Little was a broken man.

Stripping the thing starkly down to its bare bones, he saw that the scenario was as follows. Mrs Bingo was a woman with six Pekes. When she returned from Bognor Regis, she would be a woman with seven Pekes. And his knowledge of human nature told him that the first thing a six-Peke woman does, on discovering that she has suddenly become a seven-Peke woman, is to ask questions. And to those questions what would be his answer?

It would, he was convinced, be perfectly useless for him to try to pretend that the extra incumbent was one which he had bought her as a surprise during her absence. Mrs Bingo was no fool. She knew that he was not a man who frittered away his slender means buying people Pekes. She would consider the story thin. She would institute inquiries. And those inquiries must in the end lead her infallibly to this Winterbottom, or Benjafield, or whatever his name was.

It seemed to Bingo that there was only one course open to him. He must find the stowaway a comfortable home elsewhere, completely out of the Benjafield-Winterbottom zone, and he must do it immediately.

So now you understand why the poor old bird called upon you that day with the animal. And, as I said, you will probably agree that he was more to be p. than c. In this connection, he has authorized me to say that he is prepared to foot all bills for sticking-plaster, arnica, the Pasteur treatment and what not.

After your refusal to hold the baby, he appears to have lost heart. I gather that the scene was a painful one, and he did not feel like repeating it. Returning home, he decided that there was nothing to be done but somehow to dig up that name. So shortly after lunch he summoned Bagshaw to his presence.

'Bagshaw,' he said, 'mention some names.'

'Names, sir?'

'Yes. You know. Like people have. I am trying to remember a man's name, and it eludes me. I have an idea,' said Bingo, who had now begun to veer towards Jellaby, 'that it begins with a J.'

Bagshaw mused.

'J, sir?'

'Yes.'

'Smith?' said the ass.

'Not Smith,' said Bingo. 'And if you mean Jones, it's not as common as that. Rather a bit on the exotic side it struck me as, when I heard it. As it might be Jerningham or Jorkins. However, in supposing that it begins with a J, I may quite easily be mistaken. Try the A's.'

'Adams, sir? Allen? Ackworth? Anderson? Arkwright? Aarons? Abercrombie?'

'Switch to the B's.'

'Bates? Bulstrode? Burgess? Bellinger? Biggs? Bultitude?'

'Now do me a few C's.'

'Collins? Clegg? Clutterbuck? Carthew? Curley? Cabot? Cade? Cackett? Cahill? Caffrey? Cahn? Cain? Caird? Cannon? Carter? Casey? Cooley? Cuthbertson? Cope? Cork? Crowe? Cramp? Croft? Crewe? . . .'

A throbbing about the temples told Bingo that in his enfeebled state he had had enough of this. He was just waving a hand to indicate this, when the butler, carried along by his momentum, added:

'Cruickshank? Chalmers? Cutmore? Carpenter? Cheffins? Carr? Cartwright? Cadwallader?'

And something seemed to go off in Bingo's brain like a spring.

'Cadwallader!'

'Is that the gentleman's name, sir?'

'No,' said Bingo. 'But it'll do.'

He had suddenly recalled that Cadwallader was the name of the grocer from whom he had purchased the cheese. Starting from that grocer's door, he was pretty sure that he could find his way to Chez Purkiss. His position was clear. Cadwallader ho! was the watchword.

The prudent thing, of course, would have been to postpone the expedition until darkness had fallen, for it is under cover of night that these delicate operations are best performed. But at this season of the year, what with summertime and all that, darkness fell so dashed late, and he was all keyed up for rapid action. Refreshing his memory with another look at Cadwallader's address in the telephone book, he set out in the cool of the evening, hope in his heart and the Peke under his arm. And presently he found himself on familiar ground. Here was Cadwallader's grocery establishment, there was the road down which he had sauntered, and there a few moments later was the box hedge that fringed the Purkiss's domain and the gate through which he had entered.

He opened the gate, shoved the Peke in, bade it a brief farewell and legged it. And so home, arriving there shortly before six.

As he passed into the Little domain, he was feeling in some respects like a murderer who has at last succeeded in getting rid of the body and in other respects like Shadrach, Meshach and Abednego on emerging from the burning fiery furnace. It was as if a great load had been lifted from him. Once, he tells me, in the days of his boyhood, while enjoying a game of football at school, he was compelled in pursuance of his duties to fall on the ball and immediately afterwards became the base of a sort of pyramid consisting of himself and eight beefy members of the opposing team with sharp elbows and cleated boots. Even after all these years, he says, he can still recall the sense of buoyancy and relief when this mass of humanity eventually removed itself from the small of his back. He was feeling the same relief and buoyancy now. I don't know if he actually sang, but I shouldn't be at all surprised if he didn't attempt a roundelay or two.

Bingo, like Jonah, is one of those fellows who always come up smiling. You may crush him to earth, but he will rise again. Resilient is, I believe, the word. And he now found the future, if not actually bright, at least beginning to look for the first time more or less fit for human consumption. Mistily, but growing every moment more solid, there had begun to shape itself in his mind a story which might cover that business of the Boddington and Biggs ten quid. The details wanted a bit of polishing, but the broad, basic structure was there. As for the episode at Charing Cross Station, there he proposed to stick to stout denial. It might or might not get by. It was at least worth trying. And, in any event, he was now straight on the Peke situation.

Walking on the tips of his toes with his hat on the side of his head, Bingo drew near to the house. And it was at this point that something brushed against his leg with a cheery gurgle and, looking down, he saw that it was the Peke. Having conceived a warm regard for Bingo, and taking advantage of the fact that he had omitted to close the Purkiss's gate, it had decided to toddle along with him.

And while Bingo stood rooted to the spot, staring wanly at the adhesive animal, along came Bagshaw.

'Might I inquire, sir,' said Bagshaw, 'if you happen to know the telephone number of the house at which Mrs Little is temporarily residing?'

'Why?' asked Bingo absently, his gaze still gummed to the Peke.

'Mrs Little's friend, Mr Purkiss, called a short while back desirous of obtaining information. He was anxious to telephone to Mrs Little.'

The wanness with which Bingo had been staring at the Peke was as nothing compared to the wanness with which he now stared at the butler. With the mention of that name, memory had returned to him, sweeping away all the Jellabys and Winterbottoms which had been clogging up his thought processes.

'Purkiss?' he cried, tottering on his base. 'Did you say Purkiss?'

'Yes, sir.'

'He has been calling here?'

'Yes, sir.'

'He wanted to telephone to Mrs Little?'

'Yes, sir.'

'Did he . . . did Mr Purkiss . . . Had he . . . Had Mr Purkiss . . . Did Mr Purkiss convey the impression of having something on his mind?'

'Yes, sir.'

'He appeared agitated?'

'Yes, sir.'

'You gathered . . . you inferred that he had some urgent communication to make to Mrs Little?'

'Yes, sir.'

Bingo drew a deep breath.

'Bagshaw,' he said, 'bring me a whisky and soda. A large whisky and soda. One with not too much soda in it, but with the whisky stressed. In fact, practically leave the soda out altogether.'

He needed the restorative badly, and when it came lost no time in introducing it into his system. The more he contemplated Purkiss's call, the more darkly sinister did it seem to him.

Purkiss had wanted to telephone to Mrs Bingo. He had appeared agitated. Facts like these were capable of but one interpretation. Bingo remembered the hat which he had left somewhere in the bush. Obviously, Purkiss must have found that hat, observed the initials in its band, leaped to the truth and was now trying to get hold of Mrs Bingo to pour the whole story into her receptive ear.

There was only one thing to be done. Bingo shrank from doing it, but he could see that he had no other alternative. He must seek Purkiss out, explain all the circumstances and throw himself on his mercy, begging him as a sportsman and a gentleman to keep the whole thing under his hat. And what was worrying him was a grave doubt as to whether Purkiss was a sportsman and a gentleman. He had not much liked the man's looks on the occasion of their only meeting. It seemed to him, recalling that meeting, that Purkiss had had the appearance of an austere sort of bird, with that cold, distant look in his eyes which he, Bingo, had often seen in those of his bookie when he was trying to get him to let the settlement stand over till a week from Wednesday.

However, the thing had to be done, and he set forth to do it. He made his way to the Purkiss's home, and the butler conducted him to the drawing-room.

'Mr Little,' he announced, and left him. And Bingo braced himself for the ordeal before him.

He could see at a glance that Purkiss was not going to be an easy audience. There was in his manner nothing of the genial host greeting the welcome popper-in. He had been standing with his back turned, looking out of the open french window, and he spun round with sickening rapidity and fixed Bingo with a frightful stare. A glare of loathing, Bingo diagnosed it as – the natural loathing of a ratepayer who sees before him the bloke who has recently lured away his Peke with cheese. And he felt that it would be necessary for him, if anything in the nature of a happy ending was to be arrived at, to be winning and spell-binding as never before.

'Well?' said Purkiss.

Bingo started to make a manly clean breast of it without preamble.

'I've come about that Peke,' he said.

And at that moment, before he could say another word, there barged down his windpipe, wiping speech from his lips and making him cough like the dickens, some foreign substance which might have been a fly – or a gnat – or possibly a small moth. And while he was coughing he saw Purkiss give a sort of despairing gesture.

'I was expecting this,' he said.

Bingo went on coughing.

'Yes,' said Purkiss, 'I feared it. You are quite right. I stole the dog.'

Bingo had more or less dealt with the foreign substance by this time, but he still couldn't speak. Astonishment held him dumb. Purkiss was looking like somebody in a movie caught with the goods. He was no longer glaring. There was a dull, hopeless agony in his eyes.

'You are a married man, Mr Little,' he said, 'so perhaps you will understand. My wife has gone to stay with an ailing aunt at Tunbridge Wells. Shortly before she left, she bought a Pekinese dog. This she entrusted to my care, urging me on no account ever to allow it out of the house except on a lead. Last night, as the animal was merely going to step out into the garden for a few moments, I omitted the precaution. I let it run out by itself. I never saw it again.'

He gulped a bit. Bingo breathed heavily a bit. He resumed.

'It was gone, and I saw that my only course was immediately to secure a substitute of similar appearance. I spent the whole of today going round the dog-shops of London, but without avail. And then I remembered that Mrs Little owned several of these animals – all, as I recalled, singularly like the one I had lost. I thought she might possibly consent to sell me one of them.'

He sighed somewhat.

'This evening,' he went on, 'I called at your house, to find that she was away and that I could not reach her by telephone. And it would be useless to write to her, for my

wife returns tomorrow. So I turned away, and as I reached
the gate something jumped against my leg. It was a
Pekinese dog, Mr Little, and the very image of the one I
had lost. The temptation was too great . . .'

'You pinched it?' cried Bingo, shocked.

Purkiss nodded. Bingo clicked his tongue.

'A bit thick, Purkiss,' he said gravely.

'I know, I know. I am fully conscious of the
heinousness of what I did. My only excuse must be that
I was unaware that I was being observed.' He heaved
another sigh. 'The animal is in the kitchen,' he said,
'enjoying a light supper. I will ring for the butler to bring
it to you. And what my wife is going to say, I shudder to
think,' said Purkiss, doing so.

'You fancy that she will be upset when she returns and
finds no Peke to call her Mother?'

'I do, indeed.'

'Then, Purkiss,' said Bingo, slapping him on the
shoulder, 'keep this animal.'

He likes to think of himself at that moment. He was
suave, kindly, full of sweetness and light. He rather
imagines that Purkiss must have thought he had run up
against an angel in human shape or something.

'Keep it?'

'Definitely.'

'But Mrs Little – ?'

'Have no concern. My wife doesn't know from one day
to another how many Pekes she's got. Just so long as
there is a reasonable contingent messing about, she is
satisfied. Besides,' said Bingo, with quiet reproach, 'she
will have far too much on her mind, when she gets back,
to worry about Pekes. You see, Purkiss, she had set her
heart on my becoming editor of *Wee Tots*. She will be
distressed when she learns of your attitude in that
matter. You know what women are.'

Purkiss coughed. He looked at Bingo, and quivered a
bit. Then he looked at him again, and quivered a bit

more. Bingo received the impression that some sort of spiritual struggle was proceeding within him.

'Do you *want* to edit *Wee Tots*, Mr Little?' he said at length.

'I do, indeed.'

'You're sure?'

'Quite sure?'

'I should have thought that a young man in your position would have been too busy, too occupied – '

'Oh, no. I could have fitted it in.'

A touch of hope came into Purkiss's manner.

'The work is hard.'

'No doubt I shall have capable assistants.'

'The salary,' said Purkiss wistfully, 'is not large.'

'I'll tell you what,' said Bingo, inspired. 'Make it larger.'

Purkiss took another look, and quivered for the third time. Then his better self triumphed.

'I shall be delighted,' he said in a low voice, 'if you will assume the editorship of *Wee Tots*.'

Bingo patted him on the shoulder once more.

'Splendid, Purkiss,' he said. 'Capital. And now, in the matter of a small advance of salary . . .'

2 — The Amazing Hat Mystery

A Bean was in a nursing-home with a broken leg as a result of trying to drive his sports-model Poppenheim through the Marble Arch instead of round it, and a kindly Crumpet had looked in to give him the gossip of the town. He found him playing halma with the nurse, and he sat down on the bed and took a grape, and the Bean asked what was going on in the great world.

'Well,' said the Crumpet, taking another grape, 'the finest minds in the Drones are still wrestling with the great Hat mystery.'

'What's that?'

'You don't mean you haven't heard about it?'

'Not a word.'

The Crumpet was astounded. He swallowed two grapes at once in surprise.

'Why, London's seething with it. The general consensus of opinion is that it has something to do with the Fourth Dimension. You know how things do. I mean to say, something rummy occurs and you consult some big-brained bird and he wags his head and says "Ah! The Fourth Dimension!" Extraordinary nobody's told you about the great Hat mystery.'

'You're the first visitor I've had. What is it, anyway? What hat?'

'Well, there were two hats. Reading from left to right, Percy Wimbolt's and Nelson Cork's.'

The Bean nodded intelligently.

'I see what you mean. Percy had one, and Nelson had the other.'

'Exactly. Two hats in all. Top hats.'

'What was mysterious about them?'

'Why, Elizabeth Bottsworth and Diana Punter said they didn't fit.'

'Well, hats don't sometimes.'

'But these came from Bodmin's.'

The Bean shot up in bed.

'What?'

'You mustn't excite the patient,' said the nurse, who up to this point had taken no part in the conversation.

'But, dash it, nurse,' cried the Bean, 'you can't have caught what he said. If we are to give credence to his story, Percy Wimbolt and Nelson Cork bought a couple of hats at Bodmin's – at *Bodmin's*, I'll trouble you – and they didn't fit. It isn't possible.'

He spoke with strong emotion, and the Crumpet nodded understandingly. People can say what they please about the modern young man believing in nothing nowadays, but there is one thing every right-minded young man believes in, and that is the infallibility of Bodmin's hats. It is one of the eternal verities. Once admit that it is possible for a Bodmin hat not to fit, and you leave the door open for Doubt, Schism and Chaos generally.

'That's exactly how Percy and Nelson felt, and it was for that reason that they were compelled to take the strong line and they did with E. Bottsworth and D. Punter.'

'They took a strong line, did they?'

'A very strong line.'

'Won't you tell us the whole story from the beginning?' said the nurse.

'Right ho,' said the Crumpet, taking a grape. 'It'll make your head swim.'

'So mysterious?'

'So absolutely dashed uncanny from start to finish.'

You must know, to begin with, my dear old nurse (said the Crumpet), that these two blokes, Percy Wimbolt and

Nelson Cork, are fellows who have to exercise the most watchful care about their lids, because they are so situated that in their case there can be none of that business of just charging into any old hattery and grabbing the first thing in sight. Percy is one of those large, stout, outsize chaps with a head like a watermelon, while Nelson is built more on the lines of a minor jockey and has a head like a peanut.

You will readily appreciate, therefore, that it requires an artist hand to fit them properly, and that is why they have always gone to Bodmin. I have heard Percy say that his trust in Bodmin is like the unspotted faith of a young curate in his Bishop and I have no doubt that Nelson would have said the same, if he had thought of it.

It was at Bodmin's door that they ran into each other on the morning when my story begins.

'Hullo,' said Percy. 'You come to buy a hat?'

'Yes,' said Nelson. 'You come to buy a hat?'

'Yes.' Percy glanced cautiously about him, saw that he was alone (except for Nelson, of course) and unobserved, and drew closer and lowered his voice. 'There's a reason!'

'That's rummy,' said Nelson. He, also, spoke in a hushed tone. 'I have a special reason, too.'

Percy looked warily about him again, and lowered his voice another notch.

'Nelson,' he said, 'you know Elizabeth Bottsworth?'

'Intimately,' said Nelson.

'Rather a sound young potato, what?'

'Very much so.'

'Pretty?'

'I've often noticed it.'

'Me, too. She is so small, so sweet, so dainty, so lively, so viv – , what's-the-word? – that a fellow wouldn't be far out in calling her an angel in human shape.'

'Aren't all angels in human shape?'

'Are they?' said Percy, who was a bit foggy on angels. 'Well, be that as it may,' he went on, his cheeks suffused to a certain extent, 'I love that girl, Nelson, and she's coming with me to the first day of Ascot, and I'm relying on this new hat of mine to do just that extra bit that's needed in the way of making her reciprocate my passion. Having only met her so far at country houses, I've never yet flashed upon her in a topper.'

Nelson Cork was staring.

'Well, if that isn't the most remarkable coincidence I ever came across in my puff!' he exclaimed, amazed. 'I'm buying my new hat for exactly the same reason.'

A convulsive start shook Percy's massive frame. His eyes bulged.

'To fascinate Elizabeth Bottsworth?' he cried, beginning to writhe.

'No, no,' said Nelson, soothingly. 'Of course not. Elizabeth and I have always been great friends, but nothing more. What I meant was that I, like you, am counting on this forthcoming topper of mine to put me across with the girl I love.'

Percy stopped writhing.

'Who is she?' he asked, interested.

'Diana Punter, the niece of my godmother, old Ma Punter. It's an odd thing, I've known her all my life – brought up as kids together and so forth – but it's only recently that passion has burgeoned. I now worship that girl, Percy, from the top of her head to the soles of her divine feet.'

Percy looked dubious.

'That's a pretty longish distance, isn't it? Diana Punter is one of my closest friends, and a charming girl in every respect, but isn't she a bit tall for you, old man?'

'My dear chap, that's just what I admire so much about her, her superb statuesqueness. More like a Greek goddess than anything I've struck for years. Besides, she isn't any taller for me than you are for Elizabeth Bottsworth.'

'True,' admitted Percy.

'And, anyway, I love her, blast it, and I don't propose to argue the point. I love her, I love her, I love her, and we are lunching together the first day of Ascot.'

'At Ascot?'

'No. She isn't keen on racing so I shall have to give Ascot a miss.'

'That's Love,' said Percy, awed.

'The binge will take place at my godmother's house in Berkeley Square, and it won't be long after that, I feel, before you see an interesting announcement in the *Morning Post*.'

Percy extended his hand. Nelson grasped it warmly.

'These new hats are pretty well bound to do the trick, I should say, wouldn't you?'

'Infallibly. Where girls are concerned, there is nothing that brings home the gravy like a well-fitting topper.'

'Bodmin must extend himself as never before,' said Percy.

'He certainly must,' said Nelson.

They entered the shop. And Bodmin, having measured them with his own hands, promised that two of his very finest efforts should be at their respective addresses in the course of the next few days.

Now, Percy Wimbolt isn't a chap you would suspect of having nerves, but there is no doubt that in the interval which elapsed before Bodmin was scheduled to deliver he got pretty twittery. He kept having awful visions of some great disaster happening to his new hat: and, as things turned out, these visions came jolly near being fulfilled. It has made Percy feel that he is psychic.

What occurred was this. Owing to these jitters of his, he hadn't been sleeping any too well, and on the morning before Ascot he was up as early as ten-thirty, and he went to his sitting-room window to see what sort of a day it was, and the sight he beheld from that window absolutely froze the blood in his veins.

For there below him, strutting up and down the pavement, were a uniformed little blighter whom he recognized as Bodmin's errand-boy and an equally foul kid in mufti. And balanced on each child's loathsome head was a top hat. Against the railings were leaning a couple of cardboard hat-boxes.

Now, considering that Percy had only just woken from a dream in which he had been standing outside the Guildhall in his new hat, receiving the Freedom of the City from the Lord Mayor, and the Lord Mayor had suddenly taken a terrific swipe at the hat with his mace, knocking it into hash, you might have supposed that he would have been hardened to anything. But he wasn't. His reaction was terrific. There was a moment of sort of paralysis, during which he was telling himself that he had always suspected this beastly little boy of Bodmin's of having a low and frivolous outlook and being temperamentally unfitted for his high office: and then he came alive with a jerk and let out probably the juiciest yell the neighbourhood had heard for years.

It stopped the striplings like a high-powered shell. One moment, they had been swanking up and down in a mincing and affected sort of way: the next, the second kid had legged it like a streak and Bodmin's boy was shoving the hats back in the boxes and trying to do it quickly enough to enable him to be elsewhere when Percy should arrive.

And in this he was successful. By the time Percy had got to the front door and opened it, there was nothing to be seen but a hat-box standing on the steps. He took it up to his flat and removed the contents with a gingerly and reverent hand, holding his breath for fear the nap should have got rubbed the wrong way or a dent of any nature been made in the gleaming surface; but apparently all was well. Bodmin's boy might sink to taking hats out of their boxes and fooling about with them, but at least he hadn't gone to the last awful extreme of dropping them.

The lid was OK absolutely: and on the following
morning Percy, having spent the interval polishing it with
stout, assembled the boots, the spats, the trousers, the
coat, the flowered waistcoat, the collar, the shirt, the
quiet grey tie, and the good old gardenia and set off in a
taxi for the house where Elizabeth was staying. And
presently he was ringing the bell and being told she would
be down in a minute, and eventually down she came,
looking perfectly marvellous.

'What ho, what ho!' said Percy.

'Hullo, Percy,' said Elizabeth.

Now, naturally, up to this moment Percy had been
standing with bared head. At this point, he put the hat
on. He wanted her to get the full effect suddenly in a good
light. And very strategic, too. I mean to say, it would
have been the act of a juggins to have waited till they
were in the taxi, because in a taxi all toppers look much
alike.

So Percy popped the hat on his head with a meaning
glance and stood waiting for the uncontrollable round of
applause.

And instead of clapping her little hands in girlish
ecstasy and doing Spring dances round him, this young
Bottsworth gave a sort of gurgling scream not unlike a
coloratura soprano choking on a fishbone.

Then she blinked and became calmer.

'It's all right,' she said. 'The momentary weakness has
passed. Tell me, Percy, when do you open?'

'Open?' said Percy, not having the remotest.

'On the Halls. Aren't you going to sing comic songs
on the Music Halls?'

Percy's perplexity deepened.

'Me? No. How? Why? What do you mean?'

'I thought that hat must be part of the make-up and
that you were trying it on the dog. I couldn't think of
any other reason why you should wear one six sizes too
small.'

Percy gasped.

'You aren't suggesting this hat doesn't fit me?'

'It doesn't fit you by a mile.'

'But it's a Bodmin.'

'Call it that if you like. I call it a public outrage.'

Percy was appalled. I mean, naturally. A nice thing for a chap to give his heart to a girl and then find her talking in this hideous, flippant way of sacred subjects.

Then it occurred to him that, living all the time in the country, she might not have learned to appreciate the holy significance of the name Bodmin.

'Listen,' he said gently. 'Let me explain. This hat was made by Bodmin, the world-famous hatter of Vigo Street. He measured me in person and guaranteed a fit.'

'And I nearly had one.'

'And if Bodmin guarantees that a hat shall fit,' proceeded Percy, trying to fight against a sickening sort of feeling that he had been all wrong about this girl, 'it fits. I mean, saying a Bodmin hat doesn't fit is like saying . . . well, I can't think of anything awful enough.'

'That hat's awful enough. It's like something out of a two-reel comedy. Pure Chas. Chaplin. I know a joke's a joke, Percy, and I'm as fond of a laugh as anyone, but there is such a thing as cruelty to animals. Imagine the feelings of the horses at Ascot when they see that hat.'

Poets and other literary blokes talk a lot about falling in love at first sight, but it's equally possible to fall out of love just as quickly. One moment, this girl was the be-all and the end-all, as you might say, of Percy Wimbolt's life. The next, she was just a regrettable young blister with whom he wished to hold no further communication. He could stand a good deal from the sex. Insults directed to himself left him unmoved. But he was not prepared to countenance destructive criticism of a Bodmin hat.

'Possibly,' he said, coldly, 'you would prefer to go to this bally race-meeting alone?'

'You bet I'm going alone. You don't suppose I mean to be seen in broad daylight in the paddock at Ascot with a hat like that?'

Percy stepped back and bowed formally.

'Drive on, driver,' he said to the driver, and the driver drove on.

Now, you would say that that was rummy enough. A full-size mystery in itself, you might call it. But wait. Mark the sequel. You haven't heard anything yet.

We now turn to Nelson Cork. Shortly before one-thirty, Nelson had shoved over to Berkeley Square and had lunch with his godmother and Diana Punter, and Diana's manner and deportment had been absolutely all that could have been desired. In fact, so chummy had she been over the cutlets and fruit salad that it seemed to Nelson that, if she was like this now, imagination boggled at the thought of how utterly all over him she would be when he sprang his new hat on her.

So when the meal was concluded and coffee had been drunk and old Lady Punter had gone up to her boudoir with a digestive tablet and a sex-novel, he thought it would be a sound move to invite her to come for a stroll along Bond Street. There was the chance, of course, that she would fall into his arms right in the middle of the pavement: but if that happened, he told himself, they could always get into a cab. So he mooted the saunter, and she checked up, and presently they started off.

And you will scarcely believe this, but they hadn't gone more than half-way along Bruton Street when she suddenly stopped and looked at him in an odd manner.

'I don't want to be personal, Nelson,' she said, 'but really I do think you ought to take the trouble to get measured for your hats.'

If a gas main had exploded beneath Nelson's feet, he could hardly have been more taken aback.

'M-m-m-m . . .' he gasped. He could scarcely believe that he had heard aright.

'It's the only way with a head like yours. I know it's a temptation for a lazy man to go into a shop and just take whatever is offered him, but the result is so sloppy. That thing you're wearing now looks like an extinguisher.'

Nelson was telling himself that he must be strong.

'Are you endeavouring to intimate that this hat does not fit?'

'Can't you feel that it doesn't fit?'

'But it's a Bodmin.'

'I don't know what you mean. It's just an ordinary silk hat.'

'Not at all. It's a Bodmin.'

'I don't know what you are talking about.'

'The point I am trying to drive home,' said Nelson, stiffly, 'is that this hat was constructed under the personal auspices of Jno. Bodmin of Vigo Street.'

'Well, it's too big.'

'It is not too big.'

'I say it's too big.'

'And I say a Bodmin hat cannot be too big.'

'Well, I've got eyes, and I say it is.'

Nelson controlled himself with an effort.

'I would be the last person,' he said, 'to criticize your eye-sight, but on the present occasion you will permit me to say that it has let you down with a considerable bump. Myopia is indicated. Allow me,' said Nelson, hot under the collar, but still dignified, 'to tell you something about Jno. Bodmin, as the name appears new to you. Jno. is the last of a long line of Bodmins, all of whom have made hats assiduously for the nobility and gentry all their lives. Hats are in Jno. Bodmin's blood.'

'I don't . . .'

Nelson held up a restraining hand.

'Over the door of his emporium in Vigo Street the passer-by may read a significant legend. It runs:

330

"Bespoke Hatter To The Royal Family." That means, in simple language adapted to the lay intelligence, that if the King wants a new topper he simply ankles round to Bodmin's and says: "Good morning, Bodmin, we want a topper." He does not ask if it will fit. He takes it for granted that it will fit. He has bespoken Jno. Bodmin, and he trusts him blindly. You don't suppose His Gracious Majesty would bespeak a hatter whose hats did not fit. The whole essence of being a hatter is to make hats that fit, and it is to this end that Jno. Bodmin has strained every nerve for years. And that is why I say again – simply and without heat – This hat is a Bodmin.'

Diana was beginning to get a bit peeved. The blood of the Punters is hot, and very little is required to steam it up. She tapped Bruton Street with a testy foot.

'You always were an obstinate, pig-headed little fiend, Nelson, even as a child. I tell you once more, for the last time, that that hat is too big. If it were not for the fact that I can see a pair of boots and part of a pair of trousers, I should not know that there was a human being under it. I don't care how much you argue. I still think you ought to be ashamed of yourself for coming out in the thing. Even if you don't mind for your own sake, you might have considered the feelings of the pedestrians and traffic.'

Nelson quivered.

'You do, do you?'

'Yes, I do.'

'Oh, you do?'

'I said I did. Didn't you hear me? No, I suppose you could hardly be expected to, with an enormous great hat coming down over your ears.'

'You say this hat comes down over my ears?'

'Right over your ears. It's a mystery to me why you think it worth while to deny it.'

I fear that what follows does not show Nelson Cork in the role of a parfait gentil knight, but in extenuation of

his behaviour I must remind you that he and Diana Punter
had been brought up as children together, and a dispute
between a couple who have shared the same nursery is
always liable to degenerate into an exchange of
personalities and innuendoes. What starts as an academic
discussion on hats turns only too swiftly into a raking
up of old sores and a grand parade of family skeletons.

It was so in this case. At the word 'mystery,' Nelson
uttered a nasty laugh.

'A mystery, eh? As much a mystery, I suppose, as why
your uncle George suddenly left England in the year 1920
without stopping to pack up?'

Diana's eyes flashed. Her foot struck the pavement
another shrewd wallop.

'Uncle George,' she said haughtily, 'went abroad for
his health.'

'You bet he did,' retorted Nelson. 'He knew what was
good for him.'

'Anyway, he wouldn't have worn a hat like that.'

'Where they would have put him if he hadn't been off
like a scalded kitten, he wouldn't have worn a hat at all.'

A small groove was now beginning to appear in the
paving-stone on which Diana Punter stood.

'Well, Uncle George escaped one thing by going abroad,
at any rate,' she said. 'He missed the big scandal about
your aunt Clarissa in 1922.'

Nelson clenched his fists.

'The jury gave Aunt Clarissa the benefit of the doubt,'
he said hoarsely.

'Well, we all know what that means. It was
accompanied, if you recollect, by some very strong
remarks from the Bench.'

There was a pause.

'I may be wrong,' said Nelson, 'but I should have
thought it ill beseemed a girl whose brother Cyril was
warned off the Turf in 1923 to haul up her slacks about
other people's Aunt Clarissas.'

'Passing lightly over my brother Cyril in 1924,' rejoined Diana, 'what price your cousin Fred in 1927?'

They glared at one another in silence for a space, each realizing with a pang that the supply of erring relatives had now given out. Diana was still pawing the paving-stone, and Nelson was wondering what on earth he could ever have seen in a girl who, in addition to talking subversive drivel about hats, was eight feet tall and ungainly, to boot.

'While as for your brother-in-law's niece's sister-in-law Muriel . . .' began Diana, suddenly brightening.

Nelson checked her with a gesture.

'I prefer not to continue this discussion,' he said, frigidly.

'It is no pleasure to me,' replied Diana, with equal coldness, 'to have to listen to your vapid gibberings. That's the worst of a man who wears his hat over his mouth – he will talk through it.'

'I bid you a very hearty good afternoon, Miss Punter,' said Nelson.

He strode off without a backward glance.

Now, one advantage of having a row with a girl in Bruton Street is that the Drones is only just round the corner, so that you can pop in and restore the old nervous system with the minimum of trouble. Nelson was round there in what practically amounted to a trice, and the first person he saw was Percy, hunched up over a double and splash.

'Hullo,' said Percy.

'Hullo,' said Nelson.

There was a silence, broken only by the sound of Nelson ordering a mixed vermouth. Percy continued to stare before him like a man who has drained the wine-cup of life to its lees, only to discover a dead mouse at the bottom.

333

'Nelson,' he said at length, 'what are your views on the Modern Girl?'

'I think she's a mess.'

'I thoroughly agree with you,' said Percy. 'Of course, Diana Punter is a rare exception, but, apart from Diana, I wouldn't give you twopence for the Modern Girl. She lacks depth and reverence and has no sense of what is fitting. Hats, for example.'

'Exactly. But what do you mean Diana Punter is an exception? She's one of the ring-leaders – the spearhead of the movement, if you like to put it that way. Think,' said Nelson, sipping his vermouth, 'of all the unpleasant qualities of the Modern Girl, add them up, double them, and what have you got? Diana Punter. Let me tell you what took place between me and this Punter only a few minutes ago.'

'No,' said Percy. 'Let me tell you what transpired between me and Elizabeth Bottsworth this morning. Nelson, old man, she said my hat – my Bodmin hat – was too small.'

'You don't mean that?'

'Those were her very words.'

'Well, I'm dashed. Listen. Diana Punter told me my equally Bodmin hat was too large.'

They stared at one another,

'It's the Spirit of something,' said Nelson. 'I don't know what, quite, but of something. You see it on all sides. Something very serious has gone wrong with girls nowadays. There is lawlessness and licence abroad.'

'And here in England, too.'

'Well, naturally, you silly ass,' said Nelson, with some asperity. 'When I said abroad, I didn't mean abroad, I meant abroad.'

He mused for a moment.

'I must say, though,' he continued, 'I am surprised at what you tell me about Elizabeth Bottsworth, and am inclined to think there must have been some mistake. I have always been a warm admirer of Elizabeth.'

'And I have always thought Diana one of the best, and I find it hard to believe that she should have shown up in such a dubious light as you suggest. Probably there was a misunderstanding of some kind.'

'Well, I ticked her off properly, anyway.'

Percy Wimbolt shook his head.

'You shouldn't have done that, Nelson. You may have wounded her feelings. In my case, of course, I had no alternative but to be pretty crisp with Elizabeth.'

Nelson Cork clicked his tongue.

'A pity,' he said. 'Elizabeth is sensitive.'

'So is Diana.'

'Not so sensitive as Elizabeth.'

'I should say, at a venture, about five times as sensitive as Elizabeth. However, we must not quarrel about a point like that, old man. The fact that emerges is that we seem both to have been dashed badly treated. I think I shall toddle home and take an aspirin.'

'Me, too.'

They went off to the cloak-room, where their hats were, and Percy put his on.

'Surely,' he said, 'nobody but a half-witted little pipsqueak who can't see straight would say this was too small?'

'It isn't a bit too small,' said Nelson. 'And take a look at this one. Am I not right in supposing that only a female giantess with straws in her hair and astigmatism in both eyes could say it was too large?'

'It's a lovely fit.'

And the cloak-room waiter, a knowledgeable chap of the name of Robinson, said the same.

'So there you are,' said Nelson.

'Ah, well,' said Percy.

They left the club, and parted at the top of Dover Street.

*

Now, though he had not said so in so many words, Nelson Cork's heart bled for Percy Wimbolt. He knew the other's fine sensibilities and he could guess how deeply he must have been gashed by this unfortunate breaking-off of diplomatic relations with the girl he loved. For, whatever might have happened, however sorely he might have been wounded, the way Nelson Cork looked at it was that Percy loved Elizabeth Bottsworth in spite of everything. What was required here, felt Nelson, was a tactful mediator – a kindly, sensible friend of both parties who would hitch up his socks and plunge in and heal the breach.

So the moment he had got rid of Percy outside the club he hared round to the house where Elizabeth was staying and was lucky enough to catch her on the front door steps. For, naturally, Elizabeth hadn't gone off to Ascot by herself. Directly Percy was out of sight, she had told the taxi-man to drive her home, and she had been occupying the interval since the painful scene in thinking of things she wished she had said to him and taking her hostess's dog for a run – a Pekinese called Clarkson.

She seemed very pleased to see Nelson, and started to prattle of this and that, her whole demeanour that of a girl who, after having been compelled to associate for a while with the Underworld, has at last found a kindred soul. And the more he listened, the more he wanted to go on listening. And the more he looked at her, the more he felt that a lifetime spent in gazing at Elizabeth Bottsworth would be a lifetime dashed well spent.

There was something about the girl's exquisite petiteness and fragility that appealed to Nelson Cork's depths. After having wasted so much time looking at a female Carnera like Diana Punter, it was a genuine treat to him to be privileged to feast the eyes on one so small and dainty. And, what with one thing and another, he found the most extraordinary difficulty in lugging Percy into the conversation.

They strolled along, chatting. And, mark you,

Elizabeth Bottsworth was a girl a fellow could chat with without getting a crick in the neck from goggling up at her, the way you had to do when you took the air with Diana Punter. Nelson realized now that talking to Diana Punter had been like trying to exchange thoughts with a flag-pole sitter. He was surprised that this had never occurred to him before.

'You know, you're looking perfectly ripping, Elizabeth,' he said.

'How funny!' said the girl. 'I was just going to say the same thing about you.'

'Not really?'

'Yes, I was. After some of the gargoyles I've seen today – Percy Wimbolt is an example that springs to the mind – it's such a relief to be with a man who really knows how to turn himself out.'

Now that the Percy *motif* had been introduced, it should have been a simple task for Nelson to turn the talk to the subject of his absent friend. But somehow he didn't. Instead, he just simpered a bit and said: 'Oh, no, I say, really, do you mean that?'

'I do, indeed,' said Elizabeth earnestly. 'It's your hat, principally, I think. I don't know why it is, but ever since a child I have been intensely sensitive to hats, and it has always been a pleasure to me to remember that at the age of five I dropped a pot of jam out of the nursery window on to my Uncle Alexander when he came to visit us in a deerstalker cap with ear-flaps, as worn by Sherlock Holmes. I consider the hat the final test of a man. Now, yours is perfect. I never saw such a beautiful fit. I can't tell you how much I admire that hat. It gives you quite an ambassadorial look.'

Nelson Cork drew a deep breath. He was tingling from head to foot. It was as if the scales had fallen from his eyes and a new life begun for him.

'I say,' he said, trembling with emotion, 'I wonder if you would mind if I pressed your little hand?'

'Do,' said Elizabeth cordially.

'I will,' said Nelson, and did so. 'And now,' he went on, clinging to the fin like glue and hiccoughing a bit, 'how about buzzing off somewhere for a quiet cup of tea? I have a feeling that we have much to say to one another.'

It is odd how often it happens in this world that when there are two chaps and one chap's heart is bleeding for the other chap you find that all the while the second chap's heart is bleeding just as much for the first chap. Both bleeding, I mean to say, not only one. It was so in the case of Nelson Cork and Percy Wimbolt. The moment he had left Nelson, Percy charged straight off in search of Diana Punter with the intention of putting everything right with a few well-chosen words.

Because what he felt was that, although at the actual moment of going to press pique might be putting Nelson off Diana, this would pass off and love come into its own again. All that was required, he considered, was a suave go-between, a genial mutual pal who would pour oil on the troubled w's and generally fix things up.

He found Diana walking round and round Berkeley Square with her chin up, breathing tensely through the nostrils. He drew up alongside and what-hoed, and as she beheld him the cold, hard gleam in her eyes changed to a light of cordiality. She appeared charmed to see him and at once embarked on an animated conversation. And with every word she spoke his conviction deepened that of all the ways of passing a summer afternoon there were none fruitier than having a friendly hike with Diana Punter.

And it was not only her talk that enchanted him. He was equally fascinated by that wonderful physique of hers. When he considered that he had actually wasted several valuable minutes that day conversing with a young shrimp like Elizabeth Bottsworth, he could have kicked himself.

Here, he reflected, as they walked round the square, was a girl whose ear was more or less on a level with a fellow's mouth, so that such observations as he might make were enabled to get from point to point with the least possible delay. Talking to Elizabeth Bottsworth had always been like bellowing down a well in the hope of attracting the attention of one of the smaller infusoria at the bottom. It surprised him that he had been so long in coming to this conclusion.

He was awakened from this reverie by hearing his companion utter the name of Nelson Cork.

'I beg your pardon?' he said.

'I was saying,' said Diana, 'that Nelson Cork is a wretched little undersized blob who, if he were not too lazy to work, would long since have signed up with some good troupe of midgets.'

'Oh, would you say that?'

'I would say more than that,' said Diana firmly. 'I tell you, Percy, that what makes life so ghastly for girls, what causes girls to get grey hair and go into convents, is the fact that it is not always possible for them to avoid being seen in public with men like Nelson Cork. I trust I am not uncharitable. I try to view these things in a broad-minded way, saying to myself that if a man looks like something that has come out from under a flat stone it is his misfortune rather than his fault and that he is more to be pitied than censured. But on one thing I do insist, that such a man does not wantonly aggravate the natural unpleasantness of his appearance by prancing about London in a hat that reaches down to his ankles. I cannot and will not endure being escorted along Bruton Street by a sort of human bacillus the brim of whose hat bumps on the pavement with every step he takes. What I have always said and what I shall always say is that the hat is the acid test. A man who cannot buy the right-sized hat is a man one could never like or trust. Your hat, now, Percy, is exactly right. I have seen a good many hats in my time, but I really do not think that I have ever come across a more perfect specimen of all that a hat should be. Not too large, not too small, fitting snugly to the head like the skin on a sausage. And you have just the kind of head that a silk hat shows off. It gives you a sort of look . . . how shall I describe it? . . . it conveys the idea of a master of men. Leonine is the word I want. There is something about the way it rests on the brow and the almost imperceptible tilt towards the south-east . . .'

Percy Wimbolt was quivering like an Oriental muscle-dancer. Soft music seemed to be playing from the direction of Hay Hill, and Berkeley Square had begun to skip round him on one foot.

He drew a deep breath.

'I say,' he said, 'stop me if you've heard this before, but what I feel we ought to do at this juncture is to dash off somewhere where it's quiet and there aren't so many houses dancing the "Blue Danube" and shove some tea into ourselves. And over the pot and muffins I shall have something very important to say to you.'

'So that,' concluded the Crumpet, taking a grape, 'is how the thing stands; and, in a sense, of course, you could say that it is a satisfactory ending.

'The announcement of Elizabeth's engagement to Nelson Cork appeared in the Press on the same day as that of Diana's projected hitching-up with Percy Wimbolt: and it is pleasant that the happy couples should be so well matched as regards size.

'I mean to say, there will be none of that business of a six-foot girl tripping down the aisle with a five-foot-four man, or a six-feet-two man trying to keep step along the sacred edifice with a four-foot-three girl. This is always good for a laugh from the ringside pews, but it does not make for wedded bliss.

'No, as far as the principals are concerned, we may say

that all has ended well. But that doesn't seem to me the important point. What seems to me the important point is this extraordinary baffling mystery of those hats.'

'Absolutely,' said the Bean.

'I mean to say, if Percy's hat really didn't fit, as Elizabeth Bottsworth contended, why should it have registered as a winner with Diana Punter?'

'Absolutely,' said the Bean.

'And, conversely, if Nelson's hat was the total loss which Diana Punter considered it, why, only a brief while later, was it going like a breeze with Elizabeth Bottsworth?'

'Absolutely,' said the Bean.

'The whole thing is utterly inscrutable.'

It was at this point that the nurse gave signs of wishing to catch the Speaker's eye.

'Shall I tell you what I think?'

'Say on, my dear young pillow-smoother.'

'I believe Bodmin's boy must have got those hats mixed. When he was putting them back in the boxes, I mean.'

The Crumpet shook his head, and took a grape.

'And then at the club they got the right ones again.'

The Crumpet smiled indulgently.

'Ingenious,' he said, taking a grape. 'Quite ingenious. But a little far-fetched. No, I prefer to think the whole thing, as I say, has something to do with the Fourth Dimension. I am convinced that that is the true explanation, if our minds could only grasp it.'

'Absolutely,' said the Bean.

3 — Goodbye to All Cats

As the club kitten sauntered into the smoking room of the Drones Club and greeted those present with a friendly miaou, Freddie Widgeon, who had been sitting in a corner with his head between his hands, rose stiffly.

'I had supposed,' he said, in a cold, level voice, 'that this was a quiet retreat for gentlemen. As I perceive that it is a blasted zoo, I will withdraw.'

And he left the room in a marked manner.

There was a good deal of surprise, not unmixed with consternation.

'What's the trouble?' asked an Egg, concerned. Such exhibitions of the naked emotions are rare at the Drones. 'Have they had a row?'

A Crumpet, always well-informed, shook his head.

'Freddie has had no personal breach with this particular kitten,' he said. 'It is simply that since that weekend at Matcham Scratchings he can't stand the sight of a cat.'

'Matcham what?'

'Scratchings. The ancestral home of Dahlia Prenderby in Oxfordshire.'

'I met Dahlia Prenderby once,' said the Egg. 'I thought she seemed a nice girl.'

'Freddie thought so, too. He loved her madly.'

'And lost her, of course?'

'Absolutely.'

'Do you know,' said a thoughtful Bean, 'I'll bet that if all the girls Freddie Widgeon has loved and lost were placed end to end – not that I suppose one could do it – they would reach half-way down Piccadilly.'

'Further than that,' said the Egg. 'Some of them were pretty tall. What beats me is why he ever bothers to love them. They always turn him down in the end. He might just as well never begin. Better, in fact, because in the time saved he could be reading some good book.'

'I think the trouble with Freddie,' said the Crumpet, 'is that he always gets off to a flying start. He's a good-looking sort of chap who dances well and can wiggle his ears, and the girl is dazzled for the moment, and this encourages him. From what he tells me, he appears to have gone very big with this Prenderby girl at the outset. So much so, indeed, that when she invited him down to Matcham Scratchings he had already bought his copy of *What Every Young Bridegroom Ought To Know*.'

'Rummy, these old country-house names,' mused the Bean. 'Why Scratchings, I wonder?'

'Freddie wondered, too, till he got to the place. Then he tells me he felt it was absolutely the *mot juste*. This girl Dahlia's family, you see, was one of those animal-loving families, and the house, he tells me, was just a frothing maelstrom of dumb chums. As far as the eye could reach, there were dogs scratching themselves and cats scratching the furniture. I believe, though he never met it socially, there was even a tame chimpanzee somewhere on the premises, no doubt scratching away as assiduously as the rest of them. You get these conditions here and there in the depths of the country, and this Matcham place was well away from the centre of things, being about six miles from the nearest station.

'It was at this station that Dahlia Prenderby met Freddie in her two-seater, and on the way to the house there occurred a conversation which I consider significant – showing, as it does, the cordial relations existing between the young couple at that point in the proceedings. I mean, it was only later that the bitter awakening and all that sort of thing popped up.'

'I do want you to be a success, Freddie,' said the girl,

after talking a while of this and that. 'Some of the men I've asked down here have been such awful flops. The great thing is to make a good impression on Father.'

'I will,' said Freddie.

'He can be a little difficult at times.'

'Lead me to him,' said Freddie. 'That's all I ask. Lead me to him.'

'The trouble is, he doesn't much like young men.'

'He'll like me.'

'He will, will he?'

'Rather!'

'What makes you think that?'

'I'm a dashed fascinating chap.'

'Oh, you are?'

'Yes, I am.'

'You are, are you?'

'Rather!'

Upon which, she gave him a sort of push and he gave her a sort of push, and she giggled and he laughed like a paper bag bursting, and she gave him a kind of shove and he gave her a kind of shove, and she said 'You *are* a silly ass!' and he said 'What ho!' All of which shows you, I mean to say, the stage they had got to by this time. Nothing definitely settled, of course, but Love obviously beginning to burgeon in the girl's heart.

Well, naturally, Freddie gave a good deal of thought during the drive to this father of whom the girl had spoken so feelingly, and he resolved that he would not fail her. The way he would suck up to the old dad would be nobody's business. He proposed to exert upon him the full force of his magnetic personality, and looked forward to registering a very substantial hit.

Which being so, I need scarcely tell you, knowing Freddie as you do, that his first act on entering Sir Mortimer Prenderby's orbit was to make the scaliest kind of floater, hitting him on the back of the neck with a tortoiseshell cat not ten minutes after his arrival.

His train having been a bit late, there was no time on reaching the house for any stately receptions or any of that 'Welcome to Meadowsweet Hall' stuff. The girl simply shot him up to his room and told him to dress like a streak, because dinner was in a quarter of an hour, and then buzzed off to don the soup and fish herself. And Freddie was just going well when, looking round for his shirt, which he had left on the bed, he saw a large tortoiseshell cat standing on it, kneading it with its paws.

Well, you know how a fellow feels about his shirt-front. For an instant, Freddie stood spellbound. Then with a hoarse cry he bounded forward, scooped up the animal, and, carrying it out on to the balcony, flung it into the void. And an elderly gentleman, coming round the corner at this moment, received a direct hit on the back of his neck.

'Hell!' cried the elderly gentleman.

A head popped out of a window.

'Whatever is the matter, Mortimer?'

'It's raining cats.'

'Nonsense. It's a lovely evening,' said the head, and disappeared.

Freddie thought an apology would be in order.

'I say,' he said.

The old gentleman looked in every direction of the compass, and finally located Freddie on his balcony.

'I say,' said Freddie, 'I'm awfully sorry you got that nasty buffet. It was me.'

'It was not you. It was a cat.'

'I know. I threw the cat.'

'Why?'

'Well . . .'

'Dam' fool.'

'I'm sorry,' said Freddie.

'Go to blazes,' said the old gentleman.

Freddie backed into the room, and the incident closed.

Freddie is a pretty slippy dresser, as a rule, but this episode had shaken him, and he not only lost a collar-stud but made a mess of the first two ties. The result was that the gong went while he was still in his shirt-sleeves: and on emerging from his boudoir he was informed by a footman that the gang were already nuzzling their *bouillon* in the dining room. He pushed straight there, accordingly, and sank into a chair beside his hostess just in time to dead-heat with the final spoonful.

Awkward, of course, but he was feeling in pretty good form owing to the pleasantness of the thought that he was shoving his knees under the same board as the girl Dahlia: so, having nodded to his host, who was glaring at him from the head of the table, as much as to say that all would be explained in God's good time, he shot his cuffs and started to make sparkling conversation to Lady Prenderby.

'Charming place you have here, what?'

Lady Prenderby said that the local scenery was generally admired. She was one of those tall, rangy, Queen Elizabeth sort of women, with tight lips and cold, blancmangey eyes. Freddie didn't like her looks much, but he was feeling, as I say, fairly fizzy, so he carried on with a bright zip.

'Pretty good hunting country, I should think?'

'I believe there is a good deal of hunting near here, yes.'

'I thought as much,' said Freddie. 'Ah, that's the stuff, is it not? A cracking gallop across good country with a jolly fine kill at the end of it, what, what? Hark fo'ard, yoicks, tally-ho, I mean to say, and all that sort of thing.'

Lady Prenderby shivered austerely.

'I fear I cannot share your enthusiasm,' she said. 'I

346

have the strongest possible objection to hunting. I have always set my face against it, as against all similar brutalizing blood-sports.'

This was a nasty jar for poor old Freddie, who had been relying on the topic to carry him nicely through at least a couple of courses. It silenced him for the nonce. And as he paused to collect his faculties, his host, who had now been glowering for six and a half minutes practically without cessation, put a hand in front of his mouth and addressed the girl Dahlia across the table. Freddie thinks he was under the impression that he was speaking in a guarded whisper, but, as a matter of fact, the words boomed through the air as if he had been a costermonger calling attention to his Brussels sprouts.

'Dahlia!'

'Yes, Father?'

'Who's that ugly feller?'

'Hush!'

'What do you mean, hush? Who is he?'

'Mr Widgeon.'

'Mr Who?'

'Widgeon.'

'I wish you would articulate clearly and not mumble,' said Sir Mortimer fretfully. 'It sounds to me just like "Widgeon." Who asked him here?'

'I did.'

'Why?'

'He's a friend of mine.'

'Well, he looks a pretty frightful young slab of damnation to me. What I'd call a criminal face.'

'Hush!'

'Why do you keep saying "Hush"? Must be a lunatic, too. Throws cats at people.'

'Please, Father!'

'Don't say "Please, Father!" No sense in it. I tell you he does throw cats at people. He threw one at me. Half-witted, I'd call him – if that. Besides being the most offensive-looking young toad I've ever seen on the premises. How long's he staying?'

'Till Monday.'

'My God! And today's only Friday!' bellowed Sir Mortimer Prenderby.

It was an unpleasant situation for Freddie, of course, and I'm bound to admit he didn't carry it off particularly well. What he ought to have done, obviously, was to have plunged into an easy flow of small talk: but all he could think of was to ask Lady Prenderby if she was fond of shooting. Lady Prenderby having replied that, owing to being deficient in the savage instincts and wanton blood-lust that went to make up a callous and cold-hearted murderess, she was not, he relapsed into silence with his lower jaw hanging down.

All in all, he wasn't so dashed sorry when dinner came to an end.

As he and Sir Mortimer were the only men at the table, most of the seats having been filled by a covey of mildewed females whom he had classified under the general heading of Aunts, it seemed to Freddie that the moment had now arrived when they would be able to get together once more, under happier conditions than those of their last meeting, and start to learn to appreciate one another's true worth. He looked forward to a cosy *tête-à-tête* over the port, in the course of which he would smooth over that cat incident and generally do all that lay within his power to revise the unfavourable opinion of him which the other must have formed.

But apparently Sir Mortimer had his own idea of the duties and obligations of a host. Instead of clustering round Freddie with decanters, he simply gave him a long, lingering look of distaste and shot out of the french window into the garden. A moment later, his head reappeared and he uttered the words: 'You and your dam' cats!' Then the night swallowed him again.

Freddie was a good deal perplexed. All this was new

stuff to him. He had been in and out of a number of country houses in his time, but this was the first occasion on which he had ever been left flat at the conclusion of the evening meal, and he wasn't quite sure how to handle the situation. He was still wondering, when Sir Mortimer's head came into view again and its owner, after giving him another of those long, lingering looks, said: 'Cats, forsooth!' and disappeared once more.

Freddie was now definitely piqued. It was all very well, he felt, Dahlia Prenderby telling him to make himself solid with her father, but how can you make yourself solid with a fellow who doesn't stay put for a couple of consecutive seconds? If it was Sir Mortimer's intention to spend the remainder of the night flashing past like a merry-go-round, there seemed little hope of anything amounting to a genuine *rapprochement*. It was a relief to his feelings when there suddenly appeared from nowhere his old acquaintance the tortoiseshell cat. It seemed to offer to him a means of working off his spleen.

Taking from Lady Prenderby's plate, accordingly, the remains of a banana, he plugged the animal neatly at a range of two yards. It yowled and withdrew. And a moment later, there was Sir Mortimer again.

'Did you kick that cat?' said Sir Mortimer.

Freddie had half a mind to ask this old disease if he thought he was a man or a jack-in-the-box, but the breeding of the Widgeons restrained him.

'No,' he said, 'I did not kick that cat.'

'You must have done something to it to make it come charging out at forty miles an hour.'

'I merely offered the animal a piece of fruit.'

'Do it again and see what happens to you.'

'Lovely evening,' said Freddie, changing the subject.

'No, it's not, you silly ass,' said Sir Mortimer. Freddie rose. His nerve, I fancy, was a little shaken.

'I shall join the ladies,' he said, with dignity.

'God help them!' replied Sir Mortimer Prenderby in a

voice instinct with the deepest feeling, and vanished once more.

Freddie's mood, as he made for the drawing room, was thoughtful. I don't say he has much sense, but he's got enough to know when he is and when he isn't going with a bang. Tonight, he realized, he had been very far from going in such a manner. It was not, that is to say, as the Idol of Matcham Scratchings that he would enter the drawing room, but rather as a young fellow who had made an unfortunate first impression and would have to do a lot of heavy ingratiating before he could regard himself as really popular in the home.

He must bustle about, he felt, and make up leeway. And, knowing that what counts with these old-style females who have lived in the country all their lives is the exhibition of those little politenesses and attentions which were all the go in Queen Victoria's time, his first action, on entering, was to make a dive for one of the aunts who seemed to be trying to find a place to put her coffee cup.

'Permit me,' said Freddie, suave to the eyebrows.

And bounding forward with the feeling that this was the stuff to give them, he barged right into a cat.

'Oh, sorry,' he said, backing and bringing down his heel on another cat.

'I say, most frightfully sorry,' he said.

And, tottering to a chair, he sank heavily on to a third cat.

Well, he was up and about again in a jiffy, of course, but it was too late. There was the usual not-at-all-ing and don't-mention-it-ing, but he could read between the lines. Lady Prenderby's eyes had rested on his for only a brief instant, but it had been enough. His standing with her, he perceived, was now approximately what King Herod's would have been at an Israelite Mothers Social Saturday Afternoon.

The girl Dahlia during these exchanges had been

sitting on a sofa at the end of the room, turning the pages of a weekly paper, and the sight of her drew Freddie like a magnet. Her womanly sympathy was just what he felt he could do with at this juncture. Treading with infinite caution, he crossed to where she sat: and, having scanned the terrain narrowly for cats, sank down on the sofa at her side. And conceive his agony of spirit when he discovered that womanly sympathy had been turned off at the main. The girl was like a chunk of ice cream with spikes all over it.

'Please do not trouble to explain,' she said coldly, in answer to his opening words. 'I quite understand that there are people who have this odd dislike of animals.'

'But, dash it . . .' cried Freddie, waving his arm in a frenzied sort of way. 'Oh, I say, sorry,' he added, as his fist sloshed another of the menagerie in the short ribs.

Dahlia caught the animal as it flew through the air.

'I think perhaps you had better take Augustus, Mother,' she said. 'He seems to be annoying Mr Widgeon.'

'Quite,' said Lady Prenderby. 'He will be safer with me.'

'But, dash it . . .' bleated Freddie.

Dahlia Prenderby drew in her breath sharply.

'How true it is,' she said, 'that one never really knows a man till after one has seen him in one's own home.'

'What do you mean by that?'

'Oh, nothing,' said Dahlia Prenderby.

She rose and moved to the piano, where she proceeded to sing old Breton folksongs in a distant manner, leaving Freddie to make out as best he could with a family album containing faded photographs with 'Aunt Emmy bathing at Llandudno, 1893', and 'This is Cousin George at the fancy-dress ball' written under them.

And so the long, quiet, peaceful home evening wore on, till eventually Lady Prenderby mercifully blew the whistle and he was at liberty to sneak off to his bedroom.

*

You might have supposed that Freddie's thoughts, as he toddled upstairs with his candle, would have dwelt exclusively on the girl Dahlia. This, however, was not so. He did give her obvious shirtiness a certain measure of attention, of course, but what really filled his mind was the soothing reflection that at long last his path and that of the animal kingdom of Matcham Scratchings had now divided. He, so to speak, was taking the high road while they, as it were, would take the low road. For whatever might be the conditions prevailing in the dining room, the drawing room, and the rest of the house, his bedroom, he felt, must surely be a haven totally free from cats of all descriptions.

Remembering, however, that unfortunate episode before dinner, he went down on all fours and subjected the various nooks and crannies to a close examination. His eye could detect no cats. Relieved, he rose to his feet with a gay song on his lips: and he hadn't got much beyond the first couple of bars when a voice behind him suddenly started taking the bass: and, turning, he perceived on the bed a fine Alsatian dog.

Freddie looked at the dog. The dog looked at Freddie. The situation was one fraught with embarrassment. A glance at the animal was enough to convince him that it had got an entirely wrong angle on the position of affairs and was regarding him purely in the light of an intrusive stranger who had muscled in on its private sleeping quarters. Its manner was plainly resentful. It fixed Freddie with a cold, yellow eye and curled its upper lip slightly, the better to display a long, white tooth. It also twitched its nose and gave a *sotto-voce* imitation of distant thunder.

Freddie did not know quite what avenue to explore. It was impossible to climb between the sheets with a thing like that on the counterpane. To spend the night in a chair, on the other hand, would have been foreign to his policy. He did what I consider the most statesmanlike

thing by sidling out on to the balcony and squinting
along the wall of the house to see if there wasn't a lighted
window hard by, behind which might lurk somebody
who would rally round with aid and comfort.

There was a lighted window only a short distance
away, so he shoved his head out as far as it would stretch,
and said: 'I say!' There being no response, he repeated: 'I
say!'

And, finally, to drive his point home, he added: 'I say! I
say! I say!'

This time he got results. The head of Lady Prenderby
suddenly protruded from the window.

'Who,' she inquired, 'is making that abominable
noise?'

It was not precisely the attitude Freddie had hoped for,
but he could take the rough with the smooth.

'It's me. Widgeon, Frederick.'

'Must you sing on your balcony, Mr Widgeon?'

'I wasn't singing. I was saying "I say".'

'What were you saying?'

'"I say".'

'You say what?'

'I say I was saying "I say." Kind of a heart-cry, if you
know what I mean. The fact is, there's a dog in my room.'

'What sort of dog?'

'A whacking great Alsatian.'

'Ah, that would be Wilhelm. Good night, Mr Widgeon.'

The window closed. Freddie let out a heart-stricken
yip.

'But I say!'

The window reopened.

'Really, Mr Widgeon!'

'But what am I to do?'

'Do?'

'About this whacking great Alsatian!'

Lady Prenderby seemed to consider.

'No sweet biscuits,' she said. 'And when the maid

brings you your tea in the morning please do not give him sugar. Simply a little milk in the saucer. He is on a diet. Good night, Mr Widgeon.'

Freddie was now pretty well nonplussed. No matter what his hostess might say about this beastly dog being on a diet, he was convinced from its manner that its medical adviser had not forbidden it Widgeons, and once more he bent his brain to the task of ascertaining what to do next.

There were several possible methods of procedure. His balcony being not so very far from the ground, he could, if he pleased, jump down and pass a health-giving night in the nasturtium bed. Or he might curl up on the floor. Or he might get out of the room and doss downstairs somewhere.

This last scheme seemed about the best. The only obstacle in the way of its fulfilment was the fact that, when he started for the door, his room-mate would probably think he was a burglar about to loot silver from a lonely country house and pin him. Still, it had to be risked, and a moment later he might have been observed tiptoeing across the carpet with all the caution of a slack-wire artist who isn't any too sure he remembers the correct steps.

Well, it was a near thing. At the instant when he started, the dog seemed occupied with something that looked like a cushion on the bed. It was licking this object in a thoughtful way, and paid no attention to Freddie till he was half-way across No Man's Land. Then it suddenly did a sort of sitting high-jump in his direction, and two seconds later Freddie, with a draughty feeling about the seat of his trouserings, was on top of a wardrobe, with the dog underneath looking up. He tells me that if he ever moved quicker in his life it was only on the occasion when, a lad of fourteen, he was discovered by his uncle, Lord Blicester, smoking one of the latter's cigars in the library: and he rather thinks he must have clipped at least a fifth of a second off the record then set up.

It looked to him now as if his sleeping arrangements for the night had been settled for him. And the thought of having to roost on top of a wardrobe at the whim of a dog was pretty dashed offensive to his proud spirit, as you may well imagine. However, as you cannot reason with Alsatians, it seemed the only thing to be done: and he was trying to make himself as comfortable as a sharp piece of wood sticking into the fleshy part of his leg would permit, when there was a snuffling noise in the passage and through the door came an object which in the dim light he was at first not able to identify. It looked something like a pen-wiper and something like a piece of a hearthrug. A second and keener inspection revealed it as a Pekingese puppy.

The uncertainty which Freddie had felt as to the newcomer's status was shared, it appeared, by the Alsatian: for after raising its eyebrows in a puzzled manner it rose and advanced inquiringly. In a tentative way it put out a paw and rolled the intruder over. Then, advancing again, it lowered its nose and sniffed.

It was a course of action against which its best friends would have advised it. These Pekes are tough eggs, especially when, as in this case, female. They look the world in the eye, and are swift to resent familiarity. There was a sort of explosion, and the next moment the Alsatian was shooting out of the room with its tail between its legs, hotly pursued. Freddie could hear the noise of battle rolling away along the passage, and it was music to his ears. Something on these lines was precisely what that Alsatian had been asking for, and now it had got it.

Presently, the Peke returned, dashing the beads of perspiration from its forehead, and came and sat down under the wardrobe, wagging a stumpy tail. And Freddie, feeling that the All Clear had been blown and that he was now at liberty to descend, did so.

His first move was to shut the door, his second to fraternize with his preserver. Freddie is a chap who believes in giving credit where credit is due, and it seemed to him that this Peke had shown itself an ornament of its species. He spared no effort, accordingly, to entertain it. He lay down on the floor and let it lick his face two hundred and thirty-three times. He tickled it under the left ear, the right ear, and at the base of the tail, in the order named. He also scratched its stomach.

All these attentions the animal received with cordiality and marked gratification: and as it seemed still in pleasure-seeking mood and had plainly come to look upon him as the official Master of the Revels, Freddie, feeling that he could not disappoint it but must play the host no matter what the cost to himself, took off his tie and handed it over. He would not have done it for everybody, he says, but where this life-saving Peke was concerned the sky was the limit.

Well, the tie went like a breeze. It was a success from the start. The Peke chewed it and chased it and got entangled in it and dragged it about the room, and was just starting to shake it from side to side when an unfortunate thing happened. Misjudging its distance, it banged its head a nasty wallop against the leg of the bed.

There is nothing of the Red Indian at the stake about a puppy in circumstances like this. A moment later, Freddie's blood was chilled by a series of fearful shrieks that seemed to ring through the night like the dying cries of the party of the second part to a first-class murder. It amazed him that a mere Peke, and a juvenile Peke at that, should have been capable of producing such an uproar. He says that a baronet, stabbed in the back with a paper-knife in his library, could not have made half such a row.

Eventually, the agony seemed to abate. Quite

suddenly, as if nothing had happened, the Peke stopped yelling and with an amused smile started to play with the tie again. And at the same moment there was a sound of whispering outside, and then a knock at the door.

'Hullo?' said Freddie.

'It is I, sir. Biggleswade.'

'Who's Biggleswade?'

'The butler, sir.'

'What do you want?'

'Her ladyship wishes me to remove the dog which you are torturing.'

There was more whispering.

'Her ladyship also desires me to say that she will be reporting the affair in the morning to the Society for the Prevention of Cruelty to Animals.'

There was another spot of whispering.

'Her ladyship further instructs me to add that, should you prove recalcitrant, I am to strike you over the head with the poker.'

Well, you can't say this was pleasant for poor old Freddie, and he didn't think so himself. He opened the door, to perceive without, a group consisting of Lady Prenderby, her daughter Dahlia, a few assorted aunts, and the butler, with poker. And he says he met Dahlia's eyes and they went through him like a knife.

'Let me explain . . .' he began.

'Spare us the details,' said Lady Prenderby with a shiver. She scooped up the Peke and felt it for broken bones.

'But listen . . .'

'Good night, Mr Widgeon.'

The aunts said good night, too, and so did the butler. The girl Dahlia preserved a revolted silence.

'But, honestly, it was nothing, really. It banged its head against the bed . . .'

'What did he say?' asked one of the aunts, who was a little hard of hearing.

357

'He says he banged the poor creature's head against the bed,' said Lady Prenderby.

'Dreadful!' said the aunt.

'Hideous!' said a second aunt.

A third aunt opened up another line of thought. She said that with men like Freddie in the house, was anyone safe? She mooted the possibility of them all being murdered in their beds. And though Freddie offered to give her a written guarantee that he hadn't the slightest intention of going anywhere near her bed, the idea seemed to make a deep impression.

'Biggleswade' said Lady Prenderby.

'M'lady?'

'You will remain in this passage for the remainder of the night with your poker.'

'Very good, m'lady.'

'Should this man attempt to leave his room, you will strike him smartly over the head.'

'Just so, m'lady.'

'But, listen . . .' said Freddie.

'Good night, Mr Widgeon.'

The mob scene broke up. Soon the passage was empty save for Biggleswade the butler, who had begun to pace up and down, halting every now and then to flick the air with his poker as if testing the lissomness of his wrist muscles and satisfying himself that they were in a condition to ensure the right amount of follow-through.

The spectacle he presented was so unpleasant that Freddie withdrew into his room and shut the door. His bosom, as you may imagine, was surging with distressing emotions. That look which Dahlia Prenderby had given him had churned him up to no little extent. He realized that he had a lot of tense thinking to do, and to assist thought he sat down on the bed.

Or rather, to be accurate, on the dead cat which was lying on the bed. It was this cat which the Alsatian had been licking just before the final breach in his relations with Freddie – the object, if you remember, which the latter had supposed to be a cushion.

He leaped up as if the corpse, instead of being cold, had been piping hot. He stared down, hoping against hope that the animal was merely in some sort of coma. But a glance told him that it had made the great change. He had never seen a deader cat. After life's fitful fever it slept well.

You wouldn't be far out in saying that poor old Freddie was now appalled. Already his reputation in this house was at zero, his name mud. On all sides he was looked upon as Widgeon the Amateur Vivisectionist. This final disaster could not but put the tin hat on it. Before, he had had a faint hope that in the morning, when calmer moods would prevail, he might be able to explain that matter of the Peke. But who was going to listen to him if he were discovered with a dead cat on his person?

And then the thought came to him that it might be possible not to be discovered with it on his person. He had only to nip downstairs and deposit the remains in the drawing room or somewhere and suspicion might not fall upon him. After all, in a super-catted house like this, cats must always be dying like flies all over the place. A housemaid would find the animal in the morning and report to GHQ that the cat strength of the establishment had been reduced by one, and there would be a bit of tut-tutting and perhaps a silent tear or two, and then the thing would be forgotten.

The thought gave him new life. All briskness and efficiency, he picked up the body by the tail and was just about to dash out of the room when, with a silent groan, he remembered Biggleswade.

He peeped out. It might be that the butler, once the eye of authority had been removed, had departed to get the remainder of his beauty-sleep. But no. Service and Fidelity were evidently the watchwords at Matcham

Scratchings. There the fellow was, still practising half-
arm shots with the poker. Freddie closed the door.

And, as he did so, he suddenly thought of the window.
There lay the solution. Here he had been, fooling about
with doors and thinking in terms of drawing rooms, and
all the while there was the balcony staring him in the
face. All he had to do was to shoot the body out into
the silent night, and let gardeners, not housemaids,
discover it.

He hurried out. It was a moment for swift action. He
raised his burden. He swung it to and fro, working up
steam. Then he let it go, and from the dark garden there
came suddenly the cry of a strong man in his anger.

'Who threw that cat?'

It was the voice of his host, Sir Mortimer Prenderby.

'Show me the man who threw that cat!' he thundered.

Windows flew up. Heads came out. Freddie sank to
the floor of the balcony and rolled against the wall.

'Whatever is the matter, Mortimer?'

'Let me get at the man who hit me in the eye with a
cat.'

'A cat?' Lady Prenderby's voice sounded perplexed.
'Are you sure?'

'Sure? What do you mean sure? Of course I'm sure. I
was just dropping off to sleep in my hammock, when
suddenly a great beastly cat came whizzing through the
air and caught me properly in the eyeball. It's a nice
thing. A man can't sleep in hammocks in his own garden
without people pelting him with cats. I insist on the
blood of the man who threw that cat.'

'Where did it come from?'

'Must have come from that balcony there.'

'Mr Widgeon's balcony,' said Lady Prenderby in an acid
voice. 'As I might have guessed.'

Sir Mortimer uttered a cry.

'So might I have guessed! Widgeon, of course! That
ugly feller. He's been throwing cats all the evening. I've

360

got a nasty sore place on the back of my neck where he hit me with one before dinner. Somebody come and open the front door. I want my heavy cane, the one with the carved ivory handle. Or a horsewhip will do.'

'Wait, Mortimer,' said Lady Prenderby. 'Do nothing rash. The man is evidently a very dangerous lunatic. I will send Biggleswade to overpower him. He has the kitchen poker.'

Little (said the Crumpet) remains to be told. At 2.15 that morning a sombre figure in dress clothes without a tie limped into the little railway station of Lower Smattering on the Wissel, some six miles from Matcham Scratchings. At 3.47 it departed Londonwards on the up milk-train. It was Frederick Widgeon. He had a broken heart and blisters on both heels. And in that broken heart was that loathing for all cats of which you recently saw so signal a manifestation. I am revealing no secrets when I tell you that Freddie Widgeon is permanently through with cats. From now on, they cross his path at their peril.

4 — Help Yourself

(Wodehouse's notes for an unwritten Freddie Widgeon story, from the Dulwich College Archive.)

It seems as if this story should begin in the Drones with Freddie, apostate to its principles, carrying a fiery cross and generally making a bloody nuisance of himself.

The thing that has roused the reforming spirit in Freddie is a tasty dish named the Hon. Millicent Puddleford. Millicent is a red-hot progressive dedicated to the cause of social betterment. Instead of sharing in the general lamentation about the difficulty in staffing the stately homes of England, Millicent is all for telling the servants to turn to more useful employments than coddling the diehard remnant of the idle rich.

Her pet enthusiasm is a school designed to help these dependant creatures by teaching them to fend for themselves. She herself is attending it and this has inspired Freddie with the idea of joining up. What could be more delicious than sharing in a class of sock-darning with the lovely Millicent?

Whether taking with him other members of the Drones or not, Freddie enrolls and sets to work, smiled on approvingly by Millicent.

The classes include: Cooking; Washing Up; Sweeping, dusting and scrubbing; Clothes washing and ironing; shoe shining and clothes pressing; bed-making, marketing and cooking. Gardening is an extra.

Love burgeons as Freddie and the Hon. Millicent meet over adjoining wash-tubs. They discuss the varying merits of Daz, Rinso, Tide etc. and the detergents that are warranted to do the job without giving them dishpan hands.

Freddy's home, Orpington Manor, is not far distant from the Self Help Academy and he repairs there on a weekend where, zealot that he is, he preaches the gospel of self help to the family, which consists of Father, Lord Clumber, mother, Lady Ditto, sport-loving sister and formidable uncle from whom the family hope to derive testamentary benefits.

Freddie's seed falls on barren soil. Lady Clumber suffers from chronic servant trouble but she has no wish to solve her difficulties by doing the job herself. Freddie goes to inspect matters below stairs and is regarded with a jaundiced eye by the cook. The only member of the staff to give him a friendly smile is Polly the upstairs maid and when Freddie asks her for some tips on bedmaking she kindly pulls one of the beds to pieces so as to show him how to do the job properly.

Freddie has been given an A in cooking, in fact he seems to have a genuine flair for the culinary art. He fancies the gift may have come to him from an ancestor who was Groom of the Saucery and Yeoman of the Chandlery under King John. Tradition has it that it was his recipe for cooking lamphreys that did the king in. Freddie's success in the field has made him critical and his strictures on the dinner are discussed in the servants' hall with dire effect.

Unaware that he is treading on dangerous ground, Freddie explains to the cook where she went wrong. Breathing lethal fumes, the cook pushes past him and, marching into the drawing room, her kitchen maid following her, she gives notice on behalf of both of them.

This tragic event is followed by the departure of the parlour maid, Freddie having criticized the way she built the fire. The whole staff is demoralized, only Polly smiles on the self-helper as warmly as ever.

Freddie has asked some of his schoolfellows to come

for the weekend. He tells the distraught Lady C. not to worry. The guests will not only look after themselves but will take care of the domestic problems for all concerned. As for the cooking he will see to that personally.

But when Freddie's friends arrive they are far from pleased to find that the holiday on which they had been counting is nothing of the sort. Only Millicent accepts the situation cheerfully. She and Freddie are clearly moving toward an engagement.

The thought of an avant garde daughter-in-law bent on turning all of England's servant class into office and factory workers, is horrifying to the earl, his wife and the rest of the family. A conference is held at which someone expresses the thought that were Freddie himself obliged to function as a domestic he wouldn't think so well of it. As it is it's a game, with Millicent as combined cheer-leader and prize.

It is Uncle Rufus who gets the great idea. Why not let him have a taste of it? A taste of really belonging to the servant class? How? Uncle Rufus proceeds to explain.

It seems that Freddie was born in Penang when Lord Clumber was serving as governor general. He had been shipped back to England to escape the summer heat when only a month old. There he had been taken charge of by Nannie Judkins, who had an infant of the same age, now Bill Judkins the gardener. Uncle Rufus's plot is to slip Nannie a handsome present for which she is to tell a story to the effect of having switched the two infants so that hers could enjoy the privileges of an heir to an ancient title. After he had inherited she had planned, so she is to say, to reveal herself as her son's benefactor and, presumably reap a rich reward. But now her conscience has prompted her to tell the truth and undo the wrong she has done to the rightful heir. (Uncle Rufus admits he got the idea from The Baby's Vengeance in the Bab Ballads.)

When first proposed the plan seems utterly

preposterous but, as they examine it, the thing appears not only feasible but definitely promising. Besides the shock it must mean for Freddie at finding himself reduced to the servant class, it should surely dispose of Millicent. She may be 'left wing' but she will hardly want to marry a penniless gardener. And Freddie will thus be rescued from a tough minded dame who, however beautiful, would be sitting on his neck in years to come.

Of course it is necessary to take gardener Bill in on the plot as well as his mother. The job, entrusted to Uncle Rufus proves surprisingly easy of accomplishment. Naturally they want to be paid for their services. Nannie sees herself as an actress and says she will want her part written out so that she can study it properly. The big scene is when she throws herself on the bosom of the rightful heir (Bill) and begs his forgiveness for the wrong she has done him.

From rehearsal to performance. All play their allotted parts. The earl protests vigorous disbelief, the Countess collapses, overcome by the shock, Penny, Freddie's sister, professes to see an hitherto unexplained likeness between Bill and the earl. As for Uncle Rufus it is his role to pass from bewilderment to belief as he reconstructs the day when he received the infant from the Ayah and passed it on to Nannie Judkins. His is the corroborative evidence that nails the story down, while Bill clasps his head and cries out at the thought of all he has missed.

Freddie blinks, trying to get his bearings. This is certainly a bit of a facer but it now seems almost providential that he has gone some way at learning to fend for himself. He is not equipped to take over Bill's job (except the boot polishing) but he can take on the job of cook. He feels sure he can give satisfaction in that capacity.

The earl says 'nonsense, he will be given a proper allowance'. 'But Freddie – that is to say "Bill" – likes being a servant,' Penny intervenes.

The transformed Freddie suggests that he and Bill swop Christian names – it will be less confusing. He also says he would prefer to call his new parent 'Nannie' rather than 'Mum'. Bill, on the other hand, takes full advantage of the new relationship to call the earl 'Dad' and to make up for all the respectful 'your ladyships' by a warm display of filial affection toward Lady C. The conspirators find there are some features attendant on the hoax that are not altogether to their liking.

But in one respect the conspiracy works according to plan. Millicent, after the first moment of incredulity, becomes patronizing and chilly. Freddie's ardour is damped. She had insisted that rank or class meant nothing to her but it becomes increasingly clear that they do. He goes about the job of cooking the dinner in mechanical fashion. Polly tries to cheer him and insists on helping him peel the onions while her eyes are filled with tears of sympathy.

The new heir, the erstwhile respectful gardener, is metamorphosed into an over familiar, free spending pain in the neck. On the excuse of acting his part convincingly he pokes playful fun at 'Dad' and 'Uncle Rufus' (whom he addresses as 'Nunky') and insists on kissing 'Mum' and 'Sis'. Making free use of the car that once was Freddie's, he dashes off to race meetings, after touching 'the old man' (or 'the Pater') for a tenner.

The problem is, how soon will Freddie have had his lesson? When will he admit he is sick of living below stairs? The earl has made him an offer to find some berth for him that will match his education and upbringing. Freddie refuses. Cooking is the only thing for which he has a talent.

Into this disturbed household there suddenly comes a new element, a small group of movie people, seeking a background for a film called 'The Girl and The Earl'. They offer a handsome fee for a week's invasion and Penny begs her father to accept. With his usually placid life already in a state of chaos, Lord Clumber says 'what's the difference?' and goes off to spend the day on his trout stream.

The visitors consist of a rising star named Dawn O'Day, a director, Pop Peters, an American leading man (who plays the earl) and a couple of camera men. They are all enraptured with Orpington Manor and, having been invited to lunch, they declare that the customary slurs on British cooking current in America are so much claptrap.

Dawn insists on visiting the kitchen to give a tip to the cook and is overwhelmed. 'That cook would make a damn sight better earl than you do,' she tells her fellow star. Pop Peters agrees and suggests the movie earl should take a few lessons in deportment.

'I can do better than that,' the actor responds. 'Lord Bedlington, the heir to the earldom, has agreed to take me in hand and teach me what's what in the peerage.'

And 'Lord Bedlington' does. Penny's conscience is troubled at the thought of Vin Sands (the actor) modelling himself on Bill, and presenting the resulting portrait of a young peer to the American public.

Penny's conscience is shocked still further as it becomes evident that Bill is enamoured of the gorgeous Dawn and that she, with the thought of the title and all that goes with it, is warmly responsive. Something must be done. They can't let this go on.

Meanwhile Pop goes to Freddie and suggests that he come to America. He goes further and offers $200 a week on his own behalf. 'It's a pity you're not married,' he says. 'What we like in America is a married couple. They stay more contented and don't want to be running off here and there like the unmarried help do.'

This thought prompts Freddie to examine his feelings in respect to Polly. He realizes that she has been the reason he has found his changed circumstances tolerable and even pleasant. She has filled the spot in his affections left empty by the desertion of the Hon. Millicent.

'How would you like to go with me to Hollywood?' he asks.

Polly would love it but raises the question of the proprieties. Freddie explains a marriage certificate would precede their departure. Polly throws her arms around his neck and says she adores him.

Penny wonders why Polly is singing over her work and Polly confides the fact that she is in love. Penny is naturally interested and congratulates her. Polly says that the marriage is going to take place immediately. After which she and her young man are going off to America. They will be sorry to leave Orpington Manor but they have been offered $500 a week and their own car and such a chance is not to be missed. Polly asks faintly who Polly's young man is and is knocked sideways by learning that it is her own brother.

Another family conference is hastily summoned and it is quickly agreed that things must be put straight. Bill and his mother are sent for. Some story will have to be told that will save the faces of the earl, his wife, daughter and uncle. Nannie will have to admit her story was a lie for which act both she and Bill will be duly paid.

To their horror Nannie insists the story is true. She says Uncle Rufus must have suspected it and that is why he set to work to have the rightful heir acknowledged by the family! The fact that they all seemingly accepted the situation has put them in a spot. Bill, getting on toward winning the stunning Dawn O'Day as his bride, is clearly the motivating force behind Nannie's attitude. So this is what has come of Uncle Horace's crazy idea!

One thing they can do and must do at once – tell the truth to Freddie and stop him from marrying a housemaid who, however pretty and sweet can never be a suitable mistress for Orpington Manor. So Freddie is told and the reason for the hoax somewhat shamefacedly

368

admitted. Freddie says this is another facer and he goes off to think things over. Penny feels it incumbent to break the news to Polly. She does and Polly accepts the changeover without comment. Millicent pays a surprise visit and learns the news. She goes to Freddie and tries to mend her fences. But Freddie isn't having any. He is determined to go on and marry Polly whether or no. Only here he finds Polly is the difficulty. She insists she will not hold him to his proposal now that he is once more Lord Bedlington. She addresses him as 'sir', which reduces him to a state of frenzy. Polly says what the family did is cruel and unforgivable. Freddie says he is eternally grateful to them. If it weren't for this he would probably have married Millicent and certainly would never have found his true love in Polly.

The film sequence is in the can and the Americans prepare to take their departure. Pop Peters meets with a disappointment when Freddie tells him he won't be accepting his generous offer to come to his home on the slopes of Bel-Air. Why has he changed his mind? Freddie explains. It is true they may have some difficulty with the claimant but Lady Clumber at least saw enough of him in infancy to swear to a strawberry mark as identification.

But Dawn is satisfied with her peer as he is. He will be all right as one of her husbands. The title will give her a tone and Bill can serve as an expert on life as lived by the British nobility.

As for Polly, Freddie carries her off protesting for an old-fashioned, romantic Scotch elopement.

5 — A Drones Money-making Scheme

His Uncle Fred's theory that Horace Davenport, scientifically worked, would develop pay gold had impressed Pongo Twistleton a good deal both when he heard it and during the remainder of the day. Throughout the drive back to London it kept him in optimistic mood. But when he woke on the following morning the idea struck him as unsound and impractical.

It was hopeless, he felt, to expect to mace any one given person for a sum like two hundred pounds. The only possible solution of his financial worries was to open a subscription list and let the general public in on the thing. He decided to look in at the Drones immediately and test the sentiment of the investors. And having arrived there, he was gratified to note that all the indications seemed to point to a successful flotation.

The atmosphere in the smoking-room of the Drones Club on the return of its members from their annual weekend at Le Touquet was not always one of cheerfulness and gaiety – there had been years when you might have mistaken the place for the Wailing Wall of Jerusalem – but today a delightful spirit of happiness prevailed. The dingy gods who preside over the *chemin-de-fer* tables at Continental Casinos had, it appeared, been extraordinarily kind to many of the Eggs, Beans, and Crumpets revelling at the bar. And Pongo, drinking in the tales of their exploits, had just decided to raise the assessment of several of those present another ten pounds, when through the haze of cigarette smoke he caught sight of a familiar face. On a chair at the far end of the room sat Claude Pott.

It was not merely curiosity as to what Mr Pott was doing there or a fear lest he might be feeling lonely in these unaccustomed surroundings that caused Pongo to go and engage him in conversation. At the sight of the private investigator, there had floated into his mind like drifting thistledown the thought that it might be possible to start the ball rolling by obtaining a small donation from him. He crossed the room with outstretched hand.

'Why, hullo, Mr Pott. What brings you here?'

'Good morning, sir. I came with Mr Davenport. He is at the moment in the telephone booth, telephoning.'

'I didn't know old Horace ever got up as early as this.'

'He has not retired to bed yet. He went to a dance last night.'

'Of course, yes. The Bohemian Ball at the Albert Hall. I remember. Well, it's nice seeing you again, Mr Pott. You left a bit hurriedly that time we met.'

'Yes,' said Claude Pott meditatively. 'How did you come out with The Subject?'

'Not too well. She threw her weight about a bit.'

'I had an idea she would.'

'You were better away.'

'That's what I thought.'

'Still,' said Pongo heartily, 'I was very sorry you had to go, very. I could see that we were a couple of chaps who were going to get along together. Will you have a drink or something?'

'No, thank you, Mr T.'

'A cigarette or something?'

'No, thank you.'

'A chair or something? Oh, you've got one. I say, Mr Pott,' said Pongo, 'I was wondering – '

The babble at the bar had risen to a sudden crescendo. Oofy Prosser, the club's tame millionaire, was repeating for the benefit of some new arrivals the story of how he had run his bank seven times, and there had come into

Mr Pott's eyes a dull glow, like the phosphorescent gleam on the stomach of a dead fish.

'Coo!' he said, directing at Oofy the sort of look a thoughtful vulture in the Sahara casts at a dying camel. 'Seems to be a lot of money in here this morning.'

'Yes. And talking of money – '

'Now would be just the time to run the old Hat Stakes.'

'Hat Stakes?'

'Haven't you ever heard of the Hat Stakes? It sometimes seems to me they don't teach you boys nothing at your public schools. Here's the way it works. You take somebody, as it might be me, and he opens a book on the Hat Race, the finish to be wherever you like – call it that door over there. See what I mean? The punters would bet on what sort of hat the first bloke coming in through that door would be wearing. You, for instance, might feel like having a tenner – '

Pongo flicked a speck of dust from his companion's sleeve.

'Ah, but I haven't got a tenner,' he said. 'And that's precisely why I was saying that I wondered – '

' – on Top Hat. Then if a feller wearing a top hat was the first to come in, you'd cop.'

'Yes, I see the idea. Amusing. Ingenious.'

'But you can't play the Hat Stakes nowadays, with everybody wearing these Homburgs. There wouldn't be enough starters. Cor!'

'Cor' agreed Pongo sympathetically. 'You'd have to make it clothes or something, what? But you were speaking of tenners, and while on that subject . . . Stop me if you've heard this before . . .'

Claude Pott, who had seemed about to sink into a brooding reverie, came out of his meditations with a start.

'What's that you said?'

'I was saying that while on the subject of tenners – '

'Clothes!' Mr Pott rose from his chair with a

spasmodic leap, as if he had seen The Subject entering the room. 'Well, strike me pink!'

He shot for the door at a speed quite remarkable in a man of his build. A few moments later, he shot back again, and suddenly the Eggs, Beans, and Crumpets assembled at the bar were shocked to discover that some bounder, contrary to all club etiquette, was making a speech.

'Gentlemen!'

The babble died away, to be succeeded by a stunned silence, through which there came the voice of Claude Pott, speaking with all the fervour and *brio* of his Silver Ring days.

'Gentlemen and sportsmen, if I may claim your kind indulgence for one instant! Gentlemen and sportsmen, I know gentlemen and sportsmen when I see them, and what I have been privileged to overhear of your conversation since entering this room has shown me that you are all gentlemen and sportsmen who are ready at all times to take part in a little sporting flutter.'

The words 'sporting flutter' were words which never failed to touch a chord in the members of the Drones Club. Something resembling warmth and sympathy began to creep into the atmosphere of cold disapproval. How this little blister had managed to worm his way into their smoking-room they were still at a loss to understand, but the initial impulse of those present to bung him out on his ear had softened into a more friendly desire to hear what he had to say.

'Pott is my name, gentlemen – a name at one time, I venture to assert, not unfamiliar to patrons of the sport of kings, and though I have retired from active business as a turf commission agent I am still willing to make a little book from time to time to entertain sportsmen and gentlemen, and there's no time like the present. Here we all are – you with the money, me with the book – so I say again, gentlemen, let's have a little flutter.

Gentlemen all, the Clothes Stakes are about to be run.'

Few members of the Drones are at their brightest and alertest in the morning. There was a puzzled murmur. A Bean said, 'What did he say?' and a Crumpet whispered, 'The what Stakes?'

'I was explaining the how-you-do-it of the Hat Stakes to my friend Mr Twistleton over there, and the Clothes Stakes are run on precisely the same principle. There is at the present moment a gentleman in the telephone booth along the corridor, and I have just taken the precaution to instruct a page-boy to shove a wedge under the door, thus ensuring that he will remain there and so accord you all ample leisure in which to place your wagers. Coo!' said Claude Pott, struck by an unpleasant idea. 'Nobody's going to come along and let him out, are they?'

'Of course not!' cried his audience indignantly. The thought of anybody wantonly releasing a fellow member who had got stuck in the telephone booth, a thing that only happened once in a blue moon, was revolting to them.

'Then that's all right. Now then, gentlemen, the simple question you have to ask yourselves is – What is the gentleman in the telephone booth wearing? Or putting it another way – What's he got on? Hence the term Clothes Stakes. It might be one thing, or it might be another. He might be in his Sunday-go-to-meetings, or he might have been taking a dip in the Serpentine and be in his little bathing suit. Or he may have joined the Salvation Army. To give you a lead, I am offering nine to four against Blue Serge, four to one Pin Striped Grey Tweed, ten to one Golf Coat and Plus Fours, a hundred to six Gymnasium Vest and Running Shorts, twenty to one Court Dress as worn at Buckingham Palace, nine to four the field. And perhaps you, sir,' said Mr Pott, addressing an adjacent Egg, 'would be good enough to officiate as my clerk.'

'That doesn't mean I can't have a bit on?'

'By no means, sir. Follow the dictates of your heart
and fear nothing.'

'What are you giving Herringbone Cheviot Lounge?'

'Six to one Herringbone Cheviot Lounge, sir.'

'I'll have ten bob.'

'Right, sir. Six halves Herringbone Cheviot Lounge.
Ready money, if you please, sir. It's not that I don't trust
you, but I'm not allowed by law. Thank you, sir. Walk
up, walk up, my noble sportsmen. Nine to four the
field.'

The lead thus given them removed the last inhibitions
of the company. Business became brisk, and it was not
long before Mr Pott had vanished completely behind a
mass of eager punters.

Among the first to invest had been Pongo Twistleton.
Hastening to the hall porter's desk, he had written a
cheque for his last ten pounds in the world, and he was
now leaning against the bar, filled with the quiet
satisfaction of the man who has spotted the winner and
got his money down in good time.

For from the very inception of these proceedings it had
been clear to Pongo that Fortune, hitherto capricious,
had at last decided that it was no use trying to keep a
good man down and had handed him something on
a plate. To be a successful punter, what you need is
information, and this he possessed in abundant measure.
Alone of those present, he was aware of the identity of
the gentleman in the telephone booth, and he had the
additional advantage of knowing the inside facts about
the latter's wardrobe.

You take a chap like – say – Catsmeat Potter-Pirbright,
that modern Brummel, and you might guess for hours
without hitting on the precise suit he would be wearing
on any given morning. But with Horace Pendlebury-
Davenport it was different. Horace had never been a
vivacious dresser. He liked to stick to the old and tried till
they came apart on him, and it was this idiosyncrasy of

his which had caused his recent *fiancée*, just before her departure for Le Touquet, to take a drastic step.

Swooping down on Horace's flat, at a moment when Pongo was there chatting with its proprietor, and ignoring her loved one's protesting cries, Valerie Twistleton had scooped up virtually his entire outfit and borne it away in a cab, to be given to the deserving poor. She could not actually leave the unhappy man in the nude, so she had allowed him to retain the shabby grey flannel suit he stood up in and also the morning clothes which he was reserving for the wedding day. But she had got away with all the rest, and as no tailor could have delivered a fresh supply at this early date, Pongo had felt justified in plunging to the uttermost. The bulk of his fortune on Grey Flannel at ten to one and a small covering bet on Morning Suit, and there he was, sitting pretty.

And he was just sipping his cocktail and reflecting that while his winnings must necessarily fall far short of the stupendous sum which he owed to George Budd, they would at least constitute something on account and remove the dark shadow of Erb at any rate temporarily from his life, when like a blow on the base of the skull there came to him the realization that he had overlooked a vital point.

The opening words of his conversation with Claude Pott came back to him, and he remembered that Mr Pott, in addition to informing him that Horace was in the telephone booth, had stated that the latter had attended the Bohemian Ball at the Albert Hall and had not been to bed yet. And like the knell of a tolling bell there rang in his ears Horace's words: 'I am going as a Boy Scout.'

The smoking-room reeled before Pongo's eyes. He saw now why Claude Pott had leaped so enthusiastically at the idea of starting these Clothes Stakes. The man had known it would be a skinner for the book. The shrewdest and most imaginative Drone would never think of Boy Scouts in telephone booths at this hour of the morning.

He uttered a stricken cry. At the eleventh hour the road to wealth had been indicated to him, and owing to that ready-money clause he was not in a position to take advantage of the fact. And then he caught sight of Oofy Prosser at the other end of the bar, and saw how by swift, decisive action he might save his fortunes from the wreck.

The attitude of Oofy Prosser towards the Clothes Stakes had been from the first contemptuous and supercilious, like that of a Wolf of Wall Street watching small boys scrambling for pennies. This Silver Ring stuff did not interest Oofy. He held himself aloof from it, and as the latter slid down the bar and accosted him he tried to hold himself aloof from Pongo. It was only by clutching his coat sleeve and holding on to it with a fevered grip that Pongo was able to keep him rooted to the spot.

'I say, Oofy – '

'No,' replied Oofy Prosser curtly. 'Not a penny!'

Pongo danced a few frantic dance steps. Already there was a lull over by the table where Mr Pott was conducting his business, and the closing of the book seemed imminent.

'But I want to put you on to a good thing!'

'Oh?'

'A cert.'

'Ah?'

'An absolute dashed cast-iron cert.'

Oofy Prosser sneered visibly.

'I'm not betting. What's the use of winning a couple of quid? Why, last Sunday at the big table at Le Touquet – '

Pongo sped towards Claude Pott, scattering Eggs, Beans, and Crumpets from his path.

'Mr Pott!'

'Sir?'

'Any limit?'

'No, sir.'

377

'I've a friend here who wants to put on something big.'

'Ready money only, Mr T., may I remind you? It's the law.'

'Nonsense. This is Mr Prosser. You can take his cheque. You must have heard of Mr Prosser.'

'Oh, Mr Prosser? Yes, that's different. I don't mind breaking the law to oblige Mr Prosser.'

Pongo, bounding back to the bar, found there an Oofy no longer aloof and supercilious.

'Do you really know something, Pongo?'

'You bet I know something. Will you cut me in for fifty?'

'All right.'

'Then put your shirt on Boy Scout,' hissed Pongo. 'I have first-hand stable information that the bloke in the telephone booth is Horace Davenport, and I happen to know that he went to a fancy-dress dance last night as a Boy Scout and hasn't been home to change yet.'

'What! Is that right?'

'Absolutely official.'

'Then it's money for jam!'

'Money for pickles,' asserted Pongo enthusiastically. 'Follow me and fear nothing. And don't forget I'm in for the sum I mentioned.'

With a kindling eye he watched his financial backer force his way into the local Tattersall's, and it was at this tense moment that a page-boy came up and informed him that Lord Ickenham was waiting for him in the hall. He went floating out to meet him, his feet scarcely touching the carpet.

Lord Ickenham watched his approach with interest.

'Aha!' he said.

'Aha!' said Pongo, but absently, as one who has no time for formal greetings. 'Listen, Uncle Fred, slip me every bally cent you've got on you. I may just be able to get it down before the book closes. Your pal, Claude Pott, came here with Horace Davenport – '

'I wonder what Horace was doing, bringing Mustard to the Drones. Capital chap, of course, but quite the wrong person to let loose in a gathering of impressionable young men.'

Pongo's manner betrayed impatience.

'We haven't time to go into the ethics of the thing. Suffice it that Horace did bring him, and he shut Horace up in the telephone booth and started a book on what sort of clothes he had on. How much can you raise?'

'To wager against Mustard Pott?' Lord Ickenham smiled gently. 'Nothing, my dear boy, nothing. One of the hard lessons Life will teach you, as you grow to know him better, is that you can't make money out of Mustard. Hundreds have tried it, and hundreds have failed.'

Pongo shrugged his shoulders. He had done his best.

'Well, you're missing the chance of a lifetime. I happen to know that Horace went to a dance last night as a Boy Scout, and I have it from Pott's own lips that he hasn't been home to change. Oofy Prosser is carrying me for fifty.'

It was evident from his expression that Lord Ickenham was genuinely shocked.

'Horace Davenport went to a dance as a Boy Scout? What a ghastly sight he must have looked. I can't believe this. I must verify it. Bates,' said Lord Ickenham, walking over to the hall-porter's desk, 'were you here when Mr Davenport came in?'

'Yes, m'lord.'

'How did he look?'

'Terrible, m'lord.'

It seemed to Pongo that his uncle had wandered from the point.

'I concede,' he said, 'that a chap of Horace's height and skinniness ought to have been shrewder than to flaunt himself at a public dance in the costume of a Boy Scout. Involving as it does, knickerbockers and bare knees – '

'But he didn't, sir.'

379

'What!'

The hall-porter was polite, but firm.

'Mr Davenport didn't go to no dance as no Boy ruddy Scout, if you'll pardon me contradicting you, sir. More like some sort of negroid character, it seemed to me. His face was all blacked up, and he had a spear with him. Gave me a nasty turn when he come through.'

Pongo clutched the desk. The hall-porter's seventeen stone seemed to be swaying before his eyes.

'Blacked up?'

A movement along the passage attracted their attention. Claude Pott, accompanied by a small committee, was proceeding to the telephone booth. He removed the wedge from beneath the door, and as he opened it there emerged a figure.

Nature hath framed strange fellows in her time, but few stranger than the one that now whizzed out of the telephone booth, whizzed down the corridor, whizzed past the little group at the desk and, bursting through the door of the club, whizzed down the steps and into a passing cab.

The face of this individual, as the hall porter had foreshadowed, was a rich black in colour. Its long body was draped in tights of the same sombre hue, surmounted by a leopard's skin. Towering above his head was a head-dress of ostrich feathers, and in its right hand it grasped an assegai. It was wearing tortoiseshell-rimmed spectacles.

Pongo, sliding back against the desk, found his arm gripped by a kindly hand.

'Shift ho, my boy, I think, eh?' said Lord Ickenham. 'There would appear to be nothing to keep you here, and a meeting with Oofy Prosser at this moment might be fraught with pain and embarrassment. Let us follow Horace – he seemed to be homing – and hold an enquiry into this in-and-out running of his. Tell me, how much did you say Oofy Prosser was carrying you for? Fifty pounds?'

Pongo nodded bleakly.

'Then let us assemble the facts. Your assets are nil. You owe George Budd two hundred. You now owe Oofy fifty. If you don't pay Oofy, he will presumably report you to the committee and have you thrown into the street, where you will doubtless find Erb waiting for you with a knuckleduster. Well,' said Lord Ickenham, impressed, 'nobody can say you don't lead a full life. To a yokel like myself all this is very stimulating. One has the sense of being right at the pulsing heart of things.'

They came to Bloxham Mansions, and were informed by Webster that Mr Davenport was in his bath.

Psmith

1 — Mike Meets Psmith

The train, which had been stopping everywhere for the last half-hour, pulled up again, and Mike, seeing the name of the station, got up, opened the door, and hurled a bag out on to the platform in an emphatic and vindictive manner. Then he got out himself and looked about him.

'For the school, sir?' inquired the solitary porter, bustling up, as if he hoped by sheer energy to deceive the traveller into thinking that Sedleigh station was staffed by a great army of porters.

Mike nodded. A sombre nod. The nod Napoleon might have given if somebody had met him in 1812, and said, 'So you're back from Moscow, eh?' Mike was feeling thoroughly jaundiced. The future seemed wholly gloomy. And, so far from attempting to make the best of things, he had set himself deliberately to look on the dark side. He thought, for instance, that he had never seen a more repulsive porter, or one more obviously incompetent than the man who had attached himself with a firm grasp to the handle of the bag as he strode off in the direction of the luggage-van. He disliked his voice, his appearance, and the colour of his hair. Also the boots he wore. He hated the station, and the man who took his ticket.

'Young gents at the school, sir,' said the porter, perceiving from Mike's *distrait* air that the boy was a stranger to the place, 'goes up in the bus mostly. It's waiting here, sir. Hi, George!'

'I'll walk, thanks,' said Mike frigidly.

'It's a goodish step, sir.'

'Here you are.'

'Thank you, sir. I'll send up your luggage by the bus, sir. Which 'ouse was it you was going to?'

'Outwood's.'

'Right, sir. It's straight on up this road to the school. You can't miss it, sir.'

'Worse luck,' said Mike.

He walked off up the road, sorrier for himself than ever. It was such absolutely rotten luck. About now, instead of being on his way to a place where they probably ran a halma team instead of a cricket eleven, and played hunt-the-slipper in winter, he would be on the point of arriving at Wrykyn. And as captain of cricket, at that. Which was the bitter part of it. He had never been in command. For the last two seasons he had been the star man, going in first, and heading the averages easily at the end of the season; and the three captains under whom he had played during his career as a Wrykynian, Burgess, Enderby, and Henfrey, had always been sportsmen to him. But it was not the same thing. He had meant to do such a lot for Wrykyn cricket this term. He had had an entirely new system of coaching in his mind. Now it might never be used. He had handed it on in a letter to Strachan, who would be captain in his place; but probably Strachan would have some scheme of his own. There is nobody who could not edit a paper in the ideal way; and there is nobody who has not a theory of his own about cricket-coaching at school.

Wrykyn, too, would be weak this year, now that he was no longer there. Strachan was a good, free bat on his day, and, if he survived a few overs, might make a century in an hour, but he was not to be depended upon. There was no doubt that Mike's sudden withdrawal meant that Wrykyn would have a bad time that season. And it had been such a wretched athletic year for the school. The football fifteen had been hopeless, and had lost both the Ripton matches, the return by over sixty points. Sheen's

victory in the lightweights at Aldershot had been their
one success. And now, on top of all this, the captain of
cricket was removed during the Easter holidays. Mike's
heart bled for Wrykyn, and he found himself loathing
Sedleigh and all its works with a great loathing.

The only thing he could find in its favour was the fact
that it was set in very pretty country. Of a different type
from the Wrykyn country, but almost as good. For three
miles Mike made his way through woods and past fields.
Once he crossed a river. It was soon after this that he
caught sight, from the top of a hill, of a group of buildings
that wore an unmistakably school-like
look.

This must be Sedleigh.

Ten minutes' walk brought him to the school gates,
and a baker's boy directed him to Mr Outwood's.

There were three houses in a row, separated from the
school buildings by a cricket-field. Outwood's was
the middle one of these.

Mike went to the front door, and knocked. At Wrykyn
he had always charged in at the beginning of term at the
boys' entrance, but this formal reporting of himself at
Sedleigh suited his mood.

He inquired for Mr Outwood, and was shown into a
room lined with books. Presently the door opened, and the
house-master appeared.

There was something pleasant and homely about Mr
Outwood. In appearance he reminded Mike of Smee in
'Peter Pan'. He had the same eyebrows and pince-nez and
the same motherly look.

'Jackson?' he said mildly.

'Yes, sir.'

'I am very glad to see you, very glad indeed. Perhaps
you would like a cup of tea after your journey. I think
you might like a cup of tea. You come from Crofton, in
Shropshire, I understand, Jackson, near Brindleford? It
is a part of the country which I have always wished to

visit. I dare say you have frequently seen the Cluniac
Priory of St Ambrose at Brindleford?'

Mike, who would not have recognized a Cluniac
Priory if you had handed him one on a tray, said he had
not.

'Dear me! You have missed an opportunity which I
should have been glad to have. I am preparing a book on
Ruined Abbeys and Priories of England, and it has always
been my wish to see the Cluniac Priory of St Ambrose.
A deeply interesting relic of the sixteenth century. Bishop
Geoffrey 1133–40–'

'Shall I go across to the boys' part, sir?'

'What? Yes. Oh, yes. Quite so. And perhaps you would
like a cup of tea after your journey? No? Quite so. Quite
so. You should make a point of visiting the remains of
the Cluniac Priory in the summer holidays, Jackson.
You will find the matron in her room. In many respects
it is unique. The northern altar is in a state of really
wonderful preservation. It consists of a solid block of
masonry five feet long and two and a half wide, with
chamfered plinth, standing quite free from the apse wall.
It will well repay a visit. Good-bye for the present,
Jackson, good-bye.'

Mike wandered across to the other side of the house,
his gloom visibly deepened. All alone in a strange school,
where they probably played hop-scotch, with a house-
master who offered one cups of tea after one's journey and
talked about chamfered plinths and apses. It was a little
hard.

He strayed about, finding his bearings, and finally
came to a room which he took to be the equivalent of
the senior day-room at a Wrykyn house. Everywhere else
he had found nothing but emptiness. Evidently he had
come by an earlier train than was usual. But this room
was occupied.

A very long, thin youth, with a solemn face and
immaculate clothes, was leaning against the

mantelpiece. As Mike entered, he fumbled in his top left waistcoat pocket, produced an eyeglass attached to a cord, and fixed it in his right eye. With the help of this aid to vision he inspected Mike in silence for a while, then, having flicked an invisible speck of dust from the left sleeve of his coat, he spoke.

'Hullo,' he said.

He spoke in a tired voice.

'Hullo,' said Mike.

'Take a seat,' said the immaculate one. 'If you don't mind dirtying your bags, that's to say. Personally, I don't see any prospect of ever sitting down in this place. It looks to me as if they meant to use these chairs as mustard-and-cress beds. A Nursery Garden in the Home. That sort of idea. My name,' he added pensively, 'is Smith. What's yours?'

'Jackson,' said Mike.

'Are you the Bully, the Pride of the School, or the Boy who is Led Astray and takes to Drink in Chapter Sixteen?'

'The last, for choice,' said Mike, 'but I've only just arrived, so I don't know.'

'The boy – what will he become? Are you new here, too, then?'

'Yes! Why, are you new?'

'Do I look as if I belonged here? I'm the latest import. Sit down on yonder settee, and I will tell you the painful story of my life. By the way, before I start, there's just one thing. If you ever have occasion to write to me, would you mind sticking a P at the beginning of my name? P-s-m-i-t-h. See? There are too many Smiths, and I don't care for Smythe. My father's content to worry along in the old-fashioned way, but I've decided to strike out a fresh line. I shall found a new dynasty. The resolve came to me unexpectedly this morning. I jotted it down on the back of an envelope. In conversation you may address me as Rupert (though I hope you won't), or simply Smith, the

P not being sounded. Cp. the name Zbysco, in which
the Z is given a similar miss-in-baulk. See?'

Mike said he saw. Psmith thanked him with a certain
stately old-world courtesy.

'Let us start at the beginning,' he resumed. 'My
infancy. When I was but a babe, my eldest sister was
bribed with a shilling an hour by my nurse to keep an eye
on me, and see that I did not raise Cain. At the end of
the first day she struck for one-and-six, and got it. We
now pass to my boyhood. At an early age, I was sent to
Eton, everybody predicting a bright career for me. But,'
said Psmith solemnly, fixing an owl-like gaze on Mike
through the eyeglass, 'it was not to be.'

'No?' said Mike.

'No. I was superannuated last term.'

'Bad luck.'

'For Eton, yes. But what Eton loses, Sedleigh gains.'

'But why Sedleigh, of all places?'

'This is the most painful part of my narrative. It seems
that a certain scug in the next village to ours happened
last year to collar a Balliol – '

'Not Barlitt!' exclaimed Mike.

'That was the man. The son of the vicar. The vicar
told the curate, who told our curate, who told our
vicar, who told my father, who sent me off here to get a
Balliol too. Do *you* know Barlitt?'

'His father's vicar of our village. It was because his son
got a Balliol that I was sent here.'

'Do you come from Crofton?'

'Yes.'

'I've lived at Lower Benford all my life. We are
practically long-lost brothers. Cheer a little, will
you?'

Mike felt as Robinson Crusoe felt when he met Friday.
Here was a fellow human being in this desert place. He
could almost have embraced Psmith. The very sound of
the name Lower Benford was heartening. His dislike for

his new school was not diminished, but now he felt that life there might at least be tolerable.

'Where were you before you came here?' asked Psmith. 'You have heard my painful story. Now tell me yours.'

'Wrykyn. My father took me away because I got such a lot of bad reports.'

'My reports from Eton were simply scurrilous. There's a libel action in every sentence. How do you like this place from what you've seen of it?'

'Rotten.'

'I am with you, Comrade Jackson. You won't mind my calling you Comrade, will you? I've just become a Socialist. It's a great scheme. You ought to be one. You work for the equal distribution of property, and start by collaring all you can and sitting on it. We must stick together. We are companions in misfortune. Lost lambs. Sheep that have gone astray. Divided, we fall, together we may worry through. Have you seen Professor Radium yet? I should say Mr Outwood. What do you think of him?'

'He doesn't seem a bad sort of chap. Bit off his nut. Jawed about apses and things.'

'And thereby,' said Psmith, 'hangs a tale. I've been making inquiries of a stout sportsman in a sort of Salvation Army uniform, whom I met in the grounds – he's the school sergeant or something, quite a solid man – and I hear that Comrade Outwood's an archaeological cove. Goes about the country beating up old ruins and fossils and things. There's an Archaeological Society in the school, run by him. It goes out on half-holidays, prowling about, and is allowed to break bounds and generally steep itself to the eyebrows in reckless devilry. And, mark you, laddie, if you belong to the Archaeological Society you get off cricket. To get off cricket,' said Psmith, dusting his right trouser-leg, 'was the dream of my youth and the aspiration of my riper years. A noble game, but a bit too thick for me. At Eton I used to have

to field out at the nets till the soles of my boots wore
through. I suppose you are a blood at the game? Play for
the school against Loamshire, and so on.'

'I'm not going to play here, at any rate,' said Mike.

He had made up his mind on this point in the train.
There is a certain fascination about making the very
worst of a bad job. Achilles knew his business when he
sat in his tent. The determination not to play cricket for
Sedleigh as he could not play for Wrykyn gave Mike a
sort of pleasure. To stand by with folded arms and
a sombre frown, as it were, was one way of treating the
situation, and one not without its meed of comfort.

Psmith approved the resolve.

'Stout fellow,' he said. ''Tis well. You and I, hand in
hand, will search the countryside for ruined abbeys. We
will snare the elusive fossil together. Above all, we will
go out of bounds. We shall thus improve our minds, and
have a jolly good time as well. I shouldn't wonder if one
mightn't borrow a gun from some friendly native, and
do a bit of rabbit-shooting here and there. From what I
saw of Comrade Outwood during our brief interview,
I shouldn't think he was one of the lynx-eyed contingent.
With tact we ought to be able to slip away from the
merry throng of fossil-chasers, and do a bit on our own
account.'

'Good idea,' said Mike. 'We will. A chap at Wrykyn,
called Wyatt, used to break out at night and shoot at cats
with an air-pistol.'

'It would take a lot to make me do that. I am all against
anything that interferes with my sleep. But rabbits in
the daytime is a scheme. We'll nose about for a gun at the
earliest opp. Meanwhile we'd better go up to Comrade
Outwood, and get our names shoved down for the
Society.'

'I vote we get some tea first somewhere.'

'Then let's beat up a study. I suppose they have studies
here. Let's go and look.'

They went upstairs. On the first floor there was a passage with doors on either side. Psmith opened the first of these.

'This'll do us well,' he said.

It was a biggish room, looking out over the school grounds. There were a couple of deal tables, two empty bookcases, and a looking-glass, hung on a nail.

'Might have been made for us,' said Psmith approvingly.

'I suppose it belongs to some rotter.'

'Not now.'

'You aren't going to collar it!'

'That,' said Psmith, looking at himself earnestly in the mirror, and straightening his tie, 'is the exact programme. We must stake out our claims. This is practical Socialism.'

'But the real owner's bound to turn up some time or other.'

'His misfortune, not ours. You can't expect two master-minds like us to pig it in that room downstairs. There are moments when one wants to be alone. It is imperative that we have a place to retire to after a fatiguing day. And now, if you want to be really useful, come and help me fetch up my box from downstairs. It's got a gas-ring and various things in it.'

2 — Mike and Psmith visit Clapham

The department into which Mike was sent was the Cash, or, to be more exact, that section of it which was known as Paying Cashier. The important task of shooting doubloons across the counter did not belong to Mike himself, but to Mr Waller. Mike's work was less ostentatious, and was performed with pen, ink, and ledgers in the background. Occasionally, when Mr Waller was out at lunch, Mike had to act as substitute for him, and cash cheques; but Mr Waller always went out at a slack time, when few customers came in, and Mike seldom had any very startling sum to hand over.

He enjoyed being in the Cash Department. He liked Mr Waller. The work was easy; and when he did happen to make mistakes, they were corrected patiently by the grey-bearded one, and not used as levers for boosting him into the presence of Mr Bickersdyke, as they might have been in some departments.

The cashier seemed to have taken a fancy to Mike; and Mike, as was usually the way with him when people went out of their way to be friendly, was at his best. Mike at his ease and unsuspicious of hostile intentions was a different person from Mike with his prickles out.

Psmith, meanwhile, was not enjoying himself. It was an unheard-of thing, he said, depriving a man of his confidential secretary without so much as asking his leave.

'It has caused me the greatest inconvenience,' he told Mike, drifting round in a melancholy way to the Cash Department during a slack spell one afternoon. 'I miss you at every turn. Your keen intelligence and ready sympathy were invaluable to me. Now where am I? In the cart. I evolved a slightly bright thought on life just now. There was nobody to tell it to except the new man. I told it him, and the fool gaped. I tell you, Comrade Jackson, I feel like some lion that has been robbed of its cub. I feel as Marshall would feel if they took Snelgrove away from him, or as Peace might if he awoke one morning to find Plenty gone. Comrade Rossiter does his best. We still talk brokenly about Manchester United – they got outed in the first round of the Cup yesterday, and Comrade Rossiter is wearing black – but it is not the same. I try work, but that is no good either. From ledger to ledger they hurry me, to stifle my regret. And when they win a smile from me, they think that I forget. But I don't. I am a broken man. That new exhibit they've got in your place is about as near to the Extreme Edge as anything I've ever seen. One of Nature's blighters. Well, well, I must away. Comrade Rossiter awaits me.'

Mike's successor, a youth of the name of Bristow, was causing Psmith a great deal of pensive melancholy. His worst defect – which he could not help – was that he was not Mike. His others – which he could – were numerous. His clothes were cut in a way that harrowed Psmith's sensitive soul every time he looked at them. The fact that he wore detachable cuffs, which he took off on beginning work and stacked in a glistening pile on the desk in front of him, was no proof of innate viciousness of disposition, but it prejudiced the Old Etonian against him. It was part of Psmith's philosophy that a man who wore detachable cuffs had passed beyond the limit of human toleration. In addition, Bristow wore a small black moustache and a ring, and that, as Psmith informed Mike, put the lid on it.

Mike would some times stroll round to the Postage Department to listen to the conversations between the two. Bristow was always friendliness itself. He habitually addressed Psmith as Smithy, a fact which entertained

Mike greatly but did not seem to amuse Psmith to any
overwhelming extent. On the other hand, when, as he
generally did, he called Mike 'Mister Cricketer', the
humour of the thing appeared to elude Mike, though
the mode of address always drew from Psmith a pale, wan
smile, as of a broken heart made cheerful against its own
inclination.

The net result of the coming of Bristow was that
Psmith spent most of his time, when not actually
oppressed by a rush of work, in the precincts of the Cash
Department, talking to Mike and Mr Waller. The latter
did not seem to share the dislike common among the
other heads of departments of seeing his subordinates
receiving visitors. Unless the work was really heavy, in
which case a mild remonstrance escaped him, he offered
no objection to Mike being at home to Psmith. It was this
tolerance which sometimes got him into trouble with
Mr Bickersdyke. The manager did not often perambulate
the office, but he did occasionally, and the interview
which ensued upon his finding Hutchinson, the underling
in the Cash Department at that time, with his stool
tilted comfortably against the wall, reading the sporting
news from a pink paper to a friend from the Outward
Bills Department who lay luxuriously on the floor beside
him, did not rank among Mr Waller's pleasantest
memories. But Mr Waller was too soft-hearted to interfere
with his assistants unless it was absolutely necessary.
The truth of the matter was that the New Asiatic Bank
was over-staffed. There were too many men for the work.
The London Branch of the bank was really only a nursery.
New men were constantly wanted in the Eastern
branches, so they had to be put into the London branch
to learn the business, whether there was any work for
them to do or not.

It was after one of these visits of Psmith's that Mr
Waller displayed a new and unsuspected side to his
character. Psmith had come round in a state of some

depression to discuss Bristow, as usual. Bristow, it seemed, had come to the bank that morning in a fancy waistcoat of so emphatic a colour-scheme that Psmith stoutly refused to sit in the same department with it.

'What with Comrades Bristow and Bickersdyke combined,' said Psmith plaintively, 'the work is becoming too hard for me. The whisper is beginning to circulate, "Psmith's number is up. As a reformer he is merely among those present. He is losing his dash." But what can I do? I cannot keep an eye on both of them at the same time. The moment I concentrate myself on Comrade Bickersdyke for a brief spell, and seem to be doing him a bit of good, what happens? Why, Comrade Bristow sneaks off and buys a sort of woollen sunset. I saw the thing unexpectedly. I tell you I was shaken. It is the suddenness of that waistcoat which hits you. It's discouraging, this sort of thing. I try always to think well of my fellow man. As an energetic Socialist, I do my best to see the good that is in him, but it's hard. Comrade Bristow's the most striking argument against the equality of man I've ever come across.'

Mr Waller intervened at this point.

'I think you must really let Jackson go on with his work, Smith,' he said. 'There seems to be too much talking.'

'My besetting sin,' said Psmith sadly. 'Well, well, I will go back and do my best to face it, but it's a tough job.'

He tottered wearily away in the direction of the Postage Department.

'Oh, Jackson,' said Mr Waller, 'will you kindly take my place for a few minutes? I must go round and see the Inward Bills about something. I shall be back very soon.'

Mike was becoming accustomed to deputizing for the cashier for short spaces of time. It generally happened that he had to do so once or twice a day. Strictly speaking, perhaps, Mr Waller was wrong to leave such an important task as the actual cashing of cheques to an inexperienced person of Mike's standing; but the New Asiatic Bank differed from most banks in that there was not a great deal of cross-counter work. People came in fairly frequently to cash cheques of two or three pounds, but it was rare that any very large dealings took place.

Having completed his business with the Inward Bills, Mr Waller made his way back by a circuitous route, taking in the Postage desk.

He found Psmith with a pale, set face, inscribing figures in a ledger. The Old Etonian greeted him with the faint smile of a persecuted saint who is determined to be cheerful even at the stake.

'Comrade Bristow,' he said.

'Hullo, Smithy?' said the other, turning.

Psmith sadly directed Mr Waller's attention to the waistcoat, which was certainly definite in its colour.

'Nothing,' said Psmith. 'I only wanted to look at you.'

'Funny ass,' said Bristow, resuming his work. Psmith glanced at Mr Waller, as who should say, 'See what I have to put up with. And yet I do not give way.'

'Oh – er – Smith,' said Mr Waller, 'when you were talking to Jackson just now – '

'Say no more,' said Psmith. 'It shall not occur again. Why should I dislocate the work of your department in my efforts to win a sympathetic word? I will bear Comrade Bristow like a man here. After all, there are worse things at the Zoo.'

'No, no,' said Mr Waller hastily, 'I did not mean that. By all means pay us a visit now and then, if it does not interfere with your own work. But I noticed just now that you spoke to Bristow as Comrade Bristow.'

'It is too true,' said Psmith. 'I must correct myself of the habit. He will be getting above himself.'

'And when you were speaking to Jackson, you spoke of yourself as a Socialist.'

'Socialism is the passion of my life,' said Psmith.

Mr Waller's face grew animated. He stammered in his eagerness.

'I am delighted,' he said. 'Really, I am delighted. I also – '

'A fellow worker in the Cause?' said Psmith.

'Er – exactly.'

Psmith extended his hand gravely. Mr Waller shook it with enthusiasm.

'I have never liked to speak of it to anybody in the office,' said Mr Waller, 'but I, too, am heart and soul in the movement.'

'Yours for the Revolution?' said Psmith.

'Just so. Just so. Exactly. I was wondering – the fact is, I am in the habit of speaking on Sundays in the open air, and – '

'Hyde Park?'

'No. No. Clapham Common. It is – er – handier for me where I live. Now, as you are interested in the movement, I was thinking that perhaps you might care to come and hear me speak next Sunday. Of course, if you have nothing better to do.'

'I should like to excessively,' said Psmith.

'Excellent. Bring Jackson with you, and both of you come to supper afterwards, if you will.'

'Thanks very much.'

'Perhaps you would speak yourself?'

'No,' said Psmith. 'No. I think not. My Socialism is rather of the practical sort. I seldom speak. But it would be a treat to listen to you. What – er – what type of oratory is yours?'

'Oh, well,' said Mr Waller, pulling nervously at his beard, 'of course I – Well, I am perhaps a little bitter – '

'Yes, yes.'

'A little mordant and ironical.'

'You would be,' agreed Psmith. 'I shall look forward to Sunday with every fibre quivering. And Comrade Jackson shall be at my side.'

'Excellent,' said Mr Waller. 'I will go and tell him now.'

'The first thing to do,' said Psmith, 'is to ascertain that such a place as Clapham Common really exists. One has heard of it, of course, but has its existence ever been proved? I think not. Having accomplished that, we must then try to find out how to get to it. I should say at a venture that it would necessitate a sea-voyage. On the other hand, Comrade Waller, who is a native of the spot, seems to find no difficulty in rolling to the office every morning. Therefore – you follow me, Jackson? – it must be in England. In that case, we will take a taximeter cab, and go out into the unknown, hand in hand, trusting to luck.'

'I expect you could get there by tram,' said Mike.

Psmith suppressed a slight shudder.

'I fear, Comrade Jackson,' he said, 'that the old *noblesse oblige* traditions of the Psmiths would not allow me to do that. No. We will stroll gently, after a light lunch, to Trafalgar Square, and hail a taxi.'

'Beastly expensive.'

'But with what an object! Can any expenditure be called excessive which enables us to hear Comrade Waller being mordant and ironical at the other end?'

'It's a rum business,' said Mike. 'I hope the dickens he won't mix us up in it. We should look frightful fools.'

'I may possibly say a few words,' said Psmith carelessly, 'if the spirit moves me. Who am I that I should deny people a simple pleasure?'

Mike looked alarmed.

'Look here,' he said, 'I say, if you *are* going to play the goat, for goodness' sake don't go lugging me into it. I've got heaps of troubles without that.'

Psmith waved the objection aside.

'You,' he said, 'will be one of the large, and, I hope, interested audience. Nothing more. But it is quite possible that the spirit may not move me. I may not feel inspired to speak. I am not one of those who love speaking for speaking's sake. If I have no message for the many-headed, I shall remain silent.'

'Then I hope the dickens you won't have,' said Mike. Of all things he hated most being conspicuous before a crowd – except at cricket, which was a different thing – and he had an uneasy feeling that Psmith would rather like it than otherwise.

'We shall see,' said Psmith absently. 'Of course, if in the vein, I might do something big in the way of oratory. I am a plain, blunt man, but I feel convinced that, given the opportunity, I should haul up my slacks to some effect. But – well, we shall see. We shall see.'

And with this ghastly state of doubt Mike had to be content.

It was with feelings of apprehension that he accompanied Psmith from the flat to Trafalgar Square in search of a cab which should convey them to Clapham Common.

They were to meet Mr Waller at the edge of the Common nearest the old town of Clapham. On the journey down Psmith was inclined to be *débonnair*. Mike, on the other hand, was silent and apprehensive. He knew enough of Psmith to know that, if half an opportunity were offered him, he would extract entertainment from this affair after his own fashion; and then the odds were that he himself would be dragged into it. Perhaps – his scalp bristled at the mere idea – he would even be let in for a speech.

This grisly thought had hardly come into his head, when Psmith spoke.

'I'm not half sure,' he said thoughtfully, 'I sha'n't call on you for a speech, Comrade Jackson.'

'Look here, Psmith – ' began Mike agitatedly.

'I don't know. I think your solid, incisive style would rather go down with the masses. However, we shall see, we shall see.'

Mike reached the Common in a state of nervous collapse.

Mr Waller was waiting for them by the railings near the pond. The apostle of the Revolution was clad soberly in black, except for a tie of vivid crimson. His eyes shone with the light of enthusiasm, vastly different from the mild glow of amiability which they exhibited for six days in every week. The man was transformed.

'Here you are,' he said. 'Here you are. Excellent. You are in good time. Comrades Wotherspoon and Prebble have already begun to speak. I shall commence now that you have come. This is the way. Over by these trees.'

They made their way towards a small clump of trees, near which a fair-sized crowd had already begun to collect. Evidently listening to the speakers was one of Clapham's fashionable Sunday amusements. Mr Waller talked and gesticulated incessantly as he walked. Psmith's demeanour was perhaps a shade patronizing, but he displayed interest. Mike proceeded to the meeting with the air of an about-to-be-washed dog. He was loathing the whole business with a heartiness worthy of a better cause. Somehow, he felt he was going to be made to look a fool before the afternoon was over. But he registered a vow that nothing should drag him on to the small platform which had been erected for the benefit of the speaker.

As they drew nearer, the voices of Comrades Wotherspoon and Prebble became more audible. They had been audible all the time, very much so, but now they grew in volume. Comrade Wotherspoon was a tall, thin man with side-whiskers and a high voice. He scattered his aitches as a fountain its spray in a strong wind. He was very earnest. Comrade Prebble was earnest, too. Perhaps even more so than Comrade Wotherspoon. He was handicapped to some extent, however, by not having a palate. This gave to his profoundest thoughts a certain weirdness, as if they had been uttered in an unknown tongue. The crowd was thickest round his platform. The grown-up section plainly regarded him as a comedian, pure and simple, and roared with happy laughter when he urged them to march upon Park Lane and loot the same without mercy or scruple. The children were more doubtful. Several had broken down, and been led away in tears.

When Mr Waller got up to speak on platform number three, his audience consisted at first only of Psmith, Mike and a fox-terrier. Gradually, however, he attracted others. After wavering for a while, the crowd finally decided that he was worth hearing. He had a method of his own. Lacking the natural gifts which marked Comrade Prebble out as an entertainer, he made up for this by his activity. Where his colleagues stood comparatively still, Mr Waller behaved with the vivacity generally supposed to belong only to peas on shovels and cats on hot bricks. He crouched to denounce the House of Lords. He bounded from side to side while dissecting the methods of the plutocrats. During an impassioned onslaught on the monarchical system he stood on one leg and hopped. This was more the sort of thing the crowd had come to see. Comrade Wotherspoon found himself deserted, and even Comrade Prebble's shortcomings in the way of palate were insufficient to keep his flock together. The entire strength of the audience gathered in front of the third platform.

Mike, separated from Psmith by the movement of the crowd, listened with a growing depression. That feeling which attacks a sensitive person sometimes at the theatre when somebody is making himself ridiculous on the stage – the illogical feeling that it is he and not the actor who is floundering – had come over him in a wave. He liked Mr Waller, and it made his gorge rise to see him exposing himself to the jeers of a crowd. The fact that Mr Waller himself did not know that they were jeers, but mistook them for applause, made it no better. Mike felt vaguely furious.

His indignation began to take a more personal shape when the speaker, branching off from the main subject of Socialism, began to touch on temperance. There was no particular reason why Mr Waller should have introduced the subject of temperance, except that he happened to be an enthusiast. He linked it on to his remarks on Socialism by attributing the lethargy of the masses to their fondness for alcohol; and the crowd, which had been inclined rather to pat itself on the back during the assaults on Rank and Property, finding itself assailed in its turn, resented it. They were there to listen to speakers telling them that they were the finest fellows on earth, not pointing out their little failings to them. The feeling of the meeting became hostile. The jeers grew more frequent and less good-tempered.

'Comrade Waller means well,' said a voice in Mike's ear, 'but if he shoots it at them like this much more there'll be a bit of an imbroglio.'

'Look here, Psmith,' said Mike quickly, 'can't we stop him? These chaps are getting fed up, and they look bargees enough to do anything. They'll be going for him or something soon.'

'How can we switch off the flow? I don't see. The man is wound up. He means to get it off his chest if it snows. I feel we are by way of being in the soup once more, Comrade Jackson. We can only sit tight and look on.'

The crowd was becoming more threatening every minute. A group of young men of the loafer class who stood near Mike were especially fertile in comment. Psmith's eyes were on the speaker; but Mike was watching this group closely. Suddenly he saw one of them, a thick-set youth wearing a cloth cap and no collar, stoop.

When he rose again there was a stone in his hand.

The sight acted on Mike like a spur. Vague rage against nobody in particular had been simmering in him for half an hour. Now it concentrated itself on the cloth-capped one.

Mr Waller paused momentarily before renewing his harangue. The man in the cloth cap raised his hand. There was a swirl in the crowd, and the first thing that Psmith saw as he turned was Mike seizing the would-be marksman round the neck and hurling him to the ground, after the manner of a forward at football tackling an opponent during a line-out from touch.

There is one thing which will always distract the attention of a crowd from any speaker, and that is a dispute between two of its units. Mr Waller's views on temperance were forgotten in an instant. The audience surged round Mike and his opponent.

The latter had scrambled to his feet now, and was looking round for his assailant.

'That's 'im, Bill!' cried eager voices, indicating Mike.

''E's the bloke wot 'it yer, Bill,' said others, more precise in detail. Bill advanced on Mike in a sidelong, crab-like manner.

''Oo're you, I should like to know?' said Bill.

Mike, rightly holding that this was merely a rhetorical question and that Bill had no real thirst for information as to his family history, made no reply. Or, rather, the reply he made was not verbal. He waited till his questioner was within range, and then hit him in the eye. A reply far more satisfactory, if not to Bill himself, at any rate to the interested onlookers, than any flow of words.

A contented sigh went up from the crowd. Their Sunday afternoon was going to be spent just as they considered Sunday afternoons should be spent.

'Give us your coat,' said Psmith briskly, 'and try and get it over quick. Don't go in for any fancy sparring. Switch it on, all you know, from the start. I'll keep a thoughtful eye open to see that none of his friends and relations join in.'

Outwardly Psmith was unruffled, but inwardly he was not feeling so composed. An ordinary turn-up before an impartial crowd which could be relied upon to preserve the etiquette of these matters was one thing. As regards the actual little dispute with the cloth-capped Bill, he felt that he could rely on Mike to handle it satisfactorily. But there was no knowing how long the crowd would be content to remain mere spectators. There was no doubt which way its sympathies lay. Bill, now stripped of his coat and sketching out in a hoarse voice a scenario of what he intended to do – knocking Mike down and stamping him into the mud was one of the milder feats he promised to perform for the entertainment of an indulgent audience – was plainly the popular favourite.

Psmith, though he did not show it, was more than a little apprehensive.

Mike, having more to occupy his mind in the immediate present, was not anxious concerning the future. He had the great advantage over Psmith of having lost his temper. Psmith could look on the situation as a whole, and count the risks and possibilities. Mike could only see Bill shuffling towards him with his head down and shoulders bunched.

'Gow it, Bill!' said someone.

'Pliy up, the Arsenal!' urged a voice on the outskirts of the crowd. A chorus of encouragement from kind friends in front: 'Step up, Bill!'

And Bill stepped.

Bill (surname unknown) was not one of your ultra-scientific fighters. He did not favour the American crouch and the artistic feint. He had a style wholly his own. It seemed to have been modelled partly on a tortoise and partly on a windmill. His head he appeared to be trying to conceal between his shoulders, and he whirled his arms alternately in circular sweeps.

Mike, on the other hand, stood upright and hit straight, with the result that he hurt his knuckles very much on his opponent's skull, without seeming to disturb the latter to any great extent. In the process he received one of the windmill swings on the left ear. The crowd, strong pro-Billites, raised a cheer.

This maddened Mike. He assumed the offensive. Bill, satisfied for the moment with his success, had stepped back, and was indulging in some fancy sparring, when Mike sprang upon him like a panther. They clinched, and Mike, who had got the under grip, hurled Bill forcibly against a stout man who looked like a publican. The two fell in a heap, Bill underneath.

And at the same time Bill's friends joined in.

The first intimation Mike had of this was a violent blow across the shoulders with a walking-stick. Even if he had been wearing his overcoat, the blow would have hurt. As he was in his jacket it hurt more than anything he had ever experienced in his life. He leapt up with a yell, but Psmith was there before him. Mike saw his assailant lift the stick again, and then collapse as the old Etonian's right took him under the chin.

He darted to Psmith's side.

'This is no place for us,' observed the latter sadly. 'Shift ho, I think. Come on.'

They dashed simultaneously for the spot where the crowd was thinnest. The ring which had formed round Mike and Bill had broken up as the result of the intervention of Bill's allies, and at the spot for which they ran only two men were standing. And these had apparently made up their minds that neutrality was the best policy, for they made no movement to stop them. Psmith and Mike charged through the gap, and raced for the road.

The suddenness of the move gave them just the start they needed. Mike looked over his shoulder. The crowd, to a man, seemed to be following. Bill, excavated from beneath the publican, led the field. Lying a good second came a band of three, and after them the rest in a bunch.

They reached the road in this order.

Some fifty yards down the road was a stationary tram. In the ordinary course of things it would probably have moved on long before Psmith and Mike could have got to it; but the conductor, a man with sporting blood in him, seeing what appeared to be the finish of some Marathon Race, refrained from giving the signal, and moved out into the road to observe events more clearly, at the same time calling to the driver, who joined him. Passengers on the roof stood up to get a good view. There was some cheering.

Psmith and Mike reached the tram ten yards to the good; and, if it had been ready to start then, all would have been well. But Bill and his friends had arrived while the driver and conductor were both out in the road.

The affair now began to resemble the doings of Horatius on the bridge. Psmith and Mike turned at bay on the platform at the front of the tram steps. Bill, leading by three yards, sprang on to it, grabbed Mike, and fell with him on to the road. Psmith, descending with a dignity somewhat lessened by the fact that his hat was on the side of his head, was in time to engage the runners-up.

Psmith, as pugilist, lacked something of the calm majesty which characterized him in the more peaceful moments of life, but he was undoubtedly effective. Nature had given him an enormous reach and a lightness on his feet remarkable in one of his size; and at some time in his career he appeared to have learned how to use his hands. The first of the three runners, the walking-stick manipulator, had the misfortune to charge straight into the old Etonian's left. It was a well-timed blow, and the force of it, added to the speed at which the victim was running, sent him on to the pavement, where he

spun round and sat down. In the subsequent proceedings
he took no part.

The other two attacked Psmith simultaneously, one
on each side. In doing so, the one on the left tripped over
Mike and Bill, who were still in the process of sorting
themselves out, and fell, leaving Psmith free to attend
to the other. He was a tall, weedy youth. His conspicuous
features were a long nose and a light yellow waistcoat.
Psmith hit him on the former with his left and on the
latter with his right. The long youth emitted a gurgle,
and collided with Bill, who had wrenched himself free
from Mike and staggered to his feet. Bill, having received
a second blow in the eye during the course of his interview
on the road with Mike, was not feeling himself. Mistaking
the other for an enemy, he proceeded to smite him in the
parts about the jaw. He had just upset him, when a stern
official voice observed, ''Ere, now, what's all this?'

There is no more unfailing corrective to a scene of
strife than the 'What's all this?' of the London
policeman. Bill abandoned his intention of stamping on
the prostrate one, and the latter, sitting up, blinked and
was silent.

'What's all this?' asked the policeman again. Psmith,
adjusting his hat at the correct angle again, undertook
the explanations.

'A distressing scene, officer,' he said. 'A case of that
unbridled brawling which is, alas, but too common in
our London streets. These two, possibly till now the
closest friends, fall out over some point, probably of
the most trivial nature, and what happens? They brawl.
They – '

'He 'it me,' said the long youth, dabbing at his face
with a handkerchief and pointing an accusing finger at
Psmith, who regarded him through his eyeglass with a
look in which pity and censure were nicely blended.

Bill, meanwhile, circling round restlessly, in the

apparent hope of getting past the Law and having another encounter with Mike, expressed himself in a stream of language which drew stern reproof from the shocked constable. 'You 'op it,' concluded the man in blue. 'That's what you do. You 'op it.'

'I should,' said Psmith kindly. 'The officer is speaking in your best interests. A man of taste and discernment, he knows what is best. His advice is good, and should be followed.'

The constable seemed to notice Psmith for the first time. He turned and stared at him. Psmith's praise had not had the effect of softening him. His look was one of suspicion.

'And what might *you* have been up to?' he inquired coldly. 'This man says you hit him.'

Psmith waved the matter aside.

'Purely in self-defence,' he said, 'purely in self-defence. What else could the man of spirit do? A mere tap to discourage an aggressive movement.'

The policeman stood silent, weighing matters in the balance. He produced a note-book and sucked his pencil. Then he called the conductor of the tram as a witness.

'A brainy and admirable step,' said Psmith, approvingly. 'This rugged, honest man, all unused to verbal subtleties, shall give us his plain account of what happened. After which, as I presume this tram – little as I know of the habits of trams – has got to go somewhere today, I would suggest that we all separated and moved on.'

He took two half-crowns from his pocket, and began to clink them meditatively together. A slight softening of the frigidity of the constable's manner become noticeable. There was a milder beam in the eyes which gazed into Psmith's.

Nor did the conductor seem altogether uninfluenced by the sight.

The conductor deposed that he had bin on the pointing

410

of pushing on, seeing as how he'd hung abart long
enough, when he see'd them two gents, the long 'un with
the heye-glass (Psmith bowed) and t'other 'un, a-legging
of it dahn the road towards him, with the other blokes
pelting after 'em. He added that, when they reached the
trem, the two gents had got aboard, and was then set upon
by the blokes. And after that, he concluded, well, there
was a bit of a scrap, and that's how it was.

'Lucidly and excellently put,' said Psmith. 'That is
just how it was. Comrade Jackson, I fancy we leave the
court without a stain on our characters. We win through.
Er – constable, we have given you a great deal of trouble
Possibly – ?'

'Thank you, sir.' There was a musical clinking. 'Now
then, you, all of you, you 'op it. You're all bin poking
your noses in 'ere long enough. Pop off with that tram,
conductor.'

Psmith and Mike settled themselves in a seat on the
roof. When the conductor came along, Psmith gave him
half a crown, and asked after his wife and the little ones
at home. The conductor thanked goodness that he was
a bachelor, punched the tickets, and retired.

'Subject for a historical picture,' said Psmith.
'Wounded leaving the field after the Battle of Clapham
Common. How are your injuries, Comrade Jackson?'

'My back's hurting like blazes,' said Mike. 'And my
ear's all sore where that chap got me. Anything the
matter with you?'

'Physically,' said Psmith, 'no. Spiritually much. Do
you realize, Comrade Jackson, the thing that has
happened? I am riding in a tram. I, Psmith, have paid a
penny for a ticket on a tram. If this should get about the
clubs! I tell you, Comrade Jackson, no such crisis has ever
occurred before in the course of my career.'

'You can always get off, you know,' said Mike.

'He thinks of everything,' said Psmith, admiringly.
'You have touched the spot with an unerring finger. Let

us descend. I observe in the distance a cab. That looks to me more the sort of thing we want. Let us go and parley with the driver.'

Golf and Other Stories

1 — The Clicking of Cuthbert

The young man came into the smoking-room of the club-house, and flung his bag with a clatter on the floor. He sank moodily into an arm-chair and pressed the bell.

'Waiter!'

'Sir?'

The young man pointed at the bag with every evidence of distaste.

'You may have these clubs,' he said. 'Take them away. If you don't want them yourself give them to one of the caddies.'

Across the room the Oldest Member gazed at him with a grave sadness through the smoke of his pipe. His eye was deep and dreamy – the eye of a man who, as the poet says, has seen Golf steadily and seen it whole.

'You are giving up golf?' he said.

He was not altogether unprepared for such an attitude on the young man's part: for from his eyrie on the terrace above the ninth green he had observed him start out on the afternoon's round and had seen him lose a couple of balls in the lake at the second hole after taking seven strokes at the first.

'Yes!' cried the young man fiercely. 'For ever, dammit! Footling game! Blanked infernal fat-headed silly ass of a game! Nothing but a waste of time.'

The Sage winced.

'Don't say that, my boy.'

'But I do say it. What earthly good is golf? Life is stern and life is earnest. We live in a practical age. All round us we see foreign competition making itself unpleasant. And we spend our time playing golf! What do we get out

415

of it? Is golf any *use*? That's what I'm asking you. Can you name me a single case where devotion to this pestilential pastime has done a man any practical good?'

The Sage smiled gently.

'I could name a thousand.'

'One will do.'

'I will select,' said the Sage, 'from the innumerable memories that rush to my mind, the story of Cuthbert Banks.'

'Never heard of him.'

'Be of good cheer,' said the Oldest Member. 'You are going to hear of him now.'

It was in the picturesque little settlement of Wood Hills (said the Oldest Member) that the incidents occurred which I am about to relate. Even if you have never been in Wood Hills, that suburban paradise is probably familiar to you by name. Situated at a convenient distance from the city, it combines in a notable manner the advantages of town life with the pleasant surroundings and healthful air of the country. Its inhabitants live in commodious houses, standing in their own grounds, and enjoy so many luxuries – such as gravel soil, main drainage, electric light, telephone, baths (h. and c.), and company's own water, that you might be pardoned for imagining life to be so ideal for them that no possible improvement could be added to their lot. Mrs Willoughby Smethurst was under no such delusion. What Wood Hills needed to make it perfect, she realized, was Culture. Material comforts are all very well, but, if the *summum bonum* is to be achieved, the Soul also demands a look in, and it was Mrs Smethurst's unfaltering resolve that never while she had her strength should the Soul be handed the loser's end. It was her intention to make Wood Hills a centre of all that was most cultivated and refined, and, golly! how she had succeeded. Under

her presidency the Wood Hills Literary and Debating
Society had tripled its membership.

But there is always a fly in the ointment, a caterpillar
in the salad. The local golf club, an institution to which
Mrs Smethurst strongly objected, had also tripled its
membership; and the division of the community into
two rival camps, the Golfers and the Cultured, had
become more marked than ever. This division, always
acute, had attained now to the dimensions of a Schism.
The rival sects treated one another with a cold hostility.

Unfortunate episodes came to widen the breach. Mrs
Smethurst's house adjoined the links, standing to the
right of the fourth tee: and, as the Literary Society was in
the habit of entertaining visiting lecturers, many a golfer
had foozled his drive owing to sudden loud outbursts of
applause coinciding with his down-swing. And not long
before this story opens a sliced ball, whizzing in at the
open window, had come within an ace of incapacitating
Raymond Parsloe Devine, the rising young novelist (who
rose at that moment a clear foot and a half) from any
further exercise of his art. Two inches, indeed, to the right
and Raymond must inevitably have handed in his
dinner-pail.

To make matters worse, a ring at the front-door bell
followed almost immediately, and the maid ushered in
a young man of pleasing appearance in a sweater and
baggy knickerbockers who apologetically but firmly
insisted on playing his ball where it lay, and, what with
the shock of the lecturer's narrow escape and the spectacle
of the intruder standing on the table and working away
with a niblick, the afternoon's session had to be classed
as a complete frost. Mr Devine's determination, from
which no argument could swerve him, to deliver the
rest of his lecture in the coal-cellar gave the meeting a
jolt from which it never recovered.

I have dwelt upon this incident, because it was the
means of introducing Cuthbert Banks to Mrs

Smethurst's niece, Adeline. As Cuthbert, for it was he
who had so nearly reduced the muster-roll of rising
novelists by one, hopped down from the table after his
stroke, he was suddenly aware that a beautiful girl was
looking at him intently. As a matter of fact, everyone in
the room was looking at him intently, none more so than
Raymond Parsloe Devine, but none of the others were
beautiful girls. Long as the members of Wood Hills
Literary Society were on brain, they were short on looks,
and, to Cuthbert's excited eye, Adeline Smethurst stood
out like a jewel in a pile of coke.

He had never seen her before, for she had only arrived
at her aunt's house on the previous day, but he was
perfectly certain that life, even when lived in the midst
of gravel soil, main drainage, and company's own water,
was going to be a pretty poor affair if he did not see her
again. Yes, Cuthbert was in love: and it is interesting to
record, as showing the effect of the tender emotion on a
man's game, that twenty minutes after he had met
Adeline he did the short eleventh in one, and as near as a
toucher got a three on the four-hundred-yard twelfth.

I will skip lightly over the intermediate stages of
Cuthbert's courtship and come to the moment when –
at the annual ball in aid of the local Cottage Hospital, the
only occasion during the year on which the lion, so to
speak, lay down with the lamb, and the Golfers and the
Cultured met on terms of easy comradeship, their
differences temporarily laid aside – he proposed to Adeline
and was badly stymied.

That fair, soulful girl could not see him with a spy-
glass.

'Mr Banks,' she said, 'I will speak frankly.'

'Charge right ahead,' assented Cuthbert.

'Deeply sensible as I am – '

'I know. Of the honour and the compliment and all
that. But, passing lightly over all that guff, what seems
to be the trouble? I love you to distraction – '

'Love is not everything.'

'You're wrong,' said Cuthbert, earnestly. 'You're right off it. Love – ' And he was about to dilate on the theme when she interrupted him.

'I am a girl of ambition.'

'And very nice, too,' said Cuthbert.

'I am a girl of ambition,' repeated Adeline, 'and I realize that the fulfilment of my ambitions must come through my husband. I am very ordinary myself – '

'What!' cried Cuthbert. 'You ordinary? Why, you are a pearl among women, the queen of your sex. You can't have been looking in a glass lately. You stand alone. Simply alone. You make the rest look like battered repaints.'

'Well,' said Adeline, softening a trifle, 'I believe I am fairly good-looking – '

'Anybody who was content to call you fairly good-looking would describe the Taj Mahal as a pretty nifty tomb.'

'But that is not the point. What I mean is, if I marry a nonentity I shall be a nonentity myself for ever. And I would sooner die than be a nonentity.'

'And, if I follow your reasoning, you think that that lets *me* out?'

'Well, really, Mr Banks, *have* you done anything, or are you likely ever to do anything worth while?'

Cuthbert hesitated.

'It's true,' he said, 'I didn't finish in the first ten in the Open, and I was knocked out in the semi-final of the Amateur, but I won the French Open last year.'

'The – what?'

'The French Open Championship. Golf you know.'

'Golf! You waste all your time playing golf. I admire a man who is more spiritual, more intellectual.'

A pang of jealousy rent Cuthbert's bosom.

'Like What's-his-name Devine?' he said, sullenly.

'Mr Devine,' replied Adeline, blushing faintly, 'is going

to be a great man. Already he has achieved much. The critics say that he is more Russian than any other young English writer.'

'And is that good?'

'Of course it's good.'

'I should have thought the wheeze would be to be more English than any other young English writer.'

'Nonsense! Who wants an English writer to be English? You've got to be Russian or Spanish or something to be a real success. The mantle of the great Russians has descended on Mr Devine.'

'From what I've heard of Russians, I should hate to have that happen to *me*.'

'There is no danger of that,' said Adeline scornfully.

'Oh! Well, let me tell you that there is a lot more in me than you think.'

'That might easily be so.'

'You think I'm not spiritual and intellectual,' said Cuthbert, deeply moved. 'Very well. Tomorrow I join the Literary Society.'

Even as he spoke the words his leg was itching to kick himself for being such a chump, but the sudden expression of pleasure on Adeline's face soothed him; and he went home that night with the feeling that he had taken on something rather attractive. It was only in the cold, grey light of the morning that he realized what he had let himself in for.

I do not know if you have had any experience of suburban literary societies, but the one that flourished under the eye of Mrs Willoughby Smethurst at Wood Hills was rather more so than the average. With my feeble powers of narrative, I cannot hope to make clear to you all that Cuthbert Banks endured in the next few weeks. And, even if I could, I doubt if I should do so. It is all very well to excite pity and terror, as Aristotle recommends, but there are limits. In the ancient Greek tragedies it was an ironclad rule that all the real rough stuff should take place off-stage, and I shall follow this admirable principle. It will suffice if I say merely that J. Cuthbert Banks had a thin time. After attending eleven debates and fourteen lectures on *vers libre* Poetry, the Seventeenth-Century Essayists, the Neo-Scandinavian Movement in Portuguese Literature, and other subjects of a similar nature, he grew so enfeebled that, on the rare occasions when he had time for a visit to the links, he had to take a full iron for his mashie shots.

It was not simply the oppressive nature of the debates and lectures that sapped his vitality. What really got right in amongst him was the torture of seeing Adeline's adoration of Raymond Parsloe Devine. The man seemed to have made the deepest possible impression upon her plastic emotions. When he spoke, she leaned forward with parted lips and looked at him. When he was not speaking – which was seldom – she leaned back and looked at him. And when he happened to take the next seat to her, she leaned sideways and looked at him. One glance at Mr Devine would have been more than enough for Cuthbert; but Adeline found him a spectacle that never palled. She could not have gazed at him with a more rapturous intensity if she had been a small child and he a saucer of ice-cream. All this Cuthbert had to witness while still endeavouring to retain the possession of his faculties sufficiently to enable him to duck and back away if somebody suddenly asked him what he thought of the sombre realism of Vladimir Brusiloff. It is little wonder that he tossed in bed, picking at the coverlet, through sleepless nights, and had to have all his waistcoats taken in three inches to keep them from sagging.

This Vladimir Brusiloff to whom I have referred was the famous Russian novelist, and, owing to the fact of his being in the country on a lecturing tour at the moment, there had been something of a boom in his works. The Wood Hills Literary Society had been studying them for weeks, and never since his first entrance into intellectual circles had Cuthbert Banks come nearer to throwing in the towel. Vladimir specialized in grey studies of hopeless misery, where nothing happened till page three hundred and eighty, when the moujik decided to commit suicide. It was tough going for a man whose deepest reading hitherto had been Vardon on the Push-Shot, and there can be no greater proof of the magic of love than the fact that Cuthbert stuck it without a cry. But the strain was terrible and I am inclined to think that he must have cracked, had it not been for the daily reports in the papers of the internecine strife which was proceeding so briskly in Russia. Cuthbert was an optimist at heart, and it seemed to him that, at the rate at which the inhabitants of that interesting country were murdering one another, the supply of Russian novelists must eventually give out.

One morning, as he tottered down the road for the short walk which was now almost the only exercise to which he was equal, Cuthbert met Adeline. A spasm of anguish flitted through all his nerve-centres as he saw that she was accompanied by Raymond Parsloe Devine.

'Good morning, Mr Banks,' said Adeline.

'Good morning,' said Cuthbert hollowly.

'Such good news about Vladimir Brusiloff.'

'Dead?' said Cuthbert, with a touch of hope.

'Dead? Of course not. Why should he be? No, Aunt Emily met his manager after his lecture at Queen's Hall yesterday, and he has promised that Mr Brusiloff shall come to her next Wednesday reception.'

'Oh, ah!' said Cuthbert, dully.

'I don't know how she managed it. I think she must have told him that Mr Devine would be there to meet him.'

'But you said he was coming,' argued Cuthbert.

'I shall be very glad,' said Raymond Devine, 'of the opportunity of meeting Brusiloff.'

'I'm sure,' said Adeline, 'he will be very glad of the opportunity of meeting you.'

'Possibly,' said Mr Devine. 'Possibly. Competent critics have said that my work closely resembles that of the great Russian Masters.'

'Your psychology is so deep.'

'Yes, yes.'

'And your atmosphere.'

'Quite.'

Cuthbert in a perfect agony of spirit prepared to withdraw from this love-feast. The sun was shining brightly, but the world was black to him. Birds sang in the tree-tops, but he did not hear them. He might have been a moujik for all the pleasure he found in life.

'You will be there, Mr Banks?' said Adeline, as he turned away.

'Oh, all right,' said Cuthbert.

When Cuthbert had entered the drawing-room on the following Wednesday and had taken his usual place in a distant corner where, while able to feast his gaze on Adeline, he had a sporting chance of being overlooked or mistaken for a piece of furniture, he perceived the great Russian thinker seated in the midst of a circle of admiring females. Raymond Parsloe Devine had not yet arrived.

His first glance at the novelist surprised Cuthbert. Doubtless with the best motives, Vladimir Brusiloff had permitted his face to become almost entirely concealed behind a dense zareba of hair, but his eyes were visible through the undergrowth, and it seemed to Cuthbert that there was an expression in them not unlike that of a cat in a strange backyard surrounded by small boys. The man looked forlorn and hopeless, and Cuthbert wondered whether he had had bad news from home.

This was not the case. The latest news which Vladimir Brusiloff had had from Russia had been particularly cheering. Three of his principal creditors had perished in

the last massacre of the *bourgeoisie*, and a man whom
he owed for five years for a samovar and a pair of overshoes
had fled the country, and had not been heard of since. It
was not bad news from home that was depressing
Vladimir. What was wrong with him was the fact that
this was the eighty-second suburban literary reception
he had been compelled to attend since he had landed in
the country on his lecturing tour, and he was sick to death
of it. When his agent had first suggested the trip, he had
signed on the dotted line without an instant's hesitation.
Worked out in roubles, the fees offered had seemed just
about right. But now, as he peered through the brushwood
at the faces round him, and realized that eight out of ten
of those present had manuscripts of some sort concealed
on their persons, and were only waiting for an opportunity
to whip them out and start reading, he wished that he
had stayed at his quiet home in Nijni-Novgorod, where
the worst thing that could happen to a fellow was a brace
of bombs coming in through the window and mixing
themselves up with his breakfast egg.

At this point in his meditations he was aware that his
hostess was looming up before him with a pale young man
in horn-rimmed spectacles at her side. There was in Mrs
Smethurst's demeanour something of the unction of the
master-of-ceremonies at the big fight who introduces
the earnest gentleman who wishes to challenge the
winner.

'Oh, Mr Brusiloff,' said Mrs Smethurst, 'I do so want
you to meet Mr Raymond Parsloe Devine, whose work
I expect you know. He is one of our younger novelists.'

The distinguished visitor peered in a wary and
defensive manner through the shrubbery, but did not
speak. Inwardly he was thinking how exactly like Mr
Devine was to the eighty-one other younger novelists
to whom he had been introduced at various hamlets
throughout the country. Raymond Parsloe Devine

bowed courteously, while Cuthbert, wedged into his corner, glowered at him.

'The critics,' said Mr Devine, 'have been kind enough to say that my poor efforts contain a good deal of the Russian spirit. I owe much to the great Russians. I have been greatly influenced by Sovietski.'

Down in the forest something stirred. It was Vladimir Brusiloff's mouth opening, as he prepared to speak. He was not a man who prattled readily, especially in a foreign tongue. He gave the impression that each word was excavated from his interior by some up-to-date process of mining. He glared bleakly at Mr Devine, and allowed three words to drop out of him.

'Sovietski no good!'

He paused for a moment, set the machinery working again, and delivered five more at the pithead.

'I spit me of Sovietski!'

There was a painful sensation. The lot of a popular idol is in many ways an enviable one, but it has the drawback of uncertainty. Here today and gone tomorrow. Until this moment Raymond Parsloe Devine's stock had stood at something considerably over par in Wood Hills intellectual circles, but now there was a rapid slump. Hitherto he had been greatly admired for being influenced by Sovietski, but it appeared now that this was not a good thing to be. It was evidently a rotten thing to be. The law could not touch you for being influenced by Sovietski, but there is an ethical as well as a legal code, and this it was obvious that Raymond Parsloe Devine had transgressed. Women drew away from him slightly, holding their skirts. Men looked at him censoriously. Adeline Smethurst started violently, and dropped a tea-cup. And Cuthbert Banks, doing his popular imitation of a sardine in his corner, felt for the first time that life held something of sunshine.

Raymond Parsloe Devine was plainly shaken, but he made an adroit attempt to recover his lost prestige.

'When I say I have been influenced by Sovietski, I mean, of course, that I was once under his spell. A young writer commits many follies. I have long since passed through that phase. The false glamour of Sovietski has ceased to dazzle me. I now belong whole-heartedly to the school of Nastikoff.'

There was a reaction. People nodded at one another sympathetically. After all, we cannot expect old heads on young shoulders, and a lapse at the outset of one's career should not be held against one who has eventually seen the light.

'Nastikoff no good,' said Vladimir Brusiloff, coldly. He paused, listening to the machinery.

'Nastikoff worse than Sovietski.'

He paused again.

'I spit me of Nastikoff!' he said.

This time there was no doubt about it. The bottom had dropped out of the market, and Raymond Parsloe Devine Preferred were down in the cellar with no takers. It was clear to the entire assembled company that they had been all wrong about Raymond Parsloe Devine. They had allowed him to play on their innocence and sell them a pup. They had taken him at his own valuation, and had been cheated into admiring him as a man who amounted to something, and all the while he had belonged to the school of Nastikoff. You never can tell. Mrs Smethurst's guests were well-bred, and there was consequently no violent demonstration, but you could see by their faces what they felt. Those nearest Raymond Parsloe jostled to get further away. Mrs Smethurst eyed him stonily through a raised lorgnette. One or two low hisses were heard, and over at the other end of the room somebody opened the window in a marked manner.

Raymond Parsloe Devine hesitated for a moment, then, realizing his situation, turned and slunk to the door. There was an audible sigh of relief as it closed behind him.

Vladimir Brusiloff proceeded to sum up.

'No novelists any good except me. Sovietski – yah! Nastikoff – bah! I spit me of zem all. No novelists anywhere any good except me. P. G. Wodehouse and Tolstoi not bad. Not good, but not bad. No novelists any good except me.'

And, having uttered this dictum, he removed a slab of cake from a near-by plate, steered it through the jungle, and began to champ.

It is too much to say that there was a dead silence. There could never be that in any room in which Vladimir Brusiloff was eating cake. But certainly what you might call the general chit-chat was pretty well down and out. Nobody liked to be the first to speak. The members of the Wood Hills Literary Society looked at one another timidly. Cuthbert, for his part, gazed at Adeline; and Adeline gazed into space. It was plain that the girl was deeply stirred. Her eyes were opened wide, a faint flush crimsoned her cheeks, and her breath was coming quickly.

Adeline's mind was in a whirl. She felt as if she had been walking gaily along a pleasant path and had stopped suddenly on the very brink of a precipice. It would be idle to deny that Raymond Parsloe Devine had attracted her extraordinarily. She had taken him at his own valuation as an extremely hot potato, and her hero-worship had gradually been turning into love. And now her hero had been shown to have feet of clay. It was hard, I consider, on Raymond Parsloe Devine, but that is how it goes in this world. You get a following as a celebrity, and then you run up against another bigger celebrity and your admirers desert you. One could moralize on this at considerable length, but better not, perhaps. Enough to say that the glamour of Raymond Devine ceased abruptly in that moment for Adeline, and her most coherent thought at this juncture was the resolve, as soon as she got up to her room, to burn the three signed photographs he had sent her and to give the autographed presentation set of his books to the grocer's boy.

Mrs Smethurst, meanwhile, having rallied somewhat, was endeavouring to set the feast of reason and flow of soul going again.

'And how do you like England, Mr Brusiloff?' she asked.

The celebrity paused in the act of lowering another segment of cake.

'Dam good,' he replied, cordially.

'I suppose you have travelled all over the country by this time?'

'You said it,' agreed the Thinker.

'Have you met many of our great public men?'

'Yais – Yais – Quite a few of the nibs – Lloyid Gorge, I meet him. But – ' Beneath the matting a discontented expression came into his face, and his voice took on a peevish note. 'But, I not meet your *real* great men – your Arbmishel, your Arreevadon – I not meet them. That's what gives me the pipovitch. Have *you* ever met Arbmishel and Arreevadon?'

A strained, anguished look came into Mrs Smethurst's face and was reflected in the faces of the other members of the circle. The eminent Russian had sprung two entirely new ones on them, and they felt that their ignorance was about to be exposed. What would Vladimir Brusiloff think of the Wood Hills Literary Society? The reputation of the Wood Hills Literary Society was at stake, trembling in the balance, and coming up for the third time. In dumb agony Mrs Smethurst rolled her eyes about the room searching for someone capable of coming to the rescue. She drew blank.

And then, from a distant corner, there sounded a deprecating cough, and those nearest Cuthbert Banks saw that he had stopped twisting his right foot round his left ankle and his left foot round his right ankle and was sitting up with a light of almost human intelligence in his eyes.

'Er – ' said Cuthbert, blushing as every eye in the room seemed to fix itself on him, 'I think he means Abe Mitchell and Harry Vardon.'

'Abe Mitchell and Harry Vardon?' repeated Mrs Smethurst, blankly. 'I never heard of – '

'Yais! Yais! Most! Very!' shouted Vladimir Brusiloff, enthusiastically. 'Arbmishel and Arreevadon. You know them, yes, what, no, perhaps?'

'I've played with Abe Mitchell often, and I was partnered with Harry Vardon in last year's Open.'

The great Russian uttered a cry that shook the chandelier.

'You play in ze Open? Why,' he demanded reproachfully of Mrs Smethurst, 'was I not been introduced to this young man who play in opens?'

'Well, really,' faltered Mrs Smethurst. 'Well, the fact is, Mr Brusiloff – '

She broke off. She was unequal to the task of explaining, without hurting anyone's feelings, that she had always regarded Cuthbert as a piece of cheese and a blot on the landscape.

'Introduce me!' thundered the Celebrity.

'Why, certainly, certainly, of course. This is Mr – .' She looked appealingly at Cuthbert.

'Banks,' prompted Cuthbert.

'Banks!' cried Vladimir Brusiloff. 'Not Cootaboot Banks?'

'*Is* your name Cootaboot?' asked Mrs Smethurst faintly.

'Well, it's Cuthbert.'

'Yais! Yais! Cootaboot!' There was a rush and swirl, as the effervescent Muscovite burst his way through the throng and rushed to where Cuthbert sat. He stood for a moment eyeing him excitedly, then, stooping swiftly, kissed him on both cheeks before Cuthbert could get his guard up. 'My dear young man, I saw you win ze French Open. Great! Great! Grand! Superb! Hot stuff, and you can say I said so! Will you permit one who is but eighteen at Nijni-Novgorod to salute you once more?'

And he kissed Cuthbert again. Then, brushing aside one or two intellectuals who were in the way, he dragged up a chair and sat down.

'You are a great man!' he said.

'Oh, no,' said Cuthbert modestly.

'Yais! Great. Most! Very! The way you lay your approach-putts dead from anywhere!'

'Oh, I don't know.'

Mr Brusiloff drew his chair closer.

'Let me tell you one vairy funny story about putting. It was one day I play at Nijni-Novgorod with the pro. against Lenin and Trotsky, and Trotsky had a two-inch putt for the hole. But, just as he addresses the ball, someone in the crowd he tries to assassinate Lenin with a rewolwer – you know that is our great national sport, trying to assassinate Lenin with rewolwers – and the bang puts Trotsky off his stroke and he goes five yards past the hole, and then Lenin, who is rather shaken, you understand, he misses again himself, and we win the hole and match and I clean up three hundred and ninety-six thousand roubles, or fifteen shillings in your money. Some gameovitch! And now let me tell you one other vairy funny story – '

Desultory conversation had begun in murmurs over the rest of the room, as the Wood Hills intellectuals politely endeavoured to conceal the fact that they realized that they were about as much out of it at this re-union of twin souls as cats at a dog-show. From time to time they started as Vladimir Brusiloff's laugh boomed out. Perhaps it was a consolation to them to know that he was enjoying himself.

As for Adeline, how shall I describe her emotions? She

was stunned. Before her very eyes the stone which the builders had rejected had become the main thing, the hundred-to-one shot had walked away with the race. A rush of tender admiration for Cuthbert Banks flooded her heart. She saw that she had been all wrong. Cuthbert, whom she had always treated with a patronizing superiority, was really a man to be looked up to and worshipped. A deep, dreamy sigh shook Adeline's fragile form.

Half an hour later Vladimir and Cuthbert Banks rose.

'Goot-a-bye, Mrs Smet-thirst,' said the Celebrity. 'Zank you for a most charming visit. My friend Cootaboot and me we go now to shoot a few holes. You will lend me clobs, friend Cootaboot?'

'Any you want.'

'The niblicksky is what I use most. Goot-a-bye, Mrs Smet-thirst.'

They were moving to the door, when Cuthbert felt a light touch on his arm. Adeline was looking up at him tenderly.

'May I come, too, and walk round with you?'

Cuthbert's bosom heaved.

'Oh,' he said, with a tremor in his voice, 'that you would walk round with me for life!'

Her eyes met his.

'Perhaps,' she whispered, softly, 'it could be arranged.'

'And so,' (concluded the Oldest Member), 'you see that golf can be of the greatest practical assistance to a man in Life's struggle. Raymond Parsloe Devine, who was no player, had to move out of the neighbourhood immediately, and is now, I believe, writing scenarios out in California for the Flicker Film Company. Adeline is married to Cuthbert, and it was only his earnest pleading which prevented her from having their eldest son christened Abe Mitchell Ribbed-Faced Mashie Banks, for she is now as keen a devotee of the great game as her husband. Those who know them say that theirs is a union so devoted, so – '

The Sage broke off abruptly, for the young man had rushed to the door and out into the passage. Through the open door he could hear him crying passionately to the waiter to bring back his clubs.

2 — The Magic Plus Fours

'After all,' said the young man, 'golf is only a game.'
He spoke bitterly and with the air of one who has been
following a train of thought. He had come into the
smoking-room of the club-house in low spirits at the
dusky close of a November evening, and for some
minutes had been sitting, silent and moody, staring at the
log fire.

'Merely a pastime,' said the young man.

The Oldest Member, nodding in his arm-chair,
stiffened with horror, and glanced quickly over his
shoulder to make sure that none of the waiters had heard
these terrible words.

'Can this be George William Pennefather speaking!'
he said, reproachfully. 'My boy, you are not yourself.'

The young man flushed a little beneath his tan: for he
had had a good upbringing and was not bad at heart.

'Perhaps I ought not to have gone quite so far as that,'
he admitted. 'I was only thinking that a fellow's got no
right, just because he happens to have come on a bit in
his form lately, to treat a fellow as if a fellow was a leper
or something.'

The Oldest Member's face cleared, and he breathed a
relieved sigh.

'Ah! I see,' he said. 'You spoke hastily and in a sudden
fit of pique because something upset you out on the
links today. Tell me all. Let me see, you were playing
with Nathaniel Frisby this afternoon, were you not? I
gather that he beat you.'

'Yes, he did. Giving me a third. But it isn't being beaten
that I mind. What I object to is having the blighter behave

433

as if he were a sort of champion condescending to a mere mortal. Dash it, it seemed to bore him playing with me! Every time I sliced off the tee he looked at me as if I were a painful ordeal. Twice when I was having a bit of trouble in the bushes I caught him yawning. And after we had finished he started talking about what a good game croquet was, and he wondered more people didn't take it up. And it's only a month or so ago that I could play the man level!'

The Oldest Member shook his snowy head sadly.

'There is nothing to be done about it,' he said. 'We can only hope that the poison will in time work its way out of the man's system. Sudden success at golf is like the sudden acquisition of wealth. It is apt to unsettle and deteriorate the character. And, as it comes almost miraculously, so only a miracle can effect a cure. The best advice I can give you is to refrain from playing with Nathaniel Frisby till you can keep your tee-shots straight.'

'Oh, but don't run away with the idea that I wasn't pretty good off the tee this afternoon!' said the young man. 'I should like to describe to you the shot I did on the – '

'Meanwhile,' proceeded the Oldest Member, 'I will relate to you a little story which bears on what I have been saying.'

'From the very moment I addressed the ball – '

'It is the story of two loving hearts temporarily estranged owing to the sudden and unforeseen proficiency of one of the couple – '

'I waggled quickly and strongly, like Duncan. Then, swinging smoothly back, rather in the Vardon manner – '

'But as I see,' said the Oldest Member, 'that you are all impatience for me to begin, I will do so without further preamble.'

*

434

To the philosophical student of golf like myself (said the Oldest Member) perhaps the most outstanding virtue of this noble pursuit is the fact that it is a medicine for the soul. Its great service to humanity is that it teaches human beings that, whatever petty triumphs they may have achieved in other walks of life, they are after all merely human. It acts as a corrective against sinful pride. I attribute the insane arrogance of the later Roman emperors almost entirely to the fact that, never having played golf, they never knew that strange chastening humility which is engendered by a topped chip-shot. If Cleopatra had been outed in the first round of the Ladies' Singles, we should have heard a lot less of her proud imperiousness. And, coming down to modern times, it was undoubtedly his rotten golf that kept Wallace Chesney the nice unspoiled fellow he was. For in every other respect he had everything in the world calculated to make a man conceited and arrogant. He was the best-looking man for miles around; his health was perfect; and, in addition to this, he was rich; danced, rode, played bridge and polo with equal skill; and was engaged to be married to Charlotte Dix. And when you saw Charlotte Dix you realized that being engaged to her would by itself have been quite enough luck for any one man.

But Wallace, as I say, despite all his advantages, was a thoroughly nice, modest young fellow. And I attribute this to the fact that, while one of the keenest golfers in the club, he was also one of the worst players. Indeed, Charlotte Dix used to say to me in his presence that she could not understand why people paid money to go to the circus when by merely walking over the brow of a hill they could watch Wallace Chesney trying to get out of the bunker by the eleventh green. And Wallace took the gibe with perfect good humour, for there was a delightful camaraderie between them which robbed it of any sting. Often at lunch in the club-house I used to hear him and Charlotte planning the handicapping details of a proposed match between Wallace and a non-existent cripple whom Charlotte claimed to have discovered in the village – it being agreed finally that he should accept seven bisques from the cripple, but that, if the latter ever recovered the use of his arms, Wallace should get a stroke a hole.

In short, a thoroughly happy and united young couple. Two hearts, if I may coin an expression, that beat as one.

I would not have you misjudge Wallace Chesney. I may have given you the impression that his attitude towards golf was light and frivolous, but such was not the case. As I have said, he was one of the keenest members of the club. Love made him receive the joshing of his *fiancée* in the kindly spirit in which it was meant, but at heart he was as earnest as you could wish. He practised early and late; he bought golf books; and the mere sight of a patent club of any description acted on him like catnip on a cat. I remember remonstrating with him on the occasion of his purchasing a wooden-faced driving-mashie which weighed about two pounds, and was, taking it for all in all, as foul an instrument as ever came out of the workshop of a clubmaker who had been dropped on the head by his nurse when a baby.

'I know, I know,' he said, when I had finished indicating some of the weapon's more obvious defects. 'But the point is, I believe in it. It gives me confidence. I don't believe you could slice with a thing like that if you tried.'

Confidence! That was what Wallace Chesney lacked, and that, as he saw it, was the prime grand secret of golf. Like an alchemist on the track of the Philosopher's Stone, he was for ever seeking for something which would really give him confidence. I recollect that he even tried repeating to himself fifty times every morning the words, 'Every day in every way I grow better and better.' This, however, proved such a black lie that he gave it up. The fact is, the man was a visionary, and it is to auto-hypnosis of some kind that I attribute the extraordinary change that came over him at the beginning of his third season.

You may have noticed in your perambulations about the City a shop bearing above its door and upon its windows the legend:

COHEN BROS
SECOND-HAND CLOTHIERS

a statement which is borne out by endless vistas seen through the door of every variety of what is technically known as Gents' Wear. But the Brothers Cohen, though their main stock-in-trade is garments which have been rejected by their owners for one reason or another, do not confine their dealings to Gents' Wear. The place is a museum of derelict goods of every description. You can get a second-hand revolver there, or a second-hand sword, or a second-hand umbrella. You can do a cheap deal in field-glasses, trunks, dog collars, canes, photograph frames, attaché cases, and bowls for goldfish. And on the bright spring morning when Wallace Chesney happened to pass by there was exhibited in the window a putter of such pre-eminently lunatic design that he stopped dead as if he had run into an invisible wall, and then, panting like an overwrought fish, charged in through the door.

The shop was full of the Cohen family, sombre-eyed, smileless men with purposeful expressions; and two of these, instantly descending upon Wallace Chesney like leopards, began in swift silence to thrust him into a suit of yellow tweed. Having worked the coat over his shoulders with a shoe-horn, they stood back to watch the effect.

'A beautiful fit,' announced Isidore Cohen.

'A little snug under the arms,' said his brother Irving. 'But that'll give.'

437

'The warmth of the body will make it give,' said Isidore.

'Or maybe you'll lose weight in the summer,' said Irving.

Wallace, when he had struggled out of the coat and was able to breathe, said that he had come into buy a putter. Isidore therefore sold him the putter, a dog collar, and a set of studs, and Irving sold him a fireman's helmet: and he was about to leave when their elder brother Lou, who had just finished fitting out another customer, who had come in to buy a cap, with two pairs of trousers and a miniature aquarium for keeping newts in, saw that business was in progress and strolled up. His fathomless eye rested on Wallace, who was toying feebly with the putter.

'You play golf?' asked Lou. 'Then looka here!'

He dived into an alleyway of dead clothing, dug for a moment, and emerged with something at the sight of which Wallace Chesney, hardened golfer that he was, blenched and threw up an arm defensively.

'No, no!' he cried.

The object which Lou Cohen was waving insinuatingly before his eyes was a pair of those golfing breeches which are technically known as Plus Fours. A player of two years' standing, Wallace Chesney was not unfamiliar with Plus Four – all the club cracks wore them – but he had never seen Plus Fours like these. What might be termed the main *motif* of the fabric was a curious vivid pink, and with this to work on the architect had let his imagination run free, and had produced so much variety in the way of chessboard squares of white, yellow, violet, and green that the eye swam as it looked upon them.

'These were made to measure for Sandy McHoots, the Open Champion,' said Lou, stroking the left leg lovingly. 'But he sent 'em back for some reason or other.'

'Perhaps they frightened the children,' said Wallace,

recollecting having heard that Mr McHoots was a married man.

'They'll fit you nice,' said Lou.

'Sure they'll fit him nice,' said Isidore, warmly.

'Why, just take a look at yourself in the glass,' said Irving, 'and see if they don't fit you nice.'

And, as one who wakes from a trance, Wallace discovered that his lower limbs were now encased in the prismatic garment. At what point in the proceedings the brethren had slipped them on him, he could not have said. But he was undeniably in.

Wallace looked in the glass. For a moment, as he eyed his reflection, sheer horror gripped him. Then suddenly, as he gazed, he became aware that his first feelings were changing. The initial shock over, he was becoming calmer. He waggled his right leg with a certain sang-froid.

There is a certain passage in the works of the poet Pope with which you may be familiar. It runs as follows:

'Vice is a monster of so frightful mien
As to be hated needs but to be seen;
Yet seen too oft, familiar with her face,
We first endure, then pity, then embrace.'

Even so was it with Wallace Chesney and these Plus Fours. At first he had recoiled from them as any decent-minded man would have done. Then, after a while, almost abruptly he found himself in the grip of a new emotion. After an unsuccessful attempt to analyse this, he suddenly got it. Amazing as it may seem, it was pleasure that he felt. He caught his eye in the mirror, and it was smirking. Now that the things were actually on, by Hutchinson, they didn't look half bad. By Braid, they didn't. There was a sort of something about them. Take away that expanse of bare leg with its unsightly sock-suspender and substitute a woolly stocking, and you would have the lower section of a golfer. For the first time in his life, he thought, he looked like a man who could play golf.

There came to him an odd sensation of masterfulness. He was still holding the putter, and now he swung it up above his shoulder. A fine swing, all lissomness and supple grace, quite different from any swing he had ever done before.

Wallace Chesney gasped. He knew that at last he had discovered that prime grand secret of golf for which he had searched so long. It was the costume that did it. All you had to do was wear Plus Fours. He had always hitherto played in grey flannel trousers. Naturally he had not been able to do himself justice. Golf required an easy dash, and how could you be easily dashing in concertina-shaped trousers with a patch on the knee? He saw now – what he had never seen before – that it was not because they were crack players that crack players wore Plus Fours: it was because they wore Plus Fours that they were crack players. And these Plus Fours had been the property of an Open Champion. Wallace Chesney's bosom swelled, and he was filled, as by some strange gas, with joy – with excitement – with confidence. Yes, for the first time in his golfing life, he felt really confident.

True, the things might have been a shade less gaudy: they might perhaps have hit the eye with a slightly less violent punch: but what of that? True, again, he could scarcely hope to avoid the censure of his club-mates when he appeared like this on the links: but what of *that*? His club-mates must set their teeth and learn to bear these Plus Fours like men. That was what Wallace Chesney thought about it. If they did not like his Plus Fours, let them go and play golf somewhere else.

'How much?' he muttered, thickly. And the Brothers Cohen clustered grimly round with notebooks and pencils.

In predicting a stormy reception for his new apparel, Wallace Chesney had not been unduly pessimistic. The

moment he entered the club-house Disaffection reared
its ugly head. Friends of years' standing called loudly for
the committee, and there was a small and vehement party
of the left wing, headed by Raymond Gandle, who was an
artist by profession, and consequently had a sensitive eye,
which advocated the tearing off and public burial of the
obnoxious garment. But, prepared as he had been for some
such demonstration on the part of the coarser-minded,
Wallace had hoped for better things when he should meet
Charlotte Dix, the girl who loved him. Charlotte, he had
supposed, would understand and sympathize.

Instead of which, she uttered a piercing cry and
staggered to a bench, whence a moment later she
delivered her ultimatum.

'Quick!' she said. 'Before I have to look again.'

'What do you mean?'

'Pop straight back into the changing-room while I've
got my eyes shut, and remove the fancy-dress.'

'What's wrong with them?'

'Darling,' said Charlotte, 'I think it's sweet and
patriotic of you to be proud of your cycling-club colours
or whatever they are, but you mustn't wear them on the
links. It will unsettle the caddies.'

'They *are* a trifle on the bright side,' admitted Wallace.
'But it helps my game, wearing them. I was trying a few
practice-shots just now, and I couldn't go wrong. Slammed
the ball on the meat every time. They inspire me, if you
know what I mean. Come on, let's be starting.'

Charlotte opened her eyes incredulously.

'You can't seriously mean that you're really going to
play in – those? It's against the rules. There must be a
rule somewhere in the book against coming out looking
like a sunset. Won't you go and burn them for my sake?'

'But I tell you they give me confidence. I sort of squint
down at them when I'm addressing the ball, and I feel
like a pro.'

'Then the only thing to do is for me to play you for

them. Come on, Wally, be a sportsman. I'll give you a half and play you for the whole outfit – the breeches, the red jacket, the little cap, and the belt with the snake's-head buckle. I'm sure all those things must have gone with the breeches. Is it a bargain?'

Strolling on the club-house terrace some two hours later, Raymond Gandle encountered Charlotte and Wallace coming up from the eighteenth green.

'Just the girl I wanted to see,' said Raymond. 'Miss Dix, I represent a select committee of my fellow-members, and I have come to ask you on their behalf to use the influence of a good woman to induce Wally to destroy those Plus Fours of his, which we all consider nothing short of Bolshevik propaganda and a menace to the public weal. May I rely on you?'

'You may not,' retorted Charlotte. 'They are the poor boy's mascot. You've no idea how they have improved his game. He has just beaten me hollow. I am going to try to learn to bear them, so you must. Really, you've no notion how he has come on. My cripple won't be able to give him more than a couple of bisques if he keeps up this form.'

'It's something about the things,' said Wallace. 'They give me confidence.'

'They give *me* a pain in the neck,' said Raymond Gandle.

To the thinking man nothing is more remarkable in this life than the way in which Humanity adjusts itself to conditions which at their outset might well have appeared intolerable. Some great cataclysm occurs, some storm or earthquake, shaking the community to its foundations; and after the first pardonable consternation one finds the sufferers resuming their ordinary pursuits as if nothing had happened. There have been few more striking examples of this adaptability than the behaviour

of the members of our golf-club under the impact of
Wallace Chesney's Plus Fours. For the first few days it is
not too much to say that they were stunned. Nervous
players sent their caddies on in front of them at blind
holes, so that they might be warned in time of Wallace's
presence ahead and not have him happening to them all
of a sudden. And even the pro. was not unaffected.
Brought up in Scotland in an atmosphere of tartan kilts,
he nevertheless winced, and a startled 'Hoots!' was
forced from his lips when Wallace Chesney suddenly
appeared in the valley as he was about to drive from the
fifth tee.

But in about a week conditions were back to normal.
Within ten days the Plus Fours became a familiar feature
of the landscape, and were accepted as such without
comment. They were pointed out to strangers together
with the waterfall, the Lovers' Leap, and the view from
the eighth green as things you ought not to miss when
visiting the course; but apart from that one might almost
say they were ignored. And meanwhile Wallace Chesney
continued day by day to make the most extraordinary
progress in his play.

As I have said before, and I think you will agree with
me when I have told you what happened subsequently,
it was probably a case of auto-hypnosis. There is no other
sphere in which a belief in oneself has such immediate
effects as it has in golf. And Wallace, having acquired self-
confidence, went on from strength to strength. In under
a week he had ploughed his way through the Unfortunate
Incidents – of which class Peter Willard was the best
example – and was challenging the fellows who kept three
shots in five somewhere on the fairway. A month later
he was holding his own with ten-handicap men. And by
the middle of the summer he was so far advanced that
his name occasionally cropped up in speculative talks on
the subject of the July medal. One might have been
excused for supposing that, as far as Wallace Chesney was

concerned, all was for the best in the best of all possible worlds.

And yet –

The first inkling I received that anything was wrong came through a chance meeting with Raymond Gandle who happened to pass my gate on his way back from the links just as I drove up in my taxi; for I had been away from home for many weeks on a protracted business tour. I welcomed Gandle's advent and invited him in to smoke a pipe and put me abreast of local gossip. He came readily enough – and seemed, indeed to have something on his mind and to be glad of the opportunity of revealing it to a sympathetic auditor.

'And how,' I asked him, when we were comfortably settled, 'did your game this afternoon come out?'

'Oh, he beat me,' said Gandle, and it seemed to me that there was a note of bitterness in his voice.

'Then he, whoever he was, must have been an extremely competent performer,' I replied, courteously, for Gandle was one of the finest players in the club. 'Unless, of course, you were giving him some impossible handicap.'

'No; we played level.'

'Indeed! Who was your opponent?'

'Chesney.'

'Wallace Chesney! And he beat you playing level! This is the most amazing thing I have ever heard.'

'He's improved out of all knowledge.'

'He must have done. Do you think he would ever beat you again?'

'No. Because he won't have the chance.'

'You surely do not mean that you will not play him because you are afraid of being beaten?'

'It isn't being beaten I mind – '

And if I omit to report the remainder of his speech it is not merely because it contained expresssions with which I am reluctant to sully my lips, but because,

omitting these expletives, what he said was almost word
for word what you were saying to me just now about
Nathaniel Frisby. It was, it seemed, Wallace Chesney's
manner, his arrogance, his attitude of belonging to some
superior order of being that had so wounded Raymond
Gandle. Wallace Chesney had, it appeared, criticized
Gandle's mashie-play in no friendly spirit; had hung up
the game on the fourteenth tee in order to show him how
to place his feet; and on the way back to the club-house
had said that the beauty of golf was that the best player
could enjoy a round even with a dud, because, though
there might be no interest in the match, he could always
amuse himself by playing for his medal score.

I was profoundly shaken.

'Wallace Chesney!' I exclaimed. 'Was it really Wallace
Chesney who behaved in the manner you describe?'

'Unless he's got a twin brother of the same name, it
was.'

'Wallace Chesney a victim to swelled head! I can
hardly credit it.'

'Well, you needn't take my word for it unless you want
to. Ask anybody. It isn't often he can get anyone to play
with him now.'

'You horrify me!'

Raymond Gandle smoked a while in brooding
silence.

'You've heard about his engagement?' he said at
length.

'I have heard nothing, nothing. What about his
engagement?'

'Charlotte Dix has broken it off.'

'No!'

'Yes. Couldn't stand him any longer.'

I got rid of Gandle as soon as I could. I made my way
as quickly as possible to the house where Charlotte lived
with her aunt. I was determined to sift this matter to the
bottom and to do all that lay in my power to heal

445

the breach between two young people for whom I had a great affection.

'I have just heard the news,' I said, when the aunt had retired to some secret lair, as aunts do, and Charlotte and I were alone.

'What news?' said Charlotte, dully. I thought she looked pale and ill, and she had certainly grown thinner.

'This dreadful news about your engagement to Wallace Chesney. Tell me, why did you do this thing? Is there no hope of a reconciliation?'

'Not unless Wally becomes his old self again.'

'But I had always regarded you two as ideally suited to one another.'

'Wally has completely changed in the last few weeks. Haven't you heard?'

'Only sketchily, from Raymond Gandle.'

'I refuse,' said Charlotte, proudly, all the woman in her leaping to her eyes, 'to marry a man who treats me as if I were a kronen at the present rate of exchange, merely because I slice an occasional teeshot. The afternoon I broke off the engagement' – her voice shook, and I could see that her indifference was but a mask – 'the afternoon I broke off the en-gug-gug-gagement, he t-told me I ought to use an iron off the tee instead of a dud-dud-driver.'

And the stricken girl burst into an uncontrollable fit of sobbing. And realizing that, if matters had gone as far as that, there was little I could do, I pressed her hand silently and left her.

But though it seemed hopeless I decided to persevere. I turned my steps towards Wallace Chesney's bungalow, resolved to make one appeal to the man's better feelings. He was in his sitting-room when I arrived, polishing a putter; and it seemed significant to me, even in that tense moment, that the putter was quite an ordinary one, such as any capable player might use. In the brave old happy

days of his dudhood, the only putters you ever found in
the society of Wallace Chesney were patent self-adjusting
things that looked like croquet mallets that had taken the
wrong turning in childhood.

'Well, Wallace, my boy,' I said.

'Hallo!' said Wallace Chesney. 'So you're back?'

We fell into conversation, and I had not been in the
room two minutes before I realized that what I had been
told about the change in him was nothing more than the
truth. The man's bearing and his every remark were
insufferably bumptious. He spoke of his prospects in the
July medal competition as if the issue were already
settled. He scoffed at his rivals.

I had some little difficulty in bringing the talk round
to the matter which I had come to discuss.

'My boy,' I said at length, 'I have just heard the sad
news.'

'What sad news?'

'I have been talking to Charlotte – '

'Oh, that!' said Wallace Chesney.

'She was telling me – '

'Perhaps it's all for the best.'

'All for the best? What do you mean?'

'Well,' said Wallace, 'one doesn't wish, of course, to
say anything ungallant, but, after all, poor Charlotte's
handicap *is* fourteen and wouldn't appear to have much
chance of getting any lower. I mean, there's such a thing
as a fellow throwing himself away.'

Was I revolted at these callous words? For a moment,
yes. Then it struck me that, though he had uttered them
with a light laugh, that laugh had had in it more than a
touch of bravado. I looked at him keenly. There was
a bored, discontented expression in his eyes, a line of pain
about his mouth.

'My boy,' I said, gravely, 'you are not happy.'

For an instant I think he would have denied the
imputation. But my visit had coincided with one of those

447

twilight moods in which a man requires, above all else, sympathy. He uttered a weary sigh.

'I'm fed up,' he admitted. 'It's a funny thing. When I was a dud, I used to think how perfect it must be to be scratch. I used to watch the cracks buzzing round the course and envy them. It's all a fraud. The only time when you enjoy golf is when an occasional decent shot is enough to make you happy for the day. I'm plus two, and I'm bored to death. I'm too good. And what's the result? Everybody's jealous of me. Everybody's got it in for me. Nobody loves me.'

His voice rose in a note of anguish, and at the sound his terrier, which had been sleeping on the rug, crept forward and licked his hand.

'The dog loves you,' I said, gently, for I was touched.

'Yes, but I don't love the dog,' said Wallace Chesney.

'Now come, Wallace,' I said. 'Be reasonable, my boy. It is only your unfortunate manner on the links which has made you perhaps a little unpopular at the moment. Why not pull yourself up? Why ruin your whole life with this arrogance? All that you need is a little tact, a little forbearance. Charlotte, I am sure, is just as fond of you as ever, but you have wounded her pride. Why must you be unkind about her tee-shots?'

Wallace Chesney shook his head despondently.

'I can't help it,' he said. 'It exasperates me to see anyone foozling, and I have to say so.'

'Then there is nothing to be done,' I said, sadly.

All the medal competitions at our club are, as you know, important events; but, as you are also aware, none of them is looked forward to so keenly or contested so hotly as the one in July. At the beginning of the year of which I am speaking, Raymond Gandle had been considered the probable winner of the fixture; but as the season progressed and Wallace Chesney's skill developed to such a remarkable extent most of us were reluctantly inclined to put our money on the latter. Reluctantly, because Wallace's unpopularity was now so general that the thought of his winning was distasteful to all. It grieved me to see how cold his fellow-members were towards him. He drove off from the first tee without a solitary hand-clap; and, though the drive was of admirable quality and nearly carried the green, there was not a single cheer. I noticed Charlotte Dix among the spectators. The poor girl was looking sad and wan.

In the draw for partners Wallace had had Peter Willard allotted to him; and he muttered to me in a quite audible voice that it was as bad as handicapping him half a dozen strokes to make him play with such a hopeless performer. I do not think Peter heard, but it would not have made much difference to him if he had, for I doubt if anything could have had much effect for the worse on his game. Peter Willard always entered for the medal competition, because he said that competition-play was good for the nerves.

On this occasion he topped his ball badly, and Wallace lit his pipe with the exaggeratedly patient air of an irritated man. When Peter topped his second also, Wallace was moved to speech.

'For goodness' sake,' he snapped, 'what's the good of playing at all if you insist on lifting your head? Keep it down, man, keep it down. You don't need to watch to see where the ball is going. It isn't likely to go as far as all that. Make up your mind to count three before you look up.'

'Thanks,' said Peter, meekly. There was no pride in Peter to be wounded. He knew the sort of player he was.

The couples were now moving off with smooth rapidity, and the course was dotted with the figures of players and their accompanying spectators. A fair proportion of these latter had decided to follow the fortunes of Raymond Gandle, but by far the larger number were sticking to Wallace, who right from the start showed that Gandle or anyone else would have to return

449

a very fine card to beat him. He was out in thirty-seven,
two above bogey, and with the assistance of a superb
second, which landed the ball within a foot of the pin,
got a three on the tenth, where a four is considered good.
I mention this to show that by the time he arrived at the
short lake-hole Wallace Chesney was at the top of his
form. Not even the fact that he had been obliged to let the
next couple through owing to Peter Willard losing his
ball had been enough to upset him.

The course has been rearranged since, but at that time
the lake-hole, which is now the second, was the
eleventh, and was generally looked on as the crucial hole
in a medal round. Wallace no doubt realized this, but
the knowledge did not seem to affect him. He lit his pipe
with the utmost coolness: and, having replaced the
matchbox in his hip-pocket, stood smoking nonchalantly
as he waited for the couple in front to get off the green.

They holed out eventually, and Wallace walked to the
tee. As he did so, he was startled to receive a resounding
smack.

'Sorry,' said Peter Willard, apologetically. 'Hope I
didn't hurt you. A wasp.'

And he pointed to the corpse, which was lying in a
used-up attitude on the ground.

'Afraid it would sting you,' said Peter.

'Oh, thanks,' said Wallace.

He spoke a little stiffly, for Peter Willard had a large,
hard, flat hand, the impact of which had shaken him up
considerably. Also, there had been laughter in the crowd.
He was fuming as he bent to address the ball, and his
annoyance became acute when, just as he reached the top
of his swing, Peter Willard suddenly spoke.

'Just a second, old man,' said Peter. Wallace spun
round, outraged.

'What *is* it? I do wish you would wait till I've made
my shot.'

450

'Just as you like,' said Peter, humbly.

'There is no greater crime that a man can commit on the links than to speak to a fellow when he's making his stroke.'

'Of course, of course,' acquiesced Peter, crushed.

Wallace turned to his ball once more. He was vaguely conscious of a discomfort to which he could not at the moment give a name. At first he thought that he was having a spasm of lumbago, and this surprised him, for he had never in his life been subject to even a suspicion of that malady. A moment later he realized that this diagnosis had been wrong.

'Good heavens!' he cried, leaping nimbly some two feet into the air. 'I'm on fire!'

'Yes,' said Peter, delighted at his ready grasp of the situation. 'That's what I wanted to mention just now.'

Wallace slapped vigorously at the seat of his Plus Fours.

'It must have been when I killed that wasp,' said Peter, beginning to see clearly into the matter. 'You had a match-box in your pocket.'

Wallace was in no mood to stop and discuss first causes. He was springing up and down on his pyre, beating at the flames.

'Do you know what I should do if I were you?' said Peter Willard. 'I should jump into the lake.'

One of the cardinal rules of golf is that a player shall accept no advice from anyone but his own caddie; but the warmth about his lower limbs had now become so generous that Wallace was prepared to stretch a point. He took three rapid strides and entered the water with a splash.

The lake, though muddy, is not deep, and presently Wallace was to be observed standing up to his waist some few feet from the shore.

'That ought to have put it out,' said Peter Willard. 'It was a bit of luck that it happened at this hole.' He stretched out a hand to the bather. 'Catch hold, old man, and I'll pull you out.'

'No!' said Wallace Chesney.

'Why not?'

'Never mind!' said Wallace, austerely. He bent as near to Peter as he was able.

'Send a caddie up to the club-house to fetch my grey flannel trousers from my locker,' he whispered, tensely.

'Oh, ah!' said Peter.

It was some little time before Wallace, encircled by a group of male spectators, was enabled to change his costume; and during the interval he continued to stand waist-deep in the water, to the chagrin of various couples who came to the tee in the course of their round and complained with not a little bitterness that his presence there added a mental hazard to an already difficult hole. Eventually, however, he found himself back ashore, his ball before him, his mashie in his hand.

'Carry on,' said Peter Willard, as the couple in front left the green. 'All clear now.'

Wallace Chesney addressed his ball. And, even as he did so, he was suddenly aware that an odd psychological change had taken place in himself. He was aware of a strange weakness. The charred remains of the Plus Fours were lying under an adjacent bush; and, clad in the old grey flannels of his early golfing days, Wallace felt diffident, feeble, uncertain of himself. It was as though virtue had gone out of him, as if some indispensable adjunct to good play had been removed. His corrugated trouser-leg caught his eye as he waggled, and all at once he became acutely alive to the fact that many eyes were watching him. The audience seemed to press on him like a blanket. He felt as he had been wont to feel in the old days when he had had to drive off the first tee in front of a terrace-full of scoffing critics.

The next moment his ball had bounded weakly over the intervening patch of turf and was in the water.

'Hard luck!' said Peter Willard, ever a generous foe.
And the words seemed to touch some almost atrophied
chord in Wallace's breast. A sudden love for his species
flooded over him. Dashed decent of Peter, he thought,
to sympathize. Peter was a good chap. So were the
spectators good chaps. So was everybody, even his
caddie.

Peter Willard, as if resolved to make his sympathy
practical, also rolled his ball into the lake.

'Hard luck!' said Wallace Chesney, and started as he
said it; for many weeks had passed since he had
commiserated with an opponent. He felt a changed man.
A better, sweeter, kindlier man. It was as if a curse had
fallen from him.

He teed up another ball, and swung.

'Hard luck!' said Peter.

'Hard luck!' said Wallace, a moment later.

'Hard luck!' said Peter, a moment after that.

Wallace Chesney stood on the tee watching the spot
in the water where his third ball had fallen. The crowd was
now openly amused, and, as he listened to their happy
laughter, it was borne in upon Wallace that he, too, was
amused and happy. A weird, almost effervescent
exhilaration filled him. He turned and beamed upon the
spectators. He waved his mashie cheerily at them. This,
he felt, was something like golf. This was golf as it
should be – not the dull, mechanical thing which had
bored him during all these past weeks of his perfection,
but a gay, rollicking adventure. That was the soul of golf,
the thing that made it the wonderful pursuit it was –
that speculativeness, that not knowing where the dickens
your ball was going when you hit it, that eternal hoping
for the best, that never-failing chanciness. It is better to
travel hopefully than to arrive, and at last this great
truth had come home to Wallace Chesney. He realized
now why pro's. were all grave, silent men who seemed
to struggle manfully against some secret sorrow. It was

453

because they were too darned good. Golf had no surprises for them, no gallant spirit of adventure.

'I'm going to get a ball over if I stay here all night,' cried Wallace Chesney, gaily, and the crowd echoed his mirth. On the face of Charlotte Dix was the look of a mother whose prodigal son had rolled into the old home once more. She caught Wallace's eye and gesticulated to him blithely.

'The cripple says he'll give you a stroke a hole, Wally!' she shouted.

'I'm ready for him!' bellowed Wallace.

'Hard *luck*!' said Peter Willard.

Under their bush the Plus Fours, charred and dripping, lurked unnoticed. But Wallace Chesney saw them. They caught his eye as he sliced his eleventh into the marshes on the right. It seemed to him that they looked sullen. Disappointed. Baffled.

Wallace Chesney was himself again.

3 — The Eighteenth Hole

A Very Modern Golfing Romance

When William John Maxwell received the note and recognized on the envelope the handwriting of B. Rockleigh Derrick, the father of his Genevieve, hope, for the first time in many days . . . for the first time, in fact, since that painful interview in Mr Derrick's study, when the life-romance of two loving young hearts had hit the resin with a thud, as if it had been sand-bagged, began to stir within him.

It was true that at the interview referred to, Mr Derrick, basing his refusal on some trivial ground, such as the stunted nature of William's annual income, had declined, with considerable violence, to give his consent to what William regarded as a most suitable match; but, if he had not relented, why was he writing notes in this way?

It is not too much to say that, as he tore open the envelope, William expected a Father's Blessing to jump out at him. He was even surprised to find no tear-stains of remorse on the epistle.

And all it was – and in the third person, at that – was an invitation to play golf. Mr Derrick begged to inform Mr Maxwell that, by defeating Mr Saul Potter, he had qualified for the final round of the Rockport Golf Tournament, in which, he understood, Mr Maxwell, who had also survived the opening rounds, was to be his opponent.

If it would be convenient for Mr Maxwell to play off the match on the following afternoon, Mr Derrick would be obliged if he would be at the club-house at half-past two. If this hour and day were unsuitable, would he kindly arrange others. The bearer would wait.

The bearer did wait, and then trudged off with a note, in which Mr Maxwell begged to inform Mr Derrick that he would be at the clubhouse at the hour mentioned.

'And,' added Mr Maxwell, after the bearer had departed, 'I will give him such a licking that he'll brain himself with a clock.'

It is painful to write of the lower emotions, especially when exhibited by otherwise estimable young men, but the fact must be faced that, on the following afternoon, William John Maxwell looked forward to a gruesome revenge on Mr Derrick. The prospect brought a wan, faint smile to his lips.

Mr Derrick was one of those Merchant Princes who have taken to golf in middle age, of whose golf the best one can say is that they take pains. Mr Derrick took exquisite pains. He lived for golf, and it was the ambition of his life to win the Rockport Championship. He came to Rockport every year, and always went in for the Cup, and such is the magic of perseverance that for two years in succession he had been runner-up.

It was a galling thought to him that, if it had not been for the presence of William Maxwell, this year he would have brought the thing off. Nor did it make it better to remember that the presence of William Maxwell was directly due to the fact that he himself was at Rockport – for, though William had no great love for Mr Derrick, he always went where he knew Genevieve to be.

All this William knew, and he was conscious of a moody joy at the prospect of snatching the prize from Mr Derrick. He knew that he could do it. Even allowing for bad luck – and he was never a very unlucky golfer – he could rely with certainty on crushing his rival.

But he did not intend to do it abruptly. It was his intention to nurse Mr Derrick to play with him. The contest would be decided to match play, which would give him ample scope for toying with the victim. He proposed to allow Mr Derrick to get ahead, and then to catch him up. He would then forge ahead himself, and let Mr Derrick catch him up.

They would race neck and neck together to the very end, and then, when Mr Derrick's hair had turned white with the strain and he had lost forty pounds in weight and his eyes were starting out of his head, he would go ahead and beat him by a hole.

He felt ruthless towards Mr Derrick. He knew that to one whose soul is in the game, as Mr Derrick's was, the agony of being just beaten in an important match exceeds in bitterness all other agonies.

He knew that, in days to come, Mr Derrick would wake from fitful slumber moaning that, if he had only used his iron at the tenth, all would have been well; that, if he had putted more carefully on the seventh green, life would not be drear and blank; that a more judicious manipulation of his mashie throughout might have given him something to live for. All these things he knew, but they did not touch him. He was adamant.

William drove off from the first tee. It was a splendid drive, and it intimidated Mr Derrick. He addressed the ball at twice his usual length, waggling his club over it as if he were about to perform a conjuring trick. Then he struck, and topped it. The ball rolled ten yards. He got to work with a brassey. This time he hit a bunker, and the ball rolled back. He repeated the maneuver twice.

'I shall pick my ball up,' he said huskily, and they walked in silence to the second tee.

Mr Derrick did the second hole in four, which was good. William did it in three, which – unfortunately for Mr Derrick – was better.

William won the third hole.

William won the fourth hole.

William won the fifth hole.

Beads of perspiration stood out on Mr Derrick's

forehead. His play became wilder and wilder at each hole in arithmetical progression. If he had been a plow, he could hardly have turned up more soil. The imagination recoiled from the thought of what he would be doing in another half hour if he deteriorated at his present speed.

A feeling of calm and content stole over William. He was not sorry for Mr Derrick. Once, when the latter missed the ball clean at the tee, their eyes met, but William saved his life by not smiling.

The sixth hole on the Rockport links involves the player in a tricky piece of cross-country work. There is a nasty ditch to be negotiated. Many an optimist has been reduced to blank pessimism by the ditch. 'All hope abandon, ye who enter here,' might be written on a notice board over it.

Mr Derrick entered here. The unhappy man sent his ball into its very jaws, and then madness seized him. The merciful laws of golf, framed by kindly men who do not wish to see the asylums of the country overcrowded, chart that in such a case the player may take his ball and throw it over his shoulder, the same to count as one stroke. But vaulting ambition is apt to try to drive out of the ditch, thinking thereby to win through without losing a stroke. This way madness lies.

'Sixteen!' said Mr Derrick at last between his teeth. And he stooped and picked up his ball. 'I give you this hole.'

They walked on.

William won the seventh hole.

William won the eighth hole.

The ninth hole they halved, for in the black depths of William's soul a plan of fiendish subtlety had formed. He intended to allow Mr Derrick to win eight holes in succession, then, when hope was once more strong within him, he would win the last, and Mr Derrick would go mad.

William watched his opponent carefully as they trudged on. Emotions chased one another over the latter's face. When Mr Derrick won the tenth hole, he merely refrained from oaths. When he won the eleventh, a sort of sullen pleasure showed in his face.

Mr Derrick won the twelfth. It was at the thirteenth that William detected the first dawning of hope. When, with a sequence of shocking shots, he took the fourteenth, fifteenth and sixteenth and when he took the seventeeth hole in eight, he was in a parlous condition. He wanted, as it were, to flap his wings and crow. William could see dignity wrestling with talkativeness.

When he brought off an excellent drive from the eighteenth tee, Mr Derrick seemed to forget everything.

'My dear boy,' he began, and stopped abruptly in some confusion. Silence once more brooded over the pair as they played themselves up the fairway and onto the green.

Mr Derrick was on the green in four. William reached it in three. Mr Derrick's sixth stroke took him out.

William putted carefully to the very mouth of the hole. He walked up to his ball, and paused. He looked at Mr Derrick. Mr Derrick looked at him.

'Go on,' said Mr Derrick hoarsely.

And then, at the eleventh hour, William's better nature asserted itself. A wave of compassion flooded over him. He made up his mind.

'Mr Derrick,' he said.

'Go on.'

'That looks a simple shot,' said William, eyeing him steadily, 'but I might easily miss it.'

Mr Derrick started.

'And then you would win the championship.'

Mr Derrick dabbed his forehead with a wet ball of a handkerchief.

'Go on,' he said for the third time, but there was a note of hesitation in his voice.

'Sudden joy,' said William, 'would almost certainly

459

make me miss it. If, for instance, you were suddenly to give your consent to my marriage with Genevieve – '

Mr Derrick looked from William to the ball, from the ball to William, and back again to the ball. It was very, very near the hole.

'Why not?' said William.

Mr Derrick looked up, and burst into a roar of laughter.

'You young devil,' he said, 'you've beaten me.'

'On the contrary,' said William, 'you have beaten *me*, Mr Derrick.'

He swung his putter, and drove his ball far beyond the green.

From *Vanity Fair*, August 1915,
rewritten from a closing chapter in
Love Among the Chickens

4 — A Plea for Indoor Golf

And a Plaintive Dirge – By a Golfing Neophyte – for the Passing of Winter

It might be supposed, by the vapid and unreflective, that in winter, when the first snows have begun to fall and the last pro's have started flying South, the enthusiastic golfer would be to some extent up against it. The fact is, however, that of the four seasons of the golfing year – Spring, when you lose your ball in the unmown hay; Summer, when you lose it in the glare of the sun; Autumn, when you lose it under dead leaves; and Winter, when you have a sporting chance of not losing it at all – the last-named is, to the thoughtful golfer, quite the pleasantest.

It is glorious, no doubt, on a lovely afternoon in Summer, with the sun shining down and a gentle breeze tempering the heat, to slice your ball into the adjacent jungle and to feel that you are thereby doing a bit of good to a small boy who needs the money which he will get when – directly your back is turned – he finds and sells the missing globule.

It is thrilling, on one of those still, crisp days in the Fall, to drive off the tee at eleven-fifteen and potter about the course till twelve-forty-five, turning over leaves with a niblick in the hope that each leaf be the one under which your ball has elected to nestle. But both these pleasures are eclipsed by the delight of playing on a frosty morning in the winter.

In Winter You Get Good Visibility

There you stand, before you a prairie denuded of all vegetation. The trees, into which you used to send your second shot, have now no leaves, and it is quite possible to penetrate them with a well-judged stroke of the light iron. Your caddie broods dejectedly beside you. He knows that, even if you slice into the wood at the elbow-hole, you can find the ball for yourself.

And then you drive off.

It is one of your medium drives. You have violated, possibly, only eleven out of the twenty-three rules for correct driving. The ball soars in a lofty arc, edging off to the right. Sixty yards from the tee it touches earth, and bounds another fifty, when it hits the frozen surface of a puddle and skids against a tree-trunk, a further ninety yards ahead. The angle at which it hits the tree just corrects your slice to perfection, and there you are, in a dead straight line with the pin, with a two hundred and thirty yard drive to your credit.

This is Golf, in the true sense of the word.

Even now, however, your happiness is not complete. You have omitted to take into consideration the fact that you are playing what are called Winter Rules, which entitle you to tee your ball up in the fairway. So you remove the pill from the cuppy lie into which it has settled and look round you for a convenient hillock. You can usually find a worm-cast or a mole-hill of a convenient height, and from this you propel the ball on to the green.

The green is a trifle rough, perhaps, but, after all, what does that matter? Experts will try to tell you otherwise, but every beginner knows that putting is a pure game of chance, and that you are just as likely to hole out over rough ground as over smooth. I, personally, prefer a worm-cast or two on the green.

They seem to lend zip to my putting.

*

Of course, there are weeks in the Winter when golf on the links is impossible, unless you happen to be in such an advanced stage of mental decay that you can contemplate with equanimity a round in the snow with a red ball. The ordinary golfer, unequal to such excesses, will take, during these weeks, to indoor golf. There are two varieties of the indoor game, both almost equally enjoyable.

The Glories of Indoor Golf
The first, and more customary, kind of Indoor Golf is that played in department stores, where professionals live in little dens on the Toys and Sporting Goods floor and give instruction, at a dollar the half hour. You stand on a rubber mat: the ball is placed on an ordinary door-mat: and you swat it against a target painted on a mattress.

The merits of this plan are obvious.

It is almost impossible not to hit the mattress *somewhere*, and it makes just as satisfactory a thud whether you hit it in the middle or in one of the outlying suburbs. And in indoor golf, as played in department stores, the thud is everything. This indoor instruction is invaluable. I may say that I, myself, am what I am as a golfer almost entirely through indoor instruction.

In the fall of 1917 I was a steady hundred-and-twenty man. Sometimes I would get into difficulties at one or other of the holes, as the best players will do, and then my score would be a hundred and thirty. Sometimes, again, I would find my form early in the round and shoot a hundred and eighteen. But, take me for all in all, I averaged a hundred and twenty. After a steady winter of indoor instruction, I was going round, this Spring, in a hundred and twelve.

These figures speak for themselves.

Of course, the drawback to department-store golf is that it is so difficult to reproduce the same conditions when you get out on the links. I have been in a variety of lies, good and bad, in my time, but never yet have I had the luck to drop my ball on a door-mat. Why this should be so, it is hard to say. I suppose the fact is that, unless you actually pull the ball, off the first tee, at right angles between your legs, it is not easy to land on a door-mat. And, even then, it would probably be a rubber door-mat, which is not at all the same thing.

Indoor Sport for the Housewreckers' Union
The other form of indoor golf is that which is played in the home. Whether you live in a palace or a hovel, an indoor golf-course, be it only of nine holes, is well within your reach. A house offers greater facilities than an apartment, and I have found my game greatly improved since I went to live in the country. I can, perhaps, scarcely do better than give a brief description of the sporting nine-hole course which I have recently laid out in my present residence.

All authorities agree that the first hole on every links should be moderately easy, in order to give the nervous player a temporary and fictitious confidence.

At Wodehouse Manor, therefore, we drive off from the front door – in order to get the benefit of the door-mat – down an entry fairway, carpeted with rugs, and without traps. The hole – a loving-cup from the Inebriates' Daughters of Communipaw for my services in combating the drink evil – is just under the stairs; and a good player ought to have no difficulty in doing it in two.

The second hole, a short one, takes you into the telephone booth. This also is simple. Trouble begins with the third, a long dog-leg hole through the kitchen into the dining-room. This hole is well trapped with table-legs, kitchen utensils, and a moving hazard in the person of Clarence the cat, who is generally wandering about the fairway. The hole is under the glass-and-china cupboard, where you are liable to be bunkered if you loft your approach-shot excessively. It is better to take your light iron and try a running-up approach instead of becoming ambitious with the mashie-niblick.

The fourth and fifth holes call for no comment. They are straightforward holes without traps, the only danger being that you may lose a stroke through hitting the maid if she happens to be coming down the back stairs while you are taking a mashie-shot. This is a penalty under the local rule.

A Word as to the Water Hazard

The sixth is the indispensable water-hole. It is short, but tricky. Teeing off from just outside the bathroom door, you have to loft the ball over the side of the bath, holing out in the little vent pipe, at the end where the water runs out. It is apparently a simple shot, but I have known many fine players, notably Ouimet, and Chick Evans, who have taken threes and fours over it. It is a niblick shot, and to use a full swing with the brassey is courting disaster. (In the Open Championship of 1914 Ouimet broke all precedents by taking a shovel for his tee-shot, and the subsequent controversy and the final ruling of the Golf Association will be fresh in the memory of all.)

The seventh is the longest hole on the course. Starting at the entrance of the best bedroom, a full drive takes you to the head of the stairs, whence you will need at least two more strokes to put you dead on the pin in the drawing-room. In the drawing-room the fairway is trapped with photograph frames – with glass, complete – these serving as casual water: and anyone who can hole out on the piano in five or under is a player of class. Bogey is six, and I have known even such a capable exponent of the game as my Uncle Reginald, who is plus two on his home links on Park Avenue, to take twenty-seven at the hole. But on that occasion he had the misfortune to be bunkered in a photograph of my Aunt Clara and took no few than eleven strokes with his niblick to extricate himself from it.

The eighth and ninth holes are straightforward, and can be done in two and three respectively, provided you swing easily and avoid the canary's cage. Once trapped there, it is better to give up the hole without further effort. It is almost impossible to get out in less than fifty-six, and after you have taken about thirty the bird gets visibly annoyed.

5 — Bingley Crocker Learns Cricket

Poets have dealt feelingly with the emotions of practically every variety except one. They have sung of Ruth, of Israel in bondage, of slaves pining for their native Africa, and of the miner's dream of home. But the sorrows of the baseball enthusiast, compelled by fate to live three thousand miles away from the Polo Grounds, have been neglected in song. Bingley Crocker was such a one, and in summer his agonies were awful. He pined away in a country where they said 'Well played, sir!' when they meant 'At-a-boy!'

'Bayliss, do you play cricket?'

'I am a little past the age, sir. In my younger days – '

'Do you understand it?'

'Yes, sir. I frequently spend an afternoon at Lord's or the Oval when there is a good match.'

Many who enjoyed a merely casual acquaintance with the butler would have looked on this as an astonishingly unexpected revelation of humanity in Bayliss, but Mr Crocker was not surprised. To him, from the very beginning, Bayliss had been a man and a brother, who was always willing to suspend his duties in order to answer questions dealing with the thousand and one problems which the social life of England presented. Mr Crocker's mind had adjusted itself with difficulty to the niceties of class distinction, and though he had cured himself of his early tendency to address the butler as 'Bill', he never failed to consult him as man to man in his moments of perplexity. Bayliss was always eager to be of assistance. He liked Mr Crocker. True, his manner might have struck a more sensitive man than his employer as a shade too closely resembling that of an indulgent father toward a son who was not quite right in the head; but it had genuine affection in it.

Mr Crocker picked up his paper and folded it back at the sporting page, pointing with a stubby forefinger.

'Well, what does all this mean? I've kept out of watching cricket since I landed in England, but yesterday they got the poison needle to work and took me off to see Surrey play Kent at that place, Lord's, where you say you go sometimes.'

'I was there yesterday, sir. A very exciting game.'

'Exciting? How do you make that out? I sat in the bleachers all afternoon waiting for something to break loose. Doesn't anything ever happen at cricket?'

The butler winced a little, but managed to smile a tolerant smile. This man, he reflected, was but an American, and as much more to be pitied than censured. He endeavoured to explain.

'It was a sticky wicket yesterday, sir, owing to the rain.'

'Eh?'

'The wicket was sticky, sir.'

'Come again.'

'I mean that the reason why the game yesterday struck you as slow was that the wicket – I should say the turf – was sticky – that is to say, wet. Sticky is the technical term, sir. When the wicket is sticky the batsmen are obliged to exercise a great deal of caution, as the stickiness of the wicket enables the bowlers to make the ball turn more sharply in either direction as it strikes the turf than when the wicket is not sticky.'

'That's it, is it?'

'Yes, sir.'

'Thanks for telling me.

'Not at all, sir.'

Mr Crocker pointed to the paper.

'Well, now, this seems to be the boxscore of the game

we saw yesterday. If you can make sense out of that, go to it.'

The passage on which his finger rested was headed Final Score, and ran as follows:

SURREY

FIRST INNINGS

Hayward, c Wooley b Carr	67
Hobbs, run out	0
Hayes, st Huish b Fielder	12
Ducat, b Fielder	33
Harrison, not out	11
Sandham, not out	6
Extras	10
Total (for four wickets)	139

Bayliss inspected the cipher gravely.

'What is it you wish me to explain, sir?'

'Why, the whole thing. What's it all about?'

'It's perfectly simple, sir. Surrey won the toss and took first knock. Hayward and Hobbs were the opening pair. Hayward called Hobbs for a short run, but the latter was unable to get across and was thrown out by mid-on. Hayes was the next man in. He went out of his ground and was stumped. Ducat and Hayward made a capital stand considering the stickiness of the wicket, until Ducat was bowled by a good length off-break and Hayward caught at second slip off a googly. Then Harrison and Sandham played out time.'

Mr Crocker breathed heavily through his nose.

'Yes!' he said. 'Yes! I had an idea that was it. But I think I'd like to have it once again slowly. Start with these figures. What does that sixty-seven mean, opposite Hayward's name?'

'He made sixty-seven runs, sir.'

'Sixty-seven! In one game?'

469

'Yes, sir.'

'Why, Home-Run Baker couldn't do it!'

'I am not familiar with Mr Baker, sir.'

'I suppose you've never seen a ball game?'

'Ball game, sir?'

'A baseball game?'

'Never, sir.'

'Then, Bill,' said Mr Crocker, reverting in his emotion to the bad habit of his early London days, 'you haven't lived. See here!'

Whatever vestige of respect for class distinctions Mr Crocker had managed to preserve during the opening stages of the interview now definitely disappeared. His eyes shone wildly and he snorted like a warhorse. He clutched the butler by the sleeve and drew him closer to the table, then began to move forks, spoons, cups, and even the contents of his plate, about the cloth with an energy little short of feverish.

'Bayliss?'

'Sir?'

'Watch!' said Mr Crocker, with the air of an excitable high priest about to initiate a novice into the mysteries.

He removed a roll from the basket.

'You see this roll? That's the home plate. This spoon is first base. Where I'm putting this cup is second. This piece of bacon is third. There's your diamond for you. Very well then. These lumps of sugar are the infielders and the outfielders. Now we're ready. Batter up! He stands here. Catcher behind him. Umps behind catcher.'

'Umps, I take it, sir, is what we would call the umpire?'

'Call him anything you like. It's part of the game. Now here's the box, where I've put this dab of marmalade, and here's the pitcher winding up.'

'The pitcher would be equivalent to our bowler?'

'I guess so, though why you should call him a bowler gets past me.'

'The box, then, is the bowler's wicket?'

'Have it your own way. Now pay attention. Play ball! Pitcher's winding up. Put it over, Mike, put it over! Some speed, kid! Here it comes right in the groove. Bing! Batter slams it and streaks for first. Outfielder – this lump of sugar – boots it. Bonehead! Batter touches second. Third? No! Get back! Can't be done. Play it safe. Stick round the sack, old pal. Second batter up. Pitcher getting something on the ball now besides the cover. Whiffs him. Back to the bench, Cyril! Third batter up. See him rub his hands in the dirt. Watch this kid. He's good! Lets two alone, then slams the next right on the nose. Whizzes round to second. First guy, the one we left on second, comes home for one run. That's a game! Take it from me, Bill, that's a game!'

Somewhat overcome with the energy with which he had flung himself into his lecture, Mr Crocker sat down and refreshed himself with cold coffee.

'Quite an interesting game,' said Bayliss. 'But I find, now that you have explained it, sir, that it is familiar to me, though I have always known it under another name. It is played a great deal in this country.'

Mr Crocker started to his feet.

'It is? And I've been five years here without finding it out! When's the next game scheduled?'

'It is known in England as rounders, sir. Children play it with a soft ball and a racket, and derive considerable enjoyment from it. I have never heard of it before as a pastime for adults.'

Two shocked eyes stared into the butler's face.

'Children?' The word came in a whisper. 'A racket?'

'Yes, sir.'

'You – you didn't say a soft ball?'

'Yes, sir.'

A sort of spasm seemed to convulse Mr Crocker. He had lived five years in England, but not till this moment had he realized to the full how utterly alone he was in an alien land. Fate had placed him, bound and helpless, in a country where they called baseball rounders and played it with a soft ball.

6 — A Day with the Swattesmore

Whit-Monday, which to so many means merely one more
opportunity of strewing Beauty Spots with paper bags,
has a deeper significance for the hunting man. For,
if you look in your diary, you will find the following
entry:

May 20 (Whit-Monday) – *Fly Swatting Begins*.

Simple words, but how much they imply. What magic
memories of past delights they conjure up, what roseate
visions of happy days to come.

English poetry is rich in allusions to this king of sports.
Every schoolboy is familiar with those lines of
Coleridge:

It is the Ancient Mariner,
He swatteth one in three.

These have been taken by some to suggest a slur on
the efficiency of the British Merchant Service, but I do
not think that Coleridge had any such interpretation in
mind.

Mark the word 'ancient'. 'It is the *ancient* Mariner.'
That is to say, he was past his prime, possibly even of
an age when he might have been expected to abandon the
sport altogether. Yet, such was the accuracy of eye and
suppleness of limb resulting from the clean, fresh life of
the open sea that he was still bagging one out of every
three – a record which many a younger man would be
glad to achieve.

It is Chaucer who is responsible for the old saw:

When noone is highe,
Then swatte ye flye,

which has led some to hold that the proper time for a
meet is after lunch. Others, of whom I am one, prefer
the after breakfast theory. It seems to me that a fly which
has just risen from its bed and taken a cold plunge in the
milk-jug is in far better fettle for a sporting run than one
which has spent the morning gorging jam and bacon and
wants nothing more than a quiet nap on the ceiling.

The Swattesmore, the hunt to which I belong, always
meets directly after breakfast. And a jovial gathering it
is. Tough old Admiral Bludyer has his rolled-up copy of
Country Life, while young Reggie Bootle carries the lighter
and more easily wielded *Daily Mail*.

There is a good deal of genial chaff and laughter because
some youngster who is new to the game has armed
himself with a patent steel-wire swatter, for it is contrary
to all the etiquette of the chase to use these things. Your
true sportsman would as soon shoot a sitting bird.

Meanwhile Sigsbee, our host's butler – specially
engaged for his round and shiny head, which no fly has
ever been known to resist – has opened the window. There
is a hush of anticipation, and the talk and laughter are
stilled. Presently you hear a little gasp of excitement from
some newly joined member, who has not been at the
sport long enough to acquire the iron self-control on
which we of the Swattesmore pride ourselves. A fine fly
is peering in.

This is the crucial moment. Will he be lured in by
Sigsbee's bald head, or will he pursue his original
intention of going down to the potting-shed to breakfast
on the dead rat? Another moment, and he has made his
decision. He hurries in and seats himself on the butler's
glistening cupola. Instantaneously, Francis, the
footman, slams the window. The fly rockets to the ceiling.
'Gone away, sir, thank you, sir,' says Sigsbee

respectfully, and with a crashing 'Yoicks!' and 'Tally-ho!' the hunt is up.

Ah me! How many wonderful runs that old library has seen. I remember once a tough old dog fly leading us without a check from ten in the morning till five minutes before lunch.

We found on Sigsbee's head, and a moment later he had made a line across country for the south window. From there he worked round to the bookshelves. Bertie Whistler took a fearful toss over a whatnot, and poor old General Griggs, who is not so keen-sighted as he used to be, came to grief on a sunken art-nouveau footstool.

By the end of a couple of hours only 'Binks' Bodger and myself were on the active list. All the rest were nursing bruised shins in the background. At a quarter to one the fly doubled back from the portrait of our host's grandmother, and in trying to intercept him poor 'Binks' fell foul of the head of a bearskin rug and had to retire.

A few minutes later I had the good luck to come up with the brute as he rested on a magnificent Corot near the fireplace. I was using a bedroom slipper that day, and it unfortunately damaged the Corot beyond recognition. But I have my consolation in the superb brush which hangs over my mantelpiece, and the memory of one of the finest runs a swatter ever had.

There are some who claim that fly-swatting is inferior as a sport to the wasping of the English countryside. As one who has had a wide experience of both, I most emphatically deny this. Wasping is all very well in its way, but to try to compare the two is foolish.

Waspers point to the element of danger in their favourite pursuit, some going so far as to say that it really ought to come under the head of big-game hunting.

But I have always maintained that this danger is more imaginary than real. Wasps are not swift thinkers. They do not connect cause and effect. A wasp rarely has the intelligence to discover that the man in the room is responsible for his troubles, and almost never attacks him. And, even admitting that a wasp has a sting, which gives the novice a thrill, who has ever heard of any one barking his shin on a chair during a wasp hunt?

Wasping is too sedentary for me. You wait till the creature is sitting waist-high in the jam and then shove him under with a teaspoon. Is this sport in the sense the fly-swatting is sport? I do not think so. The excitement of the chase is simply non-existent. Give me a cracking two-hours' run with a fly, with plenty of jumps to take, including a grand piano and a few stiff gate-leg tables. That is the life.

Ukridge

1 — Ukridge's Dog College

'Laddie,' said Stanley Featherstonehaugh Ukridge, that much-enduring man, helping himself to my tobacco and slipping the pouch absently into his pocket, 'listen to me, you son of Belial.'

'What?' I said, retrieving the pouch.

'Do you want to make an enormous fortune?'

'I do.'

'Then write my biography. Bung it down on paper, and we'll split the proceeds. I've been making a pretty close study of your stuff lately, old horse, and it's all wrong. The trouble with you is that you don't plumb the well-springs of human nature and all that. You just think up some rotten yarn about some-dam-thing-or-other and shove it down. Now, if you tackled my life, you'd have something worth writing about. Pots of money in it, my boy – English serial rights and American serial rights and book rights, and dramatic rights and movie rights – well, you can take it from me that, at a conservative estimate, we should clean up at least fifty thousand pounds apiece.'

'As much as that?'

'Fully that. And listen, laddie, I'll tell you what. You're a good chap and we've been pals for years, so I'll let you have my share of the English serial rights for a hundred pounds down.'

'What makes you think I've got a hundred pounds?'

'Well, then, I'll make it my share of the English *and* American serial rights for fifty.'

'Your collar's come off its stud.'

'How about my complete share of the whole dashed outfit for twenty-five?'

479

'Not for me, thanks.'

'Then I'll tell you what, old horse,' said Ukridge, inspired. 'Just lend me half a crown to be going on with.'

If the leading incidents of S. F. Ukridge's disreputable career are to be given to the public – and not, as some might suggest, decently hushed up – I suppose I am the man to write them. Ukridge and I have been intimate since the days of school. Together we sported on the green, and when he was expelled no one missed him more than I. An unfortunate business, this expulsion. Ukridge's generous spirit, ever ill-attuned to school rules, caused him eventually to break the solemnest of them all by sneaking out at night to try his skill at the coconut-shies of the local village fair; and his foresight in putting on scarlet whiskers and a false nose for the expedition was completely neutralized by the fact that he absent-mindedly wore his school cap throughout the entire proceedings. He left the next morning, regretted by all.

After this there was a hiatus of some years in our friendship. I was at Cambridge, absorbing culture, and Ukridge, as far as I could gather from his rare letters and the reports of mutual acquaintances, flitting about the world like a snipe. Somebody met him in New York, just off a cattle-ship. Somebody else saw him in Buenos Aires. Somebody, again, spoke sadly of having been pounced on by him at Monte Carlo and touched for a fiver. It was not until I settled down in London that he came back into my life. We met in Piccadilly one day, and resumed our relations where they had been broken off. Old associations are strong, and the fact that he was about my build and so could wear my socks and shirts drew us very close together.

Then he disappeared again, and it was a month or more before I got news of him.

It was George Tupper who brought the news. George

was head of the school in my last year, and he has
fulfilled exactly the impeccable promise of those early
days. He is in the Foreign Office, doing well and much
respected. He has an earnest, pulpy heart and takes other
people's troubles very seriously. Often he had mourned
to me like a father over Ukridge's erratic progress through
life, and now, as he spoke, he seemed to be filled with a
solemn joy, as over a reformed prodigal.

'Have you heard about Ukridge?' said George Tupper.
'He has settled down at last. Gone to live with an aunt
of his who owns one of those big houses on Wimbledon
Common. A very rich woman. I am delighted. It will be
the making of the old chap.'

I suppose he was right in a way, but to me this tame
subsidence into companionship with a rich aunt in
Wimbledon seemed somehow an indecent, almost a
tragic, end to a colourful career like that of S. F. Ukridge.
And when I met the man a week later my heart grew
heavier still.

It was in Oxford Street at the hour when women come
up from the suburbs to shop; and he was standing among
the dogs and commissionaires outside Selfridge's. His
arms were full of parcels, his face was set in a mask of wan
discomfort, and he was so beautifully dressed that for an
instant I did not recognize him. Everything which the
Correct Man wears was assembled on his person, from
the silk hat to the patent-leather boots; and, as he confided
to me in the first minute, he was suffering the tortures of
the damned. The boots pinched him, the hat hurt his
forehead, and the collar was worse than the hat and boots
combined.

'She makes me wear them,' he said, moodily, jerking
his head towards the interior of the store and uttering a
sharp howl as the movement caused the collar to gouge
his neck.

'Still,' I said, trying to turn his mind to happier things,
'you must be having a great time. George Tupper tells

me that your aunt is rich. I suppose you're living off the fat of the land.'

'The browsing and sluicing are good,' admitted Ukridge. 'But it's a wearing life, laddie. A wearing life, old horse.'

'Why don't you come and see me sometimes?'

'I'm not allowed out at night.'

'Well, shall I come and see you?'

A look of poignant alarm shot out from under the silk hat.

'Don't dream of it, laddie,' said Ukridge, earnestly. 'Don't dream of it. You're a good chap – my best pal and all that sort of thing – but the fact is, my standing in the home's none too solid even now, and one sight of you would knock my prestige into hash. Aunt Julia would think you worldly.'

'I'm not worldly.'

'Well, you look worldly. You wear a squash hat and a soft collar. If you don't mind my suggesting it, old horse, I think, if I were you, I'd pop off now before she comes out. Goodbye, laddie.'

'Ichabod!' I murmured sadly to myself as I passed on down Oxford Street. 'Ichabod!'

I should have had more faith. I should have known my Ukridge better. I should have realized that a London suburb could no more imprison that great man permanently than Elba did Napoleon.

One afternoon, as I let myself into the house in Ebury Street of which I rented at that time the bedroom and sitting room on the first floor, I came upon Bowles, my landlord, standing in listening attitude at the foot of the stairs.

'Good afternoon, sir,' said Bowles. 'A gentleman is waiting to see you. I fancy I heard him calling me a moment ago.'

'Who is he?'

'A Mr Ukridge, sir. He – '

A vast voice boomed out from above.

'Bowles, old horse!'

Bowles, like all other proprietors of furnished apartments in the south-western district of London, was an ex-butler and about him, as about all ex-butlers, there clung like a garment an aura of dignified superiority which had never failed to crush my spirit. He was a man of portly aspect, with a bald head and prominent eyes of a lightish green – eyes that seemed to weigh me dispassionately and find me wanting. 'H'm!' they seemed to say. 'Young – very young. And not at all what I have been accustomed to in the best places.' To hear this dignitary addressed – and in a shout at that – as 'old horse' affected me with much the same sense of imminent chaos as would afflict a devout young curate if he saw his bishop slapped on the back. The shock, therefore, when he responded not merely mildly but with what almost amounted to camaraderie was numbing.

'Sir?' cooed Bowles.

'Bring me six bones and a corkscrew.'

'Very good, sir.'

Bowles retired, and I bounded upstairs and flung open the door of my sitting room.

'Great Scott!' I said, blankly.

The place was a sea of Pekingese dogs. Later investigation reduced their numbers to six, but in that first moment there seemed to be hundreds. Goggling eyes met mine wherever I looked. The room was a forest of waving tails. With his back against the mantelpiece, smoking placidly, stood Ukridge.

'Hallo, laddie!' he said, with a genial wave of the hand, as if to make me free of the place. 'You're just in time. I've got to dash off and catch a train in a quarter of an hour. Stop it, you mutts!' he bellowed, and the six Pekingese, who had been barking steadily since my arrival, stopped in mid-yap, and were still. Ukridge's personality seemed to exercise a magnetism over the animal kingdom, from ex-butlers to Pekes, which bordered on the uncanny. 'I'm off to Sheep's Cray, in Kent. Taken a cottage there.'

'Are you going to live there?'

'Yes.'

'But what about your aunt?'

'Oh, I've left her. Life is stern and life is earnest, and if I mean to make a fortune I've got to bustle about and not stay cooped up in a place like Wimbledon.'

'Something in that.'

'Besides which, she told me the very sight of me made her sick and she never wanted to see me again.'

I might have guessed, directly I saw him, that some upheaval had taken place. The sumptuous raiment which had made him such a treat to the eye at our last meeting was gone, and he was back in his pre-Wimbledon costume, which was, as the advertisements say, distinctly individual. Over grey flannel trousers, a golf coat, and a brown sweater he wore like a royal robe a bright yellow mackintosh. His collar had broken free from its stud and showed a couple of inches of bare neck. His hair was disordered, and his masterful nose was topped by a pair of steel-rimmed pince-nez cunningly attached to his flapping ears with ginger-beer wire. His whole appearance spelled revolt.

Bowles manifested himself with a plateful of bones.

'That's right. Chuck 'em down on the floor.'

'Very good, sir.'

'I like that fellow,' said Ukridge, as the door closed. 'We had a dashed interesting talk before you came in. Did you know he had a cousin on the music halls?'

'He hasn't confided in me much.'

'He's promised me an introduction to him later on. May be useful to be in touch with a man who knows the ropes. You see, laddie, I've hit on the most amazing scheme.' He swept his arm round dramatically, overturning a plaster cast of the Infant Samuel at Prayer.

'All right, all right, you can mend it with glue or something, and anyway, you're probably better without it. Yessir, I've hit on a great scheme. The idea of a thousand years.'

'What's that?'

'I'm going to train dogs.'

'Train dogs?'

'For the music-hall stage. Dog acts, you know. Performing dogs. Pots of money in it. I start in a modest way with these six. When I've taught 'em a few tricks, I sell them to a fellow in the profession for a large sum and buy twelve more. I train those, sell 'em for a large sum, and with the money buy twenty-four more. I train those – '

'Here, wait a minute.' My head was beginning to swim. I had a vision of England paved with Pekingese dogs, all doing tricks. 'How do you know you'll be able to sell them?'

'Of course I shall. The demand's enormous. Supply can't cope with it. At a conservative estimate I should think I ought to scoop in four or five thousand pounds the first year. That, of course, is before the business really starts to expand.'

'I see.'

'When I get going properly, with a dozen assistants under me and an organized establishment, I shall begin to touch the big money. What I'm aiming at is a sort of Dogs' College out in the country somewhere. Big place with a lot of ground. Regular classes and a set curriculum. Large staff, each member of it with so many dogs under his care, me looking on and superintending. Why, once the thing starts moving it'll run itself, and all I shall have to do will be to sit back and endorse the cheques. It isn't as if I would have to confine my operations to England. The demand for performing dogs is universal throughout the civilized world. America wants performing dogs. Australia wants performing dogs. Africa could do with a

few, I've no doubt. My aim, laddie, is gradually to get
a monopoly of the trade. I want everybody who needs a
performing dog of any description to come automatically
to me. And I'll tell you what, laddie. If you like to put up
a bit of capital, I'll let you in on the ground floor.'

'No, thanks.'

'All right. Have it your own way. Only don't forget
that there was a fellow who put nine hundred dollars
into the Ford Car business when it was starting and he
collected a cool forty million. I say, is that clock right?
Great Scott! I'll be missing my train. Help me mobilize
these dashed animals.'

Five minutes later, accompanied by the six Pekingese
and bearing about him a pound of my tobacco, three pairs
of my socks, and the remains of a bottle of whisky,
Ukridge departed in a taxi-cab for Charing Cross Station
to begin his life work.

Perhaps six weeks passed, six quiet Ukridgeless weeks,
and then one morning I received an agitated telegram.
Indeed, it was not so much a telegram as a cry of anguish.
In every word of it there breathed the tortured spirit of
a great man who has battled in vain against overwhelming
odds. It was the sort of telegram which Job might have
sent off after a lengthy session with Bildad the Shuhite:

> 'Come here immediately, laddie. Life and death
> matter, old horse. Desperate situation. Don't fail me.'

It stirred me like a bugle: I caught the next train.

The White Cottage, Sheep's Cray – destined,
presumably, to become in future years an historic spot
and a Mecca for dog-loving pilgrims – was a small and
battered building standing near the main road to London
at some distance from the village. I found it without
difficulty, for Ukridge seemed to have achieved a certain
celebrity in the neighbourhood; but to effect an entry was
a harder task. I rapped for a full minute without result,

then shouted; and I was about to conclude that Ukridge was not at home when the door suddenly opened. As I was just giving a final bang at the moment, I entered the house in a manner reminiscent of one of the Ballet Russe practising a new and difficult step.

'Sorry, old horse,' said Ukridge. 'Wouldn't have kept you waiting if I'd known who it was. Thought you were Gooch, the grocer – goods supplied to the value of six pounds three and a penny.'

'I see.'

'He keeps hounding me for his beastly money,' said Ukridge, bitterly, as he led the way into the sitting room. 'It's a little hard. Upon my Sam it's a little hard. I come down here to inaugurate a vast business and do the natives a bit of good by establishing a growing industry in their midst, and the first thing you know they turn round and bite the hand that was going to feed them. I've been hampered and rattled by these bloodsuckers ever since I got here. A little trust, a little sympathy, a little of the good old give-and-take spirit – that was all I asked. And what happened? They wanted a bit on account! Kept bothering me for a bit on account, I'll trouble you, just when I needed all my thoughts and all my energy and every ounce of concentration at my command for my extraordinarily difficult and delicate work. *I* couldn't give them a bit on account. Later on, if they had only exercised reasonable patience, I would no doubt have been in a position to settle their infernal bills fifty times over. But the time was not ripe. I reasoned with the men. I said, "Here am I, a busy man, trying hard to educate six Pekingese dogs for music-hall stage, and you come distracting my attention and impairing my efficiency by babbling about a bit on account. It isn't the pull-together spirit," I said. "It isn't the Spirit that wins to wealth. These narrow petty-cash ideas can never make for success." But no, they couldn't see it. They started calling here at all hours and waylaying me in the public highways till life

became an absolute curse. And now what do you think
has happened?'

'What?'

'The dogs.'

'Got distemper?'

'No. Worse. My landlord's pinched them as security
for his infernal rent! Sneaked the stock. Tied up the
assets. Crippled the business at the very outset. Have you
ever in your life heard of anything so dastardly? I know
I agreed to pay the damned rent weekly and I'm about six
weeks behind, but, my gosh! Surely a man with a huge
enterprise on his hands isn't supposed to have to worry
about these trifles when he's occupied with the most
delicate – Well, I put all that to old Nickerson, but a fat
lot of good it did. So then I wired to you.'

'Ah!' I said, and there was a brief and pregnant pause.

'I thought,' said Ukridge, meditatively, 'that you might
be able to suggest somebody I could touch.'

He spoke in a detached and almost casual way, but his
eye was gleaming at me significantly, and I avoided it
with a sense of guilt. My finances at the moment were in
their customary unsettled condition – rather more so,
in fact, than usual, owing to unsatisfactory speculations
at Kempton Park on the previous Saturday; and it seemed
to me that, if ever there was a time for passing the buck,
this was it. I mused tensely. It was an occasion for quick
thinking.

'George Tupper!' I cried, on the crest of a brain-wave.

'George Tupper?' echoed Ukridge, radiantly, his gloom
melting like a fog before the sun. 'The very man, by
Gad! It's a most amazing thing, but I never thought of
him. George Tupper, of course! Big-hearted George, the
old school-chum. He'll do it like a shot and won't miss
the money. These Foreign Office blokes have always got
a spare tenner or two tucked away in the old sock. They
pinch it out of the public funds. Rush back to town,
laddie, with all speed, get hold of Tuppy, lush him up, and

ite his ear for twenty quid. Now is the time for all good men to come to the aid of the party.'

I had been convinced that George Tupper would not fail us, nor did he. He parted without a murmur – even with enthusiasm. The consignment was one that might have been made to order for him. As a boy, George used to write sentimental poetry for the school magazine, and now he is the sort of man who is always starting subscription lists and getting up memorials and presentations. He listened to my story with the serious official air which these Foreign Office fellows put on when they are deciding whether to declare war on Switzerland or send a firm note to San Marino, and was reaching for his cheque book before I had been speaking two minutes. Ukridge's sad case seemed to move him deeply.

'Too bad,' said George. 'So he is training dogs, is he? Well, it seems very unfair that, if he has at last settled down to real work, he should be hampered by financial difficulties at the outset. We ought to do something practical for him. After all, a loan of twenty pounds cannot relieve the situation permanently.'

'I think you're a bit optimistic if you're looking on it as a loan.'

'What Ukridge needs is capital.'

'He thinks that, too. So does Gooch, the grocer.'

'Capital,' repeated George Topper, firmly, as if he were reasoning with the plenipotentiary of some Great Power. 'Every venture requires capital at first.' He frowned thoughtfully. 'Where can we obtain capital for Ukridge?'

'Rob a bank.'

George Topper's face cleared.

'I have it!' he said. 'I will go straight over to Wimbledon tonight and approach his aunt.'

'Aren't you forgetting that Ukridge is about as popular with her as a cold welsh rabbit?'

'There may be a temporary estrangement, but if I tell

her the facts and impress upon her that Ukridge is really making a genuine effort to earn a living – '

'Well, try it if you like. But she will probably set the parrot on to you.'

'It will have to be done diplomatically, of course. It might be as well if you did not tell Ukridge what I propose to do. I do not wish to arouse hopes which may not be fulfilled.'

A blaze of yellow on the platform of Sheep's Cray Station next morning informed me that Ukridge had come to meet my train. The sun poured down from a cloudless sky, but it took more than sunshine to make Stanley Featherstonehaugh Ukridge discard his mackintosh. He looked like an animated blob of mustard.

When the train rolled in, he was standing in solitary grandeur trying to light his pipe, but as I got out I perceived that he had been joined by a sad-looking man, who, from the rapid and earnest manner in which he talked and the vehemence of his gesticulations, appeared to be ventilating some theme on which he felt deeply. Ukridge was looking warm and harassed, and, as I approached, I could hear his voice booming in reply.

'My dear sir, my dear old horse, do be reasonable, do try to cultivate the big, broad flexible outlook – '

He saw me and broke away – not unwillingly; and, gripping my arm, drew me off along the platform. The sad-looking man followed irresolutely.

'Have you got the stuff, laddie?' enquired Ukridge, in a tense whisper. 'Have you got it?'

'Yes, here it is.'

'Put it back, put it back!' moaned Ukridge in agony, as I felt in my pocket. 'Do you know who that was I was talking to? Gooch, the grocer!'

'Goods supplied to the value of six pounds three and a penny?'

'Absolutely!'

'Well, now's your chance. Fling him a purse of gold. That'll make him look silly.'

'My dear old horse, I can't afford to go about the place squandering my cash simply in order to make grocers look silly. That money is earmarked for Nickerson, my landlord.'

'Oh! I say, I think the six-pounds-three-and-a-penny bird is following us.'

'Then for goodness' sake, laddie, let's get a move on! If that man knew we had twenty quid on us, our lives wouldn't be safe. He'd make one spring.'

He hurried me out of the station and led the way up a shady lane that wound off through the fields, slinking furtively 'like one that on a lonesome road doth walk in fear and dread, and having once looked back walks on and turns no more his head, because he knows a frightful fiend doth close behind him tread.' As a matter of fact, the frightful fiend had given up the pursuit after the first few steps, and a moment later I drew this fact to Ukridge's attention, for it was not the sort of day on which to break walking records unnecessarily.

He halted, relieved, and mopped his spacious brow with a handkerchief which I recognized as having once been my property.

'Thank goodness we've shaken him off,' he said. 'Not a bad chap in his way, I believe – a good husband and father, I'm told, and sings in the church choir. But no vision. That's what he lacks, old horse – vision. He can't understand that all vast industrial enterprises have been built up on a system of liberal and cheerful credit. Won't realize that credit is the life-blood of commerce. Without credit commerce has no elasticity. And if commerce has no elasticity what dam' good is it?'

'I don't know.'

'Nor does anybody else. Well, now that he's gone, you can give me that money. Did old Toppy cough up cheerfully?'

'Blithely.'

'I knew it,' said Ukridge, deeply moved, 'I knew it. A good fellow. One of the best. I've always liked Tuppy. A man you can rely on. Some day, when I get going on a big scale, he shall have this back a thousand fold. I'm glad you brought small notes.'

'Why?'

'I want to scatter 'em about on the table in front of this Nickerson blighter.'

'Is this where he lives?'

We had come to a red-roofed house, set back from the road amidst trees. Ukridge wielded the knocker forcefully.

'Tell Mr Nickerson,' he said to the maid, 'that Mr Ukridge has called and would like a word.'

About the demeanour of the man who presently entered the room into which we had been shown there was that subtle but well-marked something which stamps your creditor all the world over. Mr Nickerson was a man of medium height, almost completely surrounded by whiskers, and through the shrubbery he gazed at Ukridge with frozen eyes, shooting out waves of deleterious animal magnetism. You could see at a glance that he was not fond of Ukridge. Take him for all in all, Mr Nickerson looked like one of the less amiable prophets of the Old Testament about to interview the captive monarch of the Amalekites.

'Well?' he said, and I have never heard the word spoken in a more forbidding manner.

'I've come about the rent.'

'Ah!' said Mr Nickerson, guardedly.

'To pay it,' said Ukridge.

'To pay it!' ejaculated Mr Nickerson, incredulously.

'Here!' said Ukridge, and with a superb gesture flung money on the table.

I understood now why the massive-minded man had wanted small notes. They made a brave display. There was a light breeze blowing in through the open window, and so musical a rustling did it set up as it played about the heaped-up wealth that Mr Nickerson's austerity seemed to vanish like breath off a razorblade. For a moment a dazed look came into his eyes and he swayed slightly; then, as he started to gather up the money, he took on the benevolent air of a bishop blessing pilgrims. As far as Mr Nickerson was concerned, the sun was up.

'Why, thank you, Mr Ukridge, I'm sure,' he said. 'Thank you very much. No hard feelings, I trust?'

'Not on my side, old horse,' responded Ukridge, affably. 'Business is business.'

'Exactly.'

'Well, I may as well take those dogs now,' said Ukridge, helping himself to a cigar from a box which he had just discovered on the mantelpiece and putting a couple more in his pocket in the friendliest way. 'The sooner they're back with me, the better. They've lost a day's education as it is.'

'Why, certainly, Mr Ukridge; certainly. They are in the shed at the bottom of the garden. I will get them for you at once.'

He retreated through the door, babbling ingratiatingly.

'Amazing how fond these blokes are of money,' sighed Ukridge. 'It's a thing I don't like to see. Sordid, I call it. That blighter's eyes were gleaming, positively gleaming, laddie, as he scooped up the stuff. Good cigars these,' he added, pocketing three more.

There was a faltering footstep outside, and Mr Nickerson re-entered the room. The man appeared to have something on his mind. A glassy look was in his whisker-bordered eyes, and his mouth, though it was not easy to see it through the jungle, seemed to me to be sagging mournfully. He resembled a minor prophet who has been hit behind the ear with a stuffed eel skin.

'Mr Ukridge!'

'Hallo?'

493

'The – the little dogs!'

'Well?'

'The little dogs!'

'What about them?'

'They have gone!'

'Gone?'

'Run away!'

'Run away? How the devil could they run away?'

'There seems to have been a loose board at the back of the shed. The little dogs must have wriggled through. There is no trace of them to be found.'

Ukridge flung up his arms despairingly. He swelled like a captive balloon. His pince-nez rocked on his nose, his mackintosh flapped menacingly, and his collar sprang off its stud. He brought his fist down with a crash on the table.

'Upon my Sam!'

'I am extremely sorry – '

'Upon my Sam!' cried Ukridge. 'It's hard. It's pretty hard. I come down here to inaugurate a great business, which would eventually have brought trade and prosperity to the whole neighbourhood, and I have hardly had time to turn round and attend to the preliminary details of the enterprise when this man comes and sneaks my dogs. And now he tells me with a light laugh – '

'Mr Ukridge, I assure you – '

'Tells me with a light laugh that they've gone. Gone! Gone where? Why, dash it, they may be all over the county. A fat chance I've got of ever seeing them again. Six valuable Pekingese, already educated practically to the stage where they could have been sold at an enormous profit – '

Mr Nickerson was fumbling guiltily, and now he produced from his pocket a crumpled wad of notes, which he thrust agitatedly upon Ukridge, who waved them away with loathing.

'This gentleman,' boomed Ukridge, indicating me with a sweeping gesture, 'happens to be a lawyer. It is extremely lucky that he chanced to come down today to pay me a visit. Have you followed the proceedings closely?'

I said I had followed them very closely.

'Is it your opinion that an action will lie?'

I said it seemed highly probable, and this expert ruling appeared to put the final touch on Mr Nickerson's collapse. Almost tearfully he urged the notes on Ukridge.

'What's this?' said Ukridge, loftily.

'I – I thought, Mr Ukridge, that, if it were agreeable to you, you might consent to take your money back, and – and consider the episode closed.'

Ukridge turned to me with raised eyebrows.

'Ha!' he cried. 'Ha, ha!'

'Ha, ha!' I chorused, dutifully.

'He thinks that he can close the episode by giving my money back. Isn't that rich?'

'Fruity,' I agreed.

'Those dogs were worth hundreds of pounds, and he thinks he can square me with a rotten twenty. Would you have believed it if you hadn't heard it with your own ears, old horse?'

'Never!'

'I'll tell you what I'll do,' said Ukridge, after thought. 'I'll take this money.' Mr Nickerson thanked him. 'And there are one or two trifling accounts which want settling with some of the local tradesmen. You will square those – '

'Certainly, Mr Ukridge, certainly.'

'And after that – well, I'll have to think it over. If I decide to institute proceedings my lawyer will communicate with you in due course.'

And we left the wretched man, cowering despicably behind his whiskers.

It seemed to me, as we passed down the tree-shaded

lane and out into the white glare of the road, that Ukridge
was bearing himself in his hour of disaster with a rather
admirable fortitude. His stock-in-trade, the life-blood of
his enterprise, was scattered all over Kent, probably never
to return, and all that he had to show on the other side of
the balance-sheet was the cancelling of a few weeks' back
rent and the paying-off of Gooch, the grocer, and his
friends. It was a situation which might well have crushed
the spirit of an ordinary man, but Ukridge seemed by no
means dejected. Jaunty, rather. His eyes shone behind
their pince-nez and he whistled a rollicking air. When
presently he began to sing, I felt that it was time to create
a diversion.

'What are you going to do?' I asked.

'Who, me?' said Ukridge, buoyantly. 'Oh, I'm coming
back to town on the next train. You don't mind hoofing
into the next station, do you? It's only five miles. It might
be a trifle risky to start from Sheep's Cray.'

'Why risky?'

'Because of the dogs, of course.'

'Dogs?'

Ukridge hummed a gay strain.

'Oh, yes. I forgot to tell you about that. I've got 'em.'

'What?'

'Yes. I went out late last night and pinched them out
of the shed.' He chuckled amusedly. 'Perfectly simple.
Only needed a clear, level head. I borrowed a dead cat and
tied a string to it, legged it to old Nickerson's garden
after dark, dug a board out of the back of the shed, and
shoved my head down and chirruped. The dogs came
trickling out, and I hared off, towing old Colonel Cat on
his string. Great run while it lasted, laddie. Hounds
picked up the scent right away and started off in a bunch
at fifty miles an hour. Cat and I doing a steady fifty-five.
Thought every minute old Nickerson would hear and
start blazing away with a gun, but nothing happened. I
led the pack across country for a run of twenty minutes

without a check, parked the dogs in my sitting room, and so to bed. Took it out of me, by gosh! Not so young as I was.'

I was silent for a moment, conscious of a feeling almost of reverence. This man was undoubtedly spacious. There had always been something about Ukridge that dulled the moral sense.

'Well,' I said at length, 'you've certainly got vision.'

'Yes?' said Ukridge, gratified.

'*And* the big, broad, flexible outlook.'

'Got to, laddie, nowadays. The foundation of a successful business career.'

'And what's the next move?'

We were drawing near to the White Cottage. It stood and broiled in the sunlight, and I hoped that there might be something cool to drink inside it. The window of the sitting room was open, and through it came the yapping of Pekingese.

'Oh, I shall find another cottage somewhere else,' said Ukridge, eyeing his little home with a certain sentimentality. 'That won't be hard. Lots of cottages all over the place. And then I shall buckle down to serious work. You'll be astounded at the progress I've made already. In a minute I'll show you what those dogs can do.'

'They can bark all right.'

'Yes. They seem excited about something. You know, laddie, I've had a great idea. When I saw you at your rooms my scheme was to specialize in performing dogs for the music halls – what you might call professional dogs. But I've been thinking it over, and now I don't see why I shouldn't go in for developing amateur talent as well. Say you have a dog – Fido, the household pet – and you think it would brighten the home if he could do a few tricks from time to time. Well, you're a busy man, you haven't the time to give up to teaching him. So you just tie a label to his collar and ship him off for a month to the Ukridge Dog College, and back he comes,

497

thoroughly educated. No trouble, no worry, easy terms. Upon my Sam, I'm not sure there isn't more money in the amateur branch than in the professional. I don't see why eventually dog owners shouldn't send their dogs to me as a regular thing, just as they send their sons to Eton and Winchester. My golly! This idea's beginning to develop. I'll tell you what – how would it be to issue special collars to all dogs which have graduated from my college? Something distinctive which everybody would recognize. See what I mean? Sort of badge of honour. Fellow with a dog entitled to wear the Ukridge collar would be in a position to look down on the bloke whose dog hadn't got one. Gradually it would get so that anybody in a decent social position would be ashamed to be seen out with a non-Ukridge dog. The thing would become a landslide. Dogs would pour in from all corners of the country. More work than I could handle. Have to start branches. The scheme's colossal. Millions in it, my boy! Millions!' He paused with his fingers on the handle of the front door. 'Of course,' he went on, 'just at present it's no good blinking the fact that I'm hampered and handicapped by lack of funds and can only approach the thing on a small scale. What it amounts to, laddie, is that somehow or other I've got to get capital.'

It seemed the moment to spring the glad news. 'I promised him I wouldn't mention it,' I said, 'for fear it might lead to disappointment, but as a matter of fact George Tupper is trying to raise some capital for you. I left him last night starting out to get it.'

'George Tupper!' Ukridge's eyes dimmed with a not unmanly emotion. 'George Tupper! By Gad, that fellow is the salt of the earth. Good, loyal fellow! A true friend. A man you can rely on. Upon my Sam, if there were more fellows about like old Tuppy, there wouldn't be all this modern pessimism and unrest. Did he seem to have any idea where he could raise a bit of capital for me?'

'Yes. He went round to tell your aunt about your

coming down here to train those Pekes, and – What's the matter?'

A fearful change had come over Ukridge's jubilant front. His eyes bulged, his jaw sagged. With the addition of a few feet of grey whiskers he would have looked exactly like the recent Mr Nickerson.

'My aunt?' he mumbled, swaying on the door handle.

'Yes. What's the matter? He thought, if he told her all about it, she might relent and rally round.'

The sigh of a gallant fighter at the end of his strength forced its way up from Ukridge's mackintosh-covered bosom.

'Of all the dashed, infernal, officious, meddling, muddling, fat-headed, interfering asses,' he said, wanly, 'George Tupper is the worst.'

'What do you mean?'

'The man oughtn't to be at large. He's a public menace.'

'But – '

'Those dogs *belong* to my aunt. I pinched them when she chucked me out!'

Inside the cottage the Pekingese were still yapping industriously.

'Upon my Sam,' said Ukridge, 'it's a little hard.'

I think he would have said more, but at this point a voice spoke with a sudden and awful abruptness from the interior of the cottage. It was a woman's voice, a quiet, steely voice, a voice, it seemed to me, that suggested cold eyes, a beaky nose, and hair like gun-metal.

'Stanley!'

That was all it said, but it was enough. Ukridge's eye met mine in a wild surmise. He seemed to shrink into his mackintosh like a snail surprised while eating lettuce.

'Stanley!'

'Yes, Aunt Julia?' quavered Ukridge.

'Come here. I wish to speak to you.'

'Yes, Aunt Julia.'

I sidled out into the road. Inside the cottage the yapping

of the Pekingese had become quite hysterical. I found myself trotting, and then – though it was a warm day – running quite rapidly. I could have stayed if I had wanted to, but somehow I did not want to. Something seemed to tell me that on this holy domestic scene I should be an intruder.

What it was that gave me that impression I do not know – probably vision or the big, broad, flexible outlook.

2 — Ukridge's Accident Syndicate

'Half a minute, laddie,' said Ukridge. And, gripping my arm, he brought me to a halt on the outskirts of the little crowd which had collected about the church door.

It was a crowd such as may be seen any morning during the London mating season outside any of the churches which nestle in the quiet squares between Hyde Park and the King's Road, Chelsea.

It consisted of five women of cook-like aspect, four nurse-maids, half a dozen men of the non-producing class who had torn themselves away for the moment from their normal task of propping up the wall of the Bunch of Grapes public house on the corner, a costermonger with a barrow of vegetables, divers small boys, eleven dogs, and two or three purposeful-looking young fellows with cameras slung over their shoulders. It was plain that a wedding was in progress – and, arguing from the presence of the camera-men and the line of smart motor cars along the kerb, a fairly fashionable wedding. What was not plain – to me – was why Ukridge, sternest of bachelors, had desired to add himself to the spectators.

'What,' I enquired, 'is the thought behind this? Why are we interrupting our walk to attend the obsequies of some perfect stranger?'

Ukridge did not reply for a moment. He seemed plunged in thought. Then he uttered a hollow, mirthless laugh – a dreadful sound like the last gargle of a dying moose.

'Perfect stranger, my number eleven foot!' he responded, in his coarse way. 'Do you know who it is who's getting hitched up in there?'

'Who?'

'Teddy Weeks.'

'Teddy Weeks? Teddy Weeks? Good Lord!' I exclaimed 'Not really?'

And five years rolled away.

It was at Barolini's Italian restaurant in Beak Street that Ukridge evolved his great scheme. Barolini's was a favourite resort of our little group of earnest strugglers in the day when the philanthropic restaurateurs of Soho used to supply four courses and coffee for a shilling and sixpence; and there were present that night, besides Ukridge and myself, the following men-about-town: Teddy Weeks, the actor, fresh from a six-weeks' tour with the Number Three 'Only a Shop-Girl' Company; Victor Beamish, the artist, the man who drew that picture of the O-So-Eesi Piano-Player in the advertisement pages of the *Piccadilly Magazine*; Bertram Fox, author of *Ashes of Remorse*, and other unproduced motion-picture scenarios; and Robert Dunhill, who, being employed at a salary of eighty pounds per annum by the New Asiatic Bank, represented the sober, hard-headed commercial element. As usual, Teddy Weeks had collared the conversation, and was telling us once again how good he was and how hardly treated by a malignant fate.

There is no need to describe Teddy Weeks. Under another and a more euphonious name he has long since made his personal appearance dreadfully familiar to all who read the illustrated weekly papers. He was then, as now, a sickeningly handsome young man, possessing precisely the same melting eyes, mobile mouth, and corrugated hair so esteemed by the theatre-going public today. And yet, at this period of his career, he was wasting himself on minor touring companies of the kind which open at Barrow-in-Furness and jump to Bootle for the second half of the week. He attributed this, as Ukridge was so apt to attribute his own difficulties, to lack of capital.

'I have everything,' he said, querulously, emphasizing his remarks with a coffee spoon. 'Looks, talent, personality, a beautiful speaking voice – everything. All I need is a chance. And I can't get that because I have no clothes fit to wear. These managers are all the same, they never look below the surface, they never bother to find out if a man has genius. All they go by are his clothes. If I could afford to buy a couple of suits from a Cork Street tailor, if I could have my boots made to order by Moykoff instead of getting them ready-made and second-hand at Moses Brothers', if I could once contrive to own a decent hat, a really good pair of spats, and a gold cigarette case, all at the same time, I could walk into any manager's office in London and sign up for a West End production tomorrow.'

It was at this point that Freddie Lunt came in. Freddie, like Robert Dunhill, was a financial magnate in the making and an assiduous frequenter of Barolini's; and it suddenly occurred to us that a considerable time had passed since we had last seen him in the place. We enquired the reason for this aloofness.

'I've been in bed,' said Freddie, 'for over a fort-night.'

The statement incurred Ukridge's stern disapproval. That great man made a practice of never rising before noon, and on one occasion, when a carelessly thrown match had burned a hole in his only pair of trousers, had gone so far as to remain between the sheets for forty-eight hours; but sloth on so majestic a scale as this shocked him.

'Lazy young devil,' he commented severely. 'Letting the golden hours of youth slip by like that when you ought to have been bustling about and making a name for yourself.'

Freddie protested himself wronged by the imputation.

'I had an accident,' he explained. 'Fell off my bicycle and sprained an ankle.'

'Tough luck,' was our verdict.

'Oh, I don't know,' said Freddie. 'It wasn't bad fun getting a rest. And of course there was the fiver.'

'What fiver?'

'I got a fiver from the *Weekly Cyclist* for getting my ankle sprained.'

'You – *what*?' cried Ukridge, profoundly stirred – as ever – by a tale of easy money. 'Do you mean to sit there and tell me that some dashed paper paid you five quid simply because you sprained your ankle? Pull yourself together, old horse. Things like that don't happen.'

'It's quite true.'

'Can you show me the fiver?'

'No; because if I did you would try to borrow it.'

Ukridge ignored this slur in dignified silence.

'Would they pay a fiver to *anyone* who sprained his ankle?' he asked, sticking to the main point.

'Yes. If he was a subscriber.'

'I knew there was a catch in it,' said Ukridge, moodily.

'Lots of weekly papers are starting this wheeze,' proceeded Freddie. 'You pay a year's subscription and that entitles you to accident insurance.'

We were interested. This was in the days before every daily paper in London was competing madly against its rivals in the matter of insurance and offering princely bribes to the citizens to make a fortune by breaking their necks. Nowadays papers are paying as high as two thousand pounds for a genuine corpse and five pounds a week for a mere dislocated spine; but at that time the idea was new and it had an attractive appeal.

'How many of these rags are doing this?' asked Ukridge. You could tell from the gleam in his eyes that that great brain was whirring like a dynamo. 'As many as ten?'

'Yes, I should think so. Quite ten.'

'Then a fellow who subscribed to them all and then sprained his ankle would get fifty quid?' said Ukridge, reasoning acutely.

'More if the injury was serious,' said Freddie, the expert. 'They have a regular tariff. So much for a broken arm, so much for a broken leg, and so forth.'

Ukridge's collar leaped off its stud and his pince-nez wobbled drunkenly as he turned to us.

'How much money can you blokes raise?' he demanded.

'What do you want it for?' asked Robert Dunhill, with a banker's caution.

'My dear old horse, can't you see? Why, my gosh, I've got the idea of the century. Upon my Sam, this is the giltest-edged scheme that was ever hatched. We'll get together enough money and take out a year's subscription for every one of these dashed papers.'

'What's the good of that?' said Dunhill, coldly unenthusiastic.

They train bank clerks to stifle emotion, so that they will be able to refuse overdrafts when they become managers. 'The odds are we should none of us have an accident of any kind, and then the money would be chucked away.'

'Good heavens, ass,' snorted Ukridge, 'you don't suppose I'm suggesting that we should leave it to chance, do you? Listen! Here's the scheme. We take out subscriptions for all these papers, then we draw lots, and the fellow who gets the fatal card or whatever it is goes out and breaks his leg and draws the loot, and we split it up between us and live on it in luxury. It ought to run into hundreds of pounds.'

A long silence followed. Then Dunhill spoke again. His was a solid rather than a nimble mind.

'Suppose he couldn't break his leg?'

'My gosh!' cried Ukridge, exasperated. 'Here we are in the twentieth century, with every resource of modem civilization at our disposal, with opportunities for getting our legs broken opening about us on every side – and you ask a silly question like that! Of course he could break his leg. Any ass can break a leg. It's a little hard! We're all infernally broke – personally, unless Freddie can lend me a bit of that fiver till Saturday, I'm going to have a difficult job pulling through. We all need money like the dickens, and yet, when I point out this marvellous scheme for collecting a bit, instead of fawning on me for my ready intelligence you sit and make objections. It isn't the right spirit. It isn't the spirit that wins.'

'If you're as hard up as that,' objected Dunhill, 'how are you going to put in your share of the pool?'

A pained, almost a stunned, look came into Ukridge's eyes. He gazed at Dunhill through his lop-sided pince-nez as one who speculates as to whether his hearing has deceived him.

'Me?' he cried. 'Me? I like that! Upon my Sam, that's rich! Why, damme, if there's any justice in the world, if there's a spark of decency and good feeling in your bally bosoms, I should think you would let me in free for suggesting the idea. It's a little hard! I supply the brains and you want me to cough up cash as well. My gosh, I didn't expect this. This hurts me, by George! If anybody had told me that an old pal would – '

'Oh, all right,' said Robert Dunhill. 'All right, all right, all right. But I'll tell you one thing. If you draw the lot it'll be the happiest day of my life.'

'I shan't,' said Ukridge. 'Something tells me that I shan't.'

Nor did he. When, in a solemn silence broken only by the sound of a distant waiter quarrelling with the speaking-tube, we had completed the drawing, the man of destiny was Teddy Weeks.

I suppose that even in the springtime of Youth, when broken limbs seem a lighter matter than they become later in life, it can never be an unmixedly agreeable thing to

have to go out into the public highways and try to make
an accident happen to one. In such circumstances the
reflection that you are thereby benefiting your friends
brings but slight balm. To Teddy Weeks it appeared to
bring no balm at all. That he was experiencing a certain
disinclination to sacrifice himself for the public good
became more and more evident as the days went by and
found him still intact. Ukridge, when he called upon me
to discuss the matter, was visibly perturbed. He sank
into a chair beside the table at which I was beginning my
modest morning meal, and, having drunk half my coffee,
sighed deeply.

'Upon my Sam,' he moaned, 'it's a little disheartening.
I strain my brain to think up schemes for getting us all a
bit of money just at the moment when we are all needing
it most, and when I hit on what is probably the simplest
and yet ripest notion of our time, this blighter Weeks
goes and lets me down by shirking his plain duty. It's
just my luck that a fellow like that should have drawn
the lot. And the worst of it is, laddie, that, now we've
started with him, we've got to keep on. We can't possibly
raise enough money to pay yearly subscriptions for
anybody else. It's Weeks or nobody.'

'I suppose we must give him time.'

'That's what he says,' grunted Ukridge, morosely,
helping himself to toast. 'He says he doesn't know how
to start about it. To listen to him, you'd think that going
and having a trifling accident was the sort of delicate and
intricate job that required years of study and special
preparation. Why, a child of six could do it on his head
at five minutes' notice. The man's so infernally
particular. You make helpful suggestions, and instead of
accepting them in a broad, reasonable spirit of co-
operation he comes back at you every time with some
frivolous objection. He's so dashed fastidious. When we
were out last night, we came on a couple of navvies
scrapping. Good hefty fellows, either of them capable of

putting him in hospital for a month. I told him to jump
in and start separating them, and he said no; it was a
private dispute which was none of his business, and he
didn't feel justified in interfering. Finicky, I call it. I tell
you, laddie, this blighter is a broken reed. He has got
cold feet. We did wrong to let him into the drawing at all.
We might have known that a fellow like that would never
give results. No conscience. No sense of *esprit de corps*.
No notion of putting himself out to the most trifling
extent for the benefit of the community. Haven't you any
more marmalade, laddie?'

'I have not.'

'Then I'll be going,' said Ukridge, moodily. 'I suppose,'
he added, pausing at the door, 'you couldn't lend me five
bob?'

'How did you guess?'

'Then I'll tell you what,' said Ukridge, ever fair and
reasonable; 'you can stand me dinner tonight.' He
seemed cheered up for the moment by this happy
compromise, but gloom descended on him again. His
face clouded. 'When I think,' he said, 'of all the money
that's locked up in that poor faint-hearted fish, just
waiting to be released, I could sob. Sob, laddie, like a little
child. I never liked that man – he has a bad eye and waves
his hair. Never trust a man who waves his hair, old
horse.'

Ukridge's pessimism was not confined to himself. By
the end of a fortnight, nothing having happened to Teddy
Weeks worse than a slight cold which he shook off in a
couple of days, the general consensus of opinion among
his apprehensive colleagues in the Syndicate was that the
situation had become desperate. There were no signs
whatever of any return on the vast capital which we had
laid out, and meanwhile meals had to be bought, landladies
paid, and a reasonable supply of tobacco acquired. It was
a melancholy task in these circumstances to read one's
paper of a morning.

All over the inhabited globe, so the well-informed sheet gave one to understand, every kind of accident was happening every day to practically everybody in existence except Teddy Weeks. Farmers in Minnesota were getting mixed up with reaping-machines, peasants in India were being bisected by crocodiles; iron girders from skyscrapers were falling hourly on the heads of citizens in every town from Philadelphia to San Francisco; and the only people who were not down with ptomaine poisoning were those who had walked over cliffs, driven motors into walls, tripped over manholes, or assumed on too slight evidence that the gun was not loaded. In a crippled world, it seemed, Teddy Weeks walked alone, whole and glowing with health. It was one of those grim, ironical, hopeless, grey, despairful situations which the Russian novelists love to write about, and I could not find it in me to blame Ukridge for taking direct action in this crisis. My only regret was that bad luck caused so excellent a plan to miscarry.

My first intimation that he had been trying to hurry matters on came when he and I were walking along the King's Road one evening, and he drew me into Markham Square, a dismal backwater where he had once had rooms.

'What's the idea?' I asked, for I disliked the place.

'Teddy Weeks lives here,' said Ukridge. 'In my old rooms.' I could not see that this lent any fascination to the place. Every day and in every way I was feeling sorrier and sorrier that I had been foolish enough to put money which I could ill spare into a venture which had all the earmarks of a wash-out, and my sentiments towards Teddy Weeks were cold and hostile.

'I want to enquire after him.'

'Enquire after him? Why?'

'Well, the fact is, laddie, I have an idea that he has been bitten by a dog.'

'What makes you think that?'

'Oh, I don't know,' said Ukridge, dreamily. 'I've just got the idea. You know how one gets ideas.'

The mere contemplation of this beautiful event was so inspiring that for a while it held me silent. In each of the ten journals in which we had invested dog bites were specifically recommended as things which every subscriber ought to have. They came about half-way up the list of lucrative accidents, inferior to a broken rib or a fractured fibula, but better value than an ingrowing toenail. I was gloating happily over the picture conjured up by Ukridge's words when an exclamation brought me back with a start to the realities of life. A revolting sight met my eyes. Down the street came ambling the familiar figure of Teddy Weeks, and one glance at his elegant person was enough to tell us that our hopes had been built on sand. Not even a toy Pomeranian had chewed this man.

'Hallo, you fellows!' said Teddy Weeks.

'Hallo!' we responded, dully.

'Can't stop,' said Teddy Weeks. 'I've got to fetch a doctor.'

'A doctor?'

'Yes. Poor Victor Beamish. He's been bitten by a dog.'

Ukridge and I exchanged weary glances. It seemed as if Fate was going out of its way to have sport with us. What was the good of a dog biting Victor Beamish? What was the good of a hundred dogs biting Victor Beamish? A dog-bitten Victor Beamish had no market value whatever.

'You know that fierce brute that belongs to my landlady,' said Teddy Weeks. 'The one that always dashes out into the area and barks at people who come to the front door.' I remembered. A large mongrel with wild eyes and flashing fangs, badly in need of a haircut. I had encountered it once in the street, when visiting Ukridge, and only the presence of the latter, who knew it well and to whom all dogs were as brothers, had saved me from the doom of Victor Beamish. 'Somehow or other he got into my bedroom this evening. He was waiting there when I came home. I had brought Beamish back with me, and the animal pinned him by the leg the moment I opened the door.'

'Why didn't he pin you?' asked Ukridge, aggrieved.

'What I can't make out,' said Teddy Weeks, 'is how on earth the brute came to be in my room. Somebody must have put him there. The whole thing is very mysterious.'

'Why didn't he pin you?' demanded Ukridge again.

'Oh, I managed to climb onto the top of the wardrobe while he was biting Beamish,' said Teddy Weeks. 'And then the landlady came and took him away. But I can't stop here talking. I must go and get that doctor.'

We gazed after him in silence as he tripped down the street. We noted the careful manner in which he paused at the corner to eye the traffic before crossing the road, the wary way in which he drew back to allow a truck to rattle past.

'You heard that?' said Ukridge, tensely. 'He climbed onto the top of the wardrobe!'

'Yes.'

'And you saw the way he dodged that excellent truck?'

'Yes.'

'Something's got to be done,' said Ukridge, firmly. 'The man has got to be awakened to a sense of his responsibilities.'

Next day a deputation waited on Teddy Weeks.

Ukridge was our spokesman, and he came to the point with admirable directness.

'How about it?' asked Ukridge.

'How about what?' replied Teddy Weeks, nervously, avoiding his accusing eye.

'When do we get action?'

'Oh, you mean that accident business?'

'Yes.'

'I've been thinking about that,' said Teddy Weeks.

Ukridge drew the mackintosh which he wore indoors

511

and out of doors and in all weathers more closely around him. There was in the action something suggestive of a member of the Roman Senate about to denounce an enemy of the State. In just such a manner must Cicero have swished his toga as he took a deep breath preparatory to assailing Clodius. He toyed for a moment with the ginger-beer wire which held his pince-nez in place, and endeavoured without success to button his collar at the back. In moments of emotion Ukridge's collar always took on a sort of temperamental jumpiness which no stud could restrain.

'And about time you *were* thinking about it,' he boomed, sternly.

We shifted appreciatively in our seats, all except Victor Beamish, who had declined a chair and was standing by the mantelpiece. 'Upon my Sam, it's about time you were thinking about it. Do you realize that we've invested an enormous sum of money in you on the distinct understanding that we could rely on you to do your duty and get immediate results? Are we to be forced to the conclusion that you are so yellow and few in the pod as to want to evade your honourable obligations? We thought better of you, Weeks. Upon my Sam, we thought better of you. We took you for a two-fisted, enterprising, big-souled, one hundred-per-cent he-man who would stand by his friends to the finish.'

'Yes, but – '

'Any bloke with a sense of loyalty and an appreciation of what it meant to the rest of us would have rushed out and found some means of fulfilling his duty long ago. You don't even grasp at the opportunities that come your way. Only yesterday I saw you draw back when a single step into the road would have had a truck bumping into you.'

'Well, it's not so easy to let a truck bump into you.'

'Nonsense. It only requires a little ordinary resolution. Use your imagination, man. Try to think that a child has fallen down in the street – a little golden-haired

child,' said Ukridge, deeply affected. 'And a dashed great
cab or something comes rolling up. The kid's mother is
standing on the pavement, helpless, her hands clasped
in agony. "Dammit," she cries, "will no one save my
darling?" "Yes, by George," you shout, "*I will.*" And out
you jump and the thing's over in half a second. I don't
know what you're making such a fuss about.'

'Yes, but – ' said Teddy Weeks.

'I'm told, what's more, it isn't a bit painful. A sort of
dull shock, that's all.'

'Who told you that?'

'I forget. Someone.'

'Well, you can tell him from me that he's an ass,' said
Teddy Weeks, with asperity.

'All right. If you object to being run over by a truck
there are lots of other ways. But, upon my Sam, it's
pretty hopeless suggesting them. You seem to have no
enterprise at all. Yesterday, after I went to all the trouble
to put a dog in your room, a dog which would have done
all the work for you – all you had to do was stand still
and let him use his own judgement – what happened?
You climbed onto – '

Victor Beamish interrupted, speaking in a voice husky
with emotion.

'Was it you who put that damned dog in the room?'

'Eh?' said Ukridge. 'Why, yes. But we can have a good
talk about all that later on,' he proceeded, hastily. 'The
point at the moment is how the dickens we're going to
persuade this poor worm to collect our insurance money
for us. Why, damme, I should have thought you would
have – '

'All I can say – ' began Victor Beamish, heatedly.

'Yes, yes,' said Ukridge; 'some other time. Must stick
to business now, laddie. I was saying,' he resumed, 'that I
should have thought you would have been as keen as
mustard to put the job through for your own sake. You're
always beefing that you haven't any clothes to impress

managers with. Think of all you can buy with your share of the swag once you have summoned up a little ordinary determination and seen the thing through. Think of the suits, the boots, the hats, the spats. You're always talking about your dashed career, and how all you need to land you in a West End production is good clothes. Well, here's your chance to get them.'

His eloquence was not wasted. A wistful look came into Teddy Weeks's eye, such a look as must have come into the eye of Moses on the summit of Pisgah. He breathed heavily. You could see that the man was mentally walking along Cork Street, weighing the merits of one famous tailor against another.

'I'll tell you what I'll do,' he said, suddenly. 'It's no use asking me to put this thing through in cold blood. I simply can't do it. I haven't the nerve. But if you fellows will give me a dinner tonight with lots of champagne I think it will key me up to it.'

A heavy silence fell upon the room. Champagne! The word was like a knell.

'How on earth are we going to afford champagne?' said Victor Beamish.

'Well, there it is,' said Teddy Weeks. 'Take it or leave it.'

'Gentlemen,' said Ukridge, 'it would seem that the company requires more capital. How about it, old horses? Let's get together in a frank, businesslike cards-on-the-table spirit, and see what can be done. I can raise ten bob.'

'What!' cried the entire assembled company, amazed. 'How?'

'I'll pawn a banjo.'

'You haven't got a banjo.'

'No, but George Tupper has, and I know where he keeps it.'

Started in this spirited way, the subscriptions came pouring in. I contributed a cigarette case, Bertram Fox thought his landlady would let him owe for another week,

Robert Dunhill had an uncle in Kensington who, he fancied, if tactfully approached, would be good for a quid, and Victor Beamish said that if the advertisement manager of the O-So-Eesi Piano-Player was churlish enough to refuse an advance of five shillings against future work he misjudged him sadly. Within a few minutes, in short, the Lightning Drive had produced the impressive total of two pounds six shillings, and we asked Teddy Weeks if he thought that he could get adequately keyed up within the limits of that sum.

'I'll try,' said Teddy Weeks.

So, not unmindful of the fact that that excellent hostelry supplied champagne at eight shillings the quart bottle, we fixed the meeting for seven o'clock at Barolini's.

Considered as a social affair, Teddy Weeks's keying-up dinner was not a success. Almost from the start I think we all found it trying. It was not so much the fact that he was drinking deeply of Barolini's eight-shilling champagne while we, from lack of funds, were compelled to confine ourselves to meaner beverages; what really marred the pleasantness of the function was the extraordinary effect the stuff had on Teddy. What was actually in the champagne supplied to Barolini and purveyed by him to the public, such as were reckless enough to drink it, at eight shillings the bottle remains a secret between its maker and his Maker; but three glasses of it were enough to convert Teddy Weeks from a mild and rather oily young man into a truculent swashbuckler.

He quarrelled with us all. With the soup he was tilting at Victor Beamish's theories of Art; the fish found him ridiculing Bertram Fox's views on the future of the motion picture; and by the time the leg of chicken with dandelion salad arrived – or, as some held, string salad – opinions varied on this point – the hell-brew had so wrought on him that he had begun to lecture Ukridge on his misspent life and was urging him in accents audible across the street to go out and get a job and thus acquire sufficient self-respect to enable him to look himself in the face in a mirror without wincing. Not, added Teddy Weeks with what we all thought uncalled-for offensiveness, that any amount of self-respect was likely to do that. Having said which, he called imperiously for another eight bobs'-worth.

We gazed at one another wanly. However excellent the end towards which all this was tending, there was no denying that it was hard to bear. But policy kept us silent. We recognized that this was Teddy Weeks's evening and that he must be humoured. Victor Beamish said meekly that Teddy had cleared up a lot of points which had been troubling him for a long time. Bertram Fox agreed that there was much in what Teddy had said about the future of the close-up. And even Ukridge, though his haughty soul was seared to its foundations by the latter's personal remarks, promised to take his homily to heart and act upon it at the earliest possible moment.

'You'd better!' said Teddy Weeks, belligerently, biting off the end of one of Barolini's best cigars. 'And there's another thing – don't let me hear of your coming and sneaking people's socks again.'

'Very well, laddie,' said Ukridge, humbly.

'If there is one person in the world that I despise,' said Teddy, bending a red-eyed gaze on the offender, 'it's a snock-seeker – a seek-snocker – a – well, you know what I mean.'

We hastened to assure him that we knew what he meant and he relapsed into a lengthy stupor, from which he emerged three-quarters of an hour later to announce that he didn't know what we intended to do, but that he was going. We said that we were going too, and we paid the bill and did so.

Teddy Weeks's indignation on discovering us gathered about him upon the pavement outside the restaurant was intense, and he expressed it freely. Among other

things, he said – which was not true – that he had a
reputation to keep up in Soho.

'It's all right, Teddy, old horse,' said Ukridge,
soothingly. 'We just thought you would like to have all
your old pals round you when you did it.'

'Did it? Did what?'

'Why, had the accident.'

Teddy Weeks glared at him truculently. Then his mood
seemed to change abruptly, and he burst into a loud and
hearty laugh.

'Well, of all the silly ideas!' he cried, amusedly. 'I'm
not going to have an accident. You don't suppose I ever
seriously intended to have an accident, do you? It was
just my fun.' Then, with another sudden change of mood,
he seemed to become a victim to an acute unhappiness.
He stroked Ukridge's arm affectionately, and a tear rolled
down his cheek. 'Just my fun,' he repeated. 'You don't
mind my fun, do you?' he asked, pleadingly. 'You like
my fun, don't you? All my fun. Never meant to have an
accident at all. Just wanted dinner.' The gay humour of
it all overcame his sorrow once more. 'Funniest thing
ever heard,' he said cordially. 'Didn't want accident,
wanted dinner. Dinner daxident, danner dixident,' he
added, driving home his point. 'Well, good night all,'
he said, cheerily. And, stepping off the kerb onto a
banana skin, was instantly knocked ten feet by a passing
lorry.

'Two ribs and an arm,' said the doctor five minutes
later, superintending the removal proceedings. 'Gently
with that stretcher.'

It was two weeks before we were informed by the
authorities of Charing Cross Hospital that the patient
was in a condition to receive visitors. A whip-round
secured the price of a basket of fruit, and Ukridge and I
were deputed by the shareholders to deliver it with their
compliments and kind inquiries.

'Hallo!' we said in a hushed, bedside manner when finally admitted to his presence.

'Sit down, gentlemen,' replied the invalid.

I must confess even in that first moment to having experienced a slight feeling of surprise. It was not like Teddy Weeks to call us gentlemen. Ukridge, however, seemed to notice nothing amiss.

'Well, well, well,' he said, buoyantly. 'And how are you, laddie? We've brought you a few fragments of fruit.'

'I am getting along capitally,' replied Teddy Weeks, still in that odd precise way which had made his opening words strike me as curious. 'And I should like to say that in my opinion England has reason to be proud of the alertness and enterprise of her great journals. The excellence of their reading matter, the ingenuity of their various competitions, and, above all, the go-ahead spirit which has resulted in this accident insurance scheme are beyond praise. Have you got that down?' he enquired.

Ukridge and I looked at each other. We had been told that Teddy was practically normal again, but this sounded like delirium.

'Have we got that down, old horse?' asked Ukridge, gently.

Teddy Weeks seemed surprised.

'Aren't you reporters?'

'How do you mean, reporters?'

'I thought you had come from one of these weekly papers that have been paying me insurance money, to interview me,' said Teddy Weeks.

Ukridge and I exchanged another glance. An uneasy glance this time. I think that already a grim foreboding had begun to cast its shadow over us.

'Surely you remember me, Teddy, old horse?' said Ukridge, anxiously.

Teddy Weeks knit his brow, concentrating painfully.

'Why, of course,' he said at last. 'You're Ukridge, aren't you?'

'That's right. Ukridge.'

'Of course. Ukridge.'

'Yes. Ukridge. Funny your forgetting me!'

'Yes,' said Teddy Weeks. 'It's the effect of the shock I got when that thing bowled me over. I must have been struck on the head, I suppose. It has had the effect of rendering my memory rather uncertain. The doctors here are very interested. They say it is a most unusual case. I can remember some things perfectly, but in some ways my memory is a complete blank.'

'Oh, but I say, old horse,' quavered Ukridge. 'I suppose you haven't forgotten about that insurance, have you?'

'Oh, no, I remember that.'

Ukridge breathed a relieved sigh.

'I was a subscriber to a number of weekly papers,' went on Teddy Weeks. 'They are paying me insurance money now.'

'Yes, yes, old horse,' cried Ukridge. 'But what I mean is you remember the Syndicate, don't you?'

Teddy Weeks raised his eyebrows.

'Syndicate? What Syndicate?'

'Why, when we all got together and put up the money to pay for the subscriptions to these papers and drew lots, to choose which of us should go out and have an accident and collect the money. And you drew it, don't you remember?'

Utter astonishment, and a shocked astonishment at that, spread itself over Teddy Weeks's countenance. The man seemed outraged.

'I certainly remember nothing of the kind,' he said, severely. 'I cannot imagine myself for a moment consenting to become a party to what from your own account would appear to have been a criminal conspiracy to obtain money under false pretences from a number of weekly papers.'

'But, laddie – '

'However,' said Teddy Weeks, 'if there is any truth in

this story, no doubt you have documentary evidence to support it.'

Ukridge looked at me. I looked at Ukridge. There was a long silence.

'Shift-ho, old horse?' said Ukridge, sadly. 'No use staying on here.'

'No,' I replied, with equal gloom. 'May as well go.'

'Glad to have seen you,' said Teddy Weeks, 'and thanks for the fruit.'

The next time I saw the man he was coming out of a manager's office in the Haymarket. He had on a new Homburg hat of a delicate pearl grey, spats to match, and a new blue flannel suit, beautifully cut, with an invisible red twill. He was looking jubilant, and, as I passed him, he drew from his pocket a gold cigarette case.

It was shortly after that, if you remember, that he made a big hit as the juvenile lead in that piece at the Apollo and started on his sensational career as a *matinée* idol.

Inside the church the organ had swelled into the familiar music of the Wedding March. A verger came out and opened the doors. The five cooks ceased their reminiscences of other and smarter weddings at which they had participated. The camera-men unshipped their cameras. The costermonger moved his barrow of vegetables a pace forward. A dishevelled and unshaven man at my side uttered a disapproving growl.

'Idle rich!' said the dishevelled man.

Out of the church came a beauteous being, leading, attached to his arm, another being, somewhat less beauteous.

There was no denying the spectacular effect of Teddy Weeks. He was handsomer than ever. His sleek hair, gorgeously waved, shone in the sun, his eyes were large and bright; his lissom frame, garbed in faultless morning-coat and trousers, was that of an Apollo. But his bride gave the impression that Teddy had married money.

They paused in the doorway, and the camera-men became active and fussy.

'Have you got a shilling, laddie?' said Ukridge in a low, level voice.

'Why do you want a shilling?'

'Old horse,' said Ukridge, tensely, 'it is of the utmost vital importance that I have a shilling here and now.'

I passed it over. Ukridge turned to the dishevelled man, and I perceived that he held in his hand a large rich tomato of juicy and over-ripe appearance.

'Would you like to earn a bob?' Ukridge said.

'Would I!' replied the dishevelled man.

Ukridge sank his voice to a hoarse whisper.

The camera-men had finished their preparations. Teddy Weeks, his head thrown back in that gallant way which has endeared him to so many female hearts, was exhibiting his celebrated teeth. The cooks, in undertones, were making adverse comments on the appearance of the bride.

'Now, please,' said one of the camera-men.

Over the heads of the crowd, well and truly aimed, whizzed a large juicy tomato. It burst like a shell full between Teddy Weeks's expressive eyes, obliterating them in scarlet ruin. It spattered Teddy Weeks's collar, it dripped on Teddy Weeks's morning-coat. And the dishevelled man turned abruptly and raced off down the street.

Ukridge grasped my arm. There was a look of deep content in his eyes.

'Shift-ho?' said Ukridge.

Arm-in-arm, we strolled off in the pleasant June sunshine.

3 — The Return of Battling Billson

It was a most embarrassing moment, one of those moments which plant lines on the face and turn the hair a distinguished grey at the temples. I looked at the barman. The barman looked at me. The assembled company looked at us both impartially.

'Ho!' said the barman.

I am very quick. I could see at once that he was not in sympathy with me. He was a large, profuse man, and his eye as it met mine conveyed the impression that he regarded me as a bad dream come true. His mobile lips curved slightly, showing a gold tooth; and the muscles of his brawny arms, which were strong as iron bands, twitched a little.

'Ho!' he said.

The circumstances which had brought me into my present painful position were as follows. In writing those stories for the popular magazines which at that time were causing so many editors so much regret, I was accustomed, like one of my brother-authors, to take all mankind for my province. Thus, one day I would be dealing with dukes in their castles, the next I would turn right round and start tackling the submerged tenth in their slums. Versatile. At the moment I happened to be engaged upon a rather poignant little thing about a girl called Liz, who worked in a fried-fish shop in the Ratcliff Highway, and I had accordingly gone down there to collect local colour. For whatever Posterity may say of James Corcoran, it can never say that he shrank from inconvenience where his Art was concerned.

The Ratcliff Highway is an interesting thoroughfare,

but on a warm day it breeds thirst. After wandering about for an hour or so, therefore, I entered the Prince of Wales public house, called for a pint of beer, drained it at a draught, reached in my pocket for coin, and found emptiness. I was in a position to add to my notes on the East End of London one to the effect that pocket-pickery flourishes there as a fine art.

'I'm awfully sorry,' I said, smiling an apologetic smile and endeavouring to put a debonair winsomeness into my voice. 'I find I've got no money.'

It was at this point that the barman said 'Ho!' and moved out into the open through a trick door in the counter.

'I think my pocket must have been picked,' I said.

'Oh, do you?' said the barman.

He gave me the idea of being rather a soured man. Years of association with unscrupulous citizens who tried to get drinks for nothing had robbed him of that fine fresh young enthusiasm with which he had started out on his career of barmanship.

'I had better leave my name and address,' I suggested.

'Who,' enquired the barman, coldly, 'wants your blinking name and address?'

These practical men go straight to the heart of a thing. He had put his finger on the very hub of the matter. Who did want my blinking name and address? No one.

'I will send – ' I was proceeding, when things began to happen suddenly. An obviously expert hand gripped me by the back of the neck, another closed upon the seat of my trousers, there was a rush of air, and I was rolling across the pavement in the direction of a wet and unsavoury gutter. The barman, gigantic against the dirty white front of the public house, surveyed me grimly.

I think that, if he had confined himself to mere looks – however offensive – I would have gone no farther into the matter. After all, the man had right on his side. How could he be expected to see into my soul and note its

snowy purity? But, as I picked myself up, he could not
resist the temptation to improve the occasion.

'That's what comes of tryin' to snitch drinks,' he said,
with what seemed to me insufferable priggishness.

Those harsh words stung me to the quick. I burned
with generous wrath. I flung myself on that barman.
The futility of attacking such a Colossus never occurred
to me. I forgot entirely that he could put me out of action
with one hand.

A moment later, however, he had reminded me of this
fact. Even as I made my onslaught an enormous fist
came from nowhere and crashed into the side of my head.
I sat down again.

''Ullo!'

I was aware, dimly, that someone was speaking to me,
someone who was not the barman. That athlete had
already dismissed me as a spent force and returned to his
professional duties. I looked up and got a sort of general
impression of bigness and blue serge, and then I was lifted
lightly to my feet.

My head had begun to clear now, and I was able to look
more steadily at my sympathizer. And, as I looked, the
feeling came to me that I had seen him before somewhere.
That red hair, those glinting eyes, that impressive bulk
– it was my old friend Wilberforce Billson and no other –
Battling Billson, the coming champion, whom I had last
seen fighting at Wonderland under the personal
management of Stanley Featherstonehaugh Ukridge.

'Did 'e 'it yer?' enquired Mr Billson.

There was only one answer to this. Disordered though
my faculties were, I was clear upon this point. I said,
'Yes, he did hit me.'

''R!' said Mr Billson, and immediately passed into the
hostelry.

It was not at once that I understood the significance
of this move. The interpretation I placed upon his abrupt
departure was that, having wearied of my society, he had

decided to go and have some refreshment. Only when the sound of raised voices from within came pouring through the door did I begin to suspect that in attributing to it such callousness I might have wronged that golden nature. With the sudden reappearance of the barman – who shot out as if impelled by some imperious force and did a sort of backwards foxtrot across the pavement – suspicion became certainty.

The barman, as becomes a man plying his trade in the Ratcliff Highway, was made of stern stuff. He was no poltroon. As soon as he had managed to stop himself from pirouetting, he dabbed at his right cheekbone in a delicate manner, soliloquized for a moment, and then dashed back into the bar. And it was after the door had swung to again behind him that the proceedings may have been said formally to have begun.

What precisely was going on inside that bar I was still too enfeebled to go and see. It sounded like an earthquake, and no meagre earthquake at that. All the glassware in the world seemed to be smashing simultaneously, the populations of several cities were shouting in unison, and I could almost fancy that I saw the walls of the building shake and heave. And then somebody blew a police whistle.

There is a magic about the sound of a police whistle. It acts like oil on the most troubled waters. This one brought about an instant lull in the tumult. Glasses ceased to break, voices were hushed, and a moment later out came Mr Billson, standing not upon the order of his going. His nose was bleeding a little and there was the scenario of a black eye forming on his face, but otherwise there seemed nothing much the matter with him. He cast a wary look up and down the street and sprinted for the nearest corner. And I, shaking off the dreamy after-effects of my encounter with the barman, sprinted in his wake. I was glowing with gratitude and admiration. I wanted to catch this man up and thank him formally. I wanted to

assure him of my undying esteem. Moreover, I wanted
to borrow sixpence from him. The realization that he was
the only man in the whole wide East End of London who
was likely to lend me the money to save me having to
walk back to Ebury Street gave me a rare burst of speed.

It was not easy to overtake him, for the sound of my
pursuing feet evidently suggested to Mr Billson that the
hunt was up, and he made good going. Eventually,
however, when in addition to running I began to emit a
plaintive 'Mr Billson! I say, Mr Billson!' at every second
stride, he seemed to gather that he was among friends.

'Oh, it's you, is it?' he said, halting.

He was plainly relieved. He produced a murky pipe
and lit it. I delivered my speech of thanks. Having heard
me out, he removed his pipe and put into a few short
words the moral of the whole affair.

'Nobody don't dot no pals of mine not when I'm
around,' said Mr Billson.

'It was awfully good of you to trouble,' I said with
feeling.

'No trouble,' said Mr Billson.

'You must have hit that barman pretty hard. He came
out at forty miles an hour.

'I dotted him,' agreed Mr Billson.

'I'm afraid he has hurt your eye,' I said,
sympathetically.

'Him!' said Mr Billson, expectorating with scorn.
'That wasn't him. That was his pals. Six or seven of 'em
there was.'

'And did you dot them too?' I cried, amazed at the
prowess of this wonder man.

''R!' said Mr Billson. He smoked a while. 'But I dotted
'im most,' he proceeded. He looked at me with honest
warmth, his chivalrous heart plainly stirred to its depths.
'The idea,' he said, disgustedly, 'of a — — —'is size' –
he defined the barman crisply and, as far as I could judge

after so brief an acquaintanceship, accurately – 'goin' and
dottin' a little – like you!'

The sentiment was so admirable that I could not take
exception to its phraseology. Nor did I rebel at being
called 'little'. To a man of Mr Billson's mould I supposed
most people looked little.

'Well, I'm very much obliged,' I said.

Mr Billson smoked in silence.

'Have you been back long?' I asked, for something to
say. Outstanding as were his other merits, he was not
good at keeping a conversation alive.

'Back?' said Mr Billson.

'Back in London. Ukridge told me that you had gone
to sea again.'

'Say, mister,' exclaimed Mr Billson, for the first time
seeming to show real interest in my remarks, 'you seen
'im lately?'

'Ukridge? Oh, yes, I see him nearly every day.'

'I been tryin' to find 'im.'

'I can give you his address,' I said. And I wrote it down
on the back of an envelope. Then, having shaken his
hand, I thanked him once more for his courteous
assistance, borrowed my fare back to Civilization on the
Underground, and we parted with mutual expressions of
good will.

The next step in the march of events was what I shall
call the Episode of the Inexplicable Female. It occurred
two days later. Returning shortly after lunch to my rooms
in Ebury Street, I was met in the hall by Mrs Bowles, my
landlord's wife. I greeted her a trifle nervously, for, like
her husband, she always exercised a rather oppressive
effect on me. She lacked Bowles's ambassadorial dignity,
but made up for it by a manner so peculiarly sepulchral
that strong men quailed before her pale gaze. Scottish by
birth, she had an eye that looked as if it was for ever
searching for astral bodies wrapped in winding-sheets –

this, I believe, being a favourite indoor sport among certain sets in North Britain.

'Sir,' said Mrs Bowles, 'there is a body in your sitting room.'

'A body!' I am bound to say that this Phillips-Oppenheim-like opening to the conversation gave me something of a shock. Then I remembered her nationality. 'Oh, you mean a man?'

'A woman,' corrected Mrs Bowles. 'A body in a pink hat.'

I was conscious of a feeling of guilt. In this pure and modest house, female bodies in pink hats seemed to require explanation. I felt that the correct thing to do would have been to call upon Heaven to witness that this woman was nothing to me, nothing.

'I was to give you this letter, sir.'

I took it and opened the envelope with a sigh. I had recognized the handwriting of Ukridge, and for the hundredth time in our close acquaintanceship there smote me like a blow the sad suspicion that this man had once more gone and wished upon me some frightful thing.

MY DEAR OLD HORSE – It's not often I ask you to do anything for me . . .

I laughed hollowly.

MY DEAR OLD HORSE – It's not often I ask you to do anything for me, laddie, but I beg and implore you to rally round now and show yourself the true friend I know you are. The one thing I've always said about you, Corky my boy, is that you're a real pal who never lets a fellow down.

The bearer of this – a delightful woman, you'll like her – is Flossie's mother. She's up for the day by excursion from the North, and it is absolutely vital

that she be lushed up and seen off at Euston at six
forty-five. I can't look after her myself, as
unfortunately I'm laid up with a sprained ankle.
Otherwise I wouldn't trouble you.

This is a life and death matter, old man, and I'm
relying on you. I can't possibly tell you how important
it is that this old bird should be suitably entertained.
The gravest issues hang on it. So shove on your hat
and go to it, laddie, and blessings will reward you. Tell
you all the details when we meet.

Yours ever,
S. F. Ukridge
P. S. I will defray all expenses later.

Those last words did wring a faint, melancholy smile
from me, but apart from them this hideous document
seemed to me to be entirely free from comic relief. I
looked at my watch and found that it was barely two-
thirty. This female, therefore, was on my hands for a solid
four hours and a quarter. I breathed maledictions – futile,
of course, for it was a peculiar characteristic of the demon
Ukridge on these occasions that, unless one were strong-
minded enough to disregard his frenzied pleadings
altogether – a thing which was nearly always beyond me
– he gave one no chance of escape. He sprang his foul
schemes on one at the very last moment, leaving no
opportunity for a graceful refusal.

I proceeded slowly up the stairs to my sitting room. It
would have been a distinct advantage, I felt, if I had
known who on earth this Flossie was of whom he wrote
with such airy familiarity. The name, though Ukridge
plainly expected it to touch a chord in me, left me entirely
unresponsive. As far as I was aware, there was no Flossie
of any description in my life. I thought back through the
years. Long-forgotten Janes and Kates and Muriels and
Elizabeths rose from the murky depths of my memory as
I stirred it, but no Flossie. It occurred to me as I opened

the door that, if Ukridge was expecting pleasant reminiscences of Flossie to form a tender bond between me and her mother, he was building on sandy soil.

The first impression I got on entering the room was that Mrs Bowles possessed the true reporter's gift for picking out the detail that really mattered. One could have said many things about Flossie's mother, as, for instance, that she was stout, cheerful, and far more tightly laced than a doctor would have considered judicious; but what stood out above all the others was the fact that she was wearing a pink hat. It was the largest, gayest, most exuberantly ornate specimen of head-wear that I had ever seen, and the prospect of spending four hours and a quarter in its society added the last touch to my already poignant gloom. The only gleam of sunshine that lightened my darkness was the reflection that, if we went to a picture-palace, she would have to remove it.

'Er – how do you do?' I said, pausing in the doorway.

''Ow do you do?' said a voice from under the hat. 'Say "'Ow-do-you-do?" to the gentleman, Cecil.'

I perceived a small, shiny boy by the window. Ukridge, realizing with the true artist's instinct that the secret of all successful prose is the knowledge of what to omit, had not mentioned him in his letter; and, as he turned reluctantly to go through the necessary civilities, it seemed to me that the burden was more than I could bear. He was a rat-faced, sinister-looking boy, and he gazed at me with a frigid distaste which reminded me of the barman at the Prince of Wales public house in Ratcliff Highway.

'I brought Cecil along,' said Flossie's (and presumably Cecil's) mother, after the stripling, having growled a cautious greeting, obviously with the mental reservation that it committed him to nothing, had returned to the window, 'because I thought it would be nice for 'im to say he had seen London.'

'Quite, quite,' I replied, while Cecil, at the window,

gazed darkly out at London as if he did not think much
of it.

'Mr Ukridge said you would trot us round.'

'Delighted, delighted,' I quavered, looking at the hat
and looking swiftly away again. 'I think we had better
go to a picture-palace, don't you?'

'Naw!' said Cecil. And there was that in his manner
which suggested that when he said 'Naw!' it was final.

'Cecil wants to see the sights,' explained his mother.
'We can see all the pictures back at home. 'E's been
lookin' forward to seein' the sights of London. It'll be an
education for 'im, like, to see all the sights.'

'Westminster Abbey?' I suggested. After all, what
could be better for the lad's growing mind than to inspect
the memorials of the great past and, if disposed, pick out
a suitable site for his own burial at some later date?
Also, I had a fleeting notion, which a moment's reflection
exploded before it could bring me much comfort, that
women removed their hats in Westminster Abbey.

'Naw!' said Cecil.

''E wants to see the murders,' explained Flossie's
mother.

She spoke as if it were the most reasonable of boyish
desires, but it sounded to me impracticable. Homicides
do not publish formal programmes of their intended
activities. I had no notion what murders were scheduled
for today.

''E always reads up all the murders in the Sunday
paper,' went on the parent, throwing light on the matter.

'Oh, I understand,' I said. 'Then Madame Tussaud's is
the spot he wants. They've got all the murderers.'

'Naw!' said Cecil.

'It's the places 'e wants to see,' said Flossie's mother,
amiably tolerant of my density. 'The places where all them
murders was committed. 'E's clipped out the addresses
and 'e wants to be able to tell 'is friends when he gets
back that 'e's seen 'em.'

A profound relief surged over me.

'Why, we can do the whole thing in a cab,' I cried. 'We can stay in a cab from start to finish. No need to leave the cab at all.'

'Or a bus?'

'Not a bus,' I said firmly. I was quite decided on a cab – one with blinds that would pull down, if possible.

''Ave it your own way,' said Flossie's mother agreeably. 'Speaking as far as I'm personally concerned, I'm shaw there's nothing I would rather prefer than a nice ride in a keb. Jear what the gentleman says, Cecil? You're goin' to ride in a keb.'

'Urgh!' said Cecil, as if he would believe it when he saw it. A sceptical boy.

It was not an afternoon to which I look back as among the happiest I have spent. For one thing, the expedition far exceeded my hasty estimates in the matter of expense. Why it should be so I cannot say, but all the best murders appear to take place in remote spots like Stepney and Canning Town, and cab fares to these places run into money. Then, again, Cecil's was not one of those personalities which become more attractive with familiarity. I should say at a venture that those who liked him best were those who saw the least of him. And, finally, there was a monotony about the entire proceedings which soon began to afflict my nerves. The cab would draw up outside some mouldering house in some desolate street miles from civilization, Cecil would thrust his unpleasant head out of the window and drink the place in for a few moments of silent ecstasy, and then he would deliver his lecture. He had evidently read well and thoughtfully. He had all the information.

'The Canning Town 'Orror,' he would announce.

'Yes, dearie?' His mother cast a fond glance at him and a proud one at me. 'In this very 'ouse, was it?'

'In this very 'ouse,' said Cecil, with the gloomy importance of a confirmed bore about to hold forth on

his favourite subject. 'Jimes Potter 'is nime was. 'E was
found at seven in the morning underneaf the kitchen
sink wiv'is froat cut from ear to ear. It was the landlady's
brother done it. They 'anged 'im at Pentonville.'

Some more data from the child's inexhaustible store,
and then on to the next historic site.

'The Bing Street 'Orror!'

'In this very 'ouse, dearie?'

'In this very 'ouse. Body was found in the cellar in an
advanced stige of dee-cawm-po-sition wiv its 'ead
bashed in, prezoomably by some blunt instrument.'

At six-forty-six, ignoring the pink hat which protruded
from the window of a third-class compartment and the
stout hand that waved a rollicking farewell, I turned from
the train with a pale, set face, and, passing down the
platform of Euston Station, told a cabman to take me
with all speed to Ukridge's lodgings in Arundel Street,
Leicester Square. There had never, so far as I knew, been
a murder in Arundel Street, but I was strongly of opinion
that that time was ripe. Cecil's society and conversation
had done much to neutralize the effects of a gentle
upbringing and I toyed almost luxuriously with the
thought of supplying him with an Arundel Street Horror
for his next visit to the metropolis.

'Aha, laddie,' said Ukridge, as I entered. 'Come in, old
horse. Glad to see you. Been wondering when you would
turn up.'

He was in bed, but that did not remove the suspicion
which had been growing in me all the afternoon that he
was a low malingerer. I refused to believe for a moment
in that sprained ankle of his. My view was that he had
had the advantage of a first look at Flossie's mother and
her engaging child and had shrewdly passed them on to
me.

'I've been reading your book, old man,' said Ukridge,
breaking a pregnant silence with an overdone
carelessness. He brandished winningly the only novel I

had ever written, and I can offer no better proof of the black hostility of my soul than the statement that even this did not soften me. 'It's immense, laddie. No other word for it. Immense. Damme, I've been crying like a child.'

'It is supposed to be a humorous novel,' I pointed out, coldly.

'Crying with laughter,' explained Ukridge, hurriedly.

I eyed him with loathing.

'Where do you keep your blunt instruments?' I asked.

'My what?'

'Your blunt instruments. I want a blunt instrument. Give me a blunt instrument. My God! Don't tell me you have no blunt instrument.'

'Only a safety razor.'

I sat down wearily on the bed.

'Hi! Mind my ankle!'

'Your ankle!' I laughed a hideous laugh, the sort of laugh the landlady's brother might have emitted before beginning operations on James Potter. 'A lot there is the matter with your ankle.'

'Sprained it yesterday, old man. Nothing serious,' said Ukridge, reassuringly. 'Just enough to lay me up for a couple of days.'

'Yes, till that ghastly female and her blighted boy had got well away.'

Pained astonishment was written all over Ukridge's face.

'You don't mean to say you didn't like her? Why, I thought you two would be all over each other.'

'And I suppose you thought that Cecil and I would be twin souls?'

'Cecil?' said Ukridge, doubtfully. 'Well, to tell you the truth, old man, I'm not saying that Cecil doesn't take a bit of knowing. He's the sort of boy you have to be patient with and bring out, if you understand what I mean. I think he grows on you.'

534

'If he ever tries to grow on me, I'll have him amputated.'

'Well, putting all that on one side,' said Ukridge, 'how did things go off?'

I described the afternoon's activities in a few tense words.

'Well, I'm sorry, old horse,' said Ukridge, when I had finished. 'I can't say more than that, can I? I'm sorry. I give you my solemn word I didn't know what I was letting you in for. But it was a life and death matter. There was no other way out. Flossie insisted on it. Wouldn't budge an inch.'

In my anguish I had forgotten all about the impenetrable mystery of Flossie.

'Who the devil is Flossie?' I asked.

'What! Flossie? You don't know who Flossie is? My dear old man, collect yourself. You must remember Flossie. The barmaid at the Crown in Kennington. The girl Battling Billson is engaged to. Surely you haven't forgotten Flossie? Why, she was saying only yesterday that you had nice eyes.'

Memory awoke. I felt ashamed that I could ever have forgotten a girl so bounding and spectacular.

'Of course! The blister you brought with you that night George Tupper gave us dinner at the Regent Grill. By the way, has George ever forgiven you for that?'

'There is still a little coldness,' admitted Ukridge, ruefully. 'I'm bound to say old Tuppy seems to be letting the thing rankle a bit. He isn't a real friend like you. Delightful fellow, but lacks vision. Can't understand that there are certain occasions when it is simply imperative that a man's pals rally round him. Now you – '

'Well, I'll tell you one thing. I am hoping that what I went through this afternoon really was for some good cause. I should be sorry, now that I am in a cooler frame of mind, to have to strangle you where you lie. Would .

you mind telling me exactly what was the idea behind all this?'

'It's like this, laddie. Good old Billson blew in to see me the other day.'

'I met him down in the East End and he asked for your address.'

'Yes, he told me.'

'What's going on? Are you still managing him?'

'Yes. That's what he wanted to see me about. Apparently the contract has another year to run and he can't fix up anything without my OK. And he's just had an offer to fight a bloke called Alf Todd at the Universal.'

'That's a step up from Wonderland,' I said, for I had a solid respect for this Mecca of the boxing world. 'How much is he getting this time?'

'Two hundred quid.'

'Two hundred quid! But that's a lot for practically an unknown man.'

'Unknown man?' said Ukridge, hurt. 'What do you mean, unknown man? If you ask my opinion, I should say the whole pugilistic world is seething with excitement about old Billson. Literally seething. Didn't he slosh the middleweight champion?'

'Yes, in a rough-and-tumble in a back alley. And nobody saw him do it.'

'Well, these things get about.'

'But two hundred pounds!'

'A fleabite, laddie, a fleabite. You can take it from me that we shall be asking a lot more than a measly couple of hundred for our services pretty soon. Thousands, thousands! Still, I'm not saying it won't be something to be going on with. Well, as I say, old Billson came to me and said he had had this offer, and how about it? And when I realized that I was in halves, I jolly soon gave him my blessing and told him to go as far as he liked. So you can imagine how I felt when Flossie put her foot down like this.'

536

'Like what? About ten minutes ago when you started talking, you seemed to be on the point of explaining about Flossie. How does she come to be mixed up with the thing? What did she do?'

'Only wanted to stop the whole business, laddie, that was all. Just put the kybosh on the entire works. Said he mustn't fight!'

'Mustn't fight?'

'That was what she said. Just in that airy, careless way, as if the most stupendous issues didn't hang on his fighting as he had never fought before. Said – if you'll believe me, laddie; I shan't blame you if you don't – that she didn't want his looks spoiled.' Ukridge gazed at me with lifted eyebrows while he let this evidence of feminine perverseness sink in. 'His looks, old man! You got the word correctly? His looks! She didn't want his looks spoiled. Why, damme, he hasn't got any looks. There isn't any possible manner in which you could treat that man's face without improving it. I argued with her by the hour, but no, she couldn't see it. Avoid women, laddie, they have no intelligence.'

'Well, I'll promise to avoid Flossie's mother, if that'll satisfy you. How does she come into the thing?'

'Now, there's a woman in a million, my boy. She saved the situation. She came along at the eleventh hour and snatched your old friend out of the soup. It seems she has a habit of popping up to London at intervals, and Flossie, while she loves and respects her, finds that from ten minutes to a quarter of an hour of the old dear gives her the pip to such an extent that she's a nervous wreck for days.'

I felt my heart warm to the future Mrs Billson. Despite Ukridge's slurs, a girl, it seemed to me, of the soundest intelligence.

'So when Flossie told me – with tears in her eyes, poor girl – that Mother was due today, I had the inspiration of a lifetime. Said I would take her off her hands from

start to finish if she would agree to let Billson fight at
the Universal. Well, it shows you what family affection
is, laddie; she jumped at it. I don't mind telling you she
broke down completely and kissed me on both cheeks.
The rest, old horse, you know.'

'Yes. The rest I do know.'

'Never,' said Ukridge, solemnly, 'never, old son, till
the sands of the desert grow cold, shall I forget how you
have stood by me this day!'

'Oh, all right. I expect in about a week from now you
will be landing me with something equally foul.'

'Now, laddie – '

'When does this fight come off?'

'A week from tonight. I'm relying on you to be at my
side. Tense nervous strain, old man; shall want a pal to
see me through.'

'I wouldn't miss it for worlds. I'll give you dinner
before we go there, shall I?'

'Spoken like a true friend,' said Ukridge, warmly. 'And
on the following night I will stand you the banquet of
your life. A banquet which will ring down the ages. For,
mark you, laddie, I shall be in funds. In funds, my boy.'

'Yes, if Billson wins. What does he get if he loses?'

'Loses? He won't lose. How the deuce can he lose? I'm
surprised at you talking in that silly way when you've
seen him only a few days ago. Didn't he strike you as
being pretty fit when you saw him?'

'Yes, by Jove, he certainly did.'

'Well, then! Why, it looks to me as if the sea air had
made him tougher than ever. I've only just got my fingers
straightened out after shaking hands with him. He could
win the heavyweight championship of the world
tomorrow without taking his pipe out of his mouth. Alf
Todd,' said Ukridge, soaring to an impressive burst of
imagery, 'has about as much chance as a one-armed blind
man in a dark room trying to shove a pound of melted
butter into a wild cat's left ear with a red-hot needle.'

538

Although I knew several of the members, for one reason or another I had never been inside the Universal Sporting Club, and the atmosphere of the place when we arrived on the night of the fight impressed me a good deal. It was vastly different from Wonderland, the East End home of pugilism where I had witnessed the Battler make his *début*. There, a certain laxness in the matter of costume had been the prevailing note; here, white shirt-fronts gleamed on every side. Wonderland, moreover, had been noisy. Patrons of sport had so far forgotten themselves as to whistle through their fingers and shout badinage at distant friends. At the Universal one might have been in church. In fact, the longer I sat, the more ecclesiastical did the atmosphere seem to become. When we arrived, two acolytes in the bantam class were going devoutly through the ritual under the eye of the presiding minister, while a large congregation looked on in hushed silence. As we took our seats, this portion of the service came to an end and the priest announced that Nippy Coggs was the winner. A reverent murmur arose for an instant from the worshippers, Nippy Coggs disappeared into the vestry, and after a pause of a few minutes I perceived the familiar form of Battling Billson coming up the aisle.

There was no doubt about it, the Battler did look good. His muscles seemed more cable-like than ever, and a recent hair-cut had given a knobby, bristly appearance to his head which put him even more definitely than before in the class of those with whom the sensible man would not lightly quarrel. Mr Todd, his antagonist, who followed him a moment later, was no beauty – the almost complete absence of any division between his front hair and his eyebrows would alone have prevented him being that – but he lacked a certain *je ne sais quoi* which the Battler pre-eminently possessed. From the first instant of his appearance in the public eye our man was a warm favourite. There was a pleased flutter in the pews as he

539

took his seat, and I could hear whispered voices offering substantial bets on him.

'Six-round bout,' announced the *padre*. 'Battling Billson (Bermondsey) versus Alf Todd (Marylebone). Gentlemen will kindly stop smoking.'

The congregation relit their cigars and the fight began.

Bearing in mind how vitally Ukridge's fortunes were bound up in his protégé's success tonight, I was relieved to observe that Mr Todd opened the proceedings in a manner that seemed to offer little scope for any display of Battling Billson's fatal kindheartedness. I had not forgotten how at Wonderland our Battler, with the fight in hand, had allowed victory to be snatched from him purely through a sentimental distaste for being rough with his adversary, a man who had had a lot of trouble and had touched Mr Billson's heart thereby. Such a disaster was unlikely to occur tonight. It was difficult to see how anyone in the same ring with him could possibly be sorry for Alf Todd. A tender pity was the last thing his behaviour was calculated to rouse in the bosom of an opponent. Directly the gong sounded, he tucked away what little forehead Nature had given him beneath his fringe, breathed loudly through his nose, and galloped into the fray. He seemed to hold no bigoted views as to which hand it was best to employ as a medium of attack. Right or left, it was all one to Alf. And if he could not hit Mr Billson with his hands, he was perfectly willing, so long as the eye of authority was not too keenly vigilant, to butt him with his head. Broad-minded – that was Alf Todd.

Wilberforce Billson, veteran of a hundred fights on a hundred waterfronts, was not backward in joining the revels. In him Mr Todd found a worthy and willing playmate. As Ukridge informed me in a hoarse whisper while the vicar was reproaching Alf for placing an elbow where no elbow should have been, this sort of thing was as meat and drink to Wilberforce. It was just the kind of

warfare he had been used to all his life, and precisely the
sort most calculated to make him give of his best – a
dictum which was strikingly endorsed a moment later,
when, after some heated exchanges in which, generous
donor though he was, he had received more than he had
bestowed, Mr Todd was compelled to slither back and do
a bit of fancy side-stepping. The round came to an end
with the Battler distinctly leading on points, and so
spirited had it been that applause broke out in various
parts of the edifice.

The second round followed the same general lines as
the first. The fact that up to now he had been foiled in
his attempts to resolve Battling Billson into his
component parts had had no damping effect on Alf
Todd's ardour. He was still the same active, energetic
soul, never sparing himself in his efforts to make the
party go. There was a whole-hearted abandon in his rushes
which reminded one of a short-tempered gorilla trying
to get at its keeper. Occasionally some extra warmth on
the part of his antagonist would compel him to retire
momentarily into a clinch, but he always came out of it
as ready as ever to resume the argument. Nevertheless,
at the end of round two he was still a shade behind. Round
three added further points to the Battler's score, and at
the end of round four Alf Todd had lost so much ground
that the most liberal odds were required to induce
speculators to venture their cash on his chances.

And then the fifth round began, and those who a
minute before had taken odds of three to one on the
Battler and openly proclaimed the money as good as in
their pockets, stiffened in their seats or bent forward
with pale and anxious faces. A few brief moments back
it had seemed to them incredible that this sure thing
could come unstitched. There was only this round and
the next to go – a mere six minutes of conflict; and Mr
Billson was so far ahead on points that nothing but the
accident of his being knocked out could lose him

the decision. And you had only to look at Wilberforce
Billson to realize the absurdity of his being knocked out.
Even I, who had seen him go through the process at
Wonderland, refused to consider the possibility. If ever
there was a man in the pink, it was Wilberforce Billson.

But in boxing there is always the thousandth chance.
As he came out of his corner for round five, it suddenly
became plain that things were not well with our man.
Some chance blow in that last mêlée of round four must
have found a vital spot, for he was obviously in bad shape.
Incredible as it seemed, Battling Billson was groggy. He
shuffled rather than stepped; he blinked in a manner
damping to his supporters; he was clearly finding
increasing difficulty in foiling the boisterous attentions
of Mr Todd. Sibilant whispers arose; Ukridge clutched
my arm in an agonized grip; voices were offering to bet
on Alf; and in the Battler's corner, their heads peering
through the ropes, those members of the minor clergy
who had been told off to second our man were wan with
apprehension.

Mr Todd, for his part, was a new man. He had retired
to his corner at the end of the preceding round with the
moody step of one who sees failure looming ahead. 'I'm
always chasing rainbows,' Mr Todd's eye had seemed to
say as it rested gloomily on the resined floor. 'Another
dream shattered!' And he had come out for round five
with the sullen weariness of the man who has been
helping to amuse the kiddies at a children's party and
has had enough of it. Ordinary politeness rendered it
necessary for him to see this uncongenial business
through to the end, but his heart was no longer
in it.

And then, instead of the steel and india-rubber warrior
who had smitten him so sorely at their last meeting, he
found this sagging wreck. For an instant sheer surprise
seemed to shackle Mr Todd's limbs, then he adjusted
himself to the new conditions. It was as if somebody had

grafted monkey glands onto Alfred Todd. He leaped at
Battling Billson, and Ukridge's grip on my arm became
more painful than ever.

A sudden silence fell upon the house. It was a tense,
expectant silence, for affairs had reached a crisis. Against
the ropes near his corner the Battler was leaning, heedless
of the well-meant counsel of his seconds, and Alf Todd,
with his fringe now almost obscuring his eyes, was
feinting for an opening. There is a tide in the affairs of
men which, taken at the flood, leads on to fortune; and
Alf Todd plainly realized this. He fiddled for an instant
with his hands, as if he were trying to mesmerize Mr
Billson, then plunged forward.

A great shout went up. The congregation appeared to
have lost all sense of what place this was that they were
in. They were jumping up and down in their seats and
bellowing deplorably. For the crisis had been averted.
Somehow or other Wilberforce Billson had contrived to
escape from that corner, and now he was out in the
middle of the ring, respited.

And yet he did not seem pleased. His usually
expressionless face was contorted with pain and
displeasure. For the first time in the entire proceedings
he appeared genuinely moved. Watching him closely, I
could see his lips moving, perhaps in prayer. And as Mr
Todd, bounding from the ropes, advanced upon him, he
licked those lips. He licked them in a sinister meaning
way, and his right hand dropped slowly down below his
knee.

Alf Todd came on. He came jauntily and in the manner
of one moving to a feast or festival. This was the end of a
perfect day, and he knew it. He eyed Battling Billson as if
the latter had been a pot of beer. But for the fact that he
came of a restrained and unemotional race, he would
doubtless have burst into song. He shot out his left and
it landed on Mr Billson's nose. Nothing happened. He
drew back his right and poised it almost lovingly for a

moment. It was during this moment that Battling Billson came to life.

To Alf Todd it must have seemed like a resurrection. For the last two minutes he had been testing in every way known to science his theory that this man before him no longer possessed the shadow of a punch, and the theory had seemed proven up to the hilt. Yet here he was now behaving like an unleashed whirlwind. A disquieting experience. The ropes collided with the small of Alf Todd's back. Something else collided with his chin. He endeavoured to withdraw, but a pulpy glove took him on the odd fungoid growth which he was accustomed laughingly to call his ear. Another glove impinged upon his jaw. And there the matter ended for Alf Todd.

'Battling Billson is the winner,' intoned the vicar.

'Wow!' shouted the congregation.

'Whew!' breathed Ukridge in my ear.

It had been a near thing, but the old firm had pulled through at the finish.

Ukridge bounded off to the dressing-room to give his Battler a manager's blessing; and presently, the next fight proving something of an anti-climax after all the fevered stress of its predecessor, I left the building and went home. I was smoking a last pipe before going to bed when a violent ring at the front-door bell broke in on my meditations. It was followed by the voice of Ukridge in the hall.

I was a little surprised. I had not been expecting to see Ukridge again tonight. His intention when we parted at the Universal had been to reward Mr Billson with a bit of supper; and, as the Battler had a coy distaste for the taverns of the West End, this involved a journey to the far East, where in congenial surroundings the coming champion would drink a good deal of beer and eat more hard-boiled eggs than you would have believed possible. The fact that the host was now thundering up my stairs seemed

to indicate that the feast had fallen through. And the
fact that the feast had fallen through suggested that
something had gone wrong.

'Give me a drink, old horse,' said Ukridge, bursting
into the room.

'What on earth's the matter?'

'Nothing, old horse, nothing. I'm a ruined man, that's
all.'

He leaped feverishly at the decanter and siphon which
Bowles had placed upon the table. I watched him with
concern. This could be no ordinary tragedy that had
changed him thus from the ebullient creature of joy who
had left me at the Universal. A thought flashed through
my mind that Battling Billson must have been disqualified
– to be rejected a moment later, when I remembered that
fighters are not disqualified as an after-thought half an
hour after the fight. But what else could have brought
about this anguish? If ever there was an occasion for
solemn rejoicing, now would have seemed to be the
time.

'What's the matter?' I asked again.

'Matter? I'll tell you what's the matter,' moaned
Ukridge. He splashed seltzer into his glass. He reminded
me of King Lear. 'Do you know how much I get out of
that fight tonight? Ten quid! Just ten rotten
contemptible sovereigns! That's what's the matter.'

'I don't understand.'

'The purse was thirty pounds. Twenty for the winner.
My share is ten. Ten, I'll trouble you! What in the name
of everything infernal is the good of ten quid?'

'But you said Billson told you – '

'Yes, I know I did. Two hundred was what he told me
he was to get. And the weak-minded, furtive,
underhanded son of Belial didn't explain that he was to
get it for losing!'

'Losing?'

'Yes. He was to get it for losing. Some fellows who

545

wanted a chance to do some heavy betting persuaded
him to sell the fight.'

'But he didn't sell the fight.'

'I know that, dammit. That's the whole trouble. And
do you know why he didn't? I'll tell you. Just as he was
all ready to let himself be knocked out in that fifth round,
the other bloke happened to tread on his ingrowing
toenail, and that made him so mad that he forgot about
everything else and sailed in and hammered the stuffing
out of him. I ask you, laddie! I appeal to you as a reasonable
man. Have you ever in your life heard of such a footling,
idiotic, woollen-headed proceeding? Throwing away a
fortune, an absolute dashed fortune, purely to gratify
a momentary whim! Hurling away wealth beyond the
dreams of avarice simply because a bloke stamped on his
ingrowing toenail. His ingrowing toenail!' Ukridge
laughed raspingly. 'What right has a boxer to *have* an
ingrowing toenail? And if he has an ingrowing toenail,
surely – my gosh! – he can stand a little trifling
discomfort for half a minute. The fact of the matter is,
old horse, boxers aren't what they were. Degenerate,
laddie, absolutely degenerate. No heart. No courage. No
self-respect. No vision. The old bulldog breed has
disappeared entirely.'

And with a moody nod Stanley Featherstonehaugh
Ukridge passed out into the night.

Mr Mulliner

1 — Mulliner's Buck-U-Uppo

The village Choral Society had been giving a performance of Gilbert and Sullivan's *Sorcerer* in aid of the Church Organ Fund; and, as we sat in the window of the Anglers' Rest, smoking our pipes, the audience came streaming past us down the little street. Snatches of song floated to our ears, and Mr Mulliner began to croon in unison.

'"Ah me! I was a pa-ale you-oung curate then!",' chanted Mr Mulliner in the rather snuffling voice in which the amateur singer seems to find it necessary to render the old songs.

'Remarkable,' he said, resuming his natural tones, 'how fashions change, even in clergymen. There are very few pale young curates nowadays.'

'True,' I agreed. 'Most of them are beefy young fellows who rowed for their colleges. I don't believe I have ever seen a pale young curate.'

'You never met my nephew Augustine, I think?'

'Never.'

'The description in the song would have fitted him perfectly. You will want to hear all about my nephew Augustine.'

At the time of which I am speaking (said Mr Mulliner) my nephew Augustine was a curate, and very young and extremely pale. As a boy he had completely outgrown his strength, and I rather think at his Theological College some of the wilder spirits must have bullied him; for when he went to Lower Brisket-in-the-Midden to assist the vicar, the Rev. Stanley Brandon, in his cure of souls, he was as meek and mild a young man as you could meet

549

in a day's journey. He had flaxen hair, weak blue eyes, and the general demeanour of a saintly but timid cod-fish. Precisely, in short, the sort of young curate who seems to have been so common in the Eighties, or whenever it was that Gilbert wrote *The Sorcerer*.

The personality of his immediate superior did little or nothing to help him to overcome his native diffidence. The Rev. Stanley Brandon was a huge and sinewy man of violent temper, whose red face and glittering eyes might well have intimidated the toughest curate. The Rev. Stanley had been a heavyweight boxer at Cambridge, and I gather from Augustine that he seemed to be always on the point of introducing into debates on parish matters the methods which had made him so successful in the roped ring. I remember Augustine telling me that once, on the occasion when he had ventured to oppose the other's views in the matter of decorating the church for the Harvest Festival, he thought for a moment that the vicar was going to drop him with a right hook to the chin. It was some quite trivial point that had come up – a question as to whether the pumpkin would look better in the apse or the clerestory, if I recollect rightly – but for several seconds it seemed as if blood was about to be shed.

Such was the Rev. Stanley Brandon. And yet it was to the daughter of this formidable man that Augustine Mulliner had permitted himself to lose his heart. Truly, Cupid makes heroes of us all.

Jane was a very nice girl, and just as fond of Augustine as he was of her. But, as each lacked the nerve to go to the girl's father and put him abreast of the position of affairs, they were forced to meet surreptitiously. This jarred upon Augustine who, like all the Mulliners, loved the truth and hated any form of deception. And one evening, as they paced beside the laurels at the bottom of the vicarage garden, he rebelled.

'My dearest,' said Augustine, 'I can no longer brook

this secrecy. I shall go into the house immediately and ask your father for your hand.'

Jane paled and clung to his arm. She knew so well that it was not her hand but her father's foot which he would receive if he carried out this mad scheme.

'No, no, Augustine! You must not!'

'But, darling, it is the only straightforward course.'

'But not tonight. I beg of you, not tonight.'

'Why not?'

'Because father is in a very bad temper. He has just had a letter from the bishop, rebuking him for wearing too many orphreys on his chasuble, and it has upset him terribly. You see, he and the bishop were at school together, and father can never forget it. He said at dinner that if old Boko Bickerton thought he was going to order him about he would jolly well show him.'

'And the bishop comes here tomorrow for the Confirmation services!' gasped Augustine.

'Yes. And I'm so afraid they will quarrel. It's such a pity father hasn't some other bishop over him. He always remembers that he once hit this one in the eye for pouring ink on his collar, and this lowers his respect for his spiritual authority. So you won't go in and tell him tonight will you?'

'I will not,' Augustine assured her with a slight shiver.

'And you will be sure to put your feet in hot mustard and water when you get home? The dew has made the grass so wet.'

'I will indeed, dearest.'

'You are not strong, you know.'

'No, I am not strong.'

'You ought to take some really good tonic.'

'Perhaps I ought. Goodnight, Jane.'

'Goodnight, Augustine.'

The lovers parted. Jane slipped back into the vicarage, and Augustine made his way to his cosy rooms in the

High Street. And the first thing he noticed on entering was a parcel on the table, and beside it a letter.

He opened it listlessly, his thoughts far away.

'*My dear Augustine.*'

He turned to the last page and glanced at the signature. The letter was from his Aunt Angela, the wife of my brother, Wilfred Mulliner. You may remember that I once told you the story of how these two came together. If so, you will recall that my brother Wilfred was the eminent chemical researcher who had invented, among other specifics, such world-famous preparations as Mulliner's Raven Gipsy Face Cream and the Mulliner Snow of the Mountains Lotion. He and Augustine had never been particularly intimate, but between Augustine and his aunt there had always existed a warm friendship.

MY DEAR AUGUSTINE – [wrote Angela Mulliner] – I have been thinking so much about you lately, and I cannot forget that, when I saw you last, you seemed very fragile and deficient in vitamins. I do hope you take care of yourself.

I have been feeling for some time that you ought to take a tonic, and by a lucky chance Wilfred has just invented one which he tells me is the finest thing he has ever done. It is called Buck-U-Uppo, and acts directly on the red corpuscles. It is not yet on the market, but I have managed to smuggle a sample bottle from Wilfred's laboratory, and I want you to try it at once. I am sure it is just what you need.

Your affectionate aunt,

Angela Mulliner.

P. S. – You take a tablespoonful before going to bed, and another just before breakfast.

Augustine was not an unduly superstitious young man, but the coincidence of this tonic arriving so soon after Jane had told him that a tonic was what he needed affected him deeply. It seemed to him that this thing must have been meant. He shook the bottle, uncorked it, and, pouring out a liberal tablespoonful, shut his eyes and swallowed it.

The medicine, he was glad to find, was not unpleasant to the taste. It had a slightly pungent flavour, rather like old boot-soles beaten up in sherry. Having taken the dose, he read for a while in a book of theological essays, and then went to bed.

And as his feet slipped between the sheets, he was annoyed to find that Mrs Wardle, his housekeeper, had once more forgotten his hot-water bottle.

'Oh, dash!' said Augustine.

He was thoroughly upset. He had told the woman over and over again that he suffered from cold feet and could not get to sleep unless the dogs were properly warmed up. He sprang out of bed and went to the head of the stairs.

'Mrs Wardle!' he cried.

There was no reply.

'Mrs Wardle!' bellowed Augustine in a voice that rattled the window panes like a strong nor'-easter. Until tonight he had always been very much afraid of his housekeeper and had both walked and talked softly in her presence. But now he was conscious of a strange new fortitude. His head was singing a little, and he felt equal to a dozen Mrs Wardles.

Shuffling footsteps made themselves heard.

'Well, what is it now?' asked a querulous voice.

Augustine snorted.

'I'll tell you what it is now,' he roared. 'How many times have I told you always to put a hot-water bottle in my bed? You've forgotten it again, you old cloth-head!'

Mrs Wardle peered up, astounded and militant.

'Mr Mulliner, I am not accustomed – '

'Shut up!' thundered Augustine. 'What I want from you is less backchat and more hot-water bottles. Bring it up at once, or I leave tomorrow. Let me endeavour to get it into your concrete skull that you aren't the only person letting rooms in this village. Any more lip and I walk straight round the corner, where I'll be appreciated. Hot-water bottle ho! And look slippy about it.'

'Yes, Mr Mulliner. Certainly, Mr Mulliner. In one moment, Mr Mulliner.'

'Action! Action!' boomed Augustine. 'Show some speed. Put a little snap into it.'

'Yes, yes, most decidedly, Mr Mulliner,' replied the chastened voice from below.

An hour later, as he was dropping off to sleep, a thought crept into Augustine's mind. Had he not been a little brusque with Mrs Wardle? Had there not been in his manner something a shade abrupt – almost rude? Yes, he decided regretfully, there had. He lit a candle and reached for the diary which lay on the table at his bedside.

He made an entry.

The meek shall inherit the earth. Am I sufficiently meek? I wonder. This evening, when reproaching Mrs Wardle, my worthy housekeeper, for omitting to place a hot-water bottle in my bed, I spoke quite crossly. The provocation was severe, but still I was surely to blame for allowing my passions to run riot. Mem: Must guard agst. this.

But when he woke next morning, different feelings prevailed. He took his ante-breakfast dose of Buck-U-Uppo: and looking at the entry in the diary, could scarcely believe that it was he who had written it. 'Quite cross'? Of course he had been quite cross. Wouldn't anybody be quite cross who was for ever being persecuted by beetle-wits who forgot hot-water bottles?

Erasing the words with one strong dash of a thick-leaded pencil, he scribbled in the margin a hasty 'Mashed potatoes! Served the old idiot right!' and went down to breakfast.

He felt amazingly fit. Undoubtedly, in asserting that this tonic of his acted forcefully upon the red corpuscles, his Uncle Wilfred had been right. Until that moment Augustine had never supposed that he had any red corpuscles; but now, as he sat waiting for Mrs Wardle to bring him his fried egg, he could feel them dancing about all over him. They seemed to be forming rowdy parties and sliding down his spine. His eyes sparkled, and from sheer joy of living he sang a few bars from the hymn for those of riper years at sea.

He was still singing when Mrs Wardle entered with a dish.

'What's this?' demanded Augustine, eyeing it dangerously.

'A nice fried egg, sir.'

'And what, pray, do you mean by nice? It may be an amiable egg. It may be a civil, well-meaning egg. But if you think it is fit for human consumption, adjust that impression. Go back to your kitchen, woman; select another; and remember this time that you are a cook, not an incinerating machine. Between an egg that is fried and an egg that is cremated there is a wide and substantial difference. This difference, if you wish to retain me as a lodger in these far too expensive rooms, you will endeavour to appreciate.'

The glowing sense of well-being with which Augustine had begun the day did not diminish with the passage of time. It seemed, indeed, to increase. So full of effervescing energy did the young man feel that, departing from his usual custom of spending the morning crouched over the fire, he picked up his hat, stuck it at a rakish angle on his head, and sallied out for a healthy tramp across the fields.

It was while he was returning, flushed and rosy, that he observed a sight which is rare in the country districts of England – the spectacle of a bishop running. It is not often in a place like Lower Briskett-in-theMidden that you see a bishop at all; and when you do he is either riding in a stately car or pacing at a dignified walk. This one was sprinting like a Derby winner, and Augustine paused to drink in the sight.

The bishop was a large, burly bishop, built for endurance rather than speed; but he was making excellent going. He flashed past Augustine in a whirl of flying gaiters: and then, proving himself thereby no mere specialist but a versatile all-round athlete, suddenly dived for a tree and climbed rapidly into its branches. His motive, Augustine readily divined, was to elude a rough, hairy dog which was toiling in his wake. The dog reached the tree a moment after his quarry had climbed it, and stood there, barking.

Augustine strolled up.

'Having a little trouble with the dumb friend, bish?' he asked, genially.

The bishop peered down from his eyrie.

'Young man,' he said, 'save me!'

'Right most indubitably ho!' replied Augustine. 'Leave it to me.'

Until today he had always been terrified of dogs, but now he did not hesitate. Almost quicker than words can tell, he picked up a stone, discharged it at the animal, and whooped cheerily as it got home with a thud. The dog, knowing when he had had enough, removed himself at some forty-five mph; and the bishop, descending cautiously, clasped Augustine's hand in his.

'My preserver!' said the bishop.

'Don't give it another thought,' said Augustine, cheerily. 'Always glad to do a pal a good turn. We clergymen must stick together.'

'I thought he had me for a minute.'

'Quite a nasty customer. Full of rude energy.'

The bishop nodded.

'His eye was not dim, nor his natural force abated. Deuteronomy xxxiv. 7,' he agreed. 'I wonder if you can direct me to the vicarage? I fear I have come a little out of my way.'

'I'll take you there.'

'Thank you. Perhaps it would be as well if you did not come in. I have a serious matter to discuss with old Pieface – I mean, with the Rev. Stanley Brandon.'

'I have a serious matter to discuss with his daughter. I'll just hang about the garden.'

'You are a very excellent young man,' said the bishop, as they walked along. 'You are a curate, eh?'

'At present. But,' said Augustine, tapping his companion on the chest, 'just watch my smoke. That's all I ask you to do – just watch my smoke.'

'I will. You should rise to great heights – to the very top of the tree.'

'Like you did just now, eh? Ha, ha!'

'Ha, ha!' said the bishop. 'You young rogue!'

He poked Augustine in the ribs.

'Ha, ha, ha!' said Augustine.

He slapped the bishop on the back.

'But all joking aside,' said the bishop as they entered the vicarage grounds, 'I really shall keep my eye on you and see that you receive the swift preferment which your talents and character deserve. I say to you, my dear young friend, speaking seriously and weighing my words, that the way you picked that dog off with that stone was the smoothest thing I ever saw. And I am a man who always tells the strict truth.'

'Great is truth and mighty above all things. Esdras iv. 41,' said Augustine.

He turned away and strolled towards the laurel bushes, which were his customary meeting-place with Jane. The bishop went on to the front door and rang the bell.

Although they had made no definite appointment, Augustine was surprised when the minutes passed and no Jane appeared. He did not know that she had been told off by her father to entertain the bishop's wife that morning, and show her the sights of Lower Briskett-in-the-Midden. He waited some quarter of an hour with growing impatience, and was about to leave when suddenly from the house there came to his ears the sound of voices raised angrily.

He stopped. The voices appeared to proceed from a room on the ground floor facing the garden.

Running lightly over the turf, Augustine paused outside the window and listened. The window was open at the bottom, and he could hear quite distinctly.

The vicar was speaking in a voice that vibrated through the room.

'Is that so?' said the vicar.

'Yes, it is!' said the bishop.

'Ha, ha!'

'Ha, ha! to you, and see how you like it!' rejoined the bishop with spirit.

Augustine drew a step closer. It was plain that Jane's fears had been justified and that there was serious trouble afoot between these two old schoolfellows. He peeped in. The vicar, his hands behind his coat-tails, was striding up and down the carpet, while the bishop, his back to the fireplace, glared defiance at him from the hearthrug.

'Who ever told you you were an authority on chasubles?' demanded the vicar.

'That's all right who told me,' rejoined the bishop.

'I don't believe you know what a chasuble is.'

'Is that so?'

'Well, what is it, then?'

'It's a circular cloak hanging from the shoulders, elaborately embroidered with a pattern and with orphreys. And you can argue as much as you like, young Pieface, but you can't get away from the fact that there are too many orphreys on yours. And what I'm telling

you is that you've jolly well got to switch off a few of
these orphreys or you'll get it in the neck.'

The vicar's eyes glittered furiously.

'Is that so?' he said. 'Well, I just won't, so there! And
it's like your cheek coming here and trying to high-hat me.
You seem to have forgotten that I knew you when you
were an inky-faced kid at school, and that, if I liked, I could
tell the world one or two things about you which would
probably amuse it.'

'My past is an open book.'

'Is it?' The vicar laughed malevolently. 'Who put the
white mouse in the French master's desk?'

The bishop started.

'Who put jam in the dormitory prefect's bed?' he
retorted.

'Who couldn't keep his collar clean?'

'Who used to wear a dickey?' The bishop's wonderful
organ-like voice, whose softest whisper could be heard
throughout a vast cathedral, rang out in tones of thunder.
'Who was sick at the house supper?'

The vicar quivered from head to foot. His rubicund
face turned a deeper crimson.

'You know jolly well,' he said, in shaking accents, 'that
there was something wrong with the turkey. Might have
upset anyone.'

'The only thing wrong with the turkey was that you
ate too much of it. If you had paid as much attention to
developing your soul as you did to developing your
tummy, you might by now,' said the bishop, 'have risen
to my own eminence.'

'Oh, might I?'

'No, perhaps I am wrong. You never had the brain.'

The vicar uttered another discordant laugh.

'Brain is good! We know all about your eminence, as
you call it, and how you rose to that eminence.'

'What do you mean?'

'You are a bishop. How you became one we will not inquire.'

'What do you mean?'

'What I say. We will not inquire.'

'Why don't you inquire?'

'Because,' said the vicar, 'it is better not!'

The bishop's self-control left him. His face contorted with fury, he took a step forward. And simultaneously Augustine sprang lightly into the room.

'Now, now, now!' said Augustine. 'Now, now, now, now, now!'

The two men stood transfixed. They stared at the intruder dumbly.

'Come, come!' said Augustine.

The vicar was the first to recover. He glowered at Augustine.

'What do you mean by jumping through my window?' he thundered. 'Are you a curate or a harlequin?'

Augustine met his gaze with an unfaltering eye.

'I am a curate,' he replied, with a dignity that well became him. 'And, as a curate, I cannot stand by and see two superiors of the cloth, who are moreover old schoolfellows, forgetting themselves. It isn't right. Absolutely not right, my old superiors of the cloth.'

The vicar bit his lip. The bishop bowed his head.

'Listen,' proceeded Augustine, placing a hand on the shoulder of each. 'I hate to see you two dear good chaps quarrelling like this.'

'He started it,' said the vicar, sullenly.

'Never mind who started it.' Augustine silenced the bishop with a curt gesture as he made to speak. 'Be sensible, my dear fellows. Respect the decencies of debate. Exercise a little good-humoured give-and-take. You say,' he went on, turning to the bishop, 'that our good friend here has too many orphreys on his chasuble?'

'I do. And I stick to it.'

'Yes, yes, yes. But what,' said Augustine, soothingly,

'are a few orphreys between friends? Reflect! You and
our worthy vicar here were at school together. You are
bound by the sacred ties of the old Alma Mater. With
him you sported on the green. With him you shared
a crib and threw inked darts in the hour supposed to be
devoted to the study of French. Do these things mean
nothing to you? Do these memories touch no chord?'
He turned appealingly from one to the other. 'Vicar!
Bish!'

The vicar had moved away and was wiping his eyes.
The bishop fumbled for a pocket-handkerchief. There
was a silence.

'Sorry, Pieface,' said the bishop, in a choking voice.

'Shouldn't have spoken as I did, Boko,' mumbled the
vicar.

'If you want to know what I think,' said the bishop,
'you are right in attributing your indisposition at the
house supper to something wrong with the turkey. I
recollect saying at the time that the bird should never
have been served in such a condition.'

'And when you put that white mouse in the French
master's desk,' said the vicar, 'you performed one of the
noblest services to humanity of which there is any record.
They ought to have made you a bishop on the spot.'

'Pieface!'

'Boko!'

The two men clasped hands.

'Splendid!' said Augustine. 'Everything hotsy-totsy
now?'

'Quite, quite,' said the vicar.

'As far as I am concerned, completely hotsy-totsy,' said
the bishop. He turned to his old friend solicitously. 'You
will continue to wear all the orphreys you want – will
you not, Pieface?'

'No, no. I see now that I was wrong. From now on,
Boko, I abandon orphreys altogether.'

'But, Pieface – '

561

'It's all right,' the vicar assured him. 'I can take them or leave them alone.'

'Splendid fellow!' The bishop coughed to hide his emotion, and there was another silence. 'I think, perhaps,' he went on, after a pause, 'I should be leaving you now, my dear chap, and going in search of my wife. She is with your daughter, I believe, somewhere in the village.'

'They are coming up the drive now.'

'Ah, yes, I see them. A charming girl, your daughter.'

Augustine clapped him on the shoulder.

'Bish,' he exclaimed, 'you said a mouthful. She is the dearest, sweetest girl in the whole world. And I should be glad, vicar, if you would give your consent to our immediate union. I love Jane with a good man's fervour, and I am happy to inform you that my sentiments are returned. Assure us, therefore, of your approval, and I will go at once and have the banns put up.'

The vicar leaped as though he had been stung. Like so many vicars, he had a poor opinion of curates, and he had always regarded Augustine as rather below than above the general norm or level of the despised class.

'What!' he cried.

'A most excellent idea,' said the bishop, beaming. 'A very happy notion, I call it.'

'My daughter!' The vicar seemed dazed. 'My daughter marry a curate.'

'You were a curate once yourself, Pieface.'

'Yes, but not a curate like that.'

'No!' said the bishop. 'You were not. Nor was I. Better for us both had we been. This young man, I would have you know, is the most outstandingly excellent young man I have ever encountered. Are you aware that scarcely an hour ago he saved me with the most consummate address from a large shaggy dog with black spots and a kink in his tail? I was sorely pressed, Pieface, when this young man came up and, with a readiness of resource and an accuracy of aim which it would be impossible to over-praise, got that dog in the short ribs with a rock and sent him flying.'

The vicar seemed to be struggling with some powerful emotion. His eyes had widened.

'A dog with black spots?'

'Very black spots. But no blacker, I fear, than the heart they hid.'

'And he really plugged him in the short ribs?'

'As far as I could see, squarely in the short ribs.'

The vicar held out his hand.

'Mulliner,' he said, 'I was not aware of this. In the light of the facts which have just been drawn to my attention, I have no hesitation in saying that my objections are removed. I have had it in for that dog since the second Sunday before Septuagesima, when he pinned me by the ankle as I paced beside the river composing a sermon on Certain Alarming Manifestations of the So-called Modern Spirit. Take Jane. I give my consent freely. And may she be as happy as any girl with such a husband ought to be.'

A few more affecting words were exchanged, and then the bishop and Augustine left the house. The bishop was silent and thoughtful.

'I owe you a great deal, Mulliner,' he said at length.

'Oh, I don't know,' said Augustine. 'Would you say that?'

'A very great deal. You saved me from a terrible disaster. Had you not leaped through that window at that precise juncture and intervened, I really believe I should have pasted my dear old friend Brandon in the eye. I was sorely exasperated.'

'Our good vicar can be trying at times,' agreed Augustine.

'My fist was already clenched, and I was just hauling off for the swing when you checked me. What the result would have been, had you not exhibited a tact and discretion beyond your years, I do not like to think. I might have been unfrocked.' He shivered at the thought, though the weather was mild. 'I could never have shown my face at the Athenaeum again. But, tut, tut!' went on the bishop, patting Augustine on the shoulder, 'let us not dwell on what might have been. Speak to me of yourself. The vicar's charming daughter – you really love her?'

'I do, indeed.'

The bishop's face had grown grave.

'Think well, Mulliner,' he said. 'Marriage is a serious affair. Do not plunge into it without due reflection. I myself am a husband, and, though singularly blessed in the possession of a devoted helpmeet, cannot but feel sometimes that a man is better off as a bachelor. Women, Mulliner, are odd.'

'True,' said Augustine.

'My own dear wife is the best of women. And, as I never weary of saying, a good woman is a wondrous creature, cleaving to the right and the good under all change; lovely in youthful comeliness, lovely all her life in comeliness of heart. And yet – '

'And yet?' said Augustine.

The bishop mused for a moment. He wriggled a little with an expression of pain, and scratched himself between the shoulder blades.

'Well, I'll tell you,' said the bishop. 'It is a warm and pleasant day today, is it not?'

'Exceptionally clement,' said Augustine.

'A fair, sunny day, made gracious by a temperate westerly breeze. And yet, Mulliner, if you will credit my statement, my wife insisted on my putting on my thick winter woollies this morning. Truly,' sighed the bishop, 'as a jewel of gold in a swine's snout, so is a fair woman which is without discretion. Proverbs xi. 21.'

'Twenty-two,' corrected Augustine.

'I should have said twenty-two. They are made of thick

flannel, and I have an exceptionally sensitive skin. Oblige me, my dear fellow, by rubbing me in the small of the back with the ferrule of your stick. I think it will ease the irritation.'

'But, my poor dear old Bish,' said Augustine, sympathetically, 'this must not be.'

The bishop shook his head ruefully.

'You would not speak so hardily, Mulliner, if you knew my wife. There is no appeal from her decrees.'

'Nonsense,' cried Augustine, cheerily. He looked through the trees to where the lady bishopess, escorted by Jane, was examining a lobelia through her lorgnette with just the right blend of cordiality and condescension. 'I'll fix that for you in a second.'

The bishop clutched at his arm.

'My boy! What are you going to do?'

'I'm just going to have a word with your wife and put the matter up to her as a reasonable woman. Thick winter woollies on a day like this! Absurd!' said Augustine. 'Preposterous! I never heard such rot.'

The bishop gazed after him with a laden heart. Already he had come to love this young man like a son: and to see him charging so lightheartedly into the very jaws of destruction afflicted him with a deep and poignant sadness. He knew what his wife was like when even the highest in the land attempted to thwart her; and this brave lad was but a curate. In another moment she would be looking at him through her lorgnette: and England was littered with the shrivelled remains of curates at whom the lady bishopess had looked through her lorgnette. He had seen them wilt like salted slugs at the episcopal breakfast-table.

He held his breath. Augustine had reached the lady bishopess, and the lady bishopess was even now raising her lorgnette.

The bishop shut his eyes and turned away. And then – years afterwards, it seemed to him – a cheery voice

hailed him: and, turning, he perceived Augustine
bounding back through the trees.

'It's all right, bish,' said Augustine.

'All – all right?' faltered the bishop.

'Yes. She says you can go and change into the thin
cashmere.'

The bishop reeled.

'But – but – but what did you say to her? What
arguments did you employ?'

'Oh, I just pointed out what a warm day it was and
jollied her along a bit – '

'Jollied her along a bit!'

'And she agreed in the most friendly and cordial
manner. She has asked me to call at the Palace one of
these days.'

The bishop seized Augustine's hand.

'My boy,' he said in a broken voice, 'you shall do more
than call at the Palace. You shall come and live at the
Palace. Become my secretary, Mulliner, and name your
own salary. If you intend to marry, you will require an
increased stipend. Become my secretary, boy, and never
leave my side. I have needed somebody like you for
years.'

It was late in the afternoon when Augustine returned to
his rooms, for he had been invited to lunch at the vicarage
and had been the life and soul of the cheery little party.

'A letter for you, sir,' said Mrs Wardle, obsequiously.

Augustine took the letter.

'I am sorry to say I shall be leaving you shortly, Mrs
Wardle.'

'Oh, sir! If there's anything I can do – '

'Oh, it's not that. The fact is, the bishop has made me
his secretary, and I shall have to shift my toothbrush
and spats to the Palace, you see.'

'Well, fancy that, sir! Why, you'll be a bishop yourself
one of these days.'

'Possibly,' said Augustine. 'Possibly. And now let me read this.'

He opened the letter. A thoughtful frown appeared on his face as he read.

MY DEAR AUGUSTINE – I am writing in some haste to tell you that the impulsiveness of your aunt has led to a rather serious mistake.

She tells me that she dispatched to you yesterday by parcels post a sample bottle of my new Buck-U-Uppo, which she obtained without my knowledge from my laboratory. Had she mentioned what she was intending to do, I could have prevented a very unfortunate occurrence.

Mulliner's Buck-U-Uppo is of two grades or qualities – the A and the B. The A is a mild, but strengthening, tonic designed for human invalids. The B, on the other hand, is purely for circulation in the animal kingdom, and was invented to fill a long-felt want throughout our Indian possessions.

As you are doubtless aware, the favourite pastime of the Indian Maharajahs is the hunting of the tiger of the jungle from the backs of elephants; and it has happened frequently in the past that hunts have been spoiled by the failure of the elephant to see eye to eye with its owner in the matter of what constitutes sport.

Too often elephants, on sighting the tiger, have turned and galloped home: and it was to correct this tendency on their part that I invented Mulliner's Buck-U-Uppo B. One teaspoonful of the Buck-U-Uppo B administered in its morning bran-mash will cause the most timid elephant to trumpet loudly and charge the fiercest tiger without a qualm.

Abstain, therefore, from taking any of the contents of the bottle you now possess,

>   And believe me,
>   Your affectionate uncle,
>   Wilfred Mulliner.

Augustine remained for some time in deep thought after perusing this communication. Then, rising, he whistled a few bars of the psalm appointed for the twenty-sixth of June and left the room.

Half an hour later a telegraphic message was speeding over the wires.

It ran as follows:

>   Wilfred Mulliner,
>   The Gables,
>   Lesser Lossingham,
>   Salop.
>
>   Letter received. Send immediately, COD, three cases of the B. 'Blessed shall be thy basket and thy store' Deuteronomy xxviii 5.
>   Augustine.

2 — The Rise of Minna Nordstrom

They had been showing the latest Minna Nordstrom
picture at the Bijou Dream in the High Street, and Miss
Postlethwaite, our sensitive barmaid, who had attended
the première, was still deeply affected. She snuffled
audibly as she polished the glasses.

'It's really good, is it?' we asked, for in the bar-parlour
of the Anglers' Rest we lean heavily on Miss
Postlethwaite's opinion where the silver screen is
concerned. Her verdict can make or mar.

''Swonderful,' she assured us. 'It lays bare for all to
view the soul of a woman who dared everything for love.
A poignant and uplifting drama of life as it is lived today,
purifying the emotions with pity and terror.'

A Rum and Milk said that if it was as good as all that
he didn't know but what he might not risk ninepence on
it. A Sherry and Bitters wondered what they paid a woman
like Minna Nordstrom. A Port from the Wood, raising
the conversation from the rather sordid plane to which it
threatened to sink, speculated on how motion-picture stars
became stars.

'What I mean,' said the Port from the Wood, 'does a
studio deliberately set out to create a star? Or does it
suddenly say to itself "Hullo, here's a star. What ho!"?'

One of those cynical Dry Martinis who always know
everything said that it was all a question of influence.

'If you looked into it, you would find this Nordstrom
girl was married to one of the bosses.'

Mr Mulliner, who had been sipping his hot Scotch and
Lemon in a rather *distrait* way, glanced up.

'Did I hear you mention the name Minna Nordstrom?'

'We were arguing about how she became a star. I was saying that she must have had a pull of some kind.'

'In a sense,' said Mr Mulliner, 'you are right. She did have a pull. But it was one due solely to her own initiative and resource. I have relatives and connections in Hollywood, as you know, and I learn much of the inner history of the studio world through these channels. I happen to know that Minna Nordstrom raised herself to her present eminence by sheer enterprise and determination. If Miss Postlethwaite will mix me another hot Scotch and Lemon, this time stressing the Scotch a little more vigorously, I shall be delighted to tell you the whole story.'

When people talk with bated breath in Hollywood – and it is a place where there is always a certain amount of breath-bating going on – you will generally find, said Mr Mulliner, that the subject of their conversation is Jacob Z. Schnellenhamer, the popular president of the Perfecto-Zizzbaum Corporation. For few names are more widely revered there than that of this Napoleonic man.

Ask for an instance of his financial acumen, and his admirers will point to the great merger for which he was responsible – that merger by means of which he combined his own company, the Colossal-Exquisite, with those two other vast concerns, the Perfecto-Fishbein and the Zizzbaum-Celluloid. Demand proof of his artistic genius, his flair for recognizing talent in the raw, and it is given immediately. He was the man who discovered Minna Nordstrom.

Today when interviewers bring up the name of the world-famous star in Mr Schnellenhamer's presence, he smiles quietly.

'I had long had my eye on the little lady,' he says, 'but for one reason and another I did not consider the time ripe for her *début*. Then I brought about what you are good enough to call the epoch-making merger, and I was enabled to take the decisive step. My colleagues questioned the wisdom of elevating a totally unknown girl to stardom, but I was firm. I saw that it was the only thing to be done.'

'You had vision?'

'I had vision.'

All that Mr Schnellenhamer had, however, on the evening when this story begins was a headache. As he returned from the day's work at the studio and sank wearily into an armchair in the sitting-room of his luxurious home in Beverly Hills, he was feeling that the life of the president of a motion-picture corporation was one that he would hesitate to force on any dog of which he was fond.

A morbid meditation, of course, but not wholly unjustified. The great drawback to being the man in control of a large studio is that everybody you meet starts acting at you. Hollywood is entirely populated by those who want to get into the pictures, and they naturally feel that the best way of accomplishing their object is to catch the boss's eye and do their stuff.

Since leaving home that morning Mr Schnellenhamer had been acted at practically incessantly. First, it was the studio watchman who, having opened the gate to admit his car, proceeded to play a little scene designed to show what he would do in a heavy role. Then came his secretary, two book agents, the waitress who brought him his lunch, a life insurance man, a representative of a film weekly, and a barber. And, on leaving at the end of the day, he got the watchman again, this time in whimsical comedy.

Little wonder, then, that by the time he reached home the magnate was conscious of a throbbing sensation about the temples and an urgent desire for a restorative.

As a preliminary to obtaining the latter, he rang the bell and Vera Prebble, his parlourmaid, entered. For a moment he was surprised not to see his butler. Then he

recalled that he had dismissed him just after breakfast
for reciting 'Gunga Din' in a meaning way while bringing
the eggs and bacon.

'You rang, sir?'

'I want a drink.'

'Very good, sir.'

The girl withdrew, to return a few moments later with
a decanter and siphon. The sight caused Mr
Schnellenhamer's gloom to lighten a little. He was proud
of his cellar, and he knew that the decanter contained
liquid balm. In a sudden gush of tenderness he eyed its
bearer appreciatively, thinking what a nice girl she
looked.

Until now he had never studied Vera Prebble's
appearance to any great extent or thought about her
much in any way. When she had entered his employment
a few days before, he had noticed, of course, that she
had a sort of ethereal beauty; but then every girl you see
in Hollywood has either ethereal beauty or roguish
gaminerie or a dark, slumbrous face that hints at hidden
passion.

'Put it down there on the small table,' said Mr
Schnellenhamer, passing his tongue over his lips.

The girl did so. Then, straightening herself, she
suddenly threw her head back and clutched the sides of
it in an ecstasy of hopeless anguish.

'Oh! Oh! Oh!' she cried.

'Eh?' said Mr Schnellenhamer.

'Ah! Ah! Ah!'

'I don't get you at all,' said Mr Schnellenhamer.

She gazed at him with wide, despairing eyes.

'If you knew how sick and tired I am of it all! Tired . . .
Tired . . . Tired. The lights . . . the glitter . . . the gaiety
. . . It is so hollow, so fruitless. I want to get away from it
all, ha-ha-ha-ha-ha!'

Mr Schnellenhamer retreated behind the chesterfield.
That laugh had had an unbalanced ring. He had not liked

572

it. He was about to continue his backward progress in the direction of the door, when the girl, who had closed her eyes and was rocking to and fro as if suffering from some internal pain, became calmer.

'Just a little thing I knocked together with a view to showing myself in a dramatic role,' she said. 'Watch! I'm going to register.'

She smiled. 'Joy.'

She closed her mouth. 'Grief.'

She wiggled her ears. 'Horror.'

She raised her eyebrows. 'Hate.'

Then, taking a parcel from the tray:

'Here,' she said, 'if you would care to glance at them, are a few stills of myself. This shows my face in repose. I call it "Reverie". This is me in a bathing suit . . . riding . . . walking . . . happy among my books . . . being kind to the dog. Here is one of which my friends have been good enough to speak in terms of praise – as Cleopatra, the warrior-queen of Egypt, at the Pasadena Gas-Fitters' Ball. It brings out what is generally considered my most effective feature – the nose, seen sideways.'

During the course of these remarks, Mr Schnellenhamer had been standing breathing heavily. For a while the discovery that this parlourmaid, of whom he had just been thinking so benevolently, was simply another snake in the grass had rendered him incapable of speech. Now his aphasia left him.

'Get out!' he said.

'Pardon?' said the girl.

'Get out this minute. You're fired.'

There was a silence. Vera Prebble closed her mouth, wiggled her ears, and raised her eyebrows. It was plain that she was grieved, horror-stricken, and in the grip of a growing hate.

'What,' she demanded passionately at length, 'is the matter with all you movie magnates? Have you no hearts? Have you no compassion? No sympathy? No understanding? Do the ambitions of the struggling mean nothing to you?'

'No,' replied Mr Schnellenhamer in answer to all five questions.

Vera Prebble laughed bitterly.

'No is right!' she said. 'For months I besieged the doors of the casting directors. They refused to cast me. Then I thought that if I could find a way into your homes I might succeed where I had failed before. I secured the post of parlourmaid to Mr Fishbein of the Perfecto-Fishbein. Half-way through Rudyard Kipling's "Boots" he brutally bade me begone. I obtained a similar position with Mr Zizzbaum of the Zizzbaum-Celluloid. The opening lines of "The Wreck of the *Hesperus*" had hardly passed my lips when he was upstairs helping me pack my trunk. And now you crush my hopes. It is cruel . . . cruel . . . Oh, ha-ha-ha-ha-ha!'

She rocked to and fro in an agony of grief. Then an idea seemed to strike her.

'I wonder if you would care to see me in light comedy? . . . No? . . . Oh, very well.'

With a quick droop of the eyelids and a twitch of the muscles of the cheeks she registered resignation.

'Just as you please,' she said. Then her nostrils quivered and she bared the left canine tooth to indicate Menace. 'But one last word. Wait!'

'How do you mean, wait?'

'Just wait. That's all.'

For an instant Mr Schnellenhamer was conscious of a twinge of uneasiness. Like all motion-picture magnates, he had about forty-seven guilty secrets, many of them recorded on paper. Was it possible that . . .

Then he breathed again. All his private documents were in a safe-deposit box. It was absurd to imagine that this girl could have anything on him.

Relieved, he lay down on the chesterfield and gave himself up to daydreams. And soon, as he remembered that that morning he had put through a deal which would enable him to trim the stuffing out of two hundred and seventy-three exhibitors, his lips curved in a contented smile and Vera Prebble was forgotten.

One of the advantages of life in Hollywood is that the Servant problem is not a difficult one. Supply more than equals demand. Ten minutes after you have thrown a butler out of the back door his successor is bowling up in his sports-model car. And the same applies to parlourmaids. By the following afternoon all was well once more with the Schnellenhamer domestic machine. A new butler was cleaning the silver: a new parlourmaid was doing whatever parlourmaids do, which is very little. Peace reigned in the home.

But on the second evening, as Mr Schnellenhamer, the day's tasks over, entered his sitting-room with nothing in his mind but bright thoughts of dinner, he was met by what had all the appearance of a human whirlwind. This was Mrs Schnellenhamer. A graduate of the silent films, Mrs Schnellenhamer had been known in her day as the Queen of Stormy Emotion, and she occasionally saw to it that her husband was reminded of this.

'Now see what!' cried Mrs Schnellenhamer.

Mr Schnellenhamer was perturbed.

'Is something wrong?' he asked nervously.

'Why did you fire that girl, Vera Prebble?'

'She went ha-ha-ha-ha-ha at me.'

'Well, do you know what she has done? She has laid information with the police that we are harbouring alcoholic liquor on our premises, contrary to law, and this afternoon they came in a truck and took it all away.'

Mr Schnellenhamer reeled. The shock was severe. The good man loves his cellar.

'Not all?' he cried, almost pleadingly.

'All.'

'The Scotch?'

'Every bottle.'

'The gin?'

'Every drop.'

Mr Schnellenhamer supported himself against the chesterfield.

'Not the champagne?' he whispered.

'Every case. And here we are, with a hundred and fifty people coming tonight, including the Duke.'

Her allusion was to the Duke of Wigan, who, as so many British dukes do, was at this time passing slowly through Hollywood.

'And you know how touchy dukes are,' proceeded Mrs Schnellenhamer. 'I'm told that the Lulabelle Mahaffys invited the Duke of Kircudbrightshire for the weekend last year, and after he had been there two months he suddenly left in a huff because there was no brown sherry.'

A motion-picture magnate has to be a quick thinker. Where a lesser man would have wasted time referring to the recent Miss Prebble as a serpent whom he had to all intents and purposes nurtured in his bosom, Mr Schnellenhamer directed the whole force of his great brain on the vital problem of how to undo the evil she had wrought.

'Listen,' he said. 'It's all right. I'll get the bootlegger on the phone, and he'll have us stocked up again in no time.'

But he had overlooked the something in the air of Hollywood which urges its every inhabitant irresistibly into the pictures. When he got his bootlegger's number, it was only to discover that that life-saving tradesman was away from home. They were shooting a scene in *Sundered Hearts* on the Outstanding Screen-Favourites lot, and the bootlegger was hard at work there, playing the role of an Anglican bishop. His secretary said he could not be disturbed, as it got him all upset to be interrupted when he was working.

Mr Schellenhamer tried another bootlegger, then another. They were out on location.

And it was just as he had begun to despair that he bethought him of his old friend, Isadore Fishbein; and into his darkness there shot a gleam of hope. By the greatest good fortune it so happened that he and the president of the Perfecto-Fishbein were at the moment on excellent terms, neither having slipped anything over on the other for several weeks. Mr Fishbein, moveover, possessed as well-stocked a cellar as any man in California. It would be a simple matter to go round and borrow from him all he needed.

Patting Mrs Schnellenhamer's hand and telling her that there were still bluebirds singing in the sunshine, he ran to his car and leaped into it.

The residence of Isadore Fishbein was only a few hundred yards away, and Mr Schnellenhamer was soon whizzing in through the door. He found his friend beating his head against the wall of the sitting-room and moaning to himself in a quiet undertone.

'Is something the matter?' he asked, surprised.

'There is,' said Mr Fishbein, selecting a fresh spot on the tapestried wall and starting to beat his head against that. 'The police came round this afternoon and took away everything I had.'

'Everything?'

'Well, not Mrs Fishbein,' said the other, with a touch of regret in his voice. 'She's up in the bedroom with eight cubes of ice on her forehead in a linen bag. But they took every drop of everything else. A serpent, that's what she is.'

'Mrs Fishbein?'

'Not Mrs Fishbein. That parlourmaid. That Vera Prebble. Just because I stopped her when she got to "boots, boots, boots, boots, marching over Africa" she ups and informs the police on me. And Mrs Fishbein with a hundred and eighty people coming tonight, including the ex-King of Ruritania!'

And, crossing the room, the speaker began to bang his head against a statue of Genius Inspiring the Motion-Picture Industry.

A good man is always appalled when he is forced to contemplate the depths to which human nature can sink, and Mr Schnellenhamer's initial reaction on hearing of this fresh outrage on the part of his late parlourmaid was a sort of sick horror. Then the brain which had built up the Colossal-Exquisite began to work once more.

'Well, the only thing for us to do,' he said, 'is to go round to Ben Zizzbaum and borrow some of his stock. How do you stand with Ben?'

'I stand fine with Ben,' said Mr Fishbein, cheering up. 'I heard something about him last week which I'll bet he wouldn't care to have known.'

'Where does he live?'

'Camden Drive.'

'Then tally-ho!' said Mr Schnellenhamer, who had once produced a drama in eight reels of two strong men battling for a woman's love in the English hunting district.

They were soon at Mr Zizzbaum's address. Entering the sitting-room, they were shocked to observe a form rolling in circles round the floor with its head between its hands. It was travelling quickly, but not so quickly that they were unable to recognize it as that of the chief executive of the Zizzbaum-Celluloid Corporation. Stopped as he was completing his eleventh lap and pressed for an explanation, Mr Zizzbaum revealed that a recent parlourmaid of his, Vera Prebble by name, piqued at having been dismissed for deliberate and calculated reciting of the works of Mrs Hemans, had informed the police of his stock of wines and spirits and that the latter had gone off with the whole collection not half an hour since.

'And don't speak so loud,' added the stricken man, 'or

you'll wake Mrs Zizzbaum. She's in bed with ice on her head.'

'How many cubes?' asked Mr Fishbein.

'Six.'

'Mrs Fishbein needed eight,' said that lady's husband a little proudly.

The situation was one that might well have unmanned the stoutest motion-picture executive and there were few motion-picture executives stouter than Jacob Schnellenhamer. But it was characteristic of this man that the tightest corner was always the one to bring out the full force of his intellect. He thought of Mrs Schnellenhamer waiting for him at home, and it was as if an electric shock of high voltage had passed through him.

'I've got it,' he said. 'We must go to Glutz of the Medulla-Oblongata. He's never been a real friend of mine, but if you loan him Stella Svelte and I loan him Orlando Byng and Fishbein loans him Oscar the Wonder-Poodle on his own terms, I think he'll consent to give us enough to see us through tonight. I'll get him on the phone.'

It was some moments before Mr Schnellenhamer returned from the telephone booth. When he did so, his associates were surprised to observe in his eyes a happy gleam.

'Boys,' he said, 'Glutz is away with his family over the weekend. The butler and the rest of the help are out joy-riding. There's only a parlourmaid in the house. I've been talking to her. So there won't be any need for us to give him those stars, after all. We'll just run across in the car with a few axes and help ourselves. It won't cost us above a hundred dollars to square this girl. She can tell him she was upstairs when the burglars broke in and didn't hear anything. And there we'll be, with all the stuff we need and not a cent to pay outside of overhead connected with the maid.'

There was an awed silence.

'Mrs Fishbein will be pleased.'

'Mrs Zizzbaum will be pleased.'

'And Mrs Schnellenhamer will be pleased,' said the leader of the expedition. 'Where do you keep your axes, Zizzbaum?'

'In the cellar.'

'Fetch 'em!' said Mr Schnellenhamer in the voice a Crusader might have used in giving the signal to start against the Paynim.

In the ornate residence of Sigismund Glutz, meanwhile, Vera Prebble, who had entered the service of the head of the Medulla-Oblongata that morning and was already under sentence of dismissal for having informed him with appropriate gestures that a bunch of the boys were whooping it up in the Malemute saloon, was engaged in writing on a sheet of paper a short list of names, one of which she proposed as a *nom de théâtre* as soon as her screen career should begin.

For this girl was essentially an optimist, and not even all the rebuffs which she had suffered had been sufficient to quench the fire of ambition in her.

Wiggling her tongue as she shaped the letters, she wrote:

> Ursuline Delmaine
> Theodora Trix
> Uvula Gladwyn

None of them seemed to her quite what she wanted. She pondered. Possibly something a little more foreign and exotic . . .

> Greta Garbo

No, that had been used . . .

And then suddenly inspiration descended upon her and, trembling a little with emotion, she inscribed on the paper the one name that was absolutely and indubitably right.

Minna Nordstrom

The more she looked at it, the better she liked it. And she was still regarding it proudly when there came the sound of a car stopping at the door and a few moments later in walked Mr Schnellenhamer, Mr Zizzbaum and Mr Fishbein. They all wore Homburg hats and carried axes.

Vera Prebble drew herself up.

'All goods must be delivered in the rear,' she had begun haughtily, when she recognized her former employers and paused, surprised.

The recognition was mutual. Mr Fishbein started. So did Mr Zizzbaum.

'Serpent! said Mr Fishbein.

'Viper!' said Mr Zizzbaum.

Mr Schnellenhamer was more diplomatic. Though as deeply moved as his colleagues by the sight of this traitoress, he realized that this was no time for invective.

'Well, well, well,' he said, with a geniality which he strove to render frank and winning, 'I never dreamed it was you on the phone, my dear. Well, this certainly makes everything nice and smooth – us all being, as you might say, old friends.'

'Friends?' retorted Vera Prebble. 'Let me tell you . . .'

'I know, I know. Quite, quite. But listen. I've got to have some liquor tonight.'

'What do you mean, *you* have?' said Mr Fishbein.

'It's all right, it's all right,' said Mr Schnellenhamer soothingly. 'I was coming to that. I wasn't forgetting you. We're all in this together. The good old spirit of cooperation. You see, my dear,' he went on, 'that little joke you played on us . . . oh, I'm not blaming you. Nobody laughed more heartily than myself . . .'

'Yes, they did,' said Mr Fishbein, alive now to the fact that this girl before him must be conciliated. 'I did.'

'So did I,' said Mr Zizzbaum.

'We all laughed very heartily,' said Mr Schnellenhamer. 'You should have heard us. A girl of spirit, we said to ourselves. Still, the little pleasantry has left us in something of a difficulty, and it will be worth a hundred dollars to you, my dear, to go upstairs and put cotton wool in your ears while we get at Mr Glutz's cellar door with our axes.'

Vera Prebble raised her eyebrows.

'What do you want to break down the cellar door for? I know the combination of the lock.'

'You do?' said Mr Schnellenhamer joyfully.

'I withdraw that expression "Serpent",' said Mr Fishbein.

'When I used the term "Viper",' said Mr Zizzbaum, 'I was speaking thoughtlessly.'

'And I will tell it you,' said Vera Prebble, 'at a price.'

She drew back her head and extended an arm, twiddling the fingers at the end of it. She was plainly registering something, but they could not discern what it was.

'There is only one condition on which I will tell you the combination of Mr Glutz's cellar, and that is this. One of you has got to give me a starring contract for five years.'

The magnates started.

'Listen,' said Mr Zizzbaum, 'you don't want to star.'

'You wouldn't like it,' said Mr Fishbein.

'Of course you wouldn't,' said Mr Schnellenhamer. 'You would look silly, starring – an inexperienced girl like you. Now, if you had said a nice small part . . .'

'Star.'

'Or featured . . .'

'Star.'

The three men drew back a pace or two and put their heads together.

'She means it,' said Mr Fishbein.

'Her eyes,' said Mr Zizzbaum. 'Like stones.'

'A dozen times I could have dropped something heavy on that girl's head from an upper landing, and I didn't do it,' said Mr Schnellenhamer remorsefully.

Mr Fishbein threw up his hands.

'It's no use. I keep seeing that vision of Mrs Fishbein floating before me with eight cubes of ice on her head. I'm going to star this girl.'

'*You are?*' said Mr Zizzbaum. 'And get the stuff? And leave me to go home and tell Mrs Zizzbaum there won't be anything to drink at her party tonight for a hundred and eleven guests including the Vice-President of Switzerland? No, sir! *I* am going to star her.'

'I'll outbid you.'

'You won't outbid *me*. Not till they bring me word that Mrs Zizzbaum has lost the use of her vocal cords.'

'Listen,' said the other tensely. 'When it comes to using vocal cords, Mrs Fishbein begins where Mrs Zizzbaum leaves off.'

Mr Schnellenhamer, that cool head, saw the peril that loomed.

'Boys,' he said, 'if we once start bidding against one another, there'll be no limit. There's only one thing to be done. We must merge.'

His powerful personality carried the day. It was the President of the newly-formed Perfecto-Zizzbaum Corporation who a few moments later stepped forward and approached the girl.

'We agree.'

And, as he spoke, there came the sound of some heavy vehicle stopping in the road outside. Vera Prebble uttered a stricken exclamation.

'Well, of all the silly girls!' she cried distractedly. 'I've just remembered that an hour ago I telephoned the police, informing them of Mr Glutz's cellar. And here they are!'

Mr Fishbein uttered a cry, and began to look round for something to bang his head against. Mr Zizzbaum gave a short, sharp moan, and started to lower himself to the floor. But Mr Schnellenhamer was made of sterner stuff.

'Pull yourselves together, boys,' he begged them. 'Leave all this to me. Everything is going to be all right. Things have come to a pretty pass,' he said, with a dignity as impressive as it was simple, 'if a free-born American citizen cannot bribe the police of his native country.'

'True,' said Mr Fishbein, arresting his head when within an inch and a quarter of a handsome Oriental vase.

'True, true,' said Mr Zizzbaum, getting up and dusting his knees.

'Just let me handle the whole affair,' said Mr Schnellenhamer. 'Ah, boys!' he went on, genially.

Three policemen had entered the room – a sergeant, a patrolman, and another patrolman. Their faces wore a wooden, hard-boiled look.

'Mr Glutz?' said the sergeant.

'Mr Schnellenhamer,' corrected the great man. 'But Jacob to you, old friend.'

The sergeant seemed in no wise mollified by this amiability.

'Prebble, Vera?' he asked, addressing the girl.

'Nordstrom, Minna,' she replied.

'Got the name wrong, then. Anyway, it was you who phoned us that there was alcoholic liquor on the premises?'

Mr Schnellenhamer laughed amusedly.

'You mustn't believe everything that girl tells you, sergeant. She's a great kidder. Always was. If she said that, it was just one of her little jokes. I know Glutz. I know his views. And many is the time I have heard him say that the laws of his country are good enough for him and that he would scorn not to obey them. You will find nothing here, sergeant.'

'Well, we'll try,' said the other. 'Show us the way to the cellar,' he added, turning to Vera Prebble.

Mr Schnellenhamer smiled a winning smile.

'Now listen,' he said. 'I've just remembered I'm wrong. Silly mistake to make, and I don't know how I made it. There *is* a certain amount of the stuff in the house, but I'm sure you dear chaps don't want to cause any unpleasantness. You're broad-minded. Listen. Your name's Murphy, isn't it?'

'Donahue.'

'I thought so. Well, you'll laugh at this. Only this morning I was saying to Mrs Schnellenhamer that I must really slip down to headquarters and give my old friend Donahue that ten dollars I owed him.'

'What ten dollars?'

'I didn't say ten. I said a hundred. One hundred dollars, Donny, old man, and I'm not saying there mightn't be a little over for these two gentlemen here. How about it?'

The sergeant drew himself up. There was no sign of softening in his glance.

'Jacob Schnellenhamer,' he said coldly, 'you can't square me. When I tried for a job at the Colossal-Exquisite last spring I was turned down on account you said I had no sex appeal.'

The first patrolman, who had hitherto taken no part in the conversation, started.

'Is that so, Chief?'

'Yessir. No sex appeal.'

'Well, can you tie that!' said the first patrolman. 'When I tried to crash the Colossal-Exquisite, they said my voice wasn't right.'

'Me,' said the second patrolman, eyeing Mr Schnellenhamer sourly, 'they had the nerve to beef at my left profile. Lookut, boys,' he said, turning, 'can you see anything wrong with that profile?'

His companions studied him closely. The sergeant

raised a hand and peered between his fingers with his head tilted back and his eyes half closed.

'Not a thing,' he said.

'Why, Basil, it's a lovely profile,' said the first patrolman.

'Well, that's how it goes,' said the second patrolman moodily.

The sergeant had returned to his own grievance.

'No sex appeal!' he said with a rasping laugh. 'And me that had specially taken sex appeal in the College of Eastern Iowa course of Motion Picture acting.'

'Who says my voice ain't right?' demanded the first patrolman. 'Listen. Mi-mi-mi-mi-mi.'

'Swell,' said the sergeant.

'Like a nightingale or something,' said the second patrolman.

The sergeant flexed his muscles.

'Ready, boys?'

'Kayo, Chief.'

'Wait!' cried Mr Schnellenhamer. 'Wait! Give me one more chance. I'm sure I can find parts for you all.'

The sergeant shook his head.

'No. It's too late. You've got us mad now. You don't appreciate the sensitiveness of the artist. Does he, boys?'

'You're darned right he doesn't,' said the first patrolman.

'I wouldn't work for the Colossal-Exquisite now,' said the second patrolman with a petulant twitch of his shoulder, 'not if they wanted me to play Romeo opposite Jean Harlow.'

'Then let's go,' said the sergeant. 'Come along, lady, you show us where this cellar is.'

For some moments after the officers of the Law, preceded by Vera Prebble, had left, nothing was to be heard in the silent sitting-room but the rhythmic beating of Mr Fishbein's head against the wall and the rustling sound of Mr Zizzbaum rolling round the floor. Mr

Schnellenhamer sat brooding with his chin in his hands, merely moving his legs slightly each time Mr Zizzbaum came round. The failure of his diplomatic efforts had stunned him.

A vision rose before his eyes of Mrs Schnellenhamer waiting in their sunlit patio for his return. As clearly as if he had been there now, he could see her, swooning, slipping into the goldfish pond, and blowing bubbles with her head beneath the surface. And he was asking himself whether in such an event it would be better to raise her gently or just leave Nature to take its course. She would, he knew, be extremely full of that stormy emotion of which she had once been queen.

It was as he still debated this difficult point that a light step caught his ear. Vera Prebble was standing in the doorway.

'Mr Schnellenhamer.'

The magnate waved a weary hand.

'Leave me,' he said. 'I am thinking.'

'I thought you would like to know,' said Vera Prebble, 'that I've just locked those cops in the coal cellar.'

As in the final reel of a super-super-film eyes brighten and faces light up at the entry of the United States Marines, so at these words did Mr Schnellenhamer, Mr Fishbein and Mr Zizzbaum perk up as if after a draught of some magic elixir.

'In the coal cellar?' gasped Mr Schnellenhamer.

'In the coal cellar.'

'Then if we work quick . . .'

Vera Prebble coughed.

'One moment,' she said. 'Just one moment. Before you go, I have drawn up a little letter covering our recent agreement. Perhaps you will all three just sign it.'

Mr Schnellenhamer clicked his tongue impatiently.

'No time for that now. Come to my office tomorrow. Where are you going?' he asked, as the girl started to withdraw.

'Just to the coal cellar,' said Vera Prebble. 'I think those fellows may want to come out.'

Mr Schnellenhamer sighed. It had been worth trying, of course, but he had never really had much hope.

'Gimme,' he said resignedly.

The girl watched as the three men attached their signatures. She took the document and folded it carefully.

'Would any of you like to hear me recite "The Bells", by Edgar Allan Poe?' she asked.

'No!' said Mr Fishbein.

'No!' said Mr Zizzbaum.

'No!' said Mr Schnellenhamer. 'We have no desire to hear you recite "The Bells", Miss Prebble.'

The girl's eyes flashed haughtily.

'Miss Nordstrom,' she corrected. 'And just for that you'll get "The Charge of the Light Brigade", and like it.'

3 — The Nodder

The presentation of the super film, *Baby Boy*, at the Bijou
Dream in the High Street, had led to an animated
discussion in the bar-parlour of the Anglers' Rest. Several
of our prominent first-nighters had dropped in there for
much-needed restorative after the performance, and the
conversation had turned to the subject of child stars in
the motion-pictures.

'I understand they're all midgets, really,' said a Rum
and Milk.

'That's what I heard, too,' said a Whisky and Splash.
'Somebody told me that at every studio in Hollywood
they have a special man who does nothing but go round
the country, combing the circuses, and when he finds a
good midget he signs him up.'

Almost automatically we looked at Mr Mulliner, as if
seeking from that unfailing fount of wisdom an
authoritative pronouncement on this difficult point. The
Sage of the bar-parlour sipped his hot Scotch and Lemon
for a moment in thoughtful silence.

'The question you have raised,' he said at length, 'is
one that has occupied the minds of thinking men ever
since these little excrescences first became popular on
the screen. Some argue that mere children would scarcely
be so loathsome. Others maintain that a right-minded
midget would hardly stoop to some of the things these
child stars do. But, then, arising from that, we have to ask
ourselves: Are midgets right-minded? The whole thing
is very moot.'

'Well, this kid we saw tonight,' said the Rum and Milk.

'This Johnny Bingley. Nobody's going to tell me he's only eight years old.'

'In the case of Johnny Bingley,' assented Mr Mulliner, 'your intuition has not led you astray. I believe he is in the early forties. I happen to know all about him because it was he who played so important a part in the affairs of my distant connection, Wilmot.'

'Was your distant connection Wilmot a midget?'

'No. He was a Nodder.'

'A what?'

Mr Mulliner smiled.

'It is not easy to explain to the lay mind the extremely intricate ramifications of the personnel of a Hollywood motion-picture organization. Putting it as briefly as possible, a Nodder is something like a Yes-Man, only lower in the social scale. A Yes-Man's duty is to attend conferences and say "Yes". A Nodder's, as the name implies, is to nod. The chief executive throws out some statement of opinion, and looks about him expectantly. This is the cue for the senior Yes-Man to say yes. He is followed, in order of precedence, by the second Yes-Man – or Vice-Yesser, as he is sometimes called – and the junior Yes-Man. Only when all the Yes-Men have yessed, do the Nodders begin to function. They nod.'

A Pint of Half-and-Half said it didn't sound much of a job.

Not very exalted (agreed Mr Mulliner). It is a position which you might say, roughly, lies socially somewhere in between that of the man who works the wind machine and that of a writer of additional dialogue. There is also a class of Untouchables who are known as Nodders' assistants, but this is a technicality with which I need not trouble you. At the time when my story begins, my distant connection Wilmot was a full Nodder. Yet, even so, there is no doubt that he was aiming a little high when he ventured to aspire to the hand of Mabel Potter, the private secretary of Mr Schnellenhamer, the head of the Perfecto-Zizzbaum Corporation.

Indeed, between a girl so placed and a man in my distant connection's position there could in ordinary circumstances scarcely have been anything in the nature of friendly intercourse. Wilmot owed his entry to her good graces to a combination of two facts – the first, that in his youth he had been brought up on a farm and so was familiar with the customs and habits of birds; the second, that before coming to Hollywood, Miss Potter had been a bird-imitator in vaudeville.

Too little has been written of vaudeville bird-imitators and their passionate devotion to their art: but everybody knows the saying, Once a Bird-Imitator, Always a Bird-Imitator. The Mabel Potter of today might be a mere lovely machine for taking notes and tapping out her employer's correspondence, but within her there still burned the steady flame of those high ideals which always animate a girl who has once been accustomed to render to packed houses the liquid notes of the cuckoo, the whip-poor-will, and other songsters who are familiar to you all.

That this was so was revealed to Wilmot one morning when, wandering past an outlying set, he heard raised voices within and, recognizing the silver tones of his adored one, paused to listen. Mabel Potter seemed to be having some kind of an argument with a director.

'Considering,' she was saying, 'that I only did it to oblige and that it is in no sense a part of my regular duties for which I draw my salary, I must say . . .'

'All right, all right,' said the director.

' . . . that you have a nerve calling me down on the subject of cuckoos. Let me tell you, Mr Murgatroyd, that I have made a lifelong study of cuckoos and know them from soup to nuts. I have imitated cuckoos in every

theatre on every circuit in the land. Not to mention
urgent offers from England, Australia and . . .'

'I know, I know,' said the director.

' . . . South Africa, which I was compelled to turn down
because my dear mother, then living, disliked ocean
travel. My cuckoo is world-famous. Give me time to go
home and fetch it and I'll show you the clipping from
the *St Louis Post-Democrat* which says . . .'

'I know, I know, I know,' said the director, 'but, all the
same, I think I'll have somebody do it who'll do it my
way.'

The next moment Mabel Potter had swept out, and
Wilmot addressed her with respectful tenderness.

'Is something the matter, Miss Potter? Is there
anything I can do?'

Mabel Potter was shaking with dry sobs. Her self-
esteem had been rudely bruised.

'Well, look,' she said. 'They ask me as a special favour
to come and imitate the call of the cuckoo for this new
picture, and when I do it Mr Murgatroyd says I've done it
wrong.'

'The hound,' breathed Wilmot.

'He says a cuckoo goes Cuckoo, Cuckoo, when
everybody who has studied the question knows that what
it really goes is Wuckoo, Wuckoo.'

'Of course. Not a doubt about it. A distinct "W"
sound.'

'As if it had got something wrong with the roof of its
mouth.'

'Or had omitted to have its adenoids treated.'

'Wuckoo, Wuckoo . . . Like that.'

'Exactly like that,' said Wilmot.

The girl gazed at him with a new friendliness.

'I'll bet you've heard rafts of cuckoos.'

'Millions. I was brought up on a farm.'

'These know-it-all directors make me tired.'

'Me, too,' said Wilmot. Then, putting his fate to the

touch, to win or lose it all, 'I wonder, Miss Potter, if you would care to step round to the commissary and join me in a small coffee?'

She accepted gratefully, and from that moment their intimacy may be said to have begun. Day after day, in the weeks that followed, at such times as their duties would permit, you would see them sitting together either in the commissary or on the steps of some Oriental palace on the outskirts of the lot; he gazing silently up into her face; she, an artist's enthusiasm in her beautiful eyes, filling the air with the liquid note of the Baltimore oriole or possibly the more strident cry of the African buzzard. While ever and anon, by special request, she would hitch up the muscles of the larynx and go 'Wuckoo, Wuckoo'.

But when at length Wilmot, emboldened, asked her to be his wife, she shook her head.

'No,' she said. 'I like you, Wilmot. Sometimes I even think that I love you. But I can never marry a mere serf.'

'A what was that?'

'A serf. A peon. A man who earns his living by nodding his head at Mr Schnellenhamer. A Yes-Man would be bad enough, but a Nodder!'

She paused, and Wilmot, from sheer force of habit, nodded.

'I am ambitious,' proceeded Mabel. 'The man I marry must be a king among men . . . well, what I mean, at least a supervisor. Rather than wed a Nodder, I would starve in the gutter.'

The objection to this as a practical policy was, of course, that, owing to the weather being so uniformly fine all the year round, there are no gutters in Hollywood. But Wilmot was too distressed to point this out. He uttered a heart-stricken cry not unlike the mating-call of the Alaskan wild duck and began to plead with her. But she was not to be moved.

'We will always be friends,' she said, 'but marry a
Nodder, no.'

And with a brief 'Wuckoo' she turned away.

There is not much scope or variety of action open to a
man whose heart has been shattered and whose romance
has proved an empty dream. Practically speaking, only
two courses lie before him. He can go out West and begin
a new life, or he can drown his sorrow in drink. In Wilmot's
case, the former of these alternatives was rendered
impossible by the fact that he was out West already. Little
wonder, then, that as he sat in his lonely lodging that
night his thoughts turned ever more and more insistently
to the second.

Like all the Mulliners, my distant connection Wilmot
had always been a scrupulously temperate man. Had his
love-life but run smoothly, he would have been amply
contented with a nut sundae or a malted milk after the
day's work. But now, with desolation staring him in
the face, he felt a fierce urge toward something with a bit
more kick in it.

About half-way down Hollywood Boulevard, he knew,
there was a place where, if you knocked twice and
whistled 'My Country, 'tis of thee', a grille opened and a
whiskered face appeared. The Face said 'Well?' and you
said 'Service and Co-operation', and then the door was
unbarred and you saw before you the primrose path that
led to perdition. And as this was precisely what, in his
present mood, Wilmot most desired to locate, you will
readily understand how it came about that, some hour
and a half later, he was seated at a table in this
establishment, feeling a good deal better.

How long it was before he realized that his table had
another occupant he could not have said. But came a
moment when, raising his glass, he found himself looking
into the eyes of a small child in a Lord Fauntleroy
costume, in whom he recognized none other than Little

Johnny Bingley, the Idol of American Motherhood – the star of this picture, *Baby Boy*, which you, gentlemen, have just been witnessing at the Bijou Dream in the High Street.

To say that Wilmot was astonished at seeing this infant in such surroundings would be to overstate the case. After half an hour at this home-from-home the customer is seldom in a condition to be astonished at anything – not even a gamboge elephant in golfing costume. He was, however, sufficiently interested to say 'Hullo.'

'Hullo,' replied the child. 'Listen,' he went on, placing a cube of ice in his tumbler, 'don't tell old Schnellenhamer you saw me here. There's a morality clause in my contract.'

'Tell who?' said Wilmot.

'Schnellenhamer.'

'How do you spell it?'

'I don't know.'

'Nor do I,' said Wilmot. 'Nevertheless, be that as it may,' he continued, holding out his hand impulsively, 'he shall never learn from me.'

'Who won't?' said the child.

'He won't,' said Wilmot.

'Won't what?' asked the child.

'Learn from me,' said Wilmot.

'Learn what?' enquired the child.

'I've forgotten,' said Wilmot.

They sat for a space in silence, each busy with his own thoughts.

'You're Johnny Bingley, aren't you?' said Wilmot.

'Who is?' said the child.

'You are.'

'I'm what?'

'Listen,' said Wilmot. 'My name's Mulliner. That's what it is. Mulliner. And let them make the most of it.'

'Who?'

'I don't know,' said Wilmot.

595

He gazed at his companion affectionately. It was a little difficult to focus him, because he kept flickering, but Wilmot could take the big, broad view about that. If the heart is in the right place, he reasoned, what does it matter if the body flickers?

'You're a good chap, Bingley.'

'So are you, Mulliner.'

'Both good chaps?'

'Both good chaps.'

'Making two in all?' asked Wilmot, anxious to get this straight.

'That's how I work it out.'

'Yes, two,' agreed Wilmot, ceasing to twiddle his fingers. 'In fact, you might say both gentlemen.'

'Both gentlemen is correct.'

'Then let us see what we have got. Yes,' said Wilmot, as he laid down the pencil with which he had been writing figures on the tablecloth. 'Here are the final returns, as I get them. Two good chaps, two gentlemen. And yet,' he said, frowning in a puzzled way, 'that seems to make four, and there are only two of us. However,' he went on, 'let that go. Immaterial. Not germane to the issue. The fact we have to face, Bingley, is that my heart is heavy.'

'You don't say!'

'I do say. Heavy, Hearty. My bing is heavy.'

'What's the trouble?'

Wilmot decided to confide in this singularly sympathetic infant. He felt he had never met a child he liked better.

'Well, it's like this.'

'What is?'

'This is.'

'Like what?'

'I'm telling you. The girl I love won't marry me.'

'She won't?'

'So she says.'

'Well, well,' said the child star commiseratingly. 'That's too bad. Spurned your love, did she?'

'You're dern tooting she spurned my love,' said Wilmot. 'Spurned it good and hard. Some spurning!'

'Well, that's how it goes,' said the child star. 'What a world!'

'You're right, what a world.'

'I shouldn't wonder if it didn't make your heart heavy.'

'You bet it makes my heart heavy,' said Wilmot, crying softly. He dried his eyes on the edge of the tablecloth. 'How can I shake off this awful depression?' he asked.

The child star reflected.

'Well, I'll tell you,' he said. 'I know a better place than this one. It's out Venice way. We might give it a try.'

'We certainly might,' said Wilmot.

'And then there's another one down at Santa Monica.'

'We'll go there, too,' said Wilmot. 'The great thing is to keep moving about and seeing new scenes and fresh faces.'

'The faces are always nice and fresh down at Venice.'

'Then let's go,' said Wilmot.

It was eleven o'clock on the following morning that Mr Schnellenhamer burst in upon his fellow-executive, Mr Levitsky, with agitation written on every feature of his expressive face. The cigar trembled between his lips.

'Listen!' he said. 'Do you know what?'

'Listen!' said Mr Levitsky. 'What?'

'Johnny Bingley has just been in to see me.'

'If he wants a raise of salary, talk about the Depression.'

'Raise of salary? What's worrying me is how long is he going to be worth the salary he's getting.'

'Worth it?' Mr Levitsky stared. 'Johnny Bingley? The Child With The Tear Behind The Smile? The Idol Of American Motherhood?'

'Yes, and how long is he going to be the idol of American Motherhood after American Motherhood

597

finds out he's a midget from Connolly's Circus, and an
elderly, hardboiled midget, at that?'

'Well, nobody knows that but you and me.'

'Is that so?' said Mr Schnellenhamer. 'Well, let me tell
you, he was out on a toot last night with one of my
Nodders, and he comes to me this morning and says he
couldn't actually swear he told this guy he was a midget,
but, on the other hand, he rather thinks he must have
done. He says that between the time they were thrown
out of Mike's Place and the time he stabbed the waiter
with the pickle-fork there's a sort of gap in his memory,
a kind of blur, and he thinks it may have been then,
because by that time they had got pretty confidential
and he doesn't think he would have had any secrets from
him.'

All Mr Levitsky's nonchalance had vanished.

'But if this fellow – what's his name?'

'Mulliner.'

'If this fellow Mulliner sells this story to the Press,
Johnny Bingley won't be worth a nickel to us. And his
contract calls for two more pictures at two hundred and
fifty thousand each.'

'That's right.'

'But what are we to do?'

'You tell me.'

Mr Levitsky pondered.

'Well, first of all,' he said, 'we'll have to find out if this
Mulliner really knows.'

'We can't ask him.'

'No, but we'll be able to tell by his manner. A fellow
with a stranglehold on the Corporation like that isn't
going to be able to go on acting same as he's always done.
What sort of fellow is he?'

'The ideal Nodder,' said Mr Schnellenhamer
regretfully. 'I don't know when I've had a better. Always
on his cues. Never tries to alibi himself by saying he had

a stiff neck. Quiet . . . Respectful . . . What's that word
that begins with a "d"?'

'Damn?'

'Deferential. And what's the word beginning with an
"o"?'

'Oyster?'

'Obsequious. That's what he is. Quiet, respectful,
deferential and obsequious – that's Mulliner.'

'Well, then it'll be easy to see. If we find him suddenly
not being all what you said . . . if he suddenly ups and
starts to throw his weight about, understand what I mean
. . . why, then we'll know that he knows that Little
Johnny Bingley is a midget.'

'And then?'

'Why, then we'll have to square him. And do it right,
too. No half-measures.'

Mr Schnellenhamer tore at his hair. He seemed
disappointed that he had no straws to stick in it.

'Yes,' he agreed, the brief spasm over, 'I suppose it's
the only way. Well, it won't be long before we know.
There's a story-conference in my office at noon, and he'll
be there to nod.'

'We must watch him like a lynx.'

'Like a what?'

'Lynx. Sort of wild-cat. It watches things.'

'Ah,' said Mr Schnellenhamer, 'I get you now. What
confused me at first was that I thought you meant golf-
links.'

The fears of two magnates, had they but known it, were
quite without foundation. If Wilmot Mulliner had ever
learned the fatal secret, he had certainly not remembered
it next morning. He had woken that day with a confused
sense of having passed through some soul-testing
experience, but as regarded details his mind was a blank.
His only thought as he entered Mr Schnellenhamer's

office for the conference was a rooted conviction that, unless he kept very still, his head would come apart in the middle.

Nevertheless, Mr Schnellenhamer, alert for significant and sinister signs, plucked anxiously at Mr Levitsky's sleeve.

'Look!'

'Eh?'

'Did you see that?'

'See what?'

'That fellow Mulliner. He sort of quivered when he caught my eye, as if with unholy glee.'

'He did?'

'It seemed to me he did.'

As a matter of fact, what had happened was that Wilmot, suddenly sighting his employer, had been unable to restrain a quick shudder of agony. It seemed to him that somebody had been painting Mr Schnellenhamer yellow. Even at the best of times, the President of the Perfecto-Zizzbaum, considered as an object for the eye, was not everybody's money. Flickering at the rims and a dull orange in colour, as he appeared to be now, he had smitten Wilmot like a blow, causing him to wince like a salted snail.

Mr Levitsky was regarding the young man thoughtfully.

'I don't like his looks,' he said.

'Nor do I,' said Mr Schnellenhamer.

'There's a kind of horrid gloating in his manner.'

'I noticed it, too.'

'See how he's just buried his head in his hands, as if he were thinking out dreadful plots?'

'I believe he knows everything.'

'I shouldn't wonder if you weren't right. Well, let's start the conference and see what he does when the time comes for him to nod. That's when he'll break out, if he's going to.'

As a rule, these story-conferences were the part of his work which Wilmot most enjoyed. His own share in them was not exacting, and, as he often said, you met such interesting people.

Today, however, though there were eleven of the studio's weirdest authors present, each well worth more than a cursory inspection, he found himself unable to overcome the dull listlessness which had been gripping him since he had first gone to the refrigerator that morning to put ice on his temples. As the poet Keats put it in his 'Ode to a Nightingale', his head ached and a drowsy numbness pained his sense. And the sight of Mabel Potter, recalling to him those dreams of happiness which he had once dared to dream and which now could never come to fulfilment, plunged him still deeper into the despondency. If he had been a character in a Russian novel, he would have gone and hanged himself in the barn. As it was, he merely sat staring before him and keeping perfectly rigid.

Most people, eyeing him, would have been reminded of a corpse which had been several days in the water: but Mr Schnellenhamer thought he looked like a leopard about to spring, and he mentioned this to Mr Levitsky in an undertone.

'Bend down. I want to whisper.'

'What's the matter?'

'He looks to me just like a crouching leopard.'

'I beg your pardon,' said Mabel Potter, who, her duty being to take notes of the proceedings, was seated at her employer's side. 'Did you say "crouching leopard" or "grouchy shepherd"?'

Mr Schnellenhamer started. He had forgotten the risk of being overheard. He felt that he had been incautious.

'Don't put that down,' he said. 'It wasn't part of the conference. Well, now, come on, come on,' he proceeded, with a pitiful attempt at the bluffness which he used at conferences, 'let's get at it. Where did we leave off yesterday, Miss Potter?'

Mabel consulted her notes.

'Cabot Delancy, a scion of an old Boston family, has gone to try to reach the North Pole in a submarine, and he's on an iceberg, and the scenes of his youth are passing before his eyes.'

'What scenes?'

'You didn't get to what scenes.'

'Then that's where we begin,' said Mr Schnellenhamer. 'What scenes pass before this fellow's eyes?'

One of the authors, a weedy young man in spectacles, who had come to Hollywood to start a Gyffte Shoppe and had been scooped up in the studio's drag-net and forced into the writing-staff much against his will, said why not a scene where Cabot Delancy sees himself dressing his window with kewpie-dolls and fancy notepaper.

'Why kewpie-dolls?' asked Mr Schnellenhamer testily.

The author said they were a good selling line.

'Listen!' said Mr Schnellenhamer brusquely. 'This Delancy never sold anything in his life. He's a millionaire. What we want is something romantic.'

A diffident old gentleman suggested a polo-game.

'No good,' said Mr Schnellenhamer. 'Who cares anything about polo? When you're working on a picture you've got to bear in mind the small-town population of the Middle West. Aren't I right?'

'Yes,' said the senior Yes-Man.

'Yes,' said the Vice-Yesser.

'Yes,' said the junior Yes-Man.

And all the Nodders nodded. Wilmot, waking with a start to the realization that duty called, hurriedly inclined his throbbing head. The movement made him feel as if a red-hot spike had been thrust through it, and he winced. Mr Levitsky plucked at Mr Schnellenhamer's sleeve.

'He scowled!'

'I thought he scowled, too.'

'As it might be with sullen hate.'

'That's the way it struck me. Keep watching him.'

The conference proceeded. Each of the authors put forward a suggestion, but it was left for Mr Schnellenhamer to solve what had begun to seem an insoluble problem.

'I've got it,' said Mr Schnellenhamer. 'He sits on this iceberg and he seems to see himself – he's always been an athlete, you understand – he seems to see himself scoring the winning goal in one of these polo-games. Everybody's interested in polo nowadays. Aren't I right?'

'Yes,' said the senior Yes-Man.

'Yes,' said the Vice-Yesser.

'Yes,' said the junior Yes-Man.

Wilmot was quicker off the mark this time. A conscientious employee, he did not intend mere physical pain to cause him to fall short in his duty. He nodded quickly, and returned to the 'ready' a little surprised that his head was still attached to its moorings. He had felt so certain it was going to come off that time.

The effect of this quiet, respectful, deferential and obsequious nod on Mr Schnellenhamer was stupendous. The anxious look had passed from his eyes. He was convinced now that Wilmot knew nothing. The magnate's confidence mounted high. He proceeded briskly. There was a new strength in his voice.

'Well,' he said, 'that's set for one of the visions. We want two, and the other's got to be something that'll pull in the women. Something touching and sweet and tender.'

The young author in spectacles thought it would be kind of touching and sweet and tender if Cabot Delancy remembered the time he was in his Gyffte Shoppe and a beautiful girl came in and their eyes met as he wrapped up her order of Indian beadwork.

Mr Schnellenhamer banged the desk.

'What is all this about Gyffte Shoppes and Indian beadwork? Don't I tell you this guy is a prominent clubman? Where would he get a Gyffte Shoppe? Bring a girl into it, yes – so far you're talking sense. And let him gaze into her eyes – certainly he can gaze into her eyes. But not in any Gyffte Shoppe. It's got to be a lovely, peaceful, old-world exterior set, with bees humming and doves cooing and trees waving in the breeze. Listen!' said Mr Schnellenhamer. 'It's spring, see, and all around is the beauty of Nature in the first shy sun-glow. The grass that waves. The buds that . . . what's the word?'

'Bud?' suggested Mr Levitsky.

'No, it's two syllables,' said Mr Schnellenhamer, speaking a little self-consciously, for he was modestly proud of knowing words of two syllables.

'Burgeon?' hazarded an author who looked like a trained seal.

'I beg your pardon,' said Mabel Potter. 'A burgeon's a sort of fish.'

'You're thinking of sturgeon,' said the author.

'Excuse it, please,' murmured Mabel. 'I'm not strong on fishes. Birds are what I'm best at.'

'We'll have birds, too,' said Mr Schnellenhamer jovially. 'All the birds you want. Especially the cuckoo. And I'll tell you why. It gives us a nice little comedy touch. This fellow's with this girl in this old-world garden where everything's burgeoning and when I say burgeoning I mean burgeoning. That burgeoning's got to be done *right*, or somebody'll get fired . . . and they're locked in a close embrace. Hold as long as the Philadelphia censors'll let you, and then comes your nice comedy touch. Just as these two young folks are kissing each other without a thought of anything else in the world, suddenly a cuckoo close by goes "Cuckoo!

Cuckoo!" Meaning how goofy they are. That's good for a laugh, isn't it?'

'Yes,' said the senior Yes-Man.

'Yes,' said the Vice-Yesser.

'Yes,' said the junior Yes-Man.

And then, while the Nodders' heads – Wilmot's among them – were trembling on their stalks preparatory to the downward swoop, there spoke abruptly a clear female voice. It was the voice of Mabel Potter, and those nearest her were able to see that her face was flushed and her eyes gleaming with an almost fanatic light. All the bird-imitator in her had sprung to sudden life.

'I beg your pardon, Mr Schnellenhamer, that's wrong.'

A deadly stillness had fallen on the room. Eleven authors sat transfixed in their chairs, as if wondering if they could believe their twenty-two ears. Mr Schnellenhamer uttered a little gasp. Nothing like this had ever happened to him before in his long experience.

'What did you say?' he asked incredulously. 'Did you say that I . . . I . . . was wrong?'

Mabel met his gaze steadily. So might Joan of Arc have faced her inquisitors.

'The cuckoo,' she said, 'does not go "Cuckoo, Cuckoo" . . . it goes "Wuckoo, Wuckoo". A distinct "W" sound.'

A gasp at the girl's temerity ran through the room. In the eyes of several of those present there was something that was not far from a tear. She seemed so young, so fragile.

Mr Schnellenhamer's joviality had vanished. He breathed loudly through his nose. He was plainly mastering himself with strong effort.

'So I don't know the low-down on cuckoos?'

'Wuckoos,' corrected Mabel.

'Cuckoos!'

'Wuckoos!'

'You're fired,' said Mr Schnellenhamer.

Mabel flushed to the roots of her hair.

'It's unfair and unjust,' she cried. 'I'm right, and anybody who's studied cuckoos will tell you I'm right. When it was a matter of burgeons, I was mistaken, and I admitted that I was mistaken, and apologized. But when it comes to cuckoos, let me tell you you're talking to somebody who has imitated the call of the cuckoo from the Palace, Portland, Oregon, to the Hippodrome, Sumquamset, Maine, and taken three bows after every performance. Yes, sir, I know my cuckoos! And if you don't believe me I'll put it up to Mr Mulliner there, who was born and bred on a farm and has heard more cuckoos in his time than a month of Sundays. Mr Mulliner, how about it? Does the cuckoo go "Cuckoo "?'

Wilmot Mulliner was on his feet, and his eyes met hers with the love-light in them. The spectacle of the girl he loved in distress and appealing to him for aid had brought my distant connection's better self to the surface as if it had been jerked up on the end of a pin. For one brief instant he had been about to seek safety in a cowardly cringing to the side of those in power. He loved Mabel Potter madly, desperately, he had told himself in that short, sickening moment of poltroonery, but Mr Schnellenhamer was the man who signed the cheques; and the thought of risking his displeasure and being summarily dismissed had appalled him. For there is no spiritual anguish like that of the man who, grown accustomed to opening the crackling envelope each Saturday morning, reaches out for it one day and finds that it is not there. The thought of the Perfecto-Zizzbaum cashier ceasing to be a fount of gold and becoming just a man with a walrus moustache had turned Wilmot's spine to Jell-o. And for an instant, as I say, he had been on the point of betraying this sweet girl's trust.

But now, gazing into her eyes, he was strong again. Come what might, he would stand by her to the end.

'No!' he thundered, and his voice rang through the

room like a trumpet blast. 'No, it does not go "Cuckoo".
You have fallen into a popular error, Mr Schnellenhamer.
The bird wooks, and, by heaven, I shall never cease to
maintain that it wooks, no matter what offence I give
to powerful vested interests. I endorse Miss Potter's view
wholeheartedly and without compromise. I say the
cuckoo does not cook. It wooks, so make the most of
it!'

There was a sudden whirring noise. It was Mabel Potter
shooting through the air into his arms.

'Oh, Wilmot!' she cried.

He glared over her back-hair at the magnate.

'Wuckoo, Wuckoo!' he shouted, almost savagely.

He was surprised to observe that Mr Schnellenhamer
and Mr Levitsky were hurriedly clearing the room. Authors
had begun to stream through the door in a foaming torrent.
Presently, he and Mabel were alone with the two
directors of the destinies of the Perfecto-Zizzbaum
Corporation, and Mr Levitsky was carefully closing the
door, while Mr Schnellenhamer came towards him, a
winning, if nervous, smile upon his face.

'There, there, Mulliner,' he said.

And Mr Levitsky said 'There, there,' too.

'I can understand your warmth, Mulliner,' said Mr
Schnellenhamer. 'Nothing is more annoying to the man
who knows than to have people making these silly
mistakes. I consider the firm stand you have taken as
striking evidence of loyalty to the Corporation.'

'Me, too,' said Mr Levitsky. 'I was admiring it
myself.'

'For you are loyal to the Corporation, Mulliner, I know.
You would never do anything to prejudice its interests,
would you?'

'Sure he wouldn't,' said Mr Levitsky.

'You would not reveal the Corporation's little secrets,
thereby causing it alarm and despondency, would you,
Mulliner?'

'Certainly he wouldn't,' said Mr Levitsky. 'Especially now that we're going to make him an executive.'

'An executive?' said Mr Schnellenhamer, starting.

'An executive,' repeated Mr Levitsky firmly. 'With brevet rank as a brother-in-law.'

Mr Schnellenhamer was silent for a moment. He seemed to be having a little trouble in adjusting his mind to this extremely drastic step. But he was a man of sterling sense, who realized that there are times when only the big gesture will suffice.

'That's right,' he said. 'I'll notify the legal department and have the contract drawn up right away.

'That will be agreeable to you, Mulliner?' enquired Mr Levitsky anxiously. 'You will consent to become an executive?'

Wilmot Mulliner drew himself up. It was his moment. His head was still aching, and he would have been the last person to claim that he knew what all this was about: but this he did know – that Mabel was nestling in his arms and that his future was secure.

'I . . .'

Then words failed him, and he nodded.

Theatre/Hollywood

1 — An Encounter with W. C. Fields

The following extract from *Bring on the Girls* gives a
memorable account of the encounter between
P. G. Wodehouse and Guy Bolton, en route for Hollywood,
and W. C. Fields.

The train to the coast – the famous Chief – was rolling
along through the wide open spaces where men are men.
It was the second day out from Chicago and Guy and
Plum were finishing their lunch in the diner. Ethel was
to come on later after they had settled in.

The exodus from the East, which had begun with the
coming of sound to the motion pictures, was at its height.
Already on the train the two had met a number of authors,
composers, directors and other Broadway fauna with
whom they had worked in the days before the big crash.
Rudolf Friml was there and Vincent Youmans and
Arthur Richman and a dozen more. It was like one of
those great race movements of the middle ages.

'Well,' said Guy, 'California, here we come! How do
you feel?'

'I feel,' said Plum, 'as I should think Alice must have
felt when, after mixing with all those weird creatures in
Wonderland, she knelt on the mantelpiece preparatory to
climbing through the looking-glass.'

'I see what you mean – wondering what kind of freaks
she was going to meet this time. Still, maybe it won't
be so bad. Hollywood can't have many terrors for two
men who have survived Erlanger, Savage, a little
Plymouth, junior Breckenridge, the Sisters Duncan – not
to mention "Fabulous Felix" and Palmer.'

611

'Palmer?'

'Hank Savage's private poisoner.'

'Good Lord, I haven't thought of him for years. I wonder what became of him.'

'I hope he perished of his own cooking. I've never forgiven that bird for the supercilious way he sneered at that really excellent plot of ours about the pawnbroker.'

'I remember dimly something about a pawnbroker – '

'Good heavens, man, it was a superb plot and we might do worse than spring it on W. C. Fields when we get to Hollywood. You can't have forgotten. About a fellow who was the last of a long line of pawnbrokers and his ancestor had loaned the money to Queen Isabella to finance Columbus . . .'

'I remember! The contract turned up, and he found that he owned ten per cent of America. It was a darned good idea.'

'It was a terrific idea, and that hash-slinging sea cook crabbed it with a lot of stuff about thematic archaism.'

At this moment a man in horn-rimmed spectacles paused at their table.

'Oh, there you are,' he said. 'I'll come and have a chat in a minute or two. Can't stop now. See you later.'

He passed on, and they looked after him, puzzled.

'Now who on earth was that?' said Guy. 'He seemed to know us.'

'Probably somebody who was in one of our shows. The train's stiff with actors.'

They dismissed the man from their thoughts and returned to the subject of Hollywood.

'Have you talked to anyone who's been there?' asked Guy.

'Only Bob Benchley, and you know the sort of information you would get from him. He said I mustn't believe the stories I had heard about ill-treatment of inmates at the studios, for there was very little actual brutality. Most of the big executives, he said, were kindly men, and he had often seen Louis B. Mayer stop outside some Nodder's hutch and push a piece of lettuce through the bars.'

'What's a Nodder?'

'Bob explained that. A sort of Yes-Man, only lower in the social scale. When there is a story-conference and the supervisor throws out some suggestion or idea, the Yes-Men all say "Yes". After they have finished saying "Yes", the Nodders nod. Bob said there is also a sub-species known as Nodders' assistants, but he didn't want to get too technical.'

'What else? Is it true that they're all lunatics out in Hollywood?'

'Bob says no. He says he knows fully half a dozen people there who are practically sane – except of course at the time of the full moon . . . Good Lord!'

'What's the matter?'

'I've remembered who that chap was who spoke to us.'

'Who?'

'Palmer.'

'It can't have been.'

'It was. Palmer in person.'

Guy considered.

'I believe you're right. But we shall soon know. He's coming this way.'

It was Palmer – older and with a new and rather horrible briskness about him, but still Palmer. He reached their table and sat down, looking snappy and efficient.

'Well, well,' said Guy.

'Well, well,' said Plum. 'It's a long time since that yacht cruise. How's *Ophelia*?'

Palmer cocked a puzzled eyebrow.

'Ophelia?'

'Your play?'

'Oh, that?' Palmer's face cleared. 'I got tired of waiting for the Colonel to do something about it – he kept changing the subject to corned beef hash whenever I mentioned it

613

– so I threw up my job as cook on the *Dorinda* and came out here. Do you know something?'

'What?'

Palmer's voice was grave.

'I don't want to wrong him, but I've sometimes thought that Colonel Savage may have been stringing me along all the time.'

'Colonel *Savage*?' cried Guy and Plum, horrified.

'I know the idea sounds bizarre, but it has occasionally crossed my mind that he encouraged me to think that he was going to produce my play simply in order to get a free cook on that boat of his. We shall never know, I suppose. Well, as I was saying, after the seventh – or was it the eighth? – trip to Florida I got tired of waiting and came out here. I had a hard time of it for a year or two, but I won through in the end and am now doing extremely well. I'm a cousin by marriage.'

'A . . . what was that?'

'I married the cousin of one of the top executives and from that moment never looked back. Of course, cousins are fairly small fry, but I happen to know that there's a lot of talk going around the Front Office of giving me brevet rank as a brother-in-law before very long.'

'A brother-in-law is good, is it?'

Palmer stared.

'My dear fellow! Practically as high up as a nephew.'

The two authors offered congratulations.

'Well, now we're all going to be in Hollywood together,' said Guy, 'I hope we shall see something of one another.'

'We shall. I'm your supervisor.'

'Eh?'

'On this W. C. Fields picture. If you've finished your lunch, I'll take you along to meet him. What's the time?'

'Two-thirty.'

'Ah, then he may be sober.'

They made their way along the train to the Fields

drawing-room, Guy and Plum a little dubious and inclined to shake their heads. They were not at all sure how they were going to like being supervised by a man who thought that in writing a play – and presumably a talking-picture – the scale of values should be at once objective and rational, hence absolute and authentic. And their uneasiness was increased when their overlord said graciously that he hoped they would come to dinner at his Beverly Hills home on the following Saturday, adding that for the sake of old times he would cook the meal himself.

'I'm as good a cook as I ever was,' he said.

Just about, they imagined, and shivered a little.

In the semi-darkness of the drawing-room the first thing the authors heard was a hollow groan and the first thing they saw was a vast something bulging beneath the bedclothes. It stirred as they entered and there rose from the pillow a face rendered impressive by what must have been one of the largest and most incandescent nasal jobs ever issued to a human being. It reminded Plum – who had read his Edward Lear – of the hero of one of that eminent Victorian's best-known poems.

> And all who watch at the midnight hour
> From hall or terrace or lofty tower
> Cry, as they trace the meteor bright
> Moving along through the dreary night
> 'This is the hour when forth he goes,
> The Dong With The Luminous Nose'.

They were to learn later that the comedian was very sensitive about what he considered the only flaw in an otherwise classic countenance and permitted no facetious allusions to it even from his closest friends.

He switched on the light and regarded the visitors with aversion.

615

'And to what, my merry buzzards, do I owe this intrusion at daybreak?' he asked coldly.

Palmer explained that Mr Bolton and Mr Wodehouse were the two authors to whom had been assigned the task of assembling – under his supervision – the next Fields picture, and the great man softened visibly. He was fond of authors – being, as he often said, an author himself.

'Sit down, my little chickadees,' he said, 'and pass the aspirin. Are you in possession of aspirin?'

Palmer – who no doubt had foreseen this query – produced a small tin box.

'Thank you, thank you. Don't slam the lid. What I need this morning is kindness and understanding, for I am a little nervous. I was up late last night, seeing the new year in. Yes, I am aware,' proceeded Fields, 'that the general consensus of informed opinion in these degenerate days is that the year begins on 1st January – but what reason have we for supposing so? One only . . . that the ancient Romans said it did. But what ancient Romans? Probably a bunch of souses who were well into their fifth bottle of Falernian wine. The Phoenicians held that it began on 21st November. The medieval Christians threw celluloid balls at one another on the night of 15th March. The Greeks were broadminded. Some of them thought New Year's Day came on 20th September, while others voted for 10th June. This was good for the restaurateurs – who could count on two big nights in the year – but confusing for the Income Tax authorities, who couldn't decide when to send in their demands.'

'I never knew that before, Mr Fields,' said Palmer respectfully. There was that about the majestic comedian that made even supervisors respectful.

'Stick around me and you'll learn a lot. Well, you can readily appreciate the result of this confusion of thought, my dream-princes. It makes it difficult for a conscientious man to do the right thing. He starts out simply and straightforwardly by booking a reserved table for the last night in December, and feels that that is that. But mark the sequel. As March approaches, doubts begin to assail him. "Those medieval Christians were shrewd fellows," he says to himself. "Who knows whether they may not have had the right idea?"

'The only way he can square his conscience is by going out and investing heavily in squeakers and rattlers and paper caps on the night of 15th March. And scarcely has the doctor left his bedside next morning, when he starts to brood on the fact that the Phoenicians, who were nobody's fools, were convinced that 21st November was New Year's Eve. Many a young man in the springtime of life has developed cirrhosis of the liver simply by overdoing his researches into New Year's Eve. Last night I was pure Phoenician, and I would appreciate the loan of that aspirin once more.'

He mused in silence for a moment.

'So you're coming out to Dottyville-on-the-Pacific, are you, boys?' he said, changing the subject. 'Poor lads, poor lads! Well, let me give you a word of advice. Don't try to escape. They'll chase you across the ice with bloodhounds. And even if the bloodhounds miss you, the pitiless Californian climate drives you back. The only thing to do is to stick it out. But you'll suffer, my unhappy tenderfeet, you'll suffer. Conditions were appalling enough B S, but they're far worse now.'

'B S?'

'Before Sound – sometimes called the Stereoptician Age, rich in fossils. Pictures first learned to walk. Now they've learned to talk. But the thing they've always managed to do is smell. In this year A S confusion is rife. Not a soul at the studios but is clutching its head and walking around in circles, saying, "Where am I?" And can you blame them? Think how they must have felt at MGM when they found that Jack Gilbert could only talk soprano.

'Yes,' Fields went on, 'confusion is rife. I was out to Pathé in Culver City last month and found the place in an uproar. One of their most popular vice-presidents had just been carted off to the loony-bin, strong men sitting on his head while others rushed off to fetch strait waistcoats and ambulances. It came about thus. As you doubtless know, the Pathé trademark is a handsome white rooster. For years he's been popping up on the screen ahead of their pictures and newsreels, flapping his wings and a-gaping open his beak. And when Sound came in, of course the directors held a meeting and it was duly resolved that from now on he had got to crow right out loud.

'Well, they set to work and brought out all the fancy sound equipment into the front yard. The countryside had been scoured for the biggest, all-firedest rooster the sovereign state of California could provide. It was a beaut – pure white with a great red comb on him – and they had a swell background fixed up behind him and the sound machines all waiting to catch that mighty cock-a-doodle-do – and – what do you know? – not a yip could they get out of him. He'd strut about, he'd flap his wings, he'd scrabble with his feet, but he wouldn't crow.

'Well, sir, they tried everything. They even went back to the first principle of show business – they brought on the girls. But he wasn't interested, and they began to wonder if it wouldn't be best to send for a psychiatrist. Then one of their top idea men told them that the sure way to make a rooster crow was to get another rooster to crow. He remembered that the second vice-president was pretty good at barnyard imitations, though his crow wasn't his best number. His quack was better and his sow-with-a-litter-of-baby-pigs was his topper. But they thought his crow might get by, so they fetched him out of his office.

'"Crow," they said.

'"Crow?" said he.

'"That's right. Crow."

'"Oh, you mean *crow*?" said the vice-president, getting it. "Like a rooster?"

'And they all said that the more like a rooster he was the better they'd be pleased.

'Well, these vice-presidents don't spare themselves when duty calls. He crowed and crowed and crowed until he rasped his larynx, but not a sign of audience reaction. The rooster just looked at him and went on scrabbling his feet.

'"Now let's all be very calm and rational about this," said the director who had been assigned to shoot the scene. "I'll tell you what's wrong, Adolf. This bird's no fool. He sees you in those yellow slacks and that rainbow shirt and the crimson tie and he's on to it right away that you're no rooster. 'Something wrong here,' he says to himself, and your act don't get over."

'"So here's what you do, Adolf," said the president. 'You go out in the street round behind the studio wall where the bird can't see you and start crowing out there. That ought to do it."

'So the vice-president went out on the street and began to crow, and at last the old rooster started to perk up and take notice. He jumped on the perch they had built for him and cleared his throat, and it looked like they were all set to go, when darned if Adolf didn't stop crowing.

'"What's the matter with the fellow?" said the director, and the president yells over the wall:

'"Crow, Adolf, crow!"

'But not a yip out of Adolf, and then someone goes outside to see what's wrong, and there's two cops pushing him into the waggon. They're talking to him kinda soft and soothing.

'"Take it easy," they're saying. "Yes, yes, *sure* we understand why you were crowing. You're a rooster, aren't you? So you come with us, pal, and we'll take you back to the hen-house."'

619

It was only after they had left the drawing-room that Guy remembered that they had not told the comedian their pawnbroker plot. They had not, of course, had much opportunity, and they consoled themselves with the thought that later on there would no doubt be a formal story-conference where only business would be talked.

The long journey was coming to an end. They breakfasted next morning as the train was pulling out of San Bernadino. There was a strong scent of orange blossoms in the air, turning Guy's mind to thoughts of marriage. He mentioned this to Plum, as they sat in the diner gazing out at the mountains, at snow-capped Old Baldy and the distant shimmering peak of Mt Wilson.

'When are you getting married?' Plum asked.

'As soon as possible, now that we are both out here.'

'You'll probably settle down in Hollywood and spend the rest of your life there.'

Guy shook his head.

'Not if they paid me!'

'Well, they would pay you. Bob Benchley says that's the one redeeming feature of the place – the little man in the cage who hands you out the $100 bills each Thursday.'

'I mean, not if they paid me untold gold. Hollywood may turn out all right for a visit, but – '

'You wouldn't live there if they gave you the place?'

'Exactly. Not even if they made me a brother-in-law, like Palmer. I'm going to get back into the theatre again.'

'Me, too.'

'Vinton Freedley said he liked that story of ours about the fellow who's such a hit with women and the millionaire father who hires him to stop his daughter marrying a titled halfwit.'

'You mean *Anything Goes*?'

'Yes. You still like that title?'

'I think it's great.'

'Vinton says Cole Porter would write the score.'

'Cole does his own lyrics.'

'Yes.'

'That means I'm out. What pests these lyric-writing composers are! Taking the bread out of a man's mouth.'

'You would do the book with me.'

'Do you want me to?'

'Of course I do. You had an idea about a crook escaping on the boat from New York dressed as a clergyman.'

'Public Enemy Number Thirteen.'

'A superstitious crook. Never had any luck when he was Thirteen, so wants to murder one of the top dozen and get promoted to Twelve. We ought to start jotting down some of these ideas before we get all tangled up with Hollywood.'

'Write on the back of the menu.'

Cups and plates were pushed aside. They paid no further attention to the orange groves, the mountains, the advertisements of the secondhand-car dealers, the flaming twenty-four sheets of the picture-houses. They were working.

'I see the whole of the action taking place on a transatlantic liner.'

'Giving the hero six days to disentangle the girl.'

'There'll be another girl – a comic – who's mixed up with the hero. He was out with her on a supper-date when the heroine's father gave him the job, and she follows him aboard. You never saw *Girl Crazy*, did you?'

'No, I was in England.'

'There was a girl called Ethel Merman in it. It was her first job and she made a terrific hit, singing that "I've Got Rhythm" thing of Gershwin's. She puts a song over better than anybody and is great on comedy.'

'She sounds right for this part.'

'Exactly right. We're rolling!'

'Yes, we're rolling!'

But they were also rolling into Pasadena. They had to hurry back to their compartment for their things.

Held on the car platform while suitcases, golf-bags and typewriters were handed down by the porters, they looked out at the strange new land that was to be their home. Tall eucalyptus . . . blue-flowered jacarandas, feathery pepper trees dotted with red . . . And what looked like a thousand shiny new cars, one of which, they felt, must unquestionably belong to Palmer.

Guy saw all these things without really seeing them. His eyes were on a girl farther down the platform who was searching the faces of the passengers waiting to alight. She turned and saw him . . . smiled and waved.

'Journey's End,' felt Guy.

Palmer came bustling up.

'I wanted to see you two boys,' he said briskly. 'I've had an idea for the Bill Fields picture. Just an outline at present, but something for you to be mulling over. Bill's a pawnbroker, the last of a long line of pawnbrokers. His family have been pawnbrokers for centuries. They started originally in Spain and – get this – it was an ancestor of Bill's who loaned Queen Isabella the money to finance Columbus. She signed a regular contract – '

Guy drew a deep breath. His eyes had glazed a little. So had Plum's.

' – giving this ancestor ten per cent of anything Columbus discovered,' continued Palmer. 'Well, what he discovered – see what I mean – was America. So – this is going to slay you – there's good old Bill with a legal claim to ten per cent of America. Take it from there. Isn't that great?' said Palmer, his horn-rimmed spectacles flashing. 'Isn't that terrific? Isn't that the most colossal idea for a comedian's picture anyone ever heard?'

There was a long silence. The two authors struggled for words. Then they found them.

'Yes, Mr Palmer,' said Guy.

'Oh, *yes*, Mr Palmer,' said Plum.

And they knew they were really in Hollywood.

2 — Hollywood

The following extracts are from letters to W. Townend, reproduced in Wodehouse's *Performing Flea*, his 'Self-Portrait in Letters'. The notes are by W. Townend.

October 2nd, 1929

... So what with this and what with that it seemed to me a good idea to take a few days off and go to Hollywood. I wanted to see what the place was like before committing myself to it for an extended period. I was there three days, but having in an absent-minded moment forgotten to tell Flo [Ziegfeld] and Gilbert Miller that this was only a flying visit, I created something of an upheaval in the bosoms of both. Flo wanted to have me around as he expected Bill McGuire and Youmans to come out of their respective trances at any moment, and rehearsals of my adaptation of *Candlelight* for Gertie Lawrence were nearing their end and the out-of-town opening coming along, so Gilbert wanted me around, too. It was a nasty jar, therefore, when they were told that I had gone to Hollywood, presumably for good.

It hit Flo hardest, because he loves sending 1000-word telegrams telling people what he thinks of them, and he had no address where he could reach me. From what Billie Burke (Mrs Flo) told me later, I gather that he nearly had apoplexy. However, all was forgotten and forgiven when I returned on the ninth day. I went to Baltimore, where *Candlelight* was playing, and got a rather chilly reception from Gertie, but was eventually taken back into the fold.

Candlelight has since opened in New York and looks

like a hit. We did $18,060 the first week. Gertie is wonderful, as always. This is the first time she has done a straight show without music, but she is just as good as she was in *Oh, Kay*. I don't believe there's anybody on the stage who can do comedy better.

I liked what little I saw of Hollywood and expect to return there in the summer. I have had three offers of a year's work, but I held out for only five months.

The only person I knew really well out there was Marion Davies, who was in the show *Oh, Boy*, which Guy Bolton, Jerry Kern and I did for the Princess Theatre. She took me out to her house in Santa Monica and worked me into a big lunch at the Metro-Goldwyn which they were giving for Winston Churchill. All very pleasant. Churchill made a speech at the lunch, and when he had finished Louis B. Mayer said, 'That was a very good speech. I think we would all like to hear it again,' and it was played back from an apparatus concealed in the flowers on the table. Churchill seemed rather taken aback.

I wanted to go to Chula Vista, but of course hadn't time. I must do it when I come here again.

I have reluctantly come to the conclusion that I must have one of those meaningless faces which make no impression whatever on the beholder. This was – I think – the seventh time I had been introduced to Churchill, and I could see that I came upon him as a complete surprise once more. Not a trace of that, 'Why, of course I remember you, Mr Addison Simms of Seattle,' stuff.

December 9th, 1929
. . . I have just had a cable from Hollywood. They want me to do a picture for Evelyn Laye. This may mean a long trip out there pretty soon, but I don't expect to stay very long. I shall know more on December 21st when Sam Goldwyn arrives in England.

January 8th, 1930   *17 Norfolk Street*
. . . It looks as if Hollywood was off. I had some sessions
with Goldwyn, but he wouldn't meet my price. The poor
chump seemed to think he was doing me a favour offering
about half what I get for a serial for doing a job which
would be the most ghastly sweat. He said, when he sailed
today, that he would think things over and let me know,
but I'm hoping I have made the price too stiff for him. I
don't want to go to Hollywood just now a bit. Later on,
in the spring, I should like it. But I feel now I want to be
left alone with my novel [*Big Money*].

Four months later Plum set out for Hollywood. Ethel
Wodehouse, who had gone to New York at the end of
1929, arranged a contract for him with Metro-Goldwyn-
Mayer – six months at $2500 a week with an option for
another six months.

June 26th, 1930   *Metro-Goldwyn-Mayer Studios*
I have been meaning to write to you for ages, but I have
been in a tremendous whirl of work ever since I arrived
in Hollywood. For some obscure reason, after being
absolutely dead for months, my brain suddenly started
going like a dynamo. I got a new plot for a short story
every day for a week. Then I started writing, and in well
under a month have done three short stories, an act of a
play, and all the dialogue for a picture.
    There is something about this place that breeds work.
We have a delightful house – Norma Shearer's – with a
small but lovely garden and a big swimming-pool, the
whole enclosed in patio form. The three wings of
the house occupy three sides, a high wall, looking on to
a deserted road, the other. So that one feels quite isolated.
I have arranged with the studio to work at home, so
often I spend three or four days on end without going
out of the garden: I get up, swim, breakfast, work till two,

swim again, have a lunch-tea, work till seven, swim for the third time, then dinner and the day is over. It is wonderful. I have never had such a frenzy of composition . . .

California is all right. It's a wonderful relief not having to worry about the weather. Incidentally, it is only in the past few days that it has been really hot and sunny. We had three weeks of dull English weather. Still, it never rained.

I don't see much of the movie world. My studio is five miles from where I live, and I only go there occasionally. If I ever dine out or go to parties, it is with other exiles – New York writers, etc. Most of my New York theatre friends are here.

Odd place this. Miles and miles of one-storey bungalows, mostly Spanish, each with a little lawn in front and a pocket-handkerchief garden at the back, all jammed together in rows. Beverly Hills, where I am, is the rather aristocratic sector. Very pretty. Our house has a garden the size of the garden of any small house at Dulwich, and we pay £200 a month for it.

Metro-Goldwyn Studio,
August 18th, 1930   *Culver City*

. . . I expect to be out here till next spring. I might dash back to England for a week or two before that, but I am not counting on it, as I expect they will want me to stick on without going away.

As regards ideas I have had another barren spell. Isn't it the devil, how you get these brilliant periods when nothing seems easier than to plot our stories, and then comes the blank? Oddly enough, Hollywood hasn't inspired me in the least. I feel as if everything that could be written about it has already been done.

As a matter of fact, I don't think there is much to be written about this place. What it was like in the early days, I don't know, but nowadays the studio life is all

perfectly normal, not a bit crazy. I haven't seen any
swooning directors or temperamental stars. They seem
just to do their job, and to be quite ordinary people,
especially the directors, who are quiet, unemotional men
who just work and don't throw any fits. Same with the
stars. I don't believe I shall get a single story out of my
stay here.

This letter was written about ten months before Plum
was to shake the film industry to its foundations and,
quite unintentionally, bring about what amounted to a
major revolution. His forebodings about not getting
a single story out of his stay in Hollywood were quite
unjustified. Before he left for home he wrote the funniest
skits on film stars and the making of films ever written.
The Yes-Men of his stories became portents of the financial
storm that was to break with such devastating fury.

October 28th, 1930   *Metro-Goldwyn Studios*
. . . Well, laddie, it begins to look as if it would be some
time before I return to England. The Metro people have
taken up my option, and I am with them for another six
months and Ethel has just taken a new house for a year.
Which means that I shall probably stay that long.

 If you came over here and settled down, I think I would
spend at least six months in every year here. I like the
place. I think California scenery is the most loathsome
on earth – a cross between Coney Island and the Riviera –
but by sticking in one's garden all the time and shutting
one's eyes when one goes out, it is possible to get by.

 As life goes on, though, don't you find that all you
need is a wife, a few real friends, a regular supply of
books, and a Peke? (Make that two Pekes and add a
swimming-pool.)

 MGM bought that musical comedy *Rosalie* – the thing
Guy Bolton, Bill McGuire, George Gershwin, Sigmund
Romberg, Ira Gershwin, and I did for Ziegfeld for Marilyn

Miller – for Marion Davies. Everyone in the studio had a go at it, and then they told me to try. After I had messed about with it with no success, Irving Thalberg, the big boss (and a most charming fellow incidentally, about the nicest chap I've run into out here – he is Norma Shearer's husband), worked out a story on his own and summoned me to Santa Barbara, where he was spending a few days, to hear it. I drove down there with a stenographer from the studio, and he dictated a complete scenario. When he had finished, he leaned back and mopped his brow, and asked me if I wanted to have it read over to me. I was about to say Yes (just to make the party go), when I suddenly caught the stenographer's eye and was startled to see a look of agonized entreaty in it. I couldn't imagine what was wrong, but I gathered that for some reason she wanted me to say No, so I said No. When we were driving home, she told me that she had had a latish night the night before and had fallen asleep at the outset of the proceedings and slept peacefully throughout, not having heard or taken down a word.

Fortunately, I could remember the high spots of the thing, well enough to start working on it. Unfortunately for some inscrutable reason Thalberg wants me to write it not in picture form but as a novelette, after which I suppose it will be turned into a picture. The prospect of this appals me, and I am hoping that the whole thing will eventually blow over, as things do out here . . .

February 25th, 1931
Only time for a scribble. The studio has just given me a job which will take up all my time for weeks, though I'll bet when I've finished it, it will be pigeon-holed and never heard of again . . .

I have been away for a week at Hearst's ranch. He owns 440,000 acres, more than the whole of Long Island! We took Winks [the Wodehouses' Pekingese], who was a great hit.

628

The ranch is about half-way between Hollywood and San Francisco. It is on the top of a high hill, and just inside the entrance gates is a great pile of stones, which, if you ever put them together, would form an old abbey which Hearst bought in France and shipped over and didn't know what to do with so left lying by the wayside. The next thing you see, having driven past this, is a yak or a buffalo or something in the middle of the road. Hearst collects animals and has a zoo on the premises, and the ones considered reasonably harmless are allowed to roam at large. You're apt to meet a bear or two before you get to the house.

The house is enormous, and there are always at least fifty guests staying there. All the furniture is period, and you probably sleep on a bed originally occupied by Napoleon or somebody. Ethel and I shared the Venetian suite with Sidney Blackmer, who had blown in from one of the studios.

The train that takes guests away leaves after midnight, and the one that brings new guests arrives early in the morning, so you have dinner with one lot of people and come down to breakfast next morning and find an entirely fresh crowd.

Meals are in an enormous room, and are served at a long table, with Hearst sitting in the middle on one side and Marion Davies in the middle on the other. The longer you are there, the further you get from the middle. I sat on Marion's right the first night, then found myself being edged further and further away till I got to the extreme end, when I thought it time to leave. Another day, and I should have been feeding on the floor.

March 14th, 1931   *MGM Studio*

I wish you were here for this weather. It is as warm as summer, and I am bathing regularly. The pool is a nice 62 degrees.

I am doing a picture version of *By Candlelight* now for

629

John Gilbert. This looks as if it really might come to something. Everything else I have done so far has been scrapped. But I doubt if they intend to give me another contract. The enclosed paragraph from *Variety* can only refer to me, and it looks darned sinister. My only hope is that I have made myself so pleasant to all the studio heads that by now I may count as a cousin by marriage or something.

I must stop now, as we have to go out to dinner. Corinne Griffith.

Winks is in great form, and has got quite reconciled to having Johnnie, Maureen O'Sullivan's Peke, as a guest. We are putting Johnnie up while Maureen is in Ireland. Sex female in spite of the name, and age about a year. Very rowdy towards Winks, who disapproves rather. Johnnie is the only ugly Peke I have ever seen. She was run over by a car some months ago and has lost an eye. She looks like one of your tougher sailors.

This was the paragraph from *Variety* to which Plum refers:

> 'Following *Variety*'s report of the ludicrous writer talent situation, eastern executives interrogated the studios as to instances such as concerned one English playwright and author who has been collecting $2500 a week at one of the major studios for eleven months, without contributing anything really worth while to the screen.'

May 19th, 1931   *Metro-Goldwyn Studio*
Everything is very wobbly and depressed over here these days. We seem to be getting a sort of second instalment of the 1929 crash. The movies are in a bad state, and MGM showed no desire to engage me again when my contract lapsed last week. Meanwhile I am plugging along with *Hot Water* and have done 60,000 words, but it looks

like being one of those long ones and I doubt if I shall finish it before mid-August.

Two Hollywood stories, one previous to that interview of mine, the other more recent. The first is supposed to illustrate the Hollywood idea of poverty. A supervisor was giving a writer instructions about the picture he wanted him to work on. He said the outline was that a father has a ne'er-do-well son and gets fed up with his escapades and thinks the only thing to make a man of the young fellow is to force him to battle with the world for himself. So he cuts him off with $500 a week. The other story is quite a recent one, and has to do with the current depression. A man standing in the crowd outside a movie theatre here after a big opening hears the carriage starter calling for 'Mr Warner's automobile', 'Mr Lasky's automobile', 'Mr Louis B. Mayer's automobile', and so on, and he shakes his head. 'At an opening a year from now,' he says, 'there won't be any of this stuff about automobiles. You'll hear them call for Mr Warner's bicycle, Mr Lasky's kiddie car and Mr Louis B. Mayer's roller skates.'

I'm afraid that interview of mine has had a lot to do with the depression in the picture world. Yet I was only saying what everybody has been saying for years. Apparently what caused the explosion was my giving figures and mentioning a definite studio in print. But, damn it all, it never ought to have been in print. It was just a casual remark I happened to drop off the record (though, like an ass, I didn't say that it was off the record). It just shows that with these American reporters you must weigh every word before you speak.

Another story, not a Hollywood one. Wilton Lackaye, the actor, was playing in San Francisco and invited the editor of one of the San Francisco papers to dinner one night. The editor said he was sorry but he couldn't come, because he had a conference. 'A conference?' said Lackaye. 'What's that for?' The editor explained. 'We get together every day for an hour or so and decide what is to be in the next day's paper – matters of policy, emphasis on news and all that sort of thing.' 'Good heavens!' said Lackaye, amazed. 'Do you mean to tell me that you get out that paper *deliberately*?' . . .

Heather Thatcher has turned up to spend a couple of months with us. We gave a big party for her yesterday, which I found rather loathsome, as it seemed to pollute our nice garden. There was a mob milling round in it from four in the afternoon till eleven at night.

About twenty people in the pool at one time. The only beauty of having a party in your own home is that you can sneak away. I went upstairs to my room at five and only appeared for dinner, returning to my room at eight sharp. (The perfect host.) I re-read *Cakes and Ale*. What a masterly book it is . . .

We are toying with a scheme for going round the world in December on the *Empress of Britain*. Sometimes we feel we should like it, and then we ask ourselves if we really want to see the ruddy world. I'm darned if I know. I have never seen any spectacular spot yet that didn't disappoint me. Notably, the Grand Canyon, and also Niagara Falls.

Personally, I've always liked wandering around in the background. I mean, I get much more kick out of a place like Droitwich, which has no real merits, than out of something like the Taj Mahal.

Maureen O'Sullivan's Peke is still with us. She – the Peke, not Maureen – snores like twenty dogs and sleeps under my bed. I'm getting used to it. She is the ugliest and greediest hound I ever met, but full of charm.

The first intimation we had at home that anything had gone wrong was reading in *The Times* a brief report of the interview that was to rock Hollywood.

Although his contract had lapsed the Metro-Goldwyn-Mayer people rang Plum up one day to ask if he would give an interview to a woman reporter for the *Los Angeles Times*. Plum said he would be delighted.

The woman reporter duly arrived and was received by Plum politely and cheerfully. She asked Plum how he liked Hollywood. Plum said amiably that he liked Hollywood and its inhabitants immensely; he said how much he had enjoyed his stay and added, to fill in time and make conversation before the interview proper began, that his one regret was he had been paid such an enormous sum of money without having done anything to earn it.

And that was that.

The interview then got under way and was conducted by both parties on normal question-and-answer lines. The woman reporter withdrew, having got her scoop.

Early the next morning before Plum was out of bed the telephone rang. Someone wanted to speak to Mr P. G. Wodehouse. Plum answered: rather sleepily, I take it. A voice at the other end of the line said it was Reuter's Los Angeles correspondent speaking, and would Mr Wodehouse kindly say if the interview with him in that day's *Los Angeles Times* was authentic. Plum, rather startled at having been aroused at that hour to be asked so trite a question, said that it was. Reuter's correspondent then asked if he might have Mr Wodehouse's permission to cable it across to London and Plum, even more startled, said that he might!

A brief interval elapsed and then the telephone bell rang again. This time an agitated voice demanded if Mr Wodehouse had seen the interview in the *Los Angeles Times*, because if he had . . .

Plum dashed downstairs and grabbed the *Times* and almost the first thing he saw under scare headlines was the interview that was destined to revolutionize the motion-picture industry and put it on a sound basis and cut out the dead wood, the woman reporter having printed every word he had said about his regret at having been

paid such an enormous sum of money without having
done a thing to earn it!

Before nightfall Plum was the most talked-of man in
the United States of America and the bankers went into
action.

Some years later I read what the well-known American
writer, Rupert Hughes, had to say about this strange
episode in the *Saturday Evening Post*:

'Many authors have been badly treated in Hollywood,
but Hollywood has paid high for this idiocy. One of the
gentlest and one of the most valuable for Hollywood –
P. G. Wodehouse – quietly regretted that he had been
paid a hundred thousand dollars for doing next to nothing.
This remark was taken up, and it stirred the bankers
deeply, as it should have done. But Mr Wodehouse has
written no ferocious assaults on those who slighted him.'

September 14th, 1931   *Beverly Hills*
This business of writing to you has taken on a graver
aspect, the postal authorities here having raised the ante
to 5¢ per letter. I can bear it bravely as far as you are
concerned, but I do grudge having to spend 5¢ on a letter
to some female in East Grinstead who wants to know if
I pronounce my name Wood-house or Wode-house.

My art is not going too well at the moment. I have six
more stories to do for the *American* magazine, and ye Ed
has put me right out of my stride by asking me to make
them about American characters in an American setting,
like knowing that if I try to do American stuff, the result
is awful. Apparently he doesn't care for Mulliner stories,
though I'll swear things like 'Fate' and 'The Fiery Wooing
of Mordred' aren't bad, always provided you like my
sort of stuff. What puzzles me about it all is that when
he commissioned the series he must have known the
sort of thing I wrote. It can't have come on him as a
stunning shock to find that I was laying my scene in
England. What did he expect from me? Thoughtful studies

of life in the Arkansas foothills?

I suppose I ought to have taken a strong line and refused haughtily to change my act, but I'm all for strewing a little happiness as I go by, so I told him I would have a pop at some Hollywood stories . . .

We dined last night with Douglas Fairbanks and Mary Pickford. She is a most intelligent woman, quite unlike the usual movie star. I talked to her all the evening. (Probably bored her stiff.) . . .

Hollywood story. Couple of boxers at the American Legion stadium put on a very mild show, and a spectator, meeting one of them after the fight, reproached him for giving such an inadequate exhibition. The boxer admitted that he had not mixed it up very vigorously, but had a satisfactory explanation. 'Couldn't take no chances of getting mussed up,' he said, 'not with a part in Mae West's new picture coming along.'

A New York actress has just got back to Broadway after a year in Hollywood. She says that she has been so long among the false fronts and papier-mâché mansions on the set that nowadays she finds herself sneaking a look at her husband to see if he goes all the way round or is just a profile.

Non-Hollywood story. Inez Haynes Irwin, wife of Will Irwin, applied for a passport the other day and, assisted by Will Irwin and Wallace Irwin, started to fill up the 'description' form. One of the questions was 'Mouth?' Well, that was all right. She wrote 'Brilliant crimson Cupid's bow with delicious shadowy corners,' but the next question, 'Face?', puzzled her. 'What do I say to that?' she asked. 'Write "Yes",' said Wallace Irwin.

August 24th, 1932　　　　　　　　*Domaine de la Fréyère*
. . . Which reminds me of a story I read somewhere – by S. J. Perelman? I can't remember – about a movie magnate who had a wonderful idea for a picture, and he sends to New York for an author, telling him, when

he arrives, that every writer on the payroll has been
stumped for three months by one detail in the story. Get
that one small detail, and the thing will be set.

'We fade in on a street in London,' he says, 'and there's
a guy in rags dragging himself along through the fog, a
Lon Chaney type guy. He's all twisted and crippled up.
He comes to a colossal house in Berkeley Square and
lets himself in with a latchkey, and he's in a gorgeous hall
full of Chinese rugs and Ming vases, and the minute he's
inside he straightens up, takes off his harness and unties
his leg, and by golly, he's as normal as you and me, not
a cripple at all. Then we truck with him through a door,
and he's like in a hospital corridor, and he pulls on rubber
gloves and an operating gown and he goes into a room
where there's ten, fifteen beautiful dames chained to the
wall with practically nothing on. We follow him to a
bench that's full of test tubes and scientific stuff, and he
grabs a hypodermic needle and he goes around laughing
like a hyena and jabbing it into these beautiful dames. And
that's where you got to figure out this one thing: *What
kind of a business is this guy in*?'

June 11th, 1934   *Hôtel Prince de Galles, Paris*
I've been meaning to write for ages, but I've been tied up
with *The Luck of the Bodkins*. I find that the longer I go
on writing, the harder it becomes to get a story right
without going over and over it. I have just reached page
180 and I suppose I must have done quite 400 pages! Still,
it is in good shape now.

Paris is fine. I don't go out much, as I am working all
the time. I have been here for exactly five weeks, except
for one day at Le Touquet. I may be going to Le Touquet
again for a few days soon, to talk with Guy Bolton about
our play for Vinton Freedley *Anything Goes*. But this
address will always find me.

I had an offer from Paramount the other day to go to
Hollywood, and had to refuse. But rather gratifying after

the way Hollywood took a solemn vow three years ago
never to mention my name again. Quite the olive
branch!

Low Wood,
Le Touquet

December 4th, 1934

Lady Dudley (Gertie Millar) lives a few doors off us and
when she went to England asked me to exercise her
spotted carriage dog occasionally. Well, of course, after I
had taken it with me for two days on my walk to get the
papers, it proceeded to regard this walk as a fixed
ceremony. The day I had to go to Lille, I hear it refused
all food and would not be comforted.

I finished *The Luck of the Bodkins* on November 20th,
and ever since have been in a sort of coma. Do you get
like that after a big bout of work?

As a matter of fact, my present collapse is the result
of a strain that has gone on now for almost six months.
While in the middle of *The Luck of the Bodkins*, and just
beginning to see my way through it, I had to break off
and start plotting out that musical comedy, *Anything
Goes*, for New York with Howard Lindsay, the director.
We toiled all through that blazing weather in Paris, and
then we came down here and started all over again with
Guy Bolton. In the end we got out a plot, and I wrote a
rough version, and sent it off to Guy to rewrite.

Well, I eventually started on *The Luck of the Bodkins*
again. Then I got the commission for the novelette for
the *New York Herald-Tribune*, to be done in a hurry. So I
started sweating at that and, just as I was in the middle of
it, a cable came from America from Vinton Freedley, the
manager, saying that the stuff which Guy and I had sent
over wouldn't do, and that he was calling in two other
people to rewrite it. So there I was, presumably out of
that.

I got the novelette finished and sent it over, but was
naturally in a panic about it after the débâcle of the

637

musical comedy which, incidentally, had been preceded by the complete failure of the Bolton – Wodehouse comedy in London, because, though it was a commission, I wouldn't have felt able to stand on my rights and demand the money unless the stuff was acceptable. And for weeks I heard nothing.

Meanwhile, *The Luck of the Bodkins* was coming out with great difficulty. Have you had the experience of getting out what looks like a perfect scenario and then finding that it won't write and has to be completely changed?

And then suddenly – or, rather, not suddenly, but in a sort of series of bits of good news – everything came right. My arrangement about *Anything Goes* was that I was to get two per cent of the gross, if I was able to go to New York and attend rehearsals, but if I couldn't I was to give up half of the one per cent to Howard Lindsay. So I was looking on it all the time as a one and a half per cent job (one and a half per cent being the ordinary musical comedy royalty).

You can imagine my relief when I found that the rewriting was not going to affect my royalty very much. Russel Crouse, the rewriter, had consented to do the work for half of one per cent, so I am only down a quarter of one per cent on the normal royalty. Then we heard that the show was a huge success in Boston, and now it has been produced in New York and is the biggest hit for years and years and Cochran has bought it for London.

Meanwhile I had had a cable from the *New York Herald-Tribune*, which said, HAPPY ABOUT LORD HAVERSHOT (that was the name of the hero of the novelette), from which I inferred that it was all right – though don't you hate these ambiguous cables? I mean, the editor might quite easily really have written NOT HAPPY and the French postal officials cut out the word 'not' as not seeming to them important.

Finally, however, a letter arrived with the cheque, just

about the time I heard the news of the success of the show.

By that time, I was struggling with the last chapters of *The Luck of the Bodkins*. Usually when I get to the last fifty pages of a story, it begins to write itself. But this time everything went wrong and I had to grope my way through it all at the rate of two pages a day. I began to get superstitious about it and felt that if I could ever get it finished my luck would be in. On November 29th I was within four pages of the end and suddenly all the lights in the house went out and stayed out.

Still, I finished it next day, and it is pretty good, I think. Frightfully long – 362 pages of typescript – it must be over the 100,000 words.

In October 1936 Plum went to Hollywood for the second time.

1315 Angelo Drive,
November 7th, 1936   *Beverly Hills*
I am sending this to Watt, because I am not sure if you are still at the flat.

Well, here we are, settled in a house miles away up at the top of a mountain, surrounded by canyons in which I am told rattlesnakes abound, and employing a protection agency to guard the place at nights! We looked at a lot of houses in the valley part of Beverly Hills, where we were before, but couldn't find one we liked, so took this, which is a lovely place with a nice pool, but, as I say, remote. Still, that's an advantage in a way, as we don't get everybody dropping in on us . . .

Winky has taken on a new lease of life through association with the puppy. (Did I tell you Ethel bought a female puppy just before we sailed?) She ignored her for six weeks, and then suddenly became devoted to her. She races about the garden, chased by the puppy.

The puppy is a comedian. In New York, we had put on

Winky's lead and let it trail on the carpet, and we went out, but no Winky followed, though we called to her. When we went back, we found Winks trying hard to get out, but the puppy had seized the lead and was tugging at it.

Everything is very pleasant and placid here, and I am having a good time. But it doesn't seem as interesting as it was last time. I miss Thalberg very much, though I like Sam Katz, for whom I am working. I am collaborating on a musical picture with a man I last saw twenty years ago, when I was sympathizing with him for being chucked out of the cast of one of the Bolton-Wodehouse-Kern musical comedies. He is a wild Irishman named McGowan, who seems to be fighting the heads of the studio all the time. I get on very well with him myself . . .

I still swim every morning, but the water is beginning to get a bit chilly.

Haven't seen many celebrities yet. We don't see much of anybody except our beloved Maureen O'Sullivan and her husband, John Farrow. He is the man who likes your sea stories so much. I met Clark Gable the other day. Also Fred Astaire. I think Fred is going to do a picture of my *A Damsel in Distress*, with music by George Gershwin. I shall know more about this later.

The puppy Plum mentions in this letter, which was soon to be known as Wonder, became in due course the most travelled, the most celebrated and the longest-lived of all the Wodehouse Pekes, and the only one we never met.

March 7th, 1937   *1315 Angelo Drive*
I meant to send you a lot of clippings about the frosts here, but forgot. Anyway, the gist is that we have had a foul winter and the valley below this house has been wrapped in a dense London fog for weeks, because of the smudge pots which they have been burning to try to save the lemon crops.

Did smudge pots enter into your lemon-life at all when you were out in California? Or was it always warm here then in winter? Lemons have been practically wiped out this year.

I am leading a very quiet life here. Unless I have to go and see my producer, I stay around the house all day except for an hour's walk, and we go up to our rooms at eight-thirty and read and listen to the radio. I enjoy it, though I must say I would like to be nearer home. This place seems very far away sometimes.

Winks is very well. Also the puppy, who now has a new name – Wonder. My day starts when I hear the puppy bark in Ethel's room. I open the door, and the puppy comes leaping out. Winky then pokes her head out of my bed, in which she has been sleeping, and I take them downstairs and let them out. I bring them in when I come down to breakfast, and they then have to be out again in order to bark at the gardener, whose arrival is always a terrific surprise and shock to them, though he has turned up at the same time every morning for four months.

Woman out here has just got a divorce. Stated that her husband had not worked for months and was a pretty low-down character altogether. 'He was always going to dances,' she said, 'and when he wanted to go to one the other night, he took the only pair of silk stockings I had and cut the tops off so that he could wear them as socks.'

1315 Angelo Drive,
Beverly Hills

March 24th, 1937

I finished *Summer Moonshine* yesterday. Young Lorimer, of the *Saturday Evening Post*, called on me about two weeks ago and took away 80,000 words of it, leaving me about another 10,000 to do. I must say the SEP are extraordinary. Lorimer left on a Friday, read the thing in the train, arrived Philadelphia Monday night, presumably went to the office Tuesday morning and gave

the MS to somebody else, who must have read it Tuesday
and given it to Stout, the chief editor, on Wednesday
morning and Stout must have read it on Wednesday night,
because on Thursday morning I got a telegram saying it
had been accepted.

I don't see how they manage to be so quick. They get
75,000 MSS a year, all of which are read.

Price – $40,000.

Against this triumph I have to set the fact that Metro-
Goldwyn-Mayer are not taking up my option, which
expires in another two weeks. I have had another flop
with them. I started gaily in working on a picture with Bill
McGuire, and I gradually found myself being edged out.
Eventually, they came out into the open and said they
had wanted McGuire to write the thing by himself, all
along. There seems to be a curse over MGM, so far as I
am concerned.

Since then, I have had a number of offers from other
studios for one picture apiece. It seems pretty certain that
in about two weeks I shall be working on my *Damsel in
Distress*, which RKO bought for Fred Astaire. Selznick
wants me to do a thing called *The Earl of Chicago* and
Walter Wanger asked me to go round, as he had
something right in my line. It turned out to be Clarence
Budington Kelland's *Stand-In*. I turned it down. I got
myself in bad enough last time by criticizing Hollywood,
and I didn't want to do a picture which would have been
an indictment of the studios.

Raining in buckets today, and snow on the foothills
yesterday! The latest gag here is about the New York
man who came to Southern California for the winter –
and found it!

May 6th, 1937   *1315 Angelo Drive*
Listen. What has become of the old-fashioned California
climate? We had a couple of warm days last week, and
then went right back to winter weather again. Today is

absolutely freezing. And it's been the same ever since I got here.

I wish we had taken this house for six months instead of a year. There seems to be a probability that I shall do a four weeks' job on the *Damsel in Distress*, but except for that nothing is stirring. I was told that I was going to do *The Earl of Chicago*, but I see that Ben Hecht is doing it. The fact is, I'm not worth the money my agent insists on asking for me. After all, my record here is eighteen months, with only small bits of pictures to show for it. I'm no good to these people. Lay off old Pop Wodehouse, is the advice I would give to any studio that wants to get on in the world. There is no surer road to success.

May 7th, 1937   *1315 Angelo Drive*
I have been seeing a lot of G. O. Allen, the England cricket captain, who came home from Australia via Hollywood. He told me the inside story of the bodyline crisis. He is a bit sick about the last English team, as everybody failed enthusiastically on every occasion, and the fast bowlers had to do all the work.

Our butler got home last night tight as a drum and is still sleeping it off. Over here, the help take every Thursday off, and he employed his holiday in getting thoroughly pickled.

I can't fathom the mentality of Pekes. Yesterday Roland Young came to tea and sat on the sofa with Winks snuggling up to him on one side and Wonder on the other. The moment he got up and started to leave, both Pekes sprang down and attacked his ankles with savage snarls. You would have thought they had never seen him before, and had spotted him breaking in through a window.

Interesting that about your visit to the specialist. It's nice to know that your heart is all right. Isn't it difficult to get accustomed to the idea that one is now at the age when most people settle down and don't do a thing? I am now exactly the age my father was when I left

Dulwich, and I remember him as tottering to his armchair and settling in it for the day. That's one thing about being a writer – it does keep you young. Do you find you can't walk as far as you used to! I do out here, but I remember last year in Le Touquet I used to do my seven miles without feeling it. I think it's mainly the California climate.

Big strike now in the picture industry which may close all the studios. That'll teach them not to take up my option.

June 24th, 1937   *1315 Angelo Drive*
Life here at present is a bit like being on your *Lancing Island*. We can't go on the mountains because of the rattlesnakes, the butler killed two Black Widow spiders in the garden (deadlier than snakes), and last night and this morning the following episodes occurred. We were taking the dogs for a stroll after dinner, and Wonder didn't follow. We went back and found her playing with a tarantula on the drive! And this morning, when I came out from my swim, I heard her gruffling at something on the steps of the pool, and there was another tarantula, bigger than the first one!

I am sweating away at a picture. The Fred Astaire one, *A Damsel in Distress*, with musical score by George Gershwin. When they bought it, they gave it to one of the RKO writers to adapt, and he turned out a script all about crooks – no resemblance to the novel. Then it struck them that it might be a good thing to stick to the story, so they chucked away the other script and called me in. I think it is going to make a good picture. But what uncongenial work picture-writing is. Somebody's got to do it, I suppose, but this is the last time they'll get me.

September 4th, 1937   *1315 Angelo Drive*
I finished my work on *Damsel in Distress* three weeks

ago, and with only one day's interval started on a picture with Eddie Goulding – Englishman whom I used to know in London before the war – now a director here. I am not finding it very pleasant, because he has his own ideas about the thing and rewrites all my stuff, thus inducing a what's-the-use feeling and making it hard not to shove down just anything. Also, I don't like the story.

The money is fine – $10,000 for six weeks and $2000 a week after that – but this blasted Administration has just knocked the bottom out of everything by altering the tax laws, so that instead of paying a flat ten per cent as a non-resident alien I now have to pay ordinary citizen rates, which take away about a third of what one earns.

The taxes are fantastic here and very tough on Hollywood stars because they make so much over a short period and then go into the discard. Nelson Eddy, my neighbour, made $600,000 last year and when all his taxes and expenses were paid found that he had $50,000 left. Well, not bad, even so, one might say. But then the point is that in 1939 his income may be about tuppence! Stars shoot up and die away here before you can breathe.

I'm not enjoying life much just now. I don't like doing pictures. *A Damsel in Distress* was fun, because I was working with the best director here – George Stevens – and on my own story, but as a rule pictures are a bore. And just now I'm pining to get at a new novel, which I have all mapped out. I sneak in a page or two every now and then, but I want to concentrate on it.

October 11th, 1937   *1315 Angelo Drive*
Just a line to say that we are not staying here for the spring, after all, but are sailing on October 28th, and I shall be back at Le Touquet on November 4th.

1000 Park Avenue,
May 11th, 1952   *New York*

. . . Listen, Bill. If you want to make a pot of money, come over here and go into domestic service. You can't fail to clean up.

A man and his wife came here from England some years ago and got a job as butler and cook at $200 a month plus their board and lodging. They were able to salt away $150 each pay day. After they had been in this place for a while they accepted an offer from a wealthier family at $300. They had two rooms and bath and everything they wanted in the way of food and wines and were able to put away $250 a month.

About a year later their employer made the mistake of entertaining a Hollywood producer for the weekend, and the producer was so struck by the couple's virtuosity that he lured them away with an offer of $400, to include all expenses plus a car. They now banked $350 a month. And when a rival producer tried to snatch them, the original producer raised their salary to $500, at which figure it remains at moment of going to press. They now own an apartment house in Los Angeles.

We have had a series of blisters – both white and black – in our little home, each more incompetent than the last and each getting into our ribs for $60 a week – which tots up to something over £1000 a year – in spite of the fact that Ethel does all the real work with some slight assistance from me. Ninety per cent of them have been fiends in human shape, our star exhibit being dear old Horace, a coloured gentleman of lethargic disposition who scarcely moved except to pinch our whisky when we were out. We had laid in a stock of Haig and Haig Five Star for guests and an inferior brand for ourselves, and after it had been melting away for a week or two, we confronted Horace. 'Horace,' we said, 'you've been stealing our Haig and Haig and, what's more, you've also been stealing our . . .' He gave us a look of contempt and

646

disgust. 'Me!' he said. 'I wouldn't touch that stuff. I only drink Haig and Haig Five Star.' Well, nice to think that we had something he liked.

I heard of some people here who engaged a maid who had just come over from Finland. She seemed a nice girl and willing, but it turned out that there were chinks in her armour. 'How is your cooking?' they asked. She said she couldn't cook. At home her mother had always done all the cooking. 'How about housework?' No, she couldn't do housework – back in Finland her aunt had attended to all that sort of thing – nor could she look after children, her eldest sister's speciality. 'Well, what *can* you do?' they asked. She thought for a moment. 'I can milk reindeer,' she said brightly.

So if you can milk reindeer, come along. Wealth and fame await you.

3 — The Girl in the Pink Bathing Suit

As a matter of fact, I have been to Hollywood, though not recently. I went there in 1930. I had a year's contract, and was required to do so little work in return for the money I received that I was able in the twelve months before I became a fugitive from the chain-gang to write a novel and nine short stories, besides brushing up my golf, getting an attractive sun-tan and perfecting my Australian crawl in the swimming-pool.

It is all sadly changed now, they tell me. Once a combination of Santa Claus and Good-Time Charlie, Hollywood has become a Scrooge. The dear old days are dead and the spirit of cheerful giving a thing of the past. But in 1930 the talkies had just started, and the slogan was Come one, come all, and the more the merrier. It was an era when only a man of exceptional ability and determination could keep from getting signed up by a studio in some capacity or other. I happened to be engaged as a writer, but I might quite as easily have been scooped in as a technical adviser or a vocal instructor. (At least I had a roof to my mouth, which many vocal instructors in Hollywood at that time had not.) The heartiness and hospitality reminded one of the Jolly Innkeeper (with entrance number in Act One) of the old-style comic opera.

One can understand it, of course. The advent of sound had made the manufacture of motion pictures an infinitely more complex affair than it had been up till then. In the silent days everything had been informal and casual, just a lot of great big happy schoolboys getting together for a bit of fun. Ike would have a strip of celluloid, Spike a camera his uncle had given him for

648

Christmas, Mike would know a friend or two who liked dressing up and having their photographs taken, and with these modest assets they would club together their pocket money and start the Finer and Supremer Films Corporation. And as for bothering about getting anyone to write them a story, it never occurred to them. They made it up themselves as they went along.

The talkies changed all that. It was no longer possible just to put on a toga, have someone press a button and call the result *The Grandeur that was Rome* or *In the Days of Nero*. A whole elaborate new organization was required. You had to have a studio Boss to boss the Producer, a Producer to produce the Supervisor, a Supervisor to supervise the sub-Supervisor, a sub-Supervisor to sub-supervise the Director, a Director to direct the Cameraman and an Assistant Director to assist the Director. And, above all, you had to get hold of someone to supply the words.

The result was a terrible shortage of authors in all the world's literary centres. New York till then had been full of them. You would see them frisking in perfect masses in any editorial office you happened to enter. Their sharp, excited yapping was one of the features of the first- or second-act interval of every new play that was produced. And in places like Greenwich Village you had to watch your step very carefully to avoid treading on them.

And then all of a sudden all you saw was an occasional isolated one being shooed out of a publisher's sanctum or sitting in a speakeasy sniffing at his press clippings. Time after time fanciers would come up to you with hard-luck stories.

'You know that novelist of mine with the flapping ears and the spots on his coat? Well, he's gone.'

'Gone?'

'Absolutely vanished. I left him on the steps of the club, and when I came out there were no signs of him.'

649

'Same here,' says another fancier. 'I had a brace of playwrights to whom I was greatly attached, and they've disappeared without a word.'

Well, of course, people took it for granted that the little fellows had strayed and had got run over, for authors are notoriously dreamy in traffic and, however carefully you train them, will persist in stopping in the middle of the street to jot down strong bits of dialogue. It was only gradually that the truth came out. They had all been decoyed away to Hollywood.

What generally happened was this. A couple of the big film executives – say Mr Louis B. Mayer and Mr Adolf Zukor – would sight their quarry in the street and track him down to some bohemian eating resort. Having watched him settle, they seat themselves at a table immediately behind him, and for a few moments there is silence, broken only by the sound of the author eating corned beef hash. Then Mr Mayer addresses Mr Zukor, raising his voice slightly.

'Whatever was the name of that girl?' he says.

'What girl?' asks Mr Zukor, cleverly taking his cue.

'That tall, blonde girl with the large blue eyes.'

'The one in the pink bathing suit?'

'That's right. With the freckle in the small of her back.'

'A freckle? A mole, I always understood.'

'No, it was a freckle, eye-witnesses tell me. Just over the base of the spinal cord. Well, anyway, what was her name?'

'Now what was it? Eulalie something? Clarice something? No, it's gone. But I'll find out for you when we get home. I know her intimately.'

Here they pause, but not for long. There is a sound of quick, emotional breathing. The author is standing beside them, a rapt expression on his face.

'Pardon me, gentlemen,' he says, 'for interrupting a private conversation, but I chanced to overhear you saying that you were intimately acquainted with a tall,

blonde girl with large blue eyes, in the habit of wearing
bathing suits of just the type I like best. It is for a girl of
that description that I have been scouring the country
for years. Where may she be found?'

'In God's Back Garden – Hollywood,' says Mr Zukor.

'Pity you can't meet her,' says Mr Mayer. 'You're just
her type.'

'If you were by any chance an author,' says Mr Zukor,
'we could take you back with us tomorrow. Too bad
you're not.'

'Prepare yourself for a surprise, gentlemen,' says the
victim. 'I *am* an author. George Montague Breamworthy.
"Powerfully devised situations" – *New York Times*.
"Sheer, stark realism" – *New York Herald-Tribune*.
"Whoops!" – *Women's Wear*.'

'In that case,' says Mr Mayer, producing a contract,
'sign here.'

'Where my thumb is,' says Mr Zukor.

The trap has snapped.

That was how they got me, and it was, I understand, the
usual method of approach. But sometimes this plan failed,
and then sterner methods were employed. The demand
for authors in those early talkie days was so great that
it led to the revival of the old press gang. Nobody was safe
even if he merely looked like an author.

While having a Malted Milk Greta Garbo with some
of the old lags in the commissary one morning about half-
way through my term of sentence, I was told of one very
interesting case. It appeared that there was a man who
had gone out West hoping to locate oil. One of those men
without a thought in the world outside of oil, the last
thing he had ever dreamed of doing was being an author.
With the exception of letters and an occasional telegram
of greeting to some relative at Christmas, he had never
written anything in his life.

But by some curious chance it happened that his

651

appearance was that of one capable of the highest feats in the way of literary expression. He had a domelike head, piercing eyes, and that cynical twist of the upper lip which generally means an epigram on the way. Still, as I say, he was not a writer, and no one could have been more surprised than he when, walking along a street in Los Angeles, thinking of oil, he was suddenly set upon by masked men, chloroformed, and whisked away in a closed car. When he came to himself he was in a cell on the Perfecto-Zizzbaum lot with paper and a sharpened pencil before him, and stern-featured men in felt hats and raincoats were waggling rubber hoses at him and telling him to get busy and turn out something with lots of sex in it, but not too much, because of Will Hays.

The story has a curious sequel. A philosopher at heart, he accepted the situation. He wrenched his mind away from oil and scribbled a few sentences that happened to occur to him. He found, as so many have found, that an author's is the easiest job in existence, and soon he was scratching away as briskly as you could wish. And that is how Noël Coward got his start.

But not every kidnapped author accepted his fate so equably. The majority endeavoured to escape. But it was useless. Even if the rigours of the pitiless California climate did not drive them back to shelter, capture was inevitable. When I was in Hollywood there was much indignation among the better element of the community over the pursuit of an unfortunate woman writer whom the harshness of her supervisor, a man of the name of Legree, had driven to desperation. As I got the story, they chased her across the ice with bloodhounds.

The whole affair was very unpleasant and shocked the soft hearted greatly. So much so that a Mrs Harriet Beecher Stowe told me that if MGM would meet her terms for the movie, she intended to write a book about it which would stir the world.

'Boy,' she said to me, 'it will be a scorcher!'

I don't know if anything ever came of it.

I got away from Hollywood at the end of the year because
the gaoler's daughter smuggled me in a file in a meat
pie, but I was there long enough to realize what a terribly
demoralizing place it is. The whole atmosphere there is
one of insidious deceit and subterfuge. Nothing is what
it affects to be. What looks like a tree is really a slab of
wood backed with barrels. What appears on the screen as
the towering palace of Haroun al-Raschid is actually a
cardboard model occupying four feet by three of space.
The languorous lagoon is simply a smelly tank with a
stagehand named Ed wading about it in bathing trunks.

It is surely not difficult to imagine the effect of all this
on a sensitive-minded author. Taught at his mother's
knee to love the truth, he finds himself surrounded by
people making fortunes by what can only be called
chicanery. After a month or two in such an environment
could you trust that author to count his golf shots
correctly or to give his right sales figures?

And then there was – I am speaking of the old days. It
is possible that modern enlightened thought has brought
improvements – the inevitable sapping of his self-respect.
At the time of which I am writing authors in Hollywood
were kept in little hutches. In every studio there were
rows and rows of these, each containing an author on a
long contract at a weekly salary. You could see their
anxious little faces peering out through the bars and
hear them whining piteously to be taken for a walk. One
had to be very callous not to be touched by such a
spectacle.

I do not say that these authors were actually badly
treated. In the best studios in those early talkie days
kindness was the rule. Often you would see some high
executive stop and give one of them a lettuce. And it
was the same with the humaner type of director. In fact,
between the directors and their authors there frequently

existed a rather touching friendship. I remember one director telling a story which illustrates this.

One morning, he said, he was on his way to his office, preoccupied, as was his habit when planning out the day's work, when he felt a sudden tug at his coat-tails. He looked down and there was his pet author, Edgar Montrose (Book Society – Recommendation) Delamere. The little fellow had got him in a firm grip and was gazing up at him, in his eyes an almost human expression of warning.

Well, the director, not unnaturally, mistook this at first for mere playfulness, for it was often his kindly habit to romp with his little charges. Then something seemed to whisper to him that he was being withheld from some great peril. He remembered stories he had read as a boy – one of which he was even then directing for Rin-Tin-Tin – where faithful dogs dragged their masters back from the brink of precipices on dark nights, and, scarcely knowing why, he turned and went off to the commissary and had a Strawberry and Vanilla Nut Sundae Mary Pickford.

It was well that he did. In his office, waiting to spring, there was lurking a foreign star with a bad case of temperament, whose bite might have been fatal. You may be sure that Edgar Montrose had a good meal that night.

But that was an isolated case. Not all directors were like this one. Too many of them crushed the spirit of the captives by incessant blue-pencilling of their dialogue, causing them to become listless and lose appetite. Destructive criticism is what kills an author. Cut his material too much, make him feel that he is not a Voice, give him the impression that his big scene is all wet, and you will soon see the sparkle die out of his eyes.

I don't know how conditions are today, but at that time there were authors who had been on salary for years in Hollywood without ever having a line of their work used. All they did was attend story-conferences. There were other authors whom nobody had seen for years. It was like the Bastille. They just sat in some hutch away in a corner somewhere and grew white beards and languished. From time to time somebody would renew their contract, and then they were forgotten again.

As I say, it may be different now. After all, I am speaking of twenty-five years ago. But I do think it would be wise if authors-fanciers exercised vigilance. You never know. The press gang may still be in our midst.

So when you take your pet for a walk, keep an eye on him. If he goes sniffing after strange men, whistle him back.

And remember that the spring is the dangerous time. Around about the beginning of May, authors get restless and start dreaming about girls in abbreviated bathing suits. It is easy to detect the symptoms. The moment you hear yours muttering about the Golden West and God's Sunshine and Out There Beyond The Stifling City put sulphur in his absinthe and lock him up in the kitchenette.

4 — Letters to Ira Gershwin

April 29. 1949

1000 Park Avenue
New York

DEAR IRA – Can you help me out of a difficulty? No, wait, wait, this isn't a touch. Here are the circs.

I am planning out a novel with a Hollywood setting, and I want my hero to arrive in Hollywood and meet and have a night out with the father of the girl he loves, without knowing it is her father (or he could find that out during the proceedings). But the point is that I want them to meet plausibly and not by some strained coincidence.

Now, the father is penniless and is living on the bounty of a rich sister or sister-in-law (I haven't decided which), and he manages to sting someone for a hundred bucks or so and instantly lights out for the bright lights. And this is where you come in. What *are* the bright lights around Hollywood these days? The start of the binge ought to be at some gambling resort like the Clover Club. Does the Clover Club still exist? If so, that's fine. My hero is at a loose end and goes to the Clover Club. There he sees an impressive old gentleman playing at one of the tables. They get into conversation and both think it would be a good idea to go on and have supper somewhere . . . or dinner. (As I remember the Clover Club, it was a place where you went after dinner). Now, then, where would they go?

Here's a point to bear in mind. At any stage of the proceedings the old gentleman can duck out and leave the hero flat, as I don't want the latter in on the real orgies, just the start of them. So can you sketch out for me a route for them? All I want is some gambling place where they could start off and meet. Then they go to some other place for a bite of supper. Then the old gentleman, who is now blotto, gives the hero the slip and disappears. But where would he go after leaving the hero? To Los Angeles? Or are there night clubs nearer Beverly Hills? What happens is that the old gentleman gets into trouble at some night club and is jugged.

My difficulty is that it is thirteen years since I was in Hollywood and I don't know the present ropes. Which are the spots which keep open most of the night, and where are they, – in Los Angeles or around Hollywood? The old gentleman, by the way, lives with his sister (or sister-in-law) up at the top of Angelo Drive, in the mountains.

Well, there you are. What I want is (a) some gambling club where my characters could meet without critics raising a howl of 'Coincidence!', (b) Some reasonably respectable restaurant where they could go and get supper, (c) the locale of the joints where the old gentleman could go after leaving the hero and get into trouble. (What I want for 'c' is some lowdown night club.)

Can you help me? If your own life is so pure that you don't know anything about the local night life, could you ask around?

As you will see from the above address, I have moved from The Adams. We have taken a penthouse apartment for five years and are picnicking till our furniture arrives from France. It is a place that just suits me, having an enormous roof on which I can stroll and think, but Ethel complains of lack of closet room. Still, I think we shall be comfortable, and the great thing is to have a base.

It is now exactly two years since I came to New York, and I am still rather scratching along, though in one way and another money seems to come in all the time.

(In England, of course, I am getting richer and richer, but can't touch the stuff.) I have calculated that with the dollars I possess here I can live comfortably for at least three years without earning a cent, and I propose to earn a wad of cents. I have had a series of experiences of the sort which I suppose everybody has with the theater in its present condition. You know. Excited call from some agent. Will you do the lyrics for a big musical now in preparation? I say Yes, certainly, and there is great activity for a few days, and then nothing happens. It all seems very different from the old days, but I suppose one has got to expect a lot of that sort of thing. I can't get used to this modern business of starting out to do a musical and then passing the hat around and saying 'Brother, can you spare a dime?' to about a hundred people.

I was very pleased the other day to be asked to come on the committee of the society for boosting the music of George Gershwin. They are having a very big concert soon.

Guy sailed for England the day before yesterday, taking with him the script of a musical by him and me which he thinks he can place without difficulty there. He left me his Peke, Squeaky, and I was in a panic lest Wonder, our Peke, should start cursing about it, but fortunately they have hit if off like a couple of gobs on shore leave and all is well.

Love to Leonore
Yours ever
Plum

1000 Park Avenue
New York

May 10. 1949

DEAR IRA – Thanks awfully for prompt and lucid response. It's exactly what I wanted. As far as I can see, the meeting between the hero and the old gent will have to take place reasonably near dinner time, which will rule out the race course. I think I will start them off at Romanoff's and the old gent can give the hero the slip at any moment and go off by himself to one of the dives you mention. I don't actually have to describe the scene which follows their meeting. That is to say, I can cut whenever I please, because it is what the scene leads to rather than what actually takes place which matters. With your letter beside me I can handle the thing splendidly.

As far as I can make out, the Barkleys is a smash hit. All the notices I read were splendid, your lyrics getting special mentions. Everybody likes the story, and I am kicking myself for not having thought of the idea of the feamle member of a dance team wanting to quit and go into drama. It's the perfect idea for a stage story. (That word 'feamle' is meant to be 'female'.)

Incidentally, returning to my story, what a bore modern conditions in the magazine world are. In the old days I would just write my novel and ship it off to the *Saturday Evening Post* and they would use it as a serial in just the form in which it would later appear as a novel. But now, in order to get a chance of serial publication, you have to keep the story down to 25,000 words and then rewrite it in 80,000 words for book publication. I do hate messing about with a story.

Returning to the Barklays (what a good title The B's of Broadway is, by the way), that was certainly tough on you to have half your score cut. On the other hand, I have an idea that you have gained by having Ginger Rogers. I saw Judy Garland in *Easter Parade* and thought she was very good, but Ginger R. has something the others haven't got. She looks wonderful in the photographs in the papers.

1000 Park is going to be a success, I think. At first Ethel cursed all the time about the lack of closet space and the smuts on the roof, but she is coming round and

659

now admits that the roof is pretty heavenly. Personally,
I couldn't live in N.Y. without some sort of roof to stroll
on. This one of ours is terrific, practically an estate. I have
an idea that Ethel's real grudge against the place is that
she thinks she has been gypped and that $300 a month
is what we ought to be paying. Actually the score is as
follows. At the Adams we were paying $525 a month
and getting electric light, maid service etc thrown in, and
here we pay $450 a month and have to supply everything
else, so it's about the same. Our furniture arrives a week
from now, and I am thinking of clearing out while it is
put in. I might dash over to Beverly Hills for a few days.
It would be great seeing you again.

Love to Leonore

Yours ever

Plum

P. G. WODEHOUSE
REMSENBURG
NEW YORK

November 10. 1961

DEAR IRA – Thanks for the clipping. What a compliment!
Everything these days is giving me swelled head. The
N. Y. Times and *Herald-Tribune* celebrated my eightieth
birthday with long interviews, and there were reams of
stuff in the London papers. But what gave me the biggest
kick was the following telegram:

> On this happy day I wish to thank
> you on behalf of Larry Hart, Oscar
> Hammerstein and myself for all you
> taught us through the years. Please
> stay well and happy. Affectionately.
> RICHARD RODGERS

I nearly cried when I read it. I had only met him once
for a minute when he and Oscar passed the table where
I was lunching with Max Dreyfus, and it never occurred
to me that he would remember my existence. He must
be an awfully nice chap.

My granddaughter, Sheran Cazalet, was with us for
my birthday and she was talking of her last visit to
Beverly Hills and she said that you had been pointed out
to her but she had not had the nerve to go and fraternize.
She has just been there again and I told her if poss to get
in touch with you, but I gather from her letter that she was
moving around all over the place and was not in Beverly
Hills very long.

I do think it sad that two such sterling souls as you
and me are so far apart. I have to console myself with
reading your lyric book. What a masterly work!

Talking of lyrics, they are going to revive *Anything
Goes* off B'way and I have been revising You're The Top
and other Cole Porter lyrics. Don't you think he's terribly
uneven? He gets wonderful ideas, but he will strain for
rhymes regardless of the sense. As for instance

When Mrs Roosevelt with all her trimmins
Can broadcast a bed by Simmons,
Then Franklin knows
Anything goes.

What the hell does 'trimmins' mean? I always think,
as you do, that the first thing a lyric has to do is make
sense. As for instance

Sober or blotto,
This is the motto,
Keep muddling through.

Love to Lee
Yours ever
Plum

Essays, Verse and Thoughts on Writers and Writing

1 — My World

and what happened to it

It was always a small world – one of the smallest I ever met, as Bertie Wooster would say. In London it was bounded on the east by St James Street, on the west by Hyde Park Corner, by Oxford Street on the north, and by Piccadilly on the south, overflowing in the rural districts to country houses in Shropshire and other delectable counties. And now it is not even small, it is nonexistent.

This is pointed out to me every time a new book of mine dealing with Jeeves or Blandings Castle or the Drones Club is published in England. 'Edwardian!' the critics hiss at me. (It is not easy to hiss the word *Edwardian*, containing, as it does, no sibilant, but they manage it.) And I shuffle my feet and say, 'Yes, I suppose you're right.' After all, I tell myself, there has been no generic term for the type of young man who figures in my stories, since he used to be called a knut in the pre-First-War days, which certainly seems to suggest that the species has died out like the macaronis of the Regency and the whiskered mashers of the Victorian age.

But sometimes I am in a more defiant mood. Mine, I protest, are historical novels. Nobody objects when an author writes the sort of things that begin, 'More skilled though I am at wielding the broadsword than the quill, I will set down for all to read the tale of how I, plain John Blunt, did follow my dear liege to the wars when Harry, yclept the fifth, sat on our English throne.' Then why am I not to be allowed to set down for all to read the tale of how the Hon. J. Blunt got fined five pounds by the magistrate at Bosher Street Police Court for disorderly conduct on Boat Race Night? Unfair discrimination is the phrase that springs to the lips.

I suppose one thing that makes these drones of mine seem creatures of a dead past is that with the exception of Oofy Prosser, the club millionaire, they are genial and good-tempered, friends of all the world. In these days when everybody hates everybody else, anyone who is not snarling at something – or at everything – is an anachronism. The Edwardian knut was never an angry young man. He would get a little cross, perhaps, if his man Meadows sent him out some morning with odd spats on, but his normal outlook on life was sunny. He was a humble, kindly soul who knew he was a silly ass but hoped you wouldn't mind. Portrayed on the stage by George Grossmith and G. Huntley, he was a lovable figure, warming the hearts of stone. You might disapprove of him for not being a world's worker, but you could not help being fond of him.

Though, as a matter of fact, many of the members of the Drones Club *are* world's workers. Freddie Threepwood is vice-president at Donaldson's Dog-Joy, Inc., of Long Island City, and sells as smart a dog biscuit as the best of them. Bingo Little edits *Wee Tots*, the popular journal for the nursery and the home; Catsmeat Potter-Pirbright has played the juvenile in a number of West End drawing-room comedies, generally coming on early in Act One with a cheery 'Tennis, anyone?'; and even Bertie Wooster once wrote an article for his Aunt Dahlia's weekly, *Milady's Boudoir*, on 'What the Well-Dressed Man Is Wearing.' Your drone can always work if he feels like it. It is very seldom, of course, that he does feel like it. He prefers just to exist beautifully.

Two things caused the decline of the drone, or knut, the first of which was that hard times hit younger sons. Most knuts were younger sons, and in the reign of good

666

King Edward the position of younger son in aristocratic families was ... what's the word, Jeeves? Anomalous? You're sure? Right ho, anomalous. Thank you, Jeeves. Putting it another way, he was a trifle on the superfluous side, his standing about that of the litter of kittens which the household cat deposits in the drawer where you keep your clean shirts.

What generally happened was this. An Earl, let us say, begat an heir. So far, so good. One can always do with an heir. But then – these earls never know when to stop – he begat – absent-mindedly, as it were – a second son and this time was not any too pleased about the state of affairs. Unlike the male codfish which, becoming the father of three million five hundred thousand little codfish, cheerfully resolves to love them all, the aristocrat of those days found the younger son definitely a nuisance. Unless he went into the Church and became a curate – which as a rule he stoutly declined to do – it was difficult to see how to fit him in. But there he was, requiring his calories just the same as if he had been the first in succession. It made the Earl feel that he was up against something hard to handle.

'Can't let Algy starve,' he said to himself, and forked out a monthly allowance. And so there came into being a group of ornamental young men whom the ravens fed. Like the lilies of the field, they toiled not, neither did they spin, but lived quite contentedly on the paternal dole. Their wants were few. Provided they could secure the services of a tailor who was prepared to accept charm of manner as a substitute for hard cash – and it was extraordinary how full London was of altruistic tailors in the early nineteen hundreds – they asked for little more. In short, so long as the ravens continued to do their stuff, they were in that blissful condition known as sitting pretty. Then the economic factor reared its ugly head. There were global wars, and if you have global wars you cannot have happy well-fed younger sons. Income tax and

supertax shot up like rocketing pheasants, and the Earl
found himself doing some constructive thinking. A bright
idea occurred to him, and the more he turned it over in
his mind, the better he liked it.

'Dash it all,' he said to his Countess as they sat one
night trying to balance the budget, '*Why* can't I?'

'Why can't you what?' said she.

'Let Algy starve.'

'Algy who?'

'Our Algy.'

'You mean our second son, the Hon. Algernon Blair
Trefusis ffinch-ffinch?'

'That's right. He's getting into my ribs to the tune of
a cool thousand quid a year because I felt I couldn't let
him starve. The point I'm making is, why *not* let the
young blighter starve?'

'It's a thought,' the Countess agreed. 'Yes, a very sound
scheme. We all eat too much these days, anyway.'

So the ravens were retired from active duty, and Algy,
faced with the prospect of not getting his three square
meals a day unless he worked for them, hurried out and
found a job, with the result that as of even date any poor
hack like myself who, wishing to turn an honest penny,
writes stories about him and all the other Algys,
Freddies, Claudes, and Berties, automatically becomes
Edwardian.

The second thing that led to the elimination of the
knut was the passing of the spat. In the brave old days
spats were the hallmark of the young-feller-me-lad-about-
town, the foundation stone on which his whole policy
was based and it is sad to reflect that a generation has
arisen that does not know what spats were. I once wrote
a book called *Young Men In Spats*. I could not use that
title today.

Spatterdashes was, I believe, their full name, and they
were made of white cloth and buttoned around the
ankles partly no doubt to prevent the socks from getting

dashed with spatter but principally because they lent a sort of gay diablerie to the wearer's appearance. The monocle might or might not be worn, according to taste, but spats, like the tightly rolled umbrella, were obligatory.

I was never myself by knut standards really dressy as a young man (*circa* 1905), for a certain anaemia of the exchequer compelled me to go about my social duties in my brother's castoff frock coat and trousers, neither of which fitted me, and a top hat bequeathed to me by an uncle with a head some sizes larger than mine, but my umbrella was always rolled as tight as a drum, and though spats cost money I had mine all right. There they were, bright and gleaming, fascinating the passers-by and causing seedy strangers who hoped for largesse to address me as 'Captain' or sometimes even as 'M'lord.' Many a butler, opening the front door to me and wincing visibly at the sight of my topper, would lower his eyes, see the spats, and give a little sigh of relief, as much as to say, 'Not quite what we are accustomed to at the northern end, perhaps, but unexceptionable to the south.'

Naturally, if you cut off a fellow's allowance, he cannot afford spats, and without spats he is a spent force. Deprived of these indispensable adjuncts, the knut threw in the towel and called it a day. And just as the spat has vanished and the knut has vanished, so has the country house, in the deepest and fullest sense of the term, also ceased to exist. And it was into the country houses, if you remember, that my little world overflowed.

Mark you, the stately homes of England, of which Felicia Hemans thought so highly, still stand as beautiful as ever amidst their tall ancestral trees o'er all the pleasant land, and if you have half a crown (thirty-five cents at the present rate of exchange) you can go and ramble over them. Drop in, for instance, on the Duke of Bedford at Woburn Abbey with your half-crown in your hot little hand, and you will not only be greeted by His Grace in person and shown the house and all its artistic treasures but will get a snack lunch and be able to listen to the latest song hits on the jukebox. The same conditions prevail at Chatsworth, the Duke of Devonshire's little place up Derbyshire way, and in some three hundred other stately homes now in the side-show business.

But the country house as one used to know it in the old days, with its careless hospitality and grace of living, is a thing of the past. The trouble with all these Abbeys and Halls and Towers or whatever they called themselves was that the early ancestors who built them had such spacious ideas. Home, they considered, was not home unless you had accommodation for fifty guests and a few hundred varlets and scurvy knaves, and in recent times the supply of scurvy knaves and varlets has given out.

Just before the First World War, I was working on a novel dealing with life at a large country house *Something Fresh*, in case you missed the book, set at Blandings Castle, the Shropshire seat of Clarence, ninth Earl of Emsworth – and it was essential for me to inform myself about the personnel of the Servant's Hall at a place like that, my hero (from the best motives) having taken on the duties of a visiting valet. I knew a man who knew a lot of dukes and earls, and I asked him to give me the facts. They were as follows:

Take, my friend said, the Duke of Portland. Being a duke is sort of tough. It is not a thing you can make a success of singlehanded. You need helpers. Here is the list of the Duke of Portland's co-workers:

Chief Steward or Major Domo	Kitchen porter
Steward	Six odd men
Wine butler	Head housekeeper
Under butler	Valets
Groom of the Chambers	Lady's maids
	Head coachman

Four footmen	Second coachman
Steward's Room footmen	Ten grooms
Master of Servant's Hall	Twenty strappers
Two page boys	Head chauffeur
Head chef	Fifteen chauffeurs
Second chef	Six house gardeners
Head baker	Forty gardeners
Second baker	Fifty roadmen
Head kitchen maid	Head laundress
Two under kitchen maids	Twelve laundresses
Vegetable maid	Head window cleaner
Three scullery maids	Five window cleaners
Head stillroom maid	Six engineers
Three stillroom maids	Four firemen
Hall porter	Three night watchmen
Two hall boys	

With the assistance of these, working shoulder to shoulder like the Boys of the Old Brigade, His Grace of Portland managed to get by all right and was as happy a duke as you could wish. The only thing that bothered him was that he disliked ringing a bell when he wanted anything, and this might have embittered his life, had he not got the idea of having a footman always within earshot behind a screen, ready to spring forward when he shouted 'Hi!' which was his way of summoning the help. You can never baffle these dukes for long. They always find a way.

Lord Emsworth, my friend continued, would no doubt do things on a somewhat more modest scale – pigging it, as it were, with a butler, an under butler, a housekeeper, a groom of the chambers, a chef, a pastry cook, some footmen, a chauffeur, a head laundrymaid, a few under laundrymaids, a head stillroom maid, some lesser stillroom maids, a squad of pantry boys, hall boys and scullery maids, and a steward's room footman.

'Golly!' I said, and my friend seemed to think well of

the ejaculation. He confessed that when he allowed his mind to dwell on the human zoos he had described, he often felt like saying 'Golly!' himself.

A house like that today would be staffed, I suppose, by a cook and a strong-young-girl-from-the-village to do the cleaning, and even such an entourage would probably be considered a little ostentatious. The general rule now is that the Duchess cooks and washes the dishes and the Duke dries.

So if you have no troubles of your own to worry over, you might spare the time to worry over the disappearance of the world of which I have written so much – too much, many people say – for it is not the world it was. As Kipling puts it, all our pomp of yesterday is one with Nineveh and Tyre. In a word, it has had it.

But I have not altogether lost hope of its revival. I see by the papers that the Duke of Bedford cleaned up a hundred and fifty thousand pounds last year out of those half-crowns, which is unquestionably nice sugar. If things are proceeding on similar lines all over England, the country house ought soon to be able to resume work at the old stand. Family fortunes will be restored, and Algy will get his allowance again. In other words, we may shortly have the knut with us once more.

At the moment, of course, every member of the Drones Club – and, for that matter, of Buck's, White's, and the Bachelors' – is an earnest young man immersed in some gainful pursuit who would raise his eyebrows coldly if you suggested that he pinch a policeman's helmet on Boat Race Night, but I cannot believe that this austere attitude will be permanent. The heart of Young England is sound. Give it an allowance, dangle a pair of spats before its eyes, and all the old fires will be renewed. The knut is not dead, but sleepeth.

Already one sees signs of a coming renaissance. To take but one instance, the butler is creeping back. Extinct, it seemed, only a few short years ago, he is now repeatedly seen in his old haunts like some shy bird which, driven from its native marshes by alarums and excursions, stiffens the sinews, summons up the blood, and decides to give the old home another try. True, he wants a bit more than in the golden age – ten pounds a week instead of two – but pay his price and he will buttle. In a dozen homes I know there is buttling going on just as of yore. Who can say that ere long spats and knuts will not be with us again?

When that happens, I shall look my critics in the eye and say, 'Edwardian? Where do you get that Edwardian stuff? I write of life as it is lived today.'

2 — To the Editor, Sir . . .

If somebody were to come to me – I am not saying it is at
all likely, but one has to be prepared for everything – and
say 'Gosh, Wodehouse, you're wonderful!' – referring to
my writing, not to my personal appearance, I would be
obliged to reply: 'To a certain extent, my dear Smith or
Jones or Knatchbull-Hugessen or whatever the name
may be, but only to a certain extent. All we authors have
our limitations and I have long recognized mine. Hot
stuff though I am in many respects, I have never been
able to master the art of writing letters to the papers. I
get as far as "To the Editor, Sir" and then I go all to pieces.
Without wishing to wound, you have revealed my secret
sorrow and touched an exposed nerve.'

For I yearn to write letters to the papers. All authors
do. Novelists are merely those who have failed as
contributors to the correspondence column. Unable to
make the grade, they drop down a rung on the ladder
and write novels.

To test the truth of this, ask the man who has done
both. Ask William Faulkner what it felt like to win the
Nobel Prize. He yawns. But mention that you saw that
letter of his in last week's *Times* and watch his face light
up. 'Pretty good, I thought it was,' he says. 'Pretty good,
didn't you think?' and he takes you off and stands you
lunch.

The fact, however, that I can never be an executant
does not prevent me having helpful views on the matter.
I have made a close study of correspondence columns
over a number of years, and to any young fellow who came
to me for advice on how to make good in this most

exacting of all branches of literature I would say: 'Write plainly on one side of the paper only. Condense your ideas. And, above all, do not be too ambitious at the start. Begin – as all the big men – Constant Reader, Disgusted Liberal and the rest of them – have begun – with the cuckoo.

Nobody knows why, but editors have a weak spot for the cuckoo, and anyone who hears the first one is pretty sure of an entrée to their columns. The only trouble is that what is known in the profession as 'cuckoo work' is not as simple as it seems. It calls for the most precise timing. If you don't get your letter in early enough, some rival forestalls you, and there is for some odd reason no market whatever for the second man who hears the cuckoo. On the other hand, get in it too early, and it becomes merely silly. I mean, it is no use writing to *The Times* on January the first and saying:

> 'Sir,
> A very happy and prosperous New Year to you and all your readers. In this connection it may be of interest that shortly after midnight last night, while seeing the new year in with some of the boys, I distinctly heard the cuckoo.'

The editor simply laughs, and not a nice laugh, either.

Still, the only thing is to keep trying, and I say once more 'Begin with the cuckoo'. And be very careful that it is a cuckoo. I knew a man who wrote to the paper saying that he had heard the first chaffinch, and the letter was suppressed because it would have given offence to several powerful vested interests.

Another piece of advice I would give is this. As you become successful, watch yourself closely. Take care that letter writing does not grow upon you till it becomes a vice. In too many cases, I am sorry to say, the character of these letter writers deteriorates very noticeably as the result of their life work. As young men they may have been mild and unassuming, but later they want to spend their whole time putting everybody right. They cannot see the simplest statement in print without seizing pen and paper and contradicting it – often with the greatest acerbity – in a letter beginning:

> 'To the Editor, Sir,
>   In your yesterday's issue there appeared the astounding statement that . . .'

and getting nastier right along. It is the old story of the lion cub which, in its infancy satisfied with wholesome fruit and vegetable, becomes a public menace once it has tasted blood and swallowed its first coolie.

Such men as these, of course, are letter writers who require a peg on which to hang their efforts. The noblest contributors to the correspondence column, the men at the very top of the tree, burst forth spontaneously, like a lark breaking into song.

> 'To the Editor, Sir,
>   I wonder how many of your readers are aware that an excellent lotion for the hair may be made of crushed prunes and salad oil . . .'

Or

> 'To the Editor, Sir,
>   I am the seventh son of a seventh son, born on July 7th, 1897 at seven in the morning. I am forty-seven round the waist and have seven Siamese cats . . .'

Practically all a lesser man can do when he comes across this sort of thing is to bow his head and say 'Hail to thee, blithe spirit' and let it go at that.

3 — All About the Income-Tax

A New Parlour Game for the Family Circle
As I sit in my poverty-stricken home, looking at the place
where the piano used to be before I had to sell it to pay
my income-tax, I find myself in thoughtful mood. The
first agony of the separation from my hard-earned, so to
speak income, is over, and I can see that I was unjust in
my original opinion of the United States Government.
At first, I felt towards the U. S. G. as I would feel toward
any perfect stranger who insinuated himself into my
home and stood me on my head and went through
my pockets. The only difference I could see between the
U. S. G. and the ordinary practitioner in a black mask
was that the latter occasionally left his victim carfare.
   Gosh! I was bitter.
   Now, however, after the lapse of weeks, I begin to see
the other side. What the Government is going to do with
it, I do not know – I can only hope that they will not
spend it on foolishness and nut sundaes and the movies
– but, apparently, they needed a few billion dollars, and
you and I had to pay it. That part remains as unpleasant as
ever. But what I, like so many others, have overlooked is
the thoughtfulness of the authorities in having chosen
March for the final filling-up of their printed forms.

   The New Indoor Sport
You know how it is in the long winter evenings, if you
have nothing to occupy you. You either play auction
bridge, or you go in for one of those games played with

677

colored counters and a painted board (than which nothing is more sapping to the soul), or else you sit and scowl at each other and send the children early to bed. But, last March, with the arrival of Form 10536 X-G, dullness in the home became impossible. Our paternal government, always on the lookout for some way of brightening the lives of the Common People, had invented the greatest round-game in the world. Tiddlywinks has been completely superseded, and the Jig-Saw Puzzle people ought not to sell another jig.

In every home, during this past winter, it was possible to see the delightful spectacle of a united family concentrated on the new game. There was Father with his spectacles on, with Mother leaning over his shoulder and pointing out that, by taking Sec. 6428 H and shoving it on top of Sub-Sec. 9730, he could claim immunity from the tax mentioned in Sec. 4587 M. Clustered around the table were the children, sucking pencils and working out ways of beating the surtax.

'See, papa,' cries little Cyril, 'what I have found! You are exempt from paying tax on income derived from any public utility or the exercise of any essential governmental function accruing to any state or territory or any political subdivision thereof or to the District of Columbia, or income accruing to the government of any possession of the United States or any political subdivision thereof. That means you can knock off the price of the canary's bird-seed!'

'And, papa,' chimes in little Wilbur, 'I note that Gifts (not made as a consideration for service rendered) and money and property acquired under a will or by inheritance (but not the income derived from money or property received by gift, will, or inheritance) is taxable and must be reported. Therefore, by referring to Sub-Sec. 2864905, we find that you can skin the blighters for the price of the openwork socks you gave the janitor at Christmas.'

And so the game went on, each helping the other, all working together in that perfect harmony which one so seldom sees in families nowadays.

Nor is this all. Think how differently the head of the family regards his nearest and dearest in these days of income-tax. Many a man who has spent years wondering why on earth he was such a chump as to link his lot with a woman he has disliked from the moment they stepped out of the Niagara Falls Hotel, and a gang of children whose existence has always seemed superfluous, gratefully revises his views as he starts to fill up the printed form.

His wife may be a nuisance about the home, but she comes out strong when it is a question of married man's exemption. And the children! As the father looks at their grubby faces, and reflects that he is entitled to knock off two hundred bones per child, the austerity of his demeanor softens, and he pats them on the head and talks vaguely about jam for tea at some future and unspecified date.

There is no doubt that the income-tax, whatever else it has done, has taught the family to value one another. It is the first practical step that has been taken against the evil of race-suicide.

One beauty of this income-tax game is that it is educational. It enlarges the vocabulary and teaches one to think. Take, for instance, the clause on Amortization.

In pre-income-tax days, if anyone had talked to me of amortization, I should, no doubt, have kept up my end of the conversation adroitly and given a reasonable display of intelligence, but all the while I should have been wondering whether amortization was a new religion or a form of disease which attacks parrots.

Now, however, I know all about it. I am, so to speak, the Amortization Kid, who wrote the words and music. You should have seen me last Winter, pen in hand, gaily knocking off whatever I thought wouldn't be missed for amortization of the kitchen sink.

You would hardly believe – though I trust the income-tax authorities will – what a frightful lot of amortization there was at my little place last year. The cat got amortized four times, once by a spark from the fire, the other three times by stray dogs: and it got so bad with the goldfish that they became practically permanent amorters. The amortization where I live was nearly as bad as the depletion, and that was worse than the Spanish Influenza.

Heaven Help the Corporations!

As regards income-tax, I am, thank goodness, an individual. I pray that I may never become a corporation. It seems to me that some society for the prevention of cruelty to things ought to step in between the authorities and the corporations. I have never gone deeply into the matter, having enough troubles of my own, but a casual survey of the laws relating to the taxing of corporations convinces me that any corporation that gets away with its trousers and one collar-stud should offer up Hosannahs.

The general feeling about the income-tax appears to have been that it is all right this time, but it mustn't happen again. I was looking through a volume of *Punch*, for the year 1882, the other day, and I came across a picture of a gloomy-looking individual paying his tax.

'I can just do it this time,' he is saying, 'but I wish you would tell Her Majesty that she mustn't look on me as a source of income in the future.'

No indoor game ever achieves popularity for two successive years, and the Government must think up something new for next winter.

4 — Personal Details

In a second-hand bookshop the other day I came across a volume of articles and essays written by Israel Zangwill and published in the year 1896. The contents dealt with a variety of subjects, but treated chiefly of life as it strikes an author: and one of the essays was entitled 'The Penalties of Fame'. It began as follows:

> There is one form of persecution to which celebrity or notoriety is subject, which Ouida has omitted in her impassioned protest. (Apparently Ouida had been kicking about something.) It is interviewing carried one step further. The auto-interview, one might christen it, if the officiating purist would pass the hybrid name. You are asked to supply information about yourself by post. The ordinary interview, whatever may be said against it, is at least painless; and, annoying as it is to after-reflection to have had your brain picked of its ideas by a stranger who gets paid for them, still the mechanical vexations of literature are entirely taken over by the journalist who hangs on your lips. But when you are asked to contribute particulars about yourself to a newspaper, it is difficult, however equable your temperament, not to feel a modicum of irritation.

The emotion I, personally, feel in such circumstances is not irritation, but a sort of dazed helplessness. As far as any temptation to irritation goes, that is overcome by the implied compliment. To a retiring individual it is not unpleasant to be given the impression that a vast public is waiting eagerly for information about himself, his life story, and his personality. It is, at any rate, evidence that a certain number of people read his stuff. No, I am not annoyed, but I certainly do feel embarrassed and rattled, as if I had been asked to recite 'Gunga Din' at the church sociable and had forgotten how it began. Or as if, in response to calls of 'Author!' on the night of the opening performance of a play, I had come before the curtain and when it was too late to withdraw, had found that I was expected to make a speech.

Two recent events, happening almost simultaneously, have given me this embarrassed and helpless feeling. I have just been interviewed, and the Strenuous Life Publishing Company of a certain western city has made a request for some picturesque personal details about me. This practically amounts to a Boom. Wodehouse stock is shooting up. Pelham is going to par. In a word, Great Neck's favourite son has begun to make his presence felt.

All this is splendid. It makes me glow. I sing in my bath. But there is always a catch in these good things, and in my case it is the fact that, until this happened, it had never even crossed my mind that I was about the dullest chunk of dough that ever went through life without doing a thing except eat and sleep and tremble at the sight of a job of work. These calls upon me to stand and deliver something personal and picturesque in my past, have revealed me to myself for what I am. Previously, I had always gone about under the impression that I was a pretty likely sort of individual, removed by many parasangs from the common herd or bourgeoisie. Even now I hate to believe that I am really as dull as I seem, and yet what other explanation is there of the fact that I have lived all these years without doing anything of the slightest interest to anybody?

The interview was the worst. The man got out his note-book and sharpened his pencil and moistened the point and looked at me with a bright, trusting look in his eyes. 'This', he seemed to say, 'is going to be good. This will be something to tell the boys at the corner drugstore.' And he asked me about my career.

I let my mind wander back over the past. It was like talking a stroll through the Mojave desert.

'I came to America from England,' I said at last, 'in 1904.'

'Yes?' he said excitedly. 'And then?'

'Oh, then I went back again.'

'And when did you return to America?'

'In 1909.'

'And what happened then?'

'I stayed there.'

And that was all. There were other questions and other answers, but the answers were all just as startling as the above, no more, no less. My interviewer went away with rather a wan expression on his face, murmuring something about writing it all up as a personal feature story. Well, unless he puts a bit of jazz into it on his own account, it will read like a personal feature story of the wart-hog at the Bronx zoo. It looks to me as if the only man who could handle my life story right would be the author in George Ade's fable who wrote *The Simple Annals of John Gardensass*, in which the outstanding events were when John sold the cow and, later, sat on the fence and whittled.

Other authors are not like that. I know at least three who contributed their first story to a magazine from prison. The average author, as far as I can make out, is a fellow who ran away from home at the age of ten, sailed seven times round the world on a sailing-ship, did a bit of pearl-poaching, was a prominent figure in the Homestead Riots and the Spanish War, went on the stage, tramped for a few years, and then, when he was good and ready, took his pen in hand and started to turn out wholesome fiction for the young girl. There is something

683

to a man like that. He stands out. You feel he has established his right to live. But as for me – well, the only interesting thing that ever happened to me was when I drank the liniment in the dark by mistake for the sherry.

There is nothing to catch hold of even in my methods of writing. Hobbes, who wrote *The Leviathan*, 'mused as he walked; and he had in the head of his cane a pen and ink-horn.' That would make a paragraph in any Sunday paper. Thackeray, when he got a good idea, would jump out of bed and run round and round his room, shouting. Balzac used to wander through the streets bareheaded, clad in a dressing-gown and slippers. I just curse a bit and sit down at the typewriter.

Now, what I am driving at is this. Unless something is done about it eftsoones or right speedily, my biography is going to be a washout of the worst description. And, of course, there will be a biography. Everybody has one nowadays. Every day, when you open the literary supplement of your paper, you see among Books Received the announcement of the publication of *The Life and Letters of George W. Gubbs*, or *The Real Otis Boole*, or *Elmer Quackenboss Phipps as I Knew Him*. Nobody has ever heard of these people before, and nobody wants to hear about them now, but the biographer has gone grimly about his work just the same. And the chances are that, if you go to the length of reading one of these volumes, you will find that all Otis or George or Elmer did was to graduate at the Lemuel Sigsbee Technical University of Southern Carolina and, in after years, to contribute to the papers of the Schenectady Mutual Improvement Association a pamphlet on 'Some Vagaries in the Fin Development of the Common Sardine'.

So that one may be certain that, since these modest comforts are within the reach of all, I shall have my biography all right: and the thought makes me sorry for

my biographer. He will begin, no doubt, by looking
through such diaries as I have kept. For the chapter on
'Early Days' he will consult the one I started as a boy,
and will build up his chapter on such entries as the
following:

> Jan. 1. Have resolved to keep a diary and to set down
> every day all the important interesting events which
> happen to myself and my friends. In this way I shall
> have a complete record of my life. It will be interesting
> to read in after years and Uncle John says it will form
> a useful mental discipline. Wet day today. Nothing
> happened.
> Jan. 2 Wet day. Nothing happened.
> Jan. 3 Still cloudy. Nothing happened.
> Jan. 4 Fine. Nothing happened.
> Aug. 9 Nothing happened.
> Nov. 8 Nothing happened.

That, except for an entry on December 4 – 'Met. J. B.
Asked him about T. It isn't true about D. W.', – is all he
will have to go upon when writing up my life to the age
of twenty-seven.

He will not even be able to pad the thing out with
anecdotes. Most biographers, when their material runs
thin, are able to carry on for a page or so with stories
about the celebrities whom their hero met and the good
things they said. We read, for instance, that 'Blank never
wearied of telling the story of the Bishop of Toledo,
under whose influence he came at this period and whose
powerful personality exercised so marked an effect on
his character at the most plastic stage of his life. The
Bishop, it seems – then a young and nervous clergyman
– was invited to breakfast by a high dignitary of the
church. "I am afraid", said his host, as the meal progressed,
"that your egg is bad." "Oh, no, my lord", replied the
future bishop with the ingratiating smile that was to

685

win him so many converts in his missionary work in the
Far East, "parts of it are excellent!" This was always
one of Blank's favourite stories.'

You can spin this sort of thing out for pages – but not
in my biography. None of the celebrities I have met have
ever said a good thing. As a matter of fact, celebrities
have rather kept out of my way – I don't know why. I
am perfectly ready to meet them, but there seems to be
no enthusiasm at their end.

Not only does nothing ever happen to me: it does not
even happen to my animals. The cat that rouses the
household during a fire in the night and saves nine, is
never my cat. The hen that kills garter-snakes in defence
of its young is never part of the personnel of my poultry
yard. Even the dog that goes mad and has to be shot by a
policeman has had its licence paid by someone else. I
seem to shed a miasma of dullness around me, which
afflicts even the animal kingdom.

I don't want to seem to be complaining. After all, it is
nobody's fault but my own. It was perfectly open to me to
run away to sea if I had wanted to, and every state in the
union maintains a police force that would have been
charmed to insert me in the cooler had I shown any signs
of meeting them half-way. I am not grumbling. I have
set forth these personal defects of mine simply because I
see a way of remedying them. I am merely leading up to
the suggestion that it would be an excellent thing for
myself and others in my position if someone were to
start a bureau for supplying incidents to uneventful lives.
Chesterton had the right idea in his Club of Queer Trades.
One of his stories, if you remember, dealt with the strange
adventures of a certain Major Brown. The major, looking
over his wall one day into the next garden, saw a man
planting pansies to form the words 'Death to Major
Brown!' Later, just outside his door, a manhole opened, a
head emerged, and a sinister voice cried, 'Major Brown,
how did the jackal die?' Still later, in his own cellar, a

massive brute grappled with him and nearly strangled him. Inquiries revealed the fact that the innocent major had been supplied with the adventures ordered by another man of the same name from a firm that supplied serial stories in real life to their clients.

There is surely an opening for such a firm outside fiction. Nobody wants his existence to be one long movie-serial, but still a touch of the stuff that made Pauline famous would help a lot. I don't want actually to be sitting in a room under which somebody has stored dynamite at the moment when the stuff is touched off, but I do feel it would give my biographer a better chance if someone would arrange that an explosion should happen just after I had gone out. Nothing could be simpler for a properly organized firm than to supply material of this kind: and the moment has arrived for such a firm to come into being. Biographers need it.

The incident-supplying firm would, of course, have to run an anecdotal department as a side-line, with which would be incorporated a department for supplying biographers with letters. The public that reads biographies insists upon plenty of letters, and the average letter is so dull. You cannot hold your reader in these days of rush and hurry with a lot of letters like the strong one you wrote to the grocer about the bacon, or the one in which you accepted the Joneses' invitation to dinner and progressive whist.

Photographs, again. If there is one thing that is always demanded by people who want to write stuff about you, it is a photograph: and the trouble about most authors is that nature never really intended them to be photographed. I am no Adonis myself, but you should see some of the others. During the recent actors' strike, I attended meetings of playwrights, and was enabled to see these men of brain in the mass. An appalling sight! And yet every one of them was doubtless called upon to supply his photograph to the papers several times a year. It is not fair to the writer or to the public. One of the principal departments of the bureau which I should like to see come into existence would be the one which looked after authors' photographs. There would be on the staff a number of young and handsome men whose duty it would be to be photographed instead of their clients. When some human gargoyle with a large head but an ingrowing face had put over a best seller, and the papers were clamouring for pictures of him, he would simply call up the bureau and put the matter in their hands. The consequences would be that, instead of wondering how on earth the picture of Amos, the educated ape from the Hippodrome, had managed to get itself onto the Books and Readers page, you would see something that really looked like something.

The more I think of this bureau, the more clearly do I see that it must be founded, and founded quick. I need it in my business. In a day or two those Strenuous Life People will be growing impatient for the personal details of a picturesque nature, which they requested in such an optimistic spirit. I want about three good, snappy adventures for my early manhood, a couple of straight comic anecdotes, and something really interesting about what the Kaiser said to me in 1912.

5 — Verse from *Pigs Have Wings*

(From the *Bridgnorth, Shifnal and Albrighton Argus*, with which is incorporated the *Wheat Growers' Intelligencer and Stock Breeders' Gazetteer*.)

It isn't often, goodness knows, that we are urged to quit the prose with which we earn our daily bread and take to poetry instead. But great events come now and then which call for the poetic pen. So you will pardon us, we know, if, dealing with the Shropshire Show, we lisp in numbers to explain that Emp. of Blandings won again.

This year her chance at first appeared a slender one, for it was feared that she, alas, had had her day. On every side you heard folks say 'She's won it twice. She can't repeat. 'Twould be a super-porcine feat.' 'Twas freely whispered up and down that Fate would place the laurel crown this time on the capacious bean of Matchingham's up-and-coming Queen. For though the Emp. is fat, the latter, they felt, would prove distinctly fatter. 'Her too, too solid flesh,' they said, ''ll be sure to cop that silver medal.'

Such was the story which one heard, but nothing of the sort occurred, and, as in both the previous years, a hurricane of rousing cheers from the nobility and gentry acclaimed the Blandings Castle entry as all the judges – Colonel Brice, Sir Henry Boole and Major Price (three minds with but a single thought whose verdict none can set at naught) – announced the Fat Pigs champ to be Lord Emsworth's portly nominee.

With reference to her success, she gave a statement to the Press. 'Although,' she said, 'one hates to brag, I knew the thing was in the bag. Though I admit the Queen is stout, the issue never was in doubt. Clean living did the trick,' said she. 'To that I owe my victory.'

Ah, what a lesson does it teach to all of us, that splendid speech!

6 — Missed!

The sun in the heavens was beaming,
　　The breeze bore an odour of hay,
My flannels were spotless and gleaming,
　　My heart was unclouded and gay;
The ladies, all gaily apparelled,
　　Sat round looking on at the match,
In the tree-tops the dicky-birds carolled,
　　All was peace – till I bungled that catch.

My attention the magic of summer
　　Had lured from the game – which was wrong.
The bee (that inveterate hummer)
　　Was droning its favourite song.
I was tenderly dreaming of Clara
　　(On her not a girl is a patch),
When, ah, horror! there soared through the air a
　　Decidedly possible catch.

I heard in a stupor the bowler
　　Emit a self-satisfied 'Ah!'
The small boys who sat on the roller
　　Set up an expectant 'Hurrah!'
The batsman with grief from the wicket
　　Himself had begun to detach –
And I uttered a groan and turned sick. It
　　Was over. I'd buttered the catch.

Oh, ne'er, if I live to a million,
　　Shall I feel such a terrible pang.
From the seats in the far-off pavilion

A loud yell of ecstasy rang.
By the handful my hair (which is auburn)
 I tore with a wrench from my thatch,
And my heart was seared deep with a raw burn
 At the thought that I'd foozled that catch.

Ah, the bowler's low, querulous mutter
 Points loud, unforgettable scoff!
Oh, give me my driver and putter!
 Henceforward my game shall be golf.
If I'm asked to play cricket hereafter,
 I am wholly determined to scratch.
Life's void of all pleasure and laughter;
 I bungled the easiest catch.

7 — Printer's Error

As o'er my latest book I pored,
    Enjoying it immensely,
I suddenly exclaimed 'Good Lord!'
    And gripped the volume tensely.
'Golly!' I cried. I writhed in pain.
'They've done it on me once again!'
    And furrows creased my brow.
I'd written (which I thought quite good)
'Ruth, ripening into womanhood,
Was now a girl who knocked men flat
And frequently got whistled at,'
And some vile, careless, casual gook
Had spoiled the best thing in the book
    By printing 'not'
    (Yes, 'not', great Scott!)
      When I had written 'now'.

On murder in the first degree
    The Law, I knew, is rigid:
Its attitude, if A kills B,
    To A is always frigid.
It counts it not a trivial slip
If on behalf of authorship
You liquidate compositors.
This kind of conduct it abhors
    And seldom will allow.
Nevertheless, I deemed it best
And in the public interest
To buy a gun, to oil it well,
Inserting what is called a shell,

And go and pot
With sudden shot
The printer who had printed 'not'
   When I had written 'now'.

I tracked the bounder to his den
   Through private information:
I said 'Good afternoon' and then
   Explained the situation:
'I'm not a fussy man,' I said.
'I smile when you put "rid" for "red"
And "bad" for "bed" and "hoad" for "head"
   And "bolge" instead of "bough".
When 'wone' appears in lieu of 'wine'
Or if you alter "Cohn" to "Schine",
   I never make a row.
I know how easy errors are.
But this time you have gone too far
By printing "not" when you knew what
   I really wrote was "now".
Prepare,' I said, 'to meet your God
Or, as you'd say, your Goo or Bod
   Or possibly your Gow.'

A few weeks later into court
   I came to stand my trial.
The Judge was quite a decent sort,
   He said 'Well, cocky, I'll
Be passing sentence in a jiff,
And so, my poor unhappy stiff,
If you have anything to say,
Now is the moment. Fire away.
   You have?'
      I said 'And how!

Me lud, the facts I don't dispute.
I did, I own it freely, shoot

694

This printer through the collar stud.
What else could I have done, my lud?
    He's printed "not" . . .'
    The Judge said '*What*!
       When you had written "now"?
God bless my soul! Gadzooks!' said he.
'The blighters did that once to me.
    A dirty trick, I trow.
I hereby quash and override
The jury's verdict. Gosh!' he cried.
'Give me your hand. Yes, I insist,
You splendid fellow! Case dismissed.'
    (Cheers, and a Voice 'wow-wow!')

A statue stands against the sky,
    Lifelike and rather pretty.
'Twas recently erected by
    The PEN committee.
And many a passer-by is stirred,
For on the plinth, if that's the word,
In golden letters you may read
'This is the man who did the deed.
    His hand set to the plough,
He did not sheathe the sword, but got
A gun at great expense and shot
The human blot who'd printed "not"
      When he had written "now".'
He acted with no thought of self,
Not for advancement, not for pelf,
But just because it made him hot
To think the man had printed "not"
      When he had written "now".'

8 — Good Gnus

A Vignette in Verse
       By
CHARLOTTE MULLINER*

When cares attack and life seems black,
How sweet it is to pot a yak,
    Or puncture hares and grizzly bears,
        And others I could mention:
But in my Animals 'Who's Who'
No name stands higher than the Gnu;
    And each new gnu that comes in view
        Receives my prompt attention.

When Afric's sun is sinking low,
And shadows wander to and fro,
    And everywhere there's in the air
        A hush that's deep and solemn;
Then is the time good men and true
With View Halloo pursue the gnu:
    (The safest spot to put your shot
        Is through the spinal column).

To take the creature by surprise
We must adopt some rude disguise,
    Although deceit is never sweet,
        And falsehoods don't attract us:

---

* In Wodehouse's story 'Unpleasantness at Bludleigh Court', this poem
by Charlotte Mulliner was rejected, much to her chagrin, by the editor of
Animal-Lovers' Gazette. This story first appeared in book form in *Mr
Mulliner Speaking* (1929).

So, as with gun in hand you wait,
Remember to impersonate
    A tuft of grass, a mountain-pass,
      A kopje or a cactus.

A brief suspense, and then at last
The waiting's o'er, the vigil past:
    A careful aim. A spurt of flame.
      It's done. You've pulled the trigger,
And one more gnu, so fair and frail,
Has handed in its dinner-pail:
    (The females all are rather small,
    The males are somewhat bigger).

9 — *Extract from* Washy Steps into the Hall of Fame

> Good stuff in this boy.
> About a ton of it.
> Son of Cora Bates McCall
> famous food-reform lecturer
> wins pie-eating championship of
> West Side

My children, if you fail to shine or triumph in your special line; if, let us say, your hopes are bent on some day being President, and folks ignore your proper worth, and say you've not a chance on earth – Cheer up! for in these stirring days Fame may be won in many ways. Consider, when your spirits fall, the case of Washington McCall.

Yes, cast your eye on Washy, please! He looks just like a piece of cheese: he's not a brilliant sort of chap: he has a dull and vacant map: his eyes are blank, his face is red, his ears stick out beside his head. In fact, to end these compliments, he would be dear at thirty cents. Yet Fame has welcomed to her Hall this selfsame Washington McCall.

His mother (*née* Miss Cora Bates) is one who frequently orates upon the proper kind of food which every menu should include. With eloquence the world she weans from chops and steaks and pork and beans. Such horrid things she'd like to crush, and make us live on milk and mush. But oh! the thing that makes her sigh is when she sees us eating pie. (We heard her lecture last July upon 'The Nation's Menace – Pie.') Alas, the hit it made was small with Master Washington McCall.

For yesterday we took a trip to see the great Pie

Championships, where men with bulging cheeks and
eyes consume vast quantities of pies. A fashionable West
Side crowd beheld the champion, Spike O'Dowd,
endeavour to defend his throne against an upstart, Blake's
Unknown. He wasn't an Unknown at all. He was young
Washington

We freely own we'd give a leg if we could borrow, steal,
or beg the skill old Homer used to show. (He wrote the
Iliad, you know.) Old Homer swung a wicked pen, but
we are ordinary men, and cannot even start to dream of
doing justice to our theme. The subject of that great repast
is too magnificent and vast. We can't describe (or even
try) the way those rivals wolfed their pie. Enough to say
that, when for hours each had extended all his pow'rs,
toward the quiet evenfall O'Dowd succumbed to young
McCall.

The champion was a willing lad. He gave the public
all he had. His was a genuine fighting soul. He'd lots of
speed and much control. No yellow streak did he evince.
He tackled apple-pie and mince. This was the motto on
his shield – 'O'Dowds may burst. They never yield.' His
eyes began to start and roll. He eased his belt another
hole. Poor fellow! With a single glance one saw that he
had not a chance. A python would have had to crawl and
own defeat from young McCall.

At last, long last, the finish came. His features overcast
with shame, O'Dowd, who'd faltered once or twice,
declined to eat another slice. He tottered off, and kindly
men rallied around with oxygen. But Washy, Cora Bates's
son, seemed disappointed it was done. He somehow made
those present feel he'd barely started on his meal. We
asked him, 'Aren't you feeling bad?' 'Me!' said the lion-
hearted lad. 'Lead me' – he started for the street – 'where
I can get a bite to eat!' Oh, what a lesson does it teach to
all of us, that splendid speech! How better can the
curtain fall on Master Washington McCall!

10 — On Writers and Writing

Colette

All my favourite authors have let me down, and I've had
to fall back on the French. I've read everything by Colette
I could get hold of, including her autobiography, *Mes
Apprentissages*. In re Colette a thing I've never been able
to understand is how her husband, Willy, got away with
it. Did you ever hear of Willy? He must have been quite
a chap. He was a hack journalist of sorts, and shortly after
they were married he spotted Colette could write, so he
locked her in a room, and made her turn out the four
Claudine books, which he published under his own
name – *par Willy* – and made a fortune out of.

He would give her an occasional bit of the proceeds
and expect her to be grateful for it, and he used to tell
interviewers that his wife had been of considerable
assistance to him in these works of his, helping him
quite a bit.

Letter to W. Townend 6 March 1932

W. S. Gilbert

' . . . even a metropolitan audience likes its lyrics as much
as possible in the language of everyday. That is one of
the thousands of reasons why new Gilberts do not arise.
Gilbert had the advantage of being a genius, but he had the
additional advantage of writing for a public which permitted him to use his full vocabulary, and even to drop
into foreign languages, even Latin and a little Greek if he
felt like it. (I allude to that song in 'The Grand Duke')'

On the Writing of Lyrics. Vanity Fair, June 1917

*In August 1905, James Deane, a cousin of Wodehouse's,
took him to visit Gilbert. Wodehouse filled five pages
of his notebook with Gilbert's conversation, including
the following:*

Miss Mackintosh cowers before a wasp while playing
croquet v Gilbert, & says wasps spoil her nerves and put
her off her stroke.
    WSG: 'I know. I keep a private wasp for that special
purpose.'

  Kipling
'Pringle objected strongly to any unnecessary waste of
his brain-tissues. Besides, the best poets borrowed. Virgil
did it. Tennyson did it. Even Homer – we have it on the
authority of Mr Kipling – when he smote his blooming
lyre and went and stole what he thought he might require.
Why should Pringle of the School House refuse to follow
in such illustrious footsteps?'

A Prefect's Uncle

There is no point on which your modern author is more
touchy than this business of testimonials from the
public. You will see Galsworthy stroll up to Kipling in
the club and yawn with ill-assumed carelessness.
    'You don't happen to know of a good secretary, do you,
Rud?' he says. 'I have been caught short, confound it. Mine
has just got typist's cramp, answering letters from
admirers of my books, and more pouring in by every post.'
    'John,' says Kipling, 'you know me. If I could help you,
I would do it like a shot. But I'm in just the same fix
myself. Both my secretaries collapsed this morning and
are in hospital with ice-packs on their heads. I've never
known the fan-mail heavier.'
    'Look here,' says Galsworthy, abruptly, 'how many
fan-letters did you get last week?'

'How many did you?' says Kipling.

'I asked you first,' says Galsworthy, and they parted on bad terms.

And, over in a corner, Hugh Walpole rising and walking away in a marked manner from H. G. Wells.

Louder and Funnier

A. A. Milne

I don't know if it is proof of my saintlike nature, but I find that personal animosity against a writer never affects my opinion of what he writes. Nobody could be more anxious than myself, for instance, that Alan Alexander Milne should trip over a loose boot lace and break his bloody neck, yet I re-read all his early stuff at regular intervals with all the old enjoyment and still maintain that in *The Dover Road* he produced about the best comedy in English.

Letter to Denis Mackail 27 November 1945

(A. A. Milne had written a letter to the *Daily Telegraph* in July 1941 expressing critical views of Wodehouse's Broadcasts.)

Orwell

George Orwell calls my stuff Edwardian (for God knows it is. No argument about that, George) and says the reason for it being Edwardian is that I did not set foot in England for sixteen years and so lost touch with conditions there. Sixteen years, mark you, during most of which I was living in London and was known as Beau Wodehouse of Norfolk Street . . . Still, a thoroughly nice chap and we correspond regularly.

Letter to W. Townend 13 September 1945

I thought George Orwell's criticism of my stuff was masterly. I was tremendously impressed by his fair-mindedness in writing such an article at a time when it was taking a very unpopular view. He really is a good chap. I wonder, though, how many people read a book of essays. Ought to help me with the writing people, but I'm afraid the general public will miss it.

Letter to W. Townend 29 April 1946

Shakespeare

Golly, what rot it sounds when one writes it down! Come, come, Wodehouse is THIS the best you can do in the way of carrying on the great tradition of English Literature? Still, I'll bet the plot of Hamlet seemed just as lousy when Shakespeare was trying to tell it to Ben Jonson in the Mermaid Tavern. ('Well, Ben, see what I mean, the central character is this guy, see, who's in love with this girl, see, but her old man doesn't think he's on the level, see, so he tells her – wait a minute, I better start from the beginning. Well, so this guy's in college, see, and he sees a ghost, see. So this ghost turns out to be the guy's father . . .')

Letter to W. Townend 23 April 1932

' . . . The aunt. She thinks Bacon wrote Shakespeare.'

'Thinks who wrote what?' asked Archibald, puzzled, for the names were strange to him.

'You must have heard of Shakespeare. He's well known. Fellow who used to write plays. Only Aurelia's aunt says he didn't. She maintains that a bloke called Bacon wrote them for him.'

'Dashed decent of him,' said Archibald, approvingly. 'Of course, he may have owed Shakespeare money.'

'There's that, of course.'

'What was the name again?'

'Bacon.'

'Bacon,' said Archibald, jotting it down on his cuff. 'Right.'

The Reverent Wooing of Archibald

703

*In fact Plum read and re-read Shakespeare. On this
subject he would have been unbeatable on* Mastermind.
*He said that he marginally preferred the comedies to the
tragedies and that* Love's Labours Lost *was one of
Shakespeare's most underrated plays.*

(Sir Edward Cazalet)

Shaw

I had forgotten you knew Shaw. Everyone says he was
charming in private life. But he is the most maddening
public character I know. I met him twice, once at lunch
at Lady Astor's (another maddening louse) and again on
the platform of the Gare whatever that station is – ah yes,
du Lyon, when I was off to Cannes and he was starting on
his world tour. Ethel, silly ass, gave him an opening by
saying 'My daughter is so excited about your world tour,'
and he said 'The whole world is excited about my world
tour'. I nearly said 'I'M not, blast you.'

Letter to Denis Mackail 25 December 1950

Shelley

'Oh, ah, yes, of course, definitely.' I remembered
something Jeeves had once called Gussie. 'A sensitive
plant, what?'

'Exactly. You know your Shelley, Bertie.'

'Oh, am I?'

The Code of the Woosters

Tennyson

'It is the best thing that could have happened. From now
on, we start level, two hearts that beat as one, two drivers
that drive as one. I could not wish it otherwise. By George!
It's just like that thing of Tennyson's.'

He recited the lines softly:

My bride,
My wife, my life. Oh, we will walk the links
Yoked in all exercise of noble end,
And so thro' those dark bunkers off the course
That no man knows. Indeed, I love thee: come,
Yield thyself up: our handicaps are one;
Accomplish thou my manhood and thyself;
Lay thy sweet hands in mine and trust to me.

She laid her hands in his.

'And now, Mortie darling,' she said, 'I want to tell you all about how I did the long twelfth at Auchtermuchtie in one under bogey.'

The Clicking of Cuthbert

I'm afraid I've got one of those second-rate minds, because, while I realise that Shelley is in the Shakespeare and Milton class, I much prefer Tennyson, who isn't.

Letter to Guy Bolton 24 November 1948

Tolstoy

No wonder Freddie experienced the sort of abysmal soul-sadness which afflicts one of Tolstoy's Russian peasants when, after putting in a heavy day's work strangling his father, beating his wife, and dropping the baby into the city reservoir, he turns to the cupboard, only to find the vodka-bottle empty.

Jill The Reckless

Evelyn Waugh

I am now reading Evelyn Waugh's *Put Out More Flags* and am absolutely stunned by his brilliance. I think you said you didn't like *Brideshead Revisited*, which I haven't read, and I imagine it's different from his usual work. But I do think that as a comic satiric writer he stands

alone. That interview between Basil Seal and the Guards
Colonel is simply marvellous. And what a masterpiece
Decline and Fall was.

> Letter to W. Townend 30 August 1946

The Literary Life

On paper, Blair Eggleston was bold, cold, and ruthless.
Like so many of our younger novelists, his whole tone
was that of a disillusioned, sardonic philanderer who had
drunk the winecup of illicit love to its dregs but was always
ready to fill up again and have another. There were
passages in some of his books, notably *Worm i' the Root*
and *Offal*, which simply made you shiver, so stark was
their cynicism, so brutal the force with which they tore
away the veils and revealed Woman as she is.

Deprived of his fountain-pen, however, Blair was
rather timid with women. He had never actually found
himself alone in an incense-scented studio with a
scantily-clad princess reclining on a tiger skin, but in
such a situation he would most certainly have taken a
chair as near to the door as possible and talked about the
weather.

> *Hot Water*, 1932

'The moment my fingers clutch a pen,' said Leila Yorke,
'a great change comes over me. I descend to the depths
of goo which you with your pure mind wouldn't believe
possible. I write about stalwart men, strong but oh so
gentle, and girls with wide grey eyes and hair the colour
of ripe wheat, who are always having misunderstandings
and going to Africa. The men, that is. The girls stay at
home and marry the wrong bimbos. But there's a happy
ending. The bimbos break their necks in the hunting field
and the men come back in the last chapter and they and
the girls get together in the twilight, and all around is the

scent of English flowers and birds singing their evensong in the shrubbery. Makes me shudder to think of it.'

Ice in the Bedroom, 1961

'One of those ghastly literary lunches. I don't know why I go to them. It isn't as if I were like Jimmy Fothergill, fighting for a knighthood and not wanting to miss a trick. This one was to honour Emma Lucille Agee who wrote that dirty novel that's been selling in millions in America . . . About fifteen of the dullest speeches I ever heard. The Agee woman told us for three quarters of an hour how she came to write her beastly book, when a simple apology was all that was required . . .'

The Girl in Blue, 1970

He had a mild fondness for letters, which took the form of meaning to read right through the hundred best books one day, but actually contenting himself with the daily paper and an occasional magazine.

'A Sea of Troubles', *The Man with Two Left Feet*, 1917

The ordinary man who is paying instalments on the *Encyclopaedia Britannica* is apt to get over-excited and to skip impatiently to Volume XXVIII (Vet-Zym) to see how it all comes out in the end. Not so Henry. His was not a frivolous mind. He intended to read the 'Encyclopaedia' through, and he was not going to spoil his pleasure by peeping ahead.

'The Man with Two Left Feet', *The Man with Two Left Feet*, 1917

The Role of the P. G. Wodehouse Societies

The selection of stories for inclusion in this book was facilitated by a poll conducted by P. G. Wodehouse Societies around the world. Each carried out a survey of its members as to the most popular stories in each character grouping, and there was a surprising conformity of view among continents, let alone countries! Four of the six Societies conducting the survey voted for *Uncle Fred Flits By* as its overall favourite.

More generally, Wodehouse Societies (of which each has a modest annual subscription) have been formed to promote enjoyment of the Master's works in a variety of ways. Each provides publications to its members in the form of a regular journal, or an annual yearbook, or a republished story, and so on. The journals generally include learned articles (though always written for the purpose of enjoyment), often relating to material in a private archive, or drawing on the writer's expertise in another area and relating it to his or her Wodehouse experience. But they also include many pieces written merely to remind the reader of the breadth of Wodehouse's writings as demonstrated in this book.

The Societies undertake a variety of other activities, such as supporting film and stage productions of Wodehouse works, and arranging meetings with talks, performances and exchanges of views with other members. Several Societies hold golf days; the UK Society has an annual cricket fixture at Dulwich College. Many Societies hold dinners or similar functions. The Indian Society arranged for a commemorative postal cancellation featuring Wodehouse, on the occasion of the presentation of the P. G. Wodehouse Trophy to the Royal Calcutta Golf Club. The Drones Club of Belgium holds an annual Great Balloon Hunt in the autumn. In 1999 alone the Swedish and UK Societies each promoted or supported substantial exhibitions in city museums, and the Societies generally are always on the look-out for ways to promote the name of Wodehouse to the public.

The American Society, the largest at the time of writing, has established a number of 'Chapters' based in major cities, where local enthusiasts meet regularly. The other Societies have not yet reached this stage of maturity, although meetings are held in different places and the UK Society, for example, has held meetings in Scotland and several parts of England.

The American Society has also established a programme of weekend conventions which take place in a different city every two years and include a programme of talks, readings and songs.

If you are attracted by the idea of joining one of the Societies, the names of the individuals to contact for more information may be found below:

How to find the P. G. Wodehouse Societies

For further information about how to join the Societies, please contact one of the following:

The Drones Club Belgium
Mr Kris Smets
President
Gijmelbergstraat 32A
3201 Langdorp
Belgium

The P. G. Wodehouse Society (India) India
Mr S Kitson IPS (Retd)
President
41-A Elliott Road
Calcutta 700 016
West Bengal

The P. G. Wodehouse Society The Netherlands
Mr Jelle Otten
President
T G Gibsonstraat 15 F25
NL-7411 RN Deventer
The Netherlands

The Wodehouse Society (Sweden)
Mr Sven Sahlin
President
Katarinavagen 22
S-18451 Österskär
Sweden

The P. G. Wodehouse Society (UK) United Kingdom
Helen Murphy
Membership Secretary
16 Herbert Street
Plaistow
London E13 8BE
England

The Wodehouse Society United States of America
Marilyn MacGregor
Membership Secretary
1515 Shasta Drive #4210
Davis
California 95616–6692
USA

refresh yourself at penguin.co.uk

Visit penguin.co.uk for exclusive information and interviews with
bestselling authors, fantastic give-aways and the
inside track on all our books, from the Penguin Classics
to the latest bestsellers.

BE FIRST

first chapters, first editions, first novels

EXCLUSIVES

author chats, video interviews, biographies, special
features

EVERYONE'S A WINNER

give-aways, competitions, quizzes, ecards

READERS GROUPS

exciting features to support existing groups and
create new ones

NEWS

author events, bestsellers, awards, what's new

EBOOKS

books that click – download an ePenguin today

BROWSE AND BUY

thousands of books to investigate – search, try
and buy the perfect gift online – or treat yourself!

ABOUT US

job vacancies, advice for writers and company
history

Get Closer To Penguin ... www.penguin.co.uk